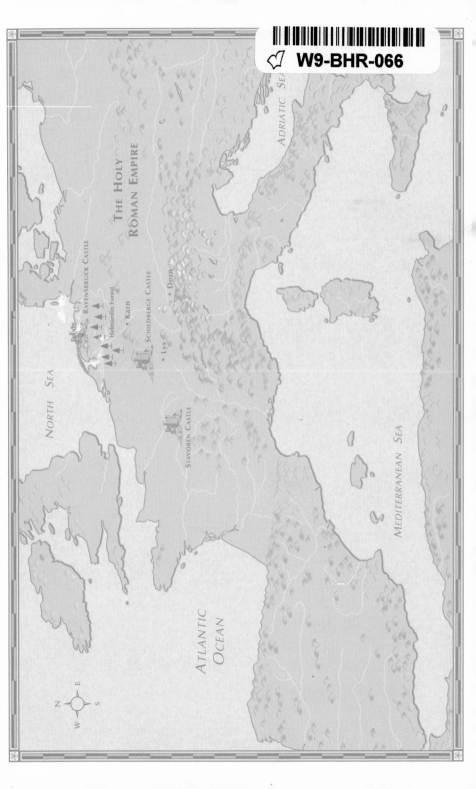

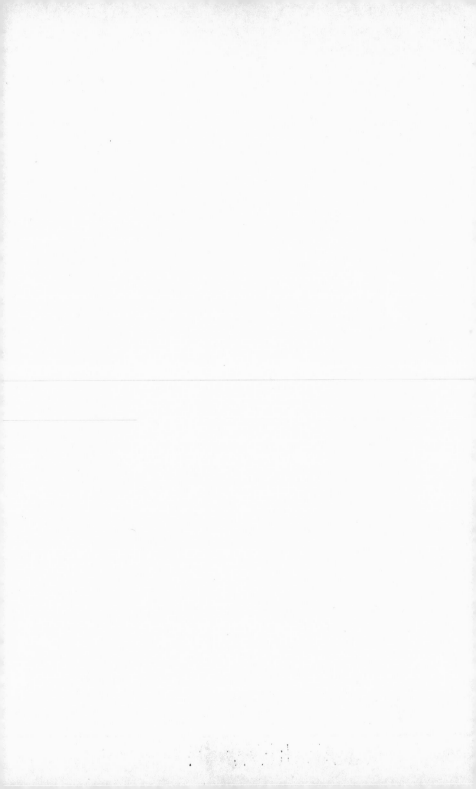

THE BLACK CHALICE

MARIE JAKOBER

THE BLACK CHALICE

Author: Marie Jakober

First published by EDGE Science Fiction and
Fantasy Publishing, Alberta,Canada.

ISBN: 1-894063-00-7

The Black Chalice is a work of fiction.

Printed in the U.S.A.

TO GALE

For introducing me to the books which formed, in part,
the inspiration for this novel;
For a hundred other things;
But mostly for being such a beautiful friend.

ACKNOWLEDGEMENTS

I wish to thank everyone who read the manuscript at various stages, and offered their comments and support. I would also like to express my appreciation for assistance received from Eli Jilek of the University of Calgary Library, and Dr. Juergen Jahn of the Department of Germanic and Slavic Studies.

CHARACTERS OF THE NOVEL

THE COUNTY OF LYS:
Karelian Brandeis, *count of Lys*
Paul von Ardiun, *his squire*
Reinhard, *his seneschal, commander of his men*
Otto, *a knight in his service*
Father Gerius, Father Thomas, *chaplains of the manor*

THE CASTLE OF CAR-IDUNA:
Raven, *Lady of the Mountain, sorceress and guardian of the Reinmark*
Marius, *her steward*

THE COUNTY OF RAVENSBRUCK:
Arnulf, *count of Ravensbruck*
Clara, *his wife*
Adelaide, *his daughter, betrothed to Karelian of Lys*
Helga, *his youngest daughter*
Rudolf of Selven, *a knight in his service*
Peter, *Arnulf's squire*
Sigune, *a Wend slave*

ELECTORAL COUNCIL OF THE HOLY ROMAN EMPIRE:
Gottfried the Golden, *duke of the Reinmark*
Ludwig, *duke of Bavaria*
Duke of Thuringia
Landgrave of Swabia
Landgrave of Franconia
Archbishop of Mainz
Archbishop of Cologne

OTHER CHARACTERS:
Ehrenfried, *Holy Roman Emperor, king of all Germany*
Prince Konrad, *his son*
Radegund, *duchess of the Reinmark, wife of Gottfried*
Theodoric, *Gottfried's eldest son*
Armund, *his younger son*
Helmuth Brandeis, *father of Karelian, former margrave of Dorn, now dead*
Ludolf Brandeis, *brother of Karelian, present margrave of Dorn*
Anselm, *a monk of Saint Benedict*
Wilhelm von Schielenberg, *an exorcist*
Cardinal Volken, *Papal legate to Germany*

Who could possess a greater prize than I have
in your high love, even if it cost him his life
and all he ever owned?

WOLFRAM VON ESCHENBACH

THE BLACK CHALICE

I

THE MONK

Nothing drags the mind of a man down from its
elevation so much as the caresses of a woman.

SAINT THOMAS AQUINAS

ON THE TWENTY-FOURTH DAY OF NOVEMBER, in the year of Our
Lord 1103, in the forests of Helmardin, there did my lord and
master Karelian of Lys, knight of the Reinmark, kinsman and vassal
of Gottfried the Golden, fall thrall to the powers of darkness. May
God have mercy on his soul!

The monk paused, squinting as the candle guttered and
almost went out. Past fifty now, and lean with fasting, his
face held a hardened serenity, his eyes the ascetic brightness
of a saint. In good light one might guess he had been handsome in his youth; he had a broad, high forehead and fine
cheekbones; where his hair was not cropped short, it still
twisted into grey curls. He dipped his quill and, bending close,
began to write again.

THERE, IN THAT FELL PLACE where no Christian may walk without peril, he was ensnared by sorcery and the foul embraces of a
woman, and so destroyed utterly his honor and his immortal soul.
I, though I sinned grievously, was by the grace of God permitted
to escape.

It is the burden of my failing years to record now all which passed there, and all which came of it: treason and war and the deaths of princes . . . .

* * *

He was aware, vaguely, of the sounds of night around him: the distant, soft lowing of the monastery cattle; a cough in the cell next to his own; the close, irritating scurry of mice; the curtain shifting at his window. None of it mattered. The world of small and common things was barely real to him at all.

I WOULD NOT WILLINGLY undertake this task. I do so out of holy obedience, and to lay bare for the world the dangers of carnal passion, and the villainy and devouring corruption which so often lie beneath the surface of a fair woman's skin. For it is in the flesh of women that the Evil One weaves his snares; by their smiles and caresses uncounted good men are brought to ruin—

He heard the flutter of a bird's wing, still unreal, still unregistered in his conscious mind, then the whisper of something moving past his shoulder. The candle tumbled, and burning wax spilled across the parchment. It flared into a gulp of bright heat, collapsed, and the room went dark.

"So." A voice spoke from the void before him: a woman's voice, bitter, mocking, utterly familiar. "You haven't changed much, Paul of Ardiun. You've been seventeen years in the house of your God, and you're still a liar."

He rose to his feet, grasping the crucifix he wore about his neck and crossing himself with his other hand. Both actions were as quick and natural as the reflexes of combat. He was not a timid man. He had fought the heathens of the east for eleven years, and he had encountered the Otherworld before. But his body was icy now with sweat, and his heart almost failed him as the darkness before him changed, and he saw her.

There was a kind of pale light about her, unsteady as firelight. Years had passed, yet everything about her was familiar, even the scar on her wrist and the gown which wrapped her body like running water, its colors never the same. She was, of course, still beautiful. Black hair spilled over her shoulders, and emeralds lay like green berries along the curves of her throat. Karelian's emeralds, heirlooms of his ancient house, lost and soiled forever now, like pearls thrown to swine. Hatred calmed his fear a little, and gave him breath.

"Begone from this place, creature of Satan!" he cried savagely. "I command you in God's name! Begone!"

It was as though he hadn't said a word. She moved towards his small wooden desk, brushed the fingertips of her graceful ringed hand through the ashes of his evening's labor, and picked up his quill.

"Those who eat the world write its histories," she said. "Some lie knowingly, and some in truth no longer remember what they did, for if they remembered they could not bear to live."

Still holding the quill, she looked directly at the monk.

"You will begin again, Paul. And this time, you will tell the truth."

She touched the quill to her lips, murmuring words he could not understand. It seemed to glow with the same pale fire surrounding her.

He tried to think, to find some way to shield himself, but his mind floundered in confusion and his body could not move. Everything was happening too quickly. He had come to feel safe, here in the monastery, safe after so many years of quietly acquired peace. Now all his knowledge as a man of God abandoned him, and his invocations of self-protection died unspoken in his throat.

She spoke to the quill again, this time in his own tongue, and aloud.

"You are bound now, feather of Reinmark," she said. "He cannot unbind you; he doesn't have the power. Write now what he truly remembers, and not what his masters expect him to say."

She laid the quill down, looked at him once, and smiled. A cold smile, pitiless, like the one she must have smiled long ago, thinking of Gottfried, closing her hand upon the stone of his destiny. A look which spoke without words: *Do what you like now; it won't matter. I have defeated you.*

She dissolved into darkness and a soft whir of wings, and the night was still.

He knelt then, one hand gripping the edge of the wooden

desk because he thought he might fall. He crossed himself.
The words of prayers formed in his mind, and scattered again
and were gone. Karelian's voice took their place, soft as it so
often was, an astonishing soft voice in such a fierce man of
war:

Pauli, Pauli, there is so much you don't understand . . . .

He was wrong, of course. It was Karelian himself who
never understood, and never saw his danger; Karelian who
was too proud, too sure of his good sword-arm and his so-
phisticated mind and—yes, one had to say it, shameful though
it was—too little the master of his own base appetites. Too
willing to take a harlot's favors, and then, ensnared by his
desires, to pay for them with any coin she named.

Paul shuddered. How could she have come here, to this
sacred place, inside these hallowed Benedictine walls, where
the footsteps of saints still whispered across the stones? How
was it possible?

"Jesus, saviour of the world, protect me . . . !"

It was so hard to pray. Memories kept intruding, sharp as
spears of light, as though thirty-one years had not passed, and
he were a youth again, in love with a dream. So splendid a
dream it was, and so quick to fade. A kingdom of heaven
upon earth. A ruler who was more than a king, more than a
conqueror, more than a man. A lord who would pass on to
his sons and his grandsons, through all the centuries of time,
a sacred heritage.

A royal house of God . . . .

Much later, in the icy darkness before lauds, he carried
the quill in a pair of tongs to the refectory fireplace and flung
it in, piling chunks of wood and kindling on it and watching
until the hearth was roaring with flame. He went to chapel
then, and afterwards to breakfast. When he returned to his
cell, the quill was lying on his desk as before. He went rigid
with shock, and yet he was not surprised.

For a week he did not touch it. He asked for a new one
from the abbot. It promptly disappeared, and he did not ask
for another. Finally, knowing how dangerous it was, and knowing also that in the end he would have no choice, he sat down
with a fresh piece of parchment, and began to write again.

On the twenty-fourth day of November, in the year of Our Lord 1103, in the forests of Helmardin, there did my lord and master Karelian of Lys, knight of the Reinmark, kinsman and vassal of Gottfried the Golden, come with his companions—

He stared at the paper. He had written the same words as before: *fall thrall to the powers of darkness.* He had framed them in his mind, and formed them with his hand.

Dear Jesus . . . !

It was not a spoken prayer. He could not speak. He was sick with fear, and not the least part of his fear was a terrible fascination, a hunger to know what the next words would be. He watched his hand moving. He watched but did not believe as the words spilled across the page like uncaged birds, like bloodstains, like tears:

. . . . There did Karelian of Lys come with his companions to the castle of the Lady of the Mountain, a castle which no one finds except those whom she will welcome there. He was the greatest knight in the Reinmark, save only for the duke himself, and he had covered himself with glory in the great victory of Christendom, when we took back Jerusalem from the dark hands of the infidel. For this and many other services the duke lavished my lord Karelian with honors, and named him count of Lys.

I was his squire then, and with us travelled some twenty knights, an escort of mounted soldiers, a baggage train, and many servants. We were five days north from the crossroads at Saint Antoninus when we met a caravan of traders, ill-tempered as hungry dogs. They told us the bridge at Karlsbruck had been swept away in a storm, and they foolishly blamed it all upon the duke, our lord Gottfried. He had been seven years in the Holy Land, valiantly serving Our Lord and the Holy Cross, but they still expected him to be tending bridges in the backwoods of the Reinmark.

The merchants, with heavy wagons and valuable cargo, had no choice except to retrace their steps, and go east again to cross the river at the great bridge of Karn. We urged the count to do the same.

God, on what tiny hinges turn the lives of men! For we lingered there, he and I, on that wild grey autumn day, and he looked to the southeast, where the wagons of the traders were winding sullenly into the valley; and he looked to the north, where the high forests of Helmardin waited dark and forbidding.

"It will cost us a fortnight to go back," he said. "More, perhaps, if the weather turns. If we took the forest road, we would scarcely lose two days."

There was a stir among the men, and quick, uncertain looks. They were good men, all of them. Two of the knights, Reinhard and Otto, had been to Palestine with Karelian. Several of the soldiers, enlisted at Gottfried's court in Stavoren, had been imperial guards, and served the emperor Ehrenfried himself.

Reinhard held the rank of seneschal, and commanded the count's escort. He was a man who always spoke bluntly, without flowery words or flattery, yet under his gruff manner he was totally devoted to his master.

"Helmardin has an evil name, my lord," he said. He was a native of the north country; he knew Helmardin's reputation very well. And he was not a youth like myself, or a foolish churl like the ones we met later at the inn. He was a brave knight and a good Christian, and when I saw Karelian was not inclined to take his arguments seriously, I swallowed my own fears, and said nothing.

So many times, in the days and the weeks which followed, I made the same decision, for which I now bear an eternal burden of guilt. I chose to say nothing. Who was I, a mere squire, to question the judgment of a lord like Karelian of Lys? He was twice my age. He had fought in the service of a dozen great kings, and in Jerusalem, too. He was afraid of nothing. More than anything in the world, I wanted him to think well of me. Even when my own heart faltered at the thought of riding into Helmardin, I admired him for it. I knew the world was full of heathen creatures and their evil, but I wanted to deny my knowledge. I wanted to believe, as my father had, that there was nothing to fear in the dark except the follies of our own minds, and nothing to fear in the woods except the wolves.

So to my shame I said nothing. But Reinhard argued with him, and some others did as well. And in the end, when he saw they were serious, he smiled—he was a beautiful man when he smiled—and took a royal coin from his pouch, and tossed it playfully in the palm of his hand.

"I will leave it to God," he said. "The crown, we go by Helmardin. The cross, we go by Karn."

The coin flew and fell. We looked down and saw the silver helm of Ehrenfried shimmering on the road.

"So be it," he laughed, and wheeled his horse into the wind. He was happy with his fate, and none of us could say anything afterwards to change his mind.

He was riding to his bride.

II

HELMARDIN

Mankind is by nature wild and strange.

WOLFRAM VON ESCHENBACH

FROM THE VERY START PAUL'S HEART MISGAVE HIM—from the very moment he reached down to sweep Karelian's coin out of the dust, and followed after him into the black November hills. Nothing thereafter was quite the same. The easy talk of the soldiers began to annoy him, and the edginess of the servants annoyed him more. He found himself looking at the sky and the forest like a fugitive watching for enemies.

He was not usually given to wild superstitions; his father had made sure of it. Unlike many of his peers, the Baron von Ardiun had learned to read and write, and to look upon the world as something which could be studied and understood. He was a practical man, hardminded and hard-souled, without a trace of weakness in his being, and deeply religious in the same practical way. He laughed at most of what passed for sorcery among the common folk. Rabbits' feet and rubbish, he called it. God disposed of matters in the world, he said, not old hags with broken teeth. God decided when it would rain. God sent sicknesses to men and beasts, and God cured them. And that was the end of it.

Mostly Paul agreed with him, for he loved his father, and he feared him. But there were times when troubling questions nudged into his mind, when it seemed to him that life was stranger than his father was willing to acknowledge—stranger and much darker. He might never have done more than wonder about it, though, if he had not gone to the Holy Land. There he saw things which his father had neither seen nor dreamt of. The east was full of magic. And the east was powerful—powerful not merely in wealth and arms, but in other, more disturbing ways. More than one good knight rode to Jerusalem a devoted Christian, and was lured there into every kind of wickedness, and came home again scarcely a Christian at all.

And from the day the count's retinue left Stavoren, and journeyed farther and farther into the hinterlands, Paul found himself wondering if the Reinmark were Christian, either, in anything but name. He thought again of all those things from his childhood which his father had ignored. The old women mouthing incantations over leather boots and hearthstones and marriage beds. The strange ointments they made, the secret potions, the amulets. The Walpurgisnacht fires. The people who lived in the woods, without crops or beasts or trades, and yet never went hungry.

Then Karelian tossed a silver coin, and left his fate to fortune, and a thousand dark things seemed to ride with them now, as if invited. Black clouds, so heavy over the forests there seemed to be no heaven there at all. Black birds in great, silent flocks, wheeling and circling. Scattered farmhouses huddled in scattered patches of ill-cleared land, more hostile, somehow, than the wilderness around them. Rough folk with ragged hair and sullen faces, staring at the passing lords without a trace of human feeling in their eyes. And the wind, howling in the dead trees, tugging at his hair, endlessly snarling and laughing. It seemed to Paul the laughter of fiends, who remembered when there had been no priests here, and no empire, and who would try with all their dark power to bring an end to both.

More than once he straightened in his saddle, and wiped his face, and took himself in hand. It was November, he reminded himself; what other weather might a man expect? And peasants were a sullen, dirty lot, and always had been. As for the wind, and the birds, and the sounds in the forest, dear God, the world was full of such things; if he saw an omen in every leaf and feather he would drive himself mad.

Then they came to the inn, and his heart misgave him again.

The inn was the last habitation along this road, the last shelter they would find until they passed through the forest and arrived at Marenfeld, beyond the hills. He did not expect it to be a pleasant lodging, or even a comfortable one, but he was appalled at the gloomy look of it. It was low and roughhewn and almost windowless, cowering against the base of a heavily wooded hill. It seemed to him less a hostel for travellers than a hideout for thieves.

The innkeeper and his servants were accommodating—indeed too much so. They fell over themselves scurrying to welcome such an extraordinary guest as the new count of Lys. But it seemed to Paul they smiled too much, and much too easily. The innkeeper had an ugly laugh and a vicious scar across his cheek. A long knife hung from his belt, and he wore a thong around his neck on which were threaded several heathen charms. All the country folk wore such things, and kept on wearing them no matter what the priests said. In some villages, Paul knew, the priests started wearing them, too. The innkeepers wife was the only woman in the place; she had a hard, unsmiling face, and sullen eyes. She rarely spoke, but when she did her words were clipped and bitter.

Karelian did not seem concerned at all. Over the years he had rubbed shoulders with many kinds of people, and he accepted his surroundings with an easy worldliness. After everyone had eaten, and the beer had flowed freely for a while, he put his feet up on the crate where the innkeeper's cat was snuggled, and asked how the north had fared during the duke's long absence.

The innkeeper shrugged and said nothing.

"We met some merchants on the way," the count persisted, "who were turned back at Karlsbruck. They said many things have suffered from neglect."

The innkeeper smiled. "That be true, my lord, but we knows the duke been fightin' heathens, and winnin' back Jerusalem. And God'll shower favors on us for it, an' make us rich in heaven. Won't he, my lord?"

He spoke with perfect humility, but his hand while he spoke fingered some horrid animal thing hanging from his neck, and his eyes were not humble at all.

But Karelian showed no resentment. The cat stretched, eyed him for a moment, and wandered onto his lap. He reached to stroke it idly.

"The duke brought many riches back from the east," he said. "He's promised to make the Reinmark into the jewel of the empire."

The innkeeper crossed himself. "Pray God I live to see it," he said.

Paul shifted irritably in his chair, wishing Karelian would object to this carefully servile insolence. In the same breath he admitted that Karelian's unruffled self-possession, his refusal to make quarrels out of trifles, his willingness to listen to almost anyone at least once—all were the qualities of a wise and steady man.

"My squire is growing weary," the count said. "And in truth, so am I. We must make an early start in the morning."

"You be headin' back to Karn, then, my lord?"

"No. We'll take the forest road, and go through Helmardin. It will be a rougher journey, but a quicker one. I was already expected in Ravensbruck some days ago."

One by one the scattered voices in the room broke off, and Paul could hear the wind howling, and the crackle of fire in the hearth, and the harsh scrape of the innkeeper's iron cup as he shoved it across the table.

"Be a strange place, Helmardin," he said. "Some as goes there don't come back."

"We are well armed," Karelian said. "Any bandits who attacked a company as large and skilled as ours would be foolish indeed."

"It isn't bandits you got to fear!" This was one of the hostlers, a young man, skinny and ill-kempt as a mongrel. "Leastways, it isn't only bandits. I been in that place once, and I wouldn't never go there again, not for all the gold on the streets of Jerusalem!"

"You'd be ill-rewarded if you went for that," Karelian said dryly. "But surely many travellers must use the road, or there'd soon be no road left at all."

"Many do," the innkeeper said. "And most pass safe. But even those will tell you things as makes you shiver. There be dead men there. And veelas."

"I wouldn't mind seeing a veela," Otto said lightly. His mind was always on lechery, and he was more than a little bit drunk. "I've heard said they're pretty, and they don't wear any clothes."

A small ripple of laughter went around the room, a mixture of bawdy amusement and very real unease.

"You don't want to see a veela," the hostler said fiercely. "Not ever you don't! They'll kill you for anything. They say the woods is theirs. All I did was sit beside a tree to rest, and she come and tried to strangle me! Look!" He pulled open his rough shirt so they could see the mark on his neck, a thin, deep-cut mark like the scar from a garotte. "Best you don't go to Helmardin, my lord! It be no place for Christian men!"

Karelian considered him in silence. It was Otto's squire Dalbert, a youth Paul's age and not easily frightened, who asked the obvious question:

"Well, if she was strangling you like that, then how come you're here, and still very much alive?"

"The Virgin saved me." Quickly and reverently the hostler crossed himself. "I called out to her with my very last breath, and she come in a flash of light, golden as the sun, and the veela screamed and let me go, and flew away."

"But you were travelling alone, weren't you?" Karelian said. "Veelas are solitary creatures. I've never yet heard of one appearing among large groups of men."

"Be a great fool if she did," the innkeeper's wife said scornfully. Her husband cast her a brief, unpleasant look.

"Veelas be the least of it, my lord," he said. "There's worse things in that devil's wood. And armed men have come to grief there, too. Near fifty good knights they were, with their sergeants and men at arms along with them, in the time of Henry II, headin' for Ravensbruck after the massacre at Dorn. They rode into Helmardin with all their banners flying, an' none was ever seen again."

"The witch got *them* in her castle," one of the servants muttered darkly.

"And the bishop of Ravensbruck, too," added another.

Paul shuddered faintly. The massacre of Dorn was nearly a hundred years ago, and the loss of the emperor's men had been made into a legend. But the bishop of Ravensbruck disappeared not long before Paul was born, and his father talked about it many times. The bishop was a brave and a saintly man. Learning of pagan practices and heresies in the regions of Karlsbruck and Helmardin, he sent two of his priests to investigate. After the priests visited many villages, and spoke to many common folk, they returned by the forest road to Ravensbruck, strangely altered, and bearing an astonishing tale.

They had, they said, become lost in a fog, and after wandering for hours they came upon a splendid castle, with high ramparts and golden banners whose crests they had never seen before. They went to bang on the gates to ask where they might be, and how they might find their way back.

Inside was music, and tables laden with food, and knights and ladies in beautiful garments, and minnesingers, and wild animals which were friendly no matter how dangerous they looked, and many other wonderful things. Ruling this castle was a black-haired queen, more beautiful than any goddess, who gave them food and wine and spoke with them—but what she spoke of, they swore they could not remember. After some days, they begged to take their leave, and return to their duties. The queen gave them gifts of food, and let them go. When they stepped out of the castle gates, the forest road was before their feet, as though they had never left it, and when they looked behind where they had come, there was only woodland, shimmering with sun.

This tale they told to the bishop of Ravensbruck, who promptly ordered an escort of soldiers, and went in search of the castle. He would exorcise it, he said, and cast the woman out, for all this kingdom belonged now to Christ. Like the triumphant ravagers of Dorn, the bishop and his escort were never seen again.

But the two priests could not forget that magic place. However much they prayed and fasted and did penance, they could not free themselves from memories, or from their longing to go back again. One at last undertook a pilgrimage to Jerusalem, and died in the journey. The other withdrew to an isolated monastery, where, according to the stories, he ended his days quite mad.

"Perhaps we shouldn't go there after all, my lord."

Paul's heart leapt at the seneschal's words, but he said nothing, his face lowered as he unfastened his master's hauberk in their small, ugly room.

Reinhard was sitting with his back to the door, his arms resting lightly on his knees. He would spend the night there, perhaps lying down for a few hours of sleep, or perhaps not; but no enemy would enter the room without killing him first. A good man, Reinhard was, loyal and solid as a rock. But he was no match for Karelian in mind or in spirit, and he never would be—a fact which pleased Paul very much, though it shamed him to admit it.

"You're very serious about this," Karelian said.

"I fear no enemy I can see, my lord," the knight said stoutly. "I think you know it well—"

"I do," Karelian interrupted him, smiling faintly.

"But these evil things . . . ! What harm would be done if we returned to Karn? Count Arnulf won't blame you for the delay, knowing the bridge is gone. And besides, the wedding won't be till after Twelfth night."

The count sat on his bed, and Paul dropped to one knee to begin tugging off his boots.

"Faithful Pauli," Karelian said to him. "You haven't said a word, but you also think we should go back to Karn, don't you?"

Paul faltered, staring at him. There was warmth in Karelian's eyes, but there was also a kind of weariness—the weariness of a man who was always stronger than the men around him, and who sometimes got tired of it.

There is no reason in the world to go back to Karn. That was what Paul wanted to say. *We are men, we are warriors, we are lords. Are we going to be scared off by wood nymphs and ghosts?*

And in another part of himself, he wanted even more desperately to say: *Oh, please, my good lord, let's turn back! It's dangerous there, and we've no reason to go, and everyone's afraid . . .*!

"It's for your lordship to decide," he said. He had meant to speak firmly like a brave knight eager to follow wherever his liege might go. But his voice was small and dry, and gave him away completely.

"I see," Karelian said. "Well then, listen, both of you, and I'll tell you something, and maybe you'll rest easier for it. Before we left the Holy Land, I went to see a mage in Acre, a man whom other knights had spoken of—"

Paul sank onto his heels, appalled. "A Saracen?" he whispered.

"He told me many extraordinary things, some of which I knew already, and some of which I still don't understand. And he also told me this: I might go safely where other men saw danger, and I should most fear danger where other men believed they were safe. So . . . ." He smiled, and tousled Paul's hair lightly. "I don't think we'll have much to fear in Helmardin."

"You trust the prophecy of a Saracen, my lord?" Reinhard asked harshly.

Karelian stood up, his easy mood broken in a breath, and the seneschal hurried on: "I'm only thinking of your welfare, my lord—"

"And so am I," the count said grimly. He walked to the window, staring out at nothing, for the night was overcast and black. "I've looked for guidance in many places over the years, my friend, and I found precious little of it anywhere. I'll take it where I can get it."

Quite suddenly Paul felt cold, as though Karelian had flung back the shutters, and the icy night was spilling in.

"Surely God has guided you in all things, my lord," he whispered.

Karelian turned then, and laughed. "Really? If he has, then men have little good to hope for in this world."

It was a terrible thing to say. Paul dropped his eyes. His master was weary, and probably a little drunk. Even the noblest and most necessary wars would leave their mark on a man, and move him sometimes to say harsh and bitter things. Only later, looking back, did Paul understand: Karelian was already falling into the doom which awaited him. Year after careless year he had disarmed himself with doubt and worldliness, and he rode into Helmardin an easy target for his enemy. Like a rich man, Paul thought bitterly, or a stranger in a foreign city, walking late along the harbor without a sword.

It was still dark when they mounted for the road. In the harsh light of torches Karelian's face was drawn and weary, and his mood was extraordinarily dark. Nothing was said about turning south again, and Paul knew nothing would be. Half asleep, the soldiers loaded the pack animals and climbed into their saddles. Reinhard approached the count, rubbing warmth back into his hands, his breath turning into coils of white fog.

"Everything is ready my lord."

For a tiny moment Paul thought he might protest one last time, but then, as if anticipating the possibility, Karelian paused, one hand on his horse's bridle, and met his vassal's eyes. The expression in his own was unyielding. *Not another word, Reini, if you value my good will. Not one more word . . . .*

This, too, was Karelian: a man whose smiles and easy words belied an astonishing hardness of resolve. He was the youngest of seven sons, bred to high rank and dismal prospects, living in war camps and trenches before Paul of Ardiun had been born. His father was Helmuth Brandeis, the margrave of Dorn, a lineage known equally for its excellent bloodlines and its unpredictable loyalties. Helmuth quarreled with the duke, and was reconciled with him again, more times than anyone could remember. Each quarrel left him poorer. Nonetheless he married three times, and had numerous children. By the time Karelian was born there were already six strapping older brothers waiting to gobble up the margravate's lands, the margravate's captaincies and baileys, the margravate's carefully arranged marriages with its neighbors' carefully guarded daughters. Karelian was going to have to make his own way in the world.

Go be a monk, his father told him. *There is nothing for you here.*

If that is so, demanded the lad of twelve or thereabouts, *why did you bother to beget me?* From this bit of insolence he acquired three broken ribs, and a taste for soldiering in other lands.

He fought Angevins in Italy, Vikings in Normandy, Capetians in Flanders. And so many others. If he gathered together all the banners he had followed, he said once, they would cover all the walls in the great hall of Stavoren.

Then Pope Urban came in splendor through the empire, calling on the warriors of Christendom to gather and march east, to take back the Holy Land and destroy the infidel. One of the first to take the cross was Gottfried the Golden, duke of the Reinmark. And a scattering of the duchy's free knights returned home to join him, Karelian among them. He was thirty-one then, and tired of the small and pointless wars which Europe's princes kept fighting among themselves. He wanted something better. He wanted a place in the world, and land, and a future with something more in it than wandering and blood.

And he had it now, earned by his own hand. He had wealth, and a splendid reputation. He had the county of Lys, a territory larger and richer than the one his brother inherited. Helmuth, the weathervane of Dorn, was dead; and though his eldest son, Ludolf, was margrave of Dorn, it was Karelian who was seen now as the leader, the favored one, the ornament of the house of Brandeis.

He had travelled a long way, but he had left many things behind him on the journey—all his innocence, and most of his faith in God, and any trace of willingness to be directed by other men. He made his choices carefully, with a good deal of thought, but once he made them, it was wiser to stay out of his way.

And he had made his choice in this. Having survived perils which the simple folk of these highlands had never dreamt of, having grown used to judging danger by the standards of the battlefield, he saw no reason not to make a short journey through Helmardin, and meet his bride, and get on with his promising new life. Paul bowed faintly and helped him to mount, and they rode silently into a day over which the sun would never rise.

Midday had barely passed when it began to snow. At first the flakes were thick and wet, and there was an eerie peacefulness in the low-hanging sky. The soldiers riding guard ahead were vague and silent shadows, fading and reappearing like horsemen in a dream.

But the land rose, and bare summits emerged here and there from the forest, and the wind began to cut like knives. They rode single-file then, bent low in their saddles, their hands and faces numbing in the cold. Grey-black clouds swept overhead, advancing and dissolving like swift-moving armies, more and still more of them rolling in behind. The trees, bare as they were, leaned in the force of the cruel wind, and howled. The innkeeper's words echoed in Paul's memory: *There be dead men there, and veelas . . . .*

He took little comfort in the fact that he rode with armed men. He would have felt safer among a horde of pilgrims, in hemp shirts with crosses sewn across their backs. But in Stavoren Karelian had removed all of his insignia from the great crusade. He wore the colors of Lys now. His shield and his high banners bore a crest of Brandeis: a black tree without leaves, poised against a pale December sky.

Paul himself had painted the shield. He thought it a strange device, that winter tree, rather stark and gloomy for so splendid a lord, for a man who always outfitted himself like a prince. Even now, on this rough journey, Karelian wore a surcoat of embroidered blue samite, a dark velvet cloak lined and trimmed with ermine, and the finest boots which could be made. And all the trappings of his horse were of satin and silver.

So Paul had asked him, back in Stavoren: *What is this crest, my lord, and why have you chosen it?*

It was, Karelian said, the winter tree of Dorn. There was a legend around it, a very old legend from pagan times. Once a magical tree had grown in the valley. It flowered in the wintertime and bore fruit in the snow. No one hungered then; the rains were soft; everyone laughed and life was long and good.

Then evil men rose up and tried to steal the tree, and so it was carried away and hidden; no one knew where. But one day, the legend said, it would be restored, and Dorn would be a paradise again.

And Paul was content. For surely this was the story of Eden lost by sin, and of the cross which restored men to everlasting life. If the story was so old, and found among a pagan people, well, it only proved how God's truth was present everywhere in the world.

Or so he had believed in Stavoren . . . .

He drew rein briefly, flexed his feet in their icy stirrups and wiped the snow from his face. It was full day now, the highlands murderous with storm. And as sane and sensible a man as he believed himself to be, he knew the storm had not happened by chance. It was not natural. Nothing here was natural, or Christian, or safe. Even Karelian's wind-flung banners looked different to him now. The winter tree which he had painted so lovingly on his master's shield was not a symbol of the cross at all. It was something from the wood of Helmardin.

He should have been glad when they left the highlands and began to move again into deep forest, where the road was shielded by close and thickly wooded hills. Yet, perversely, he felt still more afraid. A dozen times he thought he saw shapes moving in the snow-blind forest. Whether they were manshapes or beasts he was not sure, but every time he saw them they were closer.

So they travelled for many hours, and as the last light began to fail Karelian ordered lanterns to be carried all along the convoy, so no one might be lost. But he did not order a halt, and Paul was glad. He wanted nothing now, neither rest nor food nor shelter; he wanted only to be gone from here forever.

Once, for a while, when the storm seemed to have lessened for a time, some of the men began to sing. It was beautiful and strange, at once an act of defiance against the forest, and an offering to appease its anger. But the night was fiercely cold, and growing colder. Paul was afraid they soon might have to camp because it would become impossible to ride. The songs fell away, and the storm closed utterly on Helmardin.

He came alert with a start. He had not dozed, merely lost himself a little in his thoughts, and in the easy rhythm of the horse's gait. He looked up abruptly as the animal stopped. Karelian and his advance guard were clustered in front of him, blocking the road. Beyond, lovely as paradise, rose a shimmering, snow-coiled haze of lights.

Marenfeld! he thought, and for one blind and beautiful second he believed it. His body believed it, flooding with a sweat of relief, even while his mind was recoiling with bewilderment, with the terrible realization that it was not Marenfeld, it could not possibly be Marenfeld. They had passed no farms, no open fields; they were still deep in the forest. And no small, huddled peasant village showed lights like these in the depths of a wilderness, neither Marenfeld nor any other human place . . . !

He wiped his arm across his face, and forced his eyes to focus against the swirling snow. The lights outlined a fortress—a small fortress, with a single tower, with bright windows and flaming torches at its gates.

Karelian seemed as dumbfounded as the rest of them, but he recovered faster, and spoke grimly to the seneschal:

"What's the meaning of this, Reinhard?"

"As God is my witness, my lord, I don't know. I did nothing except follow the road."

Karelian did not answer. He stared at the fortress, and turned once or twice in his saddle, looking at the empty night around them as though there might be some explanation there. When the lantern's shimmer caught his face, Paul saw bits of snow clinging to his eyebrows, and ridges of it matting on the hair left uncovered by his helmet.

"Do you know this place, then?" he asked.

"There is no castle on the road to Marenfeld, my lord," the seneschal said. He kept his voice carefully even, quieting his own fear. "There never has been, save for those the stories tell of. Those which are . . . unnatural."

"We've been abroad for seven years," Karelian said.

"Aye, my lord. But I don't think we are looking at something new."

Silence closed over them, broken only by the wind and the weary shiftings of their horses. Karelian looked again towards the lighted castle. Something drew him towards it, Paul saw, something quite small perhaps, something as small as curiosity, the willingness he had always had to see another kingdom or turn another card in the deck. *How have we been lured here, and why, and how will I ever know unless I go inside?*

Reinhard saw it, too, and reached quickly to seize the bridle of Karelian's horse.

"My lord, I beg you, let's turn back! Whatever this place is, it's a place of evil! It can be nothing else! Let's go back!"

"You can't even tell me where we are," Karelian replied grimly. "To what shall we go back? It's hardly a night to be wandering about like lost children in the woods."

"My lord, I beg you—"

"Enough! Ride on, seneschal, before we are all frozen in our saddles."

"As you wish, my lord," Reinhard said, and led the way.

The castle appeared to be built into the base of a hill, as though the builders cared more for shelter from the wind than safety from their enemies. The gates were open, but a small group of armed men stood guard in front of them. One of these stepped forward as the convoy approached, and bowed very deeply.

"Welcome, my lords!" he said. He gestured broadly, generously, towards the courtyard within. "It's my lady's pleasure to offer you shelter on so bitter a night."

"What place is this?" Karelian asked.

"It's the castle of Car-Iduna, my lord. A small fortress, as you can see, but well appointed. We lack for very little."

"I regret I've never heard the name," Karelian said.

The man made a small, appeasing gesture. "It doesn't matter. You are welcome just the same."

"I thank you for your offer," the count said. "But we're bound for Marenfeld, and should be on our way. Where is the road which leads from hence?"

"You have travelled it, my lord."

For a moment even Karelian could find no suitable reply. He wiped his face with his arm, a brief gesture of frustration.

"We set out on the forest road from the south," he said, "and we didn't turn from it. And for the past hundred years or so, that road has led through Helmardin and come out on the other side. At Marenfeld."

"And so it still does, my lord. But you are no longer on that road."

"Then," Karelian said wearily, "will you tell us how we might return to it?"

"No one will pass through Helmardin tonight, my lord." The man gestured again towards the courtyard. "Come within, and take shelter. When the storm clears, we will guide you wherever you wish to go."

"As you guided me here?" Karelian said darkly.

The man said nothing, but simply waited, his manner as unyielding as it was polite.

For a moment, the count of Lys still hesitated, glancing back at the tense cluster of his men. He was spent and hungry; they all were; and the cold was growing steadily more unbearable. He seemed almost to shrug, as if saying to himself: *Well, what of it? Tonight even hell might be a nicer place than this empty road . . . .*

He nodded, and urged his horse through the open gates. Paul followed numbly, his body icy with dread, unable to find words to protest or strength to pray. Inside the courtyard, servants flocked around them, taking their horses. One of them flung open the castle doors, and stood aside as they entered.

A stairway lay within, curving upwards in a graceful sweep. From the chambers above Paul could hear music. He felt the rush of warm air, pressing his icy clothing against his body. He heard steps, and stood immobile, rooted to the stone.

Approaching them was a woman, the most exquisitely beautiful woman Paul had ever seen. She was tall and black-haired, and she wore a gown which seemed to change color with every shift of motion, shimmering blue and green and amber in the torchlight. Later, as the night wore on, he would notice a thousand tiny details: how long her nails were, and how dark her eyes. The gold belt she wore was studded with small black stones—stones which were not even pretty, and so must have been magical. She wore a bracelet carved with runes, and seven rings, each with a different jewel. Those things, and many others, he noticed later. Now he was aware only of the woman herself, the female, moving smoothly as a panther down the dark steps, torchlight glinting on her hair, her gown liquid against her body, her breasts bared to take a saint's breath away—all her beauty offered like a gift, and in the same instant demanding worship, like the smile she flashed at Karelian, like the pale ringed hand she held out for him to kiss.

"My lord of Lys, you are truly welcome here!"

Paul was staring like a witless boy but no one paid him any heed, least of all Karelian. He bowed deeply over the glittering hand, and drank in the image before him as though it were wine.

"You have the advantage, my lady."

"I always do, if I can manage it," she said wryly.

"So be it. But will you tell me, perhaps, why you've led me and my company astray?"

"It's a cruel night, as you have seen. Even the bravest woodland creatures are huddling in their dens, and some of them will die. Have I led you astray my lord, or to shelter?"

"Both, I suspect," Karelian said. He bowed again, smiling faintly. "And for the latter, at least, I thank you."

She gave a soft laugh, and met his eyes. Paul was not worldly in the ways of men and women, but even he could read the frank sexual speculation in that look, the coolly hinted possibility. *I think I'm going to like you, and if I do . . . .*

Then the woman turned to Paul, greeting him by name, and

Reinhard as well, offering welcome to them all. A dark-eyed dwarf of a man had padded quietly down the steps behind her, unnoticed by anyone until she placed her guests into his care.

His name was Marius. It was the only name in Car-Iduna which Paul would ever learn, and he never forgot it.

III

THE LADY OF THE MOUNTAIN

Such a slaughter of pagans no one has ever seen or heard of;
the pyres they made were like pyramids.

GESTA FRANCORUM—*Anonymous Chronicle of the First Crusade*

WHAT WORDS ARE THERE TO TELL OF CAR-IDUNA? It was full of witch-craft. I do not know what the others saw at first, when we followed the lady and her servants into the great hall. I think Karelian saw nothing but the black silk of her hair, and her splendid body swaying in the torchlight.

I saw a world which was not God's.

All my life, from my earliest childhood, I lived surrounded by a consciousness of God. Churches dotted the countryside, monastery bells rang the hours, windows were painted with saints, and walls were hung with crucifixes. A man did not eat, or lay down to sleep, or greet his neighbors, without mentioning God's name. On the road to Jerusalem, we carried the image of our faith upraised in our hands, and stitched on our clothing, and painted on our shields; we were a sea of crosses sweeping across the land.

Never, until I stood inside the walls of Car-Iduna, had I felt myself to be out of God's presence. Out of his favor, yes, but never out of his *presence*. But now I did. Nothing in my understanding could recognize this place, or name it. My throat was dust, and my belly knotted like a rag wrung out to dry. I had been among the Saracens, and I knew them well—better, indeed, than I ever wanted to. And I knew a Saracen would tremble walking into Car-Iduna, just as I did, and for the same reasons. This place was older than Mahomet their prophet, older than Jesus of Nazareth, older than Moses and the law, older even than Satan whom we imagined was the oldest of God's enemies . . . .

It took all the strength Paul had to put the quill down, to link his hands and press his face against their hardness and close his eyes. To say five *Pater Nosters* and open them again, and read what he had written.

It was as he feared. The words were quite clear and, in a certain sense, quite true. Those had been his thoughts, or something very near to his thoughts, his instinctive reaction to the castle in Helmardin. But they were not thoughts he meant to write. He hid the parchment carefully away and went for a walk in the fields.

It was April, the easter month, the month when a man's soul rejoiced in the resurrection of the Lord, and when his body kept drawing him to hell. Especially now, since he had begun to write, everything seemed to remind him of his flesh, and of its terrible possibilities.

Why were men so weak? he wondered. So pathetically, disgustingly weak that the smallest, most innocent thing could turn their minds to sin, and make their loins flood with shame? A dog licking his hand. The smell of sweat on a beggar woman reaching out for a gift of bread. A word in a book. The warmth of the sun pressing through his habit. The color of a stranger's tunic. The sight of a peach. Even pain, finally. Even those penances whose very objective was to silence the flesh, could awaken it instead. A man took his foul body everywhere he went; he could not escape it in prayer, or even in sleep. Dear God, what had Jesus lowered himself to, taking on a vile existence such as this?

But Jesus incarnate was not like us; he did not sin, or ever wish to sin; his body was pure, and our bodies must become like his . . . .

It had never been easy for him to control his desires, but he had, in these last years, grown a little calmer, a little less vulnerable. Age helped, as did the routine of monastery life, the endless repetition of the same labors, the same prayers, the same passing of the hours and the seasons. It made life orderly; it kept the mind occupied and the body too exhausted for lust.

Now this . . . this unbearable going back into time, to his youth and to a history filled with evil. It would have been difficult for him even if he had been in control of it, but he was not. By determining which memories he would record, that accursed quill was actually determining which memories he would remember.

Like Karelian's splendid looks: they were something he had quite forgotten over the years. What did it matter if a man's body was beautiful, if his soul was corrupt? Now, one by one, images kept tumbling out of the silent places of Paul's mind, nudged free, like desire itself, by the smallest passing thing. Knights would ride along the valley road to Karn, too far away to recognize, nothing but a bit of dust and shimmer in the distance, and he would remember the first time he saw Karelian in Acre, a proud, glittering centaur of a man, reaching over a wall to snatch an orange as he rode. A young pilgrim would stop at the monastery, or a local lord would bring his son to have him schooled, and Paul would remember: Karelian's hair was the same tawny color, and it hung to his shoulders exactly so, glinting in the torchlight . . . .

He walked for a very long time, until his feet were sodden with spring mud and numb with cold. It was Sunday, and across the river which bounded the monastery's property he could see serfs enjoying their few hours of freedom, chasing a ball around, yelling at each other, urged on by laughing women who did not hesitate to join in the game themselves now and then, simply so everyone might end in a tangle in the grass.

The people, he thought sadly, never changed. They listened to the priests. They bowed their heads and made their penances. And then a glass of rough beer, or the sound of a fife, or an hour in the summer sun, and it was as though the priests had never spoken. The Church struggled and fought and sacrificed and prayed, and the great body of men just went on living as though it weren't there.

And the evils of Car-Iduna were still unbound, still stalking the Reinmark from the wood of Helmardin. So much had been destroyed, so many good men brought to ruin, and Car-Iduna was still there. *She* was still there, her sorcery coiled in the forests and in his cell, waiting to entangle him again.

He reached the brook and halted, turning back the way he came. Woods blocked even the spire of the monastery from view. He felt utterly alone, and more afraid than he had been for many years.

It was bad enough to face his personal memories. But what of the other thing, the thing he dared not write about, not in this chronicle or any other, not even for the pope? What if she compelled those words upon his quill? What if she forced him to betray his secret, a secret he was never meant to know?

He would have to quit writing, that was all. Somehow he would have to quit.

THE HALL OF CAR-IDUNA SHIMMERED WITH LIGHT. There were torches everywhere, and voices. Many people were gathered there, yet I have not even a vague recollection of their number; and although we remained for more than a day, I can call to mind only a handful of faces. So powerful was the sorcery of the place that it could steal a man's soul, and yet elude his reason like a dream.

I understand such things now, after years of reflection. But at the time, walking pale with terror at my lord's back, I was thinking only of how we might escape unharmed.

"We must neither sleep here," Reinhard warned us, "nor touch any food or drink." But Karelian did not heed his wisdom, nor did Reinhard himself nor did any of our company except me. As soon as we were inside Car-Iduna's high-domed hall, servants came and plied us with cups of heated wine and offerings of food. The men were hungry and cold, and the Lady of the Mountain very gracious. There was nothing menacing which they could see, no trolls or dragons or headless men, and so they imagined they were safe.

Karelian took the cup, and thanked her, raising it in a gallant salute, and then he drank. Reinhard, with a small shrug of resignation, followed his lead. If his lord would hang, well then, he would hang beside him. And so one by one the company was lost to magic.

The dwarf Marius showed us to the chambers which had been set aside for us, where we might leave our belongings. Then he took us to the baths, which were tiled and had heated water. Though it was common in the east, this was a luxury which I think no lord in Europe enjoyed except the emperor, in his splendid palace at Aachen. All the men marvelled at it, but to me it seemed only further proof of the castle's fearful magic.

We were given fresh clothing to wear, all of it finely made. For Karelian there was a tunic embroidered with the emblem of the winter tree—beautifully embroidered on white linen and trimmed with cloth of gold. This gift pleased him very much, and he said again how gracious the lady was, and how he must find some gift for her in return. In the end he gave her everything he had.

Marius took us back to the great hall. There would be a feast tonight, he said, and revelry and songs; he urged us to enjoy all which might be offered us. Only remember, he added, remember always that his lady was a queen.

The hall was round and domed, and I have often wondered if the castle was a castle at all, or a cavern hollowed into the earth. Perhaps the towers and lights we had seen were only phantoms, and we walked now within the belly of the earth. Plants grew full of flowers, as though it were summer. Again and again as we moved among the gathering we saw wild creatures—foxes, snakes, strange birds who thought nothing of landing on a man's shoulder and chirping in his ear. But if they were truly creatures, tamed by the lady's magic, or if they were humans changed into beasts, I did not know, and scarcely dared to wonder.

We had been back only a short time when the ceremony began, and the clamor of voices fell still. From an open doorway on the far side of the hall, opposite from where we had entered, came the sound of music: the slow beat of a drum, the sad, sweet cry of a reed pipe, the steady shiver of a drone. It was beautiful music, beautiful and strange, and utterly hypnotic. A procession was moving out of the inner chamber, slowly, with great solemnity. First came the musicians, dressed in red and silver, and then a body of warriors, with painted helmets and shields. I will not call them knights, for some were women, and none of them were Christian, but they were splendidly dressed and armed. Behind these came dancers, all young people wearing light tunics, their hair unbound and their feet bare.

And then . . . . Even now my mind falters. I am fifty years old now, a learned man and a monk, and yet I look at the memories which coil in my mind and ask if they are not, perhaps, the leavings of an incubus. For how could those things which I saw in Car-Iduna have been possible, even in such a place, even with God's permission?

Nine women came from the sanctuary beyond the great hall, carrying a bier, and on the bier was a Chalice. Or so I call it for its

shape, but how can such a sacred word be used to describe so dark
a thing? It was neither gold nor silver, nor even bronze or fine pottery.
It looked as if it were made of mud, and yet it shimmered like a jewel.
When it passed close to me I saw that it was scabbed with moss and
hung with threads of vine.

The women who bore it were dressed in long silver robes. They
were all old women, and as they carried the bier towards us they also
turned it, forming its path into a spiral. Each person in the lady's
company bowed as it passed. We stood rigid, frozen in doubt and peril;
then Karelian, always the diplomat, bowed his head as well. Out of
sheer terror I did the same.

I have no excuse for doing so, as I have no excuse for my many
silences. I knew the thing held within it a terrible power, and I was
not mistaken. For the lady led us then to share in her feast, and to
our great amazement the servants needed only to hold our wine cups
before the Chalice, and they would fill with amber wine, or to lay
our plates before it, and they would be laden with the finest foods,
with anything we wished. Our men all marvelled at this, too, and not
one of them thought to ask: By what power is this done? Who does
this lady and her Chalice serve?

We sat at one of several long tables in the hall, Karelian at the
lady's right hand, the seneschal at her left. Our knights and various
members of her court filled the length of it. She was, of course, the
undisputed center of attention—especially Karelian's attention. She
was witty, and spoke freely on any subject she pleased, much as the
women of Constantinople had done, who dared to express opinions
even on the conduct of war. But she had a breadth of knowledge
greater than they, a knowledge which no woman could possess except
by witchcraft.

She would say astonishing, reckless things, and then laugh, waiting
for Karelian's response, pleased if he answered her well, and then
baiting him again. It was a game of seduction, I understood that, but
it was a great deal more. She was studying him, learning the ways of
his mind and finding his weaknesses. And he was trying to do the
same. For all the toasts and flattery, for all the occasions he took to
comment on her beauty or her cleverness, there was an edge sometimes
to his words, barely concealing the unspoken question: *Who are you,
and what do you want from me?*

It was an unequal contest, as such contests always are between
women and their prey. My lord was a gifted man. Gottfried ranked

him among the best of his vassals, not merely for his skill with arms, but also for his wisdom, his ability to speak well and to manoeuvre through the traps of other men's words. But here his wisdom failed him. From the start he was only half thinking of his danger, and by the night's end all he wanted was to please her, and win her to his bed.

And I could do nothing except watch it happen. In most any other hall I would have had my squire's duties, to carve my lord's meat and pour his wine, and fetch whatever he might want for his comfort. But here even the humblest of our company was placed at the tables like an honored guest. The lady's own people replenished our plates, and kept the table's great flagons filled with wine, and poured them, and carried away the bones. So I could do nothing but linger nearby almost sick with hunger at the sight of so much splendid food.

Reinhard, who had warned us not to eat, sat opposite Karelian, stuffing himself from a plate laden with different meats, roasted or stewed or baked with stuffing, and thick bread heavy with rich grains, and pastries filled with fruits. The wine flowed like water. I saw one man after another take his first sip of it and then, startled with pleasure, raise his cup eagerly for more. I was tempted to join them. What harm could there be in it? Surely food and drink were only food and drink. Surely these worldly and experienced men would not share in this feast if it were truly dangerous.

But I knew better, in my heart. I knew men were weak. I knew that experience in the world and understanding of the spirit were not the same things at all. So I held my ground, desolate and sad, while the feast passed before my eyes and disappeared.

No one bothered me about it. Once Karelian looked at me with concern, and wrapped a slab of meat in a piece of bread, and offered it to me. "Here, lad, you'll feel better if you eat a little."

I found the strength to smile. "Are you doing squire's service for me now, my lord?"

"Yes, if I must. I don't want you falling off your horse tomorrow."

"The first law of soldiering, Pauli," Reinhard said. "Never miss a chance for a good meal; God knows when you'll get another one."

And you were the one who warned us against all this, you weak-willed backwoods hireling . . . !

"I am troubled in my stomach, my lord," I said. "If I eat I fear I will disgrace you. And myself."

Karelian shrugged, and popped the food into his own mouth, and thereafter I was left in peace. He was a generous master, but he was not very interested in me just now. He ate, and sparred with the lady, and paused now and then to offer dainties to a slinky grey cat which had climbed onto the bench beside him. He was fond of small animals; and this one clearly was the lady's favorite.

"Bastet likes you," she said. "And she hardly likes anyone. She thinks she owns Car-Iduna, and everyone else is here by her leave."

"Even you?"

"Even me."

"Perhaps we should take her to Aachen, and let her try being empress."

"She wouldn't want to be bothered," the lady said, laughing.

Her laugh was soft and throaty. I wondered how old she was. This close, I could see the odd strand of grey in her black hair, and tiny lines at the corners of her eyes. Karelian's age, I thought, give or take five years.

My mother's age as well.

Nothing could have been more shattering than to think of my mother here, my mother with her high-necked gown girdled with cords and hung with heavy keys, her hair in a veil, her voice steady and her step even, moving through the manor house of Ardiun with absolute serenity. I had never seen her dressed like a wanton, or ever imagined the possibility of it. Nor could I imagine such laughter from her mouth, or such a look in her eyes as was now in the lady's, raising her cup to answer Karelian's salute. The gentle touching of their goblets was a ritual kiss. Deliberately she turned the cup to drink from the spot which had touched his.

He noticed, of course, and so did I, but no one else did. They were all too busy eating and swilling wine, and marvelling at everything, and wanting to impress her with their tales of our conquests in the east.

And I, fool that I was, encouraged the talk. For here, I thought, was something which could remind Karelian of his honor and his Christian faith. And I loved the stories, too, all those marvellous tales of a glory I had missed. I was too young to go—only twelve when they marched for Constantinople in the spring of '96. Although some very young lads went as pages and servants, my father would not hear of it. "There will always be another war," he said. It was true, but there would never be this particular war again, and I grieved bitterly to be left behind. When a second contingent left, four years later, I was with them, squire to a calm, aging knight who died of dysentery in his saddle, refusing to be carried, or to stop and rest until he had seen the walls of Jerusalem.

By then, of course, everything was over but some skirmishes. Many knights were already on their way home when I arrived. Duke Gottfried stayed another two years, helping the young king of Jerusalem secure his new realm, and I took service with his kinsman Karelian. I had missed the war, but at least I had won a place with one of its greatest heroes. For however modest Karelian's fortunes were when he left the Reinmark, he was spoken of now in the same breath as the leaders of the expedition: Raymond of Toulouse and Bohemond of Taranto and Duke Gottfried himself. Everyone told stories of his courage—how he saved Gottfried's life in Antioch, how he fought off an ambush of Seljuk Turks with only a handful of men, how he always had a plan for a crisis or a word of comfort for a wounded comrade. There was no end of the stories, but Karelian himself would never tell them. He would talk about the journey, sometimes, and about Constantinople, a city which had awed him with its splendor. But of the conquest, and his part in it, he never spoke at all.

Maybe now, I thought, maybe now, to impress this woman, he would do so . . . if the conversation ever got past the glitter of Byzantium.

"Until you've seen a city like Constantinople," he said, "you can't imagine it. I don't know how many people live there, but I am sure it's more than in the whole of the Reinmark. The churches are like palaces, and the libraries . . . ! I didn't know there were so many books in the world."

"Do you read?" she asked.

He made a small, self-deprecating gesture. "Only a little. When we settle in Lys, Paul has promised to teach me more. Though I fear he may be too gentle a teacher, and let me get away with too many mistakes." He smiled at me, and I ached with gratitude and admiration.

"I'm sure you will learn easily, my lord," I said. "But I'll throw a tantrum for you now and then, if you wish."

One of the lady's followers, sitting next to Reinhard, had a predictable question of her own.

"And the women of Byzantium? What are they like?"

"They are beautiful," Reinhard said. "But they meddle in everything."

"The emperor's daughter reads and speaks five languages, and knows a great deal about the world," Karelian said. "And she's not even twenty."

"And what did she think of all of you?" the lady wondered.

Karelian laughed. "What she thought I don't know. But her father looked at us as though we had just come riding down from the steppes, dressed in skins and drinking out of skulls. I think he sat awake more than one night, wondering if the medicine the pope sent him wasn't worse than the disease. All he'd asked for, after all, was a body of knights to help defend his eastern borders. He never asked for anyone to conquer Jerusalem. And here were fifty thousand armed men at his gates, and God alone knows how many unarmed common folk, and more than enough thugs. He was afraid his own territories might be at risk, and I must say he had cause, considering that the first thing Bohemond did when we crossed into Asia was carve out a piece of old Byzantium for himself."

"Bohemond!" Otto almost spat the Frenchman's name. "All Bohemond ever wanted out of any of this was profit."

"He wasn't alone there," Karelian replied. "And God knows the emperor could see it well enough. He would only let us into the city in groups of six, like hounds on a leash."

"It was good in a way, though," Reinhard added, "for he was in such a hurry to get rid of us, he loaded us with provisions, and we were across the Bosporus and on our way faster than we ever thought was possible."

"Farewell, Constantinople," the lady murmured.

"Yes," Karelian said. "I wish I had seen more of it."

"And more, no doubt, of those beautiful, clever, meddlesome women."

"Well, perhaps. But there are women in the Reinmark just as lovely, and just as clever. And, I suspect, even more meddlesome."

She smiled. "What did they wear?"

"Wear?"

"The Byzantine women. I'm told they are very elegant."

"Oh, they are, but I can't remember. They wore clothes . . . Paul, you notice things like that. What did they wear?"

The woman was laughing, and saved me from having to reply.

"I fear, my lord count, your only interest in a woman's clothing lies in the pleasure of taking it off."

He considered that for a moment, taking a sip of his wine.

"The more lovely a woman is in fine raiment, my lady, the more lovely still she is without it. It would be a foolish man who would look at the leaves rather than the flower."

She saluted him again with her cup, and with her eyes, and I looked away.

"So the duke of Lorraine is now the king of Jerusalem," she mused. "What a curious idea."

"He is king in fact only," Otto said, "not in name. He says he will never wear a crown of gold where our Saviour wore a crown of thorns."

"And how long will that last?" she asked dryly. "For as long as the heirs of Saint Peter made their living catching fish?"

Many of the knights smiled at her jest, for though it was irreverent, they were Germans, and they had no great love for the Franks, and even less for the Roman pope.

"It won't last," Karelian said. "And neither will the kingdom of Jerusalem itself. We might as well have gone to the beaches of Osten, and built ourselves an empire out of sand."

Reinhard stared at him appalled, drank ferociously, and wiped his hand across his mouth.

"That's—that's unthinkable, my lord! God himself gave us back Jerusalem—"

"No, Reini," the count said flatly. "Saracen squabbling gave us Jerusalem—along with some blind luck, and the advantage of surprise. They never took us seriously until it was too late. But they will from now on; you may be sure of it. We hold a string of cities along the coast; they hold an empire of hinterland. They will drive us out, and when they do, then the Christians who live there will have cause to weep. They didn't, before we came. Our last gift to the east will be the ruin of the people we claim we went to save."

I could not believe what I had heard. None of us could.

"If this is so, my lords," the lady murmured, "then why ever was it done?"

"It was done for God," Reinhard said. "And I beg to differ with you, my lord Karelian. What has been built these years in the Holy Land will last until the end of the world."

He paused, turning eagerly towards the woman.

"My lady, I don't know if you're a Christian—"

"I am not. But go on."

"We marched for three years, my lady. We starved. We burned with thirst, and choked with dust, and slogged through mud, and shiv-

ered with ague and cold. We left dead behind us with every league
we travelled. Only one thing kept us going—"

"As many things kept us going as there were men among us,"
Karelian said. "Speak for yourself, my good friend."

Reinhard flushed faintly, and plunged on: "I wanted to see the
Holy City, to walk upon its stones. To kneel by the sepulchre where
Our Lord was laid, and doing so, to know I was at peace with God.
The day we took the city, when the fighting was over, we went—I
don't know how many of us there were, lady, it was a sea of shields
and crosses!—we went to the Holy Sepulchre and prayed there. Before
we looked for food or drink or rest, we went to pray. I have never
seen so many men weep, my lady, and I have never in my life known
such joy."

"They say every man who goes to Jerusalem makes a sacred vow
there," she said.

"It is true, lady," Reinhard said. "I vowed I would go faithfully
to Mass, and pay my tithes, and live by the commandments. And I
never cared much about such things before. Our lives are different
now. The whole world is different now."

Karelian drained his wine.

"Did you make a vow in Jerusalem, my lord count?" the woman
asked him softly.

"Yes."

"Will you speak of it?"

He looked up, not at her, but at Reinhard. "I swore if I left there
alive, I would never take part in such an enterprise again, nor help
any other man to do so, not even with so much as a wooden staff or
a copper penny."

No one spoke; the crackle of torches and the cheerful talk of
guests at other tables was suddenly and painfully loud.

"It's the only vow I ever made," he went on, "and I didn't make
it in a church. I made it in a gutter, kneeling in a lake of blood.
Everything around me was dead, even the dogs and the cats. We killed
everything that crossed our path. The next day, the bodies were piled
outside the city like cordwood, and the piles were as high as the walls.
Do you remember, Reinhard?"

"My lord, it was war—!"

"Yes. It was war. A war called up by God, and fought with his
blessing. When you went to pray, I walked back through the city. Back
the way we came, through the streets where we fought. Alone. With

my sword in its scabbard and my helmet abandoned God knows where. I think I wanted someone to kill me, but there was no one left alive to do it."

"Sweet Jesus, Karelian . . . ." Reinhard whispered.

The count laughed bitterly. "Sweet? He was once, perhaps, many centuries ago. Not any more, my friend. Not any more." He raised his cup. "*Prosit.*"

Reinhard crossed himself, taking comfort, I suppose, in the fact that our lord was drinking and was surely not himself in this unnatural place. And then a thought crossed my mind which left me rigid with fear. Perhaps he was truly himself now, for the first time? Perhaps he had never been the man we thought we knew . . . ?

I shuddered. No, it couldn't be; all this wild talk was just to impress *her.* Every word had been for her, telling her he didn't care if she was not a Christian, he wasn't much of a Christian either—indeed not! He would out-heathen the heathens if it would please her, if she would just keep flashing her black eyes at him, leaning so close he could breathe the perfume of her hair, so close that if he bent his head a little he could have pressed his mouth against the pagan offering of her breasts.

But no man can play such games with his faith, and expect to get away with it . . . .

For a time the talk was trivial and strained. Karelian had gone too far, and he knew it, and he sat with his wine cup and said very little, but he looked at her sometimes. I knew the look. I had seen it on the face of my older brother, when he was besotted with a scullery maid: a dirty, wild-haired thing who was frighteningly beautiful, whom he wanted unbearably and did not want to want. In the end he bedded her, and when my father discovered it, his anger was like none I had ever seen. The girl he merely sent packing, but my brother he flogged with a whip until the blood ran. His action astonished everyone who heard of it. It was not, they said, as if the girl were high-born; everyone bedded serfs, and of course the priests said they shouldn't, but the priests did it, too, so what was all the fuss about?

But my father was a chaste man—the rarest thing which lived among the lords of the Reinmark. From the day of his marriage he had bedded no one but my mother. So he told me, some days after the encounter with my brother, and then he told me why.

If a man yielded in matters of sex, he said, he would yield in anything. If he held the line in such matters, he would hold it in anything. The measure of manhood was mastery of the flesh. My father never pampered his body, never gave in to it, never looked upon it as anything but a device for doing work, for serving God and his lord.

"Consider how women live," he said, "with their soft garments, and their perfumed baths, and their need for every dainty thing; and consider how weak they are, how easily they are led."

That was why he had beaten my brother: for being so easily led, for allowing his lust to be stronger than he was. And then, standing straight as a pillar, my father told me to hit him. "Here," he said, patting his stomach. "As hard as you can." I didn't want to do it, and I would not, until he mocked me for my softness. And then I did it, feebly, and he mocked me again, until I was angry, and hit him with all my strength. I almost broke my wrist, and he laughed.

I thought he was cruel then, but I could see now he was right. In truth, I had seen it already in Jerusalem. The crusader knights were brave and sturdy; they endured hardship as well as my father ever had. Yet in their morals they were weak, because everything they suffered was only from necessity, never from choice. When the fighting was over they forgot it all. They let the city fill up again with infidels; they reveled in the taverns and the brothels every chance they had; they dressed themselves in rich garments and hired fine Egyptian cooks, while the priests who came with them shook their heads, and the Saracens spat in the dust when they thought no one was looking: *God's people, indeed . . . .*

Thinking about all these things, I lost track of time, and did not pay attention to what passed at the table, until I heard the soft ripple of a harp, and looked up. It was the lady herself who had begun to play. Her chair was drawn back from the table and turned a little, so the harp could rest against her knee.

I knew it was the devil's work, but it was beautiful, a shimmering sorcery of music so haunting that the whole room grew still; nothing even whispered now except the torches. Later, I would learn she was a shape-shifter; this was the first of many transformations. The worldly seductress was utterly gone, and in her place was someone exquisite and strange—wanton perhaps, but also elusive, a veela who could be won but never held, a goddess whom men would kneel before, and beg to serve.

Her voice was not delicate at all, as one expected from a woman, but it was beautiful and very clear, almost eerily so, like the voices of wild birds crying across a marsh, the sound still quivering against the grey sky after the birds were still. It took all my strength to withstand its power, all my strength and the grace of Jesus Christ, just to sit unmoved, and not soften towards her, not even a little.

Her song was not really a song, but a chanted story. I have not forgotten it, nor have I forgotten Karelian's face as he listened. That brief time, I believe, was when he fell beyond hope. He saw how powerful she could be, how much she had to offer him. Her gifts were all lies, of course, all illusion, and the price was lethal to the end of time. But how enchanting she must have seemed to him, there in the torchlight, how eerily lovely, how close to his reach.

Just ask, my lord, and all of it is yours . . . .

The story she told was strange, full of foolishness, as all pagan stories are, but it must be told, for it is part of what came after. As best I can recall it, it went thus:

Long ago, in the beginning times, there was born in the far north a lady called Erce, who had care of everything which lived. It was she who taught the birds to sing, and named the flowers; and she took for her home the fairest place in all the Reinmark, the rich green valley of Dorn. There she married a lord who came from the east, a stranger who was proud and strong. He loved her dearly at first, for she was very beautiful, and they had many children.

But in time he grew bitter towards her, and his heart became filled with envy. He saw she could bring forth children and nourish them and he could not. She could take pleasure more than he could, any time she wished. She could laugh at everything, even death. He forgot his own gifts, which were many and very fine; he wanted only those he did not have. He spoke often to his brother, complaining about her; and his brother, who was a holy man living by himself, with neither wife nor children, counselled Erce's husband thus:

Clearly, he said, *she has some magic talisman inside her body, which gives her these powers. Take it from her, and the powers will be yours.*

So it was that Erce's husband led her away into the forest, promising her a gift, and he slew her, and cut open her body. But he could find no talisman, no stone, no magic thing at all, only flesh and blood and bones, no different from the animals he killed for food. And then he was more bitter still, bitter because he'd loved a creature of so little worth, and bitter too because she was gone, for now he had no wife to comfort him, and no one to care for his children.

He went back to his house, and told the children their mother no

longer wanted them, and had gone away. They were not easily convinced, but having told one lie against her he found it easy to tell
others, and in time they all lost faith in her, all except the youngest
daughter.

This girl, who was called Maris, went every day to the forest
searching for her mother. For years she searched, gathering up the
pieces of her mother's body, which had been scattered by wild beasts
and by time. When she had found them all, she placed them in a
splendid urn made of clay, and took them to the bottom of the valley,
and hid them in a cave. And from this urn grew an apple tree, and
barley, and every kind of flower; in the spring lambs would leap over
its dark edges, and in the fall it would be spread about with nuts.
When the girl was not there to tend it, the veelas took up her task,
making certain the urn was never harmed and never found. And so
the girl brought home to her father and her kindred all manner of
good things, more than they could eat, and what they could not eat
she gave to strangers and to the gods.

Then her eldest brothers took counsel among themselves, and
asked themselves how she could find all these things, even when it
was winter. They resolved to follow her. With great skill and stealth
they eluded even the veelas, and went back and told their father what
they had seen.

Our sister has a magic urn hidden in a cave, they said. *Consider,
father, what paltry use she makes of it, and what we could do if this
urn were ours! For if it makes grain and milk and every other common
thing, then surely it would make gold, and everything it makes we
could sell. With such wealth and power we would soon be kings.*

Only the youngest brother argued with them, for he loved his
sister dearly. She had found the urn herself, he said, so surely it was
hers. And she shared everything with them—was that not good
enough? But he was very young, scarcely more than a boy, and no
one listened to him. The old man told his sons: *Yes, go and take the
urn, for we are men, and wiser, and we will use it better.*

And so they armed themselves with spears, and made the long
journey deep into the valley. The veelas went to Maris then, and
warned her: *You must come now, your kinsmen are coming to steal
away the urn.* And Maris wept, for she knew she could never go home
again, or see her little brother any more. *I cannot go,* she said, *leaving
nothing good behind me.* She tore out a single branch from the sacred

urn, and left it on the ground, so life would come again to the vale
of Dorn. So there would always be a memory of the winter tree.

They fled then, Maris and the golden veelas, deep into the forests
of Helmardin, weaving behind themselves such magic that no one,
even to this day, can find their hiding place. Behind them as they fled,
all the land turned to winter, and the winds came down like death.
The brothers found themselves walking in snow, in their summer garments and with no food, and they never returned again to their father.

When the tale was finished and I looked up, the nine bearers of
the Chalice, the old women in silver samite, had placed it again on
its bier and were bearing it towards us. It was shimmering as with
marsh lights, and utterly terrible—ugly and beautiful at once, both
living and full of death. Everyone at the table stood up then, as if in
the presence of a god—myself just like the others—and bowed their
heads.

The lady of Helmardin spoke into absolute silence.

"This is what your poets seek, men of the Reinmark: the Grail
of Life, which is the loins of woman, the seed of man, the bones of
the earth, the cycle of the seasons, the gods within the world.

"Here in Car-Iduna, you look on it with awe and call it magical.
Outside, in the world, where the same magic surrounds you, you trample it into the ground. You seek gods in the sky to escape the earth,
and virtue in the mind to escape the flesh. You seek dynasty and glory,
making yourselves kings and lords in the fantasy that you can thus
live forever, and break out of the cycle of time. And it will seem so,
for a while. You will build your great churches. You will see your
names written down in scrolls. You will see men tremble when you
frown. Your sons will carry on your blood, even if you have to kill
their mothers to make sure of it. You will have your way . . . for a
little while. Till another king comes and takes your empire, and another
god who claims to be the only god leads his armies against you. Till
your bones dissolve in the earth with the bones of those you slew,
and you are as forgotten as the wind, your kings not even names in
books, and your god a bogey to frighten children.

"Such is your immortality, for which the world bleeds."

A drone began to shiver, and then a drum to beat; in the caverned
walls of Car-Iduna it seemed to tremble and echo back, until the walls
were alive with the sound. And so the Black Chalice passed from our

sight, and I thank God and his holy saints that I never laid eyes on it again.

And yet it is not gone, and nor are my memories of it, which troubled me all down the years, like old wounds. For the thing is alive, as alive as those who keep it, and as wickedly enchanting, an eternal ambush in the dark of the mind, pulling us back from God, pulling us down into death.

As Karelian was pulled down, Christ, so easily, with nothing more than the offer of her hand. He took it with a boy's smile and a brush of his own across her hair, and followed her to her sorcerous bed.

I went alone to the room which Marius had offered us—utterly alone, for Reinhard and all the rest of the company scattered into I know not what dark places. I knelt on the stone floor and prayed all night, but my prayers failed me, for God was far away and Car-Iduna was all around me. I could not block from my mind the thought of Karelian and the woman, the endlessly changing images of their coupling, and the longing which rose unbidden through all my flesh, the unbearable longing to be there in his place.

Or, more truthfully, in hers . . . .

IV

THE WRITING OF HISTORIES

What is truth?

ATTRIBUTED TO PONTIUS PILATE

"SOMETHING MUST BE DONE, ANSELM, I beg you. Something must be done."

It was painful to beg. In seventeen years Paul had never asked any of his brothers for anything. He had always been the one to help them, the one who willingly took on more tasks, more problems, or more penances.

The face of the older monk was calm, but his voice betrayed a hint of impatience.

"Three times this morning you've told me something must be done. There's only one thing which *can* be done, my friend. You must go to the abbot, and have this thing exorcised."

"And I'm telling you it's impossible."

"Then tell me why it's impossible, or let me get on with my weeding."

"Anselm . . . !"

"Listen," Anselm said, leaning on his hoe and talking to the other almost as if he were a child. "There's a limit to how much even a confessor may pry into another man's soul. But I can't advise you if you tell me nothing. You're trying to write a book, and you can't write it properly because your quill is bewitched. On the surface, that seems to me an obvious problem with an obvious solution. But I'm not a fool, Paul. I've noticed you don't take communion. And you scourge yourself so much, I fear it won't be long before the abbot reprimands you for it—"

"He already has."

"Other brothers tell me you pace at night, and cry out, and while none of us are spies, or wish to be, we live close together. They've seen your haunted looks, and the blood creeping out of your shoes, and many other things. And yet you tell me nothing. How can I help you, if I don't know what lies at the heart of your grief?"

There was a long silence.

"Let's walk down by the river, then," Paul said. "It's a long story, and I would rather not be interrupted."

Anselm nodded, and put his hoe down. They walked for a time in silence, and at last he said:

"Well, my brother?"

"It's not easy to begin."

"I would hardly expect it to be. Begin anyway. Tell me what you're writing. Is it a book of devotions which the fiend wishes to spoil?"

"No. It's a history. Of Gottfried the Golden and the war, and everything which happened there."

Anselm looked surprised. He knew his brother in Christ had once been a knight, and before that, squire to the count of Lys. He knew, but he must almost have forgotten. The world of knights and lords was a strange and distant world to him—as it had been to Paul, not very long ago.

"Why would you want to write such a book?"

"I was commanded to do so. Nothing less than a command would move me to such a thing. When I left the world all I wanted was peace. I wanted to forget, to cleanse my soul and forget. Not to write about it, and so live through all of it again."

"But if you've been commanded to do it, Paul, then you must do it. Many tasks are painful; that's how men earn their salvation. Is it the quill which is hindering you, or your own reluctance?"

"I didn't say the quill was hindering me."

"In truth, brother Paul, you've said so little I can understand, I'm beginning to lose my patience. What is the quill doing, then?"

"It's writing things which aren't true."

Anselm paused in his tracks, and crossed himself. "You must go at once to the abbot—!"

"I can't. For heaven's sake, Anselm, stop and think a moment! It was thirty years ago, but surely you haven't forgotten who won the war, and what became of those who lost? I can't speak of this to the abbot; he's nothing more than the emperor's pet. Besides, if he had the power to exorcise a wart from my backside, I'd be truly surprised."

Anselm ignored the insult to his superior. "But if he told you to write the book, then he—"

"He didn't tell me to write it. The Holy Father did."

"Oh." Anselm carefully brushed the bird dung off a fallen log and sat, wrapping his robe around his feet. He watched the ants scurry off in all directions. "That is different."

"Anselm," Paul said heavily, sitting beside him. "You know what the rest of Christendom thinks of us here in Germany. Our kings have done nothing for a century except fight with the pope, and undermine his authority, and ignore his necessities. When Urban called for the great expedition to Jerusalem, the English came, the Italians came, everyone came—Flemings, Tuscans, Normans, Greeks, Frenchmen by the thousands—everyone except the Germans. Our lords you could have counted on the fingers of one hand: Gottfried, and the knights who followed him, and William of Saxony, and two or three others. That was all, out of the whole of our Holy Roman Empire. Do you think we deserve the name? We are half Christian here, no more; and with Gottfried gone, the Reinmark is barely that."

"You're telling me nothing new," Anselm said. "But what does it have to do with your insubordinate quill?"

Paul spoke slowly, choosing his words.

"There is sorcery here, brother. Here, in the Reinmark. Not just ordinary human wickedness. Not just pride and lust and all the other things we're familiar with, but something more. There is heathen power here. As it happened, I came to know something of it, years ago. My . . . my closeness to the matter was brought to the attention of the pope; I don't know by whom. Some months ago he sent me a letter, by a special messenger, and ordered me to write the history of Karelian of Lys, and Gottfried, and the war, in all the detail I could remember. He said I should pay special attention to the use of sorcery by the German lords."

"Sorcery? By the German lords? You mean Gottfried and his allies?"

"No. I mean the other side."

Anselm pulled a branch from a tree and brushed away the ants who were now climbing over his feet.

"There was talk of that," he said. "But it was civil war, and every time a man walked into a different village, he heard a different tale, and heard someone else accused. Demonism, witchcraft, heresy— sweet Jesus, the accusations fell everywhere. But I wonder, Paul. I wondered then, and I wonder now, if there was much substance in any of it. A man of honor and good repute suddenly turns, and betrays his lawful lord, and everyone looks for some extraordinary explanation. Perhaps they should just look into the human heart."

"It was sorcery, Anselm," Paul said grimly. "I was there."

Anselm looked up, and met his eyes, and looked away again, across the greening fields. He was both a cautious and a compassionate man; he did not leap to believe evil of others. But he was not a fool.

"And this sorcery you speak of," he said at last, very softly. "You believe it's controlling your pen?"

"There's no question. The same . . . being . . . came to me when I began to write—"

"Here?" Anselm whispered, horrified. "In the monastery?"

"Yes."

Anselm knotted his hands. For the first time, he seemed truly convinced. And truly afraid.

"We must have it exorcised, Paul. And we must do so at once."

"By whom?" Paul asked simply. "And how, without telling the abbot?"

"But why shouldn't you tell the abbot?"

Paul made a small but bitter gesture, as if to say: In God's name, Anselm, aren't you *thinking* about this at all . . . ?

"The abbot is a friend of the emperor," he said pointedly. "The pope is *not* a friend of the emperor."

Anselm sighed, and nodded very faintly. He understood. When he thought about it even a little bit, he understood. The war may have been thirty years ago, but powerful men still had deeply vested interests in how the tale was told. And when politics were involved, one could not always do the simple and obvious thing.

"The abbot is a man of God," Anselm said. "It's not your place to judge him. And although it's not my place to judge the pope, he would have been wiser to arrange this through your superiors. Now, I must admit, we have a problem. Perhaps I should try an exorcism myself—"

"No!" Paul said sharply, rising. "I don't want you to come near the thing! You have no idea of the power we're dealing with."

Anselm was silent for a time. "All right. But there is something here I still don't understand. Such a great power could compel any poor fool to copy out a false history of the rebellion, if that was what it wanted. Any number of false histories. Why would it choose you?"

"So I couldn't fulfill the pope's command."

"There are easier ways to stop you from doing so."

Paul paced, glancing now and then at Anselm's tranquil head, more often at the distant western hills, beyond which lay the wood of Helmardin.

"It's not entirely a false history," he said at last, very softly.

"That's what's so terrible, Anselm!" he went on. "It is . . . oh, Christ, I can't explain . . . . The events of which it writes are true— even the words which were spoken. Often it will remember things I had completely forgotten, and yet, when I see them written, I know they took place. Only . . . ."

He shuddered, and looked away.

"It changes . . . it changes the *meaning* of everything. It changes who we were, and why we did what we did. If someone read it, someone who knew nothing of the truth, they would think . . . ."

He faltered.

"They would think ill of you?" Anselm asked gently.

Paul stared at him. *Dear God, do you think I'm so vain and worldly I would tear myself to pieces over my image in a book?*

And then he caught himself. It was better if Anselm *did* think so. Yes. Much better. Let Anselm believe the worst of him. Let Anselm never wonder if there might be another reason he was so afraid.

But the monk had already seen his bitter look.

"I only asked, my friend," he said. "Even good men take it hard sometimes, when they are made to look bad."

Paul shrugged.

"It's not about pride, Anselm. Oh, God knows there are things I'd rather not have told about myself. But it's . . . how can I say it? It's the way everything is being twisted and made different. What mattered most is ignored, and what never mattered at all is made important, and all our motives and reasons are turned upside down. It's horrible! I can't keep doing this. I swear to you I can't!"

"Then you must stop."

"It won't let me."

There was a brief, painful silence. It seemed to Paul he should feel strengthened, having shared his fear with another. Instead he was more afraid than ever.

"Your soul is in great peril," Anselm said. "No matter what you say, the thing must be exorcised. I will give thought to finding some-one—"

"Be careful, I beg you! Or I will end like a grain of wheat between two stones!"

Anselm stood up and wiped his hand across his face. "You are such a quiet, religious man, Pauli. How did you ever find yourself in the midst of something like this?"

"Karelian tossed a coin at a crossroads, and we followed where it led."

In the field above the river a bell began to ring. Anselm looked at the sun.

"Vespers," he said, and turned to go. "A coin? As small a thing as that?" And then, without missing a step or a breath, he began to pray.

V

KARELIAN

Therefore I find no love in Heaven, no light, no beauty,
A Heaven taken by storm, where none are left but the slain.

FROM THE ARABIC —*translated by Wilfrid Scawen Blunt*

H ER HAIR WAS BLACK MIST SHROUDING HER FACE, black silk whispering across his flesh. Somewhere, far away in the world, it was midday and winter. Here there was neither time nor season, only a small sheltered chamber in a castle which did not exist, and a spent fire dissolving in his blood, and this strange, enchanting creature lying in his arms.

And a question. The question which desire always silenced, and which caution always posed again. *What place is this, and what manner of woman are you, and where will all of this end?*

His hand played in her hair, slid down the smooth valley of her back. Lovely, he thought, so utterly lovely . . . . He was worse than a boy, unable to keep his eyes off her, or his hands; and recklessly unwilling to think about the consequences. He had smiled sometimes at other men who fell like this—mature men who should have known better, tangled up in the smiles of a pretty courtesan, or risking land and life for the caresses of some other man's wife. More than once he had played the prudent friend, advising a prudent retreat. It had all been babbling in the wind. And so it would be now, if his own friends came with the same excellent and utterly useless advice.

"What must I do," he murmured, "to make you tell me your name?"

She propped herself on one elbow and played a taloned finger softly across his cheek.

"My true name? Only the Nine know it, and one or two others. But I have a pet name my mother gave me. She said she was tired of chanting an invocation every time she wanted me to come to supper, or get down out of a tree. She called me Raven." She paused, studying him. "You find that strange, Karel. Why?"

He considered evading the question. For hours he had been telling her about his life, and she told him very little in return.

"I went to see a wise man in the Holy Land, in the city of Acre—"

"The great mage of Acre," she broke in. "I've heard of him. Is he as wise as they say?"

"Perhaps. He told me there were four things of great danger which lay in my path, and I should fear none of them. Dread neither forests, he said, nor dead men, nor ravens, nor storm."

He did not think it was easy to surprise a witch, but he appeared to have just done so.

"That's extraordinary," she said.

"You don't . . . communicate with him, by any chance, do you?"

She laughed. And then, quite suddenly, she grew serious again— too serious, as though something hard and bitter had moved into her thoughts.

"Things become known in the world, Karelian, by those who wish to know them. Such knowledge crosses boundaries, and passes easily through time and distance. And yet it is scattered knowledge; no one directs it, and no one can; it's simply there, like stars and water. I've never spoken with the mage of Acre, nor sent him any messages, nor did he ever send anything to me. Whatever counsel he gave you came from his own wisdom."

She spared him a small, melancholy smile.

"I am only half veela, Karelian. I was not above wishing I was wrong, wishing you might simply share my table and my bed, and ride away again, free. But if a wizard halfway across the world has helped to send you here . . . ."

The words faltered and fell still. He observed, not for the first time, that she was no longer young. There was a world of experience in her eyes, and a hardness in the lines of her mouth—a hardness which laughter and graciousness mostly hid, but which he knew would always be there, always in reach if she needed it.

It troubled him, but it did not make him want her less.

"I had hoped to capture a valiant knight, my lord of Lys. I think perhaps I've captured something better."

He shoved her away and got to his feet. "That's a compliment with a knife in its teeth, lady."

Captured . . . . Well, what had he expected? Sorcerers never lured men into their realms of power except to use them or destroy them. Any child could have told him as much. Reinhard had warned him. Poor Pauli, too loyal and too frightened to protest, had followed him shivering with fear.

Yet he had come here almost without hesitation, with his head up and his banners flying. He had never been afraid of it, not really, not even now. Was that sorcery too? Or was it something in himself, something so ravaged and so angry at the world that risks of any sort no longer mattered much?

"Why did you bring me here?" he asked bitterly.

"To save the Reinmark," she said. "If it can yet be saved."

All along she had been evasive and indirect; this sudden frank statement astonished him.

She swung her legs over the side of the bed and slid her feet gracefully into her sandals. She picked up the soft, shimmering garments abandoned on the floor, and pulled them on—like an autumn moon, he thought, full and wanton, drawing around herself whispers of cloud, so shamelessly beautiful that ordinary common sense and judgment, and all those other things a man depended on, simply failed him. They tinkled to a stop like tired bells, and all he wanted to do was look at her.

She swept her gold belt around her waist, knotted it, and confronted him.

"Do you intend to accompany me through the halls of Car-Iduna stark naked, my lord count?"

"My apologies, lady. I didn't know I was expected to accompany you anywhere."

She stood, one hand on her hip, watching him. He was unconscionably pleased by the admiration in her eyes.

"Now that I think about it," she said, "it might not be a bad idea. Consider what it would do for my prestige."

"More, I fear, than it would do for mine." Her hair was still tangled from sleep and pleasure, and his hands found their way into it all by themselves. *Christ, I am as defenseless as a baby . . . .*

"Will you tell me the truth, Raven of Car-Iduna? What do you want from me?"

She did not smile. "Everything," she said. "Everything you have in exchange for everything you want. Come."

She led him to the chamber which lay next to the great hall. It was, as he had guessed, a pagan shrine. In the center was a high dais, where the Black Chalice stood alone, dark, yet almost incandescent. Below was a stone altar with many carefully arranged objects: colored stones, sea shells, pieces of polished wood twisted into strange shapes. And among them, a small onyx cup, shaped like the great urn and crusted with jewels; over the top of it lay a splendid curved horn.

The horn in my throat, and my blood in the cup . . . is this how it ends? What a wicked irony, for a man who marched to Jerusalem and spilled so much blood for a different god . . . .

"I didn't bring you here to lop your head off, Karelian, but if you continue to scowl at me, I might consider it."

He forced himself to smile. "I've never scowled at a pretty woman in my life. I merely find all of this . . . surprising."

"I can't imagine why. You've already contemplated all the awful possibilities. That I'm a demon, a vampire, a succubus, a lamia . . . have I forgotten anything? Men are wonderfully inventive with such notions! All of it has crossed your mind, my lord, has it not?"

"Yes. Briefly. A man isn't responsible for every thought which might run across his mind."

"And what do you think now?"

"That you are still the loveliest, most desirable creature I've ever seen."

She smiled. "I must say I admire your poise."

She picked up the chalice and the horn, murmuring, raised them four times, to each corner of the world, and placed them back on the altar.

"You asked me who I am, Karelian. I am three things: guardian of the Reinmark, keeper of the Grail of Life which Maris brought here from the vale of Dorn, and high priestess of Car-Iduna. I brought you here to make a bargain with you."

She paused, her mouth crinkling with amusement. "It's not what you think. I don't bargain for my bed—at least not very often, and never with a man like you."

"Why not with a man like me?" he asked, offended.

"Because I would find myself content with pleasure, and forget to ask for anything else. My bed you have for a gift, and willingly. But my protection and my power—those are different matters. If you want to have those, you must pledge me your loyalty, and acknowledge my gods."

"Neither of those things is possible, my lady."

"Are they not? How truly do you believe in your Christ—the Christ for whose sake Jerusalem was drowned in blood?"

He looked away, to the spill of winter light falling from a curved window.

"I don't know what I believe," he said heavily. "But however many doubts I have about Christ, I have as many about Odin."

"Odin?" She made a small, dismissive gesture. "Odin is an upstart. He's like most of the sky-riders—Zeus and Yahweh and your bachelor Father Eternal, and now Allah, too, as if we needed another one. They're like spoiled princes, racing their chariots across the world, full of threats and vanity and blood-lust. I serve better gods than that, Karel."

He waited.

"The Vanir," she went on, "the ancient earth gods; and those of the high Aesir who still remember that sky belongs to earth, and is nothing but emptiness without it. Gods of the herds and the hunt, of the fields and the fires. Gods of love and pleasure, and of the winter tree which never dies. They aren't always gentle, but they don't destroy men just to prove they can."

He watched her, silent. Priestess, she had called herself, an alien word in a Christian world, so strange it lingered in the mind long after the conversation had moved to other things. Sorceress was a word a Christian recognized, yes, and catalogued instinctively, without needing to think about it. But what was a priestess? And who were these gods she claimed to serve? Were they true gods, or were they demons? Indeed, were they real at all, and would it ever be possible to know?

He had wondered about such things in his later youth, in the years before all the gods began to seem unworthy of their divinity. He had been raised staunchly Christian, as the children of the aristocracy mostly were. And he had been a bright lad, eager to excel in learning as in everything else; the teachings had gone deep. But all around him the pagan world still lingered and whispered under its breath. Men might cross themselves at the crying of a raven, but they watched its circling path for omens nonetheless. They wore holy medals and heathen charms on the same thongs around their necks. They sang the

songs of the old gods, and told their stories, and claimed them as
founders of the race.

Some Christians said it was all foolish superstition. Others called
it evil, a dangerous flirting with old, demonic powers. A long time
ago he had wondered which opinion was correct. Now both seemed
inadequate and self-serving.

The priestess spoke again.

"Whatever powers we choose to serve, Karel, those are the powers
we unleash in the world. Pagan or Christian alike; it doesn't matter;
if the lords of heaven must always have their own way, and kill and
wreak havoc to get it, the lords of earth will do the same. Odin has
his place, but it was a small place once, and it should have stayed
small. I acknowledge him, because he's there. But I do not call him
All-father, because he isn't. And I bring my gifts to others. To Iduna
of the golden apples, and to Tyr, who was earthmate and high lord of
the Germans before Thor and Odin ever came here. They call him
Aesir, too, but he's of a far older breed, and proved it.

"Do you know the story of Tyr, Karelian? Do you remember what
happened when the gods of Asgard went to bind the Fenris wolf, the
monster Loki fathered on himself?"

"Yes," he said. He knew the story; everyone did. It was Tyr who
fed the monster when he was small, because no one else had the
courage to go near him. And when Fenrir grew to be evil and dangerous, so was it Tyr who undid his power.

Loki's wolf-creature grew mean and strong—so dreadfully strong
he might soon destroy the world. The gods brought different kinds of
ropes to bind him, teasing him about his strength, wagering he could
not break free. He always won. Only the last rope was different, a
slender cord, woven from the sound of a cat's footfall, and the beard
of a woman, and the roots of a mountain, and many other things,
woven in great secrecy, and with such skill that none of those things
was ever seen again within the world. Fenrir was wary, and made them
all swear an oath: if he failed to break the cord, they must take his
wager and set him free. But even then he did not trust them. *Very
well,* he said, *you may bind me. But one of you must first put your
hand into my mouth.*

"And not one of them would do it," Raven said scornfully. "Odin
the great fighter and Thor the great boaster and Loki the great liar all
stood by, and looked at each other. Someone else could do it, sweet
heaven—what would Thor be if he couldn't pound his mighty hammer,

or Odin if he couldn't wield his sword? And so Tyr put his hand into the beast's mouth, knowing he would lose it. And they bound Fenrir, and so he will be bound till the end of time. But it hardly made a tale for the drinking halls of Valhalla. No great battle there, no fields of dead. No glory in such a small, precious sacrifice. Tyr walks lonely in the world now."

"Some would compare him to Christ, for his sacrifice."

"Why should they?" she demanded sharply. "Did Tyr say afterwards: Now the whole world must bow to me, and follow me, and all the other gods must die?"

Karelian said nothing.

"Christ was his father's son," she went on. "He was never a god of the earth; he wanted no part of it. He tried to break the sacred circles of the world. Maybe his followers talked about peace, but they looked on life as something to conquer, just as the war gods did. Where else would they finish, except in the same camp?"

He looked at her, aware even now of her body, of the long, sweet pleasure she had given him. Sinful pleasure. Or so the priests would say . . . the same priests who blessed him on the road to Jerusalem.

It was true what she said; he no longer believed much in Christianity. But it had taken years for that to happen, and even more years for him to acknowledge it. He had been well taught, after all: God was God, and revelation was absolute, and the world's order was fixed despite its bloody chaos.

But he doubted nonetheless, at first against his will, and later with a quiet, almost self-destructive defiance. And it was his own religion, not the ancient one, which fed his doubts—doubts which went far beyond the obvious contradictions of his faith, beyond the fact that the Church taught love and brotherhood while Christian men, including priests and bishops and the pontiffs themselves, dealt century after century in discord, treachery, and blood. It went beyond the scandals of Rome, where corrupt popes rose up and deposed each other in dizzying succession, each one claiming to be anointed by God. It went beyond the facile argument of original sin. He was no longer content to be told that God was good and men were wicked, that Christians knew the truth but were too weak and false to follow it. Something else was wrong—utterly wrong in the very structures of the world.

In Flanders, his liege lord hung an enemy's small children out in cages in the dead of winter, and every day the bishop walked past the cages on his way to Mass, where he thanked God for bringing the ungodly to their punishment.

In Sicily, victorious Normans sacked the fortress of Aldino; the men they hacked to pieces; the women they staked out in the courtyard and drove spears between their legs, and left them so, still living, and rode away, the cries of their victims barely heard above their songs.

It never ended. The Christian princes of Europe fought each other like dogs in the streets. Pagan Vikings sailed their high-prowed warships up the long rivers of Germany and France, and where they passed the world was wrapped in smoke, and the earth stank of corpses. The Mongols and Magyars raided from the east, and the Saracens from the south.

For some men, it was the thought of God which kept them from madness and despair. They needed God to bear it. They needed a dream of divine redemption, a hope of some other kind of life. But for Karelian, it became harder and harder to believe that God was not somehow implicated in all of it. Either God lacked the power to govern the world which he had made, or if he had the power, then he was malevolent and cruel, no God at all but a monster. Or, perhaps—and this was the last and the deepest of his doubts—perhaps God had not made the world at all. Perhaps the world was something quite different, and the order which lay over it was an order made by men, and God himself was part of their creation.

They were not mature doubts, worked out into any sort of clarity; he was not a philosopher, and he had no access to formal learning. They were simply questions which never went away. He had nothing to draw on but experience, and his increasing reluctance to accept the upside-down ethics of a Church which gave its banners to marauding armies and sent men to hell for a kiss. He rarely confessed or took the sacrament. He drank a great deal. He bedded as many women as would have him—and bedded other knights, too, now and then; in war camps strange things happened between men, and love was by no means the strangest. What was left of his faith withered to the roots.

Then Pope Urban came, preaching the great warrior pilgrimage to the east. Incredible as it seemed to Karelian now, he had believed in it. At least a little. At least enough to pray again, and dare to hope. Enough to delude himself that this war would not be like other wars. That he could wipe out, perhaps, some of the dark things of his past. That everything would be different.

And it was different. It was worse. In Jerusalem he came to the center of God's temple, and found it empty, an echoing place of blood and lies. From Jerusalem there was no way back. No way at all.

"How well did you know me, lady, before you brought me here?"

She smiled faintly. "A little. It's exhausting, reading a man's heart when he's so many leagues away. And it's not entirely reliable. So we did it three times, and burned up a great deal of sacred wood. I don't know if you'll be flattered by this or offended, but you were chosen with a great deal of care."

"Chosen for what purpose, lady? You keep promising to tell me, but you never do."

"I am about to. But first I want to explain something. It's a dark time for Europe, and growing darker. More and more power is passing into the hands of the few, into the hands of the violent. You're a man of the world, so probably you've noticed?"

"Yes," he said. "I've noticed."

"Here in Car-Iduna, our first task is to preserve the Grail of Life, and the wisdom of the earth gods which it carries. We can do little to shape the world beyond. We are too few, and many forces are ranged against us; and although we have allies, they are as vulnerable as we are. They have their own survival to consider, as we must consider ours.

"We're not gods, Karel. We have wisdom, and considerable power, but we're still capable of making fatal mistakes. So we move in the world with great care, and we let many things pass—many bitter things which will never be made right."

She moved towards him. "I can offer you so much. Armor to turn all but the most deadly blows. Potions to heal dreadful wounds. Animals to shadow your path, and give you counsel. Shields against wind and winter, against hunger and pain. Many gifts, my love, from the magic of Car-Iduna. All I ask is your fealty—the same oath any man swears to his liege, and the same loyalty."

"My lady, I am already sworn to Duke Gottfried—"

"Duke Gottfried is a viper," she said bitterly. "Such men eat the world, and spit out its bones to their dogs."

"I will not endure that, lady, not even from you."

"You will endure it from half of Germany before your hair is grey. Dear gods, are you telling me you don't fear the man?"

"I've never had any cause to fear him. He's a valiant and honorable lord."

"Karel, we're not in the courts of men."

He stared at her for a moment, and then made a small gesture of assent.

"What do you want me to say, Raven? He's a powerful man, and powerful men are always dangerous. I've seen him in combat; I know he can be pitiless. Am I a man to judge anyone else for that? He's governed well. As for our wretched enterprise in the east, if anything good can come of it, perhaps it's Gottfried's wealth; he swore he'll use it all to make the Reinmark flourish. I bound myself to him willingly enough, and I was well rewarded. I won't leave his service. I was a mercenary for twenty years, Raven. I won't go back to it, not even for you."

"I'm not asking you to leave his service."

"I can't serve you both, for God's sake!"

"No." Her voice was soft and dark as midnight rain. "You can't serve us both. But you can serve me best at Gottfried's side."

"I see."

He turned away from her, swept with anger, with a crushing sense of disillusionment and loss.

"Women have long had a reputation for treachery and cunning," he said. "I'm beginning to see why."

"And men have an equal reputation for stupidity, and it's just as well-deserved. Gottfried was a cruel and dangerous man before he went east, but he's far more dangerous now. Something happened in the Holy Land, Karel; something changed him. You say he'll make the Reinmark flourish, but I rather fear he'll make it bleed."

"But you have no evidence for it, do you?" he pointed out grimly. "And besides, you're forgetting I have lands of my own now, and vassals; I will marry soon, and hopefully have children—what of my duty to them? My father spent his whole life quarreling with Gottfried's father, and then with Gottfried himself, over one foolish thing after another. His family didn't profit from it."

"I'm not asking you to start foolish quarrels; the Reinmark has quite enough of those already. I'm asking you to stay close to him. You have his confidence already; you'll be one of the first to know if he turns his hand to something wicked. I may be wrong about him, Karel—but if I am, you'll have lost nothing. And if I'm right, you'll have all of Car-Iduna's power to shield you."

"No," he said.

"Why?"

"It's dishonorable. It's utterly unworthy, and whatever small virtues I have left to me, I am still loyal to those I serve."

"Whether they deserve it or not?"

"Yes, if you put it so. Whether they deserve it or not. We can't pick and choose in the world, as you can here in Car-Iduna; we must deal with the men who are there. Good men have served me, and you might well say I didn't deserve their loyalty either, but I got it, and if I hadn't, I would be dead. What will be left in the world, lady, when even that little bit of integrity between men is gone?"

She had no answer for him, and having no answer made her angry. She threw out one hand in a quick, impatient gesture, paced a little, and turned back.

"No one returns to Car-Iduna who is not sworn to my service, Karelian. The very stones of my walls will vanish behind you, and you'll never find them again."

And I'll never see you then, ever in my life, never lie with the silk of your hair draped against my throat, never hear your voice again, or your magic songs, not ever, till I die . . . . And all of this will be gone, too, whatever truth is here, whatever hope of truth . . . .

"I thought you didn't bargain for your bed," he said bitterly.

"It's not a matter of bargaining; it's a matter of survival. How do you think Car-Iduna is kept safe, except by desperate caution? This is not a manor house, and I'm not some country widow entertaining the gentry."

She came to him, slipped her arms lightly around his neck.

"All the eagerness you saw when I greeted you, all the pleasure I took in your talk and your company—none of it was feigned, Karelian. I often hunger for the world, more than you would believe, and more than my veela mother ever would forgive."

Her hands were soft in his hair, on his shoulders; soft and searching and utterly irresistible.

"I will miss you, if you don't come back," she said.

How sweet, those words, how perilously tempting . . . !

"I won't play Gottfried false," he said. "If that's the price of your love, Raven, then I can't pay it."

"You'll have very little happiness in the life he's offered you."

"And who shall I thank for it? You, and the magic of Car-Iduna?"

"No. I'll do nothing to harm you. Gottfried and the world are both as they are, and I did not make them so."

He turned away from her, silent, walking aimlessly. He had lost

his first love at twenty. He thought he would die, but in fact he recovered very quickly. He was no longer twenty; he knew he wouldn't
die. He also knew he was unlikely to recover at all. More things were
at stake here than love, all of them so tangled together that he no
longer knew, and indeed no longer cared, what he wanted from her
most—passion, or wisdom, or shelter, or power. He wanted everything.
And if he lost what he had found here, there was little hope he would
ever find it again.

"There was a house in Jerusalem," he said. "They lived well there,
and they had many servants. Some of them fought us, and some huddled against the walls; it made no difference. We killed them all. In
the farthest room of the house I came upon a young woman with two
small children. She was a beautiful girl, almost as lovely as you, and
very young. I suppose in the great scheme of things it didn't matter
much—the young and the old, the beautiful and the ugly—they were
all equally precious to God, or equally irrelevant. She was holding on
to her children, and crying at me in a few words of broken Greek;
for some reason she thought we were Byzantines. She tore open the
front of her dress, as if to offer herself, and said over and over again—
or so I understood—please, please don't kill my children.

"I never had a wife, or children of my own. They were pretty
youngsters she was holding—rigid with terror, but so pretty. I thought
perhaps I should keep her, and the children too; take care of them,
raise them as my own. Why not? It was a fine house, and I was weary
to death of my wars.

"I won't say the impulse was honorable or generous. I'm sure her
Saracen husband, dead somewhere on the city wall, would not have
admired me for it. But at least it was human; to slaughter them was
something less. I stood looking at her, and I lowered my sword. I saw
hope in her eyes. I wasn't thinking clearly about what I would do; I
suppose I wasn't thinking at all. I was simply unwilling to kill them . . .
so my men did it for me. They poured into the room behind me, and
my sergeant swept past me with a great cry of rage, as if I had somehow been the one in peril, and drove his sword into her body. She
fell to her knees, but she was still alive. Alive enough to see them
grab the children, and hack them to death; their blood spattered into
her face, and she let out a cry of anguish to melt the walls of Jerusalem, or the heart of any God, if he had one.

"And it was I, Raven, who couldn't bear to listen to that cry, and
struck down what was left of her life. The men took their bodies and

threw them into the street, and hung one of my banners on the lintel—for whenever a knight took a house, he needed only to mark it and no one would touch his plunder. We were very honorable about things like that . . . ."

He looked at her, wondering what he would find in her eyes. *Why am I telling you this? To make you hate me? To make it easier for me to leave?*

But her eyes were veiled. She waited for him to go on.

"It seemed an omen, that banner. Here, Karelian Brandeis, is your first fief. Your colors hang from a house of blood, and so they will again. So they will forever."

There was a long silence. Raven spoke at last, very quietly:

"What do you want from me, Karel? I can't forgive you, or make it right. No one can. Only the wounded can forgive, if they choose to. The dead can't speak, and no one can speak for them, not even the gods. Evil can't be made right, Karelian; that's why it's evil. Otherwise it would be merely inconvenience. I think perhaps you know that, inside. It's why you can't serve your Christian God anymore."

Yes, he thought, just so. She read him very well, burning all her sacred wood.

"What good has it done us," she went on darkly, "this belief in heaven and hell and eternal life? It's done nothing but unleash barbarism on the world. The God who infinitely punishes men requires it, and the God who infinitely forgives them will fix up all their mistakes. If the Saracens are truly damned, well then, we've done his work. And if by chance we were wrong, and slaughtered the innocent, he'll be right there at the gates of death: Here, poor woman, it was all a terrible misunderstanding; let me brush away your tears, and show you all my castles; look, I have fine white robes for your babies, and pretty harps for them to play with . . . !

"Don't you think it's easy enough for humankind to be cruel, my lord, without such encouragement from their gods?"

No answer was necessary. He felt defenseless against her wisdom, and yet empowered by it, too. Nothing she said surprised him very much; only her sureness surprised him, the confidence with which she could stand apart from the whole of Christian reality, and say: There is something better.

"Raven." His hands hungered over her shoulders. "Don't close the gates of Car-Iduna, Raven. Or come to me at least, now and then, somewhere in the world; I know you have the power to do so. I can't bear the thought of never seeing you again."

"Then bind yourself to Car-Iduna, and to me, and I'll never let you go!"

"That isn't possible." Why, dear God, why couldn't she understand?

"You can't bring me here," he said, "and offer me all this, and then snatch it away. So might a lighthouse call in a foundering ship, and then shut up its windows, and leave the poor devils to the rocks."

"Indeed?" she responded grimly. "God has failed to save you, and now I'm supposed to do it? Forgive me, Karelian. I like you better than I meant to, and better than I should. But none of us here in Car-Iduna are gatherers of lost sheep. If that's what you want, you'll have to go back to Christ, and pay his price instead."

"God, you are cruel!" he said bitterly.

"It's not cruel to tell a man the truth. You know what kind of world lies beyond my walls; it has almost destroyed you. It's driven even my gods underground. I have a duty to what's left there, and so do you. Why did you choose the winter tree to paint on your shield and your banners?"

"It's a device of the house of Brandeis."

"A very obscure one, as I recall. You could have chosen others."

"I liked it. Do you think I had some other reason?"

"Perhaps." Suddenly her voice was very soft, soft as her fingers whispering across his cheek. "You belong to us, Karelian, to the old gods of Dorn, to the ways of Car-Iduna. They're in your blood, and they are what drew you here, more than my magic, more than the cunning of Helmardin."

She smiled. "My gods don't ask for your soul. Or your manhood, or your blood, or your firstborn child. They won't wall up your mind, or scourge your body, or send you marching off to slaughter unbelievers. They have only one unchanging truth, and it is this: you must choose, and you must live with your choices. Why—if you want their gifts, and mine—why will you not join us?"

He did not answer. Her mouth brushed his, and he reached, pulling her close, turning the small whisper of a kiss into a long, bittersweet feast, pawing her without a care for where they were, for the gods who might not approve.

"Swear to me, Karel, here, before the Grail of Life—"

"In God's name, don't ask me any more! I can't—!"

"You can't have Gottfried's world, and mine as well!"

"Then I will die between them."

He pressed her face against his body and held her so, lost in her hair and his wish that time would stop, simply stop here and let them be. In the sudden silence he could hear the murmur of running water, a small fountain lost somewhere among the tangle of plants; and from beyond the chamber's heavy doors, the muffled keening of a pipe. Her breath burned hot through his tunic, hot and damp; she tried once to lift her face, and when he would not let her, she sighed and burrowed deeper.

He did not speak or stir. He knew how close he was to absolute surrender, to abandoning everything he had or ever hoped for, rather than abandon this. And every day, every kiss, every moment in her presence, he would draw closer still. He would find it easier to shatter the bonds which held him to the world, to discard the one unsullied virtue he had left. He had always been loyal. He had always kept his word, or formally revoked it. He had always defended his lord to the wall, and stood up for his comrades, and given faithful service for his pay. He could not betray Duke Gottfried, and in truth it was less for Gottfried's sake than for his own.

His only hope was flight—to leave now, to leave quickly and forever. At first light. A day's ride or less, and they would be gone from Helmardin. If he still had the strength to go.

All my strength, and all the courage I have, to undo the sweetest taste of happiness I have ever known . . . .

Dear God, if God is real, he has found the way to pay me for my sins.

VI

THE ROAD TO RAVENSBRUCK

For the castle and all that was therein
had been swallowed by the earth.

LIBER EXEMPLORUM—*Medieval Book of Sermons*

DAWN ROSE GREY OVER HELMARDIN. From the castle's windows I could see only a wilderness of falling snow. I went eagerly to the great hall, thinking the others would be gathering there and readying to leave. I should have known better. No one was about at all, except some of the lady's servants, and that wretched creature Marius, who came slithering over to me like a small, oily fiend. He said good morning several times, and bowed and smiled, showing crooked buck teeth. His hair was neatly cropped in a bowl around his head; his eyes were black just like hers.

Was I feeling better? he wanted to know. Could he send me some nice breakfast? Eggs, perhaps? Salt meats? Or something lighter? Stewed fruit sat well on a troubled stomach. I refused each offering as politely as I could, and then of course I had to be plied with tonics and medicines. His mistress brewed the most splendid herbal drinks, he assured me, fine-tasting, and very good for the blood.

When nothing else worked, he tried to entice me into a game. Chess, he suggested, or dice, or any sort of cards; he knew them all.

"Something to pass the time, yes? Your master will be very late in rising, I think."

He smiled, saying it, and I wanted to kill him.

"I don't gamble," I said.

A fox trotted over to us, and pushed its nose into the dwarf's hand.

"Yes, yes, Hansli," he said. "I know you're hungry, but you have to wait; I need to cook this youngster first."

Then he looked at me, and laughed. "My lady doesn't care for the monkish types," he said. "But I do. They're such good sport. Are you sure you wouldn't like a game? We could dice for your virginity."

"I wonder," I said coldly, "how well your lady cares for your despicable bad manners."

"Oh, she doesn't. She thinks I'm a wretch. But I take such good care of everything, so she puts up with me. Also, I read people very well, and that's useful to her." He smiled again, and winked. "You are singularly readable, squire Paul."

I flushed red, which was exactly what the scoundrel wanted. I turned away from him, and found a chair at the far side of the hall, and sat. How many hours passed thus I cannot say, but the dwarf was never far away. He busied himself feeding the animals and the birds, talking to them all the while, teasing them and making jokes. I wondered grimly if they were wild creatures at all, or poor ensnared Christian souls.

We might all end up so, mewling and chirping, without minds or wills or any hope of heaven . . . .

I heard a small, scurrying sound, and looked up. Marius was before me, holding a cage; inside was a huge, horrid, baleful-looking mouse.

"Look," he said. "The bishop of Ravensbruck."

And he all but collapsed with laughter at the look on my face. It was impossible to tell then if he had spoken honestly, or if he was simply playing me for a fool. He slipped small pieces of cheese into the cage, and the mouse nibbled them greedily from his fingers.

"I must say he made a splendid pet," he went on. "Though Bastet is going to get him one of these days . . . and Bastet is so *mean.*"

He smiled wickedly, but when he got no further reaction from me, he went away. Thereafter I ignored him completely. I sat like a stone, longing for Karelian to return.

There was no ceremony that night. Great platters of food and flagons of wine were laid out on a long table at the side of the hall, and the night was given over to song and dancing. A longer night, if it were possible, than the one I had already endured.

Karelian never left the lady's side. He seemed to have forgotten all of us, forgotten the world. But something had changed. There was tension between them now, a tension which at times edged close to anger, and at other times smoldered with lust.

I was glad, at first, to think they might have quarreled—until I thought about the reason for it. What must surely be the reason, with such a woman, in such a place.

She wanted him to stay.

There is no terror like the terrors of the soul. I faced death before I went to Car-Iduna, and I have faced it since. But nothing compared to my dread of being trapped there. Such terror is surely what the damned will feel on the final day, when they are dragged to the pit's edge and look down at the coiling fire, and feel the demons already tugging on their ankles, and see the wires and the whips and the knives. When they know there will be no end to it, and no escape. Ever.

But no one knew my dark thoughts, and no one would have cared—except perhaps to cuff my ears, and tell me to have a drink and mind my own affairs. I took what small comfort I could from my faith in Karelian's honor. Whatever wickedness he might personally embrace, surely he would never bind the rest of us. *I will stay, lady,* he would say to her, *but you must let them go . . . .*

I watched her every gesture and his every response; it seemed he was still refusing. She would lean close, and murmur something very soft, and he would look away. They would dance together, and then stand talking quietly, and it would end the same way in conflict. Once I swear I saw him beg, and she just tossed her head a little, like an irritated mare, and walked away.

I thought surely he would be a man, and say Enough! He would shout for his arms and his men and be damned, let all the devils in hell try to stand in his way! But no. He followed her back to the table, and sat at her elbow. If men were born with tails, he would have wagged his then, waiting for her to smile again. Which she did, very graciously, the back of her hand brushing across his cheek.

"I'm sorry, Karel."

And he was won over again in a breath, bending his mouth to her hand, holding it for a long moment, so his lowered gaze could linger on her breasts.

How could a woman so utterly undo a man's wits? A bit of silk, a pretty laugh, an offering of bared flesh—how could he trade his soul for so little? She wasn't even young. Dozens of other men must have rutted on her—aye, and not just men, I thought. She was a witch; God alone knew what strange and unnatural creatures she had lured into her bed.

How could Karelian not see?

"God's blood, you're a sour-looking wretch tonight, Pauli."

It was Otto, speaking lightly at my shoulder. I looked up. He had a cup of wine in his hand, and at least a flagon of it in his stomach; he spoke with an easy, half-drunk slur. He looked disapprovingly at my spot on the table, where there was no plate and no leavings.

"You fasting again? You shouldn't, you know. It's bad for you, too much fasting. And the food is marvelously fine. She's some lady, this queen of Car-Iduna."

I said nothing, but I followed his gaze across the hall, where Karelian was dancing with the queen of Car-Iduna. The count was a big man, hardened from a life of warfare and not especially graceful, but he danced with her beautifully. Their bodies moved in a single space, bonded by a single rhythm of desire.

"He'll be well bedded tonight," Otto said. He grinned at me. "You should snaffle yourself one of her pretty followers. They're a proud bunch, but they're mostly willing."

He took a huge drink, and went on with his lecture.

"A man fasts too much, Pauli, his stomach shrivels up. Same thing can happen to his cock."

I said nothing. I had read the works of the saints, and I knew how hard they struggled. Many would have looked on such shrivelling as a gift from God. Those nights in Car-Iduna, so would have I.

I thought we would never leave the place. But with day the sun returned to Helmardin, so blinding we could hardly see. I did not care. I would have ridden into flood and fire to be gone.

I will not dwell on our leave-takings. In truth I scarcely remember them, for I was raw with impatience and desperately afraid we might still somehow be forced to stay. It was clear the lady did not want us to go. But Karelian had set his mind to it, and he was as stubborn about leaving as he had been about coming. And I, young and innocent as I was, marvelled because she let him have his way—so small, so limited was my grasp of her designs! Keeping us, she would have undone the hope of some fourscore human souls. Letting us go, she undid the hope of the world.

My last memory of Car-Iduna is of the courtyard, of how happy
I was to be on my horse. How happy we all were. We were fighting
men once more, and armored, and fretting to be gone. All of us except
Karelian, who still would not give the order to ride. Who sat motionless, looking down at the woman standing by his stirrup. I could have
wept for the pain in his eyes.

"The gates will be closed, then?" he said.

"Yes," she said. "As you know they must be. But there's always
a way back. Did you think I would let you go without one?"

She reached up, holding out to him a black feather, long and
shimmering, taken I think from a raven's wing.

"Burn this by moonlight, in a circle of seven stones, within sight
and sound of the Maren. And I will come to claim what I have asked
for, and bring you the keys to Car-Iduna."

"You'll come only for that, lady?"

"Only for that."

"So be it," he said darkly. I thought he would fling the feather
into the trampled snow, but instead he put it carefully away, and looked
at her again.

"Farewell, Lady of the Mountain. I'll try only to remember your
beauty, and forget that you are cruel."

"You will forget nothing, Karelian of Lys."

She smiled, a melancholy smile, all the more enchanting for its
sadness. She brushed her hand across his thigh.

"Ride safe, fair one. I will wait till the snow passes twice from
the hills. And then I'll wait no longer."

He looked away, and signalled only with his hand, and so we rode
through the open gate, into the white pitiless shimmer of Helmardin.
He did not look back, not even once. I imagined it was sternness on
his part, but it was sorrow, for he knew what he would see. Even as
the last of our sutlers passed through the castle gates, the drawbridge
melted, the walls quivered and dissolved into light, and as I stared
with open mouth and rubbed my burning eyes, there remained nothing
behind us but forest—dense, pathless forest without a trace of human
habitation, without a breath of smoke, without a footprint, without a
whisper of sound except the wind.

But she was not yet done with her sorcery. For even as I stood
staring, men and horses marching past me, crunching the fresh snow,
I seemed to be alone in my astonishment. The others noticed nothing.
I grabbed the arm of one of the sergeants, crying at him: "Look!"

He swivelled obediently in his saddle and looked, and then turned back to me, bewildered.

"What is it, Paul? What have you spotted? Is it wolves?"

"It's gone!" I said harshly.

"What's gone?" he said. "You look ill, lad. What's the matter?"

I did not answer. I crossed myself, and turned again along the road to Marenfeld, the road which had been there for a hundred years, from which we had never parted, and where now, far ahead, inaccessible and silent, my lord Karelian rode like a man who had lost his soul.

The other knights were untroubled; they had perfectly clear and perfectly credible memories of our adventure. As they recalled it, we had left the inn early and travelled most of the day, until the storm grew too severe, and it was dangerous to continue. By sheer good fortune we came upon a cave, and took shelter there. They slept well, considering the cold, and many had wonderful dreams—dreams of summer flowers, of tables laden with food, of pretty women lying in their arms. *Pity it wasn't true,* one of them murmured. I might have doubted my own sanity, if it had not been for Karelian. He had more memories than enough, and he meant to keep them, along with his precious, evil feather.

That very night, in the inn at Marenfeld, he asked me to fashion him a pouch. Of good calfskin, he said, and well-sewn, held on a thong which he could wear around his neck.

My good lord, why don't you throw the horrid thing away . . . ?

I was weary, but I had slept most of the day in my saddle, an art I learned on the road to the Holy Land. So I dug about in my pack to find my sewing gear, while he brooded in his chair.

"You remember everything, Pauli, don't you?"

"Yes, my lord."

"And yet no one else does. It's very strange. I recall you never ate, or drank anything. Is that why the magic never touched you?"

"I believe so, my lord." I paused, and added: "It was Reinhard's advice, but he never followed it."

"Then why did you?"

"To try to shield you from . . . from whatever might have been there . . . ."

Many times, since I had entered his service, he had been kind to me, and looked at me with warmth in his eyes. But never more than now.

"There was no need, my friend. There is no evil in Car-Iduna. But I thank you."

He was silent for a moment, thoughtful. Then he went on very quietly:

"No one must know what passed on this journey. I will depend on you for it. No one. Will you give me your word?"

"But my lord, we'll have to confess—!"

"Confess what you please. Your sins are between you and God, if you have any, which I truly doubt. Do not mention Car-Iduna, and do not mention her." His eyes held mine. "Your word, Pauli."

"And what of you?" I whispered. "You were bewitched, I know, but still you must be shriven—"

"Must I? The last time I asked to be shriven, the priest assured me I had no sins worth mentioning. That was in Jerusalem, the day after we sacked it. If I was sinless then, I've been a veritable angel ever since."

"My lord . . . ."

"I loved her," he said. "I regret only that it ended. Let's leave it so. Give me your word you will be silent."

It is astonishing, really, how men can delude themselves. I should have reported our adventure to the archbishop at Stavoren, perhaps to the duke, perhaps even to the pope. But instead I found every possible excuse for being silent. If I spoke he would be angry, I told myself, and he would harden in his sin. This way, with time, he would repent. He would marry and live a Christian life, and forget her, and repent.

My true reason, if I had known it, I could not have borne to face.

It was four days' ride to Ravensbruck. The sun stayed with us for two; then the clouds returned, hanging almost on our banners, and the fogs sent knives into our bones. Karelian's moods were as melancholy as the weather. He sought me out sometimes, in ways he had never done before, and told me things about his life. Dark things, as if to make me understand: *See, that was why I went to Car-Iduna, why I didn't care what happened, why I loved her . . . .* I didn't argue with him, or tell him he had everything turned upside down. I listened, and was content to be chosen.

Before Car-Iduna, I almost worshiped the count of Lys. I thought him the finest man in the world, a man with every grace and virtue, a man whom it honored me greatly to serve. Now I saw he was only a flawed human being, cynical, debauched, and profoundly unhappy, a worldling without faith or purpose in his life. I saw, to my great bewilderment at the mere age of nineteen, that I was in many ways a stronger man than he was, and wiser about the world, and more honest.

It seemed indecent to have such thoughts, and terribly arrogant. I tried to put them aside. I tried to pray them away. But they remained, and I had to face them. Karelian was not the splendid, shining hero I had imagined him to be.

But he still could be, if he chose, and if I helped him. I could bring him back to God. But I mustn't quarrel with him; no one ever got anywhere quarreling with Karelian. I would have to do it by example—by loyalty, by unfailing devotion, by having always the right words at the most appropriate moments . . . .

Oh, I flattered myself. I had fantasies of his gratitude for the renewed gift of faith, fantasies of him kneeling in midnight vigils with tears running down his face, adoring the cross which he had served but never understood. I had fantasies of the honors he would receive in the world, of his praise on the lips of every Christian lord, God's true knight at last, as he was meant to be.

And finally, when some years had passed and he had sons, he would make a last, perfect renunciation, and we would ride together in the vanguard of Gottfried's new band of chaste knights, fighting wherever Christian men might need us, sworn to neither wife nor liege lord, only to God alone.

So I dreamt, crossing the ragged wilds of the northern mark, lying by his side in chilly manors with the wind tugging at the roofs, looking up finally at the bleak stone heights of Ravensbruck, at the castle which brooded like a sullen eagle over all its lonely world.

If there is a drearier place on earth than the one we found there, I never want to see it. It was border country, a harsh land made almost unlivable by war. Every village we passed was fortified, every farmstead walled or braced against a hill. Between settlements, we saw everywhere long stretches of abandoned land, overgrowing with scrub, scattered here and there with the charred skeletons of houses, with stark wooden crosses driven into the ground. Here men lived once, and here the Prussians came, the Frisians, the Latvians, the Danes. Or some angry vassal, spurred to rebellion by an insult. Or merely a kinsman, greedy for his brother's power. Count Arnulf's own son had warred against him here—and died, so the stories said, chained in a cellar without food.

We could see the castle for hours before we reached it, and the closer we came, the more forbidding it appeared. A few ragged banners flew from the turrets; unsmiling pikemen guarded the gates; rubbish and leaves clotted in the black waters of the moat. The knights who met us, even to the highest born, were splendidly armed, but otherwise ragged as barbarians.

"The border lords have a hard life." So Duke Gottfried had said to us in Stavoren, speaking of Ravensbruck and Arnulf, the man they called the Iron Count. "But if they are loyal, they are the very bones of the land."

I knew we would find no luxury here, no soft graces, and I didn't especially care. My father thought every man alive should bathe, and cut his hair, and sweep away his leavings. "There is no excuse," he used to say, "ever, for living like a pig." But my father lived in the south, in a proper manor house, and I had come to judge the matter less harshly than he did. Still, I noticed the disorder in the courtyard, the stench, the snarling, ill-fed dogs. The tension. That I noticed most of all: the edge in men's voices, the coldness in their eyes, the hints of savagery hanging in the air like bracken.

But I was still too thankful for our escape from Car-Iduna to mind anything very much, or to be half as alert as I should have been. Otherwise I might have paid more attention to the man who stood apart from the others, and did not come to greet us. A dark-haired man, rare enough among the Germans. Not much older than me in years, but a full-fledged knight, already perilous and steeped in blood. A dog without a shred of honor, whose name I will not write here because he does not deserve to be remembered.

Today—in the world I will no longer live in—today his son is count of Lys.

VII

SIGUNE

Thus shall all my sorrows be utterly avenged.

The Nibelungelied

S IGUNE CHOSE THE DAY VERY CAREFULLY. As it happened, it was the day
on which the count of Lys and his escort encountered the merchants on the road to Karlsbruck, and decided to continue on through
Helmardin. She knew nothing of this, although the count and his
intended marriage were very much on her mind. She chose the day
by the moon; it would be full that night, hidden beyond the heavy
northern clouds. Among her own people, this was judged an especially good time for sorcery—a time when the currents of power in
the world were unsteady, and sensible men did not take unnecessary
risks.

Arnulf of Ravensbruck had never been a man to worry much about
risks. She would always give him credit for it; he was brave. But
courage was a double-edged virtue; it could shade so easily into arrogance, into a brazen self-importance which refused to admit that
other, lesser beings might be dangerous. Beings such as horses, and
servants, and women . . . .

They had warned him about the horse. Probably, over the years,
some of them had warned him about her. *Get rid of that creature;
there's something strange about her, something deadly* . . . . Her face
alone was enough to do it, with its twisted nose and caved-in cheekbone, with scars all over half of it. Anyone with a face like hers was
probably a witch.

It was cold on the castle wall. The wind whipped her hair around her face, fine flaxen hair with the odd strand of white. She was forty, or something near to it. She counted the years indifferently. They varied little for a slave, until today.

Today everything would change. It began to change the moment Arnulf of Ravensbruck called for his hunting gear and his favorite stallion—the stallion they had warned him about, the one who was acting so strangely. From the ramparts she watched the count stride out with his squire and his best men, Rudolf of Selven among them, dark Rudolf who could hate almost as well as she could, which was saying a great deal.

Her eyes followed Arnulf, a great beast of a man in ragged skins and iron. He was not handsome. He was not even awesome, the way his liege lord Duke Gottfried was awesome. Arnulf was merely brutish and hard, the kind of man who was admired on a battlefield and hated everywhere else. The grooms brought out his horse, a splendid grey already fighting its bridle and tossing its head.

Signune ignored the count now, watching the animal, calling to it with her thoughts. It was time now at last. All the spells had been cast, all the dark charms slipped into the creature's grain, so many times, with so much care.

I am here, Silverwind. I am Sigune, do you remember me? Sigune who comes by night, and speaks a tongue you've never heard. Look at him, your master! See how ugly he is, and how cruel; see the sharp spurs on his boots, the iron in his eyes! I know you hate him, just as I do; our hatred is our strength.

A groom held the count's stirrup. He vaulted into his saddle with impressive ease, considering his age and the armor he was wearing. He sawed at the horse's reins, turning towards the open gates.

It happened very quickly—too quickly, after so many years of waiting. The animal reared and plunged, squealing with rage, slashing out with hooves and teeth at everything in reach. Sigune leaned forward; her fingers clawed at the stone battlement as the courtyard below her exploded into chaos. The grooms scattered with shouts of alarm; one of them, stumbling, was almost trampled. Chickens bounded in all directions, squawking and flapping. Men shouted commands and counter-commands, their own mounts panicking as the stallion lunged and screamed and struck.

Arnulf of Ravensbruck could ride anything that ran on four legs; so the talk went in the drinking halls. For a few brief moments it seemed true; he seemed rooted to his saddle. Even from here she could hear his curses. He was a Christian man, but he could curse to make his Christian devil blush. Then the horse went down, and the curses ended. The men of Ravensbruck never agreed, neither then nor ever after, if it fell from its own lunatic plunging, or if Arnulf, great brute that he was, had jerked its head back too far as it reared, and pulled it off its feet. She heard him scream—a long, agonized scream from somewhere on the ground, somewhere behind the heaving grey mass. The horse flailed to its feet and turned with a neigh of triumph. It would have reared again, and trampled him, but six hunter knights with crossbows brought it down. The stallion stumbled to its knees, speared with arrows. Only Sigune, from her vantage point on the wall, saw that Rudolf of Selven, the fastest and the finest shot in Ravensbruck, fired last of all . . . when it no longer mattered.

How they ran about then, shouting and blaming each other, shouting for a litter, for a surgeon, for the countess, for God and the Virgin Mary and whomever else they thought might be useful. Finally, of course, they would remember to shout for Sigune. She wiped her face, surprised in this cold weather to find it spattered with sweat, and went back to the wash-house where they would come to fetch her.

Like always, it was cold there, and bone-rotting damp. She filled the great hanging cauldrons with water, and laid wood carefully on the braziers—only a little wood, to make the water a little tempered. It was quite enough, the steward said. Why should she have more, when the countess herself had to beg for what she needed?

Maybe now, with the master shivering on his death bed, they would spend a few coins on wood.

He was not on his death bed, however; not nearly. His back was injured, and one leg was wrenched from its knee socket and horribly broken. The surgeon went on at great length that he would live, oh, certainly he would live, he would probably ride again, it was amazing how a strong man could recover from nearly anything.

What was really amazing, Sigune thought, was how fear made perfectly sensible people babble.

She drew as close as she dared among the cluster of huddling servants. Once, for a brief time long ago, she would have been the one to tend him, to cut away the mud-spattered garments and bathe his wounds, to hold him while the doctor bound his bones, to brew the herbs, and sit through the long night and hold the cup to his lips.

The countess did it now, the third countess, dutiful as a nun, flinching at the sight of his smashed leg, at the splinters of his bones sticking out like spikes of broken wood, wiping away the blood and crossing herself at his blasphemies. Sigune watched her without sympathy. Women came and went here—three wedded wives and God alone knew how many concubines and captives of war, all of them bedded and most of them made mothers and some of them dead. She had cared about a few of them over the years, but not this one. This one could go to the dark realms of Hel with her barbarous lord, and nothing furred or feathered or finned in the world would ever trouble itself to fetch her back.

She heard steps, a flurry of whispers. Adelaide was hurrying down the stairs, across the stone hall. The circle of armed men and servants parted respectfully to let her pass.

She was a slender girl, pale from too little sun, always fragile, and pretty the way fragile things always were. In another, gentler world she might have fashioned herself some kind of life. Here she would live as bluebells lived on rocks, flowering before the snow was gone— and dead, likely as not, before the trees were green.

She brushed past Sigune, pausing to stare at the bloodied wreckage of her father's leg, creeping closer, her eyes wide with question and fear.

Everywhere, on every face, Sigune saw the same fear. He was lord over all of them. Nothing could happen to him without it mattering to them, and the mattering was likely to be hard.

He turned his face a little, saw Adelaide, and lifted his hand.

"Come here, girl."

She edged to his side, took the outstretched hand obediently.

"Father . . . ?"

"God damned horse," he said roughly. "Don't worry; I'll see you wedded before I die. Aye, and with brats too, if this count of Lys is half his father's son."

She smiled. It was a small, obedient smile, the best she could manage, and all which was required. She was well-schooled at seventeen in the art of seeming, better known to women as the art of survival.

Sturdy men seized Arnulf's limbs and head, pinning him to the table like a felon to be tortured. His squire placed a piece of wood between Arnulf's teeth. The surgeon began his work, carefully, without haste. Small grunts broke from the count's mouth; then, finally, a long, clenched wail of pain. The countess looked away.

Sigune did not.

She had wanted him dead. But the gods had been wiser, as they always were. It was much better this way. Better he should lie here for a while, and learn what it meant to be defenseless, and see everything go, see his world splintering shard by shard. Right here in his drinking hall. He was too injured, the surgeon said, to be carried up the steep and narrow staircase to his chambers. Yes, right here, without even privacy to shatter in, among dogs and brawling men and nothing else; what else was there in life for a warrior lord?

The ultimate vengeance, she reflected, was neither death nor maiming. It was knowledge. And indeed she should have guessed as much, even from the little she knew of Christianity. What God saved for his damned, even beyond the torments of fire, was the agony of truth.

All night, as the moon rose full behind the clouds, and even the most devoted of Arnulf's kin and caretakers fell one by one asleep, Sigune sat near him and reflected on his truth.

No more battles for you, Arnulf of Ravensbruck. No more booty. No more glorious tales to tell, no more women to capture. It's all over but the long dying. And I will be here till the end.

I will do everything they tell me. I will fetch the water, and drag in the wood. I will pack hot bricks at your feet, and clean up your vomit, and pour hot drinks for your countess, and listen to her sorrows. What better way could I find to watch you suffer?

How strange you all are, in your amazing arrogance! You think everything you did to me was simply forgotten—erased, like the wood huts of Kevra, swallowed in a gulp of flame. Nothing left but the plunder—a few cattle, a few sacks of grain, a few handfuls of jewelry. Seven women. Young enough to lust for, old enough to survive the terrible journey west. How far was it, Arnulf of Ravensbruck? I do not remember. Across two great rivers, I've been told, there live the Wends. The wild people, you call them; I wonder who you use to judge them by. You liked my looks, you said; you liked my spirit. It is with women as with horses, is it not, my lord? The sport is in breaking them. After that a horse is just another horse.

Do you have any notion how I hated you? No, you couldn't have; such hatred is a man's privilege. Malice we females are supposed to be capable of, oh yes, malice and spite, but the pure, deep-souled hatred of an enemy who lives to kill—you don't think a woman strong enough for that. It wasn't why you kept me so carefully under guard. You guarded me like you guard Adelaide, to keep me pure, to keep me away from other men. Or maybe you thought I would kill myself. A woman should, after all, should she not, since her honor is her life? And I did think about it, not for honor but for grief. For hating the tread of your boots in the hall, and the sound of your voice in the courtyard, and the weight of your body in my bed.

The wounded man shifted and groaned in his sleep, and a dog lying near perked up its head and whimpered. Sigune looked at the count, at the fire, at the scatter of bodies lying in the hall.

You never knew anything about me, not one of you in all your arrogance and armor. You least of all, my lord—I must call you lord, even in my thoughts; they are a slave's thoughts still. Who else but a slave would have loved you in the end?

How do I explain it, even to myself? I know it happened, but I do not want to believe it, and I would not believe it, only I remember and I know I'm not mad. All I can say is this: finally I wanted to live, and there are things no one can live with. I could not look at my own life and believe it had been reduced to nothing. To less than nothing, just a slave's bed and a dog's whimper for bread. And so I came to love you—look, my lord, surprise! I can still choose, I can still be something human, it's not so bad, I'm not a dog, I am your woman.

Madness? Yes, perhaps, a kind of madness. I don't know who made the choice—myself or something else inside myself, maybe a soul, maybe an animal, something which said: I will act, because I must. I will choose, because I must. And if there is only one choice possible, then I will choose it, and I will call it a choice, even though it isn't . . . because I must.

But you never knew. When I began to smile and try to please you, I was just a slave learning to be good. When I began to take pleasure in your bed, well, it just proved what you always knew: women were all whores, and after they wept and struggled for awhile they came around to liking it, all of them; some just played the game longer than others, that was all. And no, I never told you; I had some pride left, and some sense. You would have found it amusing, such a word in my mouth. Love. I find it amusing now myself, dear gods. Look at you, stinking and blood-spattered, nothing but a pirate, a butcher. You murdered my family and I forgave you; I marked it down to fate and the fortunes of war. I even came to admire your glittering ferocity. Everyone feared you—didn't

*that prove how bold you were, how splendidly male? I could take pride
in it, and pride in myself. I was a match for you, I was your shield
woman, your Brunhilde, your lioness . . . .*

*Gods, how you would have laughed! Yes, I say gods. I bowed my
head to your holy water but I kept the gods of my people, too. You
never knew that, either . . . .*

The fire was failing. Wearily she went to the hearth, knelt, settled
the coals, and piled on fresh wood. The heat burned against her face.
She sat back on her heels, played one hand briefly over the old, un-
forgotten injuries. She had been pretty once, wonderfully pretty, the
fairest girl in Kevra, they said; all the men wanted her. No one did
now.

Strange, she thought, that after so many worse things, it hurt so
much to have lost her beauty. So much she could lift the poker from
the fire, and consider walking over to Arnulf's cot, and pressing the
red hot iron into his face.

*It would almost be worth it, just to hear you scream. But I will
wait. You whimpered a good bit today, for a man who once held a
burning candle against his arm and counted to twenty, just to prove
how well he could handle pain.*

*How could I ever have cared for you, even a little? Even in mad-
ness? You gave me nothing. A few gifts, a bit of passion, and then you
rode away to fight and whore wherever the wind took you. And brought
home that plaster-faced wench with the breasts of a goddess and the
brains of a flower. She didn't last either, but I suppose she was a
novelty after me. And when I screamed at you, you smashed my face.
You beat me until I couldn't stand, and then you used your feet. When
I could work again, and say yes my lord and no my lord, like a proper
servant, you sent me to the scrub-house, and thought that was the end
of it.*

*All these years you thought so, you thought it was all forgotten,
it never even mattered. I had nothing left, no people, no pride, no
decency, not even you, worthless though you were. I had only my
pretty face, which might at least have won me a servant's warm bed.
And you took it away on purpose, for sheer cruelty, and imagined I
forgot . . . .*

"Sigune . . . ?"

She jumped with terror, bashing her ankle against the chair, whirling to see Adelaide standing in her nightdress, holding a candle.

"How is my father?" the girl asked, softly but aloud.

"He's sleeping."

They walked to the count's cot. Adelaide bent, laid her hand for a moment on his forehead, straightened his blankets, looked up once, very briefly, at the slave woman. It was a look Sigune knew very well.

Like a rabbit in a snare, she thought, *frightened and sharp-toothed, but neither old enough nor hard enough to deal with the hunters. Everywhere you turn you see only more danger. And I, whom you trust at least a little . . . . I am the most dangerous of all.*

She gave the count's pillow a last, token pat, and they moved away from him towards the fire. The girl was shivering. Sigune did not think it was only from the chill.

"Keep good watch then," Adelaide said. "And do not sleep."

She did not wait for an answer. Sigune watched her flee from the hall, a ghost melting into the flicker of her own candle. When the last light was gone, the slave woman sat again, her arms folded over her belly, looking at the count.

What a pity I can't tell you all of it, my lord; you would have to give me credit. No lone warrior, scouting an enemy encampment, ever trod more secretly or more silently than I. No merchant, made wise by shipwreck, ever weighed his risks with better care. And if there is a man alive more patient in his vengeance than I have been, I would like to meet him, and drink him a toast.

You care for very little in this world. Warfare and glory, your pride of strength and manhood, your good name. And your daughter. Why this one God knows, you never cared much for the others, or for their mothers. But Adelaide is precious to you.

And precious to me, too, in my fashion. I will not sleep tonight, and I will keep good watch, as I have done so many times before.

How old was she when young Rudolf started courting her—twelve maybe? Of course no one saw it as courtship; he was only a lad himself. It was only a game, only gallantry; he would pick her a flower on a hunt; she would give him a ribbon to wear on a raid. All of it very open, very playful, a promising young vassal being nice to his liege lord's favorite child. And of course you took your power for granted—your power over Rudi, your power over her.

It was I who dusted love powders into his clothing in the wash-house—you never thought about such things, did you, when you made me a scrub-woman? I suppose I used too much; he ended with a rash, and had to see the physician; but it will take more than a doctor to cure him of the itch he has now. And it was I who told her stories when the days were long and no one was there to comfort her. I chose the stories very carefully, always tales of forbidden love, and hidden messages, and secret hiding places. She was a bright little thing; she put to use everything I taught her, and rather quickly, I must say; no doubt she inherited your splendid appetites.

She's probably with him now—wouldn't it tickle your proud lordship's heart? In the room behind the barley stores which no one uses any more, in her little nightdress, with your most faithful vassal. The one who leapt to fulfill your every command, even the worst of them, imagining he would finally be rewarded. Poor Rudi.

We are come all but full circle, lord Arnulf of Ravensbruck. You robbed me of everything I loved. You broke my honor, you broke my heart; you made me an animal, with nothing to live for but death. Now it is your turn . . . but I suppose, even to the very end, you will see everything in your dying except the truth.

Karelian of Lys and his company arrived a week later. By then the Iron Count—who indeed seemed to be made of something much harder and more indestructible than mere flesh—was able sit up in his chair, eat a full meal with plenty of beer, and give orders as usual. For the first time in months the great hall was actually swept clean, though of course it did not stay that way more than a day. There was a great flurry of hunting and butchering and baking, and piles of clothing dumped into the wash-house. It was a good thing, Sigune reflected, that people in Ravensbruck occasionally died or got married. It was the only time the countess might hope for something new to wear, or the servants for something extra to eat. However barbarous the count was in other ways, he had a well-developed sense of rank and honor. When highborn guests came to his fortress, they were treated like royalty.

This guest actually *was* royalty, in Arnulf's opinion. Karelian Brandeis was a kinsman of Duke Gottfried, and it was common knowledge in the Reinmark that Gottfried claimed ancestry back to the first Frankish kings. The very first, the Merovingians, who ruled before Charlemagne, and who were usurped by Charlemagne's father. Unfortunately for Gottfried, there was nothing to support his claim but legend. Four hundred years had passed, after all; there wasn't a royal house anywhere in Christendom which could trace its genealogy back so far, through so many wars and upheavals. Some people scoffed at the duke's claim, but others merely added it to his already extraordinary prestige. Of course he has royal blood, they would say; look at his magnificent appearance; look at his courage, his prowess in war, his splendid leadership . . . such a man was surely born of kings!

Sigune would not have cared in the least who Gottfried thought his ancestors were, if the same ancestry had not belonged to Karelian of Lys. But it was the reason Arnulf leapt at the offer of a marriage between Karelian and his daughter. There were other lords he might have chosen—among them young Rudolf of Selven—other lords equally endowed with property, and much more suitable in age for a girl of seventeen.

But royal blood was royal blood. It did not matter how many hundred years the Merovingian kings were dead. It did not matter if three separate lines had since replaced them. It did not even matter that Gottfried's claim might well be false. Karelian stood apart among Adelaide's suitors for reason of his blood alone, and he was welcomed with endless feasting and drinking, and endless tales of war.

Sigune had no place at the great feast tables, or anywhere near them. But now and then, amidst the scrubbing and the carrying, or when the count of Ravensbruck needed tending and the physician was elsewhere and the countess was busy, she had her moments to study the count of Lys, and to plan her next move.

She would get rid of this stallion Arnulf had chosen for Adelaide's bed. She would get rid of him, royal blood and all, him and however many others Arnulf was able to entice, until there were none left. Perhaps this was how the stories began, all those marvellous stories about suitors who had to guess impossible riddles or have their heads taken off. There was never a riddle, Sigune thought. There was never a princess with so much power. For if a woman had the right to set such deadly challenges, surely she had the right to just say no. What there was instead of riddles, probably, was a witch in the corner whom no one even noticed.

It was late; the room stank of torch-smoke and sweat; half the men at Arnulf's table were drunk. The count's women had long ago retired, as they were expected to do. The real storytelling never started until they were gone. There were so many things women were not supposed to hear spoken of—an astonishing thing, Sigune thought, when women were so often the ones who endured them.

She was quite far from the count's table; his exchanges with Karelian were mostly lost in the general drunken babble. Except sometimes when he raised his voice to drive home a point: "Why are we sending armies to Palestine, that's what I would like to know?"

Or when he laughed, and roared out the triumphant end of a story, how he killed some Swede, or some Prussian, or some Reinmark rebel, man to man and blow by blow, until those listening could hear the clashing of their swords, and almost see the enemy's severed head rolling across the feast table and tumbling onto the floor.

Whatever the count of Lys said in reply to any of this, Sigune could not hear. She studied him patiently and with care, as a warrior might study an enemy before combat, noting everything without emotion and without self-deceit.

He was a fine-looking man, for those to whom it mattered. His body was solid and powerful, so well-proportioned that he seemed neither tall nor heavy, though in fact he was both. He had a good nose and fine, high cheekbones. Rich hair fell curling to his shoulders, the color of a stag in August. There were no scars on his face. He was lucky in battle then, or very good. And although he looked his thirty-eight years, maturity gave him presence, and served to hone his natural gifts rather than diminish them. He smiled easily, a courteous smile which charmed men like a caress. But when once or twice she had been close enough to see his eyes, they were cool and watchful. Even now, sitting at Arnulf's right hand in the midst of all the clamor and vainglory, he seemed faintly aloof, drinking a great deal and not saying very much.

Arrogant as the devil, she thought. *You think you're too good for these wild border folk. Or maybe you're just bored. You've heard it all, you've done it all, why don't they just get on with the wedding and give you the bedchamber key . . . .*

What shall I do to you, proud Karelian of Lys, supposedly heir of all those dead kings? Maybe you should drop your trenchers all over your lap? Or start to fart like an old gelding climbing up a long hill . . . but then, in Ravensbruck, would anybody notice?

He was raising his cup to his mouth—one of Arnulf's great silver stems, freshly brimming with beer. *Well, why not?* she thought, and tipped it.

And watched, astonished and slowly tensing with fear, as he drank, and wiped the foam from his mouth, and went on listening to Arnulf's tales with the same polite exhaustion as before.

She withdrew deep into the shadows, made herself wait, breathe quietly, concentrate. A huge, mangy dog was lying against the wall.

She pressed her thought against its leg—harder than she realized. It woke yelping, scrambled to its feet with a snarl, saw her, and slunk away.

So. It's not me, then. It's him. He is a sorcerer, too . . . .

Days passed; she was afraid to try again; afraid he would notice even the smallest flicker of her power, the way magnets noticed iron, the way hawks noticed rabbits in the grass. But every day, sometime in the day she would encounter Adelaide's bleak, frightened eyes. She would see Arnulf of Ravensbruck mastering his pain as he mastered everything else in his path, growing strong again, ruling the world. Nothing had changed, really; she had plotted her vengeance all these years and nothing had changed.

She tested Karelian of Lys again. And again. She worked the most powerful spells she knew, in the deepest dead of night, and nothing happened. He did not seem to be aware of her actions; he was simply out of their reach.

Someone else was shielding him.

VIII

IN THE WOMEN'S QUARTERS

O see how narrow are our days,
How full of fear our bed.

RAINER MARIA RILKE

BLOOD WELLED INTO A GREAT RED DROP on the ball of Adelaide's thumb. It stung, but she hardly noticed; her fingers were cold, and the tiny wound was only one of many. She wiped it furtively on a handkerchief, but Helga noticed anyway.

"You've pricked yourself again, have you?" Helga smiled. "You know, you're really lucky you were born a girl, and only get to use needles. Think what would happen if they ever turned you loose with a sword."

The first thing I'd do is cut your nose off and hang it on a string around your neck. Then you'd have something of your own to meddle with . . . .

Adelaide's eyes burned from pitch smoke, from hours of trying and trying to see. The sewing lay forgotten on her lap, stiff and white, icy to the touch. There was no end to it. Pillow cloths. Table cloths. Shifts. Aprons. Shawls. Blankets. Quilts. Cloths to sit on and to sleep on, cloths for the chapel, cloths for the windows, cloths to blow your nose. The women of Ravensbruck had done nothing for months but sew, till the world had shrunk to a room, and the room to a chair and a needle. It was December; the windows were boarded shut against the winter. Their only light came from torches; their only warmth from an ill-burning hearth. Sometimes for hours she thought of nothing but running away. She would somehow run away, and become a bandit, or a veela's familiar. They said the wood nymphs stole young girls away sometimes. They carried them off to the forest, to tend their long golden hair, and learn their wild veela ways. She would go willingly; they wouldn't have to steal her. And one day she would come back, secret and powerful, and do something to Clara of Ravensbruck and her red mouthed brat. Something they would never, never forget.

Rudi said it was no better to be a man. He said you were just sent hither and thither like a dog for his master's bones, and died if you made a single mistake. But he was wrong; it had to be better than walls, better than days so endlessly alike she could not remember them, better than Clara hoping she would die. Rudi had a horse, and weapons, and the wind and the sun in his hair. And he had the possibility, the exquisite, unthinkable possibility of simply riding away, of saying, *No more, I won't endure it any more,* and turning his horse to the dawn, and never looking back.

"Really mother," Helga said. "If Adelaide isn't going to work on her own things, I don't see why I should have to."

Adelaide picked up the sewing again, quickly, but not before the countess had risen to her feet. She was almost crippled with the sickness in her joints; she moved slowly, yet in every movement was a terrible ferocity, as though she could take her lost strength back from the world by force.

They said she had been pretty in her girlhood, as Helga was now: full-bodied and vital, with a tempting, flesh-warm sweetness. Adelaide did not believe it. The woman's face was carved of shale, tight and passionless. She never laughed. She detested almost everything that lived. She limped across the room, and Adelaide's stomach knotted into a tiny ball of pain.

"What's the matter with you?" Clara demanded.

"Nothing, my lady," Adelaide said.

Clara did not seem to notice the reply or even to want a reply at all. She went on, harshly:

"You don't care about anything, do you? All your father's concern for you, and all of mine, year after year, and what's it worth to you? Nothing!" She wrenched the sewing out of Adelaide's hand. "Look at this! It's all crooked! Can't you even make a decent hem?"

"Lady, the light is so bad today—"

She should never have said it. She shouldn't have said anything at all. Clara seized a handful of her hair and jerked it viciously, snapping her head back, forcing out a small yelp of pain.

"So now even the light isn't good enough for you! I suppose you think we should burn fifty marks' worth of wood a day, and leave the windows wide open? Do you think Karelian of Lys will be able to afford that? Oh, he'll rue the day he ever took you for a wife. You can't even sew your wedding garments properly.

"I swear I don't understand your father. I served him faithfully all these years, and I gave him four good sons. But does he arrange a good marriage like this for my daughter? Oh, no, he arranges it for you, and like as not he'll send poor Helga to some dirty border fortress to be married to a brute. And all you can do is idle away your time and pull a long face! Stupid, that's what you are. Worthless and stupid!"

Adelaide turned her face away from her step-mother's wrath, and saw Helga busy herself with her sewing. On the younger girl's face was a familiar look of satisfaction and dismay. She always made trouble. She always felt guilty afterwards for doing it. Or pretended to.

Helga, she knew, would sell her soul to marry a man like Karelian of Lys. Her hard little eyes burned with longing when she saw the gifts he brought, when he talked about his lands and his splendid manor house. And he was a hero besides. He had been to Jerusalem and fought the infidels; he was descended from ancient kings.

Helga should have had him, Adelaide reflected bitterly. Then everyone would be happy. But it wasn't God's business to make people happy, was it? Life was hard. Life was supposed to be hard, the countess said. How else would a Christian deserve heaven?

The countess ripped open the hem Adelaide had made, and shoved the garment into her face.

"Do it again, and do it right, or you'll sit there until morning."

She swallowed; she did not cry. It did no good to cry; it only made things worse. It did no good, either, to complain to her father. She had done so once or twice, long ago. He had been furious, and had beaten the countess, and called her names, and that felt good for a while. But it was Clara she had to live with, day after day, Clara who controlled every waking moment of her life, Clara who did not grow kinder towards her, merely more skilful in her choice of cruelties. If she complained to the count, Clara would pay once—and then, for a very long time after, Adelaide would pay over and over. It was better to be silent. Just be silent and dream.

In the forests of Jutland, very long ago, there lived a king who was very stern and cold. He had a beautiful daughter, but he kept her in his stone fortress all alone. He did not want anyone to marry her. No one came to see her except the birds, who all sang very wonderfully. She learned to imitate them, and to sing in all their different languages.

One day a prince came, wandering lost and wounded from a distant war, and heard her singing. What bird is this, he asked, that sings so sweetly, and makes my heart so glad? If only I could tame it, I would take it home with me, and I would never be sorrowful again. And at once the princess was transformed into a bird, and flew into his hand . . . .

The smaller the world grew, the tinier were the things on which it turned. She could live a week on the glance Rudi might cast towards her window as he strode across the courtyard or mounted his horse—a seemingly idle glance, unnoticed by anyone but her, a gift, the only gift he had: *I am still here, Heidi; I still adore you . . . .* A week on that, a month on a stolen word, a year on the memory of a kiss.

A lifetime, if need be, on the quick, silent sharing of their bodies, those few times. It was hard for them to be together in this pitilessly guarded world, this world of stone and eyes; so hard and so desperately dangerous, so little pleasure in it amidst the fear, only the dark pleasure of defiance itself. They had loved each other, and nothing could ever take that away. Not the walls and the black winter, not Clara, not God. Not even death, if it came—the retribution which seemed sometimes too terrible to imagine, and sometimes held a strange compelling beauty. There would be stories about them, perhaps, stories the minnesingers would carry all across the land, love's last revenge against the law's revengers: We are the ones who are remembered. We are the ones who made the choice which mattered.

There were worse things to die for than Rudi's black eyes, and his hawk's grace, and his courage. How could Helga think Karelian of Lys was handsome? Dear God, he was old, almost as old as her father. Rudi was only twenty-one, and dark as the hunter elves, and utterly without fear. There was nothing he wouldn't do for love of her, nothing. She did not care if other men called him ruthless, and wondered about his honor, and stayed carefully out of his way. They did not know why he acted so, and if they had, they would have thought less of him than before. Such love as his was lunacy.

But Melusine took the prince upon her horse, and rode with him to the very edges of the sea. She threw away her fine garments, and he saw that her body glistened silver as the water touched it, and her loins were the loins of a fish. There, she said, pointing seaward, there lies the realm of my people. I have castles of coral, and forests of green kelp, and the sea maidens play by my side. Come now, and live with me there.

And he said to her: What of my kingdom?

And she answered him: Kingdoms will always have kings. What of me?

IX

THE IRON COUNT

He who believes that anything comes out
favorably or unfavorably because of the crying of
a raven shall do penance for seven days.

PENITENTIAL OF BARTHOLOMEOW ISCANUS

FOR YEARS AFTER, PAUL WOULD LOOK BACK to those first days and
weeks in Ravensbruck and try to remember when he first began
to be afraid. When he first began to notice that something was wrong.
Something beyond the ordinary darkness of a sinful world, beyond
the ordinary savagery of a border lord's life. The first whispers of
unease he brushed aside, thinking them carry-overs from Car-Iduna.
They came again. And again. And again.

There was the Wend woman, a horrible creature who hung about
in the shadows of the hall, and tended the count sometimes, never
speaking. The people of Ravensbruck hardly noticed her any more;
she had been there so long. It took a stranger's eye to see the malevolence in her, to realize those always lowered eyes hid pools of
hatred.

There was Peter, the count's squire, bored to distraction since his
master was injured, following Paul around like a dog, wanting stories
of the Holy Land, whispering the tale of Sigune in the shadows of
the stable, as though it were a secret no one knew but himself: *She
was his lordship's concubine; they say she tried to kill him, years
ago . . . .* Whispering other things, too, always vague, always full of
possibilities which he never explained: *Oh, I know things, if I chose
to tell you, things nobody would believe . . . .* A pretentious little

scoundrel, Paul thought, always looking for favors and for gifts, yet with just enough real knowledge to make one wonder what he might be keeping back.

There was Rudolf of Selven, whom Paul noticed at first simply because he was dark. Peter had other reasons for noticing him.

"Nobody messes with that one," Peter said. "Not since Reisdorf."

Silence. Feigning infinite indifference, Paul turned Karelian's saddle about on his knee, and began polishing the other side.

"He met his best friend under a flag of truce," Peter went on, "and then he betrayed him. Oh, it was the right thing to do, of course. Nicholas was a rebel. He'd killed the count's son, and he was living like a bandit, stealing and plundering. But a lot of the men thought he had cause for it, and they didn't want to go after him—"

"Why did they think he had cause?"

"Well, it's just gossip of course, no one knows if it's true. But they say the count's son lost a wager to Nicholas, and they quarreled. Some days afterwards, they found Nicholas's young page in the woods, dead—well, worse than dead, if you know what I mean. Nicholas blamed the count's son, and killed him like a dog, and went to war against the count. He had a lot of friends; it would have been a hard fight.

"So Rudi slipped off into the hills, with just a few men, and sent out word to arrange a meeting at a farm near Reisdorf, hinting he would join the rebels. There wasn't another soul in the world Nicholas would have trusted, not even Jesus Christ, but he trusted Rudi. And Rudi brought him back for Arnulf to hang."

"No wonder he's so high in Arnulf's favor."

"Not nearly as high as he'd like to be."

"What do you mean?"

"Oh, nothing. Everybody wants more than they have, don't they?"

And that was all Peter would say on the subject for almost a fortnight—a fortnight which passed with a wearying sameness of grey winter days, and long winter nights of boasting and drink.

"Why are we sending armies to Palestine, that's what I would like to know?" Count Arnulf's voice boomed across the great hall; men at the far end of his long table broke off their conversations and looked up. The man was amazing, hardly a man at all, but a force of nature. He had been gravely injured; he could not walk at all, or stand up without a cane. And yet he sat here, hour after hour, night after night, indifferent to pain, indifferent to time, drinking unimaginable quantities of beer and talking everyone around him to blank exhaustion.

"We should be sending our men east," he went on fiercely, "to Prussia, to Latvia—the whole damned Baltic could be ours for the taking. Why the devil doesn't the pope think about that?"

"I have no idea," Karelian replied. "He doesn't make a habit of asking my advice."

Arnulf chuckled. "No, I am sure he doesn't. Not yours, or mine, or any other German's." He waved at Peter to fetch him more beer.

"Well, at least you brought something worthwhile back from that damnable desert. The rumors say Gottfried needed a ship to bring home his booty. Is it true?"

"It's true. And he paid off his men first, all of them—and generously too, for seven years of service."

"How in God's name did he come by such a treasure?"

"He stripped the temple of Jerusalem."

Arnulf paused with his cup almost at his mouth. "He did what?"

"He plundered the great temple. We learned from some spies that it was laden with treasure—gold, silver, precious stones, everything. Once we were over the walls, he made a point of being the first man there."

Arnulf banged his fist on the table in delight. "Yes, he would, by God! But it must have been more than the Franks could swallow, when he got there ahead of them. I'll wager they howled like babies, wanting their own fistful."

"They wanted a fistful; the priests wanted it all. They said it should belong to the Church. There was no end of quarreling over it, but in the end Gottfried kept the lion's share."

"As the lion should."

Arnulf shifted in his chair, wincing briefly against the pain.

"God knows, maybe I should have gone, if the pickings were so rich. To say nothing of all those pretty heathen girls to choose from, wearing nothing but their perfumes and their veils. What were they like, Karel, tell me—and for Christ's sake don't pretend to be a saint, just because you're marrying my daughter! I wouldn't expect any man to pass up a chance like that—four women for every infidel in the city, Christ, it must have been a feast!"

Arnulf waited, watching him with expectation, but the reply came from Reinhard instead.

"You misjudge us, my lord count," he said. "We did no evil with the Saracen women. We killed them wherever we found them."

"You're not serious."

The lord of Ravensbruck was not easily surprised, but this time, Paul thought, he truly did not believe what he had heard. "He's not serious, Karelian? You're not going to tell me it's true?"

Karelian looked at his cup for a time, and then met Arnulf's eyes levelly, grimly.

"When the sun went down that day, my lord, every Saracen in Jerusalem was dead, and every Jew, and most every other living thing except ourselves. So, yes, it is true."

"You didn't even hump them first?"

"Some did, I expect. The knights mostly did not."

"And you took no slaves? Even a plain woman is worth a few marks if she's young and can work."

"They were infidels, my lord," Reinhard said.

"They were plunder, for Christ's sake! You kept the gold, didn't you? Wasn't it infidel gold? God's blood, you take this business of holy war entirely too far!"

Karelian downed another stein, wiped his mouth with the back of his hand, and stared at a spot on the table where a sharp object—a dagger, perhaps, or a spear—had left a deep, ugly gouge. Then he laid his head back against the wooden chair. Paul's hand had been resting there, idly, only a whisper of distance now from the fine, tawny head. Without noticing, Paul drew his hand away and held it for a long time clenched by his side.

"We need some minstrels," Karelian said dreamily. "Minnesingers. Dancing girls. Fools. Lots and lots of fools. What do you think, Pauli? Where can we find some fools?"

Arnulf was staring at him in absolute bewilderment.

"My lord," Paul whispered. "You're very drunk."

"Not nearly drunk enough. Doesn't anyone in the whole of Ravensbruck know how to sing? Give me some beer, Pauli."

He held out his cup unsteadily, but as Paul bent to fill it, he saw that the count's fingers were closed firmly on the handle, and his eyes were not muddy at all. Only bitter and tired.

Arnulf was talking again. There was clearly no point discussing the great crusade any further; Karelian was too drunk, and Reinhard too misguided, and Otto was playing dice. But there were other wars to talk about; indeed, he preferred to talk about his own. There were so many. It would take years to tell of every battle, every warrior slain blow by blow in single combat, every house burned, every village, every ship. Every woman taken, and every horse, and every sack of coin.

"Sit down, lad, for God's sake, before you fall," Karelian murmured.

So Paul sat by the count's chair as Arnulf talked on, and the night dissolved into a space without borders or meaning. Servants took away the leftover food and sat in huddles in the background, sleeping or gossiping, waiting for commands, waiting for it to end. Dogs fought over bones in the rushes on the floor. Men bloated with beer staggered off to a corner and threw up, or wrapped themselves in their cloaks and found a place to sleep. The room stank of smoke and sweat, and yet it was desolately cold. Wind guttered the torches, and snow blowing in from the cracks of high windows gathered in small ridges along the walls.

Mostly it was Vikings Arnulf did battle with. Occasionally Prussians. Once, apparently, it had been the Wends. But the Vikings were his enemies of choice. He had travelled the whole of the North Sea coast to meet them wherever they came, and he remembered it all with the pleasure of a man remembering sex.

"We caught up with them half a mile from the river. They'd have made it back to their ships, but they were loaded with booty. They'd plundered half the valley; Christ, they had cartloads of pigs, they had cattle, and I don't know how many sacks of grain, and all the women they could find. And do you know what the heathen devils did, when they saw we were on them, and they'd have to abandon everything? They destroyed it. Everything. They slashed the grain sacks, they killed the animals, they cut the women's throats—that's Vikings for you, they were bred in hell, the lot of them. But there wasn't one of them made it home to their heathen altars, not this time. We got between them and the river, and I sent a small party to fire the ships, and the rest of us dealt with the dogs. By luck we took the chief's son alive. Some of the men wanted to ransom him, to try and get some of our own captives back. But I wouldn't even consider it. What is the worst death you ever saw a man die, Karelian?"

Karelian pulled his fur cloak close around his neck. "Don't know," he muttered.

"We torched his balls and the soles of his feet, till they were black. We put out his eyes. We smashed every one of his fingers with a stone club, and every one of his toes, and then his arms and his legs. We drove nails into both sides of his jaws. It took about a week, all of that, and then we finished him off with a burning iron rod, lodged in what I will leave you to judge was the most appropriate place."

"You're an extraordinary man, my lord."

"Aye." Arnulf took a long drink. He was tiring, but only a little. "I can be generous to a fault, Karelian, to those who deserve it. But any man who earns my enmity, God help him. He'll rue the day he was born."

Somewhere down the table a chair scraped, a man cursed, an iron cup smashed against the table. For a moment Paul thought it was only a drunken vassal stumbling to his feet to find the privy or a bed. But men all around were springing to their feet; he heard scuffling, and then a yelp of pain.

"Stand aside!"

Arnulf's voice was a thunderclap, awesome not only for its power, but for the weight of authority it carried. He had risen from his chair, clinging to his cane with one hand and to his squire's arm with the other; and wounded though he was, Paul knew, no man there was likely to defy him.

The cluster of men parted, and he saw one of Arnulf's knights, a man called Franz, swaying drunkenly and daubing at his side with his fingers, completely bewildered, as though he could not understand where the blood was coming from. Rudolf of Selven stood in front of him, grappled to standstill by his comrades, still holding a stained dagger in his hand.

Arnulf of Ravensbruck chuckled.

"Is it blood or ale you're losing there, Franzli?"

The wounded knight, drunk to a stupor, looked at him, grinned, and collapsed. They heaved him onto the table; someone ran for the surgeon. Carefully, they let Rudi go. He wiped his blade clean and strode without a word towards the door.

This time the count did not have to shout to be heard. He barely had to murmur.

"Selven."

For a moment Paul thought the young man would simply keep on walking. Then he stopped and turned. He was, except for Paul himself, the only sober man in the place, but it did not seem like a virtue just now. It seemed rather like a demonstration of power, something icy and calculated. This man kept his wits about him for reasons which had nothing to do with Christian moderation.

"My lord?"

"There's a rule in this hall, Rudi. You leave your weapons by the door when you come in. All of them."

Selven wiped his face with the back of his hand. Then, for no reason Paul could imagine, he glanced once, with a terrible bitterness, towards Karelian of Lys.

"I forgot I was carrying it, my lord."

"You remembered again right quickly when you wanted to. Give it here."

Unwillingly, Selven approached his lord. From the day of his arrival Paul disliked the man, though at first he could not have said why. Now perhaps he could. Rudi's arrogance, for one thing: the hard-edged, chip-on-his-shoulder arrogance which bristled against everything it met. The sullen demeanor as well; the watchfulness, the thin face hung with ragged hair, too young a face to be so knife-like and hard. The threat of coiled violence in his body, which made even his most innocent movements seem predatory and dangerous. He was a man to walk circles around, just like his liege.

He handed the dagger to Count Arnulf, casually, hilt first.

Arnulf examined it as though it were a gift.

"Pretty," he said. "You've always wanted one of these, Peter. You can have it."

The count's squire, greedy little rat that he was, took it eagerly.

Rudolf's face tightened a fraction more, but he only bowed faintly, said good night, and stalked away.

Arnulf sank into his chair.

"Best man I have," he said to Karelian, wearily. "But always pushing the edges. Always. And snarly as hell. He's got nerve, though, Christ. There's only one man in the Reinmark with more balls than Rudi Selven. And that one is me."

It was not the German way for men and women to live or work apart. From the smallest serf's hut to the great palace at Aachen, the sexes mingled freely. They ate at the same board, and often from the same plate. They did their different tasks side by side, and slept in the same rooms. Squires and pages bedded down on pallets beside their masters' marriage beds. Any man rich enough to own a bath was served there by the household maids; they washed his hair and scrubbed his back and draped him in his towels. Paul's own father, being a singularly chaste man, kept a linen cloth tied around his loins in his bath, and the canopy closed around his bed, but otherwise he lived as did his peers, and thought nothing of it.

Neither did Paul think anything of it until he saw something of the world. Even infidels were appalled by the Germans' disgraceful lack of modesty. They assumed, as the Byzantines had, that every man in the Roman west was a savage, and every woman a whore—an outrageous assumption, considering their own decadence. At least the Europeans kept only one wife, and utterly forbade perversions against nature.

But Paul learned one thing from the eastern world nonetheless: the appearance of virtue mattered as well as the substance. It created a climate of morality. It made the idea of sin more unacceptable, and the possibility of it more difficult. Human carnality and wickedness being what they were, men were wise to keep their women sheltered.

How Arnulf of Ravensbruck reached the same conclusion Paul could not imagine. Perhaps it was because of his very shamelessness, his own intensely predatory sexuality. He knew better than anyone why his daughters should not sit through the long evenings in his feast hall with a horde of drunken knights; why they should not go hunting and riding all over the countryside like the daughters of his peers did; why they went nowhere, not even to the cathedral of Ravensbruck for Christmas Mass, without armed guards. The violence of the borderlands was a factor, of course: the insecurity, the possibility of sudden and pitiless attack. But the world everywhere was dangerous—surely nowhere more dangerous than on the long march to Jerusalem, where hundreds of men, even many of the highest rank, took along their wives.

Fear alone did not account for Arnulf's caution. He kept his women from the world because he knew the world. Every time he looked at it, he saw himself.

Because of this, Karelian had very little contact with his bride. Once, very discreetly, he asked if they might spend an afternoon together—with servants present, of course, or the countess herself. He was nearly forty, he said, and the girl but seventeen; he had spent most of his life abroad; they had a great deal to learn about each other.

He did not mention it, of course, but he was also thoroughly bored with Arnulf's company.

The count of Ravensbruck laughed.

"God's blood, Karelian, it is clear you've never been married. You'll see more than enough of her in the years to come."

"That may be, my lord. Still, I would rather we didn't marry as total strangers."

"Why on earth not? There are only two things you need to know which matter, and you won't learn either of them sitting by the window."

The women, he went on, had a great deal of work to do preparing for the wedding, and the countess was not well.

"Yes, of course, I understand," Karelian said. "It was a frivolous request. Forgive me."

They went hunting instead. They exercised their horses in the count's huge barracks yard, and practiced their swordplay. The days passed, short days heavy with low-hanging cloud, long evenings endless with war-talk. The winter closed, falling towards the solstice.

Karelian tried, without success, to drink himself into oblivion.

Maybe, Paul told himself, maybe it was just the season after all, the heaviness of winter. Maybe it was just his memories of Car-Iduna making him see evil everywhere, making him afraid. For today the sun was out, and their horses raced across the frozen ground with boundless energy, and they laughed, watching the pack animals grow laden with hares and partridges and small deer, riding and shooting and wishing the sun might never go down.

Karelian reined in his horse, letting the others go. He pulled a chunk of bread out his saddle pack, broke off half and gave it to Paul, and bit heartily into the other.

"They will lose us," Paul said.

"Good." The count chewed off another mouthful, and pointed casually to the southwest. "Look."

For a moment Paul saw nothing except forest, bits of clearing, the lines of the distant hills. Then his eyes caught motion, and focused. Far away, almost too far to identify, a great stag moved among the scattered, naked trees.

"That one," Karelian said quietly, "is mine."

"Is there anything you don't see, my lord?" Paul asked.

"Not much."

They rode on slowly, quietly. A brisk wind was in their faces, carrying off the sound of their approach. Closer now, Paul could see the stag was magnificent, and his breath quickened with excitement. This would be a prize to set all of Ravensbruck a-marveling. Karelian slowed his horse and reached for his bow.

That was when the raven came. It swung in a soft black arc across the valley, graceful and silent. For a moment Karelian was distracted, his eyes following the bird. He smiled faintly, taking its appearance as an omen of good luck.

But for Paul the brightness of the day vanished in a breath, as though a huge black cloud had rolled across the sky. The tug in the pit of his stomach was no longer simply the thrill of the hunt; it was a soft whisper of fear. The same fear as before, the same certainty of danger which followed him everywhere in Ravensbruck.

Without haste, Karelian dismounted, braced the crossbow with his feet and drew it taut, aimed it, following the restless motions of the animal with infinite patience.

The raven circled, stark and shimmering against the winter sky.

For Christ's sake, my lord, take your stag, and let us be gone from here . . . !

Karelian pulled the trigger. It was a splendid shot; the deer bolted, took two great leaps into the trees, and crashed to the earth. The count leapt onto his horse with a shout of triumph; and they raced towards their prey, ducking branches and bounding over deadfall.

"God, would you look at him!" Karelian said proudly as they approached. "We'll feast like kings tonight."

The raven screamed.

It was a terrible sound, a cry almost human in its ferocity. Karelian reared his mount to a halt, looking skyward for the bird. The smile of triumph vanished from his face and his hand closed on the hilt of his sword.

"My lord, what is it?" Paul whispered, every drop of his blood turning into ice.

The count did not answer. The raven shrieked again, then broke from its lazy flight like an arrow, diving low above a patch of heavy woods.

And so they saw in those woods a shadow, a fallen pine, the bent form of a man leveling a crossbow, other shadows close around him . . . .

Karelian cursed, whirling his horse and bending low across its back.

"Ride, lad!" he shouted. "Ride for your life!"

Paul did not answer, or question, or look back. He lunged after Karelian, spurring his mount and praying without knowing that he did so. How foolish they had been, going off alone in this perilous country for such a frivolous prize as a stag; dear God, what empty vanity . . . ! Then an arrow whistled past his shoulder and he thought only of wanting to live.

But they were not shooting at him. The first arrow thudded into Karelian's saddle. Several others flew wild. The last (from a careful marksman, like Karelian himself?) struck the count high in the back. He faltered a little, but kept going; it was Paul who cried out, a blind cry to God that it could not be, a man like Karelian could not die like this, after so many glories, after Jerusalem itself, not like this, in a wretched little ambush in a miserable border mark, for the sake of a stag.

No! He was sobbing in his throat, over and over, *no, no, no . . . !* Then the trees were around them, hundreds of trees, great black firs shutting out the sun and the arrows. They rode on for some time more, until they were sure they were not being followed. Karelian pulled up then, straightening, his face rigid with pain.

"Oh, my lord . . . here, let me help you . . . !" Paul started to dismount, meaning to draw the count from his saddle and tend his wound, but Karelian stopped him with a gesture.

"Break the damn thing off Pauli. I don't want to bleed all the way back to Ravensbruck."

His voice was surprisingly strong; indeed he looked angry more than hurt. The shaft had struck high—too high to kill, unless the tip was poisoned or the wound went bad. And his heavy leather hauberk had absorbed most of the arrow's force. Paul reached for the hideous thing, and suddenly he could not bear to touch it.

"A quick snap, Pauli, that's the easy way," Karelian said.

He wanted to do it. It was a perfectly reasonable, necessary thing, and no more painful than the surgeon's care would be later. Instead he slid his hand over Karelian's shoulder, and bending, pressed his face against his back.

It was only for a moment, the tiniest of moments. It meant nothing, only thankfulness. Why should he not be thankful that his lord was safe, and feel pity for his pain? It meant nothing evil, and if Karelian thought it did, well, that was Karelian's own cynicism. Worldly men read sin into everything.

He felt tears against his face. He straightened, and broke off the arrow. He said inane things: "It's just a tiny wound, my lord, are you sure you can ride?" He did not look at Karelian's face, or meet his eyes, but it was only because he was ashamed of being maudlin. Only because of that.

They met up with the rest of the hunting party less than a league away. Rudolf of Selven was not with them; nobody knew where he was.

Karelian made light of the attack, blaming it on bandits, and asked if some of the men would be so kind as to fetch in his stag.

"You know where it is, Paul; show them. We can wait for you here."

"My lord, let's go back to Ravensbruck, and have your wound tended."

"I want that stag." He smiled then, his wonderfully charming smile which no one ever could resist. "It cost me enough."

He wanted also to wait for Rudolf of Selven, Paul thought; to see from which direction he came, and what he might have to say for himself.

He came from the east, nearly an hour later, with lathered horses and no game. He had nothing to explain, and he did not much like being asked. He had picked up the trail of a boar, he said, and he did the same thing Karelian did. He went after a prize kill—only he hadn't been as lucky.

Having said that, he sat on his horse with his thin face arrogantly set, his manner and his mood both defying Karelian, or anyone else who had any doubts about him, to go ahead and make something of it. No one did.

X

THE MARRIAGE

How much time did Adam and Eve spend in paradise?
Seven hours.

Why not any longer?
Because hardly was woman created when she sinned.

HONORIUS OF AUTUN

WE HUNTED NO MORE THAT DAY. We took Karelian back to Ravensbruck, where his wound was carefully tended. Arnulf was furious. He swore a group of armed men would go out the next day and look for any sign of bandits, and hunt them down. But it snowed overnight, and the searchers found nothing, and the matter was soon brushed aside. Karelian accused no one. There was no evidence other than circumstance, and Ravensbruck was too tense and violent a place to make unfounded charges against anyone. But he watched his back very carefully thereafter, and he went nowhere without his men.

I was not entirely satisfied with Arnulf's response. So I lured Peter into the back of the stable with the promise of a gold buckle from Damascus, and questioned him again, and found myself more troubled than before.

Karelian was not in his quarters where I sought him, after I had spoken with Peter. Nor was he with Arnulf in the great hall, or anywhere in the courtyard. The day was nearly gone by then; the last light failing. Finally one of the servants, laden down with a great armful of wood, made a simple gesture with his head towards the towering ramparts.

I ran all the way up, and when I came out on the roof the icy wind all but took my breath away. He was standing alone by the wall, staring to the southwest, to the distant hills of Helmardin. Wind rippled the furs on his collar and tugged at his hair. He heard my footsteps, and turned, and I saw the black feather trembling in his hand.

Strangely, it was I who felt embarrassed. He put the talisman away, without haste, without a trace of shame, and leaned both elbows on the castle wall, looking off towards the hills as before. I went to stand beside him.

"It will snow tonight, I think," I said.

"Probably."

I waited for him to speak further, to give me some kind of opening, but he did not, and finally I began again.

"I've just had a long talk with Peter, my lord."

"And what does Peter have to say?"

"He says Rudolf of Selven had his heart set on marrying Adelaide himself."

Karelian turned quickly. Too quickly, I thought. "Was there an agreement?" he demanded.

"No. None whatever. But Arnulf married three of his other daughters to local lords, and since the count always favored Rudi, apparently he took it for granted he'd have the same privilege. God knows he has a singular opinion of himself."

Karelian turned back to the hills. He looked cold, and I thought perhaps he was in pain.

"How is it possible," he brooded, "that a man can reach the age of nearly forty, and live through all manner of dangers, and see much of the world, and still be as naive as a boy?"

"Naive, my lord?" I protested, even though I had described him the same way in my private thoughts, more than once.

"Yes. To leap into one folly after another, and tell himself each time it's going to be different. I haven't even made this alliance yet, and already I regret it. I wish to God I had thanked Gottfried for his trouble, and ridden home to Lys, and found myself a widow with a pretty laugh and a big feather bed and a tavern."

"You're not serious, my lord."

"I have rarely been more serious." He paused, brushing fallen branches off the wall, into the tumbling wind. "This place stinks of death."

"My lord, there are reckless, ambitious men everywhere—"

He looked at me, and looked away, and I could read his thoughts as clearly as if he had spoken them aloud: *You don't know what in God name I'm talking about, do you, lad?*

Stung, I tried to pursue it. "My lord, I don't like it here, either. It's disputed land, as most borders are, and Arnulf is a harsh and vulgar man. And if it was Selven who attacked us, then he's nothing but a cutthroat. Even so, I don't think it's very different from a lot of other places—"

"Precisely," he said.

"My lord, the world is the world. There is nowhere it's different, except in a monastery."

"Is that our choice, then? To be eunuchs or killers? My father said as much when I was twelve, every time I wanted something: Go be a monk. I never cared for the idea at the time, and I still don't.

"Do you have any idea how weary I am of it, Pauli? Since Jerusalem I've been waiting for it to end. Waiting to live, to go home and spend the rest of my days listening to minstrels and admiring my apple trees."

I lowered my eyes quickly, for I did not want him to see my disappointment—indeed, my disbelief. This was the greatest knight in the land, save for Gottfried himself. Past his prime as a fighting man, perhaps, but not by much, and what he had lost with age he more than made up for with experience. How could such a man be thinking about apple trees?

"I know," he went on. "It all sounds strange to you, what I'm saying. You can't wait to be a knight yourself, and ride off to some scarred field and earn your own glory. I was the same for a long time. I wanted to fight. And God knows I was good at it. So what if I had nothing but my horse and the mail shirt on my back? So what if I was only the last leftover son of a fool? I was better than any of them, and one day they would all know it."

He smiled, a cold, drawn smile in the failing light. "There's one great advantage in being good, Pauli. You might stay alive long enough to finally figure out what's going on. We were just another breed of serfs, the lot of us. Highborn serfs in shining armor, killing each other for our keep, for the hope of a noble marriage or a piece of land. Only a handful of the wars I fought in were honest wars, led by good men with a good cause to fight. A handful, Pauli. The rest were for gain, or for malice, or for the sheer love of fighting."

But my good lord, no one forced the sword into your hand. No one bound you to serve evil men. You bound yourself for payment, for those things of the world which you are still attached to, quite as much as ever . . . .

"My lord, that is the way of men, and it always has been. If you would offer your sword only to God—"

He laughed, harshly and scornfully, and the rest of my words dissolved in my throat.

"God's swords are the bloodiest of all," he said. "And the most dishonest."

I studied the cracks in the grey stone wall.

"Then all those things you said in Car-Iduna, my lord—you meant them?" My words were part question, part statement, part blind pleading.

"Meant them?" He was genuinely astonished. "Of course I meant them! Whatever did you think?"

I did not answer, and he laughed again, but softly.

"I was not ensorceled, Pauli. My mind was quite my own, and it still is."

He took out the feather once more, ran one finger softly over the black silk.

"She saved my life today, Pauli. You realize that, don't you?"

"My lord, you can't possibly believe—"

"How do you see it, then? Do you think the raven's coming, and its warning, was all a singular coincidence?"

"I think if you were saved, my lord, it was God's doing, and God's will."

"God and I are no longer on very good terms."

"You may see it so. God may not."

"God is a realist, I think. He knows me for what I am."

I was never going to be close to him. And I understood it for the first time, I think, there on the windblown tower of Ravensbruck. The distance between us was too great—not the distance of years or rank, but the moral distance.

He told me once, not long before we left the Holy Land, that nearly every close friend he'd ever had was dead. He was drunk, and somewhat maudlin, but his loneliness was real enough. And I imagined I would be his friend. Not just his squire, not just a vassal or a comrade-in-arms, but a friend, the man to whom he would pour out his heart, with whom he would share his cloak in the rain, and his last crust of bread.

I marvel now, here in the quiet of my monastery cell, I marvel at my own continuing innocence. He was not the only one who was naive. A handful of our stumbling conversations should have been enough to make me see the truth, for every time we spoke it was the same. Every time we reached out to each other, we crashed against the walls of his worldliness and his dark unbelief. And each time, he turned away. He withdrew into his disappointment in me, his shrugging assumption that I was just a boy—an overzealous boy with a lot of monkish rhetoric and not much knowledge of the world. And yet I kept believing I could reach him, and earn his love, and bring him back to God. Such is the presumption, the terrible blindness of youth.

It was dawn. The candle guttered in its own ruins. Outside, it was June, the valley quivering with birdsong. In Paul's cell it was dead winter, pitiless and cold, and death birds circled endlessly over the black towers of Ravensbruck.

They were all gone now, to God or to darkness: Arnulf and his wretched women, and Selven, and the Golden Duke who, that very winter, had been only months away from the dazzling center of their lives. All dead, or worse than dead.

Karelian too.

Paul's body ached from hunger, from lashings, from cold, and yet all those hurts could not silence the other hurt. All those years, thirty-one of them, spent first in warfare and then in solitude—nothing, neither time nor prayer nor the undoing of worlds, would erase from his consciousness the face or the voice of Karelian Brandeis.

Twice during the long night he flung the quill away, and took the pages he had written and held them to his candle. They fluttered there, shimmering, the words only clearer for being framed against the light. They would not burn.

How terrible was sorcery, when it could violate the laws of nature, and compel him to remember things which had never been, and to experience in his memories monstrous desires which he had never felt. If he ever doubted the devil's power, he could not doubt it now.

And the outcome for himself was inevitable. He saw it again and again in the horrors which came with his sleep. Fire. Billowing, windblown fire, like the long-ago burning of Ravensbruck. Fire and black terror, men and horses in flames, and Karelian with the arrow in his back, riding towards him, fire in his hair, reaching for him, laughing, their bodies meeting, mating, entangled in a horrid, irresistible embrace.

He slept as little now as his flesh could endure. More than once, groping for consciousness in panic and dismay, in the half-world between dream and waking, he had seen the succubi scurrying away—the demons who came and defiled men in their sleep. But he did not have to see them to know they had come. There was proof enough in the bed, and in the desolate, icy weakness of his body.

He found no respite in prayer. The sacred words dissolved into other words, the images of divine things into other images. Even the slow Gregorian chants, which to his brothers seemed so peaceful, so utterly monastic and pure and not of this world—to him they were sensual now, an exquisitely seductive rising and falling of sound which made him both languorous and tense. It made him think of dancers: lean, slow-moving dancers whose faces kept changing, whose naked bodies sank into the music and emerged again, always different. And always with Karelian. Circling his hard, tawny body and writhing against him and pulling him down, right there in the chapel, right in front of Paul. He would shudder and fling the images away, and they would come back. He would press his knees into the stone until they screamed with pain, and fasten his eyes on the crucifix, and it would be all right for a moment, a small moment, until the singing washed over him again and the face on the crucifix smiled and it was Karelian's face, Karelian's voice, soft amidst the chanting:

It's no great matter, Pauli; I've known for a long time . . . .

Week after week it went on like that. Finally, in early May, Anselm had given him some hope. There was a priest in Mainz who was known to have remarkable success in exorcising demons; he was also politically safe.

"He's been one of the staunchest supporters of the great reform," Anselm said. "He's devoted to the pope. I am sure he'll have no qualms about acting behind the abbot's back. I've sent for him to come as soon as he can manage it."

"You didn't . . . ?" Paul faltered. "You didn't write anything down, I trust?"

"I sent a messenger, who will somehow have to be infi-

nitely persuasive without saying much. Fortunately Father Wilhelm knows me slightly. I'm sure he will come, Paul."

Anselm looked at him then, very hard, and went on:
"Why don't you ask to go to the infirmary for a few days?
Bleeding might help, and some rest certainly would. You look
quite terrible, my friend."

"Nothing will help," Paul said. "Not until it's gone."

That had been weeks ago. Six weeks, to be exact; he
knew because the church counted the days, allotting a special
ritual to each. Otherwise he would not have known. The days
and hours he lived by were those of a distant winter; they
were days of storm, of wind and witchcraft and darkfall at
Ravensbruck.

THERE IS SO LITTLE GOOD IN THE SOULS OF WOMEN.

Yes, I know some of you will say I am unjust, and some will
want to argue with me, as Karelian did once. I have neither wife nor
mistress, you will say, and so I speak without experience. But that is
nonsense. A man does not need to be bitten by a snake to know it's
poisonous. Nor did I need a wife or daughters of my own to see how
much enduring grief could be brought upon a man by the women of
his house.

I was as much deceived by Adelaide as the others were; I admit
it. She was pleasing in appearance, although not strikingly beautiful.
She spoke softly, and kept her eyes down; she behaved always with
the utmost delicacy. She did not thrust herself into men's conversations,
or act flirtatiously to attract their attention. More than one of our men,
commenting quietly among themselves, thought Karelian had done
very well for himself, and I was the first to agree.

I do not know what Karelian thought of her at the outset, for other
than saying she was sweet and pretty and—as he put it—rather too
young, he told us nothing. Why he seemed surprised at her youth I
cannot imagine, for Gottfried told him everything about her, including
her age. Perhaps after so many years of warfare and wandering he
had forgotten what youth and innocence were like.

But whatever he thought of her, or of his future kin, he treated
Adelaide with courtesy and charm. He was a polished man, and he
knew that he was handsome; all his life he had enjoyed the admiration
of women. He courted her as much as the restraints of Arnulf's harsh
world permitted. She smiled at him sometimes; she never laughed.

Only afterwards did we know why. She was terrified of Karelian, of any man who might come to her as husband, and so find her un-virgin and despoiled.

Quite soon after we arrived—before the ambush in the forest—Arnulf summoned his chaplain, and a lawyer and two scribes from the town, and gathered his family around his table so the marriage contract could be drawn up and signed.

Countess Clara was there, splendidly dressed; a heavy, slow-moving woman with unfeeling blue eyes. Helga was with her, the youngest of her living children, a pretty girl of fourteen. She was not precisely flirtatious—no daughter of Count Arnulf would have dared to be flirtatious in his presence—but she was bold enough to steal repeated and admiring glances at Karelian of Lys.

First at Karelian. Then, even more covetously, at his gifts. He had brought splendid presents for his bride. Jewels for her throat and gold plate for her table. Bolts of silk, shimmering with colors the grey northern marches had never seen. Strange treasures from the east: jewel cases and carvings of exquisite materials and bewildering design, so lovely that soft ohhhs went all around the table, and even Arnulf of Ravensbruck, roughhewn soldier though he was, reached out once or twice to pick up one object or another, and turn it approvingly in his calloused hands.

Countess Clara's thin line of mouth grew thinner. I watched her for a moment, remembering Peter's words to me the day before, when I told him she looked ill.

"The countess is angry about the marriage," he said. It was his first of many indiscretions.

"But it's an excellent match," I had protested.

"Of course. That's why she's angry. She wanted Lord Karelian for her own daughter, for little Helga. The one with the greedy eyes."

I listened to him, of course, but I didn't think much about it at the time. Mothers always preferred the advancement of their own children, rather than those of some other, earlier wife.

But there was real bitterness in Clara's expression, I saw now. Even Arnulf, who otherwise paid little attention to her, noticed it, and gave her a scowl or two of his own.

Karelian detailed for them his holdings at Lys. The county lay along the Maren, in one of the Reinmark's safest and most sheltered regions. He had in fief over three hundred knights, and God alone knew how many serfs, and a magnificent manor house to live in.

Nearby in the Schildberge was the splendid fortress of Otto the Great, a stronghold which had never yet fallen in any war. In the valley were sheep and cattle and swine; there was a mill and a brewery; there were apple trees, and streams full of fish, and acres of gardens . . . .

Karelian had his faults, God knew, but puffing himself up was not one of them. I knew he wasn't trying to brag, or to make an impression on Count Arnulf; he wanted to reassure Adelaide. She sat by her father's side with the pale face of a nun, and the uncertain glances of a bewildered child. It was for her benefit, this catalog of riches. It occurred to me, ungenerously, that in a certain sense he was trying to buy her affection.

Look. All these things are mine to offer you. God knows I came by them hard, but they are mine now; you will have a good life there.

Will you not smile at me, then, not even once?

They were married eight days after the New Year, on a stormy, winterswept morning. It was a wedding much like any other, with plenty of revelry and improper jokes, so I will not say much about it. The exchange of vows was brief and simple, but after there was feasting and dancing long into the night, in which all of Arnulf's knights and their ladies took part. Rudolf of Selven was there, too, in such black and sullen humor that everyone must have noticed. But when I commented on it once or twice, discreetly, all I got for answer was a shrug. *Rudi's always like that . . . .*

Two weeks later, to my unutterable relief, he would be summoned home to Selven. His father the baron had died; he was to return to take care of the family and take possession of his lands. My only regret was that it had not happened sooner. His mere presence in a room made me tense, and through the whole long day of Karelian's wedding I was troubled and on edge.

It is the only day I can remember when the castle of Ravensbruck was truly cheerful. The count of Lys, to my considerable surprise, drank very sparingly. He paid a great deal of attention to his bride, now that he was finally allowed to do so. Whenever I glanced at her I saw the same fragile image as before, the same modest grace over-laying fear. Yet, when she sat at Karelian's side, she seemed different to me, and to my own great bewilderment, I no longer thought well of her. I cannot say why. I suspected her of no wrongdoing, not then— at least not in my conscious mind. She was behaving perfectly; she listened to everything he said; she thanked him for his compliments, and returned his toasts. She looked up sometimes, very briefly, to study him, and even I could read the question in her eyes: *What kind of man is this? What manner of life will I have with him?*

When he caught that look, as he mostly did, he would smile at her, a wonderful smile which might have melted rocks and glaciers, and once he reached and touched her cheek with the back of his hand, very softly. I felt his presence wrap itself around her like a shield, as though her youth and her terrible vulnerability had caught something in himself, and closed on it, and was holding it fast. The look in his eyes was not love, nor even lust; I had seen both in him, more than once, and I knew the difference.

It was . . . it was a kind of keeping, of sheltering, and it had in it something of Karelian's power, of his lordship, something new which I had never seen before.

I knew men were expected to offer such protectiveness to women, but I could see he was offering too much, and offering it much too readily. Already I was afraid he would waste himself on her—in a totally different fashion than he would have wasted himself on the witch of Helmardin—but waste himself nonetheless, because she was female, and by that very fact had the power to demand more than she deserved.

After, when she betrayed him, I was only half surprised.

XI

DARKFALL AT RAVENSBRUCK

Would I might go far over sea,
My love, or high above the air,
And come to land or heaven with thee
Where no law is, and none shall be
Against beholding the most rare
Strange beauty that thou hast for me.

MARIE DE FRANCE

THE STRANGE THING ABOUT FEAR was the way it could matter more than anything, and yet not matter at all. Through all of Adelaide's life, fear was present everywhere: in the wind, in the shadows of the fire, in the sounds which tore up the quiet of the night—so many sounds, war talk and drunken laughter and fights and sometimes killings. And the other sound, the one no one ever talked about, the sound she heard most often when they came back from a war, when they brought women with them. Long into the night she could hear it, down below in the great hall and up here too, in the chamber just next to their own, just next to where Clara slept with her daughters and her women servants. She would cover her head at the screaming, cover it with her pillows and her arms and everything she could find. And then she would think about the stories Sigune told her. She would think about the hunter elves, and the women who lived in the sea, and the warriors who could never be defeated, not ever, not by anybody; and one of them would find the princess in the castle and she would go with him to his own lands and no one would take her away again, there would be walls there as high as the moon . . . .

She used Sigune's stories to shut out the sounds. And after a couple of weeks, the worst of the sounds would stop. The strange young women learned not to scream, just like she learned not to tell on Clara. They learned it was better to be quiet and dream about getting away, or getting even, or maybe just getting old.

But the watching in Clara's eyes never stopped at all. And that was another fear, those bitter eyes, those eyes which always followed her, hunting like hungry falcons for her smallest mistakes and her tiniest insubordinations. And then struck, and struck again. Clara wanted her to die. Oh, she pretended not to, she pretended to be concerned: *You look so sickly, child, do you have a fever again? Perhaps you shouldn't eat anything, it will make you throw up. My sister died of plague when she was your age . . . .* Clara had witch things in her jewel box, hidden way at the bottom where she thought no one would know. For a long time Adelaide believed she was using them to make her sick. Clara wanted her to die because she was pretty, because one day she would ride away with the hunter elves and Clara would have to stay behind; they would just laugh at her: *Wicked, wicked, stay there and die!*

But when finally she told Sigune, the scarred woman only laughed.

"Clara can't do anything to you," Sigune said. "Not that way. She doesn't have the power."

"How do you know?"

"I just know, that's all."

"Then why does she have those things?"

"Everybody has them. They're charms, that's all, like a medal of the Virgin."

"Then why does she hide them?"

"Because the priests say it's bad. They say everything is bad. They say there are no elves, no women in the sea. They say it's wrong to talk about them; all you should talk about is Jesus up there on his cross."

"I'm afraid of him."

Sigune looked away then, far away into some dark place where Adelaide had never been and did not want to go. When she spoke again it was not to the child; it was to herself.

"Aye, and so am I. So are we all."

So many things to fear, and one far greater than them all, and that was her father. Nothing made a dent in her terror of him. His gifts, his occasional expressions of bluff affection, his brazen favoring of herself over Helga—they were all irrelevant, as meaningless as old leaves blowing over the cage of a rabbit.

Arnulf was simply brute force to her, the absolute principle of violence at the center of the world. He was the bellow shattering the hall, the fist crunching bone, the certainty of destruction which awaited any man's defiance—or any woman's.

Arnulf would kill her for smaller things than loving Rudi Selven.

She loved him nonetheless. And that was the strangest thing of all: amidst so much fear, there could still be things over which fear had no power. Rudi was the son of the hunter elves, the warrior who would never be defeated, the prince who would take her to the sea. She was very young the first time he gave her a flower. She smiled and thanked him and went away again just as she was supposed to, and they all were pleased and said what a pretty child she was and forgot about it. Only she took the flower and sat alone with it in a corner where no one would find her, and smelled its sweetness and stroked its small petals one by one, and they changed into silver swords, they changed into birds, they changed into veils of coral silk which she would wrap around herself when she went with him into the forest.

No one could be allowed to know. She understood that from the first. So it was weeks until she managed to catch him by himself, in the courtyard, just for a moment. Long enough to ask him if he would be her knight, and love her and serve her faithfully forever.

He looked at her very strangely. She was small for her age, and delicate, but she was not a child, not inside. Maybe he realized it when she spoke to him, or maybe he had already known.

He rarely smiled; he was dark-souled even then, a stranger, a prince from some other, perilous land. But he smiled at her that day.

"I will always be your knight, lady Adelaide."

For a long time she thought she would marry him. Then the messengers came from Stavoren; and Arnulf, beaming like a bandit with a bag full of gold, told her he had found a husband for her, a kinsman of the Golden Duke, a man with royal blood. She thanked him, as she was expected to do, and crept away. It was late October. The yellow hills were turning bare and dead leaves rattled all night against the stones of Ravensbruck, all night while the moon wept and the elves marched west into the forest, utterly silent, their faces bent and hooded. She knew they would not come back again.

Some nights she cried till the moon went down; some nights she lay shivering with fear. Who was this strange man who would come for her? A knight, but not like Rudi at all. Like her father, old and probably cruel. He would know he was not the first. They said a man could always tell. He would know and he would kill her.

She pleaded with Sigune: *You can do things, I know you can . . . !* She did not know, precisely, what things Sigune could do, but in the depths of her terror she did not care. Sigune was a witch. Sigune herself had those forbidden powers she once feared in Clara, which Clara did not have. Sigune would make him go away, make him change his mind, make him drown in the river.

But Sigune did not do it. She took Arnulf down instead. And the man from Lys did not kill her; he smiled, and gave her presents. The story turned strange, twisting like a deer path in a forest. Neither death nor life had any certainty now; either could melt in a moment like snow against her hand.

How was it possible, after all that black fear, to go to Rudi again? To walk to their secret room, holding her life like cupped water in her hands, one small stumble and it would be gone? It should not have been possible. It was simply necessary. She cringed at every shadow in the long passageway and listened for every tiny sound beyond. Her stomach hurt and her breathing was ragged; twenty times she thought of going back, but going back was equally unbearable.

It was over between them, even the stolen words, the gift of a look. It was a tale for the minnesingers now. He was leaving, and by spring the whole of the Reinmark would lie between them. Once in a while, in strange courts, in Stavoren perhaps, they would smile across a crowded room, or share a dance. Only that would be left, only that and his promise: *I will always love you, Heidi.*

But they would say good-bye. They would touch each other this one last time. It was possible, just barely possible, with the countess shivering with ague in her bed, and Karelian and her father's men all gone hunting halfway to Helmardin, and no one thinking anything of it that Rudi stayed behind. Of course he would stay; he was preparing for his long journey home, to take charge of his kindred and his duties.

She slid the storeroom door open very slowly, stepped inside. There was not even a flicker of light. She did not speak; she could not. What if someone else were there instead of him?

But it was Rudi, his arms circling her, hard animal warmth in the darkness, beautiful although she could not see him, utterly beautiful and graceful and wild, kissing her, his hands hungering inside her garments, opening them to a twin shock of fire and cold. They did not speak much; they never had. Time was always precious and brief, and words could be overheard. They lay on his cloak on the stone floor and mated. He was greedy, always greedy like beggars were for sweets, but he never hurt her. For a while there was no fear.

"Did he say anything?" His voice was a murmur in the darkness, troubled and hard-edged. "On your wedding night?"

"Nothing at all."

"Probably he was too drunk to notice. Is he nice to you?"

"Yes. Very nice. He seems . . . kind. Generous and kind."

There was a long silence.

"Do you wish he weren't?" she whispered.

"Yes."

Then, after a small time, she could feel him shaking his head. "No, I don't. I don't know what I wish, except to have married you myself."

She burrowed her face into his neck, but said nothing. Twice she had begged him to run away with her, and each time his answer had been the same. *Run where, and to what?*

Do you know what a man is who has no land, Adelaide? He is a beggar, a bandit, or a mercenary. Nothing more. And do you know what such a man's wife is, if she's young and pretty? She's prey for every scoundrel, every band of robbers, every bullying lord who crosses his path. And if he has the bad luck to die, she'd better find another man before his bones are cold, or she'll end in a brothel. I haven't loved you all these years for that!

Still she would have run. She would have thrown their lives to fortune, to the gods of love and defiance. It seemed strange to her that Rudi, who would take so many other risks, would not take this one. Perhaps he knew the world too well. Or perhaps it was too terrible a surrender to let the lord of Ravensbruck drive him into exile, after so many other wrongs.

"There is one other thing I wish for," he said. "I wish your father were dead and in hell. But I will settle with him one day."

She knew what she should say, what the world expected of her— certainly the Christian world, and maybe all the others, too. She should defend her father. *No, you mustn't say such things. He is your lord. He did what he thought best . . . .* She should lie as the world lied, endlessly, kneeling before the feet of power.

"Don't," she whispered. "Not ever—not unless you're sure of winning."

"I'm not a fool, Heidi."

"No. But you're reckless sometimes."

He laughed softly, ran his fingers down her throat to the tip of her breast. "God knows that is true. Or I wouldn't be here."

He was reckless beyond words, beyond all men's forgiveness. Reckless to the death he had promised to die for her, because he was her knight and he would serve her forever. The door crashed open; torchlight spilled over them, torchlight and curses and the sound of iron striking flesh, and another sound which only long after could she identify, the sound of her own voice screaming, of her own body crashing into a wall of shelves, of pottery shattering around her, the last pieces falling with sad small tinkles into a sudden, inhuman silence.

And then the thud, scrape, thud of Arnulf of Ravensbruck moving from the doorway into the circle of light, dragging his lame foot and leaning on his cane.

She pulled herself to her knees, gulping terror, the scream still howling in her throat, voiceless now. She had no breath to scream, and no strength. She saw Rudi pinned against the wall, blood running from his face. Three men were holding him, one with a mailed arm around his neck. She saw his sword still lying on the floor beside his cloak, where he had so carefully placed it and then somehow not found it in the darkness. He was dishevelled and almost naked, his trousers clinging in a huddle around one foot.

Arnulf looked at her. The hatred in his eyes blackened into absolute contempt.

"Cover yourself, you damnable whore."

She fumbled at the lacings of her dress, helplessly. Then, sobbing, she groped out for Rudi's cloak, and dragged it around her shoulders—and she saw her lover, with his unutterable defiance, smile to see her do it.

Arnulf turned back to him. "You bastard," he said bitterly. "I trusted you. More than any man alive, I trusted you."

"That makes us even," Selven said.

The count waved at one of his soldiers. "Bring me a brazier and some iron spars. Lots of coals, too, and my chair. We're going to be here for a while."

Adelaide moved unsteadily towards him, trying to find words and the courage to use them.

"Father . . . ."

The blow cracked her cheekbone and spun her back like a rag doll, into the broken shelving.

"Don't call me father, you whore! And don't beg for your life. Beg for a priest."

She knelt, tasting blood in her mouth, feeling it trickle from cuts on her hands and her knees.

"Please," she whispered. "Please . . . !"

They were coming already; she heard the tramp of feet, the smell of fire. Was hell so close then, already? What answer could she give to God and his judges when they stood before her? *We never knew* . . . . Oh, but you did! *We never meant it* . . . . Oh, but you did!

She shook her head, the motion turning into a slow, blind rocking on her knees. There was no use appealing to God. It was God who made the laws, God who condemned her, God who was waiting for it to end, so the real punishment could begin . . . .

"Rudi . . . ."

Arnulf shoved the iron spars deep into the fire. She knew what they were for.

"Let him go. Please let him go."

Arnulf laughed. "Do you think I should? I'll tell you what I'll do, whore. I'll give him back to you, one piece at a time. Nicely roasted. The best parts first."

The men chuckled. She stared at them. Rudi's fellow knights, his comrades in arms, *chuckled* . . . ?

She tasted bile in her throat, burning, mixed with tears. It was barely possible to speak.

"Let him go, and I'll tell you what happened to Silverwind."

For the first time in her life, she had her father's absolute, undivided attention. It terrified her as nothing else had.

"What did you say?" he asked. He was always dangerous, but most dangerous of all when he spoke quietly.

She backed away without even noticing, tearing her knees on the broken pottery.

"It wasn't an accident," she whispered. "Someone . . . bewitched him."

"Really? How can you possibly know that?"

"I saw things. I heard things. I know."

"Why didn't you tell me?"

She could not look at him. "I was afraid."

"You were afraid, when my life was at stake? But not afraid now, for this dog of a traitor? What a loving child you've grown up to be. Very well. Tell me what you know, and I'll let him go."

She swallowed, and lifted her head, and tried to keep her voice from shattering. "Not here. At the gates. When he's gone, and out of bowshot, with his horse and his arms—then I'll tell you."

The silence was devouring. No one moved. No one dared to. She shot a brief, desperate glance towards her lover, wanting to see hope in his face, and not finding it.

Arnulf took one lumbering step towards her.

"You mean to bargain with me, girl?" He laughed. It was a laugh of raw fury and absolute astonishment. "I killed a thousand men before you were born, and every one of them was smarter than you. I've bested every breed of man there is. Vikings. Prussians. Wends. Frisians. For damn near forty years, in mud and rain and blood and fury. Every emperor since Otto the Great swore these borders could not be held, and I held them. I held them, when God himself couldn't! And you think you can bargain me out of my honor, as though I were a stupid boy haggling over a tin whistle? *You?* God's blood, I'll show you how to bargain!"

He moved another step towards her. She could not back away any further; the wall was at her back.

"I will set the terms here, and I won't debate them. This man will die. If an enemy were standing here with a drawn bow, ready to kill me, and God himself were standing beside me, and God said to me: You may strike one more blow in your life, and then never strike again, I would kill Rudolf of Selven.

"This is my bargain, whore: tell me what you know, and I'll kill him with a single blow. Refuse, and I'll roast him alive. And then we'll see who is stronger. We'll see if you can listen to his screams longer than I can listen to your silence."

She did not answer him. It was Rudi who answered him, shouting despite the arm pressed against his throat, the brutal plunge of a knee into his groin.

"It doesn't matter, Heidi! Nothing is going to matter! Save yourself, if you can—!" The voice ended in a choked snarl.

"That's enough, Franz!" Arnulf said sharply. "I don't want him strangled."

He picked up one of the iron spars and handed it to a soldier.

She scrambled to her feet, sobbing. She tried to run to him, but armed men blocked her way. The iron glowed a handbreadth from Rudi's thigh.

She had always known they might die. She had even known they might die hard, but she had never imagined it would be like this, so shamefully, without even being allowed to do up their clothing first. They were not people any more, not lovers from the shining songs. They were only objects of sport, caged animals to whimper and howl until they were dead.

"Don't! Oh, God, please don't, I'll tell you!"

Arnulf raised his hand, and the iron stopped moving.

"Well?" he said.

"The countess bewitched your horse. Lady Clara. To kill you."

He stared at her, disbelieving.

"My wife? She wouldn't dare."

But nobody would dare; that was the problem. He was Arnulf of Ravensbruck, the man who fought half the northern world and walked away laughing.

"I saw her. She has . . . things . . . in her jewel box. Horrible things. I heard her calling devils into the horse, asking them to break your neck. She hates you. You know she hates you, and you know why!"

He was still staring at her. She went on, frantically. "I swear to you, I heard her . . . !"

He was tottering a little on his cane. For a moment she thought he was going to fall.

"And you never told me?" he said.

"I never thought . . . I didn't know . . . !"

He turned slowly, spoke to the men. "Bind him. On his feet. Those pillars should do."

Horror knotted her throat and dissolved the last of her strength.

"No!" she sobbed. "No, father, you can't, dear God, you can't, you promised!"

"I promised I would kill him with a single blow. And so I will."

"What did you expect, Heidi?" Rudi said bitterly. "That he would keep his word to you any better than he kept it to me?"

And so she stood, prisoned between two soldiers who would neither let her fall, nor run, nor die, and watched her father take a lance, and balance it a moment in his hands, and walk forward on the steady arm of his squire, and drive the weapon through Rudi's belly, low and hard—so hard that it lodged in the wall behind him.

She screamed. She did not know what the words were, or if they were words at all or only cries. Something hit her in the stomach, a fist, a club, she did not know which, she did not care. She buckled, vomiting, and the darkness took her down.

XII

A MATTER OF HONOR

The adulteress Swanhild, he said, ought to suffer a
shameful end, trampled under the hoofs of beasts.

SAXO GRAMMATICUS

"I HAVE LEFT IT TO YOUR HANDS, KARELIAN—unwillingly , I must
admit. I don't bear shame well, least of all in my own house.
But you are her husband, and I have deferred to your rights."

No, Karelian thought grimly. *You have deferred to my kinship with
Gottfried, and to nothing else.*

"You may be sure," the lord of Ravensbruck continued, "whatever
punishment you choose, you need have no fear of offending me."

Arnulf had aged. They had ridden out three mornings ago with
their horns and their hounds, and he had stood in the courtyard with
only a cape flung around his shoulders and naked envy in his eyes.
"By God," he had said, "next time I'll be riding with you!"

Now he sat leaning both elbows on his wooden table, as though
even his chair would no longer hold up his sagging body. His eyes
were hollows of bitterness, and he drank without ceasing. The great
hall was empty; even their squires had been sent away. The whole
world knew what had happened, but he would not speak of it in front
of others, and no sane man, after today, would ever speak of it in
front of him.

"When I was ten," he said, "my father told me to trust no one—
not ever. No man, he said, and still less any woman. I heeded him for
most of my life. And then I forgot."

Arnulf's wounded feelings were not something Karelian wanted to discuss.

"Where is Adelaide?" he asked.

Arnulf gestured vaguely. "In the prison. The men will take you."

"Selven?"

"He died last night."

Last night. He had lived two and half days then, shackled to a pillar, with a lance in his bowels . . . . Karelian rose, pulled his cloak around his body, looked again at his father-in-law, who was no longer looking at anything.

"You were here," he said, "and the countess was confined to her bed. How did they come to be discovered?"

"I have one honest daughter left," Arnulf said. With great difficulty, like a man forced to remember that the world was still with him, he straightened a little. "I hope you won't hold this against me. Against our friendship. The duke wouldn't wish it so, and nor would I. When this is over, I trust we can discuss a new alliance."

"I am honored, my lord."

There was no warmth in Karelian's voice. There was barely respect. Arnulf, ill and weary as he was, still noticed, and a spark of anger ignited in his eyes.

"Don't judge me until you've raised your own brood, Karelian. You may find it's harder than you think."

"So I may." He bowed faintly. "Good day, my lord."

It was a fine afternoon. So often, in the very depths of the winter, the northern lands enjoyed these days of quiet warmth. It was a favorite time for visiting, for festivals, for great, far-ranging hunts. They had come home laden with game, singing. It was a fool, Karelian thought, who ever sang in Ravensbruck.

She was such a gentle thing. So young, so afraid of the world and everything in it. At times he wanted to shake her, and other times he wanted to wrap her under his cloak like a starving kitten and wait for her to purr.

He was a worldly man; he knew the physical evidence of virginity was sometimes very slight, and could be lost in completely innocent ways, often when the girl was still a child. He knew all things were possible in Ravensbruck, rape and incest among them. Whatever had happened to Adelaide, he was prepared to consider her innocent, and to go on doing so until he had a reason not to.

He knew she did not love him, or even trust him much. But she had tried to please him. She liked stories; she enjoyed it when he told her about his travels, about the cities he had seen, and the marvels he had found in strange lands. After the first few nights, she did not turn away when he slept, to huddle alone on the far side of the bed. He would wake to find her nestled against him, like a wary cat who nonetheless knew enough to stay where it was warm.

And all the while she was in love with Rudolf of Selven. Thinking of him. Wanting him. Bedding with him. Nothing, he thought, was ever as it seemed, and human creatures least of all.

The soldiers who led him across the courtyard kept their eyes straight ahead, and did not speak. What did you say to a man who was not married a month, and was already a cuckold? Reinhard walked beside him, his face ashen and set, and Pauli shadowed them in mute yet eloquent despair.

They went through a narrow gate into the western bastion. The soldiers took torches from the wall, and lit them, and they went down a long stone staircase. He heard shouts, a man's voice babbling somewhere in the caverns beyond. Their breath turned into puffs of fog, grey and scattering in the torchlight.

This is my life then, the same life still, the life of a man who never mattered, except to those he killed . . . .

The men stopped before an iron door, mauled it roughly with a twisted key, and yanked it open.

There was a huddle lying in the corner; a very small huddle. He thought they had made a mistake, it was only a child, and what on earth was a child doing here? But the child wore Adelaide's clothes; he recognized the dress, recognized the face lifting from the straw, fever-eyed, hung about with tangles of matted hair.

She sat up. For a moment it seemed she did not know him. Her sight was never good, and the torchlight was flickering in her eyes. Her mouth trembled faintly, but she did not speak. She waited. He stood over her, and found he had no words, either; they dissolved against the terror in her eyes. He had seen such terror before, many times, but always on the faces of enemies, always in a sea of blood. This was his own wife, a woman barely grown, looking at him the way fallen soldiers looked at an advancing foe, knowing the next blow would kill.

So many of those faces. Jerusalem had been full of them—faces backed against walls, against the edges of roofs, against rings of iron-clad men, always with the same wild, empty, bitter look.

She had on nothing but her dress and her shoes, and she was shivering. Shivering and dirty; her face was bruised and there were smears of blood on it, as though she had touched it with bleeding hands. *Whore . . . deceiving wife . . . unfaithful . . . without faith . . . infidel . . . .*

He was swept by vertigo, and found himself reaching to steady himself against Reinhard's shoulder. *My own house . . . . Is this where it ends, then, or where it all begins?*

He had not known what he would feel, walking across the courtyard. But his judgment came easily now, so easily it surprised him. He knew what he would do, and he knew he would live with it. After Jerusalem nothing would be hard to live with, not ever again.

"Your cloak, Reini."

The seneschal surrendered his garment without a word.

He lifted Adelaide to her feet, and wrapped the cloak around her.

"Can you walk?"

She did not answer. There was nothing but fear in her eyes, fear and a black, wild grief. She did not make it even to the cell door without stumbling, and would have fallen except for Karelian's arm. He picked her up and carried her like a child.

Everything stopped where they passed. The world stood frozen into watching statues: servants and soldiers and men-at-arms. A few crossed themselves, and their eyes followed him, but otherwise they did not move or speak. As each door closed behind him, he knew, there would be an outburst of question and dispute:

—Is she dead?

—What are they going to do?

—Maybe he'll forgive her; she's only a child.

—She's old enough; she knew what she was doing; she should pay.

—You're heartless; what if she were your daughter?

—I would wield the knife myself.

—Aye, and go to the brothel afterwards, just like you've been doing for the last twenty years, you damn hypocrite . . . .

Adelaide's chambermaid was a steady young woman named Matilde.

"Oh, my lady . . . !" One glance, and she was reaching for the reeling girl, shouting for hot bricks and broth, stripping off Adelaide's fouled clothing, slipping a gown over her head, wiping the blood from her face, all the while talking softly like a mother to a child: "There now, my lady it's all right, it's all right . . . ."

In better light, he could see that Adelaide was very sick. Her face and throat were flushed with fever, and when she tried once to speak— whether to thank him or to plead he did not know—all she could manage was a harsh whisper and a broken cough. Matilde tucked her into the canopied bed, and she curled there into a shivering ball.

"She's burning up, my lord," the maid said. "Shall I send for Sigune?"

"Sigune?"

"The Wend woman. The scarred one. She's better than the doctor, if I may say so."

"Get her then—quietly. And send Reinhard in here, too."

"At once, my lord."

The seneschal, waiting outside the door, entered immediately. He said nothing. He would rarely comment on anything concerning his lord's personal life unless he were asked. But he carefully did not look at Adelaide, and that was comment enough.

"Nobody comes into this room when I'm not here, Reini, except Matilde and the Wend woman. I will depend on you for it."

"We are in Count Arnulf's house, my lord." It was not an objection; it was simply a fact.

"I will deal with Count Arnulf." Karelian hesitated before he spoke again, not because he was unsure of his decision, but because he did not know how Reinhard would react. It was painful to be thought a fool.

"If it comes to a fight, Reini, I will defend her."

"That is your choice, my lord. I made mine in Stavoren." Bent on one knee, with his raised hands held between those of the count of Lys, swearing his allegiance . . . .

"Thank you, my good friend."

He touched Reinhard's shoulder briefly, fondly, and went back to Arnulf's hall, dreading the encounter more than he dreaded most of the battles he had ever faced, even the nasty, outnumbered ones. He was not afraid of Arnulf, at least not in any personal, physical sense. But he was afraid of chaos. He knew how little he or anyone could control the lunacies of other men.

He sat down by Arnulf's elbow. A mute servant brought beer, served them both, and withdrew to the far reaches of the hall. Arnulf looked up from his dark brooding; their eyes met and held. Whatever else, the count of Ravensbruck was an intelligent man; intelligent and shrewd. He was rarely mistaken in his judgment of others. When it happened, he did not take it well.

"Why," he asked flatly, "did you bring that whore back into my house?"

"There would be little point in trying to punish her now," Karelian said. "She's too sick to notice."

"And when she's better?"

"We will return to Lys." Karelian drained his beer. It annoyed him to realize how much he depended on it for strength. "I'll deal with my domestic affairs in my own house, my lord, and according to my own judgment."

"I wonder," Arnulf said, "if you have the balls to deal with it at all."

"You presume on your infirmity, my lord."

"You may challenge me any time you wish. I have three hundred men in range of my voice. Any one of them will stand good for my honor—better than you seem willing to do!"

"Keep throwing your men to the wolves, my lord, and one day you'll wake up and find you haven't any left."

Arnulf knotted his hands together on the table before him— whether to prevent himself from reaching for a weapon, or to hide their trembling, Karelian did not know.

"When I was on my feet, you wouldn't have crossed me like this, in my own house! By God, you wouldn't have!"

He was finished, Karelian thought. He was done and shredding like an old cloak. But he was still dangerous. Evil men were the most dangerous of all when they were going down.

"I mean you no offense, my lord. But I won't kill Adelaide. She's only a child."

Why am I apologizing? I'm under no damned obligation to kill anyone, not any more, and please God not ever again . . . .

"You're a guest in my house," Arnulf said grimly. "One word from me, Karelian, one single word and by God's blood it will be done with! I won't sit here in my own house unavenged!"

"If you speak that word, my lord, there'll be a bloodbath."

Arnulf stared at him. His hands were gripping the edge of the table, as though he were about to heave himself to his feet. "You would fight over it?"

"Yes."

"Why?"

"Because I choose to."

"You will lose."

"No, my lord. I will die. You will lose." Karelian reached, poured more beer from the flagon. "You'll lose your ally in Lys. More important, you'll lose your ally in Stavoren."

"Duke Gottfried would never take your side in a matter like this! There isn't a man in Christendom who would!"

"Indeed? Your first words to me, as I recall, were that you put the matter in my hands. Because I was her husband. You know yourself where the right of it lies. So will Gottfried. Besides . . . ." Karelian had the edge now, and he knew it. He paused, deliberately. "Besides, Duke Gottfried owes me his life. *And* the temple of Jerusalem. Had we not been blood kin, he would have given me one of his own daughters to marry."

"And he owes me the north of the Reinmark!"

"Yes. We're his best-loved vassals, the two of us. He wanted this alliance very much; he'll never forgive you if you destroy it. And a man who earns Gottfried's enmity is as much to be pitied as a man who earns yours. Don't forget, my lord: I'm not the only man who came back from Palestine in high favor. There are others—young men, brave men, as willing to fight and hold these borders as you have been."

He rose. "We are, as you said, guests in your house. We won't stay long. You may slaughter us; the choice is yours. But I swear to you, it will cost you Ravensbruck."

"For a whore? And a whoremonger? For a whelp of the weather-vane of Dorn?" Arnulf laughed, and then spat. "Your father was a spineless fool, and you're nothing but a mercenary with a purchased fief and purchased honors. Gottfried will spit on you as I do."

"Are you sure?" Karelian said softly. Darkly. The power in his voice surprised him; it was almost sorcerous. "That is the question, is it not, my lord? *Are you sure?"*

Adelaide recovered slowly. She was pitiably grateful for her life, yet she didn't really seem to want it much. Her life was a shadow to her now, a story with no further meaning. One quiet afternoon, when the fever was gone, and she could sit up comfortably and speak without coughing, he sent the others from the room—and immediately the fear leapt back into her eyes, the fear and the voiceless, numb waiting.

She judged the whole world by Arnulf of Ravensbruck, and why should she not? It was all of the world she had ever seen.

"Will you tell me what happened?" he asked.

The question bewildered her. "Did his lordship not tell you?"

"He told me what he chose to tell me. I want to hear what you have to say."

She looked at her hands. "I wronged you, my lord. I have nothing to say."

"Was I so unworthy a mate for you, then?"

"Unworthy?" For the first time, there was a flicker of something in her eyes besides fear. "It was never that, my lord. I thought you were kind and generous; I admired you . . . ."

She fell silent, and the flicker went out.

"And Rudolf of Selven?"

"He's dead," she whispered.

Dear Jesus, I know he's dead . . . .

"They said his father was not the lord of Selven," she went on softly, almost as if she were speaking to herself. "They said he was sired by one of the hunter elves. The dark ones, who don't need light to see. No one really believed it, only me. I knew he was different; he wasn't one of them at all."

"You could scarcely have known him," Karelian said, "living as you did."

She looked at him as though he were a fool. He did not know whether to be angry about it, or to wonder if perhaps he was.

"I knew him," she said. "He loved me more than the world."

"Did he ask to marry you?"

"Yes. Years ago. My father never said yes or no; he said it was too soon, I was too young. He let Rudi hope; he encouraged him to hope. He used him. He used him and used him, and then he killed him."

Tears spilled from the corners of her eyes and spattered onto her nightdress. She seemed unaware of them.

"When his friend Nicholas rebelled, Rudi would have joined with him, except for me. Instead he brought him back. Because my father promised. He said: bring him back, and you can name your own reward—"

"But I was assured there had been no other betrothal," Karelian said. "The duke had your father's word on it."

"It wasn't a betrothal. It was only a promise, and no one else was there. My father knew how Rudi would take the promise, but it was easy enough, afterwards, to say he'd never meant it so. He just laughed about it. 'Come now,' he said, 'you know such a promise has limits; suppose you asked for my castle and my lands—would I have to give them to you?' He had a better offer for me now. He could marry me to one of Gottfried's favorites, to a man with royal blood. He offered Rudi twenty marks and one of his bastards."

Karelian said nothing. It was a lord's right, of course, to arrange his affairs as he judged best. It was the duty of his vassals and his children to accept his decisions. But there was also such a thing as justice.

"He used to leave me things," she went on. Her voice was soft now, drifting. "Colored stones, flowers, pieces of driftwood . . . we had places to leave things, behind tapestries, and in cracks in the walls. Once he left me two flowers, all knotted together, I don't know where he found them, there was still snow everywhere. He said he would take me to the sea one day; there are castles there, under the water . . . . Do you know where they buried him?"

"No." *But his head is on a pike on the northern wall; pray God you never have to see it there . . . .*

"Sigune says the hunter elves come sometimes and take their children back. When they're still little. I wish they had taken him . . . . Father sent messengers to the prison . . . three times . . . to tell me he was still alive . . . still alive . . . like that . . . ."

She was choking with sobs, wrenching sobs that convulsed her body like a seizure. She turned away from Karelian and wrapped herself into a ball on the bed. She did not want comfort. She did not believe comfort was possible, and perhaps it was not—at least not for a very long time.

He knew he should feel deeply wronged—by her, and even more so by Rudolf of Selven, who apart from everything else had tried to murder him in cold blood. But he felt only empty. Betrayed yes, but less by them than by his own unfolding reality. He had fought for twenty years so he might come to Ravensbruck, or somewhere like it, with land and rank and bridal gifts, and this was what he had come to.

Raven had warned him. *You know what kind of world lies outside my walls . . . .* Yes, dear God, he knew, and every time he forgot, the world reminded him with a club.

He thought of her now with unbearable regret. Raven the sorceress, the dreamer of other worlds. Raven kneeling over him in the depths of Car-Iduna, her splendid body swaying in the curtain of her hair, her eyes and her voice dark with knowing. Beautiful Raven who still shadowed his path, who sent her witch-birds out to shield him from the treachery he himself—however innocently—had set afoot. His longing to see her now, to wrap her in his arms, was so bitter he could have wept.

Rudolf of Selven abandoned his honor for love, and I my love for honor. Which one of us, in the end, will prove to have been the greater fool?

XIII

SHADOWS

Hard and fell am I to him, though I hide it from others.

VOLSUNGA SAGA

IT WAS LONG PAST MIDNIGHT, the sky clear above the northern mark, the white land lit with a waxing moon. In the great hall men slept restlessly with troubled dreams, or did not sleep at all. Sigune heard their silence, their quiet waiting for blood. She heard the moon pass shimmering; she heard the snow crunch beneath the feet of the hunter elves.

Arnulf sat by his table, waiting for a sign.

He had not returned his guests' greetings at the supper feast. He had neither spoken nor eaten. He refused to be laid to bed. He was the ruler of Ravensbruck, and he ruled it absolutely. Alone.

"Sigune."

She took the candle and walked to the table. "My lord?"

"It's cold here."

"I'll put more wood on the fire, my lord." She began to turn away but instead he motioned her to sit.

"Will she die?" he asked. She hated his voice when he shouted. She hated it more when it was soft like this.

"Not of her sickness, my lord."

"Then poison her."

She said nothing.

"If you disobey me, I'll kill you."

"It's a grievous sin, my lord. What you ask of me."

"To kill a whore like her? It's no sin at all."

Across the hall, a man shifted, groaning in his sleep. Idly, Sigune moved the candle, easing its light away from her face, towards his own.

"The count of Lys will know, my lord."

"Don't be a fool, woman. How could he know?"

"He is watching, my lord. He warned me. He knows I'm your slave. If she dies, he said, I will judge it murder, and both you and your master will answer for it."

Arnulf sucked in his breath. "He has a devil in him, that one. God damn him."

She was silent, watching him. She had never seen the count of Ravensbruck react like this before. He was a man who vented anger readily, a man who struck and cursed and killed as his passions moved him. His pride was inhuman; people who wounded it usually died. He took pleasure in his own immense capacity for cruelty. He waited sometimes to strike, when it was tactically wise to do so, but he rarely waited long, and he never worried about the consequences.

Now he was faltering. He was genuinely unsure. He was—as much as Arnulf of Ravensbruck ever could be—afraid.

And it was beautiful to see.

"Won't you try to sleep a little, my lord?"

He looked at her, and she saw time shift in his eyes, saw him remember, actually consciously remember who she was: Sigune the Wend, the pretty one. He had liked her the best of his mistresses; after her, they had been only playthings, only cunt.

"I should have kept you," he said.

He seized her wrist, pulling her towards him, drawing her hand to his loins. She did not protest. She was a slave, and in any case it did not matter; nothing mattered now except watching him go down.

You misjudged Karelian of Lys, did you not, my lord? A warrior hero, a favorite of the Golden Duke—you were so sure he'd be exactly like yourself.

The count of Ravensbruck slept, his head resting on one arm on his wooden table. The candle had burned out; his body was only a shadow against the faint light of the hearth.

Well, we have both been wrong before, about men. I wish I knew who has wrapped that shield around him. A woman, I'm sure of it, and a stronger one than I. It is her power you fear. Oh, he's a match for you, and more; he's earned his reputation. But there's something else, and you know it, only you don't know what it is. Your instincts are good, Arnulf of Ravensbruck. So many wars, so many enemies, and you've never walked into an ambush, never trusted a lying messenger, never drank from a poisoned cup.

You sense danger. Real danger, not just the threat in an enemy's good sword arm. And it's killing you. Tearing your bowels out because you aren't sure. He has barely fifty armed men and a handful of servants. He was nothing before the crusade, just a knight errant making war for his bread. How can you hesitate—you of all men, lord of the north, bane of the Vikings and terror of the world?

Is it that wounded body, my lord? The knowledge it has given you of limitations? Oh, you can give orders, your men still fear you, but it's no longer quite the same, is it? Deep in your bones you know it's not the same. They can turn on you now, or they can just smile and walk away. You haven't even sent for your sons because you're safer without them.

You have begun to die as a man. Perhaps one day you'll know what it means to live as a woman. Standing in a broken house with no armor, no weapons worth mentioning, no men to command. And nowhere to run. With only your body and its bottomless capacity for pain, watching your enemies come on . . . .

May the gods keep me living and beside you until then!

XIV

DEPARTURE

There are in the world a great many situations that weaken the conscientiousness of the soul. First and foremost of these is dealings with women.

SAINT JOHN CHRYSOSTOM

ALL DURING MY TIME OF SERVICE with Karelian of Lys, he only once did a thing which I failed utterly to understand. I knew why he chose to ride into Helmardin, and why he came to love its sorcerous queen. And later, after our fateful gathering at Stavoren, I knew also why he turned to darkness. But I never understood why he chose to shelter Adelaide of Ravensbruck.

Neither did anyone else.

"It's the Christian thing to do," Reinhard said. It was the best answer he could come up with, and it was a rather weak one, considering Karelian's not very Christian life. "He will leave it to God to judge her, and that's the Christian thing."

Otto regarded him without much sympathy. "The point is, Reini, he isn't leaving it to God. Whatever God's will for her might be, Karelian's sword is in the way of it. And so is everybody's neck. Including yours."

"He's a good man. Are you going to condemn him for it?"

Otto ran his hands through his long, ill-kempt hair. "No," he said heavily. "No, I'm not. But how long do you think Arnulf will put up with this? Dear Christ, our lord is Arnulf's son-in-law, and we're in Arnulf's house, and that Wendish crone is Arnulf's slave . . . ." He shook his head, and then, quite suddenly, he laughed. "I must say, if

I weren't afraid of the outcome, I would rather enjoy watching it. I'll wager no man has ever stood up to Arnulf like this before, not ever. Pity it wasn't for a better reason."

He looked at me then, wondering if he had said too much. I looked down, and said nothing. It was the middle of the morning, and we were gathered in a huddle near the main stairwell of the castle of Ravensbruck, throwing a few dice around and otherwise pretending we did this sort of thing every day.

"It's a bit like Constantinople, actually," Otto said dryly. "Bowing and scraping and waiting to see if old Alexis would pile gold in our laps, or take us out and hang us."

I had not been with them in Constantinople, but except for the tension, I could not imagine why he would make such a comparison. The other had been a confrontation worthy of kings. This one . . . I shook my head. It was bad enough that Adelaide had betrayed Karelian's honor, and her own. But there was the dreadful matter of her father's accident, and the murderous sorcery she had concealed. There was the attack against Karelian in the forest. So much wickedness already, and she was only seventeen. Surely any man in his right mind would leave such a woman to her fate. At least leave her to the justice of others, if he had no wish to punish her himself.

But no. Karelian meant to keep the wench, and even to defend her if he had to. It was beyond comprehending. And there was nothing Christian about it. Reinhard was wrong there, as he was about so many things.

I would have understood Karelian's decision if he loved her. I might even have understood if it had been only a matter of personal arrogance, a battle of wills against a man he frankly detested. But the count of Lys did not love his wife; and he was too sensible to endanger himself and all of us merely out of foolish pride.

Then what moved him to take such a risk?—for a risk it surely was. From hour to hour we could not predict how Arnulf's moods would swing, or how the county itself might divide in the face of them. The lord of Ravensbruck had always held his power in large part by fear. He was faltering visibly now, and a void of chaos was opening around him. Old hatreds began to surface everywhere, and whispers of mutiny were in the air. More than once I was certain that he would turn on us, or that his followers would turn on him. Either way we would find ourselves in the midst of a slaughter, with no allies on either side to count on.

It did not happen. We lived to ride safely out of Ravensbruck, and we owed it to God's will, and to the distant but always acknowledged power of the duke, golden Gottfried with his fame and his ship full of eastern treasure, Gottfried who was Karelian's cousin and who looked upon him almost as a son. But if this is to be an honest chronicle, then I must tell you we owed it also to the count of Lys himself. We did not approve of his decision, or comprehend his motives, but there wasn't a man among us—and few, I think, among the knights of Ravensbruck—who did not end by admiring his mastery of an impossible situation.

He carried the argument by never opening it, refusing to justify himself, refusing to be baited by anyone. He was Adelaide's lord. Arnulf himself had acknowledged the fact, and was bound to stand by his original and proper decision. No one else had anything to say about it. The matter was closed.

He left the count of Ravensbruck with no opening short of a full-scale, unprovoked attack. He ignored innuendo; he used cunning words to turn other men's words around, till they themselves did not know whether they had insulted him or praised him. He refused utterly to be drawn into the divisive politics of the county. If he was Adelaide's lord, he was also Arnulf's ally, and the one bond was no more open to discussion than the other.

I watched, fascinated, as the men of Ravensbruck faltered, every one of them, not least the count himself, watching his neighbor and smelling the wind, waiting to be just a little bit surer of his position in the face of a man who was so flawlessly sure of his own. And the course of inaction, once begun, became harder and harder to reverse. The world jolted like a cart on a rough mountain road, tottered horribly . . . and righted itself and went on.

That was my first clear understanding of the meaning of personal power. The strength which a man might carry inside himself was a strength which could shape worlds. Although his rank and his reputation and his fighting skill might all seem part of it, in its essence it was different from those things; it was separate and strange. And it was in no way moral, no more than a magnet was. The man who possessed it might be good or evil; his strength drew men to him just the same, or held them at bay.

We lived those last days as though we were under siege, and we left as soon as we could—much sooner than we might otherwise have chosen. It was still deep winter; the roads were barely passable, and the weather was foul. We loaded the pack beasts in freezing darkness and gulped down our last meal by torchlight, wrapped in layers of wool and booted to our thighs.

The servants moved around us like shadows, and kept their eyes down, not looking at their lord who sat with both elbows on the table, staring at the smoke-blackened wall. They stepped carefully over the bodies of fighting men who lay near the braziers pretending to be asleep. I saw the Wend woman watching us, always watching from places where the light would never reach her face; every time I looked at her I shuddered.

Then a door from a side chamber opened, spilling out light and, God help us, music: a reed pipe and bells, both played painfully ill; the lads who carried them were frightened half to death. Behind the boys came a priest. And behind him came Arnulf's daughter, the lady Helga, veiled and gowned as for a bridal.

We had not seen her since our return from the ill-fated hunt— neither her nor her mother, who was now in the same dungeon which had prisoned Adelaide. Perhaps Arnulf had forbidden her to appear, or perhaps she was too frightened to face the chaos she unleashed when she betrayed her sister. She was pale now; her gown looked hastily and shabbily made.

My heart stopped. I saw, vaguely, several of Arnulf's men scrambling to their feet, as bewildered as we were, looking at each other, looking at the girl, looking at the count of Ravensbruck who was rising as well, leaning on the arm of his squire.

"My lord of Lys," he said. He was actually smiling, like a proud father about to yield his daughter's hand in marriage.

He's mad, I thought frantically. *He is utterly gone, and oh Jesus, sweet Jesus, help us now . . . !*

Karelian's face was ash.

"What is the meaning of this, my lord?"

Arnulf did not answer him. He made an impatient gesture towards Helga.

"Come here, girl. Give him your hand."

She moved towards Karelian. There was something quite horrible in her face, a mixture of terror and dark slyness and greed. No doubt she knew how ghastly it was, how shameful, but she would do it, oh yes, she would do almost anything, to have so fine a life for herself to be lady of Lys.

Karelian did not take her hand.

"My lord," he said, "I have a wife."

"Your marriage is invalid," Arnulf said irritably. He looked at the priest, who licked his lips nervously, and looked no man in the eye, neither his lord nor anyone else.

"Well, tell him!" Arnulf snapped.

"If a bride is found to be debauched, my lord," the priest said, "then the marriage was made under false pretenses, and is invalid."

"Really?" said Karelian softly. "That is canon law?"

"Yes, my lord," the priest said, swallowing again. "Or at least, the law can be interpreted so. There have been . . . other cases."

"Well. I must say, I grow more and more impressed with the Church's capacity for adaptation. However . . . ." He paused and smiled. "It has no relevance here. My wife committed adultery, true enough, but she came to her marriage bed a virgin."

"That's a lie!" Arnulf hissed. "And we all know it's a lie! Selven boasted that he'd had her! He was dying, and he boasted of it, right in front of me, in front of my knights!"

"No doubt he did," Karelian said. "He was a traitor and an assassin. You favored him in every way possible, yet he betrayed you. Whose word will you take in the matter, his or mine?"

So absolute was the silence then, I think even the flames in the hearth froze in mid-air. Arnulf's mouth was slightly open; I saw confusion in his eyes. And I saw something else, something which made me realize he was not mad. Oh, perhaps a little bit: there was a kind of driven desperation in him which was real enough. But his irrationality was mostly self-indulgence. It was just another way of being absolute lord, and doing anything he wished, and keeping everyone around him afraid.

All he seemed to feel now was hatred, and it was not because of Adelaide—not any more. It wasn't even because he had lost. In his long lifetime of conflict, he must have lost occasionally before. But this time he had encountered a man who no longer allowed him to make the rules, who changed the very terms on which they fought. Who did it in Arnulf's own house, in front of Arnulf's own vassals.

It was something the count of Ravensbruck would never, never forgive.

"You will swear a sacred oath on it?" he demanded. "The girl was a virgin?"

A sacred oath, if perjured, was a very grave mortal sin.

"I think my word of honor is oath enough in this hall . . . ."
Karelian looked around, at the human statues gathered in the torchlight.
"In this hall, or in any other. But if you insist, yes, I will swear."

That he would offer to do so was enough. Even I believed him
then, although I no longer do.

Arnulf glared at the priest, who moved quickly to save his lordship's face.

"If this is true, my lord, then we cannot—"

"Yes, yes, you damned fool, get out of here." Arnulf sat down,
slowly, looking over at Helga who waited rigid and utterly humiliated.
Just now, she must have wished she were dead.

"Such a pretty bride," Arnulf said. "You insult my lovely daughter,
Karelian."

"With all due respect, my lord, I do not. I would insult her if I
married her when I already have a wife."

Arnulf knotted his great hands together over the table, and glared
at us. He would have liked nothing better than to call out his men,
and have us cut to pieces. He would have done it in a moment, I
think, if he had been sure they would obey.

Karelian allowed him little time to wonder about it. He gave us
the signal to leave, and moved closer to the count's chair.

"The day advances, my lord, and we must be gone. I thank you
for your hospitality, and for your good will." He bowed, formally perhaps, but nonetheless graciously. "I wish you good health, and good
fortune. Farewell, lady Helga."

Arnulf did not soften to his courtesy, not even a whisper.

"Are you taking the whore with you?" he asked.

"Yes."

"You will regret it."

"Perhaps."

"The duke wanted this alliance," Arnulf said, "and for the duke's
sake I will honor it." It was not yet dawn, but he had a beer stein by
his elbow. He raised it in a mock salute. "You'll be well advised, count
of Lys, to never, *never* fall out of favor with the duke." He smiled,
and my blood ran cold. He drank then, and put the cup down, and
wiped his mouth. "And don't ever bring that creature near me again,
do you understand?"

"As you wish, my lord."

Footsteps were coming down the staircase, careful steps, slow and
unsteady. Everyone glanced towards them except Arnulf. He knew.

Adelaide walked between her servants, both of them supporting her, all three bundled in furs. Only their eyes showed, frightened eyes, and small wedges of nose.

"Farewell, my lord," Karelian said. He bowed again, and nodded to the rest of us to take our leave; we passed before the count of Ravensbruck one by one, mouthing empty courtesies; by the time the last of us had said good-bye Adelaide was at the doorway.

And Count Arnulf was on his feet.

"Harlot!" he shouted. "Treacherous whore, I'm not done with you yet!"

Karelian spun around like a cat, as if expecting a death-blow. More than one man's eyes swept to the lines of weapons hanging by the door—theirs and ours—but no one moved. Except Adelaide, who neither paused nor looked back, who did not even seem to hear. I wondered then if she still walked within this world.

We strapped on our arms and followed her into the snow.

XV

OF LOVE AND MEMORY

He who defiles himself with a male shall do penance for fifteen years. He who murders, ten or seven years.

PENITENTIAL OF THEODORE

WE HAD COME TO RAVENSBRUCK throbbing with drums and glittering with banners. We left like thieves in the night, with only lanterns raised against a black and starless sky. Adelaide and her servants rode in a small sleigh, with heated bricks piled under their feet, and ermine robes wrapped all around their bodies. She was better, but she was not well. I knew Karelian was sorely troubled, torn between his desire to get away before some small thing blew Ravensbruck apart, and ourselves with it, and his fear that she was unready for the journey.

But he had little cause for fear, as it turned out. We were not three hours out of Ravensbruck when the weather changed. The dawn clouds lifted and broke into patches of blue light. Soft winds came from the south; by mid-morning water was dripping from the branches of the trees, and the men rode with their cloaks flung back across their shoulders.

"God is with us," Reinhard said. More than one man smiled and nodded and agreed with him. I was the only one who remembered Helmardin, who understood that strange and unnatural weather was not necessarily the work of God.

Karn was a market town, crowded and wild and far older than the Reinmark itself. Before the Germans came, Frankish tribes had traded here, and feasted, and built walls, and before them the Huns and even earlier the Celts. Small remnants of each race remained—bits of ruin, scraps of language, strange colorings of eyes and hair. When I first came to Karn as a boy, I had marvelled at its bewildering clamor, its pushing and shoving and endlessly acquisitive humanity, its dangerousness. It was the place where young men of the Reinmark went to find debauchery, where good fighting men and assassins both waited to hire out their swords, where thieves and prostitutes and jongleurs filled the taverns and the streets.

I saw bigger and more glittering cities afterwards, on my long journey to the Holy Land. But Karn still possessed for me an aura of excitement and worldliness and peril. We stayed there till the end of the winter. Our host was a baron named Lehelin. He was a kinsman of Karelian's by virtue of having married a Brandeis cousin from somewhere in the Silverwald. Kinship was a formality, however; what they really had in common was soldiering. They had fought together in at least a dozen foreign wars, and while neither of them was especially interested in remembering the bloodshed, they positively reveled in remembering everything else, especially the taverns and the courtesans.

Lehelin's barony was close to the city, and I swear we spent more time in Karn than in his manor house, most of it in a place called the White Ram, where the beer was particularly good and the entertainment often scandalous.

This was a side of Karelian I had already seen in the Holy Land, but which I had quietly forgotten. He loved revelry, be it a half-naked infidel dancing to a reed pipe in a perfumed room, or an inn full of drunken soldiers roaring out bawdy songs. He loved it all. And I suppose that is how men get, when they live so close to death, and have no solid core of faith to hold them steady. They rush to lose themselves in drink, in laughter, and above all in lust.

It was an evening in March when the jongleurs came to the White Ram, a particular group of jongleurs whom I will remember until I die. They entertained us well, I will admit; but that is not why I remember them.

I remember because of what happened after.

They were ratty people, dirty and ill-kempt, yet with a powerful and fascinating energy. At first we did not even realize they were acting out a play. A woman simply ambled in through the tavern door, hunched and dressed in black, wearing a witch's cone hat and carrying a basket. Moments later a man stormed in after her, cursing at the top of his lungs.

"Damn you, woman!" he was shouting. "Damn you, I want it back!"

Conversations broke off; men turned in their chairs to see what was the matter. The woman paused and turned, peering at her pursuer as though she could not remember where she had seen him before.

"You want what back?" she asked.

"You know perfectly well!" He patted his crotch. "You miserable thieving hag, I want it back!"

"Oh, that. What a fuss you men make over trifles."

"Trifles? God's teeth, you call it a trifle? I might as well be dead. What am I supposed to tell my wife?"

"Tell her you lost it in a dice game. She'll believe you."

The man made as if to leap at her, and then thought better of it. He paced frantically, waving his arms about and cursing more.

Then he stopped.

"I'll put an end to you, woman! I'll tell the archbishop about you, just see if I won't!"

"Go ahead; it won't do you any good. Better you give me three copper pennies, and you can have your dinkle back."

"Three pennies? God's blood, you're a thief twice over!"

"Well, there's some aren't worth three pennies, that be true. Never mind. I'll keep it, and give it to some poor sot what's lost it in the wars." She shifted the basket on her arm, and began to walk away.

"No, you don't!" He sprang past her, and stood square in her path. "I want it back!"

"Then shell out your three pennies. Nobody pays me any more; how's an old whore supposed to live, will you tell me?"

"I can't spare three pennies," he wailed. "I'll starve."

"One way or the other," she said. "You decide."

The man looked about, as if expecting help from the tavern crowd. He received only laughter and rude joshing.

"All right," he said. "Take your cursed money!"

She tucked away the coins he offered her, and opened her basket.

"Here," she said. "Take your pick." And spilled out on a table several dozen male members.

I could not tell how they had been made, but they looked quite lifelike from a distance. A few poor fools in the audience gulped with shock, but most of them roared with laughter, and kept on laughing harder and harder as the man picked up one cock after another, turning them in his hands, and trying them on for size, joking all the while. He held up a tiny wizened member, not much bigger than a boy's thumb: "Bet I know who this belongs to . . . ." The tavern howled. Another one, long and stretched: "This fellow's been in some strange places, don't you think?" Then a great thick one, massive enough to equip a horse.

"Ah, yes. This will suit me just fine."

The witch slapped him over the wrist, so hard that he yelped and dropped his prize. "No, you don't," she said grimly. "That one belongs to the archbishop."

Everyone laughed harder than ever, and applauded the players as they went around the tavern accepting coins or offers of food and drink. The woman took off her cone hat and her cape, and flirted with the men like any other tavern whore. She was past her youth and rather shapeless, but there was an earthy sensuality about her; she would earn a few more coins before the night was over. Otto looked, and thought it over, and passed.

When she had moved on, Lehelin smiled and asked him:

"Did you recognize her?"

"No. Should I have?"

"I just wondered. She was on the crusade, you know. With the people's army. She made it all the way, too. Claims she did a roaring business in Jerusalem, when it was all over."

"Actually, you know who she reminds me of?" Karelian said. "The one in Rouen. The one Armand and Aric were always fighting over—do you remember—the one who emptied the chamber pots on people's heads in the morning when they wouldn't let her sleep?"

"Oh, yes, Jesus . . . . Bellefleur her name was, wasn't it? Nothing very belle about that one."

And they were off again.

It went on for hours. They talked, and the jongleurs entertained us more. Karelian laughed harder than anyone at their jokes, and drummed his fingers on the table in time with their songs. He was hungry for laughter, I knew; hungry for an escape from the dark things in his mind, and the thought of the woman he had married. A woman who laughed at inappropriate things and wept at even more inappropriate ones, who stared across roomfuls of strangers looking for a face which was never there, who went up to men sometimes with the innocence of a child, calling them by other people's names, asking if they had seen the hunter elves, if they knew where the dark-haired ones had gone. A woman who smiled at him and stayed close by his side—and wedged colored stones into cracks in her hostess's walls, and twisted the first spring flowers into tangled knots and hung them behind the tapestries.

He did not share her bed. She was still ill, the flush of fever still bright in her cheeks. She had the manor's best room, and her maids with her day and night; the physician came every second day with fresh medicines and fresh advice. But it was not her illness, I think, which kept Karelian from her embrace; it was the ghost who walked beside her, the strange light burning in her eyes.

I was sorry for him, and yet in another part of my mind I was glad. She was not worthy of him. It was better if there was nothing between them, better if he would never love her, never be lured into trusting her again. Better if his heart and his mind could stay free to choose another, cleaner, and eternal love.

We returned to Lehelin's manor in high spirits. After another flagon or two had been finished off there, and all the good nights had been spoken three times over, we found ourselves in our chamber without a thought in our minds of sleep; we were past it.

"All those places you were with Lehelin, fighting," I said. "It must have been a long time ago."

"A very long time ago. When we were both young and innocent." He looked up, and added dryly: "And don't look so skeptical, my friend. Hard as you may find it to believe, there was a time when I was young and innocent."

He looked so very splendid then. I imagined him as a young knight, without the guilt and the cynicism. I envied Lehelin for knowing him then.

I suppose it was too many mugs of beer which put the next words into my mouth; I have no other excuse.

"Can I ask you something, my lord? I know it's not my business, and I will quite understand if you tell me so. Only . . . only I keep wondering why you . . . why you did what you did at Ravensbruck."

As soon as I had spoken I realized how outrageous it was, and I was afraid he might be terribly angry. But he was not angry at all. Neither was he honest.

He smiled. "Quite apart from any other consideration, Pauli, it was one of Count Arnulf's daughters or the other. Imagine me married to little Helga."

I did not want to imagine it at all.

"There is a story about Lehelin I must tell you," he said, changing the subject rather obviously. "We were in Burgundy. We didn't have a copper sou between us, and we'd borrowed to the point where no one would lend us anything more. We wondered if we'd have to start selling off our horses and equipment—after a man does that, God knows, he might as well carve himself a begging bowl.

"We heard about a tournament outside La Tour, so we went. It was absolute chaos; I have been in far more orderly real battles. All I managed to capture was three horses, and not very good ones, either. Lehelin got nothing. He was unhorsed, and lost his mount and his weapons. They were dragging him off by his feet when I rescued him.

"He wasn't happy. We took a room in a ratty little inn in the town. All evening he pouted, and walked around feeling sorry for himself, until I was ready to heave him out the window. Then all at once he leaned out into the street, and shouted at me: 'Come, Karel, come quickly!' and went tearing down the stairs. I followed him, thinking either the Vikings had landed or Lady Godiva was riding through town.

"It was nearly dark; the tournament had been over for hours. And there, ambling down the street on a completely exhausted horse, was a wounded knight. He had lost both helmet and shield; he was bleeding all over his mount, and barely conscious. Lehelin grabs the bridle, and says to him very formally: 'Sir, you are my prisoner; yield or die!' "

"My lord, you didn't . . . !"

"Oh, but we did. We dragged the poor devil off his horse, and up the stairs, and into our room, and shackled him to the bed. We fetched him a surgeon, and we fed him, but we kept him prisoner there until he paid his ransom. Five hundred silver marks we got, too; he was a man of substance."

Karelian was laughing at the memory.

"The best part of all was that he couldn't remember a thing after his helmet was battered off his head. He really believed Lehelin had beaten him in combat, and he was very respectful to us. It seems no one had ever beaten him before. He even gave us presents when he left."

"Which you took?"

"Which we took."

I was laughing, too; I could not help it. I don't know why I would

scarcely find the story amusing now. But at the time I was almost
doubled over with giddiness.

"And that, my lord . . . was when you were . . . young . . .
and . . . innocent . . . ?"

We laughed over it the way he must have laughed with Lehelin,
long ago in Burgundy, mauling each other and shouting like children
in a summer field, being complete fools, complete friends, rank forgotten, everything forgotten except delight and triumph and sheer flam-
boyant energy.

And then we stopped laughing. His hand was still in my hair, his
gaze still fixed on my face. But something had changed.

The camaraderie was gone. Our hilarity had melted into absolute
silence. I could not think or speak or breathe. His hand played like a
whisper of wind through my hair, searching and drawing away and
searching again, the touch unlike anything I had experienced, not
friendship at all now, something very different, tender and subtle and
possessive.

"Pauli . . . ."

His other hand, which had rested on my shoulder, was no longer
resting there; it was opening and closing softly, wandering down my
forearm and then across my back, every tiny shift of motion turning
into a caress, an invitation . . . .

I could not believe it was happening. I could not believe he would
touch me so, and smile, and let his eyes grow smoky as they did when
he went after a pretty whore—God knows I had seen the look before—*Yes, this one is nice; maybe she'll come upstairs with me* . . . .

My breath choked in my throat; my flesh turned to water; so overwhelming was my outrage, my grief. It was not possible. It could not
be happening. It simply could not.

My lord, no . . . !

I do not know if I spoke, or if the words died strangled on my
lips. I had no strength, and it seemed I had no will; I was paralyzed
with shame.

No man who is impure will enter the kingdom of God . . . .

Years later, in one of the darkest hours of my life, I would speak
to a holy man in the Alban Hills, in the great monastery of San Giuseppe.
It was a great sin to entertain foul desires, he would warn me, and a far
greater sin to act on them. But to stir up such desires in others was the
greatest sin of all. More women would fall to damnation for it, he said,
than for all the other evils in the world.

And what of men who do evil with men? I asked him.

The greatest sin done according to nature, he said, was less than the smallest sin done against it.

I bowed my head and said nothing, knowing it was true. I had known since my earliest boyhood. Even on my father's strictly governed manor there were corruptions, some so vile they had no names; they were known only as negations.

Unnatural. Unspeakable. Unimaginable.

Unmale.

A man who did such a thing was more wicked than a murderer, more hated by God than a heretic, more despised by men than a traitor. He was no longer a man at all.

I ducked away from Karelian's arm and almost ran across the room, grabbing at tasks I had already completed hours ago, the way a drowning man might grab at the wreckage of his ship. I seized upon anything which was handy to clean, or brush, or fold, or put away. He came and sat near me, saying nothing for a time, and finally I looked at him. I could not help it. He was always beautiful, more than any man I would ever know, and I understood now that part of his beauty had always been his powerful sensuality. Another man might have had the same fine features, the same splendid body, and yet not have seemed so desperately fair. Karelian's flesh was unmastered, unconsecrated, free. It was not a temple to the Holy Spirit or to anything else; it was an animal, alive in its own right, and full of dark promise. The witch of Helmardin had seen it. She wanted his soul, yes, but she wanted his body, too.

"I'm sorry if I have offended you, Pauli," he said. "But don't wear such a dark face. There's no harm done. I've known for a long time."

"I have no idea what you're talking about, my lord."

He made a small, assenting gesture. "As you wish. But it's nothing to grieve over, my friend, believe me. If we ever made public the names of all the high-born, glory-laden men who've warmed themselves in a comrade's tent at least once in their lives, the world would go spinning off its moorings from the shock. And for what? In a life as full of pain as this one, a bit of pleasure is no great matter to the gods."

No great matter?

The count smiled. He wanted to erase it, to make it into nothing, a small mistake of judgment for which a small apology would suffice.

I said nothing, and it was he who finally turned away from the anger in my eyes. From my outrage that he, lord or not, would have dared. Would have spoken so. Would have expected *that!*

Of me!

He stood up. When he spoke again there was an edge in his voice—not, I think, because I refused him, but because I blamed him, because I would not allow him to pretend it did not matter.

"Which do you think is a darker thing for a man, Pauli?" he asked bitterly. "To share his bed with a living man, or with a dead one?"

I did not answer. I was not going to be drawn in by his shabby excuses, his willingness to always find something or someone to blame for his sins: war and other men's greed and the Church and probably God himself, and now of course his marriage, the same marriage which he could and should have ended in Ravensbruck where it began . . . . No, dear God, he was not going to get anywhere with that argument!

I did not know it at the time, nor for a long time after, but it was then, I think—that very night—when I began to hate him.

Lauds had rung, and then nones; Paul did not go to chapel. He sat as a man condemned, unaware of the moonset, or of the pink dawn lightening the walls of his cell.

The exorcist from Mainz had arrived eight days ago: a tall, robust man with steady eyes, riding on a mule. He was not just an ordinary priest, but a monsignor, and he arrived with a perfectly credible story. The Church, he said, was growing troubled about the practice of sorcery among the common folk, a practice which it no longer considered harmless. It was too easy for monks, shut away in the quiet sanctity of their lives, to ignore such things, or fail to notice them. They must become more aware, he said. He spoke in the chapel; he led prayers in the refectory; he heard confessions. And so, when the time came to sit alone with Brother Paul in his cell, no one thought anything about it.

He sat with his elbows on the small wooden table, his fingers carefully poised into a pinnacle. His name was Wilhelm von Schielenberg. He was the son of a Rhineland baron, and he might well have aspired to a bishop's miter, or at the very least an abbey of his own.

"Well, Brother Paul?"

Paul knotted and unknotted his hands. He brushed dirt from his robe, and from the scarred wooden table. He was almost overwhelmed by panic, by a desperate wish to back away and run.

It is nothing, Monsignor. I'm a foolish man; I alarmed Brother Anselm over nothing. I had a few bad dreams, that's all; it is nothing . . . .

But if he sent this man away, he was finished, and he knew it. He could not defend himself—not against them, not against her. And no one else would listen to him after this, not even Anselm. The servants of darkness would come triumphant and howling with laughter. They would pull him down, and always further down, into the depths of his own corruption. And finally into eternal pain.

He had to speak to this man; he had to save himself. Only the risk was so terribly great . . . .

He saw with sickening clarity what the witch of Car-Iduna had done to him. She had caught him between two pits, each more black and terrifying than the other. All he could do was stumble back and forth between them, like a rat in a burning cage.

"You wished to speak to me, Brother Paul?"

The priest had a strong face, with a clean line of jaw and deep, knowing eyes. It was a face to inspire confidence in anyone, even those who were utterly desperate. Those whose souls were no longer their own.

Paul began slowly, haltingly. He had served, many years ago, as squire to Count Karelian of Lys. He had been in the war—

"Which war, my son? There have been many."

"The war against the Salian kings."

"Ah, yes. Gottfried's war. Go on."

"I was asked to write a history of it. By the Holy Father. Only when I began—"

"Forgive me, Brother Paul. I mean no offense. But why would the pope ask you to write such a history? You were hardly one of the principals in the affair."

"I wasn't one of the principals, Monsignor. But because of my years of service with Karelian Brandeis, I knew things about him which most of the principals didn't know—at least they didn't know for sure. He served the powers of darkness,

Monsignor, and he used sorcery and other abominations against his enemies. This was what the pope wanted me to write about. Only when I began, they . . . they put a spell on my quill. So now it writes what they wish."

"They?"

"The witch of Car-Iduna. And her demons."

Father Wilhelm linked his fingers briefly and then steepled them again. "And who is this witch of . . . of Carduna? What is her name?"

"I don't know her name. She's the witch of Helmardin. The Lady of the Mountain."

The priest's face did not change, but Paul could sense the fierce quickening of his interest.

"You're saying it is she who bewitched you? How do you know? Many people say she's only a legend."

"I met her. I was there, inside her fortress in Helmardin. With Karelian of Lys. And she came here also, to my cell. The night I began my history. She took up my quill in her hand and she cursed it."

"How extraordinary!" Wilhelm murmured. "Go on."

"Please." Paul wanted to kneel, to place his head between Father Wilhelm's hands, and weep. "Please, will you rid me of them? Drive them out of my quill, out of this cell, out of me? My soul is in mortal peril."

He looked up, half expecting the priest to rise, and wrap his stole around his neck, and take out the crucifix and the hyssop, and begin. But Monsignor von Schielenberg sat as calmly as before, and when Paul did not say anything further, he repeated his soft command.

"Go on, Brother Paul."

"They torment me day and night," Paul said desperately. "I dare not sleep for the evil things they put into my mind. I dare not close my eyes. I've even thought . . . I've even thought of self-destruction—oh, not willingly, dear God, no! They put the thought in my head; they whisper it in my ear: End it, Paul of Ardiun, end it and sleep . . . !" He shuddered. "Can't you help me? In the name of God, can't you help me?"

Wilhelm shifted a little in his chair.

"What is the nature of the torments they inflict on you?" he asked. "Do the demons cause you pain?"

"No." Paul shook his head. "They fill my mind with evil thoughts?"

"What manner of thoughts?"

Paul looked at his hands. "Unclean desires. Images . . . vile images of the vilest deeds. I can't speak of them, Father."

"You must speak of them. How else can we learn how devils come into men's souls? Or how to defend against them? Tell me exactly what happens when they appear, and what they do."

Exactly? How was it possible, when their coming was all nightmare and fire, all shadow and mist? Voices in darkness, demon flesh melting even as the eye wakened to discover it? Heat rising up in his own loins, night after night unbidden? Dead men walking into his cell, laughing, brushing their hands through his hair, their blood spilling over him while his own flesh burst in a hideous mating of hatred and desire?

There were no words for such things.

But he had to answer the priest. He needed help. He had to find the words somehow.

"They . . . they provoke in me a terrible concupiscence. I can't control it. They fill my mind with thoughts of sin— every kind of sin there is, Monsignor, between men and women, men and beasts, men and men. And then they . . . ." It took all his strength to finish. "And then they . . . take me."

"In what fashion?"

"Every fashion."

"They assume human bodies?"

"Yes."

"Women's bodies?"

"Yes." His head fell lower. "Sometimes."

"And the other times?" Wilhelm asked.

"They have the bodies of men."

"Most times, perhaps?"

"Yes. Most times."

There was a brief, unbearable silence. Wilhelm got to his feet and walked to the window.

"The devil," he said, "is an excellent strategist. It's always his way to attack the soul at its weakest point. What have you done to draw this evil into your life? Are you one of those who foul themselves with their own kind? Who come on purpose into monasteries to live among their brothers and corrupt them?"

"Never! I swear to you, never—!"

"But you have been tempted," Wilhelm said, turning back to him. "Sorely tempted."

"No."

No. To be tempted was to desire, and he had never been guilty of it; never. He had loved them purely, both of them. It was Karelian who saw everything through his own corrupted eyes . . . .

"You have lived chastely in the monastery?" Wilhelm asked.

"Yes. Always."

"And before?"

"Yes. Almost always. I tried very hard."

The exorcist sat down again, and drummed his fingers softly on the table.

"It's remarkable, you know, how many times I hear the same stories. Lust is in all men the great corrupter."

He paused thoughtfully, and looked up. "Corruption begins with the passions of the body; it doesn't end with them. There's a great deal you're not telling me, Brother Paul."

Paul sat rigid, barely able to breathe. The exorcist picked up the quill and turned it in his hands.

"The Holy Father asked you to write an account of the war, of the sorcery practiced by Karelian of Lys and his allies?"

"Yes."

"At the time, many men accused Karelian of such crimes. Those accusations reflected on the highest lords of the land— even on the king himself. If you knew the truth, Brother Paul, why didn't you reveal it then?"

"I did speak of it, Monsignor, to such men as would listen. But I was only a knight of modest station. As you say, many other men accused him, and most of them were far more powerful than I. If the lords of Germany would not listen to their peers, or believe the evidence of their own eyes, nothing I could have said would have made any difference."

"I'm not talking about the lords of Germany, Brother Paul. I know what they believe, and what they don't believe. They do not concern me right now. I want to know why you didn't take your knowledge to the Church."

He paused. His voice was soft, almost fatherly, yet there was a threat in it, and a terrifying power. He spoke as one who spoke for God.

"You should have taken this information directly to the archbishop of Mainz," he went on. "To the papal legate, perhaps even to Rome itself. Yet you were silent. You were silent then, and for thirty years thereafter. Tell me why, Brother Paul. Why did it take all these years, and a command from the pope himself, to make you speak to the Church?"

Paul did not know what to say. In a matter of moments the exorcist had penetrated all his defenses. He had found the lethal question, the one question Paul could not answer with the truth.

"I was confused and afraid."

Yes, he thought. Let it seem so. Let Wilhelm think he was weak, or vain, or stupid. Let him jump to any shabby, wrong conclusion, just as Anselm did. *You don't want to look bad; you don't want people to know about your sins . . . .*

"I was terribly afraid, Monsignor. And after, when the war was over, I wanted only to forget, and dedicate my life to God."

"But surely, Brother Paul, the highest service you could have offered God was to confirm those terrible accusations, if you knew they were true. To confirm them at the time, when it would have done the most good. Instead you joined an obscure band of knights and fled to the Holy Land. And you stayed there for eleven years, until Germany had forgotten all about you.

"You had things to hide. Your own involvement, perhaps? Did you obtain such a thorough knowledge of your master's sorceries by taking part in them yourself?"

Paul stared at him, appalled. "Dear Jesus, Monsignor! Never! As God is my witness, I never once—!"

"Then why were you silent?"

Paul made a brief, helpless gesture. "I don't know. It was . . . easier. To say nothing. To just . . . run away."

"Yes. But what were you running away from? That is the question, isn't it?"

Paul had seen strength in von Schielenberg, and found it comforting. How foolish he had been! The face across the table had no warmth in it, no priestly concern. It was a face of raw power.

"Brother Paul." Wilhelm paused, choosing his words. "You tell me you've been bewitched, against your will, and through no fault of your own. It may be so. Or it may be that your own folly and corruption have finally caught up with you. Until I know which, I can't begin to help you. Where is the manuscript?"

"The manuscript?" Paul whispered.

"Yes, Brother Paul. The manuscript."

"It's hidden. Under the floor."

"I want to see it."

It was unbearable to think of anyone reading it, seeing those words from his own hand, those memories of his own life so twisted and befouled. But he knew he could not refuse. He retrieved the parchments from their hiding place, and handed them to the priest.

"You must understand, Monsignor," he said. "I had no power over this. It's the devil's work, full of contradictions and lies."

"We shall see."

Wilhelm von Shielenberg rose, tucking the bundle under his arm.

"You must pray, Brother Paul. Pray and do penance. Throw yourself utterly on God's mercy; it's your only hope of salvation. When we speak again, I will expect you to tell me everything."

The pink dawn turned to golden daylight. A faint smell of wood smoke drifted in through Paul's window, reminding him instinctively of food. He did not know when he had last eaten anything but crusts of bread. He felt a brief tug of longing. As a boy he had lived well in Ardiun. They had eaten meat whenever it was permitted. They always had butter and cheese, and pastries sweetened with honey. His father had such a stern view of human flesh; why did he not fast more?

But Paul knew why, when he thought about it. His father did not have to fast in order to learn mastery of self; the mastery was already there, the absolute will. He, Paul, was only a shabby echo of the man who had sired him. Could his father see him now, he wondered, looking down from his place in heaven? Could his father see him and know what he had become—a plaything for devils, a weakling who stank of sin? It did not bear thinking about. It was worse than God knowing, or the whole world.

The priest from Mainz returned the following day. He looked as though he had not slept at all. He laid the manuscript on Paul's wooden table and sat down across from him. He did not even bother to hide his distaste. False though it was, the chronicle had done its work. It had marked Paul forever in Wilhelm's mind as cowardly and sexually corrupt.

"Your writing," he said, "is full of heresy and abominations."

"I know, Monsignor—"

"But it's interesting nonetheless. As long as it's not allowed to fall into the wrong hands, I think it will prove singularly useful to the Church."

The room spun. Paul closed his eyes, gripping the side of the table, cold sweat spilling over his face and drenching his habit.

"Forgive me," he whispered. "I'm weak from fasting."

"No, Paul. You're afraid." The priest smiled; it was the calculated, knowing smile of the born interrogator. "You're afraid of damnation, but you're even more afraid of the truth. And since we already know the truth about your . . . concupiscence . . . it's clear you must be hiding something else."

"I'm hiding nothing," Paul said desperately. "I want to be free of this . . . this horrible entrapment."

"No doubt you do. God knows what you might be compelled to reveal. I'm not a fool, Brother Paul. I know when men are lying to me; it's my business to know. Left to your own devices, you would never fulfill the pope's command. You would write what you wished him to know, and conceal the rest. Only now it appears the devil's minions have come to blows—just as they did thirty years ago. And when thieves fall out, honest men can sometimes prosper."

As they spoke, Wilhelm had been watching him with cold and relentless eyes, and it occurred to Paul what the exorcist really was—what any exorcist had to be. He was a Christian sorcerer, wielding all the same gifts of power, practicing all the same skills, merely doing so from the other side of the fence. The thought was unexpected, and utterly horrifying.

"Let me be blunt," Wilhelm went on. "The Church has had little except grief from her German subjects. You do nothing about the paganism in your midst. Your highest lords hang witch-charms around their necks, and call on the old gods in battle. And your people hold them up as heroes. It's reached the point where good Christians can no longer pick their way through the muddle. They will come to blows quarreling over Gottfried and the count of Lys, claiming one was a sorcerer and the other a saint, but from house to house and village to village they will not agree on which was which.

"The archbishop of Mainz was in Stavoren when it ended," he went on. "Many times afterwards, he said the same thing: 'They were all evil,' he said, 'all three, and they trampled down the will of God between them.' I think he was right. And I think you know something about them even the archbishop didn't know."

Paul could not believe what he was seeing. The priest was gathering up the sheaves of parchment, as if the interview were over. As if he were about to leave.

"Monsignor . . . ?"

"Your chronicle has a certain ring of truth to it. A perverted, malevolent truth, but a truth nonetheless. That's what troubles you, I think. It might not be a mistake to hear what the witch of Helmardin has to say about all of these things."

"You can't be serious?" Paul whispered. "You would trust a document written like this? A devil's chronicle? Dear Jesus, you expect it to be true?"

"No. I expect it to be revealing. There is a difference."

He paused, looking grimly at the monk. "Two things you are forgetting, Brother. First, God's will is absolute. Nothing passes in the world without his consent, not even this. And second, you forget that evil often works to its own destruction.

What better weapon might we wish for to combat sorcery than the testament of sorcerers? I could have spent a lifetime searching out their ways, and found nothing better than this."

"But when they constantly mingle truth with lies, how will you make sense of it? How will you know what is true?"

"God will give us the wisdom to know. Why else did he send his Church into the world?"

Paul sat numb. It had been a terrible risk, asking for help. He had always known it. But even in his darkest moments he had not feared an outcome as perilous as this.

"You can't mean to leave me to them?" he said harshly. "My soul is utterly in their hands!"

"Your soul is in your own hands, as are those of all men. I can't exorcise a man who isn't sincerely penitent, who will not in full humility lay bare his soul. Truly, I marvel at your arrogance in sending for me. Did you think you could escape them and still hold yourself back from God?

"If you want to be saved—if you really mean it—you know exactly what to do. Renounce all your sorceries and corruptions, not just the ones you've grown afraid of. Come with me to Rome. Dictate your history to the Holy Father's scribes, under oath and in the presence of witnesses. Answer truthfully every question that's put to you, and confess every sin. You will be forgiven."

"Come with you to Rome, Monsignor?" Paul said numbly. "That isn't possible."

"If it isn't possible, then clearly your soul is not your first concern. So how can I or anyone possibly help you?"

He stood up. "I'm keeping the document you've produced so far. I will take it with me, and I will suggest to the Holy Father that you be called before the Inquisition. You have a great deal of knowledge—knowledge which could advance the Church's work, and save countless Christian souls. Knowledge you must share with us, if you're to have any hope of God's mercy."

He paused at the door of Paul's cell, and looked back.

"I will pray for you, my son."

Then he was gone, stern and upright into a stillborn day. Paul sat for a long time, letting the summons of the monastery bells pass unheeded. He missed lauds; he missed nones. It did not matter. He would be reprimanded and punished. It did not matter.

He was alone now. He had no allies in the world; he had abandoned it. He had no allies in the Church; it had abandoned him. They would pursue him now on an uncontested field, all of them, like Saracens chasing a single, beaten knight across the sand.

They would pursue him, but they would not close and kill . . . not yet. The desert was vast, and he had nowhere to hide, and the story was only just begun.

XVI

STAVOREN

Leave Babylon behind you and fight
for the kingdom of heaven.

CARMINA BURANA

TWICE EVERY DECADE THE HOLY ROMAN EMPEROR made the long journey across his empire, through all his feudal domains to visit all
of his chief vassals. The *Königsritt* took months; it was high summer
when he came to Stavoren to be feasted and honored in the palace
of Duke Gottfried. All of the duke's vassals were there, too, summoned by his command, so he might, in the full glory of his court,
offer proper homage to his king.

There they met again, Gottfried and Karelian, and there the dream
was born, the dream I have carried all these years in the silence of
my heart. The dream I dare not speak of, not even to the Church
where it finally and properly belongs. It is too late now, and too soon.
For in the great affairs of history, as in all other things, there is a
time and a season, an hour when the tide is at flood, the ship in full
sail, the captain chosen and peerless among men, the wind right and
the stars in their places. If it sails, the world will be changed forever.
If it is run aground, years will pass, or centuries, before the hour
comes again.

A few months earlier, we left Karn, and arrived at Lys in the
flower of its spring. There is no fairer place in all the Reinmark, not
even the vale of Ardiun where I was raised. The trees were hung with
blossom; small creeks were singing everywhere, running headlong into

the deep embrace of the Maren. Lambs bounded in the fields, and the sun burned warm in our faces. For a while it seemed as if the world was good.

Karelian loved his lands. Day after day he was out walking in the orchards in the first morning light, or hunting in the woodlands, or visiting with the master brewer and the master miller, with the stewards and the gamekeepers, with the gardeners and the serfs, wanting to know everything they did, and how they might do it better.

As for my lord's wife, I would as soon not speak of her. Everyone, of course, knew of the scandal in Ravensbruck, or soon was told about it. There was a good deal of whispering in the sculleries and the stables, but Karelian went about his life as though nothing whatever was wrong with it. He turned the household and the running of the manor over to Adelaide. He made her generous gifts. He accepted her strange, soul-scarred moods, her whispers of madness, her sudden offerings of passion, when she would embrace him in full view of anyone who might be about, and kiss his mouth and hang her arms around his neck like a besotted courtesan. What he thought of it he did not say, and no one else dared to say anything at all.

Did she truly come to care for him? Or did she merely offer him the same perfected sham of loyalty she once had offered to her father? To this day I do not know, and I do not think Karelian knew, either. At unexpected moments I would see him looking at her, uncertain and a little sad, as though he did not entirely understand how he had gotten himself into such a strange situation, or where it would lead him, or how he would ever get out.

She did not come with us to Stavoren. She was by now visibly with child, and more fragile than ever. She wept when we left, and stood in the open gate until we were lost in a whisper of dust across the valley. Every night while we were gone—so I learned later from the servants—she burned lights in the chapel, and spread flowers and witch-charms and medals of the Virgin all over Karelian's pillow. But when she rose, and walked in the sleep of madness from her bed, the name she murmured to the shadows was not his.

It is enough; I will speak of her no more.

As for myself, between me and my lord nothing changed on the surface, and I think for him nothing changed at all. He was as kind to me as always. He never spoke of what passed that night in Karn, not even once; nor did he offend against my honor again, not in the smallest word or deed. It was as though none of it had happened. I had all but forgiven him when we raised our banners yet again, and marched southwest to Stavoren to pay our homage to the king.

Gottfried entertained us with lavish generosity. As lord of all the Reinmark, he was one of the five great German princes whose domains made up the empire. This was the first *Königsritt* since his return from Jerusalem, and thus it was his first opportunity to impress upon both his vassals and his liege how much he had accomplished in the east, how magnificent he was now, and how well served.

I have spoken little of him in this chronicle, for in truth until the meeting in Stavoren he was to me a stern and distant figure, majestic and revered, but distant, a lord so far above me in rank and so outstanding in his achievements that I simply felt awed in his presence, like a stableboy in the presence of a king. I had met him several times in the Holy Land, and as Karelian's squire I made the long journey home in his retinue, yet I never overcame my feeling of awe. The Golden Duke was always a man apart, a man above the common measure of his peers.

I realize now, with the wisdom of long years, that my sense of his superiority rested only partly on his rank and his accomplishments. There were other highborn dukes in the world, after all. There were other knights whose shields were hung with laurels, whose names were known in every court in Europe. There was Ehrenfried himself, emperor of all the Germans, who stirred no such awe in me, even on the first day I met him.

Gottfried was different from them all. Everything about him stood in contrast to the qualities of lesser men, even the fact that he was difficult to know. He had nothing of Karelian's common touch. He would never sit in a rough chair in a dirty inn, and laugh at crude jokes and put his feet up and pet the innkeeper's cat. He was not arrogant, but he never lowered himself, even for a moment; he never forgot who he was.

He was a man of immense physical stature, well over six feet, with massive shoulders and a great, leonine head. Not beautiful at all, in the immediate, sensual way we think of beauty. His neck was too thick, and his nose too large. His mouth was a hard slash across a plain, blunt face. His golden hair was straight and thinning from the forehead. Yet he needed only to walk into a room to be admired. He needed only to speak and conversations around him would fall silent, and men would turn and listen.

It was an evening late in June, the first evening of our arrival.

Others had come before us. The summergreen fields below the duke's castle were now a city of tents, crowded to bewilderment with high-born guests and their retinues. And though the duke was gracious to everyone, from the very first Karelian was favored more than any man there. Gottfried greeted him as a brother, and honored him with several splendid gifts, not least a beautiful grey stallion, an Arabian, one of the finest horses I have ever seen.

"He loves the chase even more than you do," the duke told Karelian. "I think you will enjoy him."

Karelian was pleased, and very flattered. It always surprised him a little, I think, to be reminded that he'd finally made his place in the world.

"You are very generous, my lord. Thank you."

"We'll go hunting tomorrow, and you can try him out," Gottfried said. "The emperor will not arrive for a few more days."

Karelian handed the horse's reins to me, and fell in step beside his liege.

"He's bringing over two hundred knights," the duke went on. "And of course Prince Konrad will be here. So it will be a particularly good tournament, this one. Since I can't take part, we will all look to you to cover the Reinmark with glory."

The emperor Ehrenfried arrived with his queen and his court about a week later. I had never seen him before, and I suppose it was unfair of me to expect him to be physically magnificent, or to be disappointed because he was not. But I was very disappointed. He did not look like a king. He was only of medium height, plump as a merchant, with stubby pink fingers and very little hair. He liked to laugh.

Sometimes, when he had passed out of earshot, I would hear the occasional sullen whisper against him, or see men exchange dark looks. The civil wars had been over for some years, but the wounds they left were still raw. On the surface, all was friendship, but there was more than one lord visiting at Gottfried's court who hated the king.

He wore splendid garments, and he always behaved with dignity. Yet from the day he came until the long festival was over, I could never stop feeling that it was Gottfried, and not the king, who was the greatest lord. More and more it was Gottfried I found myself watching. I began to admire the very qualities which had intimidated me when I was younger—his separateness, his personal reserve, his extraordinary power. He dwarfed the men around him, princes and champions and emperor alike. All of them, and Karelian too.

It saddened me a little to admit it. But Gottfried was lord to me, too, lord to all of us. I thought myself a very fortunate young man, being able to serve and honor them both.

Oh, there was glitter that summer in Stavoren! It was the last joyful summer of my life, and, until it ended in one black hour, it was the best. There was feast after feast in the duke's great hall, with such food as I have never tasted since; there were minstrels and dancing; there were magnificent, clamorous hunts along the wild edges of the Silverwald.

And, a few days after Ehrenfried arrived, there was the birth of a new order of knighthood. Gottfried planned it before he ever left the Holy Land. Years later the Church would carry on the idea, creating first the Knights of Saint John and then the Templars, but it was Gottfried who first saw the possibility—the glorious possibility of finally linking warfare and faith. Of creating a true Church Militant, an army of warrior monks.

Only seven to start with, hardly an army, but oh, God, I envied them, those chaste, golden-haired youths in their white garments, keeping vigil through the long night in the chapel of Stavoren. They were the first of the Order of Saint David. In the end Gottfried would drop the word "saint" from the name, and call them, at least among his friends, simply the Order of David, which was what he had always had in mind: the followers of David who slew Goliath, and swept the heathen lands, and took them for God.

The emperor did not approve.

"A warrior monk is a contradiction in terms," he said. He sat at the head of Gottfried's feast table. When he sat thus, greying and thoughtful, with his elbows on the table, he looked far more like a scholar than a king.

They said he was a fine soldier in his prime, and I believe it, for he fought two civil wars to keep his crown, both of them under the ban of excommunication. He was very bitter now against the pope. He sent no men on the great crusade, and offered its leaders only token gifts of money. Thus Germany, largest of all the Christian nations, took almost no part in Christianity's greatest adventure.

"I don't understand how they think in Rome," the emperor went on. "For a thousand years the Church said warfare was wrong. Oh,

God knows we Christians haven't always lived by it, but it's what we were taught. Thou shalt not kill. Blessed are the peacemakers. If thy enemy smite thee on one cheek, turn him the other."

Gottfried's son could barely contain himself. He was the eldest son, the duke's heir, a golden-haired giant named Theodoric who seemed an exact, youthful copy of his father.

"And if we lived by such principles, my lord," he demanded, "how many Christians would be left in the world? The pagans slaughter us, the infidels slaughter us—"

"And we slaughter each other," the emperor interrupted calmly. "It's beside the point."

"How can it be beside the point?" Gottfried demanded.

"Because the Church's business is men's souls. Not warfare. Not politics. The popes are no longer interested in souls, it seems to me. They're interested in power. Power here, in the world. And they're turning Christ's teaching on its head in order to get it. In thirty years we went from 'Thou shalt not kill' to a holy war, and in ten years more to an order of warrior monks. That's not a Church any more, it's a rival empire."

He paused, looking grimly at the faces which lined his table.

"Am I the only one who's noticing a pattern here? God knows some of you are old enough to remember the Saxons who fled to us after William took England. They filled our courts for twenty years. They were scattered all over the world, driven from their lands with nothing but the cloaks on their backs. All because an ambitious Norman poured sacks of gold into the coffers of the Church, and an even more ambitious priest decided that he, and not the people of England, should choose the English king."

Ehrenfried's bitterness was almost physical; it darkened his face, and made his voice hard as granite.

"The same priest who sat behind the papal throne and urged his pope to support the invasion of England and overthrow King Harold— that same priest became pope himself, and then did the same thing to me! My crown was promised to another, just like Harold's. I was excommunicated, just like he was—I and every man who might dare to raise a sword in my defense. What's an honest citizen to do, faced with such a choice—turn against his lawful king, or turn against his God? Whatever choice he makes he must feel himself condemned.

"That's not religion any more, it is tyranny. It's not the pope's place to make such judgments, to bring whole nations to such a pass."

He took a peach which a servant offered to him and broke it in half, speaking more calmly.

"The Church is forgetting God, my friends, and setting its eyes on the world. They may call it reform, but it's really a drive for power. And that's why, after a thousand years of teaching peace, now we're teaching war, and telling men it's Christian to fight. It's never Christian. It's sometimes necessary, but it is never Christian."

"My lord," Gottfried said, "you spoke earlier of a contradiction in terms. Surely to say a thing is necessary, and then to say it's not Christian—surely that's the greatest contradiction in terms we could imagine. Wait—I beg you, my lord, let me finish—I think you're right; there is a pattern here. A pattern which has been unfolding ever since the days of Constantine.

"Why shouldn't the Church turn its eyes to the world? Charlemagne brought half of Europe under his rule, and so to the rule of Christ. Was that unchristian? We took back Jerusalem; was that unchristian? If it's honorable and worthy to go to war for one's king, isn't it a thousand times more honorable and worthy to go to war for the king of heaven? The popes aren't overturning Christian teaching, my lord; they are finally acknowledging what has always been Christian practice. We are men who fight for God."

"And who was Charlemagne, Duke Gottfried?" Ehrenfried demanded. "Was he the king or was he the pope? There used to be a difference, you know. Christ told us to render to Caesar the things which are Caesar's, and to God the things which are God's. The popes want to rule over God's things, and over Caesar's, too."

The abbot of Saint Stephen's leapt into the fray. "But God must always be the final authority in the world, my lord," he said.

"Yes," agreed Ehrenfried. "Acting through his lawful and anointed agent, the Christian king."

"No, my lord," said the abbot. "With all due respect. Acting through the authority of Peter, who is Christ's heir, and lord over all kings."

"I think," Karelian said dryly, "we are on the brink of another twenty years of war."

Everyone laughed, willing to let the tension dissolve. It was a feast, and the matter had been argued over many times before. Only Gottfried, I noticed, did not let it drop, following on quietly with his duchess and his son, with the circle of men around them. I heard only his first comment, before a fresh conversation and women's laughter drowned him out.

"There is no contradiction," he said. "God's power is one. There can be no contradiction."

All during the long evening of revelry, I found my thoughts going back to his words, and to his new band of knights. They would be dressed all in white, except for a black cross sewn across their surcoats and painted on their shields. Its shape was their Christian icon; its color would remind them they were God's unto death, vowed to chastity, obedience, and the defense of the Church.

It took a great deal of money to become a knight—money I did not have, although I knew I could borrow it from my father. One had to buy horses and weapons and mail, and this last especially cost a small fortune. There was my poverty, holding me back. There was also Karelian. I did not want to leave his service, not even for the Knights of Saint David.

Night after night, when the feasting and dancing was finally over, and the duke's court was scattered with bodies like a battlefield, when even Karelian had found his bed—his own bed, I mean, which was rarely the first one he fell into—even then I would sit awake, with my arms around my knees, and think about those white-clad knights, and wonder why I could want so much to follow them, and still want to stay here.

Loyalty, I told myself was the highest of all virtues. It was right for me to honor my liege, and choose to stay with him.

But was it really loyalty? asked another part of my mind—the harder, colder part. Or was it simply worldliness? Life in Lys was good. The count was generous, and moreover he was mowing down his rivals on the tournament field like so many blades of grass. Everyone envied me, serving so splendid a lord.

Was I weak, perhaps, weak and nothing more? Weak like I had always been, like my father always told me? *Your spine is made of porridge, Pauli. Get some iron into you, or you will never amount to anything.*

Better than all the feasts of the summer, and all the wild hunts, best of everything we enjoyed in Stavoren was the great tournament of the emperor. For two weeks Gottfried's court was centered on the jousting field, a narrow stretch of flatland beyond the castle, ringed about with banners and a small, splendid city of tents. There the knights of the Reinmark tested their valor and their skills against each other, and against all who came to challenge them: from the royal court in Aachen, from Bavaria, from Saxony, even from the courts of the Franks. More than two hundred knights had followed Ehrenfried's long journey across the empire, hungry for fame and silver marks and the kisses of women.

Gottfried himself did not take part. It was a tradition in the Reinmark that a host never competed against his own guests, for no matter which man won, he would seem to offer a discourtesy to the other. The emperor, of course, was too old now for jousting, but his personal champion was there to win honor on his behalf, and so was his son Prince Konrad.

It was not the sort of tournament Karelian fought in during his youth with Lehelin. Those had been sheer wild melees, with few rules and less honor, and with no object except profit: the capture of horses and equipment, and the taking of captives for ransom. They had been mock battles with all the chaos of real battles, not least the victimization of the innocent. More than one peasant saw his crops trampled to ruin; more than one village saw a tourney end in a wholesale rampage of rape and plunder; and more than one honest man judged the word knight as nothing but another word for bandit.

This was different. The knights here fought in an enclosed field, according to the strictest rules of chivalry. They used blunted weapons, but it was still desperately perilous, and every man rode onto the field knowing he might be carried from it gravely hurt, or dead.

God, I was proud of Karelian those long, fierce days, proud to aching in the depths of my bones. There was no man there who looked more splendid than he did, all in blue and black and silver, with the winter tree stark on his shield and that strange black ribbon flying from the tip of his lance. It was Acre all over again, the sun burning, all the horizons shimmering with heat, the ground rocking with the sound of hooves. Lances shattered like dry reeds against the painted shields. Men went down, and horses. I think I prayed; I know my heart stopped more than once before it was over. But day after day it was the same; no one broke more lances than he did, or left more rivals lying on the field. And no one unhorsed him, not even once.

We will all look to you to cover the Reinmark in glory . . . !

He had never fought in the emperor's lists before, in such high company and for such high stakes. And now he wanted to win. Though he claimed he had his fill of warfare, all the things which made him good at warfare were still with him: the daring, and the cool judgment, and the will to win. He was thirty-eight, and he was still good, and he took a surprisingly fierce pleasure in demonstrating it. *So what if I was only the last left-over son of a fool? I was better than any of them, and one day they would all know it . . . !*

And yes, I gloried in it with him. I polished his shield and his trappings until they glistened. I followed him everywhere, in case he might need me for some small service. I strutted like a little godling among the other squires: *Just wait! Just you wait until my lord meets yours . . . !* I handed him his shield and his lance as I might have handed a priest the vessels of the Eucharist. And when he smiled at me, as he did sometimes, before he veered the horse away—*Wish me luck, Pauli!*—I felt like I carried the world in the curve of my fingers.

There were women everywhere, all of them loving the ferocity of it. Any man who thinks females are the gentler sex has never seen them at a tournament. Their eyes hung on their favorites with the adoration of lovers, and glittered like the swords on the field. As far as they were concerned, each knight fought for one thing only—for the woman whose token he carried, for the smile she would give him, or the kiss, or the hour in her bed. Every shattered lance was a tribute to her beauty. Every man who knelt on the field had been brought to his knees for her. And it was the same no matter who the woman was. They all chose some man to honor with a token, and they gloried in the certainty that he would dare for her more than he would dare for himself, or for his king, or for his God.

The sad thing was, they were so often right.

Karelian never told me why he wrapped that piece of black silk around his lance, and I never asked. I never had to. He smiled at the women in Stavoren, and wore their favors, and he took more than one of them to bed. But she was there, always there in some quiet place in his mind, in some always unsated hunger of his body. *You will forget nothing, Karelian of Lys . . . .*

It was for her that he fought in Stavoren. For the glory of it, yes, and for the pride of coming home a hero and a lord, and flaunting it to all of Germany—a man who had been nobody, who had bought his first knightly accouterments with money borrowed from a prostitute, and spent most of his life trading his sword in the same fashion—oh, yes, he was letting the whole world know he was no longer just a whelp of the weathervane of Dorn. There was all of that. But there was something else, too, something softer and darker which I noticed in his unguarded moments. A confusion. A sense of indirection, of loss, of empty longing, which his triumphs on the field did not assuage—quite the opposite. The closer he came to victory the more I knew what he really wanted from it, more than the bag of golden coins or the adulation of all Germany. He wanted to offer it to her.

All of what I have written here is true: I was happy in Stavoren, and filled with admiration for my lord. But I was also troubled, and neither my happiness nor my admiration was complete. Doubts hung often in the back of my mind—doubts and guilt and wondering, and a growing ambivalence about who I was, and what I was going to become.

The Church forbade tournaments. Gottfried's fresh-dubbed Knights of Saint David did not take part. Monks and bishops spoke openly against the practice, mocking the lords of Christendom for turning combat into a game, and knighthood into a mere badge of rank:

What are you doing here, fighting among yourselves? Dressing yourselves in fine silks, and feasting, and letting your hair grow long like women, and wearing perfumes? You are the swordsmen of God; why are you not abroad with your swords in your hands, riding against his enemies?

I thought about those questions, too, sometimes, and I did not like the answers. I liked them least of all the day I found my master in his tent with the margravine von Uhland.

It was the second last day of the tournament. Karelian had done well, defeating among others the duke of Thuringia, who had been many times a champion himself. But it was a hard-won victory. He had been battered to raw exhaustion, and we had to help him from the field, Reinhard on one side of him and I on the other, a whole band of our men following, all of them clamorous with triumph.

In the tent, I quickly removed his helmet and heavy armor. He almost groaned with relief, and sank wearily onto the cot. His hair was dank and stained with rust. He no longer looked like a tawny German at all, but like one of those carrot-colored Irishmen with flaming locks and freckles.

I brought a huge basin of water and some towels, and he washed off the worst of it and took a long, grateful drink of water.

"Thank God the emperor only comes once every five years," he said.

"I thought you were enjoying this, my lord," Otto said.

He laughed roughly. "I'm enjoying every minute of it. Just don't hold your breath until I do it again."

He was hurting, and quite a lot. I helped him out of his shirt and his boots; his body was savaged with bruises, gathered over days of combat. The worst of them were fresh, and for the first time he was no longer moving easily. His experience was one of his finest assets, but the years which allowed him to acquire it were beginning to show."

He did not want well-wishers, just then; he did not even want wine; he wanted nothing except rest. We left him and went to eat.

"Shall I bring something back for you, my lord?" I asked, just as I was going out.

"The margravine," he said. "But later. Much, much later."

I did not have to bring him the margravine. She found her way there all by herself. When I went back to his tent just after vespers, I found him lying on his cot, entirely naked, his body gleaming with oil. The margravine knelt beside him, bending as she kneaded his shoulders and back with long, supple fingers, over and over, moving with exquisite slowness—a movement which would take her right to his feet. And back again, searching out all the hurts, all the spent and knotted muscles, coaxing back their grace, their potency, all without haste, without a trace of uncertainty. She glanced up at me as I came in, without much interest. She might have been playing cards for all the difference my presence made. My presence, or that of her serving woman, or that of Otto, sprawling in a chair and nursing a cup of wine with brazen envy in his eyes.

Karelian moaned once or twice, with sheer gratitude for the gift. "An hour of that," he sighed, "and I might live to joust again."

She laughed softly, and kept on, her hands slipping over his ribs, very gently, yet still pressing—hungering almost, as if she could find the pain and pluck it away like a thorn.

"You had better live to joust again," she said.

Yes, I thought bitterly, *so afterwards you can dance and smile and strut around before the whole court of Germany, finally, on the arm of a champion!*

We all knew about her, Arthea von Uhland, a whore who was no less a whore for being a lady, who had slept with half of the Holy Roman Empire, and still had a place in the courts.

Her husband doesn't care. It was Otto's squire who told me, the knowledge garnered no doubt from his master, who had a taste for scandal. *Why should he care?* he went on. *He's slept with half the empire, too, and apparently it's pretty much the same half . . . .*

I looked around the tent. There were maybe a dozen men there, all talking of the jousts, sitting on the floor, drinking, making wagers perhaps, as if they were nothing more than peasants at a bear-pit.

And I thought of Rome.

Not our Rome, the sacred city of the popes, but the old Rome, pagan and corrupt, with its circuses and its glittering champions. Its gladiators. Men who fought for the pleasure of it, or for the price of a good whore. Most of them had been soldiers once, mercenaries; gold was gold, after all. A good day in the arena, and then wine and camaraderie and the hero tended, his fine body oiled and massaged and honed for fresh glories—and why not? Without it he was nothing.

The margravine's hands were edging downwards from the small of Karelian's back. I turned without a word and left them.

Outside, people were everywhere, walking, sitting in clusters, gathered around chess boards or minstrels, talking about everything under the sun but mostly talking about the tournament. About the count of Lys. I left them too, and finding no place where I could be alone, I went finally to the chapel.

The stained glass windows were muted brilliance against the early evening sun; light fell through them in high poised spears, but everywhere else the chapel was dark. The sanctuary at the far end was a cave with a single unsteady crimson light, the kneeling worshipers were only silhouettes of black on grey. Then slowly, as my eyes adapted to the dimness, I made out the forms of two servants, the face of a duchess from Bern, who was said to be gravely ill. And, close to the altar, kneeling utterly alone and in the deepest stillness of prayer, Gottfried von Heyden, duke of the Reinmark.

How can I describe what I felt then? Everything around me seemed to stop, and turn, and become something different. The bright day shrouded, and this dark place became suffused with light. The silence filled with meaning, and the thousand voices beyond dissolved into a babble of stupidity, just dust and clashing swords and drunkenness and lust. Just the world, the same world as always, failing us as it failed us in Jerusalem. Angels led us to the Holy City, angels and visions and the prayers of all Christendom—but once we had taken it, once the infidels were slain and the city was ours, we filled it with taverns and brothels and market stalls and baths, with all the foulness of the world, as though it were merely another captured town, as though Christ had never walked upon its stones.

Why?

I wanted to weep with longing. Why could men not *be* what they were meant to be, chaste and devoted and true? Why was Karelian not here, kneeling in prayer like his liege, instead of lying in his tent with a whore? He had so much courage, so much strength of hand and will. Yet what did he earn with his gifts? A bit of gold, a bit of glory, some harlot's hands between his thighs. That was all. It was such a waste.

I watched Gottfried. How serene he looked—troubled, in a fashion, and yet serene. For weeks I thought nothing could be more splendid than being part of the tournament, and yet now, suddenly, I was glad he was not in it. He was above it, untouched by all its gaudy violence.

Men could be different, I thought wistfully. They could be like Gottfried, like the young knights he was training to follow him, with their white surcoats and their shining faces. Ehrenfried was wrong. The warrior monk was not a contradiction in terms. The warrior monk was the only warrior in whom there was no contradiction at all. Worldly men did violence for pleasure, or gold, or self-advancement. Only a man who fought for God could be whole and sound and clean. He could be more than a man; he could be the very arm of God. He could be the man Karelian should have been, the man I always wanted to serve.

Did I really think those things, thirty years ago, on a melancholy afternoon in the chapel of Stavoren? Or do I now merely imagine I did, because of everything which happened afterwards? I know the heart can play strange tricks upon the memory.

But it was that day, I think, that strange and beautiful and troubled day, when I first began to hear a whisper, like grasses trembling in a summer wind. A whisper new and different in the quiet of my soul. A name, stern and majestic and separate from all the world around it.

Gottfried.

XVII

THE GOLDEN DUKE

Then he thought of how Parzival once said
it was better to trust women than God.

WOLFRAM VON ESCHENBACH

I FELL INTO SIN IN STAVOREN. One single mortal sin, in all the history
of the world, was enough to cause the suffering and death of Jesus
Christ. Who can say what my sin caused? Because of it I learned a
thing I was never meant to know, and everything I did thereafter was
shaped by my knowledge.

I do not remember the wench's name; she belonged to the retinue
of the Empress Theresa. She had a very fine body, and a way of
moving which constantly drew attention to it. If the empress had permitted such shamelessness, I am sure she would have dressed herself
like the witch of Helmardin.

She was always smiling at me, following me about, asking me
questions, finding excuses to move close to me. Once as I sat in the
courtyard engrossed in my own duties, she came over to me, flirting
with me and teasing me about my virtue. She pretended to catch sight
of a pretty butterfly, and leaned across me to reach for it, so that her
breast touched the side of my face. I reddened with shame, and she
laughed.

"Poor Pauli," she said. "You're in sore need of tending."

She could not have been a day past sixteen, yet she set out deliberately to seduce me. Twice she pursued me so as to find me alone,
and the second time I fell. I can blame this only on my weakness, for

I did not like her. I did not even want her. She never lingered in my thoughts, neither before nor after; it was the darkness of a moment.

She found me, the second time, in a hallway in the duke's palace; I was returning from delivering a message for Karelian. It was nearly dusk. The light was failing, and I was absorbed in my own thoughts. A door opened just ahead of me; I recognized her voice and her scent before I could make out her face in the dim light.

"Pauli? Oh, I am so glad it's you! Can you help me?"

You may well call me a fool for believing her. She said there was a kitten trapped in a closet, and I followed her into the room to rescue it. Of course, there was no kitten. There was only her laughter, her body pressing against me, her mouth all over my face and her hands sliding over my back. The suddenness of it, the rawness, was both compelling and awful. I found the strength to seize her wrists and push them back, trying to shove her away.

"Am I not pretty, Pauli?" she said. Her voice was soft, mocking. "Are you really so sated you don't find me pretty? Or do you like little page boys better?"

The soul eager for sin can persuade itself of anything. I should have flung her aside and stalked away: *I don't care what you think, you little whore! And anyone who does care what you think is too stupid to concern me!*

It's what I should have done. But instead I stood frozen, appalled by her words, appalled that anyone would say such a thing about me, even in mockery. Dear Christ, what if she said it to others? She was pressing against me again, laughing, and because I did not know what to do I did nothing, and she did as she wished. There was an astonishing power to the encounter, yet I did not enjoy it. Through it all I was aware of how animal it was, how meaningless. Her writhing body disgusted me, and my own disgusted me more. I could hardly believe it was my own, behaving so, burning and heaving, caring about nothing except itself.

This was the burden of original sin. Through Eve we were lowered to this, and through Eve's daughters we were dragged back to it again and again . . . .

She wanted to kiss me after, and play with me, but I could not bear her presence, or the foul sweetness of her perfume. I went alone to the chapel, and there, sick with shame and self-contempt, I wept.

It was the first time, and the last. I never sinned with a woman again. For no matter how much they tried to tempt me—and they did, sometimes, before I left the world—I never yielded, remembering how ugly it was, and how shameful.

There was another unlikely outcome from my sin. Six days later, while walking in Duke Gottfried's orchard, I avoided a meeting with her by hiding myself in one of his private pavilions, and so learned the future of the world.

It was two days after the tournament ended. The finish was glorious. Until the last, Karelian and Prince Konrad had outshone everyone else. There was barely any difference between them in the scoring, and neither was prepared to concede victory to the other.

A great deal has been said and written about Prince Konrad through the years; I would just as soon write nothing more. I never thought well of him. Like so many young men raised to power, he thought uncommonly well of himself. He was impulsive and cocky, and tended to say whatever was on his mind without thinking of the consequences.

Those who liked him admired his outspoken manner; they called him honest. Those who saw more clearly judged him reckless, for he respected neither fate, nor his father, nor his God. Certainly he was fearless. As heir to the imperial throne, he was not expected to take part in tournaments; they endangered not merely his own life, but the future of the dynasty and the security of the state. But in this as in most things Konrad did as he pleased. He enjoyed combat; he loved to win. And there were some who whispered, even then, that he fought so boldly because he had so much to prove.

I do not know the truth of those rumors. Powerful men always have enemies, and terrible lies can be fashioned out of innocent truths. But the prince was still unmarried, and seemed inclined to remain so as long as possible. All of his close friends were young men, some of them quite beautiful, one of them a minnesinger with amber eyes and a voice which could have melted granite. This youth went everywhere with the prince; he even sang in Gottfried's court. The enemies of the Salian kings watched him, and smiled, and nudged each other's ribs.

But Konrad was a warrior, a very good one. And at the jousting field it was the friends of the Salian kings who smiled and nudged each other; they knew a man when they saw one.

For myself I was never sure, though I admit I was inclined to think the worst of Konrad from the beginning. As the tournament drew to a finish, and he kept winning, just like Karelian, I liked him less and less. I wanted to see him beaten.

So, I think, did Gottfried, though he was much too wise to say so. What he did say—and most everyone agreed—was that a point or two of difference in the scoring proved nothing in a match like this. Whichever man won, the victory would satisfy no one. They had to meet in a duel, and settle it, just the two of them. Three passes with the lance, and then swords, until one or the other yielded.

Nearly everyone expected Konrad to win. Even I, in my most honest moments, thought it likely. There was nothing to choose between them in strength, and very little in skill. But after days and days of exhausting combat, youth was now Konrad's great advantage. Karelian was tired, so tired that I grieved for him. I knew he was asking himself what in God's name he had begun this for, surely not for a hundred gold marks and a wreath of pretty flowers?

He dressed slowly that morning; every careful motion betrayed his pain. When I had buckled on his sword, and pulled the hem of his surcoat to make it neat and straight, he took a little wine, raising the cup briefly before he drank.

"The last time," he said.

Something cold went all through my bones. For a reason I could not name, I believed him: it was the last time.

His head and throat were wrapped close in his coif of ring mail. Armor though it was, this garment could give even hardened warriors a strangely youthful look, almost . . . yes, I will say it: almost feminine . . . before the helmet was fitted over it. A transformation I always noticed, and which always disturbed me.

"You will ride in many tournaments yet, my lord," I said. "You are younger than Duke Gottfried."

He ignored the comparison.

"No," he said. "I will not." Then he smiled, beautifully. "That's why I intend to win this one."

And he did, the only way he could have won it: by being wiser, cooler, more experienced than his opponent. At least, that's what everyone said at the time, myself most of all. We marveled at his steadiness, his ability to wait; we marveled especially at his gift of anticipation. He did not outfight Konrad. Strictly speaking, he could not have done so. He outthought him. He seemed to know everything Konrad was going to do before the prince did it. Three times I was certain Karelian was finished; three times I saw the blow coming which should have ended it; each time, at the lethal moment, Karelian was somehow not there.

A year later, I would reflect on the encounter again, in a less worshipful frame of mind, and wonder if it was purely skill. No doubt the witch of Car-Iduna wanted him to win. She wanted him raised to the greatest possible heights in Gottfried's confidence. He was good, God knows, but he was just a man, and he fought that day like something more.

Alas, it is all hindsight now, like so much of my wisdom. At the time I was exactly like the others, caught up in the excitement like a twig in a whirlpool, flung back and forth between triumph and dismay. They rode at each other and broke both their lances, and we cheered. They rode again, and crashed together, and went down. Neither had been unhorsed, not even once, in all the tournament; now both were tumbled into the dirt. Karelian got to one knee and faltered there, reeling as the prince strode towards him. That was the first time I thought it was over. But he recovered in time to parry Konrad's blow. And then he led him slowly, pitilessly, to defeat.

Slowly? In truth, I do not know if it was slow, or very quick. It seemed forever, an unending, brilliant masque; not mortal, and yet perilous enough, a dance of splendor and darkness. I am a monk now; I know the vanity of it; and I know, too, how evil both men really were. Yet still I feel a tug of admiration. Their swords struck sparks off the sky; they attacked, parried, stumbled, missed ruin by a breath more times than we could afterwards remember. They stood poised, sword caught against sword and neither yielding, and we held our own breaths until one or the other swung free, and struck again.

Almost from the start, from the moment he had seen Karelian dazed and on his knees, Konrad believed he had the best of it, and he fought accordingly, with daring and confidence, pressing what he believed was his advantage. He never understood that in everything except youth he was outmatched; he grew angry and ever so slightly desperate as victory eluded him. As Karelian eluded him, and continued to return his blows—not as many blows, perhaps, all counted, but just as many dangerous ones. As Karelian began finally to lead, to set the pace and the style of the fight.

I never saw the raven; I was too busy watching the field. But some others did, and mentioned it later. It had drifted across the plain of Stavoren in a smooth, high arc, safely distant from the massed gathering of fighting men and weapons. Without haste, they said, and wonderfully graceful, its wings stark and black against the summer sky. Drifting away again, as though it had only come there out of idle curiosity.

As perhaps it had. Perhaps it was just a bird, an ordinary raven of the forest. That's what my father would have said, shaking his head at me. At the moment I might have said so myself; the ordinary world was very real just then, very bright and loud, all harsh voices and iron and dust. Konrad suddenly attacking, Karelian circling away, the prince's sword flashing out like the jaws of an adder, too quick to follow with the eye, just a blur of menace, but the count's shield was there, breaking its force. Konrad stuck again, in pure fury, all of his strength and weight behind the blow. Karelian swung his blade upward, catching the other in mid-air. For a tiny moment nothing moved at all; they stood like stags in autumn, feet braced and weapons locked. But Konrad had put too much into his massive blow; he was off balance—just a little, just for a breath.

A breath was all Karelian needed. A sudden shift of his weight, a savage whiplash motion of his wrist, and Konrad's sword was gone, spinning like a silver trinket across the field.

After, there would be clamor and chaos and cheering and dismay but for one long moment there was pure silence. Even the king was struck dumb, leaning forward from his fenced and guarded dais as the young prince recovered his footing and backed away, disarmed and bewildered.

I remember the moment as clearly as if it were painted on my wall. I remember how good I felt. None of us knew the future. None of us imagined that these two men, meeting for the first time here in a game of chivalry, would soon meet again in a war camp in Mainz. They would regard each other once again across a small, charged patch of ground, and smile.

Konrad wiped his arm across his face. He did not like losing, and it showed.

"Are you going to insist on my oath of surrender?" he demanded.

"No, my lord," Karelian said.

And then, before Konrad's squire could hurry out to help his master, the count bent and picked up his rival's sword himself and offered it to him with a small bow.

It was a singularly courteous gesture. But it was more, and a soft, awed murmur passed over the gathering. Karelian was a profoundly political man. He knew how much bitterness remained against Ehren-

fried after twenty years of civil war. He knew how many of the watching lords were pleased to see the Salian prince humbled. Some would
have been pleased to see him killed. For Karelian, this was no simple
act of chivalry; it was a clear political statement. The game had been
a game, and now it was over. Victorious or not, he was still the loyal
servant of his king.

Konrad took the weapon, held it for a moment, his eyes hard—
neither angry nor admiring, just hard.

"I have lost jousts before, Karelian of Lys. But never to a man
worthier than you."

So it was my lord who knelt before the whole of Germany, just
as the sun was setting, to receive the wreath of victory from Ehrenfried's hands, and who sat after at his elbow, in the place of highest
honor. I was drunk with pride, and, for the first time in my life, I
ended the evening drunk silly on wine as well.

I was still suffering from it two days later; I suppose that's why
I fell asleep in Duke Gottfried's pavilion.

It was a pleasant place, raised in the middle of the garden like a
small tower. I had no idea it was a place the duke favored for private
meetings. Even so, I would not have gone inside except for the girl.

The same girl, the empress's little whore. She was still halfway
across the garden when I saw her, and there were some trees between
us. She was coming in my direction, but she had not seen me yet.
She was walking idly; she looked bored. I knew what would happen
if she spotted me, and I did not want to deal with it. My head still
hurt. I was tired, and even thinking about her made me more tired.
The door into the pavilion was open, and so I simply went inside, and
closed it behind me.

It was dim inside. I remembered the room with the non-existent
kitten. If she had seen me come in here, I reflected, I was worse off
than before. So I went up the long staircase to the open bower. I was
sure it was empty. And it was—for the moment.

It was a lovely, peaceful place, entirely open to the wind and the
sun. There was a small marble table and some chairs, and a locked
cupboard where I supposed they kept silverware and perhaps a stock
of wine. For all its plainness, it felt very regal; the duke's arms hung
on one wall, and were inlaid in the glistening surface of the table.

What in God's name am I doing here?

Even as the thought occurred to me, I heard steps on the stairs.
I had not walked into a stable or a storeroom or even some casual

bower set out for the casual use of guests. I had no right to be here uninvited, and I did not want to be found.

The only place to hide was the privy, enclosed behind a heavy arras. So I hid there, peeking out to see who came.

Servants came, and still more servants. They swept and scrubbed the floor. They polished the gleaming marble table until it gleamed even brighter. The privy, I saw with infinite relief was unused and needed no attention. I waited for them to finish and go away and when they had done so, I waited longer, just to be safe. It was quiet there; the breezes wafting through were just enough to mellow the day's heat. I waited too long, and I fell asleep.

I did not hear steps the second time; I heard voices. They were already in the room. I looked out again in dismay, though I had recognized both voices: Duke Gottfried himself, and Karelian of Lys. They were moving towards the marble table, where a great carafe of wine and two gold cups had been laid out for them.

God help me . . . !

I could not believe my own folly. Oh, I was tired, I was half sick, I utterly *detested* that girl, but how could I have gotten myself into this? And how was I going to get out?

Gottfried settled into a chair, and motioned his guest to sit across from him. I expected a servant to appear at once to serve them, but instead the Golden Duke filled the cups himself, and handed one to Karelian with a smile.

I knew what that meant. They had come here to speak in absolute privacy, and my small folly was turning rapidly into a great one. I cringed back behind the arras, wishing to God I had let the servants catch me. No, dear God, I should have come out on my own, I should have gone to them and apologized: "Please forgive me, I wandered in here by mistake, I am leaving this instant . . . !" At worst I would have been taken for an ill-bred fool; now, if I were discovered, I might well be taken for a spy.

"Your health, Karel."

"And yours, my good lord."

I did not want to listen. I wanted to change myself into a beetle and crawl away.

"That was a magnificent demonstration of prowess," Gottfried went on. "I've always thought well of you, but you continue to impress me. I couldn't wish for a better man at my right hand."

"You honor me too much, my lord."

"I have only begun to honor you."

Gottfried fell silent for so long I began to wonder if he had forgotten what he came here to say. When he spoke again, his voice was soft, meditative.

"I'm concerned about the future, Karelian—the future of Europe, and the future of Christendom. Our conquests in the east are very fragile; unless something extraordinary is done, we will not hold them."

I was astonished; I had never expected such a comment from the duke.

"Raising money," he went on, "sending a few more ragtag armies like the one we marched in—that's not going to do it. Would you agree?"

"Entirely, my lord."

"And I don't believe such a magnificent victory was won for nothing. I will never believe it. Do you not think, Karel, God must surely have a plan for the world?"

"That has always been at the heart of Christian teaching."

"Well, if we look at history, we see there are pivotal moments in the unfolding of God's plan—moments when everything depended on one person. Moses had to lead the Israelites out of Egypt. Mary had to accept her destiny as the mother of Jesus. Constantine had to turn the empire to God. If any of those persons had failed—if they had refused to do their duty—our history would be very different.

"Wait! I know what you're going to say—God's plan can't possibly be so vulnerable. And you're right. He *knows* the individuals he chooses for his tasks. He knew Moses, and Mary, and Constantine. He chooses those who will not fail him. Nonetheless, Karel, history turns on their actions. Their choices and their tasks are real."

There was a brief silence. When the duke spoke again, all the softness was gone from his voice.

"Ehrenfried is not the man to lead the empire now. It troubles me to say so; he was a good man in his day. But he's lost his edge. He doesn't see the world as it is."

"Ehrenfried is the lawfully elected and anointed king, my lord."

"He's a fool. Oh, come my friend, we're quite alone. We both know what he's become: a prattling dreamer with his head full of scrolls, good for nothing but chess games and prayers. Christendom must be led, in God's name, not tinkered with!"

"Meaning precisely what, my lord?"

On my knees, barely daring to breathe, I watched Duke Gottfried lean forward across the marble table.

"A new empire, Karel. A different kind of empire, a different kind of world. I spoke a moment ago about turning points in history; this is one of them." He paused, not to choose his words, I think, but simply to make them more compelling.

"The Holy Roman emperor will be replaced. I will replace him as high king of Germany and leader of Christendom."

Karelian poured himself more wine.

"You, my good friend and kinsman," Gottfried went on, "will have first place at my side. Every honor a king can offer to his best-loved vassal—every one of those honors will be yours. Other men will follow me; I know because I've already spoken with them. But to you will go the richest fiefs, and the highest rank among my captains. And that, I admit frankly, is quite selfish on my part; you're the best man in a fight I've ever seen."

"My lord—"

"One word more. I have given this a great deal of thought, and a great deal of prayer. Christendom needs leadership now, as it hasn't for centuries. God gave us Jerusalem as a sign, Karelian, as a portent of his will. This is not the time for strong men to stand idle, and let his kingdom go to wrack and ruin."

"More than one man in history believed he was doing the will of God, and turned out to be deceived."

The duke shook his massive golden head.

"God does not deceive men. Such men deceive themselves."

"Exactly so. And why—saving my respect for your lordship—why should I think you aren't one of them?"

"You know my line is descended from Clovis," Gottfried snapped. "From the very first Frankish kings."

"Your pardon, my lord, but I don't know it. I know only that you and your father and your grandfather always said so. Many men make similar claims, yet there isn't a house in Christendom which can trace its lineage back so far except in legend. I will not consent to treason on the authority of a legend."

Gottfried was on his feet.

"Damn you, Karel—!"

Karelian rose as well, and continued heedlessly. "And even if you were descended from the Merovingian kings, I wouldn't consider it

THE GOLDEN DUKE   183

reason enough to plunge the empire into civil war, and to unleash upon the Reinmark God knows what flood of misery and ruin."

Very slowly, Karelian reached across his body with his left hand, pulled his sword from its scabbard, and placed it on the table, the hilt turned to Gottfried's hand. He bowed faintly.

"Judge the matter as you see fit, my lord."

Gottfried turned away from him with an angry gesture, paced briefly and settled back into his chair.

"When God sent Noah's flood, Karelian, he should have left the vale of Dorn under a thousand feet of water. Nothing grows there but trouble. Put your sword away, for Christ's sake, and sit down."

The count obeyed. I stared at Gottfried, bewildered by his manner. He did not seem especially angry and he certainly did not seem surprised. If he had known how Karelian would respond, why had he opened the discussion at all? And what would he do now to a man who knew he was plotting rebellion, and would not join him?

"I have offered you great honor, and the highest place among my followers. Isn't that enough?"

"I've already answered you, my lord."

"God's blood, you are pretentious!"

"No," Karelian said. "I'm tired. I'm damnably tired, and I'm disillusioned with men's ambitions. And most of all, though you may not believe it, I am loyal to you, and unwilling to see you make a tragic and irrevocable mistake."

There was another long silence. I could hear my own heart pounding, so loudly I feared they might hear it, too.

"And suppose I could prove it's not a mistake?" Gottfried said at last. "Suppose I could show you it's both wise and necessary?"

"We don't know the future, my lord, and short of knowing it, I don't see how such proof is possible."

"But if it were?"

"Then . . . ." Karelian made a small, appeasing gesture. "Then I suppose I would look at the matter differently, my lord."

Gottfried relaxed a little, then, and picked up his wine cup.

"I would as soon lay siege to Jerusalem again, as to that piece of rock you call your honor. I hope you realize there's not another man in all the world I would argue with like this?"

"I know how much you favor me, my lord. And I've always been grateful."

"You have an odd way of showing it. But never mind. You want proof, so be it. I will give you proof. And it's not by knowing the future, my friend; it's by knowing the past."

Silence. I was aware of the roughness of my own breathing, of the sweat running down my body. At first I had not wanted to listen; now if God had appeared and offered me a miraculous escape, I might well have refused it.

"You're not a man whose mind needs to be coddled," Gottfried said. "So I will tell the matter straight. I learned many things in the Holy Land, many things about its history, and about the Church which was born there. Jesus was not a carpenter's son. That's a lot of poor people's nonsense—rather like the Christmas song where Mary rocks her baby to sleep on a Silesian mountaintop. Jesus was a prince, an heir to the house of David, and his goal was not merely a new faith, but a whole new kingdom of Israel.

"That's one thing I learned. I also learned it was unheard of for a Jewish rabbi not to have a wife. If Jesus had been unmarried when he began to teach, he would have been criticized for it as he was for so many other things, like healing on the sabbath and keeping company with low life. Yet we don't hear a word about it in the gospels. Or anywhere else. Therefore it's reasonable to think he was a married man, without any further evidence.

"But there *is* further evidence. There are traditions, legends, secret books, knowledge treasured from generation to generation, from century to century, more carefully and more faithfully than any knowledge has ever been preserved in the history of the world. Not only was he married, but he had children. The marriage feast at Cana was the wedding of Jesus Christ himself. His wife was Mary Magdalene; like Jesus she was descended from the house of David, and David himself was of an even older blood. But that is another story.

"After the Crucifixion, the followers of Jesus scattered all over the world. His mother, with Joseph of Arimathea and Magdalene, came by sea to Gaul. His children came with them; we know there were at least two. And there, in great secrecy, the sacred line was preserved. In very great secrecy, as you may imagine. First from imperial Rome, which feared the prospect of yet another Jewish king challenging the empire. And then in even greater secrecy from the popes, who could hardly go on claiming to be Christ's heirs if his real heirs were still living in the world.

"This line established itself with great care among the highborn of Gaul. Clovis, the first of the Merovingian kings, was one of its sons."

Karelian's breath caught as though he had been struck. He unclenched his hands from his goblet, and placed it carefully back on the table. His face was pale.

"My lord . . . ." He paused, shaking his head. "My lord, forgive me, but do you really expect anyone to believe that?"

Gottfried laughed, wonderfully, like a boy.

"All the time we've been having this argument, I've been asking myself: Why did I bother? Why did I bring this arrogant, stubborn man here and open my heart to him? Now I see why. Half the men I know would be jumping up and down, pointing their fingers at me and yelling 'Heretic!' at the top of their lungs. And the other half would be stammering and slithering and wondering what it might be safe to say. You look me cold in the eye and say: 'Really my lord, do you expect anyone to believe it?' "

He leaned back, smiling. "That's what I admire in you, Karel. You have a mind like a crossbow and nerve to match it. So tell me, of all the things I've just told you, which do you not believe?"

"Without proof, I believe none of it."

"What would you accept as proof?"

Karelian moved as if to speak, and paused. "I'm not sure. God coming down out of heaven, perhaps, with scrolls and trumpets. Anything less . . . ." He shook his head. "The past is gone, my lord. It's buried under centuries of war and plague and migration; under lies told out of fear and lies told out of love; under the manipulations of every pope and king and rebel who had a reason to manipulate it— which is all of them. You can't hope to prove a thing like this."

"To men who are determined not to believe, Karel, no proof is ever proof enough. Why else would the world be full of pagans and infidels? But men who want to know the truth, and who are willing to look honestly at the facts—they will find much to consider here. Do you think I was easy to convince? It's my life in the balance, after all, and my soul.

"I have documents, more than fifty of them. Most of them came to me in the Holy Land, in a manner too unusual to be a coincidence. I believe I was meant to have them. A few more have been acquired since, in the south of France, by a trusted friend.

"One of these documents speaks of Clovis's ancient and sacred lineage, of his having ancestors among the chosen of God. It's a letter written in the year 483, from an abbot in Mont Clair to a local lord, urging him to support Clovis for the kingship. I see you're smiling. Of course. Men write such letters all the time, urging support for one lord or another, and listing all his virtues to make their case.

"But this is what's so remarkable. The letter hardly mentions his virtues; it talks about his blood, his lineage. A sacred lineage, Karel. Not noble or valiant or honorable or any of those other things we usually say, and which would seem a great deal more reasonable. Men aren't usually described as sacred; why this man? And why the references to an ancient and distant kingdom?

"I have another document, a marriage contract between a certain Louise Meire, a knight's daughter, and a young lord named Jacques of Arles. There is a curious clause in this contract; it stipulates that if Louise Meire does not bear children, her husband—notwithstanding the laws of the Church—shall take a concubine, and her issue shall be his legitimate heirs, raised in his house. No blame or censure shall fall on him for this, neither from his wife nor from her family. The reason given: his line, which is most ancient and especially blessed by God, must be preserved. His grandfather was the illegitimate son of a Merovingian prince."

"Men do all sorts of things to assure their inheritance and lineage," Karelian said. "Taking a concubine is hardly unusual."

"But writing it into the marriage contract? In advance? Assuring, so to speak, that it would be done, done openly and even honorably, with no blame or censure? Come, Karelian! That is most unusual!"

The count shrugged. "So be it. It's unusual. What does it prove?"

"It doesn't *prove* anything. It's merely a link in the chain." The duke leaned forward. "Both of these documents were in a sealed casket in Jerusalem, along with thirty-one others. Three of them deal with matters in the east; all the rest deal with Gaul. All of them, in one way or another, deal with questions of dynasty. Now tell me, my good friend, what are they doing in the Holy Land? Why would anyone in Palestine care who had married whom, or was allied to whom, or gave birth to whom, among a bunch of warring barbarians on the other side of the world? And why was I, Clovis's heir—why was I, by the sheerest chance, the one who found them?

"Wait before you answer," the duke went on quickly. "What you said a moment ago is true. Much of the past is gone. Hard proof I don't have, and I may never have it. There are gaps in the record. But I have a great deal of evidence, and I haven't made any of it up. The first time a man told me Christ's descendants still lived in the west, I laughed in his face. I have come to this slowly, with many doubts and fears, and many prayers.

"The point is not to ask what evidence is missing. The point is to realize how much evidence is left—evidence which has survived against all the odds, across enormous passages of distance and time. Evidence for which no other credible explanation is possible, except strings of endless and overwhelming coincidence."

"Then let me suggest some explanations," Karelian said. "People migrate. They scatter in wars, taking their treasures with them. They bury gold under their houses, and seal parchments in their foundation stones. They die in plague, they're slaughtered by invaders, they're carried off as slaves. The gold, the documents, the lock of somebody's hair, lie under a pile of ruins, preserved for centuries by simple fate. In Lorraine my men went out to dig a privy and found a tin box with a hundred Roman eagles in it, fresh minted by the emperor Trajan; I don't think they were left there for us.

"Maybe Christ was married and had children. In this whole wild tale, it's the one thing which seems to me halfway possible. But to say the line endured, and can still be traced? No. That I don't believe.

"In our own world, every detail of a prince's birth is a public matter—the marriage, the pregnancy, the confinement, everything—so there can be no errors, no uncertainties, no deceptions. And even so, now and then, strange things happen. Very strange things, which cast the leadership of an entire kingdom in doubt.

"How do you maintain a royal genealogy in secret, my lord? If too many people know, the heirs will be betrayed. If too few know, a single accident, a single epidemic, a single massacre in a small war, and it's all over. Even if one or another of the children survives, what will it matter, if no one knows who they are? I have seen enough wars, my lord; I know what happens in them."

Karelian picked up his cup, drank briefly. The duke waited, watching him with riveted attention.

"Consider what you must assume, my lord," the count went on. "You must assume that in every generation for eleven hundred years, at least one child of this line grew up, and had children in turn. You must assume that no wife upon whom the line depended ever bore a bastard. That no dead infant was ever replaced with someone else's child. That every person entrusted with the knowledge of a child's lineage lived and passed the knowledge on. You must assume that

Clovis was in fact born from this line, and that your ancestors were born from his. One mistaken assumption among all of them—only one—and the entire structure collapses like a house of cards."

"Easy, Karel," Gottfried said sharply. "Don't put words in my mouth. The knowledge wasn't always passed on among the heirs—though it was preserved elsewhere. Some of the later Merovingian princes were headstrong and violent, and they could not be trusted with the secret of their ancestry.

"I knew I was bred of the house of Clovis, but I knew nothing of the rest until I went to Jerusalem. There were hints, of course—whispers and legends. We were always said to be different, a much older, a much more revered and splendid house, even when we held no crown, when we held nothing at all but a few provincial fiefs. We all grew up knowing of a treasure in Jerusalem which belonged to us. My father assumed it was an ordinary treasure, and so did I, until I was shown the documents."

Even from where I hid, I could see the disbelief on Karelian's face.

"You're telling me," he said, "that the line itself was preserved in Europe, but its identity was preserved in Palestine? On the other side of the world, among people of another culture, another language, another faith? For bloody centuries until you, the rightful heir, happened to march to Jerusalem and discover it? From documents which you admit are not proof but merely links in a chain? Your case depends on that, on top of all the other improbabilities I've just mentioned? No. Forgive me, my lord, but no. It will not hold. You assume too much."

I was not prepared for Gottfried's answer, although it was the only answer possible.

"And you, Karelian of Lys, are assuming God took no interest whatever in the matter. You think the Holy Family is no different from any batch of peasants in a hut."

He stood up, began to walk a little, restlessly. I could feel his frustration like a wound.

"The world always asks the same questions," he went on. "Why did God make so sinful a human race? Why did he wait thousands of years to send a redeemer? Why is the Church beset on all sides with enemies? I don't know the answer to those questions. God does what he does for reasons of his own. I don't know why the truth was hidden for so long, why this hour was chosen for its discovery, why it fell to me to pick it up. I know only what I've seen. I didn't seek this out, my friend; I fled from it. And it pursued me."

His voice held me motionless, like blinding light. I had looked upon many splendid men, but never before upon one who seemed so utterly and so effortlessly a king.

"You marched with us to Jerusalem," he said. "You remember how many times we acted on faith. We were finished a dozen times over—finished and beaten by the standards of any reasonable man, except the one who judges by his heart. The one who says: I know this is right. Not because I can prove it, but because I *know*. Either God works in history or he doesn't, Karel. And if he does, then nothing I'm assuming is difficult to believe. The line is unbroken. I know it in my blood. I know it as I know my name, as I know the sun rises in the east."

There was no arrogance in his assertion, and no uncertainty. Whatever doubts he had had—and surely he must have had many—he had worked them through before he spoke to anyone.

"The whole of Christendom will call it heresy, my lord," Karelian said.

"We shall see. It's obvious we can't throw this willy-nilly into the world. Many lords have joined me against Ehrenfried, but only you and two others know my true reasons. The others are my sons. That should tell you where you stand in my esteem."

Karelian wrapped his hands around the stem of his cup and stared at the patterns in the marble.

"Don't you think the empire has had enough of war, my lord?" he said at last, softly and bitterly.

"Yes," Gottfried said. "More than enough." He walked back to the table, and placed his hand on the count's shoulder.

"But this will be the last war," he said. "Of all my purposes, my friend, this is the greatest—to create peace. Stability and peace. Not just here. Everywhere, across the length and breadth of the world. Byzantium as well, and the Saracen lands, and all the pagan lands, wherever they may be. We will build God's kingdom, and this time it will last. No more petty kings, no more ravening hordes spoiling for war, no more cities turned into armed camps, hating each other across empty roads and burning fields. No more. We'll have one Christendom, one king, and one law—God's peace over all the earth. Are you with me, Karel?"

"What you speak of is impossible, my lord."

"Suppose it were not."

"History is full of men who supposed it," Karelian said. "They were the ones you spoke of just now, the petty kings, the ravening hordes, the makers of empty roads and burning fields."

"You're forgetting something, Karel."

"What am I forgetting?"

"God. And your own cynicism. It's all very well to be worldly and reasonable, but a man is a great fool when he believes in nothing at all. I want to show you something."

After all the duke had said, I could hardly believe he had still another astonishing revelation to make. But he did. He went to the cabinet on the far side of the room, unlocked it, and took out an object. It was perhaps twice the size of a man's head, shaped like a pyramid and made of splendid crystal.

"This also came to me in Jerusalem," Gottfried said. "In the same mysterious fashion as the documents—all of which I will tell you about later, by the way. It's more than three thousand years old, and it belonged to the kings of Israel."

Karelian turned the stone in his hands. There were mottled colors in it, and when the sun caught it briefly, the brightness hurt my eyes.

"What is it?" Karelian asked.

"It's called a willstone. He who has the gift to use it can call up any image he wishes, past or present, as if it were alive before your eyes. Watch. You'll see your own arrival at my gates three weeks ago!"

I forgot myself in eagerness and leaned forward, brushing the arras. To my great good fortune neither of them saw it move; they were too absorbed in their own encounter. But I, horrified at my folly, huddled back against the wall, and so I saw nothing at all. I only heard Karelian's single, soft exclamation.

"Jesus!"

"With this stone," Gottfried said, "I can show the world as it is, in a way which cannot be disbelieved. It was one of God's gifts to his chosen people, and many things we read of in the Bible were wrought with its power. When the Romans destroyed Jerusalem in the first century, it was taken and hidden away, till the time was right to show it to the world again."

He went again to his chair and sat, and took a drink of wine.

"Karelian, I'm not a foolish man. I know Ehrenfried fought two wars to keep his crown, and won them both, with half of Germany and the wrath of Rome against him. I understand your caution; it's one of the things about you I admire. I'm as unwilling as you are to start a futile war. But surely you must see: if this sacred object came to me, then I am meant to use it, and I will not fail. Not because I'm personally incapable of failure, but because this is God's will."

I watched the count of Lys. I had never seen him so shaken. He had fought in a hundred wars; he had shrugged off the dangers of Car-Iduna, and walked smiling into a witch's embrace. Now he seemed devastated and unmanned.

"Let me be clear about this, my lord. If I understand you correctly, the stone contains no truth within itself. It will convey whatever images, whatever . . . reality . . . its user wants others to see—"

"Yes. And I know what you're going to say. Such an object is very dangerous. In the hands of an evil man it could be used for dreadful things. That's why it was hidden for so long, and why we must guard it so carefully."

"Actually, my lord, I was going to say something different—though I do agree the thing is dangerous. I was going to ask why we should call sacred an oracle which merely repeats whatever a man tells it to say."

"Why should we call anything sacred? The Bible was written down by men, too. How then do we know it's true? How do we know that God made the world, and that Jesus Christ was his son?"

"The fact is, my lord, we don't know."

It was Gottfried's turn to be surprised. And troubled.

"You're a dangerous man, Karelian of Lys. I truly wonder if I should have brought you here."

"That is precisely *why* you brought me here."

Gottfried laughed, and some of the tension went out of him then. Out of both of them.

"I like you, do you know that?" the duke said. "Quite apart from anything else, I like you enormously."

His face grew serious again, as it mostly was, all traces of laughter fading from it.

"The stone is not a toy which any fool can play with," he said quietly. "I tested it before I ever thought of bringing it home. I encouraged others to try it. To some I offered gold; with others I made wagers. I even suggested images they might want to call up: lovely women bathing in a lake, or lying on the sand. Images of their homes, their families.

"No one could use it, Karelian. They couldn't raise so much as a shadow on its face. You fear the message may be untrue because any man could tell it what to say. Yet it speaks for no one but me. Is there no truth in that? No argument for who I am?"

He gestured towards the pyramid which lay between them.

"Take it up, Karelian. You have a splendid mind and a powerful will. Use it. Call up whatever truth you please."

The count hesitated, and then closed his hands about the stone.

"You won't use your own will to block me?"

"I'd be a fool to so deceive myself. Go on. Try your best."

I knelt rigid, barely breathing. What did I hope for then? That the stone would speak to Karelian, or that it wouldn't? Tension whitened his fingers and turned his face to shale. But there was no look of wonder, no cry of surprise, only desperate concentration, ending finally in an exhausted sigh of defeat. He laid his head back against his chair. Even from this distance, I could see his temples gleaming with sweat.

"Are you convinced?" Gottfried murmured, reaching across the table to take the pyramid back.

Karelian wiped his face and took a long draught of wine.

"Do you think I alone would have this power," Gottfried went on, "if I were not who I am?"

How splendid he looked then, poised with the godstone in his hands, a great rough-hewn man, not beautiful as Karelian was beautiful, and yet a hundred times more so, his gold hair like a halo around his lion's head: emperor of Christendom and lord of all the world.

Karelian smiled faintly, and saluted him with his cup.

"I am convinced, my lord. You batter a man down like a curtain wall, one stone at a time. I am convinced."

"Then you will ride with me?"

The count's eyes fell. "To war?" he asked unhappily.

"To one last war, my friend, and then to peace for all the world. Such a war is worth fighting. And you, my dear doubting Thomas, will be worth more to me than twenty of these tail-wagging fools I have around me, who need merely to be given a whiff of gold, or a whisper of power, and they are all scrambling to follow. Truly now, will you back me in this?"

I did not breathe until Karelian answered him. With every hammer of my heart I was pleading: *Yes, yes, yes, you must tell him yes!*

"I will." His voice was heavy, but he met Gottfried's eyes unflinching. "With some regrets and some misgivings. But yes, I will back you."

"On the cross? For many men will judge it treason, and dearly though I love you, I must have an oath."

"On the cross, my lord, and on my hope of heaven."

XVIII

OF TREASON AND FAITH

When a man has carnal knowledge of his wife
and the pleasure
of it in no way pleases him, but rather is hateful to him,
then such commerce is without sin.

WILLIAM OF AUXERRE

He who feels nothing does not sin.

HUGUCCIO, CARDINAL OF FERRARA

I KNOW WHAT MOST MEN WILL THINK, reading this chronicle. They will cry heresy and treason—all the while forgetting that Christ himself was condemned on the same charge. I have no better answer than the one Gottfried gave Karelian:

It is only heresy if it is not true.

And on what, you ask me, do I judge its truth? Not on argument, although Gottfried's arguments were good. Not on miracles, although his power was awesome. I judge his truth—as I believe Christ's followers judged his—by the man himself, his own magnificence, his own unyielding virtue. Never once, even from his bitterest enemies, was a word ever said against his personal honor. There was no lewdness in the man, no cowardice, no false ambition. He was jealous of his greatness, but how could he not be, being who he was? Unlike the selfish of the world, who will sit back and tuck their worldly goods around them, and ask only to be left alone, he rode into fire and blood to seek the will of God.

He was not beautiful, but the world stopped when he walked into a room. He was a king in every gesture, in every thread of raiment; his power followed him like grace. He might have captured all the world for God, had he never trusted Karelian of Lys.

Why did he do so? The question has turned in my soul for thirty years, and there is no answer. Gottfried was not a youth like me, caught up in the folly of the world, admiring a man for nothing but his fine looks and the glitter of his sword. Oh, I still remember myself in Acre, standing in the burning sun and staring until my eyes watered, tugging at the sleeve of my companion who was trying to buy a melon, demanding he pay attention and answer me: *Who is that knight?* The one in samite and silver, with sapphire fringes hanging to the fetlocks of his horse, and the sun shining in his hair, and an orange in his hand?

"Who? Oh. That one. Karelian Brandeis," he said irritably, and went back to his bargaining. I watched Karelian Brandeis until the turning street hid him from my view, and I vowed I would find a place in his service if it took me all my days.

But Gottfried was not a boy, admiring heroes from a distance. He was a king, and the heir of a godly house of kings. He did not look up to men like the count of Lys, but rather down. He was experienced and wise; he knew the risk of treachery. Why then did he take for his closest confederate a man who would shamelessly betray him?

How could he not have known?

The news came to the monastery of Saint Benedict late in the winter, the way news usually came—late and mostly by accident, along with gifts for the abbot and a small satchel of letters. Monsignor Wilhelm von Schielenberg, the great exorcist from Mainz, had fallen with two companions in Lombardy. They died as men often did on the lonely roads of Europe, slain by brigands for nothing more than the horses they were riding, and the garments on their backs.

The bodies had been found naked, Anselm told Paul. And less than a league away was found what must have been the bandits' camp, with the remains of the horse they had eaten, and a few scraps of charred parchment scattered around the fire—the holy men's books and breviaries torn apart and used for kindling.

"This is what our world is come to," Anselm said, and crossed himself and said no more.

Paul walked in the snow. He did not notice that his toes were slowly freezing; he would not have cared. He had come to love the winter, for the same reason other people dreaded it: for the cold. For the purity, the infinite absence, the unlife which was true life, where no birds sang, where God alone existed and God was the only thing which mattered.

Almost a year had passed since it began, and several months since the priest from Mainz had come and gone. His horrid dreams had almost ceased. As the focus of the chronicle shifted to the Golden Duke, so did the world shift: winter came, and his soul lifted itself to a quiet polar silence, all of its passions burned to ice. Every night he wrote; every day he fasted and labored and did penance. The whispers had begun, passing as whispers did from house to house, from town to town. Whispers of sanctity, of a man who lived without food and did not die, a man who took upon his body more of the sufferings of mankind and the lord Jesus than any human flesh could hope to bear, and yet had strength to work and pray. Just whispers. Just wind in the grass.

He walked on, and thought of what Anselm had told him. The man who might have unravelled his secret was dead. The perilous manuscript was ash in the mountains of Lombardy.

Nothing passed in the world which was not God's will. Once again, in yet another strange and unfathomable way, Gottfried had been protected. Or rather, his memory, his inheritance had been protected, from a world still too fouled to welcome it.

It was not possible to be happy, not ever, not with everything ruined and undone. But it was possible, sometimes, to close his hands upon a measure of peace, of acceptance, as he did now in this world of silence, of white crystal and pain.

Gottfried was what he had claimed to be, the heir of Jesus and the son of God. Paul had known it from the first. He had reached out to it instinctively, without needing to be asked. He had been among the first to say 'Yes, lord.' He could have been a chosen one, one of those who sat at Gottfried's right hand, and rested his head upon his shoulder.

Except for them, those two, who destroyed it all . . . .

He stumbled and fell. Only then, groping to rise again, did he realize he could no longer feel his hands or his feet.

NONE OF IT MATTERS. Perhaps Gottfried could not foresee what Karelian would do. Perhaps in his humanness he was limited to human knowledge, just as he was compelled to die a human death. Or perhaps he did see it, and followed his destiny as Christ followed his: *This is what must happen; it is part of God's plan.*

I do not know which is true, and although I long to know, I must always remind myself it doesn't matter.

It is so hard to write. I lost three fingers in January, and I've had to break the quill, and press a small piece of it into the palm of my hand, and clutch it there with all my strength. When I quit, my hand is bleeding, but the letters are very clear. I know I must finish this chronicle, but it no longer distresses me. I have ceased to grieve for the world, for there is nothing good in it.

God's only purpose here is to exalt his chosen ones. There is no other reason for anything which happens. We must struggle to do good in the world, as Gottfried did, and yet by its very nature the world cannot be saved. It has taken me so long to understand these things, and yet they are all here, in the book of Honorius, the marvelous Elucidarium, which I read every night, till I know its words almost by memory.

If none but the predestined are saved, for what purpose were the rest created, and what is the fault for which they perish?

The damned were made for the sake of the chosen, so they might be perfected in their virtues and corrected from their vices. So the chosen few would appear more glorious hereafter, and, seeing the torments of the many, rejoice in their own salvation.

For this Karelian Brandeis was born. For this he made the fire in which the Golden Duke was forged to his divinest glory . . . and in the same fire he will burn till the end of time.

Paul did not hear her come into his cell. Perhaps he slept, for when he first heard her speak his head was resting on his hands, and his mind was empty of thought. Dazed, he stared at her, unable to say a word. There were parchments in her hand. Even before he recognized the script, he knew it was his manuscript. All of his manuscript—the new pages he had hidden under the floor, the old pages he thought had been taken to Rome.

What a fool a man was, who ever thought he understood the ways of sorcerers . . . !

She let the manuscript fall idly onto his desk.

"Really, squire Paul, a god like the one you speak of here should never be turned loose on an unsuspecting world."

"You have no right to speak of my God," he whispered.

"I will speak," she said coldly, "of anything I please. And your god repels me. So do you. Though I must say you are an amazing man. Even when you lie, you reveal the truth. And even when you're compelled to tell the truth, you still manage to lie."

"If I repel you, then why don't you let me go?" he demanded. He was surprised at the strength in his voice, the boldness.

She smiled. She looked windblown and weary, as though she had travelled a long distance. So had she come to Karelian on the banks of the Maren—just so, with tangled hair, and her breasts shining in the moonlight.

"You know why," she said. "I am half veela, Paul of Ardiun. Half veela and half Russian Cossack. Do you think a creature such as myself would ever forgive?"

"I seek forgiveness only from God, not from any whore of Babylon?"

"Car-Iduna. Please, if we must be so righteous, let's be a little more precise. And while we're on the subject of sin, perhaps you can explain something to me. If your Jesus had children, how did he manage it? Without feeling any of that dreadful concupiscence you're so concerned about? And darling Gottfried, too—he had seven or eight of them, didn't he? How did it happen, do you suppose? Haven't you ever wondered?"

"No. I never did."

"Why not?"

He stared at her, hating her for asking. Why would anyone do so, except to mock the sons of God, to drag them down and diminish them merely by asking? Christ ate, but he never felt gluttony. He was offended, but he never felt anger. He needed material things to live, but he never felt avarice. So why even ask if he ever felt lust? Only out of malice, that was all, out of malice and wickedness.

"What is divine is untainted by sin," he said coldly. "As you know very well, witch."

She shrugged. "You're growing very cocky. You learned it from Gottfried, I suppose. So be it. I don't mind at all how cocky you become. And however you sort out your poor muddled soul, it's entirely your own affair. But don't underestimate my power."

She leaned slightly across his desk, and he caught the hot, lascivious scent of perfume. He was swept with nausea and hatred—the bitter hatred which always came back when he remembered her body in Karelian's embrace.

"It wasn't your god who crossed the path of Wilhelm von Schielenberg," she said. "It was me. And believe me, protecting your Golden Duke had nothing to do with it."

He knew; he had known from the moment he saw the manuscript in her hand. And yet the spoken words were a naked threat.

"What do you want from me?" he whispered.

"Justice," she replied. "Justice for the Reinmark, and for Karelian Brandeis. A measure of justice is not a great deal to ask, from a man who wants to be a saint."

"What do you know or care about justice?" he said bitterly.

"Truth is a kind of justice. Sometimes no other kind is left."

She gathered up the pages of his manuscript and tied a ribbon around them.

"This will be safer in Car-Iduna," she said. And she stood looking at him, with neither pity nor malice in her eyes. She had aged, he thought. Not much. Not as much as thirty years required, but enough to notice.

"Remember one thing, Paul of Ardiun. I did not command you to write this history. Your Church did. Bitterly as I hated you, I would have let you be. I have too little strength to waste it pursuing enemies merely for the pleasure of revenge.

"But when you set your hand to this, I thought: By the

gods, it's enough! I am a guardian of the Reinmark, and you have done enough. We don't need whatever wretched little treatise on sorcery you would have written, filling men with fear and hatred of everything that isn't Christian, of everything earthborn and free.

"But I thought it fitting you should obey your pope. Obedience, after all, is what your fathergod loves most. Go ahead and write your history. But write it as you lived it, through every fear, every desire, every dark betrayal. Think about it day and night, and maybe you'll discover what you are.

"That's what I hoped for, squire Paul, but I fear I was wrong. Once men like you invest their souls in a false first premise, thinking will not lead them out of it. The more they think, the wilder and wilder will be the fantasies they devise to make the premise hold. So be it. You will die a liar. But your chronicle I will keep; the future will understand it better. At Walpurgis I'll come back for more."

She turned as if to go, and looked back.

"He was beautiful, wasn't he, Paul? Beautiful as fire and winter moon and running stag. Beautiful to make a woman's bones melt . . . or a man's. And you will never forget it, no matter how many lies you tell, or how many mangods you worship. You went to astonishing lengths to find a lover too sacred to lust after. And yet that one is still in your blood, and in your deepest memories. When you die, it will be his face you see, his name you whisper in your pain. A lovely name, Karelian; it plays on the tongue like a kiss. You will remember it."

She left him. Afterwards he could not remember how, if she changed into another creature or simply walked out the door.

He tried to pray, but the words were empty and mechanical; they were dry mouthings into a dry void. He took off his habit, took the lash of knotted thongs beside his bed and scourged himself until he could not bear it; it made no difference. God did not hear him, or see him, or care. God was as distant as the stars.

He went to his table, took fresh parchment, pressed the quill into his palm and began to write again.

IT WAS AUGUST WHEN WE RETURNED TO LYS. We made a quick journey, despite the summer heat. Karelian was often lost in his own thoughts, and the men whispered that he was thinking of his wife, wondering about the child she would bear soon. He was worried about her, said some. No, said others darkly, he was worried about what the nestling would look like when it hatched.

But I knew he wasn't thinking about her at all. He was thinking about Gottfried, about the destiny which lay before us. It troubled me to see his mood so dark, although I fancied I knew why. He was tired of war. Only surely, I thought, surely he could see this was different. The life of a good knight was an honorable life. It was he himself who had soiled it, making war as he was paid to do, without conscience, like a whore who opened her legs to any scoundrel with a coin, until finally she could no longer see the difference between her own corruption and the sanctity of a marriage.

He would come to value his knighthood again; I was sure of it. I still had faith in him; indeed, when he smiled at Gottfried, and raised his cup, and made his promise, I loved him almost as fiercely as before.

At times I could barely contain my soaring excitement. I longed to tell him I knew, to sit with him beside a night fire and talk about it, softly and perilously, talk about how strange and wonderful it was, how glad I was that Gottfried had chosen him, and he had chosen Gottfried.

I was a boy then; what more can I say? I was a boy who could forget in an hour every dark thing he had learned about his master, and remember only that he was a hero.

The child was three days in the world when we came to Lys. They tried to smile when they told him, and to say all the happy things: "The countess was delivered of a boy, my lord, a fine, healthy son . . . ." But few would meet his eyes. And when he had gone, arms and dust and all up the narrow staircase to their chamber, Otto almost took the steward by the throat.

"Well?" he demanded.

The man shook his head. "Dark as a Turk," he said sadly. "And enough black hair on his head to cover yours."

"Damn little bitch," Otto said bitterly—and not very softly either.

To my considerable surprise, the steward called him for it.

"She is mistress here, my lord," he said calmly. "You won't speak ill of her in my presence.

"I won't *what?*"

In another context I might have grinned at them. An armed knight looming over an aging willow of a servant, slender enough for Otto to snap in pieces with his huge arms. The steward looked up at the warrior without a flicker in his eyes, as if to say: Well, and what precisely are you going to do to me? Remember, I answer to *them.*

"Get us some beer," Otto said.

Most of the household was protective of Adelaide; I never understood why. Her extreme youth was a reason, perhaps: her strange moods, her gratitude to Karelian—a gratitude which I found too shamelessly flaunted to be real, but which others admired, particularly the women. She was generous with gifts and favors, too, small trinkets, a handful of coin on a saint's day, a free afternoon to meet a lover in the village . . . oh, yes, she knew how to survive.

Karelian did not say a word about the child. Everyone assumed he would quietly send it away, and we waited for the thankful whisper from whoever would be the first to know: *Yes, it is gone. Last night, to the monks in Brochen . . . .*

Instead we heard nothing but rumors of war.

That very night, Karelian addressed his household and his men. There was concern, he said, over growing unrest beyond the Reinmark's eastern borders. There might be a new invasion from the Baltic. The tribes there fought in snow as though they were born to it—which indeed they were—and when they came west they came in wintertime, when the great barrier rivers were sheets of ice and the armies of Christendom huddled in their castles.

It was only talk, the count said. But he would prepare nonetheless. By noon the next day his armorers were on the road to Karn to order weapons and mail, and Reinhard himself was sent out to the taverns and the tournament fields to look for men. The best men you can find, Karelian told him, for honor or for gold. Messengers went out to all the knights who held land under his authority, ordering them to report to him within the fortnight. The serfs were called in from their fields to build up the walls of the manor, and to carry food stores and supplies to the fortress in the Schildberge.

Gottfried's plan was already underway—wonderfully, gloriously underway. And so when my lord left the manor house of Lys late at night, four days after we came there, without taking myself or any other man along, I knew without a doubt that he was going to meet one of Gottfried's allies, or someone else who was in some way bound to our great enterprise.

Nothing had ever touched me as this did. I had wept to go along on the eastern crusade, but its splendor and promise were small compared to Gottfried's hope. That had been Jerusalem; this would be the world. I was determined to be part of it, as much a part of it as I possibly could be.

So I followed the count of Lys to the Maren that night, under a brilliant three quarters moon. I did not intend to be discovered, but if by chance I were, I would throw myself at his feet. I would swear loyalty, secrecy, absolute obedience, anything he wanted, just to have a place with him, to be allowed to serve.

I was not surprised when he went to the river, rather than to another manor house or to the town. Everything would of course be desperately secret. Nor was I surprised when no one waited for him there; whoever was meeting him would soon come.

But then he did a strange thing. He took something from the pack behind his saddle—several things, one of them a spear. It was too dark to see what the other things were. He cleared a place beside a great fir tree and put the smaller things there, kneeling to arrange them very carefully—I would have said reverently, if I could have thought of any reason for using the word. Then he rose, gripping the spear in both hands, holding it high above his head. He shouted—one single word, one defiant cry in the shimmering darkness.

"Tyr!"

And then again, and once again. Three times he shouted it, and all my blood ran cold.

I knew then. Even before I watched him gather the stones and make the fire, I knew what he would do. My mind fought against it. *No,* I told myself, *it's only a campfire, the night is chill* . . . . The fire leapt high in its circle of stones, and its glitter caught the gold in his armbands as he reached and took the black feather from the pouch around his neck. He held it a moment, as if swept by doubt, by a terrible unwillingness to give up his talisman, his lady's gift. Then he touched it to his lips and threw it in the fire.

I don't know what I thought would happen, but for a long time nothing happened at all. He crouched beside the fire, turning at every small sound in the night, waiting, turning back to the fire again when no one came, poking at it with a purposeless, weary unease. The moon arched slowly westward, yet he clearly did not mean to leave.

I shared that long vigil with him, and through it all I fought against believing what I saw. It was not happening. He could not have come here to summon the witch of Car-Iduna. He simply could not, not *now . . . !*

I knew he lusted after her; he had never stopped lusting after her. But dear God, he was not a fool. It had been one thing to amuse himself with her in Helmardin; all he risked there was his soul. But kingdoms were at stake now, and history itself. It was reckless beyond imagining to send for her now.

Then I thought why he might do so, and I caught my breath as though I had been struck with an arrow. Even today I can't say which overwhelmed me more: the horror of it, or the drenching relief.

The child!

Of course! Oh yes, of course, the child. He had something now to trade for her favors: Rudi Selven's sin-begotten bastard. Maybe he had brought the boy with him. Maybe that was what he had lain so carefully beside the fir tree.

It was a chilling thought, chilling and utterly evil, and it sickened me; yet even as I cringed from it and crossed myself and said no, he wouldn't do it, he wouldn't give a child to witches, he would kill it first—even then I was glad. Because it was an answer, and once I had one answer I did not need to seek another.

She emerged from the woods without a sound, a lithe shadow moving into the firelight, within reach of his hand before he saw her, so intent was he on his own thoughts, and so silent her approach.

He rose quickly, eagerly. She was as I remembered her—and no doubt as he did—all shimmer, all pale flesh and pale silk, reaching to embrace him, pressing herself into his arms before a word could be said, staying there and staying there, coiling against his mouth and his loins until I thought they would mate where they stood.

But no. She drew away, pulled her loose shawl up over her shoulders and wrapped it close. They spoke then, quietly, too quietly for me to hear. I did not want to hear. I wanted him to go and fetch the child from where he had lain it—for by now I was as certain of its presence as if I heard it cry. He would give her the child, and she would take it and go. Bed with him first, maybe, but go. And then, horrible though it was, it would be over. He would go back to Lys and to Gottfried and it would be over.

He drew his sword.

Oh, how my heart leapt with hope then! He wouldn't give her the child, he wouldn't give her anything, he would kill her where she stood . . . !

He dropped to one knee, and placed the weapon at her feet.

No!

He raised both hands, his palms pressed together. Her own hands closed over them. It was an action as familiar in our lands as the signing of the cross, and almost as meaningful—the action by which men swore allegiance to their lords.

No no no no no, it was not possible, no . . . !

Not this.

Not Karelian. Not after he had promised: On the cross, my lord, and on my hope of heaven!

Not this, not ever, and, dear God, not *now* . . . !

I think I wept. I know my youth died that night, and all my love for him, and all my loyalty. His promise to Gottfried was a lie. Everything he had ever been was a lie, ruined and betrayed in Car-Iduna. He sold himself to her, and then he came bold and smiling to Gottfried, pretending loyalty, pretending opposition, pretending consent, drawing out of him his most dear and desperate secrets, so he could betray them to her.

Or so he could, perhaps, use them for himself . . . ?

I went colder still, thinking thus. However fiercely the heathen powers would crave Gottfried's defeat, there was one thing they would crave even more—a lord of their own to take his place. One who had the same blood, who could claim the same powers and the same dominion. Oh, how Karelian would love that, God damn him, with his taste for ermine and silver, with his insatiable appetite for whores!

I thought my mind would break. I went plunging down a bottomless shaft, tumbling from darkness to darkness. Never before or since have I felt such hatred. I wish to God my crossbow had been hanging from my saddle that night, as it often was when I went abroad. I might well have killed him then, and the world would now be different.

But I had no bow. I had only my hatred and my tears. I crawled away, cursing him over and over, calling him every foul name I knew and finding there were none foul enough. I made my way back to the manor house of Lys, slowly, as the witch moon fell into the western hills and the dawn began to redden.

I did not see the serfs already dragging rocks to his walls in the first morning light, or the sweep of hills beyond, black with pathless forest. I saw only the road, the road which went on forever, to Stavoren and Aachen and Rome and Jerusalem, to heaven and to hell. One road, one God, one duty for us all. My mind had calmed by then, and I knew what I would do. It was no sin to work harm against the wicked; no betrayal to turn treason back against the treasonous. I rode through the gates of Lys with my head held high, the thought of Gottfried pure and shining in my mind.

XIX

IN A CIRCLE OF SEVEN STONES

Those who commit perjury and practice sorcery
shall be cast out forever from the fellowship of God . . . .

LAWS OF EDMUND—10TH CENTURY

THE MAID MATILDE WAS A STEADY WOMAN, too steady to be going
on like this, lifting the blankets piece by piece and folding them
fussily, gathering up the little handful of wrapped baby and babbling
like a market wife:

"Oh, he's a lovely tyke, my lord, just a darling little boy, healthy
as can be, and always laughing. A bit dark, but that's babies for you,
my youngest sister was black-haired as a gypsy when she was born,
and you ought to see her now, she's fairer than I am. Isn't he just a
little princeling, my lord?"

Karelian took the child from her arms, and then, uncertain what
to do with it, laid it down again on the foot of the bed. He unwrapped
the swaddling clothes and watched the baby kick and grin at him. A
fine boy, like she said, pretty and perfectly made. Without a trace of
Brandeis in his eyes or his coloring. With so much dark hair—not
wisps of it, like most babies had, but a fine headful, as though it were
nothing to be ashamed of. As though he were flaunting himself to the
world.

"He hardly cries at all, my lord," Matilde went on. "He's a sturdy
one, he'll grow up brave as a stag and just as tawny, I'll bet on it,
I've seen it twenty times before—"

"For Christ's sake, stop prattling," he said.

The silence fell like ash. He ignored it. He was exhausted. The dust of the long road from Stavoren still clung to his clothing and burned against his eyes, and his bitterness was raw as a wound. It would be war again, nothing but war, damn Gottfried von Heyden, damn the world.

Damn Adelaide.

A girl child he could have borne with, or a second child—dear Christ, he could have borne with almost anything, he was hungry enough to just live. But a firstborn son was the heir. Everything Karelian had, his rank, his wealth, his rich fields and orchards and cattle, would all go to this boy. The crystal streams shimmering with fish, the apple trees, the deer. The life he had bought at so high a price he could rarely bear to think about it . . . all for this black-haired stranger.

He looked across the child's body towards Adelaide. She was small as a child herself in the big, canopied bed, small and unmoving with fear.

Your first fief, Karelian Brandeis; your colors hang from a house of blood; so they will again; so they will forever . . . .

Gottfried. And now this. He had sworn no road on earth would lead him back to Jerusalem. He wondered now if any road existed which would lead him away.

"Matilde, if you will be so kind, put the child back in his cradle, and leave us," he said.

She obeyed like a ghost.

He went to sit on the edge of the bed beside Adelaide. She looked feverish and exhausted. All her strength had gone into making her child; she had nothing left now. She watched him with the soft, darting eyes of a cornered animal.

It was impossible to hate her; it always had been. The abyss of power between them was too great. It was impossible to love her, probably, for the same reason.

"Are you all right?" he asked.

"Yes, my lord. Thank you."

He wiped his face. He wanted to berate her, but it would be like clubbing a wounded man lying on the ground. Anything he might say to her she already knew. She had no right to do this to him. She could not expect him to accept it. He ought to throw her out on the road, and her brat with her.

She already knew. She acknowledged it with a pitiless honesty, as one acknowledged the existence of the sky. She had made a choice, and the rest followed. And she did not regret her choice. Deep down, in the private core of herself which the world had never touched and never would touch, she did not regret anything. That required courage, a courage all the more proud and astonishing because she was only a young girl.

Another reason it was impossible to hate her.

She spoke again, so softly he could barely hear. "What are you going to do, my lord?"

"I don't know," he said.

"You won't kill him? Please? Please, my lord, give him away to someone, to the holy sisters, they'll take care of him, please—!"

He stood up. This much at least he could answer.

"I won't kill him," he said. He would kill no more children, not for any cause on earth.

But what would he do? He could send it away. No one would blame him, not in the least; they would judge him a better man than most for never having used his sword. Only what if Matilde was right?

The child might, after all, grow up tawny as a stag. And even if it didn't, it might still be his. Europe was full of mingling tribes. Rudi Selven got his own dark looks from somewhere; who could say what strange blood might also run in the veins of Brandeis? Karelian had not spent all those hours arguing with Gottfried for nothing. His own stubborn logic was still lying soft in the back of his mind: *You can't be sure about blood, you can't ever be absolutely sure . . . !*

What if he sent the child away and it was his? The thought made him cold to his bones.

There was that. A tiny, tiny thing, a remote possibility, but enough to make him pause. There was Adelaide, who would grieve to lose her child. The right and wrong of it was quite beside the point, she would grieve. And that made him pause, too, because he would have to live with it.

And there was Gottfried . . . .

He walked towards the window, aware of her eyes following him. He looked back, and said it again. "I give you my word, Adelaide, I won't kill him."

He needed to bathe. He needed food and twenty hours of sleep. Whatever choice he made he would not make it now.

Or tomorrow either, probably.

The broad sweep of the valley of Lys lay golden with August; the Schildberge were beginning to darken as the sun moved west. He stood for a long time by the window, letting his eyes caress the fields and wander to the woods and the wilderness. Southwards, across the curving mountains, lay Dorn, and the ducal lands of Stavoren. To the north, far beyond the edges of the world, lay the wood of Helmardin.

He was not a fool; he knew where his inclinations were leading him. To refuse to act was to act nonetheless. A decision made by default was still a decision. He would probably never send the child away, because there would always be a reason for not doing it today.

And maybe that was all right. There was only war ahead of him now, war and darkness and very little time. Maybe there wouldn't be any other children, only this one, and this one was whole and healthy and grinning at him, and really, did it matter so very much? He would have raised Saracen babes once and thought nothing of it. Life was too precious to throw away now; he was almost forty and going to war with the lord of the world . . . .

No, probably he would never send the child away. And it wouldn't matter much, not even to his honor. The world would soon have darker things to judge him for.

He tried to wait for the full moon, but his days dragged intolerably, and his nights were raw with longing. Once he knew he would go to her—and he knew it the moment he looked into the willstone—every delay became unbearable. Her love was his only hope of happiness, her power his only hope of life.

He rode to the great river in a waxing moon. He thought about her, and about Car-Iduna; and all the time, even when he was thinking about her, he was thinking also about Gottfried.

He had hated men before, and more than one of them. But the hatred he bore now towards his liege astonished even himself. It was villainy enough for Gottfried to plunge the Reinmark and the whole German empire into civil war for the sake of his own real or imaginary royal lineage. But this other thing—this fantasy of holy blood and world dominion, woven not out of madness but out of arrogance and sheer self-worship, with a perfectly rational mind—this made Karelian's head spin, and made him angry as few things had made him angry in his life.

Gottfried had so many gifts. He was healthy and strong; he had a large and prosperous domain. He had the treasure of the great temple of Jerusalem, plundered with his kinsman's considerable help. He had promised: *I will make the Reinmark into the jewel of the empire.* And Karelian had believed him. All those eighteen months in the Holy

Land, after the sack of Jerusalem, when all he wanted in his despair and revulsion was to go home, he stayed with Gottfried because it still seemed worthwhile. Worthwhile to secure the fledgling state— having taken it at such cost, he thought, the least they could do was keep it. Worthwhile to strengthen his own bonds with his liege, a man he did not trust entirely or like very much at all, but for whom he felt a genuine respect. Worthwhile to finally have a place in the world, to have the valley of Lys and a woman sitting at his table and an end to the wandering and the blood.

And now Gottfried would take it all away again. Because no matter what happened, the count of Lys was still just a pawn on a game board. Still expendable. If Gottfried went down, all his chief supporters would go down with him. And if he won it would be worse, because then there would only be more wars—against the Franks, perhaps, or the Lombards, or the Byzantines. And Karelian could fight those wars for Gottfried, one after another. *(We will all look to you to cover the Reinmark with glory!)* He could kill and burn and plunder for Gottfried until finally, in one muddy field or another, he was struck down. Or until, in spite of all the odds, he went home battered and exhausted to a wife who no longer knew him, children he had hardly ever seen, apple trees he had never eaten from, to watch the golden fields of Lys pour their harvests into Gottfried's war coffers, summer after summer, so it could go on. And on. And on.

No.

No, and again no. He wanted nothing more to do with war, any war at all, but if Gottfried forced him into one, then it was Gottfried he would fight, Gottfried who would discover just how good a knight he was, and how dangerous a man.

The river was black and silver, with pieces of scattered moonlight dancing on its back. It was a warm night, and the smells of the forest were rich and musky. The Maren sang as though it were alive—alive, and restless with melancholy, like an abandoned nymph.

The moon was high now. By its light he made his offerings and built the fire, and laid upon it the talisman the queen of Car-Iduna had given him. *Burn this by moonlight, in a circle of seven stones, within sight and sound of the Maren . . . .*

And then he waited, wondering desperately if she would come. Or if, when she came, he would be sorry. Perhaps it had all been sorcery and delusion, and now she would show herself to him as she really was, monstrous and evil, or perhaps just pathetic, just an aging whore who knew a few tricks. What if he looked at her now and saw someone he no longer wanted and dared not trust? He felt vulnerable as a babe, prisoned between darkness and darkness, between Gottfried and the unknown—but the unknown was still Car-Iduna, was still Raven, was still possible . . . .

Was she truly beautiful?

She moved through the shadows towards him, more beautiful than anything that lived. Utterly as he remembered her; there was no delusion, she was all grace, all goddess, her black hair tangled in the wind, her breasts shimmering in the moonlight, her silken garments clinging to the curves of her loins.

"Karel."

Perhaps there was a catch in her voice, a tiny sob of desire. He did not know and he did not care. Her arms closed around him, and he held her as he would have held his life.

"That was a lovely way to say hello, my lord count." She stood away from him, wrapped in her power and the heavy shawl she wound deliberately, protectively about her shoulders. "But why have you sent for me?"

"Because I want to make love to you. Right here under the fir trees."

"Is that all?"

"Isn't it enough?"

"In a better world, it would have been. In this world, no."

So be it.

"I sent for you to offer you my fealty. And my heart. And my sword?" He looked at her, sorcerous and splendid in the moonlight, and left nothing unsaid. "And to ask for your help. I need your help, queen of Car-Iduna."

"For what purpose?"

"To stop Gottfried."

She smiled. It troubled him, her smile of raw triumph, but there was nowhere else for him to go, no one else to trust at all.

"Swear then," she said softly.

He knelt, and swore his fealty, and then he truly would have bedded her under the fir trees, but she laughed, and pulled away from him again. She was no longer twenty, she said, she preferred a bed. Marius was setting up her tent less than a bowshot down the river.

"I will stay for three days. If you will be my guest there . . . ."

She smiled, and offered him her hand. The shawl had fallen loose again, and she left it so, the gesture even more an offering than her words.

"If you will be my guest there, any pleasure you might wish for will be yours."

He took her arm as they began to walk. "I find it marvelous, lady, that you could come from Helmardin in so little time."

"And is it the fighting man who finds it marvelous, I wonder, or the lover?"

"Both."

"I could come from Helmardin faster than you might imagine, Karel. But not this fast. And not with my steward and my tent. We've been in the Schildberge for several days. I wanted to be here when you came back from Stavoren." She reached, and brushed her fingers across his cheek. "Just in case."

Her tent was small but beautifully appointed, close to the river-bank, lying in a circle of seven stones. Marius fished for them, and trapped small birds, and gathered berries. Once or twice Karelian saw water veelas prowling the green banks, and other watchers deep in the trees, but most times it was as if they were utterly alone.

The sun rose, and fell, and rose again; he had no sense of time. He took her in her silken bed, and on the riverbank, and against the trunks of trees, and it was not enough. He took her with his hands and with his mouth, and gave himself up to the worship of her own, and it was not enough. His body kindled again and again, with a marvelous potency he had not enjoyed since his early youth. Maybe it was sorcery; they said veelas would sometimes do that for a man, if they liked him especially well. But they said a lot of things about veelas. Maybe it was sorcery. Or maybe flesh itself could turn sorcerous sometimes, and pull fire from the sun and the earth and the burning wind, and turn it into passion.

They swam naked in the Maren, and sat by its banks as the moon rose, wrapped only in their cloaks. They wandered in the dead heat of noon into the forest, the air heavy with roses and humming with drunken bumblebees rolling from flower to flower. Once she took off her gown there, and the great shifting oaks patterned light and shadow on her flesh until he would have sworn she was a hind, or a wild cat.

And then quite suddenly she was. He caught his breath as the edges of light around her began to ripple, to dissolve. She was no longer there, and a golden creature was padding through the grass, supple and powerful and perilously fanged, moving towards him as if he were prey.

"Jesus!"

He backed away; for a moment he was terrified and utterly appalled; then Raven's arm was slipping around his neck, and she was laughing, a woman again, her dark eyes wantonly amused.

"Did I frighten you, my lord?" she said.

"A little." He closed his hands on her soft bare shoulders, wondering how they could possibly be anything but what they were now, graceful and vulnerable. "If you have it in mind to eat me, lady, I hope you choose to do it in a more conventional fashion."

She smiled. "I'll say one thing for you, Karelian Brandeis. You're a steady man under fire."

"So I have been told."

"What are you going to do about Gottfried?"

"Raise an army, and place it and myself at the emperor's disposal. There's not much else I can do."

"You think like a soldier."

"Well, you'll have to forgive me for it. I've been one for twenty-two years?"

"If you want to defeat a man like Gottfried von Heyden, you'll have to start thinking like a witch."

But he was not thinking like either at the moment; he was thinking like a hot-blooded boy in a grove with a shepherdess. The sun played strange shades of blue into her hair, and glitters of silver. The trees moved forest shadows across her throat, across the ivory grace of her thighs. He followed the shifting patterns with his fingertips, slowly, wherever they led. First with his fingertips, and then with his mouth.

"You are insatiable, Karel."

Her breasts were exquisite, thrust out like a wanton girl's, with a faint upward curve. They leaned into his hands like purring cats, the sweet copper tips rising delightfully to his tongue.

"I am insatiable?" he said. "Now the raven is calling the poor, muddled magpie black."

"Magpie indeed. You don't have a whisper of white plumage on you anywhere."

"How would you know?"

"Do you think there's any bit of you I haven't already seen, and touched, and tasted?"

"That was hours ago. The world is very changeable. You're a shapeshifter; for all you know I might be one, too."

She laughed and pressed close to him, kissing his mouth for a very long, delicious time.

"Tell me," he murmured, "how a witch would make war against the lord of the world."

They spoke of him the first time over Marius's offerings of fresh trout and bread, in the smoky dawn of the first of those three days. Karelian was tired from his vigil, and she from her long journey. But they were not tired enough to sleep, not just yet, with the excitement of pleasure still clinging to their bodies, and so many things needing to be said.

"So what has he done, our Golden Duke?" she asked.

Marius knelt beside them, opening the slender fishes with great care, peeling away the nets of bones and carving the flesh into pieces small enough to eat.

Karelian hesitated, and she said, with a smile towards the steward, "You may speak freely, Karel. Marius is more loyal than my shadow."

"It seems our duke is a blood descendant of Jesus Christ, and therefore should be king. First of the empire, and then of the world."

Raven—may all the gods cherish her forever—Raven did what he had longed to do in the pavilion at Stavoren. She laughed. It spilled out almost before he'd finished speaking, a wonderful fit of helpless, shameless, dark-in-the-throat laughter.

"Karel, no?" she whispered between gulps of it.

"Yes."

"Jesus Christ? The original, one and only Jesus of Nazareth? Gottfried is his son and heir?"

"Well, his many times great great grandson and heir. By way of the Merovingians, needless to say."

"Oh, tell me, Karel! Tell me how he's worked all this out!"

She seized a piece of fish and bit into it eagerly, her eyes equally eager on his face.

"Well, as best as I can remember it; it wasn't too clear to start with . . . ."

He had been hungry as a wolf smelling the fire, the rich promise of frying fish. He was, quite suddenly, no longer hungry. He told her everything Gottfried had said, aware of the scorn in his voice, of the coil of hatred knotting in his belly.

When he finished, she said simply:

"He can't possibly get away with it. Against the Church, the whole of Christendom, a Christian emperor? There's not a hope of it; they'll burn him at the stake before a week is out. Gottfried is not a fool, Karelian; there's something wrong here—"

"He's not going to make that part of it public yet—the holy blood part."

"But then he's just a traitor. They won't burn him, they'll hang him—and the Reinmark can pay in blood for his ambition."

"He thinks he can win."

"All traitors think so."

"He has some grounds for it."

She looked up sharply. "The princes of Germany won't back him in an unprovoked rebellion. Some may, but not enough of them to topple Ehrenfried. The pope tried twice, and he couldn't raise enough support to topple Ehrenfried."

"He has a . . . a device he brought back from Palestine. A crystal pyramid; he can call up images in it—"

"The willstone? *He has the willstone?*" Raven's face turned ashen in the pale dawn light. "So that's it, dear gods! No wonder he's become so bold."

He was as astonished as she had been a moment earlier. "You know about this stone?"

"Yes. I know about it."

"What is it then, can you tell me? He said it belonged to the kings of Israel, and many things in the Bible were done by its power."

"He may well be right. The stone is very old, Karel; even in Car-Iduna we don't know its origins. But we think it was made far in the east, by men who served a sky god like Yahweh. The pyramid was the most sacred of all their sacred symbols. It was the shape of the world they were building: linear, unyielding, and ruled by an absolute power."

She fell silent for a moment; a piece of bread lay unnoticed in her hand; after a moment she put it back on the plate. The curve of her mouth was hard and bitter.

"Are you sure he has it, Karel? Did you see it?"

"Yes, I saw it. I saw him use it to conjure images."

She was a powerful woman; he was not used to seeing fear in her eyes. But fear was there now, quiet and icy.

"It's very evil, then, this stone," he said. The words were not quite a statement, not quite a question.

She shook her head. "It's not evil in itself; it's only a thing. And things do no evil, Karel; they simply are. Only . . . only as it is in the nature of the circle to connect, and of the spiral to return, so it is in the nature of the pyramid to do neither. The pyramid knows only how to layer and to climb, to press more and more of the world beneath its weight for the glory of an ever smaller and more distant pinnacle.

"The willstone is rightly named; it's a thing of pure power, power which is not connected to anything except its user. And so it has served far more often for evil than for good. The kings of Israel may well have used it. They waged a long and bitter war there against Astarte, against the gods in the world and the world of circled magic. The willstone would have suited them, as it suits Gottfried. But all magic can be turned back on itself by those who know how."

"He says no one can use the crystal but himself; he considers it the proof of his divinity—"

"He may say so, but he'd never dare to let anyone try."

"Actually, he has. Several different men, in fact."

"Really? He's a good deal bolder than I judged him, then."

"And very shrewd. I can see why he'd want to know, no matter what the risk. He even gave it to me."

She seemed almost to freeze, like a woodland creature in the shadow of a hawk.

"Did it make images for you?"

"No." He paused, savoring his next words. "But it took every fragment of strength I had to prevent it."

"You can command it?" she whispered.

"I think so. I would have to be able to use it freely to be sure, but yes, I think so."

She laughed, softly and triumphantly. "By all the gods, Karel, you delight me. You utterly delight me."

She reached impulsively to run her hand into his hair, across the line of his cheekbone. And then, quite suddenly her smile was gone.

"He would have killed you, you know that?" she said. "If the surface of the stone had shown so much as a ripple, you'd have never left Stavoren alive."

"Yes. I know." He was moved by the warmth in her warning, the

tenderness. He caught her still lingering hand and kissed it even more
lingeringly.

"If I hadn't known it, lady, I couldn't possibly have resisted the
image I wanted to call up."

"Which was?"

"Yourself. Without a thread of raiment on, I might add."

She smiled. She was very pleased with him, and the taste of it
was good. Too good. He might be willing to do most anything, he
reflected, to keep such fierce admiration kindled in her eyes. For as
long as he could. For as long as there might be of days and hours
before they brought him down.

Sunrise fell to moonrise, moonrise to day. For a while it rained,
small drops pattering endlessly on the roof of the tent and running in
small rivers down its sides. Sexual languor melted into voluptuous
sleep, and sleep into waking languor. The world smelled of water and
flowers and wind. They went swimming, and ate again. They sat by
the Maren as the sun rose to noon. Sometimes, for as much as an
hour, she would fall silent, lost in her own sorcerous thoughts, searching out answers, and he would go off by himself, or chat with Marius
if he was nearby.

Marius, as it happened, was plucking the last feathers out of a
pair of partridges he had trapped. He held up the naked birds with a
smile of satisfaction.

"Supper, my lord. Nice and fat and tasty."

Karelian smiled. "You take very good care of us, Marius."

The dwarf smiled, too. His smile was sly and worldly and ever
so slightly sad.

"I'm deformed, my lord count. Even in Car-Iduna. There are many
things I wanted in my life which I will never have." He spoke without
self-pity; a fact was simply a fact. "So I take my pleasure in seeing
other people happy. Especially my lady, and those who delight her.
Which you must do, my lord, singularly well; I can't remember when
she ever spent so much time in bed."

To Karelian's own surprise he flushed faintly, and the dwarf
laughed with mischievous glee.

"You are presumptuous," Karelian said, but he said it without ran-
cor.

"Dreadfully so," Marius agreed. "But I'm also irreplaceable.
Would you like these baked, my lord, or shall I roast them on a spit?"

One day passed, and then another. There were only two things they cared about very much, here in the circle of seven stones: their hunger for each other, and their hatred for the Golden Duke, around whose name they brooded like hunting falcons, circling and moving off and circling back again.

"There's one thing in this I still don't understand," he said.

"Only one?" she responded dryly.

He ignored her reply. From the start his mind had snagged on this question. He considered it a dozen times, only to abandon it in pure bewilderment.

"Gottfried is a Christian, Raven; I know him well enough to know that. He may have gone to Jerusalem for glory and power, but he also went for the Church and for God. Nothing he's ever said, or ever done, has caused me to wonder about his faith.

"He told me he prayed over this, and frankly, I believe him. He told me he didn't want to accept it. It's completely heretical, after all. Something in all of it . . . ." Karelian made a brief but eloquent gesture of frustration. "Something just doesn't make sense."

"The trouble with you, my lord of Lys, is your admirable and uncommon tendency to think straight."

She smiled. "A little too straight, sometimes. Why can a Christian not be sorcerer?"

He stared at her. "A sorcerer? Gottfried?"

"Yes. He imagines he has royal blood from the Merovingians, and sacred blood from Jesus Christ. What he has, in fact, is witch blood from Dorn."

"You're going to have to explain that."

"Your lines are crossed twice, Karelian. Three generations back, your great grandfather married Maria von Heyden, which makes you an heir of Gottfried's house—"

"And of the Merovingians," he added dryly. "And of God knows who else."

"Never mind. Two generations earlier, a very remarkable sorceress named Cundrie Brandeis married Martin of Helm. She had only one child, a daughter, and died on her childbed, so no one thinks about her much. Her daughter had a daughter, who married a Frankish count, and they had a daughter, who married Wolfram of Thuringia, and they had a daughter who married Albrecht von Heyden. The father of our Golden Duke."

"But surely Gottfried knows all that."

"Oh, he knows it, of course—when he thinks about it. But why

should he think about it? It's the female line. And who are the mar-
graves of Dorn in any case? Impoverished gentry on the edges of the
Silverwald, famous for nothing except their political unreliability—no
offense, my love—"

He shrugged.

"It would never occur to Gottfried to think he owes anything to
those ancestors. But he does.

"He has sorcerous powers, Karel. I've known it for years. It's why
I've watched him so closely, and feared him so much. But how can
a Christian possibly interpret such a gift? Your God allows only for
the demonic or the divine, nothing else. And he can hardly believe
himself demonic. He's Gottfried the Golden, he's a knight and a prince,
he goes to Mass and to the sacraments, he's been blessed by God with
a faithful wife and fine sons. Your saints do works of magic and call
them miracles, but they are priests and missionaries; they have some
kind of excuse. He has no excuse; he's a man of the world, a soldier,
the ruler of a duchy.

"I don't believe he was unwilling to accept this. I rather think he
stared at it for a minute, and then he put it down, and said 'No, really,
it's not possible.' And then he walked about two steps away, and turned
around and picked it up again.

"It was an answer made for him. He didn't want to give up his
powers, or his faith. Quite apart from his own inclinations, it's dangerous these days to be anything except a Christian. But he had all
these gifts, he knew he did, and they had to come from somewhere—
why not from the blood of Christ? With his terrible pride, his daring,
his belief in his own superiority—oh, yes, Karel, the more he would
look at it, the more obvious it would seem."

Karelian was not giving up just yet. "But . . . but damn it, Raven,
it's heresy. To a Christian it has to be heresy."

"Only if it isn't true."

He stared at her. And then he laughed, unamused. "That's what
he said, too?" He picked up small stones, one after another, and threw
them in the river.

"It may look like heresy to you," she said softly. "From where
I'm sitting, it looks very Christian. Your whole world is full of men
who claim to speak for God. They bind you in the smallest and most
personal aspects of your lives, till you scarcely know what food you
dare put into your mouths, or what garments on your backs. Till every
human thought is dangerous and every human pleasure sin—except

of course the exercise of power. Controlling others is a great Christian virtue, if only you can seem to be doing it for the Lord. You must admit our Golden Duke has solved *that* problem singularly well.

"This is where the pyramid leads, Karel. Where it has to lead: to an endless scramble for the pinnacle, for the place where men can speak for God. And finally for the place where one man doesn't need to."

There was a long silence.

"And your gods, Raven," he said at last, "does no one claim to speak for them?"

She smiled. "All the time. It's a good day for planting today, the moon is right. The deer have moved west, into the hills. This child will grow up strong, give it a hunter's name. This one has the gift of poetry, treat it gently. The winter will be long and cold, we must take offerings to the forest. The enemy advances; here is the place to wait, and make an ambush . . . . So do the gods of Car-Iduna speak, my love. Only so."

She brushed her hand across his face. "Perhaps they will speak to us tonight."

She built a small stone altar at the edge of the river, and when the moon was high they burned offerings there, mating while the flames leapt and shimmered, a long, wild mating which she would not allow to end: *No, Karel, no, not yet, the longer we are bound, the more fiercely we burn, the stronger will be the spells I work here . . . .* He thought he would die in her embrace, die of the fire in his loins and the fire in his mind, each kindling the other in an endless spiral of desire, a wildness which swept him deeper and deeper without direction or time. And then it steadied, and it held. He heard her laugh, softly, triumphantly; he heard his own name like an incantation in the wind, Karel, Karel, Karel . . . . He could have stayed so forever then, just so, aflame inside of her, content to burn, content with her wild kisses and her hair all over him, content with the knowledge that she was his—gods knew for how long or even for what reason, but his.

So wild, so beautiful in the firelight, kneeling over him, bending to give him her mouth, her breasts, everything she could give and all of it animal with wanting; rocking against him for a reckless, unmeasured time, her breath hot and ragged, his name a sob in her throat as she came and kindled and came again, each time more quickly, until his own drowning surrender finally ended it. And the world returned, slowly, the sound of wind and water, the slow caress of her fingers stroking his hair. Her voice, warm and languorous against his throat, and faintly amused.

"Sorcerer."

She dressed and knelt by the fire. Before he could protest, she had taken her dagger and pressed the point into her wrist; blood ran into the flames.

"Raven . . . !"

"Not a word, my lord," she said harshly. "Bind this for me now, and then say nothing more, nothing until I'm done!"

She swayed beside the leaping fire, chanted over it, sang to it, tossed into its black and red and golden mouth many strange things— some of them he truly hoped were not the things they seemed. Then, as the fire burned out and turned slowly into ash, she played her harp, until he thought the stars would be plucked from the sky and his heart would break. He ached to touch her, just a little, to stroke her hair or her pale cheek, just ever so little, with the back of his hand. But she was priestess now, and he knew he dared not.

The fire was cold. She touched the ash to his face, all over him, ran it down the blade of his sword, over his helmet and the brightly painted iron of his shield. All the while she chanted spells, spells against the wood of lances and the iron of swords, spells against dagger and poison, spells against cold, spells to shield his strength and his cunning and his potency.

Her palms lingered on his face. "I promised you all the gifts of Car-Iduna, Karelian of Lys. You have them now. You are not invulnerable; don't ever dare to think so. But you are shielded with many strengths. Use them well."

From a small pouch she drew out three bright, smooth objects, tiny as wrens' eggs, and offered them to him.

"The red is of wolfsblood," she said. "The green is of thorn. The black is the belly of the world. They say the first of these were made by Gullveig, before the days of men, and used in the great war between the Vanir and the Aesir."

He took them wonderingly, turned them in his hands. They felt hard as polished stone.

"What are they for?"

She smiled and kissed him. "When you need them, you will know."

Last of all she gave him another feather, black and shimmering like the first.

"Use this only if you're desperate, if there is no other hope. Toss it into the sky, that is all; I will come to you."

She kissed him yet again, softly. "I promise I will come."

She slept spent, tangling him in her limbs, in the black silk of her hair. He lay awake for a long time, listening to the river and the melancholy owls, to the easy wanderings of Marius who stood guard for them at night, out of courtesy more than out of need; there was more power here than any ordinary mortals were likely to disturb.

He thought about his fate.

Tell me, he had asked her, how a witch would make war against the lord of the world.

Her answer had been clear, and pitiless, and sound. Every word lingered in his mind, as if they were speaking now.

—*Don't go to Aachen, Karel. Don't give Gottfried the smallest reason to mistrust you.*

—*The emperor must be warned. Gottfried is perfectly capable of having him murdered in his bed.*

—*I will see to it he's warned. Stay with the duke. Learn everything you can about his plans.*

They were in the glade where she had changed herself, where she had rippled into that splendid golden predator. She was still naked; had she been younger, she might have seemed elfin there, and playful; instead she only seemed shamelessly beautiful. And perilous, he thought, more perilous than twenty knights in armor.

—*Most of all, Karelian, learn everything you can about the stone. I doubt we can steal it from him, but we may discover ways to block its power, or destroy it. And then we'll see how divine he really is, our Golden Duke!*

It was night now; the glade where they had lingered was shadowed with foxes, the moon high, the altar stone black with ash, the woman spent and soft in his arms.

And he was damned.

If it was true. If the God of Rome and Jerusalem was real, then he was damned now, irrevocably and absolutely damned to those caverns of hellfire churning at the bottom of the world. All his other sins were forgivable—at least in the eyes of the Church, if not in his own. But from this circle of seven stones there would be no way back, even if he should ever halfway wish for one. She would never let him go.

More importantly, he had made his own choice, his own irrevo-

cable act of unfaith and disobedience. He was not even sure when he
had made it, if it had been in Stavoren or in Lys or here with her.
But it was made, and it lay in his mind as a spear might have lain
against his hand, pitiless and comforting.

All he had wanted was to live. To have yet some kind of life, to
live it in some measure of human decency.

Gottfried von Heyden had forgotten what it meant to a man to
sell his soul for a night's good lodging, for a promise of land, for a
handful of coins to pay for a bit of pleasure, to shut out the memory
of how the coins were earned. Or rather, Gottfried von Heyden had
never known those things; he had never needed to know them. He
was one of those with lands to give away, and promises, and coins;
he could buy a man and scarcely notice that he'd done so, and then
smile and cross himself and walk away.

Therefore Gottfried von Heyden could rob such a man of his last
hope of peace, and never imagine he might be hated for it. Never
imagine he might unleash against himself an enemy with absolutely
nothing to lose, not even honor. Karelian's honor had been bought and
sold too many times for it to matter. Allegiance counted for nothing
now, and rank for less; and as for God, he had not counted much for
years.

If it was treason, then so be it. If it was death on the field or on
the gallows, then so be it. If it was hellfire, then so be it. He would
bring Gottfried down. He would tear out his golden throat, and drag
his banners in the mud, and ride his horse across his bones.

And she would help him. She would shield him and counsel him
and pour her sweet, dark passion into his blood; she would call forth
the old gods, the gods of the earth who were all the gods any man
needed to live.

And he would take her gift of sorcery, take it with both hands,
triumphantly, and love her better for it. It was magic and wildness and
shimmering power; it was strength in his body and cunning in his
mind; it was the hunger to live and the hope to win and it was sweet,
sweet, sweet . . . sweet as her harpsongs, sweet as the taste of her
flesh against his mouth. He would never go back to the other who
was called a God, not ever; and there was fear in his resolve, like the
fear which lay over the morning of a battle. *Maybe this is my last
sun, my last drink of water, my last word of friendship.*

My last chance to turn and ride away . . . .

He knew the meaning of what he did then, and he did it because he knew. He slid out of the tangle of her arms and eased her onto her back. She purred softly, briefly, but she was too spent to waken. He kissed her throat, and took the copper tips of her breasts into his mouth, first one, and then the other, and knelt over her, and took her as she slept.

XX

BETRAYAL

Among them that broke their vows I saw a young knight
brenning in the fire whom I knew sometime full well.

REVELATION TO A MONK OF EVESHAM

FOR WEEKS I HAVE AVOIDED putting these words to paper. And no,
I did not hesitate because I care what you think—whoever you
may be who come to read this. I never cared about the small opinions
of the world, not even in my youth. Still less do I care now, at the
edge of death, in this place where the world is nothing. I fear one
thing only, and that is my own despair.

It had rained for days. Sodden grey clouds lay across the
whole of the Reinmark. Northward, in the wild march of Ravensbruck, they were wind-blown and cold; here, in the valley
of the Maren, some twenty-eight leagues from the great city
of Karn, they were sleepy and warm. Rain slithered softly
over the monastery walls, and ran down the cobbled paths,
whispering of bursting grapes and flowers, whispering of life:
boundless life, spilling out forever from the black loins of the
earth.

Always more life . . . and still more . . . and yet still
more. Paul shook his head. He acknowledged God's generosity, the marvelous abundance of creation, yet he was sickened
by this endless glut of life, this growing over of everything
by the weeds of indiscriminate existence.

To the black fecund earth, the bones of a king and the

leavings of a rat were no different. They were both just offal, just matter to chew up and spit out again in still another form—another weed, another drop of rain, another rat. Why did God permit it? Why did all this life exist, when all but a few tiny fragments of it were meaningless and befouled? Why did it continue, all of it mindlessly clamoring, and then afterwards mindlessly still, disappearing forever into the never-was, the never-mattered, burying the little which was good under its sheer, overwhelming mass?

In Stavoren, he had heard, the tombs of von Heyden were cracking, and briars were growing from their bones.

The cell where he sat was lit with a tiny candle, just enough to write by. He picked up his quill, slowly, hatefully. He did not want to write any more—not this damned and despicable chronicle, dictated by an incubus, turning everything he did into folly, everything he loved into delusion. And yet he could not resist. His hand was restless without the quill in it, and his mind was sick with memories. Writing them was unbearable; resisting them was worse.

BETRAYAL DID NOT COME EASY TO ME, whatever anyone may think. I was a baron's son, taught from childhood to respect the bonds of rank. I was a German, born to a world of passionate tribal loyalties, where treachery, though not uncommon, was bitterly condemned. I was a Christian. I knew that Our Lord obeyed his divine Father in all things, even to the point of death, and that he demanded of us the same submission to authority.

And finally, I was young and powerless. To go behind my own lord's back and accuse him of witchcraft and treason, with no proof except my word—you may well ask how I could have dared to do it, for it was likely to earn me nothing except my own death, or a dungeon cell without a key.

For weeks my knowledge tormented me, yet I could not bring myself to act. Every day I decided I would speak; every night I huddled in my bed, and decided I could not. It was too dangerous, too futile. Gottfried would never believe me.

And yet in the end I went to him, because I had to.

You may say I was treacherous, and a fool. You may say, too, that I should have left the matter in God's hands. It was for God to unfold the history of Gottfried and Karelian, and not for me to interfere. God would have revealed his truth in his own way, and accomplished his design. How can I answer you? How can I answer God? I did what I did, and the rest followed.

All of the rest of it, ruin by ruin to the end. Was I God's agent, or was I theirs?

There were at least a dozen people in the room, counting the guards and the scribe who sat at the duke's elbow, ready to note down whatever he might command. I walked stiffly across acres of stone floor, trying to swallow my fear, trying to ignore my horrible sense of wrong-doing. I was just twenty. In all my life I had never lied about anything, except the trivial deceptions of childhood—claiming an apple was windfall, perhaps, when in fact I had snatched it off a tree. Things even the priest had smiled at, though of course he told me not to do it again.

Now I stood wrapped in lies, in a peasant woman's filthy dress, with black cinders in my hair, and old rags covering my hands, so no one would notice how big they were, or how callused from swordplay. I was deception given bones and flesh, a pretender bowing almost to the floor to hide my panic.

They looked at me without much interest. To them I was just another peasant, a pleader for favors or a dreamer of folly. But they would listen to me, if only for a moment, because I claimed to have knowledge concerning the duke's safety.

"Well?" Gottfried said.

It was three months since I had seen him, and in spite of my love for him, I had forgotten how magnificent he was. Tall and broad, his square face hardened with wisdom, his eyes steady, as though he looked right through men's flesh into their souls, and feared nothing he might see there.

I held out a folded, sealed paper. Only one sentence was written inside it: I am Paul von Ardiun, squire to the count of Lys.

A servant took the paper and passed it to the duke. He opened it. His face never changed. He folded it and put it carefully away, and glanced at the attendants, who waited patient and bored.

"Leave us," he said.

When everyone had gone, he waved me to approach him, and smiled.

"What is Karel up to then," he asked, "that he must resort to such nonsense as this? Surely he knows he can send me messengers at any hour of the day or night, and I will see them?"

"I am not here on the count's behalf, my lord."

"Then on whose?"

"Yours, my lord."

"You will have to explain yourself," he said.

So I told him everything. How it began the autumn before, as we journeyed to Ravensbruck for Karelian's marriage. How the bridge was gone at Karlsbruck, and how Karelian had decided, against the advice of all his men, to pass through the perilous forest of Helmardin.

As soon as I mentioned that name, I noticed the tightening of Gottfried's hand on the arm of his chair, the sudden, riveted attention of his gaze.

"And what befell you in Helmardin?" he asked, very softly.

"A storm came, my lord, a terrible storm, unnatural for the season, and we were lost in it. We came finally upon a castle, a place full of sorcery, kept by a witch queen. They called it Car-Iduna."

Even now, many months later, I shivered remembering it. Plants grew there without sun, and men were turned into animals, and lust coiled in the air like scented smoke.

"This witch queen you speak of," Gottfried demanded. "Do you know her name? What did she look like?"

"I never learned her name. But she had black hair. She was tall, and very beautiful, the way a harlot is beautiful. She wore many rings, and a gold belt studded with black stones, and a gown which only pretended to cover her. All she had to do was smile at Karelian, and he was undone."

"The same one, then," Gottfried murmured, more to himself than to me.

"Do you know this witch, my lord?" I whispered.

"Of her," he said. "I know of her." He gave me a hard, searching look. "They say everyone who enters her realm either remains there captive, or, if they return to the world, they can't remember anything that happened."

"It was so for the others, my lord—all the count's men, except me. Because I did not eat, or drink, or touch any of the women. All the others have forgotten. They think we passed the night in a cave."

"And why didn't *you* eat or drink or pleasure yourself? You were the youngest, the least worldly, and you saw the danger of it, when your betters did not?"

"It was the seneschal who warned me, my lord. Reinhard. He warned us all. But once we were inside, and they saw her, and heard the music, and had cups of hot wine pressed into their hands . . . my lord, the power of the place . . . ! It was like nothing I can describe. It was as if God himself wasn't present in the world any more, inside those walls."

"And yet you did not falter," he said coldly. "How very extraordinary."

I swallowed. I knew it sounded arrogant and righteous. Surviving always did.

"I was so terrified of them, my lord, I wasn't much tempted."

My answer surprised Gottfried, but I think it satisfied him. It was perhaps the only answer he would have considered honest.

"Go on," he said.

"She wanted something from him; I don't know what. They quarreled—or at least I thought they did. Then we left, and even as we passed through the gates, my lord, Car-Iduna disappeared. One moment it was there, and the next moment there was only forest. I thought it was over then; I thought we were safe. We went on to Ravensbruck, and afterwards to Lys. Karelian kept the black feather she gave him, but I never thought he'd use it. I never thought he'd call her back. And then he did."

"When?" the duke asked sharply.

"In August, my lord. After we left your court here in Stavoren."

After you told him your true identity, and your destiny, and your plans . . . .

"He went to the banks of the Maren, and made offerings to the pagan god Tyr, and burned the feather in the manner she commanded. When she came, he knelt to her and swore allegiance."

"And he took you along, I suppose, to hold his cloak, and gather the wood for the fire."

His mockery hurt bitterly. I knew he had to doubt me, test me, trap me in any lie or malice I might be guilty of. But still it hurt.

"He went alone, my lord. I followed him secretly."

"Do you make a habit of spying on your master?"

"No, my lord, never! Only that one time—!"

"And why, Paul of Ardiun? Why that one time?"

I stared at the duke's boots; they were heavy and brown, laced to his knees; he had huge feet. I had no idea what to say. Till this moment

I had spoken honestly. But I could not tell the truth now. I could not admit to knowing who he was.

"Ever since Helmardin, my lord, ever since he met . . . *her* . . . I was afraid for him, afraid he would . . . do something. He never stopped thinking about her. He cherished the raven's feather she gave him. He kept it in a pouch hung around his neck, as a man might keep a sacred relic. He carried her colors at the tournament, right here in Stavoren—"

"A moment ago," Gottfried reminded me grimly, "you told me you were sure it was over. You were sure he'd never call her back."

Christ, those eyes . . . ! He knew I was lying, and his eyes were pitiless, as the eyes of God will be at the hour of our judgment.

If he had simply sat, and gone on staring at me, God alone knows what I might finally have said, if only to free myself from his look, from the awful knowledge that he despised me for a plotter and a fool. But he reached to the table beside him, and poured himself a small bit of wine, and began to speak.

"What injury has passed between you and the count of Lys, squire Paul?"

"Injury, my lord? None."

"Karelian is a well bred and well spoken man," he went on. "An easy man to like. And generous. Last autumn, as I recall, before you left for Ravensbruck, he made you some very fine gifts. And when you came here for the *Königsritt,* we all could see you thought the world of him.

"Now you come to me with a tale which would mean his death—if I decided to believe it. Such a change of heart must surely have a reason. Either he has wronged you, or . . . ." He paused, and considered me again. "Or you have done some wrong against him, and hope to cover your guilt with treachery. Which is it, squire Paul?"

"It is neither, my lord. I am—"

He cut me short with a single blunt gesture. "Listen to me, you babbling whelp! No one knows you're here; you made sure of it yourself. You may wish you hadn't been half as clever. You walked in here as a peasant drab—who will care if you walk out again? Who will even *notice?* I can have your liar's throat cut before you open it to scream! Now tell me the truth. What is your quarrel with the count of Lys?"

My courage almost failed me then. It was as bad as I had feared. He did not believe me. He thought me nothing more than a foolish,

dishonorable young man with a grudge. I would die for it, and that
was horrible enough. But what would become of him?

I threw myself to my knees at his feet.

"My lord, please, I beg you, let me speak! I haven't lied to you.
I thought the world of Count Karelian, it's true. And because I did, I
blinded myself. Every chance he gave me to think well of him, I took
it. And so yes, I believed it was over when we left Helmardin; I believed he would come back to God; I believed he was honorable at
heart. Over and over I believed it—because I wanted to. Only . . .
only a part of me was always afraid. And the last while, before he
sent for her, he was . . . he was so dark and silent . . . ! I thought
surely something must have happened in Stavoren. Something must
be turning his mind back—"

"Did he speak of any such . . . *happening?*"

"No, my lord. He spoke of nothing but his plans for war. He said
there was talk of invasion from the east. He is already hiring men,
and replenishing his fortress—"

Gottfried waved me to silence.

"Then he's doing nothing more than following my advice."

He turned the wine glass slowly in his hand. When he spoke again
his voice was warm, almost a purr.

"You still haven't told me why, Paul. Why you left him, and came
to me."

The future of the world, I thought, might hang upon my answer.

"Because he is evil, my lord, and you are good."

There was a long and heavy silence. I don't think Gottfried expected such an answer, or quite knew what to make of it.

"You're doing this," he said at last, "for no ulterior motive whatever? You've come to me at the command of your conscience, only
because you want to do what is right?"

"Yes, my lord. Is that so unbelievable?"

"Not unbelievable. Merely unusual."

"I am a Christian, my lord. I cannot serve a man who deals with
sorcerers, and offers sacrifice to pagan gods."

"Agreed. You could, however, merely walk away. It's what most
men would do, especially young men without power. You've taken an
extraordinary risk."

"I had to warn you, my lord."

"Yes, but of what? Perhaps you haven't noticed the fact, lad, but
your warning has no substance whatever. Karelian is besotted with a

sorceress, and has offered her some act of service. I am appalled by it, of course, but it hardly proves he is my enemy. Many men still secretly serve the old gods, and have dealings with diviners and witches. It doesn't follow that every one of them is plotting against his lord. If you know your master at all well, you know he's never been particularly . . . devout. If this is all you can tell me, Paul, you must surely admit it isn't much."

He shifted a little in his chair, like a busy man who was losing interest in the subject of discussion. I had persuaded him of my sincerity, perhaps, but of very little else. And in the world of princes and power, a fool was no less a fool for being sincere.

So I lied. If a small lie is needed to make clear a great truth, it can hardly be a sin. She was evil, and there was no doubt in my mind that she hated Gottfried. She must hate him, being who she was. I did not have to hear her say so.

"The sorceress spoke against you, my lord. In Car-Iduna. She said the Reinmark belonged to her gods. She called you many evil names. She said she'd never be content until you were broken and brought to your knees."

"She spoke so in front of Karelian?"

"Yes, my lord."

"And he did not object?"

It took all my strength to continue meeting his eyes, but I did so. I had to.

"No, my lord. He cared for nothing but pleasing her."

"But you said they quarreled," he reminded me.

"Yes, my lord. Or so it seemed to me. Perhaps she wanted him to be her ally then, and he wouldn't. Not until he'd thought about it."

I didn't have to say the rest of it aloud: *Not until he knew, until you told him you were the heir of Christ and the son of God.*

The duke did not respond to my words at all. Instead he waved me to my feet, and changed the subject completely.

"Where does the count of Lys think you are at the moment?"

"Still at home in Ardiun. I hadn't seen my parents since we returned from the Holy Land. He gave me a month's leave to visit them."

"And what do you mean to do now?"

"I will go back to Lys, and take my leave of him. I will tell him I've thought about changing the direction of my life—which in fact is true. I even discussed it with my father. I was hoping, my lord, that you might accept me into the Knights of Saint David—"

"So you want a reward, after all. How surprising."

"Only one reward, my lord. To be allowed to serve my God, and to serve you."

"The heart of service is obedience, Paul. If what you tell me is true—and I am by no means convinced of it—then you'll be more than willing to serve me in whatever manner I think best."

"I am ready, my lord," I said eagerly.

"Very well. You said you always thought well of Count Karelian; you believed he would come back to God. If it's still possible, if he can be . . . dissuaded . . . from his attachment to this sorceress, then you're the one person who can do it."

"Me, my lord? Everything I say to him, he laughs at—"

"Not with words. God doesn't always touch men's hearts with words. Often the words come after, merely to explain what has already been made clear by faith.

"I have a relic which came into my possession in Jerusalem. I do not part with it willingly, and yet for the good of a man's soul—for a kinsman who's served me as faithfully as Karelian—I will give it up. You are his squire; all his belongings are in your care. You must conceal it in such a way that he will carry it on his person. It has extraordinary grace. No devil can come near it, and no summons from any devil. No conjuring, no spells, no evil of any sort can cross its barriers."

He went to a cabinet and unlocked it, and took out a fine, jeweled chest which was also locked. From this he brought out a tiny cross. He touched it to his lips, reverently and placed it in my hands.

It was made of wood, but very thin, and shorter than my smallest fingernail. In its center was a tiny piece of crystal. I thought at once of the godstone I had seen him holding in Stavoren, the glittering pyramid he had brought back from the Holy Land. I knew there must be some connection between them.

"It will be God's shield around Karelian," the duke said. "If he has still some love for Christ, some wish to save himself, this will give him strength. If he has fallen totally, beyond recall, then it still will lessen the evil he is able to do. Now go back to Lys, and stay there. Say nothing to anyone. Go on with your life exactly as before.

"You may go now," he added.

For a moment I could only stare at him, holding the tiny, awesome thing, appalled at what he had asked me to do—utterly appalled and utterly admiring. If even now, confronted with peril and betrayal, he could think first of Karelian's soul, then he was truly the man I believed him to be.

"It will save him?" I said. "It will turn him away from her?"

"Only he can do that," Gottfried said. "But it will help."

If Karelian were saved, I thought desperately, if he came back to God, back to his liege lord and his rightful place, then I was not betraying him! And once he knew, once he understood, he would be grateful, we would be friends again, and everything would be like before . . . .

I saw Gottfried watching me curiously.

"You are truly good, my lord," I said. "I thank you for this. Pray God one day the count will thank you, too."

"We shall see."

"My lord, will you perhaps send for me later—?"

He waved me to silence.

"You are either very brave," he said, "or unconscionably evil. One day I will know which. Believe me, lad, I will. And when I do, I will deal with you accordingly."

"Thank you, my lord. God keep you, my lord."

I bowed—I do not know how many times—and blundered away. I went into the woods and found a stream, and washed the peasant filth from my body and changed back into my own clothing.

And then for a long time I sat, clutching the tiny cross in my palm. It was so small, and so beautiful. *No conjuring, no spells, no evil of any sort can cross its barriers.* Could it save Karelian? And even if it could, how would I be able to fulfill Gottfried's command, and conceal it somehow in my lord's most personal belongings? Suppose he found it? How would I live, day after day by his side, waiting for him to find it?

The night closed deeper and darker, and its whisperings began to trouble me—owls mourning in the treetops, and the small feet of night hunters rustling in the shrubs. I knew if I stayed there I would grow more and more afraid. I pulled myself together and fetched my horse, and headed back towards Dorn. From there I would cross the Schildberge mountains into Lys. I was exhausted, but I did not stop to eat or rest until the sun was high. I would do what the duke asked, however dangerous it was. I would do it for my soul's sake, and for Karelian, too.

But above all, I would do it for Gottfried himself. *He* was now my lord, my true lord, the one I would serve before all others. His was the image I held before me as I rode. I would do it for him . . . and for his favor, for the divine certainty of my reward.

The monastery lay wrapped in fog; thick mists shut away every sound of the valley beyond, and sent their small white ghosts slipping in through the cell windows and wandering across the floors.

Paul's hand was bleeding. He put the quill down and watched the fog wisps endlessly dissolve and endlessly return—like guilt, he thought, like the unending, irremediable evil of the world. Only an infinitely good God could care about such a place, or about the vile creatures who lived in it.

The night was cold, and its dampness had gone deep into his bones. He rose stiffly, and walked a bit to ease himself. He was in pain all the time; he only noticed when it grew worse.

He had been strong and sturdy in his youth. He journeyed twice to the Holy Land to make war, and came home without wounds. Now his health was utterly gone. During the past winter he had frozen both his feet, and they festered where the toes were lost, stinking and horrible to look at. His right hand was completely crippled. He could not eat solid food unless it was cooked to mush. His bowels tormented him with alternating periods of constipation and flux. He rarely slept without evil dreams.

Yet he took comfort from the fact that God continued to burden him, to break him down still farther into his human nothingness. It meant that God still loved him. God still judged him worthy of redemption. No, not worthy; no one was ever *worthy* of redemption. But still, at least, redeemable. Still capable of breaking free, of severing himself finally and forever from his despicable body and its passions, and soaring skyward to his Lord.

It happened sometimes, briefly. Sometimes he caught the barest glimpse, gone in the catch of a breath. A glimpse of infinite peace, of infinite purity, a central stillness where nothing existed except God, and God was only soul. No flesh at all, no bones, no blood, no filth. Only soul. But the vision never lasted—or rather, it never really focused at all. It was always a shadow behind a shadow of something else, and he would yearn after it with the craving of a lover. He would meditate and pray, but always it eluded him.

If only once, just once, he could actually *see it* . . . *!*

He looked up sharply at the sound of movement, and caught his breath. A man was sitting in his cell—no, a devil, surely, a splendid devil wearing a surcoat of blue velvet, who put his feet up on the table as though he were entirely at home, and leaned back in his chair, and smiled.

"Don't you understand yet, Pauli?" he said. "You can't see it because it isn't there."

He had seen devils before. They came to him often, and took many shapes. This one seemed a knight, well-dressed and fully armed, in every way a man, except for a softly burning darkness where his face ought to have been. His voice was soft, and utterly familiar. Paul stumbled closer.

"Karelian . . . ?"

The devil answered only with a smile, as if to say: If you know me, Pauli, why do you trouble yourself to ask?

"Are you in hell, then?" Paul whispered, and wondered why the thought so utterly devastated him. It was only justice, after all.

"There is no hell. There is no heaven, either. There is only this." The devil waved his arm in an elegant, sweeping arc. "It's all here, Pauli: the flesh and the spirit, the world and the gods. There is no otherwhere, only this. But why do I go on talking to you? It never made any difference before." He paused. The smoldering image cleared a little, and Paul could see his eyes, dark with bitterness and a strange, remote pity.

"It never made any difference at all."

"Go away from here!" Weakly, foolishly, Paul shoved at the table. "In the name of God, go, and leave me in peace!"

The devil merely smiled, and crossed his boots.

"Think about it," he said. It's what Karelian always said, in the same soft, seductive, relentless voice. Think about it. Consider the possibility. What if you have it wrong? What if you've always had it wrong, all of it, all these long years . . . ?"

XXI

THE DEMON LORD OF LYS

He attacked our religion in a very villainous and ungenerous way,
introducing into his persecution the traps and snares of argument.

SAINT GREGORY OF NAZIANZUS

*What if there is no absolute, omnipotent God? No, Pauli, don't
close your mind yet, don't tell me what we all think we know.
Just consider it. The possibility. The tiny possibility that divinity,
whatever it may be, is not outside the world, but in it. That there is
no otherwhere. That the gods are bound up with the fate of the world:
those we choose to serve grow powerful, and those we abandon grow
weak, and so the world and the gods both become, in the end, what
we make of them—*

My lord . . . !

*Just consider it, that's all. For if it's true, Pauli, then for more
than a thousand years we've been chasing a phantom, and for its sake
we have made bitter war against the finest things we have: our minds,
our bodies, and the bounty of the earth.*

I went back to the manor house at Lys, and passed on to the count
the good wishes of my father. I told him how the crops were in the
south, and how my family fared. I acted for all the world like the
devoted young squire he believed me to be.

It was a dark time for me. I could neither overcome my guilt—and
my willingness, because of it, to do him every possible kindness—nor
could I silence my simple longing to be elsewhere. I yearned to be

with Gottfried, or perhaps in some distant, silent monastery, where I would be done with it all, and safe.

For days I brooded over the relic, wondering how I might conceal it. It was my only consolation, my hope that things might yet turn out well. If it could, as Gottfried promised, block every demonic impulse, if the sorceries of Car-Iduna could no longer reach my lord and corrupt his mind, then he might yet retrieve his soul. In the end he would thank me. He would know I hadn't really betrayed him.

As it happened, his own vanity provided me with the opportunity I needed. He still wore the pouch I made for him on the road to Ravensbruck, where he had hidden the witch's feather. What charms he kept in it now I did not know, but he never took it off, not even to sleep. It was soiled now, and showing wear. Would I, he asked, be so kind as to make him a new one?

Which I did. A very fine one, and sturdy as he requested, with the tiny cross stitched inside a folded seam, so subtly and perfectly hidden that only sorcery, or the most unlikely chance, was ever going to discover it. He thanked me for the pouch, and gave me a coin because it was so beautifully made, and hung it around his neck without a second thought.

Nonetheless I was terrified, and for a while I slept very badly, and jumped like a kitchen maid at mice and shadows. I thought his every frown or moment of thoughtful silence meant he had noticed something wrong. But as the weeks passed I grew less afraid. Gottfried had been right. No deviltry was stronger than the cross. Just as the relic could shield Karelian from the powers of evil, so could it shield itself from discovery and harm.

But it could not turn a man back to God, unless he wished it so.

Karelian never flaunted his unbelief. It was unwise, even for a highborn lord, to become known as an apostate. But I was his squire, bound to him in a singular relationship of personal service and mentorship; we had for a time been very close. Indeed, he seemed to think we still were. He barely noticed how his own follies had wrecked the bond between us. And so he spoke to me sometimes of his thoughts of God and the world. There was no way I could escape those discussions; all I could do was shut my mind to them.

What if there was no absolute, omnipotent God? he would ask me, moodily. What if there were many gods, or none at all? Why were all our virtues said to be God's doing, when all our sins were said to be our own? Why were there so many sins? He had traveled a great deal, he said; he had known many kinds of men, good men, honorable and just, and some of them doubled over and howled with laughter at the Church's list of sins. And how was it, he asked me, that a perfect, loving God created hell?

"My lord, forgive me, but you must not think such things!"

"Why mustn't I?"

"Because all God's truth has already been revealed through Jesus and the Church, and proven by the resurrection, and by the miracles of the saints! It's all there, my lord! We have the word of God himself!"

"So do the Jews. So do the infidels. So, I suppose, does most everyone else. Either God is very confused, Pauli, or else we have only the words of men."

Then Karelian did a thing which raised questions in other minds besides my own. The summer had ripened into fall, and all over the golden fields of Lys the serfs and freeholders were gathering the crops. It had been a good year. The granaries were bursting; the wine presses running day and night. We lived well. For all his thoughts of war—or perhaps because of them—Karelian made sure we lived exceptionally well.

It was, I remember, a Friday. We ate no meat, and the countess Adelaide ate nothing at all.

She had turned eighteen that summer. She had also given birth to her first child, a black-haired boy-child fathered by her dead lover, Rudolf of Selven. Everyone knew about it, though of course in the count's presence everyone pretended to forget. The girl was fragile and pretty; if he wished to keep her, and forgive her because of her youth, few men thought worse of him for it. But his decision to keep the child bewildered everyone. He seemed willing to turn the whole world upside down, I thought sometimes, merely for the pleasure of seeing it on its head.

Our dinner was a lavish one, as usual. The servants carried in huge plates with fine baked fishes, and great pots of stew, and pasties stuffed with nuts and fruits; everything smelled of honey and garlic and butter. Adelaide sat with her hands on her lap. As each splendid dish was offered, she refused it—firmly at first, and then with greater and greater reluctance. Her last refusals were only small, sorrowful shakes of her pale blond head.

I wondered about it, but only fleetingly. I did not like her, and my duty in any case was to serve my master, to fill his wine cup and his plate, to peel the skeleton from his trout and carve it into pieces.

Karelian had put away the first fish and was starting on the second when he noticed his wife, at the far end of the table, still sitting before an empty plate.

"You're not eating, Adelaide."

"No, my lord."

"Are you ill?"

The concern in his voice was real. He had brought her from Ravensbruck dazed with fever. He had sheltered her all winter in Karn, and ordered all manner of small luxuries for her here in Lys, so she would regain her health. It was not untypical. Whatever his vices, he took good care of his people.

But in Adelaide's case, there was something more than his usual sense of duty. I never quite knew what. He certainly did not love her. She had after all betrayed him, and his own heart was locked in Car-Iduna. But there was a stubborn loyalty between them, and sometimes a strange, uneasy kind of passion. She was halfway mad; sometimes she lived as though he were not there, as though none of us were there. Other times she followed him about and pleasured with him like a courtesan—once even in the apple orchard, not caring in the least if they were seen, giving shameless scandal to the peasants.

"I'm not ill, my lord," Adelaide said. "I'm fasting."

The count put his fish back onto his plate and his elbows onto the table.

"Why," he demanded, "are you fasting?"

"Father Gerius said I must. For twenty-one days."

"Twenty-one days? That was my penance once for killing a man in a duel." He paused, and looked around the table. "I see no one missing from the household, lady."

Everyone laughed—not least the countess herself. Karelian spoke again, and I sensed more than heard the hint of anger in his voice.

"You're not strong enough to fast, Adelaide. Surely Father Gerius can see that."

The pale fox face looked up very quickly. Very eagerly. "Do you forbid it, my lord?"

"Yes. I forbid it. Greta, give the countess her dinner. I will speak with Father Gerius tomorrow. He will have to assign you some other kind of penance."

"Thank you, my lord."

He watched until Greta had served her and she began to eat, greedy as a starving child, playing on his sympathy as she played on that of the servants. *Poor little thing, she's barely had a mouthful all day, and she's so pale . . . .*

Karelian spoke to the manor chaplain the next day, as he promised. But first he spoke to Adelaide, and in the privacy of their bedchamber he learned the reason for her penance. (All this I was told later by the servants, who had it from Adelaide's maid.) I have no idea what Karelian imagined, perhaps that the three-week fast had been imposed for her adultery, or for some secret, long-ago offense.

But Father Gerius had, in the course of her confession, questioned her about her married life—as of course he had to do. Married life was the ordinary Christian's primary occasion of sin.

Did they engage in the carnal act on Wednesdays? On Fridays? On Sundays between midnight and Mass? In daylight? During her unclean times? During Lent or Advent, or on any Ember Day? Did they seek pleasure from it, rather than merely obey the requirements for bearing children? Did she allow her husband to see her unclothed body? Did they engage in lewd or unnatural acts?

At this point the countess, already much distressed, asked him what was unnatural. He responded very carefully: "Describe to me what you do, and I will tell you if it is unnatural." She did so, and was corrected sadly, each time with greater firmness: "My child, you and his lordship have gravely offended God."

Long before they finished, she began to cry.

Karelian did not cry. He sat at his breakfast like a man contemplating murder, and the moment he had eaten, the tables were cleared and the manor chaplain was ordered to appear before him.

Everyone else was sent away, even Adelaide herself; but as I rose to follow, Karelian waved me to a chair.

"Stay," he said bluntly. "I want someone here who can read better than I can."

I obeyed with considerable reluctance. I did not know, at that point, what the nature of his confrontation with the priest would be, but whatever it was going to be, I did not want to be part of it.

Father Gerius came promptly. He was a man of forty or so, town-born and modestly educated. He had been chaplain at Lys for over ten years, and no doubt expected to end his days there.

He bowed deeply and smiled. "Good morning, and God bless your lordship."

Even when he was angry, Karelian most always let others say their piece. It was in part a basic fairness in the man, but it was also ruthless strategy. If you ever want to hang a man, he told me once, be sure to give him plenty of his own rope.

"I understand," the count said, "you have been questioning my wife in confession. About her personal relationship with me."

Father Gerius lost nothing of his benign composure. He explained politely, lucidly. No doubt other husbands had challenged him before, and wives, too.

"My lord, it would never be my wish to ask such questions. But sadly, people are not well educated in the teachings of the Church, regarding carnal matters or any other. Many of my parishioners know little more than pagans. Sometimes even priests do not know precisely what is forbidden by Christian law, and what is not. Which sort of untruth is a venial sin, for example, and which a mortal sin? Is it wrong to wear a charm if you wear it in memory of your mother, who gave it to you, and not for any magical purposes? And so on and so on.

"Because of this, the Church has commanded us to teach people when they come to confess. They cannot tell us their sins until they know what is sinful. So it is our duty to ask—gently and discreetly, of course; we don't wish to introduce them to sins they haven't yet thought of committing.

"It was never my intention, my lord, to cause embarrassment to her ladyship, or to yourself, but rather to do my duty for the welfare of her soul."

"The questions you asked her," Karelian said, "and the penances you imposed—I understand they're from a book?"

"Yes, my lord. As I said, sometimes priests themselves do not know as much as they should about the law. And even those who do might wonder how to say things properly. So we are given a book to guide us, a penitential—"

"Do you have it?"

For the first time, the priest looked troubled.

"Yes, my lord. But it is intended only for the use of the clergy—"

"Show it to me."

"It is in my quarters, my lord."

"Then send someone to fetch it."

With some dismay, the priest obeyed, and a small, leather-bound volume was brought to the count. Karelian leafed through it briefly and passed it on to me. It was arranged according to the commandments. Those questions dealing with the first commandment, and those dealing with the sixth, were carefully marked and much worn with use.

"Heresy and sex," Karelian murmured. "I should have known. Read it to me, Paul. I want to know wherein I've sinned."

"Were you not instructed in these matters in Ravensbruck, my lord?" the priest wondered. "Before your marriage? It is the custom."

"I was instructed in many strange things in Ravensbruck, Father Gerius. But surprisingly, this got missed. Read, lad."

I was terribly embarrassed by the whole affair, but I read out, carefully, what the sins were, and what penances were recommended for each. About halfway through the chapter, Karelian waved me impatiently to silence, and sat for a while looking at a scratch on the wooden table. Another man might have imagined he was overcome with shame. I knew better.

"I understand now," he said at last, looking up. "I've wondered and wondered why the Church is so determined that its priests shouldn't marry. I could never see why it should matter. But if you had a woman of your own, my friend, you wouldn't be able to lower yourself to this.

"It's a mortal sin to see my wife naked. To make love to her in daylight. To lie behind her—or even worse, beneath her. You would give me a harsher penance for it than for going out to rape my vassals' daughters. Can you explain that, priest?"

"My lord, both actions are of course most evil. But even in sin there is the natural and the unnatural, and the unnatural is always much worse, for it overturns the order of things as prescribed by God. The woman is by nature subordinate, and must lie below the man—"

"Suppose I'm tired? Suppose I have a broken arm?"

"My lord, I beg you, do not mock the holy faith—"

"I can't imagine what connection this has to the holy faith," Karelian said, "but if there is one, it deserves to be mocked. You are relieved of your duties, Father Gerius. My steward will pay you, and give you a small stipend to see you on your way. I want you out of my demesne before the sun goes down tomorrow."

"My good lord . . . ?"

The man was devastated. He opened his mouth, closed it again. He looked at me, and I looked carefully at the floor.

"My lord, please . . . ! I assure you, I meant no offense! I sought only the good of my lady's soul—!"

"The countess has a body and a mind as well as a soul, Father Gerius. After a few years in your judicious care, I wonder how much would be left of either. Go. Before I start believing you're something worse than just a fool."

"My lord, I beg you . . . !"

Karelian said nothing; he merely met the man's eyes. The chaplain flinched. Visibly.

"Very well, my lord. May I take all of my belongings?"

"Please take all of your belongings."

"Thank you, my lord. I will pray for you, my lord." The priest bowed faintly and turned to go. For the first time, from the unevenness of his step, I realized he limped.

Karelian settled back into his chair with a considerable air of weariness.

"Do you believe the presumption, Pauli?" he murmured. "I thought princes were arrogant; they are lambs compared to churchmen."

I scrambled for something to say.

"My lord, you can't mean to leave the manor without a chaplain. There will be no Masses, and no one to fetch if people fall ill. It's too far to the village—"

"Yes, I know. I will replace him. The bishop would have my head if I didn't."

And then he smiled, the quick winsome smile which I used to find so enchanting, and which now seemed only cynical to me—cynical and frightening, like the soft, dark smile of a sorcerer.

"He said there are many priests who aren't well educated in the teachings of the Church. I'm sure with a bit of effort I can find one."

So it was that Father Thomas came to Lys. He came from Karn, the worldly mercantile city where whores and thieves thrived alongside silk merchants and slavers and lenders of gold. He came with a personal recommendation from Karelian's old friend Baron Lehelin, and he brought with him his Provençal lyre, his treasured library of seven books, a basket with two yellow cats, and his wife.

He was not the first married priest I had ever met, nor would he be the last. Rome had been struggling for centuries against the practice, and failing over and over because most of Europe still refused to recognize the authority of the pope. Some bishops enforced celibacy on their priests; some did not think it mattered. Some were themselves married, and used their links with powerful families as a way of advancing their own position in the Church. As for the kings and lords, most of them were like our own Emperor Ehrenfried. He was first of all a German, and no Roman pope was going to tell his German bishops what to do.

Married priests were often criticized, but they were not rare, and the arrival of Father Thomas raised few eyebrows. Indeed, the women of the manor were mostly glad he had a wife. "He will understand us better," they said, and other such nonsense, as if the laws of God were social niceties, to be chatted over and served around a fire.

Karelian had spoken cynically about wanting an ignorant priest; in fact, from his perspective he did better. Father Thomas had an excellent education in the teachings of the Church. He simply did not take most of the teachings seriously. All books were sacred to him, and all brave men were godly. Being a priest was simply a way for him to be a scholar, and a dreamer, and a teller of pretty tales.

It must have taken him only a few days to learn what was expected of him. Quite possibly Karelian sat him down and told him. *Baptize the babies. Marry the young people. Say Mass every day. Console the sorrowful and bury the dead. And otherwise mind your own business. I am a wealthy man; you can have a good life here until the end of your days if you're sensible . . . .*

Christendom was full of men who wanted that kind of priest, and full of priests willing to accommodate them. I watched and said nothing. I waited for Gottfried to send for me.

For weeks no news worth mentioning came from the world beyond Lys, and then came news I did not want to hear. Ehrenfried, king of the Germans and lord of the Holy Roman Empire, was summoning all the princes of the land. They were to gather in Mainz in the spring, so they might confirm the succession of his son, Prince Konrad. Ehrenfried meant to see his son crowned king while he still lived.

I was devastated by the news. At best, it meant the Salian kings would strengthen their position and their dynasty. At worst, it meant Gottfried had already been betrayed.

My faith almost failed me then. Perhaps the dream I had encountered in Stavoren was only a dream. Perhaps I had imagined it all. Perhaps Gottfried was the Golden Duke, and nothing more, and Helmardin was nothing but a forest, and Karelian an ordinary worldling, no worse to serve than most, and better than many.

You have a good place there, Pauli, my father had cautioned me. *Take care you keep it.* At the most unexpected moments his words would come back, like the memory of his iron hands, his iron faith. He was a man to whom everything in the world, including God, made perfect, rational sense.

I remembered his words, and I wavered. I called myself a child, an overzealous and deluded child. I wished more than once that I could undo my journey to Stavoren.

But never for long. I took to spending hours in the chapel, and always my certainty returned there. I would remember Gottfried bent before the altar in Stavoren, wrapped in shadows and drenched in light. The image was exact in my mind, unchanging, even to the curve of his great shoulders as he knelt, the paleness of his hair, the power of his closing hands, the presence of God all about him, omnipotent and still. *This is my beloved son, in whom I am well pleased . . . .*

When I saw him so, in my mind, all the world was stripped of its illusions. I saw Lys for what it was—a corrupted, half-pagan world with a bit of Christian glitter on its face. In the morning there was Mass, and that was God's business for the day; the rest went to Mammon. Karelian spent hours with the brewers and the tanners and the master of horse. He spent whole days with Reinhard, who was his seneschal and military commander. He had no time left to think about his soul.

Jongleurs and minnesingers came daily to our gates, lured by quick-spreading rumors that the new count of Lys was fond of his pleasures and free with his coins. Father Thomas played his lyre, and spun tales of the heathens and tales of the Church side by side, until you couldn't tell the saints from the sorcerers, or Balder from Christ. Wagon trains crawled across the autumn landscape, carrying supplies up the winding mountain road to the fortress of Schildberge. Only our demon lord himself knew why he was sending so many men there, and so much food. He was preparing for war—for war and black rebellion—but hardly anyone noticed except me. The knights rode into the village to find whores, and came back by dawn light, wine-soaked and exhausted. The servants rutted in the stables and the sculleries, and lied and brawled and pleaded for forgiveness. Father Thomas smiled and forgave them all, and went back to his lyre and his books.

And every night I prayed—more than once until the tears came—I prayed Duke Gottfried would send for me, so I might live again with honorable men, in a clean and different kind of world.

XXII

FATHER AND SON

The clergy placed on the altar three books, namely those
of the Prophets, the Epistles, and the Gospels, and
prayed the Lord to reveal what should befall Chramm.

SAINT GREGORY OF TOURS

THEODORIC VON HEYDEN WAS, like his sire, a large man, imposing
on horseback, massive in armor, perilous even when asleep. His
face was pleasantly youthful, a rugged, sharp-eyed Teuton face hung
about with thin blond hair.

Among the warriors of the Reinmark, neither his size nor his looks
set him noticeably apart. What made men instantly aware of him was
his restlessness. He rarely sat, and he never sat still. His feet would
scrape constantly forward and back, and his weight would shift in his
chair. His eyes, even while he was engrossed in serious conversation,
were always glancing elsewhere, less out of watchfulness than out of
what seemed a permanent state of irritation. He made sober men ner-
vous and drunken men weary.

He paced now, his boots crunching deadfall and leaves. He was
almost wordless with anger, and desperate with the need to control it.
Finally he stopped, and turned to his father the duke. His words were
harsh and clipped.

"Will you just tell me why?" he demanded. "Why did you trust
that accursed spawn of Dorn? In God's name, my lord, tell me why!"

For a time Gottfried did not speak. Stray drops of rain fell here
and there against his face, and vanished almost as they landed. The

face was made of rock, rough-hewn and ageless. He was forty-seven; he might have been sixty, or a tired twenty-eight.

"I saw him in the willstone," he said at last, very quietly.

Theodoric tensed, like a man about to draw his sword.

"You what?"

"I saw him. On Holy Saturday, early in the morning—"

"There is nothing to see in the willstone, for Christ's sake! It's nothing but a mirror of your own thoughts. You said so yourself—!"

"Not that time. I didn't call up the image, Theo. I was exhausted with fasting, and Karelian Brandeis was the farthest man on earth from my mind. I wasn't even touching the stone." He paused, looking hard at his eldest son. "There is only one who can move the stone besides me, Theo. Only one."

"It's God's doing, then, is it? God's decision to place a sacred trust into the hands of a barbarian, and your future with it? *My future?* God's holy blood, my lord, how could you be so reckless! He's nothing but an adventurer—"

"He is our kinsman."

"At some damned remove, my lord, and from a line which never could be trusted. You know that, in God's name; it was your own father who called Helmuth Brandeis the weathervane of Dorn. And what was his son, before you gave him a place? Nothing but a wandering mercenary. He fought for any man who'd pay him. When he thought God might pay, he fought for God. He didn't come to Jerusalem to save the holy places, or destroy the infidels. He came to carve himself a name, and make his fortune—"

"Perhaps. But such men also have a role to play. We marched into Palestine with infidel guides, have you forgotten? It was an infidel who told us of the treasure in the temple of Jerusalem—my treasure now, Theodoric, and yours. God uses many stones to grind his knives."

Theodoric could no longer contain his fury. He planted himself before his father and shouted into his face.

"And did you make those infidels your friends?" he cried. "Did you put your life in their hands? *Did you tell them who you were?"*

"You forget yourself, Theo," the duke said grimly.

Theodoric growled something, and spun away, tramping brown October grass.

"Wasn't it enough to make him landgrave?" he said at last, bitterly. "To give him the Reinmark's richest county and its finest fortress? Wasn't that enough? Why did you have to tell him everything?"

"He's an intelligent man," Gottfried said. "And a survivor. And while it's true he fought for men of dubious merit, he's known to have a stubborn sense of honor. He's of my generation, remember, not yours; I know the stories better than you.

"I watched him at the *Königsritt,* Theo. I watched him very, very carefully. He admires the emperor, not least because Ehrenfried has grown peaceful and scholarly. If I didn't give him a reason to prefer us—an unusually good reason, I might add—I thought it likely he'd go over to the Salian camp."

"I should think, my lord, for a man who was once a landless adventurer, the county of Lys would be more than reason enough."

"Reason to stay with the man who gave it to him—or with the man most likely to see him keep it? Our cause may not look strong at the outset. Many of the men who say they're with me may change their minds when promise comes to payment. And there's no way of knowing which way the Church will jump. When the killing starts, the Salian camp may look like a good place to be. Ehrenfried has won two civil wars, and fought even the pope to a standstill. Unless Karelian knew the truth, he might well have judged his hard-won fortune safer in the emperor's hands than in mine."

"It seems he's done so anyway, doesn't it, my lord? Or do you think it's just a coincidence that Ehrenfried, at the height of his power and in the prime of his health, suddenly wants to see his son elected and crowned king? Karelian has warned him of your intentions."

"It may be. We simply don't know."

"Oh, Christ!" Theodoric said bitterly. He looked at the sky, at the ground, at his father's unyielding face.

"Couldn't you just have let it be? Who'd care in the end if the bastard was with us or not? Let him go over to the Salians and be damned!"

"I would have," Gottfried said simply. "I would have let him ride the whirlwind, and live or go down as he chose, except for his image in the willstone. His image armed for combat, with the ducal chain of the Reinmark on his breast, and a glowing sword upraised in his hand."

The young man went absolutely rigid. He was beyond further anger. Had he been facing anyone except the man who was both his father and his liege, he would have struck him.

"You saw Karelian as duke of the Reinmark? *In my place?* And you took it as a sign from God?"

"You have too little faith, my son. In truth, sometimes I think you don't have any. We're speaking of kingdoms here, of worlds. What is the duchy of the Reinmark? One small German state; there are fifty like it in Europe alone. Long before I make a man like Karelian a duke, I will have made you a king."

Theodoric began pacing again.

"You never wondered, father," he said finally, "if the image might have been some kind of warning?"

"Why should God warn me against something I never thought of doing?" The duke shook his head. "No. It was . . . it was an invitation. The offering of a possibility. I couldn't ignore it."

"And now?" Theodoric snapped. "Does it seem like such an attractive possibility now?"

Gottfried made a small, dismissive gesture. "The squire may be lying. There is something foul about the little wretch; I can all but smell it. I'll wager you five marks he's a catamite, and has fallen out with Karelian because of it."

"And if he's told the truth?"

Gottfried looked at his son. Hard.

"Do you think the ways of God are always clear? To any of us? Do you think the path is always straight? If God has given Karelian a role to play in this, then he will play his role, and the plan will still unfold as it should."

"In other words, any decision you make becomes the right decision, simply because you're the one who made it? That may be fine religion, my lord, but it's damnable strategy!"

"Strategy will not restore God's kingdom," the duke said. "Not by itself. Everyone seems to have forgotten that, even the popes. God's kingdom is God's will. Nothing more, and nothing less. You will see as much one day. So will Karelian of Lys."

He flung his cape back across his shoulder, and waved at the distant grooms to bring their horses.

"For three days we will fast and pray, and I will cast the *sortes sanctorum*. Then we will know."

The younger man met his eyes, and looked away.

"Don't you trust God to guide us?" the duke asked calmly.

"We're speaking of treason here, my lord. It might be wiser to trust heated iron."

"And when men are put to the question, who do you suppose

gives the innocent the strength to endure, and breaks the will of the guilty? It is still God."

Theodoric said nothing.

"I counted the years," Gottfried said. "Exactly one thousand, from the birth of the first heir with Frankish blood, to the spring of 1105. Exactly a millennium. The kingdom looks to dawn, my son."

In the west, black clouds were sinking fast, drowning the light, dissolving the boundaries of earth and sky. He spoke again, as if to himself, or to God. He was not looking at Theo.

"It may be harder this way, if he is against us. Harder and bloodier, but cleaner in the end. When they are all gone. When all the enemies of God have spoken, and identified themselves, and fallen still. There will be no true kingdom until then."

It was dawn of the third day. Outside the duke's private chapel in the castle of Stavoren, the white-clad knights of Saint David kept an armed vigil. Within, two men knelt before the altar. For three days they had knelt, wearing only pilgrims' hemp shifts, their feet bare and their knees raw against the stone. Now they were bathed and anointed and dressed in clean garments, waiting to hear God's words of judgment.

The sun was not yet risen. The only light in the chapel was from candles, the ever-burning lights which once the heathens placed in their wayside temples, and which burned now only to the glory of God.

So would all things be brought under his dominion, Gottfried reflected. So would unbelief surrender to truth, and flesh to the eternal soul. So would the earth be ruled by the sky.

Father, we do not come to you in pride, demanding to know your hidden things. We do not come as the heathens do, to work foul magic with the rot of tombs on their garments, and the filthy bones of animals in their hands. We do not call the dead from their unrest so they might speak to us. We seek truth only where you yourself have placed it, in your eternal words.

Gottfried picked up the sacred books, one by one, and pressed them against his body.

You have shown me I am your son. Tell me your will, that I might fulfill it. Speak your blessing upon your servant Karelian, or speak your curse. We will hear. We will obey. Guide the blind man's hands, and let him touch your truth. Amen.

No priest was present at the ritual, for none was needed. The door opened, the blind servant stepped inside, and stood uncertainly as the door closed behind him. He was a young man, blind from birth, and considered simple. He was bewildered by his fine new garments, for he kept touching them, and smiling.

Theodoric went to him and took his arm.

"You are in the chapel, Hansli. Show proper respect."

The lad genuflected quickly and stopped smiling.

"Do you believe in God, Hansli?" the duke's son asked.

"Oh, yes, my lord."

"Then come with me. I will place into your hands the sacred books of the Proverbs, the Prophets, and the New Testament. You will hold each one for a moment, and ask God to guide you, and then you will open it. Anywhere, Hansli, on the first page or the middle or the end, it doesn't matter. Open it where God tells you to open it, and place your finger on the page. I will read the passage you have chosen. And then you will do it again, with each book. Three times you will do this. Do you understand me?"

"Yes, my lord."

"Come then."

They moved slowly towards the altar. They knelt. For a small time nothing moved, not even the wind, or the sun creeping slowly towards the edge of the world. It seemed God himself was poised and waiting.

"Rise," Theodoric said, "and take the first book, and open it."

Gottfried did not look at either of them. He knelt a small distance away, his face pressed against his knotted hands.

God, maker of the world and lord of the universe, you who scattered the infidels like broken reeds, and spilled their blood like water on the sand; you who brought us safely to our own lands again, and filled our hands with riches; I beg you, God and father, out of the same infinity of power, out of the same unfailing justice towards the righteous and the false, name him as he deserves, as enemy or friend!

Theodoric read aloud.

"For at the window of my house I looked through my casement, and I beheld among the simple ones a young man void of understanding, passing through the street near her corner; and he went the way to her house. In the twilight, in the evening, in the black and dark night: behold there met with him a woman attired like a harlot, and subtle of heart."

Gottfried lifted his head, but he did not look at the others, only at the cross high above his head.

So, it is true then. They went to Helmardin, and found her there . . . or she found them—lured them there, perhaps? I know her ways, and her hatred of Christian men. But which of the two is the youth void of understanding? The squire Paul, who is in truth a lad? Or the count who despite his years knows as much of God as a half-taught boy, and cares less? Which one was seduced there to betray his lord?

"Again," he said.

Soft rustling as the book closed and another was taken up; a tiny, breathless silence. Theodoric read again.

"And the prince that is among them shall bear upon his shoulder in the twilight, and shall go forth; he shall cover his face that he see not the ground with his eyes. My net will I spread upon him, and he will be taken in my snare: and I will bring him to Babylon to the land of the Chaldeans; yet shall he not see it, though he shall die there."

Gottfried looked down. No ambiguity remained, none whatever, neither to guilt nor to punishment. It was not the boy then, but the lord, the prince. And he would die for it.

For the first time, Gottfried allowed himself to feel the anger of a king betrayed. And the bewilderment of a man who had made, in absolute certainty of his good judgment, a serious mistake.

Or had he?

Did I overtrust you, spawn of Dorn? Did I—for all my knowing better—did I come to admire you, as others do, for your beauty and your skill with arms and your graceful, cunning words? Did I want you as my warleader because it would enhance my honor in the world? Or was it myself I overtrusted, my own subtlety, my knowledge of your worldliness, my certainty that you would serve the highest bidder as every whore will do? Perhaps I forgot how much my enemy can offer . . . .

Or was I led to this because God wills it so? Because your treachery, like that of Judas, must yet fulfill the law?

"One last time, my friends," the duke whispered.

The blind lad took into his hands the New Testament, and opened it, and Theo read as he was bidden.

"Who shall lay any thing to the charge of God's elect? It is God who justifies."

Only to my Father, then, will I answer for what I do now . . . .

Silence again, and small shafts of dawn light lying in spears across the altar. He heard his son's voice, low but harsh: "Go now, and hold your foolish tongue; this is God's affair, and not a matter for servants' talk." He heard the young man's clumsy, groping steps, the opening and closing of the door, Theodoric coming to stand beside him. The young man's face was drained and bitter.

"Are you satisfied, my lord?"

Gottfried rose. He was aging; he had spent three days without food, ill-clothed and on his knees. Yet his body straightened like a bowstring, easily, gracefully. He was still one of the most feared fighting men in the empire, and that was in itself a miracle.

"Yes," he said. "I am satisfied."

"Then I would ask you a favor, my lord."

"Yes?"

"Give me the charge of bringing him in."

"Why do you hate him so much?"

"He's a viper in your bosom, my lord. Are you telling me I shouldn't hate him?"

"You hated him before you knew that."

"Give me some credit, my lord," Theodoric said coldly. "Consider the possibility that I've always known it."

I am considering it. I'm also considering how he shone at the Königsritt. *How everyone admired him. How the women, especially, admired him, and offered him their tokens. You are still worldly, Theodoric. Worldly in your pride, and in your flesh. You hate him because, as the world judges things, he has all its gifts, and you hunger for them entirely too much. In a part of your soul, you would still rather have his gifts than mine. Worse, for all your hatred, you do not see the danger in him, even now . . . .*

He placed a hand on Theo's shoulder.

"He will be lawfully taken and lawfully tried—not for personal vengeance, but for the honor and righteousness of God. And God's wrath is wrath enough for any man."

"And after he is tried?"

"I will fulfill the law. To the last word and letter. I will bring him to Babylon to the land of the Chaldeans; and he shall not see it, though he shall die there."

"My lord?"

The duke did not answer. He genuflected, and then turned and walked purposefully towards the door.

XXIII

THE QUEEN OF CAR-IDUNA

No man has ever beheld me but that I could have had his service.

WOLFRAM VON ESCHENBACH

THEY GATHERED IN THE HIGH-DOMED CHAMBER OF THE GODS, on the day which in the Christian world was called the Feast of Saint Callistus. It was mid-October, autumn in the Reinmark, but there were no seasons here, or rather, the seasons passed unmarked by the ordinary sun. The air was sweet with roses; the fountains laughed among budding gentians which would never see the fall of snow.

They were a fearsome gathering—or so the world would have judged it—for they were without exception women and men of extraordinary power. The aging Nine in their sheaths of silver, the Seven in arms, the Five young and eager to be proven, the Three without rank.

And she the One, crowned and potent, Lady of the Mountain, guardian of the Reinmark, keeper of the Grail of Life, Raven the sorceress, queen of Car-Iduna. She wore a gown of mottled and dissolving colors; gold wrapped her wrists and her loins; seven stones flashed rainbows from her hands. No person of her own world or the Other ever looked at her and judged her anything but beautiful. Only a few failed to entertain—at least for a few unguarded moments—some image of their own surrender, some wish to yield up whatever treasure they had to hand, in return for her favor, or even just the hope of it. She had many gifts, and this was not the least of them: she kindled desire in all its shapes and forms. She embodied it, and so held it out as infinite and barely imagined possibility.

They gathered in silence. They bowed to the Black Chalice high on its bier, the Grail of Life which Maris brought to safety from the vale of Dorn, so long ago that no one remembered exactly when, even in their stories. They bowed to their shimmering, power-wrapped queen. And then, with great solemnity, they closed the circle.

It was said that when they met so, storms broke across the empire, and ships went down at sea, and great men blundered into death, and even the pope could neither sleep nor pray. It was said also that the crops flourished after, and lovers were reconciled, and prisoners unexpectedly set free. But many things were said of Car-Iduna. Perhaps none of them were true, or perhaps they all were.

A small fire burned in a stone at the heart of their circle. Each one knelt, and cast into it an offering of their own choosing. Beside the fire was a flower-draped altar. Raven lifted from it the ceremonial cup, and the horn which lay over it, and held them between her jeweled hands.

Down through the years they thought of her more as veela than as woman. It was an easy mistake to make, for she had the Other-world's uncanny beauty, and powers far beyond the scope of ordinary human sorcery. But she had been bred of a human father—they remembered it quite clearly now—a black-haired man from the steppes, with a taste for wandering and strange adventures. He could neither stay with his inconstant mistress nor forget her, and so he came back, and came back again, haunting the wild Maren like a ghost, until time and despair took him to his death.

They watched her, and they remembered him now, and they knew. It was human eyes which held such bitter shadows, human fingers which closed around the cup like talons of steel. She had not slept for days. She had spent herself to breaking, and after all the reasons of politics and power had been accounted for, there was still another reason.

She raised the cup high. Her voice was harsh—and that, most of all, was how they knew.

"May the gods keep safe the world, and may the world keep safe the gods!"

They spoke after her, all of them, in a single voice:

"So let it be."

She dipped the horn into the cup and drank from it, and passed it on. The wine was dark and bitter.

She sought for words to begin, and could not find them. It was Aldis, first of the Nine, who finally spoke:

"Lady Raven, you have called us here for counsel. I know why, but some of us do not. And time is short now. Shall we not begin?"

"Yes," Raven said, and then still said nothing more.

What is power in the heart of the circle is death on the cliffs of the pyramid. I have always known that. But what are we to do who are caught between them?

She let her eyes travel around the circle. She did not love them all, but every one of them she trusted. She began then, quietly leaving nothing unsaid.

"I've tried, with all my strength and skill, to contact the count of Lys, and I cannot do so. Either Gottfried has cast a net around him more powerful than either of us can break . . . or else Karelian himself has turned against us, and refuses my command."

"Or he is dead," added Helrand, first of the Seven.

"No," she said. "If he were dead, I would know."

No one disagreed, though two or three of them exchanged glances of surprise. *So. It's as serious as that, then? She hasn't loved anyone for so long . . . but of course, those are always the ones who break their necks when they fall . . . .*

"There is more," she went on grimly. "Gottfried is riding north from Stavoren, with upwards of a thousand men. They are moving quickly, and they are armed for war. The ravens followed him deep into the pass of Dorn; he can be heading nowhere now except to Lys."

"Then it has begun," murmured Marius.

"If Gottfried is powerful enough to detect Karelian's bond with us," the queen went on, "and then to block our contact, even from the castle of Stavoren, then he is far more powerful than we knew, and the danger he presents is desperate."

"He may think he is a god," Aldis said archly. "I for one don't believe it. He doesn't have such power, lady."

"We never thought so," Raven agreed. "We may have been wrong."

"Wrong about him? Or wrong, perhaps, about our ally in Lys?"

There was a brief silence. They had all shared in the decision to lure Karelian to Helmardin, but it was Raven, most of all, who had insisted on it. It was Raven who had seen in his ensorceled image a man who could be won, a man already halfway theirs, who was skilful, and experienced, and dangerous. "He belongs to us!" she had insisted. "He is blood heir to all the great witches of Dorn, and soul heir to its enduring history of defiance. I tell you, he is ours!"

Aldis spoke again.

"Karelian Brandeis spent his life at war, serving any lord who'd offer him a place. Serving even in that utterly savage and unprovoked campaign of butchery they call their great crusade. And for his service there Duke Gottfried gave him Lys. Is it not so, Lady Raven?"

"It is."

"Then it's no great leap of the imagination, I think, to wonder if he has gone back to Gottfried's standard. Or indeed, if he ever left it. The great problem with turncoats, lady, is keeping track of how many times they've turned."

You objected to his coming from the first—you and Helrand both. His reasons I understand; he's a fighting cock like any other, and jealous of his place. But you are too old for such foolishness, and too wise . . . . Were you right then, from the start? Was I the fool? He was beautiful, tawny and proud-limbed as a stag. Was his beauty the only thing I saw?

"You may be right," the queen agreed. "But whatever the facts turn out to be, we must act now. If Gottfried is riding to war against the emperor, and if Karelian means to ride with him, then the Reinmark and all of Germany is at risk. And if Karelian is still loyal, then he must be warned, and if necessary, defended. We have to know. We can't stay here in Car-Iduna and wait for events to unravel."

"It is late in the year, lady," offered Riande, who like Helrand was one of the Seven, the warriors of Car-Iduna. "Too late, I would think, to begin a war against the emperor. And surely he won't take on King Ehrenfried with just a thousand men?"

"Well, he's not riding to Aachen, we may be sure of that," Helrand agreed. "An open uprising can't possibly succeed. He has no grounds for it, and no matter how many men he can put into the field from among his own allies, most of the German princes will oppose him. Whatever he is planning against Ehrenfried, I'm sure it's something different, and for that, a thousand men may be quite enough. Indeed, they may be too many.

"I won't pretend to know what the count of Lys is thinking, or where his loyalties are. But as for Gottfried, this sudden march to Lys does not strike me as the beginning of his rebellion. I think it has to do with affairs in the Reinmark itself—something between the duke and Karelian, or between them and someone else. Unfortunately, it was Karelian's task to tell us all these things, and he is silent.

"I agree with you in this much, lady. We can't wait any longer; we must act. Let me take a party to Lys—"

"You can't get there before Gottfried," Raven said grimly. "Not any more. He is two days' march away, or less."

"Two days? Perhaps an elf can ride across the Reinmark in two days, if he has a mind to. But no one else can."

"I can."

Every gaze fastened on her, each with a different, unbelieving look of protest.

"Lady," Helrand said, "there is but one way you can make so swift a journey, and if you choose that way, none of us can go with you. None of us have the power. And you can't possibly go into such danger alone."

"Can I not?"

"You are the queen," Aldis said grimly. "Your duty is to Car-Iduna. All your gifts were given you so you might keep this castle safe, and shield its powers!"

"I know my duty, by the gods!" the queen cried. "If all we were meant to do was shield the Grail, we wouldn't have it! The elves would, or the veelas. Their lairs are safer, and their hearts yield to nothing. But it was given to us, because we care about the world! Or we used to. What would you have us be now, lady Aldis—just a band of vine-draped sorcerers hiding in the woods?"

There was a long and painful silence.

"That was uncalled for, High One," the crone said quietly.

Raven looked at the Chalice before her, black as the fecund earth, studded with jewels, embracing the curved horn. In that image of female and male were the images of all difference, of all the divine contradictions which made possible the richness of the world.

"We had power once," she said. "All our kind, whether we came to our power by blood or by learning. The gifted ones, they called us, before the priests of the empire came, and claimed all our gifts for themselves. Or broke them.

"The world had a place for us. It had a place for many things— many gods, and many ways of knowing, and many kinds of truth. Now there is only one. One God, one priesthood, one people, one right way to pray and to think and to dress and to couple and to wipe your miserable nose.

"And for what? Love, they said, and promptly made love a crime. Peace, they said, and we have wars now such as Odin never dreamt of. There is no end to the empire's greed for land, and no bottom to Rome's craving for dominion in the empire. We've seen centuries of it, and we'll see more.

"Yet however ruinous it is to have Church and empire tearing the world apart between them, it will be worse if they are made one. That is what Gottfried von Heyden wants. And if it happens, then I think we'll all wish for chaos again, for priests and kings snarling at each other's throats. Whatever else, they check each other's power, and a few things slip from their grasp, and go free. When there is only one power left, and that one claims to speak for God—where does anyone turn then? Who will even believe, after a while, that any other kind of world is possible?

"Gottfried must be stopped, and I will leave nothing undone—nothing!—which may serve to bring him down!"

"You see the matter rightly lady," Aldis said. "But—"

"Then I am going to Lys. Whatever the duke's purpose is, he's moving with extraordinary speed. Why such haste, unless he knows we are watching him? Unless he's afraid we can still warn Karelian before he gets there?"

"You assume the count's innocence," Marius observed. He spoke without a hint of criticism in his voice; he was stating a simple fact.

"Yes," Raven said. "I do. And as for my being the queen, and having no right to fly off on such a reckless enterprise alone, I will say only this. It's true that I'm bound to protect Car-Iduna. From many things, my friends—and quite possibly from myself. Wait! This time you will listen till I'm finished.

"When we chose Karelian Brandeis for this task, to be our agent in the camp of the duke, some of you disagreed with our choice, and you had good reasons. Others of us, mostly for the same reasons, judged him the best man we could hope to find. I haven't wavered from my judgment."

She paused, looking from one to the other. Her voice softened to a riveting purr.

"Let me be very clear. I have no doubts about Karelian Brandeis. None whatever—and I have delved deep to find them. Yet neither fire, nor absinthe, nor dreams, nor the smallest whisper in my blood—nothing speaks of anything except his bond to me. I'm well aware of such facts as we have. I will say aloud that the harshest of your judgments may be right. But inside, I say no. Inside I know him as he is, my lover and my ally, a man I would trust with any weapon, and any secret. If he walked through the door this moment, it would scarcely matter what strange tale he might tell to explain his silence, I would believe it.

"So I will go to Lys. Because if I'm right, then he is truly one of us, and there's a bond between us worth saving at any price. And if I'm wrong . . . ."

She stood up, motioning them all to remain. "If I'm wrong, then my instincts are gone, and my judgment, and every claim I ever had to the wisdom of a sorceress. Then I no longer have the gifts of one who would be queen of Car-Iduna, and you should look to someone else."

They stared at each other, and some of them stared at the fire, or at the floor, but none of them disputed the truth of her words.

"Helrand," she added, "if you will bring a party to Lys, as quickly as you can, I would be grateful. Bring Marius, and as many of the Seven as you think best. And send word to Wulfstan, if you can find him; he has his own ties to the house of Dorn."

Aldis spoke again, with obvious reluctance.

"Lady, if you're determined to do this, and it seems you are, there is something we must know. What secrets and what powers have you entrusted to the count of Lys?"

"He knows how to find this castle. He has a talisman to summon me, without spells. He has healing potions, and all the charms against the weapons of enemies I could give him. And he has the shells of deception; I thought he might have need of them."

"The wyrdshells? You gave him those? Sweet gods of Valhalla, you have been generous!"

"Yes." To their considerable surprise, the queen of Car-Iduna smiled. "I tried to be. Now, let us unclose the circle, and be gone."

"You are too weary for this journey lady," Marius said.

She did not answer, but she made herself eat the food he placed carefully before her, and drink the potent brew of herbs.

"Why don't you sleep for a few hours?" he persisted. "You'll travel better for it after."

"If I *could* sleep, Marius, I would be tempted. But there's no hope of it. And you know that, so be quiet."

"Yes, lady. May I ask you something?"

"If I said no, you'd ask me anyway."

"Are you as sure of him as you said in council?"

"I'm not a fool," she said. "He may well have done exactly what Aldis thinks he's done: thought it over, and decided that a privileged place with the would-be king of the world might be a very nice place to have."

"And if it turns out to be so?"

She stopped eating, and he looked away.

"I'm sorry," he murmured. "I've said too much again, as usual."

"If it turns out to be so, then he'll wish he were still Gottfried's enemy instead of mine."

She drained the cup, and got slowly to her feet. "But I won't believe it until I must. And perhaps not even then."

"For what it's worth to you, lady. I liked him uncommonly well myself."

"You should learn to shape-shift," she said. "What good is a steward I have to leave behind whenever I'm in a hurry?"

He chuckled, but there was a note of sadness in it. "If I could shape-shift, I would soon find myself a better shape than this one, and keep it."

"You couldn't, my friend. When our strength fails we change back again, whether we want to or not. A great peril, that—and sometimes a great protection."

She wrapped her cloak around her shoulders. "I will see you in the vale of Lys."

He bowed his small, humped body very low. "Iduna keep you, Lady Raven." And then he walked with her to the east rampart of Car-Iduna, and watched as the autumn light around her melted and changed, and her cloak fell away, and the soft silk which draped her shimmered into blackness, blacker than her hair, a soft blur of blackness and smallness and power. And then she was no more. A raven stood there, perched for the briefest moment on the wall. Then it flew, making a slow spiral above the fortress, and turning southeastwards like an arrow.

For a time she was aware of the world below, of the rabbits and the birds; of the soft hum of life in the forests, and the passions in the houses of men. She was aware of the altars, Christian and pagan both, where the presence of their deities still lingered. She felt the quiet sorceries, fashioned over pools and fires and deathbeds, some evil and some good, all of them touching an echo in her, as images hit mirrors, seen but unchanged. The Reinmark was alive with mysteries, with hungerings and secrets, with dreams. In a peasant house, a girl-woman wound strands of her hair around the clasp of her lover's tunic, so he would not leave her. Priests blessed the filling granaries, and cast out devils from the sick, and the devils shrugged and looked for otherwhere to go. Old women rocked infants to sleep with tales of war among the gods, and young women begged fertility from the virgin of Jerusalem.

For a long time she heard their whisperings, and saw their ritual places, and felt the power in their yearnings. Then she grew weary, and no longer noticed. There was only distance in the world now, only forest and rivers and villages and endless forest again. She rested sometimes in the arms of a great tree, or on a high outcropping of rock, and while her body restored itself, her mind strained against the distance. She sought him, searching and hungering, and found only silence.

Karel, why? I gave you everything I promised you, and more. Why do you not answer me?

Finally, against her will, she had to return to human shape, and sleep. Thereafter she flew with all her strength, until at last the heights of the Schildberge lay to her right. She followed them for what seemed like hours. Late in the afternoon she saw, still far away, the first scattered villages as the land leveled off into the broad valley of the Maren. Rich fields followed, and high-steepled churches, then an abbey and winding roads scattered with carts and horsemen. All this was the domain of Lys: Karelian's lands, Karelian's forests, Karelian's vassals in their walled manors and quiet, tucked-in towns. And still he did not answer her.

It was half-dusk when she came over the last of many woodlands and saw the town of Lys itself, and some leagues beyond it, the famous manor of its lord.

Had she not been so weary, she would have known before she saw the place that Gottfried was already there. She would have felt his presence a thousand times more strongly than the small sorceries of the common folk, or the god-breaths from their altars. But she was spent to exhaustion; every fragment of her strength was pounding in her wings, holding in the boundaries of her altered self.

So she saw it unexpecting: the great field of tents, the cook-fires of fighting men, the guarded enclosures filled with huddled people, too far away to identify even as male or female, only as heaps of ragged fear.

The ravens.

Not the ravens of Helmardin, who served her, but the common ravens of the world, circling idly, resentfully, waiting for the endless coming and going of men and horses to stop, for the dead to be abandoned. They lay in piles outside the walls of the manor, quietly guarded until the living would have time to bury them.

Inside, in the heart of its stables and granaries and tanneries and huts, the splendid great-house of the lord of Lys still smoldered in its ruins.

XXIV

IN THE SCHILDBERGE

And imagine to yourself just how ridiculous,
how completely monstrous it is to be in love.

ERASMUS

WE WERE HUNTING THE DAY GOTTFRIED CAME TO LYS—hunting
in the hills below the great fortress of Schildberge. It was one
of the most famous warrior castles of the empire, built more than a
hundred years before by Otto the Great. In those years the Maren
had been his eastern border—by summer a highway for Danish warships, by winter a frozen plain over which any army could march,
without so much as a tree to bar the way.

Now a different and distant river lay at the edges of Christendom,
between the hunger of the west for dominion, and the hunger of the
east for land. But the great fortress remained, built on a splendid and
solitary cliff, with a single narrow road climbing hard to its gates.
From its seven towers, Otto once boasted, a hundred men could hold
off an army. He called it the Shield of the Reinmark, and in a strange
reversal of custom, the mountains came to be named for the castle
built among them.

They were not high mountains, as Germans would judge the matter: nothing like the Alps, or even the Pyrenees. But they were wild
and unpredictable, given to strange storms and stranger legends. Men
tended to avoid them, as they avoided the forest of Helmardin.

They were pretty that day. Above Karelian's fortress the sky was
blue and clear. And on the mountain beneath it, the wind-twisted firs

stood almost black among faces of grey rock and scatterings of flowers. The flowers were the last of the season, bright flashes of color rivaled by the first turning leaves.

It was a splendid day, chilly with the first taste of autumn, but invigorating; a day when ordinary folk could ride and sing and laugh without a care in the world, simply for the pleasure of being alive. But I was sorely troubled. It was growing harder and harder to live divided as I was, committed to God and bound to Karelian, torn apart with guilt no matter what I did.

Earlier in this chronicle, I said he did not change at all, but it isn't really true. He was strengthening in evil, shoring up the walls of his soul even as he strengthened the castles of his domain, using the power of his rank to fashion himself a world where God mattered less and less. And he was enjoying it, taking pleasure in what he thought of as his freedom. I think it was the hardest thing of all for me to bear—that he felt no guilt. I, who tried so hard to be good, suffered such unbearable distress, while he, having sold his soul, had no regrets at all.

We hunted all morning, and then as the sun turned westerly we built a great fire to roast the rabbits we had killed, and warmed ourselves around it, and told stories. Except for myself, everyone was in the best of spirits, especially the countess Adelaide. Frail though she was, she loved to ride and hunt. The wind and the open sky put color in her face, and the closest thing to happiness any of us ever saw in her eyes.

Father Thomas slid off his horse with some difficulty, and sank against the trunk of the nearest tree.

"A pleasant little rabbit shoot you called this, my lord? Really I'm half starved, and I'm cold, and I'm covered with bruises. If you ever undertake a journey you expect to be *un*pleasant, please don't invite me along."

Karelian laughed, and pulled a flask of mead from his saddle pack. It was good mead, sweet and strong, passed from hand to hand without much regard for rank, until it was gone. By then the fire was roaring and the rabbits spitted and beginning to turn brown. Thomas felt much better.

"The trouble with you, Thomas," Karelian said, "is you spend too much time with your books and your lyre."

"No, my lord. I don't. The trouble is, there isn't enough time in the world. A man ought to have all the time he wants for books, and time for hunting, too. Unfortunately, God decided otherwise."

"You should become an elf," the countess said lightly. "Then you'd live for hundreds of years, and have time enough for everything."

"I know a marvelous tale about a man who became an elf," the priest said. "And it's from these mountains, too. From the Schildberge."

"Is there any place from where you *don't* know a marvelous tale?" Reinhard asked dryly.

"Oh, one or two, perhaps. But in the Schildberge are the lairs of the hunter elves—the caves where they first were made, and where they go to die. Did you know that?"

Adelaide's pale face went rigid—all except her eyes, which leapt towards Thomas with the quickness and ferocity of an arrow. Only those of us who had made the journey from Ravensbruck knew why—Reini and Otto and me. And Karelian, who looked darkly at the priest, and then at the fire. I thought for a moment he might silence the storyteller, but it was too late. Thomas had already begun.

"They say there is one among the hunter elves who was born human," he was saying. "I won't claim it's true, for it's difficult to know how such a thing is possible. But I'll tell you the story, and you may judge it for yourselves.

"You all know, of course, about the great massacre at Dorn, when the soldiers of Henry the Second wiped out the last supporters of the Saxon rebel Wulfstan. Wulfstan himself had been flayed and hanged outside the castle gates the summer before, and his body carried in a cart through all the valley for everyone to see—a stupid thing it was, for it only made the resistance worse. So in the end they put all of Dorn to the sword. All the pagans were killed, as well as many Christians who were their friends and kinsmen. And the emperor's men rode on towards Ravensbruck to deal with some trouble there, and disappeared in the forest of Helmardin, and were never seen again."

"But some of the pagans from Dorn survived," Karelian said. "They fled into the mountains—or so it was always said, though no one knew what became of them after."

"Yes. There were three, according to this story. Two men, whose names were Rudolf and Widemar, and a woman named Alanas, who was Wulfstan's wife; she was a priestess and a witch. They lived for a time in great misery, for they had nothing but the garments on their backs, and Widemar was injured, and the woman was with child. And by October it was already snowing in the mountains. It was a fell year, when even strong men died of cold."

I will give Thomas credit for one thing: his voice was riveting. He could tell a story so it came to life all around you. If he spoke of a cold wind blowing, you felt it shiver on your neck; if he spoke of treachery, your own hand crept unwitting to your sword, as if to ward off a secret blow.

"One night," he went on, "in a bitter storm, Widemar gave up his soul to death, and they could do nothing but leave him for the wolves. Sick of heart, and certain they would die before the morning, the others went deep into a ravine, hoping to find a bit of shelter from the wind. And they saw, faintly through the trees, a glow of light, muted and faint. They sought it out, not caring whose it might be; it was their only hope of life.

"The light came from deep inside a cave. It was a cave such as you and I have never seen, for the floors and walls were all of polished stone, like the inside of a great cathedral, and the fire which burned there gave no smoke. It was empty, but it was clearly inhabited; cloaks and weapons hung on the wall, and there were fresh-killed rabbits lying by the fire, waiting to be skinned and roasted.

"Needless to say the fugitives did not ask whose cave it was, or whose meat. They warmed themselves and ate like ravens. But the shelter came too late for Alanas. In the night she gave birth to her child, and died of her bearing. Rudolf put the babe beneath his cloak and fell asleep, exhausted. When he woke the elves had returned, and stood before him with their swords in their hands.

"Now elves are very proud, and hunter elves more than any. It's a very foolish human who goes into their demesnes uninvited, and eats their food, and scatters about the disorder of a birthing and a death. They were all for killing Rudolf, or at the very least driving him out to starve, when the child was wakened by their voices and began to cry 'What is that?' demanded the elf leader. Rudolf took out the babe to show to them, a boy-child, fair-haired and beautiful. 'Who does it belong to?' asked the elf. 'It is the son of the woman who died,' he said, 'and of Wulfstan the Saxon.'

"Elves have few children, as you know, because they live so long. And those they father on the veelas they can't keep; the nymphs will never give them up. So they take human babies when they can, and raise them, and teach them to hunt and to ride the night wind. They feed them on nothing but flesh, and the spirits they make from bracken, so they grow lean and fierce, and can see in the dark, and become in every way like elves, except they have a human life span, and the hunger for a human mate. Or at least, that's what is said."

"Pagan rubbish," one of the knights said. "It makes for great storytelling," he added quickly as several faces turned to him at once, all of them scowling. "But there are no such creatures, and never have been."

"Who can tell?" the priest replied amiably. "In my father's house, they say, are many mansions—"

"Please," said the countess. "Go on with the story."

He bowed towards her, faintly.

"Thank you, my lady. Rudolf knew he was in the greatest danger. So he tried to bargain with the elves: 'Let me shelter here for the winter,' he pleaded, 'myself and the child. I'll be your servant, and do whatever tasks you set me. I'll fetch the wood, and make the fires. I'll mend your garments and your bows. I'll do anything you wish. In the spring, when the snow is gone, we'll go away and leave you in peace.'

" 'We have no need of servants,' the elf said. 'We would scarcely trust a human among our sacred trees with an axe, and as for mending our bows, they don't break. You have only one thing we want. Let us have the child to raise, and you may live. We'll let you keep this cave; we have many others. We'll hunt for you and bring you game, until the winter breaks. Then you must go and not come back.'

"Rudolf had no choice but to agree. The elves took the infant, and went away. True to their word, they brought him food, and so he lived all winter in the cave, sharing their bounty. But he never saw them again. They would leave their kills outside the cave, silently and the wind would cover their tracks. When the spring returned, they were gone. They vanished as only those of the Otherworld can vanish, without a trace, almost without a memory. I don't know if Rudolf grieved because the child was gone forever, or if he thought it for the best, for the story says no more of him.

"The child of Wulfstan grew up fierce and brave. His human name was that of his father, which Rudolf gave him, but what the elves called him is known to no one. He loved the forest, and the life of the wild hunters. They taught him everything they knew, and soon he was as skilful as they were. But he aged quickly like a human, and he was flaxen haired and fair beside those dark and secret bodies. And they laughed at him for it. 'Look at you,' they said. 'A star's light is enough to see you by. You might as well go hunting with torches and shawms as with that hair of yours.' "

Otto interrupted the storytelling with a rough chuckle. "He may have been a hunter, that one, but he was no fighting man. It's a simple enough thing to spread your hair and face with dirt for camouflage."

"Aye, it is," Father Thomas agreed. "But no elf ever born would lower himself so. They are beautiful and proud. They would die before they'd make themselves dirty on purpose.

"There was only one thing for the lad. He began to dream of becoming an elf. A real elf. Needless to say he didn't tell his comrades, for they would have laughed all the more. He left the mountains and came down to the Maren, to search for the veelas, who were said to have many strange and magical powers. He found one soon enough, for he was half grown by then, and singularly beautiful. She followed him, and courted him, and offered to pleasure him as much as he wished.

"He was dreadfully tempted, but he refused to lay with her until she made him a gift. 'So be it,' she said. 'I will make you any gift you like. You please me very well.'

"So he said to her: 'I want to be an elf.' She laughed so hard she fell into the river. But she wanted him nonetheless. We know how determined a woman can be when she chooses a man. Imagine then what a veela is like. It's said they will tear down mountains, and overturn castles, and stop armies in their tracks . . . what's the matter, Pauli? Do you doubt the powers of the female?"

"Not in the least, Father Thomas," I said. And I tried to compose my face, for I was thinking of Helmardin, of how beautiful she had been, how resolute. How little chance Karelian ever had.

"Well," the priest went on, "the lad was stubborn, as heroes must be. Finally she stopped laughing, and grew angry with him. 'You're a fool,' she said. 'Do you really imagine I have the power to make you into an elf? No one could do that except the gods!' 'Well then,' he said, 'you must tell me how to summon the gods.'

"Weeks passed, and the lad would not give up; so at last she showed him how to make an altar, and what sacrifices he must bring, and what spells to cast upon them, and all the other things which only veelas know. And he called forth Tyr the hunter, who is the keeper of the elves. Some say great Tyr appeared as a stag, and others say he came as wind, or marsh lights, or mounted on the clouds, which shimmered with a strange orange light. But come he did, and he spoke to the son of Wulfstan the Saxon:

" 'What you ask of me,' he said, 'is only half possible. I can give you an elf's appearance, and an elf's great speed, and the years of living which make human life seem as brief as a whisper. But you have grown up human, and I can't undo it. You will never love as elves do, but as a man. You will suffer always from the passions of the world; you will never stop caring what becomes of it. You will dream of the smiles of women. You will give life to the sons and daughters of Wulfstan the Saxon and Alanas the priestess of Tyr. They will scatter across the forests of the Reinmark, and beyond its borders, for years yet uncounted, until the gods take back their own. Such is your gift, hunter elf . . . and my justice.' "

Silence fell, briefly but absolutely. I could not help but look at Karelian, wondering what he might be thinking, wondering what possessed Father Thomas to tell such a tale, to such a man, in such a circumstance as his. There was a black-haired bastard in my lord's own house, after all, fathered by Rudolf of Selven. And many said Rudolf himself was the secret offspring of an elf . . . .

"Priest," Otto said grimly, "you have an overworked imagination and an undisciplined tongue."

"Granted," Thomas said. "Is there a storyteller in all the world who doesn't?"

He took a bite of rabbit, and added softly: "I didn't make the tale up, Sir Otto. Go to Dorn, and ask the people there—the ones who'll still talk about such things. Ask the mountain folk—"

"They're a bunch of superstitious fools—!"

"That's enough, Otto," Karelian said. "I have no quarrel with the friar's storytelling. Nor should you."

He smiled, and if the smile was a trifle forced, it was nonetheless warm. Deliberate. *I make my own judgments now; I decide what offends me, and what doesn't . . . .*

And then a thought struck me, one of those thoughts which always came out of the darkest terrors of my soul, which I never wanted to think or to believe, but which came to me nonetheless. Perhaps the story didn't trouble him because there was more to the story—things he already knew, and we did not? Suppose Adelaide had not been guilty of ordinary adultery? Suppose Rudolf of Selven had been a sorcerer, or something worse? And suppose the child, dear God, the child . . . ? Why was Karelian keeping it, raising it? Why would any man keep another man's bastard, when he knew the truth about it, when the whole world knew, when the child looked exactly like the dark villain who had fathered him? Was there some kind of pact, some dreadful purpose to be fulfilled?

I gave the half-eaten haunch of rabbit in my hand to one of the dogs, and fled into the trees, fighting nausea. I tried to put the questions out of my mind, but I could only halfway manage it. I could only halfway still believe the world was rational and ordered, like my father thought—full of trouble and evil, yes, but still rational and ordered. My father would have laughed at my questions. He would have howled with laughter, and then boxed my ears and told me to go and work it off in the barracks yard.

"You dream too much," he told me when I saw him last, before I went to Gottfried. "I thought going to the Holy Land would show you something of the world, and make a man of you. In truth, I think you've gotten sillier . . . ."

My father knew exactly why Karelian was keeping Adelaide, and apparently keeping her child. Karelian was almost forty, and in love, and passion had made him soft. It was obvious, so obvious that every man in Germany understood it. They laughed at it, or shrugged at it, or admired it, but they were certain they understood.

"It's not your affair," my father reminded me bluntly. "Don't forget it, lad, and don't presume. You must learn to keep your place."

My father was a wise man, but it was the wisdom of the world, and I was losing patience with it. Why should I keep my place? Why should I keep pretending I had no conscience, and no eyes? Why should men like Karelian have so much power, and men like Gottfried so little?

I never heard his steps. The ground was dry, and scattered with leaves and fallen branches, and yet I never heard his steps. Only his voice, soft and troubled, not an arm's reach from my shoulder.

"Pauli."

I spun about, startled, reaching for my sword, and caught myself before I could draw it.

"My lord . . . ! Forgive me, my lord, I didn't hear you. I was lost in my thoughts—"

"Yes, I can see that."

He had left his cloak by the campfire. His hair seemed to flicker different colors as he moved, brown and gold and ochre, hair made of light and October leaves and the soft back of a running stag.

My glance shifted, caught by the high, sharp line of his cheekbone. I saw it as I imagined a painter would see it, perfect, so perfect the brush would surely linger there, and go over it and over it and never get it right. I looked away again and saw his eyes, not blue as northern eyes mostly were, but hazel mottled with green. I saw his body, the jeweled belt clasping his tunic at the waist, the hard belly and the splendid thighs of a horseman, all a blur of blue silk and brown leather which dissolved in my own sudden and burning loss of sight. Men described him as kingly, after, in the war. But he was never so to me. He had about him nothing of a king's distance, or a king's sense of destiny. All of his power was personal. He was a soldier and a sorcerer; I had loved the one and learned to fear the other, but always the man himself seemed in reach of my hand.

"What happened in Ardiun?" he asked softly.

"Ardiun?" I stared at him, completely bewildered. His tunic was open at the neck; I saw the thong which held the pouch I had made. I wondered what else besides my cross was hidden there.

"You've been brooding ever since you came back from your father's house, Pauli. What happened there?"

"Nothing happened, my lord."

He made a small gesture. "Well, I won't pry. But you're less than good company of late, lad, and I'm not the only one who thinks so."

My head cleared sufficiently to frighten me. It was unwise to draw attention to myself. And since I had already done so, I knew I had to offer him a reason for it.

I turned away. I hated lying, and so I mixed lies and truth as carefully as I could.

"My father is . . . disappointed in me, my lord."

"Disappointed? Why? What on earth does he expect?"

"I'm not sure, my lord. He's always thought me somewhat . . . soft. He hasn't actually come out and said so, but he thinks I should be a knight by now, and have some laurels, maybe even a small fief. He made a point of reminding me that my master was the youngest son, not the second eldest like myself, and nonetheless was knighted at sixteen."

"Your master was a savage at sixteen, Pauli. Starving for glory and too angry to think straight. I wouldn't want you or anyone else to be like him."

I forgot myself, and stared at him. He smiled.

"I've surprised you again, I see," he said. "Since we're sharing histories, let me remind you of mine. My mother had two stillborn sons before me, and three daughters. By the time I was born she meant nothing to my father, and neither did her children. After all, he already had eleven others—six of them healthy boys.

"When I was a child, my eldest brothers were grown men. They hated my mother, and they took their hatred out on me. She was beautiful and clever, and she knew it. Her children were of no dynastic worth, perhaps, but they were special; she knew that, too. We had her beauty and her courage, and our father's Brandeis passions, and the whole house of Dorn's legendary talent for getting into trouble. We were the best of the brood. But we had nothing, not even safety in our own house. I learned fast, Pauli. I had to, if I wanted to survive. So yes, I was knighted at sixteen.

"And I spent most of my life thereafter proving that I was worth as much as my brothers were. That I had a right to a piece of land and a woman and a future, just like the precious heirs. And yes, I proved it all, though my mother never lived long enough to see it. Nor did most of my friends.

"No doubt your father is impressed, and holds me up as some kind of shining example of what young men should achieve. But the truth is, Pauli, if I could go back to being sixteen, I wouldn't do it again."

"What would you do, my lord?" I whispered.

"I'm not sure. Probably wander around by the Maren, and see if I could get myself changed into an elf."

He laughed as he said it. He was jesting, but not entirely; under the jest was a hard kernel of pure, unflinching rebellion.

"Don't take your father's words too much to heart," he said. "I have nothing but good to say about your service—and if you wish, I'll write to him and tell him so."

I was all but overcome with guilt, and the pain of it made me reckless.

"Will you knight me, then, my lord? I don't want a fief, I haven't earned it, but if I were at least a knight . . . !"

If I were at least a knight, perhaps Gottfried would not think me just a foolish boy; perhaps the warrior monks of Saint David would accept me into their ranks.

He was silent for a moment, and then he shook his head. "You're not ready."

"You agree with my father, then," I said bitterly.

"No. It has nothing to do with that."

"Then what has it to do with?"

He seemed to have no answer—at least no answer he would tell me to my face. And I struck out at him then. Anything seemed better than going on as I was. Anything, even his hatred. Even dismissal and disgrace.

"Do you imagine I will change my mind one day, my lord? If you keep me beside you long enough, and close enough?"

"Change your mind—?" The words broke off in mid-breath, as if silenced with a club. He went pale. I faltered a little, afraid he would do something terrible. But he only stared at me for a time, and then threw out one hand in a frustrated, empty gesture.

"God, you can be a fool sometimes," he said. And turned, and walked back to the camp.

And I reached—no one saw me but God—I reached towards him with both hands, blind and despairing and without thought, trying to call him back, to wind my fingers finally and forever in the mortal fires of his hair.

I walked deep into the trees, until I was certain no one could see me, and I slashed a sturdy branch from a birch tree, and took off my leather hauberk, and flogged myself across the shoulders until I could not bear it any more. It did not help at all.

It was then, I think, when I first decided I would be a monk. I would put an end to this, and live out my life as far from the world and its temptations as I could go. I might have gone that very afternoon—simply climbed on my horse and ridden away, abandoning Karelian and Gottfried alike, and my father too: *Think what you please, my lords, farewell . . . .*

Only they were shouting for me, and even I could hear the urgency in their voices. Someone was yelling, "The duke! It's the duke!" I ran back to the camp with my heart in my throat, and saw them clustered, staring across the valley.

And oh, it was lovely! It was what I had longed for, night after desolate night, wondering if any of my dreams could yet be real. Wondering if he would ever come, if there would ever be the kingdom he was born to conquer.

We were far away, an hour's ride, or more; they were only dust at this distance, dust and high-borne banners and the silver glint of armor in the sun. My shame dissolved, my despair, my longing for the silence of a cloister. There was, after all, another way to master the demons of the world.

Gottfried was riding to war.

XXV

THE WARRIOR

I ride through a dark, dark land by night . . . .

LUDWIG UHLAND

KARELIAN STOOD WITH A HANDFUL OF HIS MEN on a high knoll, reduced to silence by the scene in the valley below.

"He rides with half an army, my lord," Reinhard said. He frowned, turning towards the count. "And in full armor, too. What can it mean?"

"Wends or Prussians is what it means," Otto said grimly.

The seneschal shook his head. "We would have heard. We would have heard before he did, being closer to the borders. It took him some time to gather so many men, and march them through the Schildberge."

Otto did not answer. He had spoken out of malice and old, established prejudices. He knew Reinhard was right.

"There is war in the empire," Reinhard went on. "It can be nothing else."

He looked at Karelian, who looked only at the ranks of men moving in dark waves across the broad vale of Lys, glinting with armor in the afternoon sun.

Why wasn't I warned?

Leaves crunched softly as Adelaide edged her way to his side.

"Is it really the duke, my lord?" she asked. Although the sun was behind them, she was shielding her eyes with her hand, trying to see. Her vision had always been poor; probably the fields below held only a vaguely moving blur.

"Yes. It's Gottfried."

"It's a splendid sight, lady," her maid Matilde offered cheerfully. "They have hundreds of banners, and the most magnificent horses."

"He came to Ravensbruck once," Adelaide said. "I thought he was the king."

She slid her arm around Karelian's waist. Perhaps—strange, uncanny creature that she was—perhaps she read his fear then, just from touching him. Or perhaps, being the daughter of Arnulf of Ravensbruck, she knew armies such as this one never marched except to war. She went very quiet, and when he looked at her, there was neither light nor color in her face.

"You're leaving," she said.

"I may have to."

"Don't." She spoke softly without emotion. "Not with them."

He saw Otto and Reinhard exchanging quick looks—looks he recognized all too well. *Think what you like, my friends; but this time I'll wager her instincts are sounder than yours.*

"Reini," he said sharply. "A word."

He motioned the seneschal to follow him, and moved a distance down the hill. Below, the duke's men still advanced, less than a mile now from the manor house of Lys. Reinhard chewed thoughtfully on his lip.

"It's strange, my lord, that he sent no heralds."

"Nor did my border guards," Karelian added. "And that is stranger still."

As for my lady's silence, that is the strangest of all. Perhaps it was all a dream, and there are no gods, and this is just another war . . . .

"Reini, I have a task for you. You're not going to like it much, I fear, but if you ever loved me, or thought me worthy of your service, you will do it. Without much argument, for we don't have much time."

"I'm at your command, my lord."

"Take the countess to Schildberge castle, and send someone to fetch the babe, and bring him there, too. You're castellan from this moment on. You will take command of all defenses, and you will surrender to no one, not to the duke nor to God himself, as long as you have the smallest hope that I'm alive."

"My good lord—!"

"Wait! I'm not finished! I have no right to ask you more, but I will. If I'm killed, try to get Adelaide and her child to some kind of safety. She has no kin now, and no protectors."

"If you will forgive me for saying so, my lord, that misfortune is entirely of her own making."

"Perhaps. The world will say the same of me. Your word, Reini— will you do it? There is no one else I can trust as much as you."

The seneschal met his eye levelly. He was a plain man, plainly made and plainly spoken. But his eyes just then were wet.

"Then I, more than anyone, should be by your side."

"No," Karelian said. "One man more or less by my side—even the best of men—will not matter much. The fortress may matter desperately."

He looked again towards Gottfried's glittering advance.

"Gather the men now and go. I'll take Pauli and Otto with me; you take the others."

The seneschal stepped boldly and yet uncertainly into his path. "Wait! My lord, may I speak freely?"

"When have you ever done otherwise?"

"There is something wrong, isn't there? Something you won't speak of? You make these plans as if you were riding to your death!"

"Wars are always dangerous."

"We've been in many. Even I can see this one looks different." Reinhard hesitated, and then said outright, harshly:

"You don't trust him much, I think. The Golden Duke."

Trust him? I trust the devil better, and the paid cutthroats in the gutters of Karn.

"Reini, I don't know why he's come, or where we're going. I don't know who he means to fight. That's reason enough to be uneasy. But there is more. I can't tell you anything, just now, but there is more."

He held out his hand. "I hope we meet again, my friend. But if not, then I thank you, and farewell."

Adelaide did not weep. She kissed him without passion, and smiled without meaning it. Her eyes were empty. She had dared, for a little while, to trust him, and now he was going away. They all went away or were killed or were left behind, everyone beautiful, everyone who mattered. Rudi was murdered and gone, and all the dark elves were fled. Sigune was alone in Ravensbruck; sick, they said, and maybe dying. And now Karelian was going, too. He tried to lie, to make it seem like a small thing, a three-day raid on an unimportant enemy, but she had seen the duke's army, and she had felt their power, felt it like a cold fog rising out of the valley. They cared nothing for her lord, or for her, not even the small bit that Arnulf of Ravensbruck had once cared.

"You will come back to me, my lord?" she whispered. "You'll come back safe?"

"Of course I will," he said.

He only half believed it, and she did not believe it at all.

He stood alone and silent after the others were gone. There was no time to make even the smallest sacrifice, to attempt even the simplest divination. Yet he stood nonetheless, impotent as a five-year-old, and entirely aware of it, waiting for someone to tell him what to do. Tyr, or Raven, or the wind or a blade of grass or a bird. Or his own utterly divided judgment, which commanded him in one heartbeat to flee, and in the next to ride smiling into Gottfried's mailed embrace.

You are a sorcerer, too. So Raven had assured him, in those days by the Maren. *All these years you never guessed it. You called it instinct, and your soldier comrades called it luck, and your enemies probably called it the devil's favor. But you always acted faster than you could think, and judged better than the evidence allowed for. Gottfried honed his gifts, and you did not, but you have them just the same.*

All his gifts—whatever gifts they were—told him something was desperately wrong. Yet what it might be eluded him entirely. Gottfried's unannounced arrival, in the full panoply of war, could mean absolutely anything: he might be riding against a rebellious vassal or rising in mutiny against the king.

Or else he has come to cut my throat . . . .

A real possibility, Karelian thought, and every bit as likely as the others. Why had the duke sent no word of his approach? Haste did not explain it, at least not if he expected his warleader to join him on the march. Karelian would need some time to gather and mobilize his own men; all the more reason, then, to send a messenger ahead.

But if there was danger, why had Raven not warned him?

He looked at the sky. It had been easy, on the banks of the Maren, to believe in her power, and in her gods. Now they both seemed very far away, and the world a mere world of men, violent, unpredictable, and irremediably unsafe.

He wiped his arm across his face. There was no help for it. Whatever the risks, he had to ride down and meet his lord. He could not throw away the alliance Gottfried had offered him, the singular opportunity to be the sword of his grand ambition, and the unexpected dagger in his heart. He had to stay with Gottfried until he had a reason not to, and he had no reason yet. None at all, except the ice in his blood, and the ashes in his throat.

Do I fear because there is something real to fear? Or only because I am his enemy? Men with secrets always jump at shadows. He cannot know my heart, except by sorcery, and then he would have known it from the first, and never invited me to join him.

Raven, why don't you answer me?

He opened the pouch which hung about his neck. He touched the feather lightly, but he left it there, and took out the small egg-shaped shells. "The red is of wolfsblood," she had told him; "the green is of thorn; the black is the belly of the world. They say the first of these were made by Gullveig, before the days of men, and used in the great war between the Vanir and the Aesir."

He asked what they were for, but she had only smiled and kissed him. "When you need them," she said, "you will know."

He slipped them into the packet at his belt, in easy reach. He glanced once, regretfully, towards Schildberge fortress, and mounted his horse, remembering his own words to Pauli, just a little while ago, on the house of Dorn's legendary capacity for getting into trouble. And then he laughed softly. What else was there to do but laugh, riding into the teeth of a thousand spears, without so much as armor on his back, with nothing but these trinkets and a sword?

The army waited in unbroken ranks outside the walls of the manor, mounted, like men who had come to settle something briefly and then ride on. Inside the gates, more knights filled the courtyard with rings of iron shields and iron spears. At their head, towering and utterly magnificent, was the Golden Duke.

It was clear he had not come as a guest. The house guards would have rushed out to greet him, would have offered to take his horse and escort him into the manor, would have plied him with wine and food and any comfort he might have wished. He had obviously refused all their offers. He had not even dismounted.

Otto, riding close at Karelian's side, was a trifle sweaty at the temples.

"Were you not his lordship's favorite vassal, and his kinsman, I confess I wouldn't like the look of this."

"I don't like it in any case," Karelian said.

Nonetheless he went on, until he had ridden through the gates and the two lords were a dozen feet apart. Still no word had been offered, and no gesture—not a hint of greeting or a whisper of hostility. The duke waited like a god. A red and quickly falling sun shot flashes of crimson off his helm, and gave his white surcoat a majestic hint of gold.

Karelian smiled and bowed deeply, but he did not dismount, either. "My good lord, welcome!"

He met Gottfried's eyes, and then he knew.

He let his gaze flicker briefly to the stern-faced men at Gottfried's side. The duke's standard-bearer and three of his escort wore the insignia of the Knights of Saint David, God's new soldiers, sworn to obedience, chastity, and the service of the Church. Holy men in arms. All four were thin-faced and young, with wintry eyes which seemed to hunger for religious death.

And I rode right into their hands . . . .

He could not entirely believe it. He had come here of his own choosing. An hour ago he had been free, and out of reach. By sheerest chance Gottfried had arrived to find him gone, and he, out of his own blind folly and defiance, had thrown that gift of chance away.

"Was the hunting good, kinsman?" Gottfried asked.

"It was exceptional, my lord."

"And your fair lady Adelaide? Why did she not come to greet me? I've heard so much about her; I was quite looking forward to it."

So. First the knives, my godly lord, and then the axe . . . .

"We saw your host, my lord. It seemed obvious there is war at hand, so I sent her to my fortress. Where she will be safe."

"The fortress is no longer yours, Karelian; nor is the county of Lys. You will accompany me to Stavoren to stand trial. Herald, read out the charges, so when the citizens of Lys see their lord carried off in irons, they will know the reason why."

A man moved forward from Gottfried's ranks and stood beside his lord. He unrolled a parchment, but he spoke as though he knew every word by heart.

"Karelian Brandeis, heretofore count of Lys, you stand accused before all of Christendom as an apostate, a sorcerer, and a traitor against your lawful lord. You are from this moment placed under arrest, and hereafter shall be brought before the ducal court at Stavoren for judgment. You will now yield up your weapons, and accompany us, or you will be taken hence by force."

"You have no grounds for this!" Karelian cried savagely. "I've done nothing against you!"

"You offered sacrifice to pagan gods, and bound yourself to the witch of Car-Iduna. You promised her my death."

Karelian laughed. "Is that all? Who told you this drivel, my lord,

and how much did you pay him? Pay him a bit more, he'll tell you
I have a horse that flies, and a candlestick that farts, and a dog that
says the Credo backwards!"

The young standard-bearer lunged forward, gripping the pole of
the banner with both hands and driving it savagely into Karelian's
midsection. He buckled over the horse's neck, vomiting, and the wood
clubbed a second time against the side of his face.

"Enough," Gottfried said. "He will be treated like a nobleman
until he has been tried. After that . . . ."

Karelian straightened, slowly and painfully. The white-clad knight
leaned close again, spotting the thong around his neck.

"Ha! And what sacred relic is this, I wonder?" He reached, as
the count was still reeling, and slashed it free.

And the power of Car-Iduna exploded out of the forests of Helmardin, out of the wild-running Maren, out of the sky and the wind
and the trees. A thousand searchings, circling and crying, hit against
a sudden emptiness and shot through it, like lightning through a crack
of sky, and found him. The impact was almost physical, too brief to
identify, but he knew it for sorcery, some kind of sorcery, Raven's
creatures, Raven herself perhaps, reaching out to him with a driven,
single-minded power. It only lasted for a moment, before the crack
was closed again. But the moment was enough for him to know, and
knowing was enough to make him fight.

The young knight of Saint David tore open the pouch, and pulled
out the raven's feather, holding it up triumphantly:

"Look, my lord! Where we bear a cross, he bears the token of
Odin!"

Karelian laughed—for whatever else they were, they were a pack
of fools—and then he flung the red shell down among them. It
smashed into fragments, and out of every scattering fragment leapt a
wolf. One after another they leapt, already ravening, wolves of some
other, darker world, black and lean, wild with a thousand years of
hunger. They leapt for the throats of horses, for the flailing arms of
knights with swords and crossbows. Men and animals screamed, colliding and falling in their panic. Karelian drove at the white knight's
rearing horse, and in a single motion swept away his shield and
slammed it into the face of another who came at him. A black mass
leapt past him. The young knight screamed as a wolf sprang upon his
thigh, its jaws closing through ring mail as if it were parchment. Karelian snatched pouch and feather from his hand, drew his sword, and
wheeled his mount towards the gates.

He had been in a thousand fights, and most of them were chaos. But he had never been in a fight more mad than this one. Sometimes he could do nothing at all except try to control his plunging horse. That it did not fling him into some enemy's flailing sword, or into the path of a panic-fired arrow, he could credit only to blind luck, or to his lady's astonishing magic. He saw Otto from time to time, fighting desperately beyond his reach. He saw the manor's house-guard in the thick of it. The serfs had mostly fled, but some were throwing rocks, and running at Gottfried's fallen men with clubs. And all of it fed his black and singing fury. He had neither helmet nor armor, only his sword and the shield he had snatched in the fray, yet men were falling back from him—falling back or going down. He caught the full sweep of a mace on his shield; he leaned forward and struck, and the mace-wielder tumbled over the neck of his horse, and disappeared among the wolves and trampling hoofs. Karelian laughed. Even chaos no longer mattered. He was happy. He was drunk with happiness and ferocity, with the joy he had always taken in his own skill: body and judgment and will all bonded in a dazzling unity, and courage bottomless because nothing could hurt him; even if he died nothing could hurt him. He was a warrior of the Reinmark. Whatever he should have been or would have been in some other kind of world, it made no difference now He had learned to fight, and he had learned, sometimes, to love it. And when he truly loved it, nothing living could stand in his path.

A blade slashed deep across his side; he never felt it. He struck the man down. He noticed, briefly, the blood still running fresh from the other's sword, and wondered where it came from, for no one else was there. No one else at all. The gate was clear. He bent low over the beast's neck and rode. Like a mountain stag, they said after—those few who saw him—or like the elves on their horses of wind.

Until the moon rose twice and went down again, the duke and his men rode after him.

A long time passed before he became aware of pain, of a great wetness running down his side and soaking into his boot. He groped at his side, and found the gash in his tunic; his hand came up blackened and drenched.

"Christ . . . ."

It was a deep wound, still bleeding. It was quite enough to kill him if he went on like this. And he would have to go on like this if he hoped to reach any place of safety.

He bandaged himself as best he could. His hands shook with exhaustion; he could hardly knot the strips of cloth. He was a whisper from collapsing, and he was quite alone. Wherever her people were, however they were hunting for him, they had lost him again, and their power was gone.

"Raven . . . ."

He looked back. He could not see his pursuers in the darkness, but he knew they were there. Hundreds of them, Gottfried's whole army, perhaps, fanning out across the hills, pitiless as hounds.

He took out the feather, touched it with his fingertip, and put it away again. He was desperate enough to use it now, but he did not trust its magic to reach her. She was too far away, and Gottfried too close. But he could use the shells. Whatever their power was, whoever had fashioned it, it was present and immediate, locked within them, a power which depended on nothing but itself.

He took the green shell from his packet, and threw it against a rock. Nothing happened. Or so it seemed to him, but it was dark now, and the world no longer steady. He sighed and rode on, too weary and in too much pain to look back.

So he only heard tales, after, of the great thorn hedge which suddenly appeared on the plain of Lys. It grew right across the pastures and the barley fields, so deep and tangled a mouse could scarcely scramble through it. It reached for miles, even over streams and roads; Gottfried's men rode half the night to get around it. It died soon after, and the peasants cut it down for bonfires. By the time the war was over, only the stories about it would remain.

Karelian knew nothing of this. He rode almost till moonset, walking his horse and barely conscious on its back, and Gottfried did not catch him. By then he was deep in the Schildberge. He might have thought it elf country, if he had been awake enough to think about anything at all. He found a ravine, and followed it down to its depths. There, by a pool among some fallen trees, he slid from his horse, and drank, and broke the last black egg-shell in his hand. And the dark of the earth closed around him, and wrapped him against its heart. The sun rose, and men came, quite a lot of men, armed with a trampling, insatiable rage. They were certain they had found his trail, and for hours they would not give up searching.

But in the end they cursed and shook their heads and rode away, for there was simply nothing there, nothing human at all, only deadfall and dark pines and shadows.

XXVI

ALL FOR GOD'S KINGDOM

When we are stripping a man of the lawlessness of sin,
it is good for him to be vanquished, since nothing is
more hopeless than the happiness of sinners.

SAINT THOMAS AQUINAS

ANOTHER MAN THAN GOTTFRIED might have taken Karelian's splendid
manor house for himself, and commanded the scouring of Lys
from its warm and well-wrought halls. "It is a den of sorcery," he
said, and had it burned, and lodged himself in a silken tent outside
the walls. There, as darkness approached on the second day, I was
dragged to him in irons.

The weather had turned heavy and overcast. The Schildberge rose
beyond the valley in a dark, impenetrable ridge. It did not rain properly,
but bits of wetness would flick now and then against our faces; the
air smelled misty and restless and cold. It was common enough
weather for the season, yet it troubled me. I knew Karelian had escaped; the guards and the other prisoners talked about it all the time.
How useful it would be to him, this melancholy, darkly descending
sky. And how cold and judgmental it felt to me.

Gottfried's men went about with hard-set faces, questioning the
people, searching their houses, riding off in small groups into the forest. They found everywhere—as they would have found in any village
in the Reinmark in those years—ample evidence of superstition, sorcery, and pagan worship. (Had the soldiers troubled to search each
other, they would have found more.) A great pile of objects began to
gather in the yard for burning. Years after, the people still were bitter

about it. They said most of the things the soldiers took were harmless: jewelry and keepsakes, simple medicines, children's toys.

"They took my father's cane," one of them said to me, spitting. "What sorcery is there in having a stick to lean on, tell me that?"

But I've seen many such innocent things in my life, including a cane with a demon's face carved in it, cunningly hidden in the whorls of the wood, where only a knowing eye would see it. The Christian world was vigilant, and so of course the pagans masked their charms and idols. As time passed, and the Church grew more vigilant and more concerned, they found ever more devious ways to do so.

Yet the ugliness of the day distressed me: the sense of pervading terror, the bewilderment. The common people were a stupid lot, ignorant rather than bad; most of them meant no harm.

Worst of all was the pity I saw in their eyes as I stumbled through the mangled yard, dragging my chains. There was blood on my face and my clothing, and the soldiers were deliberately brutal towards me, for reasons which I only afterwards understood. And I saw how the people of Lys reacted. Most of them spoke only with their eyes, but a few muttered aloud, after we were past: *What are they doing, God curse them, he's just a squire . . . !* Squires were highly privileged young men. Always of noble birth, we were valued far more than civilians; yet because we did not fight, we had all the rights of noncombatants. A knight could kill a defeated soldier without dishonor, but it was judged despicable to kill a squire.

It occurred to me, then, looking into the faces of Karelian's housecarles and tanners and serfs, and seeing their outrage—it occurred to me why my lord might have refused to knight me.

I stumbled, and threw up on the ground like a dog.

Gottfried's tent was large but spartan. Theodoric was there when I was brought in, and a number of other knights, most of whom I did not recognize.

Never since I left the Holy Land had I been in a place which felt so utterly a place of war. And it was not simply the presence of so many armed men; one could find those at any jousting field. It was something quite different: a rawness, a sense of permanent urgency, and above all, a complete absence of women and all the small encroachments of the world. I knew, without having to be told, that Gottfried had begun his sacred mission, and hereafter nothing and no one would distract him from it, even for an hour.

He looked up when I was brought in, briefly, without apparent interest, and went on speaking with the men before him.

"You are telling me, then, that no one will accuse Karelian?"

The knights glanced at each other; one of them shrugged slightly.

"They will accuse him of anything we might wish, my lord," he said, "but in the next breath they'll contradict themselves, and say they never saw it, they only heard about it. Or thought they did. As for the pagan altars we found, everyone I've spoken to says they were here before he came."

"But he did nothing to remove them."

"Neither did the count before him. Or the priests. These things are still common, my lord, all over Germany."

"Well, it's time they stopped being common. We have seen where they lead—to barbarism and treason."

He stood up. "Keep on with it. And remember, we must be just. Any of them who willingly give up their sorceries, and undertake to live as proper Christians, are to be treated gently. Whatever they say or don't say, Karelian has already convicted himself."

He dismissed them all except Theodoric, and then turned his attention to my guards.

"Unchain him," he said. "And then leave us."

The guards gave him a long and dubious look, but they obeyed.

"My lords," I said hesitantly, and bowed. For a time neither spoke. They watched me, and my thoughts returned to the courtyard, to the demonic moment when Karelian conjured up the wolves against his captors.

Never before in my life had I seen, or even imagined, such blind, out-of-control terror. All around me, men were being thrown from maddened horses, slain by random, ill-directed arrows, dragged from their mounts by jaws already streaming with blood. I could not believe it was happening. No one could. Men screamed to God for mercy, and one of them, right beside me on a plunging horse, slashing wildly at everything in reach, shouted over and over: "What are they? What are they?" as though it weren't perfectly obvious what they were.

I never tried to answer him. I looked about for Gottfried, desperately. As a shipwrecked sailor flails about for a timber to cling to, so I searched the tumult for a sight of the Golden Duke. Gottfried had to stop it.

And I saw to my horror that he could not. He was standing in his stirrups, shouting, the willstone shimmering in his hand. He held neither sword nor shield, only the crystal pyramid; it caught all the colors of the falling sun. The wolves raged towards him, and veered, and raged away. It was as though a circle of grace were wrapped around him. They could not pierce it, but neither could he reach beyond it. I could see he tried; he crashed against their power like a flood against a cliff. The wolves leapt and howled and slaughtered as though he were not there.

No! They aren't stronger than you! They can't be! They can't . . . !

Then my horse threw me into a stone wall, and I saw nothing more.

The duke moved towards the table, and I remembered where I was. He looked weary, I thought, and ever so slightly disconcerted, like a man who had begun a difficult task with the utmost care, only to discover, in the very thick of it, that he'd forgotten something essential.

I had been so certain of his power. I had expected him to fling out a single, riveting command, and the creatures of hell would crumble into dust at his feet. But all he had been able to do was shield himself.

Suppose he is just a man? Suppose it is they who have all the power . . . ?

No, I told myself, *it isn't possible, God would never allow it.* But I felt cold in all my bones.

He poured a cup of wine, and brought it to me.

"You need this, I think."

I took it eagerly. I had not eaten since I walked away from our hunting camp in the Schildberge. "Thank you, my lord."

"I hardly need tell you I believe you now," he went on. "And I thank you for the warning. There is food on the table; sit and eat. I want you cared for, but no one must see you favored."

I thanked him, half dazed with gratitude. There was a great bowl of roasted chicken waiting for me, and slabs of bread, and wine. The duke sat opposite. Theodoric did not sit at all, but paced about the tent as though he wished he were somewhere else.

The duke let me sate the worst of my hunger, and then he spoke again.

"You offered once to serve me, Paul of Ardiun. Are you still willing to do so?"

My heart leapt, but I could only nod, for my mouth was full of chicken.

"Good," he said. He did not wait until I could answer him properly. "You're still in the former count's favor, I take it? You've kept his trust?"

"Yes, my lord."

His eyes held me like spears. "Was it difficult?" he asked.

I swallowed, and put the chicken down. Suddenly, I wasn't hungry any more. I knew I was being tested, but I did not know for what.

"Yes," I said, and then realizing the implications, I added quickly: "No. What I mean is, he's never suspected me of anything, not ever, that was easy enough, only—"

"Never mind."

Why did he look at me so, with such . . . distaste? I had only done what was necessary.

"The traitor is wounded," Gottfried went on. "He left a trail of blood into the hills. In fact, he may be dead by now, but I don't think so. He's gone to ground somewhere. I want you to find him."

I stared at him. Once, years after in the Levant, I lived through an earthquake, and experienced the sensation, unlike any other which can be imagined, of rock-hard earth dissolving under me. A feeling of bottomlessness, at once horrifying and impossibly unreal. So I felt now, hearing Gottfried's command.

"My lord . . . ? But I thought . . . . My good lord, please, will you not accept me into your service?"

"You *are* in my service. Or so you keep telling me."

I could find no words to answer him. My stomach was all in knots. I wished I had not eaten. I wished I had never been born.

Theodoric paused in his pacing, and looked at us. "I'll wager he wants gold, my lord. Give him a hundred marks, and send him back to his mother."

I looked bitterly at Theodoric. He was the duke's son, and shared his sacred blood. It had to be so, but I could never quite believe it, except by an act of will.

"I do not want gold, my lord," I said, with all the dignity I could muster. "I never have."

"I believe that, Pauli," the duke said. "But as for what you do want, you'll have to earn it. Find Karelian Brandeis, and lead me to him."

"But my lord . . . how can I possibly find him? And if I do . . . surely he will know, my lord? He'll know I went to you—!"

"There's no reason he should know."

"But he must know someone betrayed him, and I'm the only one who could have! I'm the only one who remembers Helmardin!"

"You're very young, Paul, and this matter is more complex than you think. There are many ways I might have come to know of the count's treachery. You may be quite unaware of them, but I assure you, he is not. A betrayal from you, his unworldly and faithful young squire? No; it's the last possibility he'll consider."

As it happened, I knew a great deal more about the matter than Gottfried imagined, and I understood at once what he was saying. He thought Karelian would blame the power of God.

And no doubt Karelian would. But he himself had the power of a sorcerer. Suppose he merely needed to look at me to know?

"He's been looking at you for quite some time now," Gottfried said dryly, "and he hasn't noticed anything."

"You read my mind, my lord," I whispered.

"You will escape tonight," he said. "I'll make sure it's easy for you. I expect the villain will go to Karn, to his friend Lehelin; or he will go to Aachen, to plead against me with the emperor; or he will go to Helmardin."

I knew without thinking about it where Karelian would go; he would go to *her.*

"And if I find him, my lord, what then?"

"I leave it to your judgment. You may simply send me word; an ordinary messenger will serve. You are Brother Fortunatus, on a pilgrimage to Compostela. You have fallen ill in such and such a place. Write to me of your misfortunes. However many days you have been ill, so many men he has with him. If she is there, tell me you are dying. That is one possibility."

He paused, and added quietly: "The other possibility is to kill him where you find him. Though I warn you, I'll accept no one's word that he is dead—neither yours nor any man's—without proof."

Kill him where I find him? You had a thousand men in arms, and you couldn't manage it . . . .

"My lord . . . ?" How could I say it, without seeming a coward? "How can I kill him, my lord? He's a sorcerer! We saw what he did in Lys—!"

"No. We saw what the demons of Car-Iduna did. He didn't conjure up those hell-hounds, Pauli. He brought them with him, prisoned in a wyrdshell. Or so Father Mathias assures me, and he has made a study of such things. Karelian doesn't have that kind of power. He's nothing but their minion."

"But they will protect him—!"

"Perhaps."

He stood up. His eyes were as they had been when I faced him in Stavoren—relentless and prisoning.

"You dream of greatness," he said. "You dream of God and his glory. But we didn't take back Jerusalem with dreams, Paul von Ardiun; we took it back with blood.

"You want to be a knight of Saint David. And so you may one day. But only the best men in the kingdom will be permitted to carry that banner. They will be men who don't look back—not ever—at anything which tempted them in the world.

"You loved him once, this traitor who fouls our altars and plots against our faith. You didn't know what he was—of course you didn't know—or perhaps you did, just a little? It doesn't matter. It's left tracks on your soul just the same. And you're the one who must erase them. If you truly want to."

"I do want to, my lord."

"Then do it. Depending where you find him, and in what circumstances, find a way to put him in my hands. If you don't . . . ." He paused, and I withered under the power of his eyes.

"If you don't, then no matter what you say in words, Pauli, we will know where your heart is."

Everything grew suddenly and intensely still. I felt as though the whole world had listened, and taken note. *We will know where your heart is.* Everyone, lords and princes, the priests in their chapels and the beggars in the streets, my father, and God in heaven too: *He's left tracks on your soul, and every one of us will know . . . .*

"My lord," I whispered, "I would not have come to Stavoren if my heart were anywhere except with you."

"Coming to Stavoren was a single step down a long and difficult road. Did you think it would end there? That all you'd have to do afterwards was smile at me, and hold my cloak, and ride behind me into heaven?"

I looked at the floor.

"God gives none of us a gentle path, Paul von Ardiun," he said then, quietly. "I won't pretend the task I've set you is easy or safe. But the powers of good are stronger than the powers of evil. Remember that. And remember this also: for a Christian nothing matters except the will of God."

He did not even smile at me. He shouted for the guard, and I stood numb and desolate, waiting for them to come and drag me away. I don't know what I had imagined, what I had dared to hope for. But surely he would give me more than this, after so terrible a risk, so terrible a sacrifice? But he was already turning away, already busy with the burdens of the world. I drank my sorrow down like gall, and went where I was taken.

The escape was, as the duke had promised me, an easy one; and Gottfried's man was waiting where he said, with simple traveling clothes, a good horse, and a small purse for my needs. It must have been midnight by then, though there were no stars to judge by. I rode some distance towards the west, merely to be rid of him. Then I found a grove of birch trees, and sheltered there, waiting for daylight.

Or so I told myself, but what I truly waited for was a miracle, for time to unravel or the world to end, for Karelian to come stumbling out of the forest begging for God's mercy for Gottfried's messenger to come riding after me: *His lordship has reconsidered, Pauli, and wants you to return.*

Slowly, as the night went on, I grew numb with cold, and all my courage left me. Never in my life had I felt so alone, or so unworthy. I understood now, here in my solitude, where I could hide from everything except myself, I understood perfectly well what I wanted from Gottfried. What I'd wanted from the start, what held me to my perilous course when nothing else could have done so. I wanted his friendship. I wanted him to smile, and welcome me; to raise me to my feet, and order wine and fatted calves; to praise me in the sight of everyone, and place me by his side.

I wanted to be the favorite of the king.

So was I drawn to Karelian, long ago in Acre. So did I go out of my way to find him and offer him my service. I admired his fine looks and glittering reputation; I wanted to stand in his reflected glory. I ran after him, blindly, only to discover that he was just an adventurer—a false crusader, a false Christian, a false vassal to his lord.

I turned to Gottfried then, because he was different. But I, God forgive me, I was no different at all. When Gottfried did not flatter me as Karelian once did, when he did not smile and play the worldling and offer me its snares, I was disappointed in him. I judged my lord by the standards of his enemy and when he did not meet those standards, *I was disappointed in him . . . !*

There was that, staring at me like a snake in a mirror, making me sick with self-loathing. But there was something else, too, something even more unforgivable. I confess it willingly; I have no vanity left. My sins lay strewn across these pages in endless number. Yet of them all, this one was the worst.

I regretted what I had done.

Yes. In some ungovernable part of myself, deep and shivering and primal, I was sorry. It did not seem like such a dark life now, serving Karelian in Lys, sleeping under a good roof every night, with a fire in the hearth and no enemies to fear. Now the house was burnt, and the manor a war camp, and Karelian a wounded fugitive, Karelian dying perhaps, alone and in bitter pain. *He left a trail of blood into the hills . . . .*

It did no good to remember he had brought it on himself, or to say my treachery was right and just. It did no good at all to think of Gottfried or of Christendom. I had betrayed Karelian—perhaps to his death—and I was sorry.

I hated myself that night to the point of despair. Everything I had done for Gottfried seemed irrevocably spoiled, made small by the smallness of my motives, made shameful by my unsilenceable, personal regret.

With sunrise, too exhausted to think any more, I climbed on my horse and began my lonely search. Some days later, unknown to anyone, I began to wear a hair shirt. No matter what it cost me, I was determined to conquer my soul, to make pure my commitment to my lord.

Thirty-two years have passed now, and I have not done so.

XXVII

IN THE BELLY OF THE WORLD

I seemed to be lost
Between the worlds
While around me
Burned the fires.

POETIC EDDA

KARELIAN WOKE IN DARKNESS, a strange darkness, thick and bottomless, yet flickering with light. He moved slightly, and a shadowed face bent close to his own, its black hair hanging long and trimmed with fire.

"Raven . . . ?"

The voice which answered was amused, strange, unquestionably male.

"You're in a bad way, worldling, if you think I'm a bird."

"No . . . bird . . . ." It was difficult to speak, too impossibly difficult to explain. "Who . . . are you?"

"You wouldn't recognize my real name. As for the others, I've had many. Drink this, and be quiet."

He lifted Karelian's head, held a cup to his lips. His hands were long and slender as a woman's, but powerful as those of an archer. The potion was bitter; for a moment, before Karelian slept again, it flooded him with strength. He remembered the black womb which had embraced him, through which he had heard, sometimes, the crash of men and horses, and the howls of hunting dogs.

"The duke . . . ?" he whispered.

"He won't find you."

"You did."

The stranger laughed. "I can see in the dark. Sleep now; I'll fetch us some food."

Sleep was already closing, unsteady and unsheltering, a sleep raw with fever and dreams. The man returned. Karelian heard the soft keening of a flute, and he tried to lift himself, to call out: *Don't, in God's name, don't! They'll hear you!* But he had no strength at all. Even as he formed the words, they dissolved. The world dissolved. Battle raged around him, battle and battle madness, men scaling walls and screaming, and then the streets of an ancient city, not golden at all, just cobblestone and blood, (we marched a thousand leagues for this?) even the sun was murderous, mirroring hate off everything and everything was crimson, everything was burning, even solid stone. There was no end to the streets, no end to the slaughtered houses, there was a Saracen woman fair as a gazelle, tearing open her dress, *Don't . . . !* her breasts amber like wine, like the soft faces of her children, *Please don't . . . !* amber spattered crimson, color of the western sky, *Please don't kill them, please . . . !* their bodies crumpling, hacked into pieces, the world into pieces, the whole world into small bloodied pieces while the churches filled with song . . . .

"Easy . . . easy worldling, easy, it's just a dream . . . ."

One lean hand pinned him to his bed, the other brushed across his hair. "Just a dream."

Sweet gods, if only it were . . . !

The dark man bathed his face, pressed fresh poultices against his wounds, spooned broth between his teeth. Clarity came again, for a small while.

"I've never even seen you before," Karelian said. "Why are you doing this for me?"

"I have a certain affection for the blood heirs of Dorn. And a definite distaste for that golden *graflein* of yours. These mountains are mine; I watch them carefully. When I saw him riding to Lys with so many knights, and in such haste, I grew curious. And it's well I did, don't you think? Here, another mouthful, you need strength."

"Who are you?"

"As I said, you wouldn't recognize my name. But my father was the young Saxon chieftain of Dorn, whom Henry put so cruelly to death. To make him Christian."

"Wulfstan?"

"Aye."

"But that was . . . that was a hundred years ago!"

"Aye. As men count them. Stop asking questions. You'll learn many things, when I'm ready to tell them to you."

He placed the bowl of broth aside, and picked up his flute.

"Will no one hear you?" Karelian protested.

"Aye. Old roots and deep-buried stones and sleeping volcanoes. Maybe the odd ghost."

And he played then, exquisitely. He played to make the mountains bend close to listen, and the stars turn away to weep. From the coils of his delirium Karelian heard rain patter softly against leaves, and run in rivulets across the rocks; he felt the clean scent of it against his burning throat.

"Thirsty . . . ."

But there was no water, there was only desert, Gottfried with a thousand knights in armor, shimmering, riding towards him, a circle of polished steel and white silk, white painted shields, everything white, scarred with black crosses. Crusaders unto death.

Gottfried smiled. *I have your witch,* he said.

The desert shimmered and dissolved, melted into the towers of Stavoren which shimmered and dissolved, *waffeled,* as ships did against the sunset, the night before they sank . . . .

"You are bred of generations of sorcery, Karelian Brandeis. The princes of Dorn were the high priests and priestesses of old, the keepers of the sacred groves and fires. Some are secret witches now in the days of conquest, and some are as ignorant of their gifts as you have been of yours."

"That's what she said, too."

"She?"

"Raven. The Lady of the Mountain."

"Ah. So that's the bird you talk to in your sleep. A bird with many names, I see, rather like myself."

"Do you serve her, too?"

"I serve no one, worldling. You are born of the clan of Alanas my mother—for this I shelter you. For this I will teach you how to be a sorcerer."

There was no measure of time in the depths of the world. When Karelian looked again across the wilds of the Schildberge, all the leaves were gone, all the summer birds were gone; patches of snow lay scattered about the forest, and the wind was sharp as slivered ice.

But in Wulfstan's lair there was only sleep and waking, both confused, both utterly devoid of boundaries.

"Where is there a fire," the elf questioned, "without the brand it burns? Where is there a dancer without the dance?"

"Nowhere."

"Precisely. So there is no maker without the made, no life without the living. All power rests upon exchange. You cannot take from the world, not ever; you can only trade."

"Tell that to the pirates and the princes—aye, and to the popes as well."

"They know it better than I do. They have traded everything for a lie."

The elf's voice was soft as running water, and mostly comprehensible. The images were different. They were warnings and memories and maybe just phantoms born of fever and pain, drawn in an unending stream from the was and the never-was, the might-be and the cannot-be and the must-never-be. He saw Gottfried crowned king. He saw Gottfried lying dead on the streets of Jerusalem. He saw wars, but the armies changed; they became other armies even as they rode, and the walled cities melted into each other with lunatic ease. And everywhere, everywhere, he saw crosses. Crosses painted and made of wood, crosses forged of gold, crosses sewn on banners, crosses held in upraised screaming hands, crosses appearing suddenly on grey stone walls, in the shapes of trees and clouds, in the meeting of roads and rivers, on public gibbets where dead men hung in rows.

He never saw Raven.

"Why is she hidden from me, hunter elf? Can your powers not tell you? Why did she send me no warning?"

"I can read the signs which are sent to me. Those which are sent to you, you must learn to read for yourself. She is strange, and dangerous, and anyone who thinks different is a fool. But she gave you the wyrdshells, and those aren't gifts she would give lightly. She gave you the potions which are healing you. Your wound was mortal, didn't you know?"

"Mortal . . . ?"

"Aye. To any ordinary physician. And certainly to an elf. We're seldom wounded or sick, so we don't learn much about healing. I could have done very little for you without her gifts. So it may be she's abandoned you, worldling, but I wouldn't break my heart about it yet. Not just yet."

Not just yet . . . . The long, slender fingers lingered on his hair, and darkness came again.

It came and went, and finally it came less often, less terribly. Then, for long quiet hours they talked—or rather the elf stranger talked, arms clasped around his knees, the fire shimmering on a face still beautiful with youth. But his eyes were not youthful. The dark of the northern winter was in them, and the cunning of the hunter, and the power of a man who had dared to bargain with a god.

And he spoke of the god he had bargained with, of Tyr the hunter, Tyr who nurtured the wolf cub and bound fast the destroying wolf, Tyr who was god of the Althing and so the god of counsel and of justice, Tyr the paradox, mighty and already fading, shrugged aside by the arrogant Odin, condemned entirely by the jealous, all-demanding Christ.

There were many gods, the elf reminded him, for many and differing realities. But Tyr was the god they needed now. For he was also the ancient god of battle. Not Odin who provoked strife to fill his drinking halls with slaughtered warriors. Not Jehovah who demanded endless wars of conquest, and would go on demanding them until the whole world knelt at his feet. Tyr turned away from both of them, and from the men who served them. He went back to the forests and the mists, back to dreams: *This is not what living is, or what I am, or even what war is. Farewell. I will return when you are wise enough to want me.*

"Play the paradox, worldling, if you want to win. The world is round, and the straightest journey is the one which comes back soonest to the place where it began. Therein lies the fatal weakness of the pyramid: it is bound by the circle, and it doesn't know it.

"The veelas taught me many things, but of them all, this was the most valuable: they taught me to look for connections. Magic doesn't lie in objects, however sacred; nor in spells, however powerful; nor in sorcerers themselves, however gifted. The holiest amulet, lost in the desert with no one to wield it, is only a piece of wood or glass or stone. The greatest spell, babbled by witless mimic, is just a branch rattling in the wind. There are some who'll tell you otherwise, but it isn't true. Where there are no connections, there is no magic. Magic is rooted in the bonds between things, and the sorcerer's gift is to see where those bonds lie—where the world touches, and where it doesn't; where things hold together, and where they don't. Even the gods are held in those bonds. That is how they are summoned, and that is why they answer—because they, like all things, are part of other things, and they must.

"Learn to listen, worldling, and to look."

Listen to the rain and the snap of fire, to the whispering of leaves, to the whispering of blood. Not as ordinary sounds—all men do that—but as the voices of another kind of being. Listen until you can hear the chanting in the shimmer of a star . . . .

Days passed, and nights; Karelian did not count them. Twice, the elf gave him potions, and after he drank them the world was unimaginably altered—or perhaps he was, he could not have said for certain which. The walls of the cave were filled with images like those of dreams. Dead men came out of the earth wielding swords. A bishop laden with robes stumbled onto a battlefield, and two knights rode to combat across his body. A great, glittering procession passed through the streets of a city, but as it approached him its colors turned all to black; it carried a bier, and on the bier was a grey-haired king. The procession stopped; armed men approached the bier, and took the dead king's crown and tossed it from one to the other like schoolboys playing with an apple . . . until it fell, and began to roll across the city, across the fields, across the whole of Germany and everything it touched turned to fire.

"Can't you help me get to Helmardin? Before that villain Gottfried undoes us all?"

"I rarely leave my mountains," the elf said. "Besides . . . ." He paused, and smiled faintly. "You have many things to learn, and you can't learn them all in a day. Gottfried isn't a deity yet. He isn't even a king—"

"When he is, it will be too late."

"It's been too late for a couple of thousand years. We can't undo it all. You're a warrior, Karelian. You know there's such a thing as an army too big to fight."

"So we should sit by our fire and let Gottfried devour the world?"

"No. We sit by our fire until you can fight him with something a bit more lethal than your voice. Then you can make your own way west. You won't, in any case, be alone for long."

Karelian looked sharply at him, but the elf's face did not change, nor did his voice.

"Don't misunderstand me," he went on. "I fear Gottfried as much as you do. More, perhaps, because I've lived longer, and I know more. That is precisely why I'm telling you to be patient. To hone every skill you have, and build every possible alliance. Because believe me, worldling, you're going to need them."

"Have you . . . have you seen our . . . future?"

The elf smiled. "Which one?"

"You're a very difficult man to talk to sometimes."

"Do you really think the future is fixed? In a world with millions of beings, all of them colliding and changing and learning, becoming wise, becoming corrupt—aye, and not a few of them becoming mad? A single, pre-determined future with every gnat flying in his place, eaten at precisely the intended moment by the right, divinely chosen sparrow? Really, Karel."

"I didn't say that."

"No. But it is that, or there are a million futures. If the gnat's fate is uncertain, so is the sparrow's. If the sparrow, so the hawk. If the hawk, so the hunter. Every place the gnat can fly is a future, and when he dies, every one of those futures has changed, and become another."

Karelian thought about his answer for a long time. It was one of the most frightening ideas he had ever contemplated, and at the same time, one of the most empowering. For it both affirmed the importance of human responsibility, and limited the responsibility to livable proportions.

"There is no original sin, then," he murmured. "No one damned the world, and no one saved it. And Christ wasn't chosen—not for death nor for anything else. All of it could have been different."

"Aye. All different. And it can be yet. And it will be."

But not in our lifetime. I am only one hunter, and Gottfried a single hawk. Yet when one of us is fallen, a million futures will have changed, and become different. Forever. And there is the only eternity which matters.

It was the following morning when he heard the partridges—the following morning or another; time was irremediably uncertain. He wakened, heard the wind fluttering dead leaves beside his head, and partridges clucking in the bushes. Bewildered, he dragged himself to sit upright against a tree, and saw that he still sheltered where he had fallen, in the depths of a gully, in a hollow shielded by deadfall. He could see the sky now; the sun had moved southerly a month or more. His pack was open, his belongings disordered, the balms and potions mostly gone, but there were no tracks in the woods around him—not of human nor of any other feet. No traces of the hunter elf, no sign that anyone had been there at all.

But I live . . . wounded to death, and alone, and yet I live . . . more sign there, I think, than in anything else he might have left me.

He was desperately hungry. He found his knife still safe in its sheath; he drew it, and waited for the partridges to grow used to his presence, and wander close again.

It was a week before he could feed himself properly, a fortnight before he left the gully and began the long journey to Helmardin. He tired quickly, and covered very little distance in the first few days.

But his body strengthened. And something else was happening, too, something he became aware of only slowly. It came first as a changing mood, like a lightening of the sky, even as the Reinmark darkened into winter. It sharpened as the days passed, becoming more and more distinct. Something was drawing away from him, something hard and evil. It was passing into distance like a caravan on an impossibly flat and unclouded plain, diminishing into ripples at the edges of the world.

And then it was gone.

Gottfried had left the Reinmark.

There was no comfort in it once he thought about it, for almost certainly it meant mutiny and war. Yet for a moment he felt a rush of triumph more dazzling than in any victory he had ever won. Because he knew. It was as if he stood on the high border pass of Saint Martin and watched them go, their banners drenched with early winter rain. He could hear the hoofbeats sharp against the stones, the soldiers' grumbling at their master's unrelenting haste. And it was not instinct, or what he would have called instinct in his youth. It was the sharp, clear certainty of sight.

He *knew*.

That night, by a sheltered fire, he tried to summon Raven. But the sky remained empty, the forest melancholy and aloof. Owls cried, and distant wolves, and gusts of aimless, icy wind. There was nothing else abroad. His loneliness burned like a wound, deepening as his other wounds healed. *Raven, Raven, Raven, I loved you beyond reason, I love you still, why don't you answer me, why don't you come?*

He sat for a long time, staring at the fire, wanting her with a double-edged, extravagant desire, as he had from the beginning. Wanting the sorceress as ally, the woman as lover, power and pleasure hopelessly entangled, as perhaps they were supposed to be, as perhaps they once were, long ages back, when power was not the measure of a man's existence and pleasure was not a sin.

The pouch felt heavy hanging from his neck, strangely heavy, for there was nothing in it now except a feather. He lifted it over his head, took out the talisman, black and shimmering like her hair, and touched it against his lips. The temptation to use it—to waste its potency simply to see her now, this very moment—was almost unbearable.

He had not, he reminded himself, survived twenty years of soldiering by giving in to reckless impulses. He put it carefully back and tied the bag shut, noticing again how heavy it felt, almost as though . . . as though some power were pulling it down, pulling it away from him. He remembered with a flash of bitter anger how it had been slashed from his throat, snatched away by that white-clad puppy with a snarling face: *Ha! And what sacred relic is this, I wonder?*

And for one moment, the one tiny moment when it was gone, when it did not touch his body, the powers of Car-Iduna had found him. Their searching, circling, hungering energies had leapt through some unknown opening and found him.

And lost him again.

Because he took the pouch back . . . ?

A gust of cold wind rippled the hair against his neck. He pulled his hood up, feeling cold to his bones. He would have paid a solid gold mark for a cup of heated wine, and twenty to have someone he trusted sitting by his fire.

He laid the pouch flat across his thigh. *Not this. This which I treasured above all my possessions, and shielded from every risk of harm or loss? It isn't possible . . . .*

But it was entirely possible. Now that he thought about it, it was one of the few possibilities which made sense, and the only possibility he wanted to face. Raven had not abandoned him. And Gottfried, powerful though he was, had not placed a barrier between them by the sheer force of will; he was not a god.

He took out Raven's feather and tucked it carefully into his pack. Then, with great care, he searched the bag for what else it might contain, and finally turned it inside out. There was nothing in it, only rubbish from his travels: dirt and scraps of leaf, a dead bug, the odors of sweat and bracken and blood.

Nothing. No secret amulet, no charm, no *thing* of any kind. It had to be the pouch itself which was ensorceled.

And if that were so, then by whom? No one had ever touched it except Pauli and himself. And Adelaide, perhaps, in the dead of night, while he slept.

Adelaide . . . .

The old mage in Acre had warned him. *You may go safely where most men fear danger, and you must fear danger most where other men believe they are safe* . . . .

Adelaide who still mourned for her dead lover, slain so cruelly in Ravensbruck, because of Karelian Brandeis—neither by Karelian's hand nor by his wish, but nonetheless because of him. Adelaide who kept silent while a sorceress plotted against her father's life. Who kept silent also, perhaps, while Rudi Selven plotted against *his*.

He fingered the pouch, thinking how easy it would have been. He had wakened so many times at unknown hours to find her cold and unsleeping, and blamed it on her strangeness, her youth, her bitter memories. What did he know about her, really except that she was a liar and a whore?

But even as the accusations took shape in his mind, they collided against his judgment, his experience. He had seen the savagery of Ravensbruck, the ongoing terror of living anywhere near Count Arnulf, even for a man. For a woman . . . . For a woman, God's blood, what was left except recklessness and cunning? She had proven untrustworthy to those who left her no options. So would Raven, cornered thus. So would Karelian Brandeis.

This was very different. This was raw treachery—not the desperate act of a frightened girl surrounded by peril and cruelty, but a calculated act of hatred. Had it succeeded, he would have fallen defenseless into Gottfried's hands, and borne the full penalties for sorcery and treason: loss of lands and rank, degradation from knighthood, death by fire. And she would have been swept to ruin with him, she and her child both, for neither had an ally in the world.

He shook his head. She did not hate him so much. In truth, he did not believe she hated him at all.

Which left Pauli, and that was even more absurd. Pauli would never *use* sorcery. He was terrified of it; he considered it mortally sinful. And Pauli would never do him harm; it took an act of will merely to entertain the possibility. Pauli nursed him through fever in the Holy Land, kept vigil for his safety in Helmardin, wept when he was wounded in Ravensbruck. Pauli worshipped him. And he trusted Pauli more than he trusted anyone. Anyone at all.

He ran his fingers softly over the pouch. It was finely made, like everything the boy did. He wondered where he might be, if he were Gottfried's prisoner in Lys, or wounded, perhaps even dead. It seemed unjust even to suspect him. If he could not believe Adelaide guilty of this much hatred, how could he believe Pauli guilty of it?

Perhaps the pouch was not ensorceled at all. Perhaps that moment in the courtyard of Lys had happened by chance. Perhaps it meant nothing. Perhaps Raven only mocked him with the promise of powers she did not have, powers which did not even exist.

And if that is so, Karelian Brandeis, then you are finished; you are neither lord nor sorcerer nor lover; you are what you were as a boy, but without a boy's hopes: a landless adventurer, trading blood for lodging and wine, your father's true son at last: Go be a monk, in God's name; there is nothing for you here . . . .

He nursed his melancholy for a time, because he could not make it go away. And then, as he had done so many times in his father's house, and after in the traps and misfortunes of war, he wrapped it up like a wound, and pulled his thoughts down over it, and went on.

Not yet. He wasn't beaten *yet*. He had to work it through.

You have many things to learn, and you can't learn them all in a day. And this, no doubt, was one of the things he had to learn, one of the reasons Wulfstan left him to make his own way to Car-Iduna. Damned clever elf . . . . He began again. Was there someone else? Someone, anyone, in the household of Lys, with an old, half-forgotten grudge? Someone who might be a secret enemy, or a spy?

Quite possibly there was, but no one had ever touched the pouch except Pauli and Adelaide.

Suppose they had never touched it, had only seen it, and made another like it, and worked the spell upon the copy?

Perhaps. Such things were done. But spells fashioned thus were always weaker; the object itself was always the most potent source of power. And this spell was potent indeed. The more he thought about the pouch, the more aware of its power he became, as though the thing pulsed here in the darkness, half alive.

No, he thought. It had not been done by distance, nor by anything except contact—immediate, direct, and murderously personal, like a dagger in his back.

One of them or the other. Pauli or Adelaide.

Adelaide at least had a reason to turn on him. Pauli had none.

Yet Pauli had gone home to Ardiun, and come back silent and

troubled. Even Reini noticed it. "Something's gnawing on the lad," he had said. "I don't like it." And Reini was not a subtle man.

Then there was the power of the spell itself. If it could stand between him and all of Car-Iduna, it surely carried more than ordinary magic, and therefore wasn't fashioned by any ordinary witch. Did Adelaide, or anyone she knew, have powers which Raven could not overwhelm? Could Adelaide have done this, even if she hated him? Even if she were fey and wicked and utterly hated him?

The question, once stated, answered itself. She could not have done it, and neither could Pauli. Only one person in the Reinmark had such extraordinary power. This was somehow Gottfried's work.

Ardiun was across the mountains from Lys, deep in the margravate of Dorn. A day's hard ride from the ducal seat at Stavoren . . . .

But no, he thought, opportunity be damned. Pauli had no reason to do this. None. Pauli loved him. Indeed, Pauli loved him far too well, as the world would judge the matter.

Play the paradox, worldling, if you want to win.

Was it the sorcerer in him then who thought once more of Dorn? The dark, smoke-blackened manor house, the impoverished villages, the high house of Brandeis collapsing into a bitter and violent shadow of itself. His father Helmuth, drunken and coarse and unpredictable, fathering children like rabbits and caring about none of them, forgetting even their names. And Ludolf, the eldest, his half brother, always watching him, with eyes as cruel as sharpened stones. Not even a clean cruelty, or an honest hate. Something worse. Ludolf watching Karelian and finding ways to make him hurt. Or not finding them, and watching still more carefully, until there was only one way left.

And all of it was born of love . . . or what might have been love, had it not sickened and rotted in the cellars of Ludolf's mind. Ludolf wanted Karelian's mother, and could not have her. And because he could not have her, he began, day by day, to find fault with her, to suspect her of wrongdoing, to strike out at her in any way he could. He learned to hate her, and to hate especially the boy she cherished, simply because that boy was not himself.

Karelian was truly cold now. He built up the fire again, but it did not warm him much. He knew this situation was not the same, not the same at all. It was a different place, different circumstances, profoundly different men. But he knew now there was a reason Pauli might have turned on him. A reason the boy would never acknowledge, no more than Ludolf ever had. What kind of man desired his father's wife . . . or the love-bed of his liege?

Not I, whispered the high-born Christian son, the high-minded Christian squire. *Not I, not I, dear God, certainly not I . . . !*

Sweat ran down the sides of Karelian's face and trickled onto his sleeves. He wiped it away. He was too exhausted to think any more, and almost too exhausted to care.

He stood up, and carried the pouch some distance from his fire, and placed it under a heavy rock at the base of a tree. And then he waited as the sky closed ever more deep around him. Perhaps she would answer him now. But only owls spoke in the night, and distant wolves, and sparks exploding briefly against the darkness.

Just a trifle more briefly, perhaps, than the proud-borne life of a man . . . .

XXVIII

THE MEETING

My face was pale and my frame chilled with fasting;
yet my mind was burning with desire, and the fires of lust
kept bubbling up before me when my flesh was as good as dead.

SAINT JEROME

THERE WERE MANY DAYS IN MY LIFE I would willingly forget, but those days when I searched for Karelian were the worst I ever lived through. I was not good at hunting, not even for hares. I had no eye for the forest, and no heart for it, either. Even at the best of times it seemed to me an alien place: mysterious, unpredictable, and dangerous.

Sometimes I saw bands of Gottfried's knights; they were hunting for him, too. And day upon day I saw ravens, great black and wheeling ravens, circling the forest (searching for carrion, my father would have said; I knew better). But Karelian had vanished utterly, and finally I began to believe that he was dead.

Oh, there were stories enough. The whole of the Reinmark was alive with stories, each one stranger than the last, and all of them third-hand or worse. "Oh, no, my lord, I didn't see it myself, my lord. It was in Karn I heard it." Or in Schafsburg, or Saint Magdalene, or the little inn by the abbey of Dorn. The demon lord of Lys, I was told, had been fetched out of the Schildberge by Lucifer himself, and carried off to hell. On All Soul's night, at midnight exactly; there was a long path of burnt forest where the prince of darkness had dragged him. Others laughed at the stories, and said surely he must have gone to Aachen, like any wronged lord would do, to appeal to their common liege the king. Still others assured me he had gone to Compostela, to beg forgiveness for his sins. Aye, and with his head shorn bare, and in rags, and eating only thorns. He had gone to the Holy Land, too, of course, and depending who was telling the tale, he had gone as a crusader to defend the Christian kingdom, or as a rebel to lead the infidel in a great uprising against God.

I learned only one useful thing from all those stories. I learned that people will believe anything about a man—good or evil as it suits them, but anything at all—once he has sparked their passions, once he is seen as someone different from themselves.

I wandered about the Schildberge for more than a fortnight, but I found no trace of the man I sought. Finally, in desperation, I circled around to Karn. I did not expect to find him there, either, but I wanted to be sure. His friend Lehelin fed me and gave me fresh supplies, and cursed Gottfried for a butcher and a dog—in the privacy of a bolted room, of course, and in the dead of night. But it was clear he knew nothing of his old comrade in arms, and I went back to the wilderness.

It was mid-November by then: a mild autumn by Reinmark standards, but still autumn, edging hard into winter. The trees were naked; in the high country, clouds drifted southward just above their tips; in the valleys, little herds of grey fog huddled among them until noon.

It was a day like any other when the dirge bell began. I thought nothing of it at first, thinking someone must have died in a village nearby. I walked on, and heard from the west another bell, distant, carried faintly on the wind. I ignored it, too, at first, but it went on all day. And in the morning it began again, before the Angelus, a steady tolling which clamored against the overcast sky and the dark hills, and hung in the air with a pitiless, hammering melancholy: Doom . . . doom . . . doom . . . . The bells were rung thus only when a great lord was dead.

Gottfried . . . ?

The thought came with a gulp of fear, and a collapsing in the pit of my stomach. I ran down into the valley, sliding on wet rocks and stumbling over broken trees, praying that Gottfried wasn't dead, he could not be, he could not! Even to imagine it was to imagine the world utterly undone.

The first man I met was a peasant dragging bundles of firewood, walking with his head down, bent against the wind. He knew the reason for the mourning bell. The whole world knew, I think, except me.

Ehrenfried, lord of the Holy Roman Empire and king of the Germans, was dead.

"Oh."

Oh, thank God, it isn't Gottfried, thank the Lord . . . ! I tried to hide my shattering relief, but I don't think I succeeded, for the peasant was looking at me oddly. I lowered my eyes and quickly signed the cross.

"God have mercy on him," I said.

"Aye, master," the peasant said. "And on us all."

I barely heard him, overwhelmed by my own emotions. First that simple animal flood of thankfulness, so intense I almost cried. And then surprise, remembering the stocky, scholarly-looking man who sat just a few months ago at Gottfried's feast table, not yet fifty, and hale as a well-fed merchant. None of us, I thought, knew the hour of our going, not even kings.

And even with those reactions came the other, the sudden wild leap of possibility, the moment of breath-catching hope. Was this the time? Would Gottfried be king now, just as he had promised in the pavilion of Stavoren? *Ehrenfried is a fool, a prattling dreamer with his head full of scrolls, good for nothing but chess games and prayers. I will replace him!*

But Ehrenfried had a son, I reminded myself, young and skillful in arms, with no taste for chess games and less for prayers. He was highly thought of among the high lords of Germany.

My heart sank into my boots, remembering Prince Konrad. Gottfried might have had some hope of deposing Ehrenfried, an aging king whose moral authority had been permanently weakened by his defiance of Rome, and by the resulting twenty years of civil war. But a young king? A legitimate heir whom no one hated, with the warrior talents and the warrior temperament Germans so admired . . . dear God, I thought, what hope would my lord have now?

"Konrad will be elected king, then," I said.

"Might be," the peasant said. He fidgeted with the harness straps on his shoulders, and made as if to move on with his burden.

He looked . . . afraid. Afraid the way men are in the presence of great evil or terrible uncertainty. It was contagious. The question leapt into my mind like an arrow.

"Wait!" I said. "How did the king come to die?"

"You haven't heard, master?"

"I've heard what you just told me, nothing else."

"They say he was murdered." He crossed himself. "In his own chamber, they say."

"Murdered? Dear God, by whom?"

"How could I know that, master?"

I could get nothing more from him. I had to find an inn, and some men who had been drinking for an hour or two, before anyone would repeat what was clearly being whispered from one border of the empire to the other. Ehrenfried had indeed been murdered in his chamber, by someone he must have trusted, someone who could get close enough to stab him in the back while he drank a cup of wine. And Prince Konrad had quarreled with his father—bitterly, publicly, repeatedly. He was in the palace at the time the king was attacked, but no one seemed to know where.

None of these lowly folk, even with their bellies full of ale, would say anything more in public. But it was clear enough what they were wondering, what everyone in Germany must be wondering. Was it the prince, perhaps, who had slain his father? And if he had—or even if he hadn't—what would such a possibility do to the succession?

Gottfried and the other princes of Germany had already been summoned, and were already traveling to Mainz with all possible haste to choose a new king. Normally, if the emperor left behind a worthy son, the crown passed to him without much question. But there would be questions now. And if the questions were not resolved, there was likely to be blood. For one thing was well-known, even among the common folk: the young prince was arrogant, strong-willed, and hungry for power.

One man sat, with two huge hands knotted around his tankard, and his elbows on the table, glowering at a spot somewhere beyond us on the wall.

"It be Konrad," he said, "or it be war."

He was grim and troubled. But my own heart rose the more I thought on these events, the more I listened. I saw in all of it the clear hand of God, the shape of an inevitable pattern unfolding, where even the worst deeds by the worst of men fell into place like pieces of mosaic. I felt sorry for these grumbling peasants, dull-witted people thinking of nothing but their crops, their little jars of coin. They were so afraid of what a war might cost them; they could not imagine what splendors it might bring.

I was never bloodthirsty. I never wanted war for its own sake, as some men did. But I was not afraid, and I wanted to tell the people so, and I wanted to tell them why. *It will be a war like no other, and after it will come the kingdom! It's all part of God's design, and the last thing we should wish for is to stop it!*

But I couldn't say a word. I could only listen, and wrap myself at last in a filthy blanket, and wait for morning. Then I went back to my bitter searching, to the one place left for me to go. I took the road for Ravensbruck, as we had all done one fateful dark November, and I haunted the ragged hills below the wood of Helmardin.

Karelian would come there sooner or later. If he still lived at all, he would come.

It was snowing the night I found him. I was cold and hungry, and my courage was almost gone. I had been in the area for weeks, and I had found nothing. Oh, there were occasional abandoned campsites, but they could have been made by any forester or bandit. And there was talk sometimes of strangers. Lone travelers passed through the inns, ate their meals with half-hooded faces and went away, but what of it? They had been doing so for a hundred years. Once I found a peasant who remembered selling bread and sausages to a traveler who paid him in gold. This seemed promising, for a while, but the traveler left no traces thereafter, neither in the wilds nor on the roads.

Through every hour of it I lived in terror. Even as humans traveled it, I was only a few day's journey from the edge of Helmardin. From the very lair of witches and demon-creatures who could fly and change their shapes; who rode on the night winds and trod the darkness with feet which never made a sound; who did not die from the wounds of ordinary weapons; who stalked men, and strangled them with vines and drowned them in marshes. Who sought always and especially to undo their souls, to make them numb or blind, to lure them with music or lust or promises of gold into a dark and endless enslavement.

Many a night I sat shivering and sleepless, catching my breath at every sound, swearing that with the first hint of daylight I would go back to Stavoren, and throw myself on Gottfried's mercy: *Do with me as you will, my lord, but please don't send me back there; I will go mad!* But with daylight it was always a little easier. *Maybe,* I would tell myself, *maybe I'll find him this very day. Maybe tonight I'll sleep in an inn. Maybe I'll find out he's already been captured.* I had to go on. If I wanted to ever have Gottfried's favor, I had to go on.

I did not sleep that night in an inn. It began to snow late in the afternoon: a light snow, the flakes small and hard-edged, spun about in bitter gusts of wind. I sought what shelter I could in a gully under the lee of a cliff. I made an ill-burning fire, and scorched a bit of meat on it, and ate it without noticing what it was. Finally, too frightened to sleep and too exhausted to stay properly awake, I curled into a ball beside my fire and dreamt of dying.

And woke to the whisper of steps on the frozen earth, the glint of a sword in the firelight, a very real sword, poised mortal inches from my throat.

"Get up," a voice said.

I was dazed with sleep and terror, and the wind was gusting snow into my face. I stumbled to my feet. The man with the sword stayed carefully back from the fire; he was just a darker shape against the darkness.

"Please," I said. "I have nothing to steal, I'm a pilgrim . . . ."

"Pauli . . . ?"

He did not sheathe his weapon, but with his other hand he reached and flung the hood back from my face, and then he laughed.

"Pauli! What in God's name are you doing here, lad? I all but cut your throat for one of Gottfried's hounds!"

And even then, though I knew his voice, and his laughter, and even the scent of his body, and though my eyes were waking to the light, still it took me a moment to recognize him. Because of the wind lashing snow in my face. Because I had been waiting so long, and seen him so many times when he was not there. Because he no longer looked like a nobleman at all, but like a common bandit.

"My lord . . . ?"

His cloak was dark-stained and torn in many places; ridges of snow clung in the fouled and matted tangles of his hair. His boots were in ruins, and the rest of his garments looked as though he had been chased by hounds through a hundred leagues of swamps and rocks and briars.

"Pauli." His voice was warm as I had rarely heard it, and it all but undid me with guilt. "I've never been so glad to see anyone in my life. But how did you get here? What's happening in Lys?"

"I escaped, my lord." I could not keep my voice from shaking. It was better so, perhaps. "I knew you were wounded. The duke's men boasted of it; they said you were probably dead. But I didn't believe it."

"You are the best of lads, my friend. The very best. Come, there's no need . . . I'm all right now."

Why did I weep then, like a stupid boy? Why did I let him wrap me in his arms, even for a moment? I was cold and frightened and raw with loneliness, with all those weeks of wandering and dread. And I forgot. That is all I can say in my defense: I forgot. He was Gottfried's enemy, and mine. He was a sorcerer, a thousand times more perilous than death. And I forgot.

"Sit, lad, come sit, and tell me everything. Has Reinhard kept my fortress safe?"

"Yes, the last I've heard. Duke Gottfried has given the county to his second son, to young Armund, and he has the castle under siege. But Reini swears he won't surrender. It'll take a year to starve him out."

"Longer," Karelian said. "It's well provisioned; I saw to that. And what of my lady, and the babe? Are they safe?"

"They're with Reinhard in the castle. It was your priest, Father Thomas, who fetched the child there, and he is with them."

"Good. One card, at least, the duke can't play against me."

"Otto is dead, my lord," I said.

His only reaction was a troubled frown. He had lost weight, I saw, and he was so weary. Yet there was a hardness in him I had never seen before, even in the war camps of the Holy Land.

Did he know?

I swallowed, and tried not to think about it. I made myself ask the questions I had to ask, the questions anyone in my place would ask if he were innocent.

"My lord, I don't understand what happened—why Gottfried turned against you so. You were his most favored vassal. Why would he accuse you of such dreadful things? It makes no sense at all."

He did not answer me for a time. The fire burned poorly, and he played with it, wondering, I suppose, how much he should confide in me.

"Gottfried himself is guilty of all the things he accused me of. He is a sorcerer, although he would deny it, and claim his power comes from God. But he is a sorcerer nonetheless."

I stared at him, astonished. Gottfried a sorcerer? Yes, but of course; he would have to say it. Perhaps he would even believe it.

"He plotted mutiny against our common lord, the emperor Ehrenfried," Karelian went on. "Now that Ehrenfried is dead, I am sure he'll try to block Konrad's succession, and take the crown for himself. And if you want to know how I know, it's quite simple. He told me. He

invited me to join him, to be his ally and his warleader, first against
the king, and then against whomever he chose to conquer next."

"God in heaven . . . !" I whispered. "But if he asked you to join
him, then why—?"

"Why did he withdraw the invitation?" Karelian said dryly. "I'm
not sure. But obviously he discovered I'm against him, though I pretended not to be. His powers of sorcery are exceptional, more than
we ever guessed."

"But . . . ." I threw out my hands. "I can hardly believe it. The
duke always seemed so . . . so Christian."

"What of it? The history of the Church is full of magic. Dying
men rise cured from their beds. Dead trees fill with flowers. Stones
talk. Sound bridges collapse for no reason, and broken ones mend.
People walk through fire without so much as a blister. The list could
go on forever—"

"But those were miracles! Are you trying to say the holy saints
were nothing more than sorcerers?"

"Nothing more?" He smiled faintly. "To be good at sorcery is a
considerable achievement, Paul. But yes, those who worked miracles
were magicians. That's what magic is: doing what seems impossible,
by using powers other people don't have, or never learn to use."

"But there are only two powers beyond the common world, my
lord: those of God, and those of Satan—!"

He laughed. "There are a million powers, and everyone uses them
who can. Power is, Pauli. That's all. It just is. It exists, and the Church
didn't stop it from existing. All the Church did was lay claim to everything which served its own advancement, and pour guilt and damnation on the rest. If a priest heals a wounded man to prove God's
power to the heathen, he's likely to be canonized. If a witch does the
same because she loves him, she's likely to be burnt. And it has nothing to do with God or Satan. It has to do with who runs things in
the world."

"You can't believe that, my lord."

He looked at me, and then at the fire, and then at me again. "Tell
me something," he said. "We've crossed words on things like this
before. You know I've left the Church. I left it in Jerusalem, and I'll
never go back. Have you never considered . . . serving another lord?
One more suited to your heart and conscience?"

It felt like the most dangerous moment of my life.

"You've always been good to me, my lord . . . ." I faltered. And the words placed themselves in my throat, without conscious thought or judgment, the words I knew I had to say, the words I knew he would believe because he wanted to believe them. Everyone did. It was every man's eternal, irremediable weakness. Mine as well . . . .

"And I . . . I could never love any other lord as much, no matter how good he was. I would always wish I were still by your side."

Yes, I did say it. I said all of it, and even as I spoke I knew it was true. Which was also why he would believe it. He was the one who made it so.

He watched me for a moment. I could not read his eyes, only the dance of firelight on his face, playing over every sharp and well remembered line.

"And besides," he said at last, with a faint smile, "if you argue with me long enough, and well enough, I might come to see the folly of my ways."

"That too, my lord," I agreed, and smiled in return. For the moment, I knew I was safe.

He slept peacefully against the small shelter of the cliff, comforted perhaps by my presence, by my unexpected and exaggerated gift of loyalty. And you might well ask why I did not kill him then, why I did not simply take my dagger and drive it into his heart.

I could not do it, and you may judge it as you wish. I was only a boy, and he was a man who had lived through every kind of violence, who probably knew every kind of trick. The knight was perilous enough to deal with. The sorcerer . . . no, dear God, it was quite beyond me. Who could say what he might observe even in his sleep? Or what evil things hovered there beside him, unseen, ready to wake him at the smallest danger?

I could not kill him, not like this. But if I did not, then I had to get the cross back. Every passing hour increased my danger. We were too close to Helmardin now, too close to *her*. She would find it in a moment. She would sense its power like a burned hand sensed a flame. And once either of them knew, and had me in their power . . . . I could not bear to think of it, and yet I had no courage to act against him. Worse, I didn't even want to.

I huddled against the wind, wrapped in my cloak. For the first time in my life, I felt bitter against Gottfried. Why had he sent me here? Didn't he know how terrible it would be? Didn't he know that the darker Karelian's image became for me, the more I was held in its power? Everything about him now possessed a sordid fascination, not least the fact that he belonged to *them*. I did not will it so, and I could not control it. All the time we sat by the fire and talked of Lys and politics and saints, my loins were hot and throbbing. With a part of my consciousness I listened to his questions and responded, and with another part I remembered his body against my own, the harsh smell of sweat and bracken, the rush of blood which sickened me and took my breath away. I'd been all but overcome by the impulse to continue, to begin again. Even now—oh yes, now more than ever as he slept beside me, as I wondered what I should do, and how I might hope to save myself—even now I wanted to thrust myself against him like a rutting dog.

I say wanted, but it is the wrong word, for I didn't want to. There was no real desire in it, nor any thought of pleasure. No conscious will. Only a driven impulse, crude and feverish, as a man might feel towards a harlot in the street. I could not make it stop, and finally I used my hands—one of the gravest sins I could commit, save for the one I dreaded more. Then I wept, thinking of Gottfried, and of how he would despise me if he knew. How everyone would despise me, and believe of me things which were not true. I never had a carnal nature, never, not like other youths my age, not like my brother, who was always in difficulty, always in the confessional begging God's forgiveness. I avoided the snares of wanton girls. In truth, I found it easy to avoid them, most times. And when I first entered Karelian's service, when I was with him in the Holy Land, those other thoughts had never crossed my mind.

Not until we passed through Helmardin. Not until he met *her*, and began to change . . . .

I wrapped my arms around my knees, shivering from the cold. It was then, in that black wilderness, in that black night, when I first began to perceive how immense, how encompassing was the power of sorcery. To conjure up a demon, or cause a storm, or make a woman barren—these were small things, the kinds of witchery everyone understood.

There was another kind, one which crept into the most secret places of our souls, in silence and with no warning at all, coaxing to life sins which we in our ordinary human frailty would have rejected, if not out of goodness then out of shame, still refusing to lower ourselves to *that*.

It was all their work, this sickness in my blood, this terrible attraction which made him ever more beautiful as he fell. It was they who filled my mind with foul images, with offers of permission, with the possibility of limitless unrestraint. *You can have anything. Do anything. Can you even imagine what is possible with me? Come here, and I will show you.*

His thoughts, not mine. His power . . . or really hers, the power of what she made him into. A power which could undo me utterly, until my body slavered like a dog after something I never wanted, until my body no longer belonged to me at all. Everything Karelian touched became entangled in sorcery, captivated by the promise of his dazzling corruption. *Come here, and I will show you . . . .*

It crept back through the silence even as I prayed. Teasing me, whispering in the corners of my mind, telling me Gottfried was less than he was, telling me I should not go back.

I could stay, and serve him again, serve him better than before. I could go missing from the world. Who would know, and in the end who would care? It would be so easy, easy as finding a fire in the darkness, a fire already in reach of my hand.

Paul stood up dizzily, wiped one arm across his face. It was all sorcery—those words carved on parchment as if on stone, lying scattered on the monastery floor. The words, and the memory, too. Both of them were lies, fashioned in his brain and in his loins by the malice of his enemies.

He had thrown the parchments across the room. Long ago, when it first began, he tried burning them. He knew better now. Fire only made the words brighter, seared them more permanently into the deepest places of his mind.

God, why do you compel me to suffer this? Pain I can bear, and hunger, and every kind of hardship. I have even learned to endure your abandonment of me, for I know I'm unworthy of your favor. But why this, after all these years? Why do you allow them to befoul my memory with sins I never wanted to commit? I loved him purely; I cared only for his soul, and for mine, and for the good of the Reinmark and of Christendom—

Soft laughter lapped across the room, like water against pebbles. Even before he looked up, he knew the voice, the silken malevolence, the half-clothed body leaning serpentine against his rough-hewn desk. He was no longer much surprised when she came, or even much frightened. Nor did he try to make her leave; he knew it was beyond his strength.

"Really, Paul," she said. "You do lie marvelously well. But if your Christian God is as omniscient as you say, surely he will know?"

"There is nothing to know," the monk said. "I am the lowest of sinners, but I was never that kind of man. It was all your doing—yours, and the evil ones you serve."

"Mine?" She smiled. "You fell in love with Karelian in Acre, before either of you knew I existed. And please, stifle your protests; they grow boring. Especially since I never had the slightest objection. He was mine from the moment he rode into Helmardin. What pleasures he might have taken with you, or with his countess—they were just strawberries in the grass. Those who find them smile, and eat, and go their way."

He stared at her. Did she really think her jealousy, or the lack of it, mattered to him in the least?

"Do you care about anything," he asked coldly, "except your lusts?"

"Never," she said. "And my lusts, as you have already decided, are many and insatiable."

She bent, and with her own ringed hand picked up the scattered pages of his manuscript.

"You're getting too old for temper tantrums, Brother Paul. Finish your book."

"Suppose I choose not to?" he said.

"You might. When hailstones choose not to fall, and dead men choose not to decay." She handed him the quill. "I'm not inclined to offer you even the smallest kindness, Paul of Ardiun, but for my own purposes I will. Finish the story, to the last drop of blood and the last cry of triumph, and you will be free to die."

"My death is in God's hands."

"No, little fool," she said softly. "It's in mine. The Reinmark is not very Christian, remember? You keep saying so yourself. Veelas haunt the riverbanks, and elves stalk wild in the mountains. The people go to your Masses, maybe, but all week long they pay reverence to Odin and Freya and Thor; Tyr's altars are laden with game. Your God is as proud as any other, Pauli; he knows where he's not wanted. You can pray until your monk's heart breaks; it won't matter. He is far away from here, and he'll never come to set you free." She paused, and added darkly: "I am the only one who can."

Many times in his life he thought he had reached the bottom of human despair, and nothing more terrible was left to befall him, short of damnation itself. Yet this was a new and utterly overwhelming terror.

"Why are you surprised?" she went on. "You've seen the powers of Car-Iduna. You know within the Grail of Life is the death of every living thing. It comes to all, even to your priests who imagine they'll recover from it. *When* it comes, depends on fate—and, if they choose to involve themselves, on the gods. Iduna has given me the apple of your life—at great cost, I will admit; she doesn't give any of them lightly. But it's mine now. You will live, and endure my power over you, until I give you leave to go."

She picked up the last page, scarred with the words she had made him write, with the passions she had made him remember.

"Finish the story," she said, "and I will let you be."

For a long time he said nothing. He knew it was an act of unfaith more terrible than any sin he had ever committed, but he believed her. Maybe God permitted it, or maybe, as she said, God was far away. But his life was in her hands, and there was nothing he could do about it.

I am damned. If they can persuade me of this, then I am truly and utterly damned . . . .

That was why he asked the question; if he was damned it did not matter. He had longed to ask so many times. It had been in the back of his mind almost from the first, creeping closer and ever closer to the boundaries of his will. Always he resisted. It was a great sin to seek knowledge from a witch. But he was so tired of resisting. And it would mean so much to know.

"Will you answer me a question, sorceress?"

"I might."

"What became of Karelian . . . after . . . after that day . . . ?"

"Your God is omniscient, Brother Paul, and your Jesus is

all-loving and all-kind. You will have to ask them. You haven't deserved an answer from me."

So. Not even that, to carry with him to his darkness. Neither God's comfort, nor any other. Only memories, memories so clear they lived before his eyes, and reduced both God and the world to shadows.

XXIX

THE PARTING

And anon after that, I was had forth through
dark places by the cruel and incredible madness of
wicked spirits . . . .

REVELATION TO A MONK OF EVESHAM

I SLEPT FINALLY, I MUST HAVE, for when I saw the world again the sun
was pouring gold all over me, and the air smelled of smoke and
roasting meat. Karelian had his crossbow propped against a tree, and
three rabbits gutted and browning on the fire.

I scrambled to my feet, glancing at the sky. It was late, almost
noon.

"Forgive me, my lord. You should have wakened me."

"There was no need," he said. "And you looked like you hadn't
slept for a year."

"I suppose I haven't, to tell the truth. I have no talent for living
in the woods."

"Yes, I've noticed," he said dryly.

I was piqued in spite of myself. "What do you mean, my lord?"

"When the prey catches the hunter, the hunter is out of his element. Or don't you think so?"

He smiled. He was teasing me. Of course he was teasing me, but
a cold shiver went all through my bones.

"Even in my element, I would hardly be a match for you, my
lord," I said. In the sunlight I saw how haggard he really was. I wondered if he had slept any more than I had, and I felt colder still.

But he only reached to turn the shimmering rabbits on their spits, and fed the fire.

"Hungry?" he asked.

"Starving." I brought more wood up, and then settled on the ground nearby.

"Where will you go now, my lord?"

He shrugged. "Wherever I can do Gottfried the most damage."

Yes, of course; that is your mission on this earth, is it not?

"Wherever I go," he added, "it will be a dangerous journey. I won't blame you if you choose not to come."

"I swore an oath to serve you, my lord."

"I'll release you from your oath, if you wish. Freely, and with thanks."

"Are you sending me away?"

"No. I'm asking you to be sure. Where I'm going now, I'll compel no one to follow."

"Car-Iduna?" I whispered.

"No, Pauli. Not simply Car-Iduna. You've been there, and you survived it. This time, I may well go to hell . . . as the priests would look on it, and men like Gottfried. I mean to destroy him, and I'll do it any way I can. Do you understand me, Pauli? There's no weapon I won't raise against him. And if I must find my strength in darkness, then that's where I will go."

"My lord . . . ."

"You needn't follow me. But if you do . . . ." He paused. "If you do, my friend, you probably won't be able to get back. Not because I'd wish it so, but because there are patterns in the world, and they unfold as they are fashioned. You must choose carefully."

"I've already chosen, my lord. I will serve you faithfully in all things, saving only the good of my immortal soul."

He looked at me bemused, and then he laughed.

"You're a jewel of a lad, Pauli, but you don't listen. Never mind. We'll talk about it later. Have some rabbit."

He pulled one of the haunches off the spit, and handed it to me. I was hungry in spite of everything, and I gobbled it, wondering precisely what it was that we would talk about later, and what I would say or do if he demanded some horrid oath, some dreadful ritual of surrender to his masters and himself.

Even now I wonder. For we had barely begun to eat when we

heard the intruder, and dropped our food and pulled our swords, springing to our feet like cornered thieves.

The woman was not twenty feet away, and I swear—I swear as God is my witness and the keeper of my soul—I swear she landed there, even as we whirled to challenge her, landed like an angel in a painting, without a breath of effort.

"Well," she said.

For the briefest moment I thought it was *her*, the lady of Car-Iduna, for her smooth and scornful voice, her smooth and shameless body. But this woman was younger, much younger and fair-haired; and although there was perhaps the faintest resemblance in their eyes and in the lines of their mouths, this was someone very different.

She moved towards us. She was very slender. She wore a garment I had never seen before on anyone, all furry and wrapping every part of her, even her throat and her fingers. She looked like a white and golden cat.

"Lord Karelian Brandeis, I take it?" Her eyes raked him, amused and insolent.

He bowed politely. "My lady."

The woman unwrapped a long rabbit scarf from around her shoulders and played with it idly. Her gaze never left Karelian.

"She told me you were the finest looking man in the empire. I can't imagine what else she has been looking at."

"I'm flattered, my lady," Karelian said. "But of whom are we speaking?"

"Her highness of Helmardin. My sister. My *baby* sister." She spoke, I thought, like one of those whores in the brothels of Jerusalem, where Karelian had dragged me once or twice when there was no one else to watch his coin-pouch or his back. *Look at me! Can't you see I'm prettier than she is, more experienced, more desirable . . . .*

"Baby sister?" Karelian murmured. The lady of Car-Iduna was his own age or more, and this creature looked all of seventeen. "You surprise me, lady."

She tossed her head. "I am veela, Lord Karelian. So was my mother. I had children myself when she took that wandering Cossack for a lover; what she saw in him I never did understand. Your queen was the last of her babes—though of course she doesn't look it. Humans *age* so ridiculously fast."

"And how fares my queen, lady veela?"

The creature shrugged. "She's besotted. But I'm sure she'll get over it."

She scrutinized him again. She obviously found her sister's choices as bewildering as she had once found her mother's.

"She should be thankful I discovered you, in any case. I passed your camp twice, my lord, and didn't bother stopping. I thought you were just a bandit."

This was too much. I stepped forward, surprised at my own anger.

"There's no need to insult his lordship," I said harshly. "He was gravely wounded, and he's been journeying in the wilderness for weeks—"

"I've been in the wilderness since I was born," she said archly, "and I don't look like a rag."

"Never mind, Pauli," Karelian said. "I beg you, lady tell me where the queen is, or take me to her! It's urgent that I see her!"

"Yes, I'm sure it is," she said. "My sister may be a brat, but she does have a way with men. They may leave her, but they're always eager to go back. Never fear, my lord, I'll tell her where you are, and then, gods willing, she'll leave me in peace. Twenty-nine years, would you believe it, twenty-nine years she sat on a little favor she did me, and then she summoned me halfway across the empire, and demanded that I pay her back! In the middle of winter, for Frigg's sake, without a shred of pity. Look till you find him, she said—or I'll strangle you. Being queen has gone to her head.

"Don't worry, my lord count, I'm sure she'll be here to fetch you before the sun goes down tomorrow."

"Then I thank you, lady . . . ?" He paused hopefully, and she smiled.

"Lady Malanthine. First of the veelas of Reinmark and Franconia, daughter of Ursula the Fair, heiress of the immortal Iduna. At your most humble service, my lord."

"I thank you, Lady Malanthine, and I beg you to tell the queen—"

"Yes, of course. You adore her and kiss her feet and can't wait to explain where the devil you've been all this time. I'll tell her, my lord, with the greatest of delight. Farewell!"

"Wait! Surely she knows what happened at Lys—!"

"She knows you failed her. Gottfried is in Mainz, getting himself made king, and you're playing in the woods like a peasant lad on a Sunday afternoon. That will take some accounting for, I expect."

And then, with the smallest of curtseys, and a toss of the fur she had flung over her shoulder, she swept away, so lightly and so quickly it's possible she flew; I wouldn't want to say. But in a few heartbeats there was only woods about us, and winter birds chattering at the sun, and nothing more.

And so I had my chance to get the cross. Karelian was like an animal in a cage, torn between happiness and dismay. *I was afraid I'd never find her again, Pauli; I tried every way I knew to reach her, and I couldn't.* He was happy, but half desperate as well, as men are always desperate when they depend on the favor of a woman. Would she be angry? Would she blame him for his absence, berate him, mock him as her sister did, wonder why she ever thought him beautiful?

It was a fine day, and since it seemed the lady of Car-Iduna would come to us, we had nothing to do but stay in our camp.

"My lord," I said. "Why don't I take your things down to the brook and wash them? They will dry by the fire before dark."

He smiled faintly, ruefully. "And then I will look like a *clean* bandit . . . ? I don't think it will help much, Pauli, but all right. Christ knows they need a scrubbing."

He wrapped his cloak close around his shoulders and took off his clothing, all but his trousers and his boots. I was shocked by the blood-stains on his tunic, by the three ugly, half-healed wounds he bore. I wondered how he ever survived.

I drew all the breath I had to keep my voice calm.

"Give me the pouch, too, my lord; it's all blood-stained. I'll wash it and soften it again with tallow."

He hesitated, but only for a second. He slipped it over his head, and took the feather out, and gave me the bag.

And I carried it to the edge of the brook with his garments, trying to control the pounding of my heart, the wish to run in my driven eagerness: *Oh, God, only a few moments, only a few moments alone and I will have it, I'll be safe!*

I threw his clothes into a pile beside me and seized the pouch in both hands, turning it inside out and groping at the bottom of the seam. But it had stiffened from being soaked over and over in sweat and rain and blood, and I was clumsy with haste. And I had forgotten, too, how tiny the cross was. Even when I first placed it there, and knew exactly in which spot, I could barely feel it between my fingers.

There was no help for it. I would have to take the pouch entirely apart. I sat, spreading my cloak across my lap and making a valley in it. Then, very carefully, I sliced the stitching with my dagger, and opened the folded seam. I thought I would see the cross at once, with its brilliant crystal, but there was dirt on everything, and bits of grass, and caked blood. I felt slowly with one finger, very slowly, tracing the length of the opened seam, once, then again. It had to be there. It was so small, perhaps it had even broken, but it had to still be there, oh, dear God, let it still be there . . . ! Sweat ran into my eyes, and I had to stop to brush it away. My searching began to grow frantic. I was scrabbling at the pouch like a rat at a wall, scraping away the detritus and shaking it into my lap, rubbing it between my fingers, oh, Jesus, if you love me, help me now, please help me find it . . . ! But there was nothing, only dirt and so much mark of blood.

And then I heard his voice, heard it maybe in my soul before I heard it in my flesh, soft and close by, without the whisper of a foot-step to warn me.

"Is this what you're looking for, Pauli?"

I turned, scrambling to my feet. He stood about ten feet away, his left hand slightly outstretched. The cross was too tiny to recognize even at such a brief distance, but as he moved the afternoon sun caught the crystal, and it shimmered. I made myself look at his face, and then at his other hand, holding his naked sword.

"My lord . . . ?"

There are no words for my fear. It was so overwhelming and yet so ambivalent, so mixed with feelings of guilt, with outrage at my own stupidity, and also, with something very close to relief. It was over. Whatever happened now, it was finally over.

Would things have turned out different in the world, if it really had been over? If I had faced him bravely and said: *Yes, I have be-trayed you; yes, I belong to Gottfried, yes!* If he had used his sword, and truly ended it, I would have had no further part to play in the story. I would not have been there when it all was decided. I could not have done what I did.

Would it have mattered?

The wondering is a pain which never leaves me. All I know is what I did: I threw myself upon my knees and pleaded.

"My good lord, forgive me, I didn't know, they told me it would help you, I swear to you I didn't know . . . !"

"Who told you? Stand on your feet, damn you! You had the gall to do this, you should have gall enough to answer for it! Get up! And tell me who put you up to this, and how, while you still have breath to do it!"

I stood. I tried to compose myself.

"Two priests, my lord. They came to me in Ardiun. They said there was talk all over the Reinmark about you, that you were turning apostate. And they asked me how it was possible, when you had served so well in the great crusade—!"

"And you didn't defend me?" he asked scornfully. "My good and faithful squire?"

"I did at first, but . . . ."

"But what?"

"They knew a great deal about you, my lord."

"Go on."

"They asked me if I might know why you had . . . changed. They said there must be some dark influence in your life, because those who had gone to Jerusalem were especially favored by God's grace, and should be the last to falter. I wanted only to help you, my lord, I swear it—!"

"What did you tell them?"

"That you had been to Car-Iduna. That you were . . . seduced there."

"You gave your word you'd never speak of Car-Iduna!"

"They were priests, my lord, and concerned for your welfare—"

"Yes, obviously. Go on."

"They gave me the cross. They said it was especially blessed, and very powerful. They said it would protect you from . . . from sorcery. I never thought it was evil, my lord. I swear to you I didn't!"

"Then why—" He took a small, perilous step closer. "Why were you searching for it? Tell me, Pauli. If you believed it was protecting me, then why would you want to take it away?"

I backed away. I could not help it. And I think it was less from fear than from despair, from the knowledge I read in his eyes. He would never trust me again, never care about me, never want me near him. I should have been glad. I was glad. And yet it had the sharpness of a knife being driven in my flesh—driven and turned there, and turned again.

"Because of what you told me, my lord," I whispered. "About Gottfried being a sorcerer. Because of what happened. I realized it had to be . . . that it wasn't . . . what they said."

He said nothing. I don't think he believed me. What was important was that he didn't entirely disbelieve me. I confess to feeling a small

tug of pride, because I had fashioned a credible story with no time
at all to consider it. I could, sometimes, think very well on my feet.

"I beg your forgiveness, my lord."

"You I may yet forgive," he said. "Your God I will not."

I shuddered at the blasphemy, and I suppose he saw it, for he
made a brief, savage gesture of contempt.

"You still don't see it, do you? What men do for this God of
yours, and what it turns them into? Jerusalem is butchered, and Lys
burned, and the empire ready to shatter into pieces, and all of it for
God, and you can't even see it! You've turned into a liar and a traitor,
and you can't see that, either. All you have left for a mind is an echo.
You'd send me to the stake and call it love, protesting your virtue
every step of the way! With so much love in the world, men hardly
need to bother hating, do they?"

There was nothing I could say, nothing I could do except steel
myself against his suddenly unleashed rage. I understood now why the
veela had dismissed him as a bandit. He had hardened since our days
in Lys. Or perhaps, without the glamour of fine garments and knightly
rituals, he was simply revealing a hardness which had always been
there. *Your master was a savage at sixteen, starving for glory and too
angry to think straight . . . .*

Always angry, year after bloodswept year, the rage transferred
from his father to other proud and powerful men, one after another,
and finally to his liege lord and to God.

"Did you ever care about me at all, Pauli?" he asked bitterly.
"Myself—the man, the knight, the soldier you rode beside? Or just
that little abstraction you call my soul? Which isn't really mine at all,
it seems, since I'm to have no lordship over it. It's just ransom money
for men like you to buy their place in heaven. Look, Lord Father,
here's another one I've brought you, all shivering and gelded, drowning
in guilt for merely being born!

"Isn't that more or less what you had in mind, Pauli? Dragging
me back to your priestlings like a hound on a chain?"

"I meant you no evil, my lord—"

He cut me off with a rough gesture. "I'm quite aware of it, lad.
You wouldn't recognize evil if it tore you into pieces, as long as it
wore a cross around its neck! Take out your sword, and drop it on the
ground."

I obeyed, dry-mouthed with fear.

"What are you going to do to me, my lord?"

"By the laws of fealty your life is forfeit, Pauli, as you know. I could kill you where you stand. I could take you prisoner to Car-Iduna, and let my lady deal with you . . . ."

He paused, letting those dark threats hang long in the air.

"Or," he added finally, "I could bind you and let you go."

"Bind me, my lord?" I whispered.

"Yes." And then he smiled, the smile I used to love, which could have melted the moon. Only there was darkness in it now. It was not malice; it went infinitely beyond malice, as though he simply looked upon something which he knew to be true, and knowing it, was satisfied.

"Yes," he said again. "You shall be bound to do no further harm, neither to me, nor to her whom I serve. By your own cross, Paul von Ardiun, by your own lord, whichever one he is—"

The smile was gone, the soft voice turned to granite. "You have your life back, but under this mortal ban: Any wrong you seek to do us shall return to you. Come to us with fire, and you will burn in it; with poison, and you will drink it; with cunning, and you'll be snared in it. I've spared you once. Neither the gods themselves, nor the winds nor the seas nor the turning of the stars will spare you a second time!"

And then, without a shred of fear, for he knew his own strength, he sheathed his sword and stepped close to me, taking my face between his palms.

"So may it be," he said.

He drew his hands away, and I saw that he held in one of them the raven's feather, and in the other Gottfried's cross.

"By your gods or by mine, Pauli, it will be so."

That was how we parted. And though I would see him many times thereafter, it was always from a distance, across the camps and council rooms of war. We never met as friends again. Oh, there is an apparition which comes into my cell in the dead of night, and speaks as he used to do, but it is only a demon she sends to torment me. In the world of men those were his words of farewell, and they were truthful: *By your gods or by mine, it will be so.* All my deeds thereafter undid themselves, like a rope unraveling from one end even as it was braided from the other.

Now in this chronicle I must finally undo myself.

XXX

A KNIGHT AND HIS LADY

A noble man must not resist love,
for love will help to make him well.

WOLFRAM VON ESCHENBACH

THE TENT WAS WARM, and the first taste of heated wine was a rush of pure pleasure. Karelian drank it all, and lowered the cup to see her smiling at him. No matter how many times he saw her smile, he would turn to see it again, to be reminded once again that she loved him. That she blamed him for nothing.

She made it quite clear when she rode into his camp, jumping off her horse and wrapping him in her arms: "Karel, Karel, Karel . . . !" She barely noticed her escort, barely responded to their deferential and slightly amused requests. "Put the tent anywhere, I don't care . . . . What, Marius? Food? Yes, make us some food. Karel, where were you, my love, we searched and we searched and we couldn't find you . . . !" No blame at all, only desperate questions and a still more desperate tenderness.

"Are you all right, Karel? You look weary to death."

"I'm all right."

She was beautifully dressed, in hunting garments of rich leather trimmed with fur; her elegance only made him more aware of his own disreputable state. In the shelter of the tent she had taken off her hooded cape, and her hair spilled black and wanton over her shoulders.

"We must talk," she had said. "The electors are already in Mainz, meeting to choose a new king."

He filled his cup again, and toasted her. He did not want to talk—

not about Gottfried, not about the world. He wanted to disarrange her hair. First her hair, then the soft tunic lacings which gathered at her throat.

"What happened, Raven?" he asked. "You promised me you'd warn the king. Didn't he heed the warnings at all?"

"Yes and no."

She paced a little, as she did when she was deeply troubled. "Things have gone . . . strangely. It shouldn't surprise us, considering who we're dealing with. And considering your own fate in Lys.

"I sent messengers to Ehrenfried—good men, clever and trustworthy. They told him he was in danger, that the duke of the Reinmark meant to usurp his crown. And he seemed to believe them at first. He said he would guarantee the succession by having Konrad crowned in the spring. And then, as we all know, he sent his envoys out to summon the electors.

"Something you must remember about the emperor, Karel: he's always been very much a Christian. His long fight against the pope was never a fight against the Church—or at least, he never saw it that way at the time.

"In the fall, a few months after my messengers spoke to him, he went hunting and was tumbled from his horse. It was the tiniest of mishaps. They say he only bruised his shoulder, but I think he must have hit his head on a rock. For after that he stopped talking about the succession, and went on instead about dying and the afterlife, and spent endless hours in the chapel worrying about his sins. When my messengers spoke to him again, to remind him that his problems in this life might be of more immediate concern—do you want to know what he said, Karel? You will not believe it."

"Try me."

"He said our warning was a warning from God. It made him realize he had to mend his life, and more precisely, he had to mend his relationship with Rome. If he were once again a true and obedient son of Christ's vicar the pope, the danger would pass; his kingdom would be safe. And that's how he set about protecting himself. By going to confession, and writing long, self-abasing letters to the pope."

Karelian drained his cup, and filled it yet again.

"Everything we do turns back on us," he said bitterly. "Like spit blown into the wind."

"Needless to say, my love, Konrad wasn't happy with his father's change of heart. He didn't want the empire tucked under the pope's belt buckle before he had a chance to inherit it. And Konrad, for all his faults, has at least one solid virtue: he thinks for himself. They quarreled—several times in private, and finally in public."

"If Gottfried set all of this up," Karelian murmured, "he did it extraordinarily well."

"Yes. It seems the last quarrel was particularly ugly. Konrad is never careful what he says. He cursed his father, and said he wasn't fit to be a king. Two days later the emperor was stabbed in his chamber. He was still alive when they found him. They say he whispered his son's name over and over, but whether he was accusing him, or asking for him, or naming him as his successor, no one can say."

"And there's no trace of the murderer, I suppose."

"None whatever. But it must have been someone close to the king, someone with easy access to his quarters."

"Probably, but not necessarily. I've slipped into a few well-guarded chambers in my life, and out again—and don't smile so knowingly, my lady; it wasn't always for pleasure."

She regarded him a moment, thoughtfully.

"Anyone might have killed the emperor, Raven," he went on. "Anyone who planned it carefully enough. A servant, a courtier, a hired assassin—anyone. But of course they will blame the prince."

"Not openly—at least not yet. There are no grounds for blaming him, except the quarrel, and his father's incoherent words. There's only a cloud of suspicion. And for a man like Konrad, whispers and doubts may prove worse than an open accusation. He's reckless, Karel; reckless and arrogant. It may be easy for his enemies to bait him into doing something stupid."

"Christ . . . ." He shook his head, and said nothing more. He reached for the wine, and then let his hand fall; he was already light-headed, and she was far too beautiful.

"The princes are already meeting?" he said.

"Yes."

"Have you . . . sent anyone?"

"To the electoral council of the Holy Roman Empire? You jest, my love."

He smiled. "I didn't mean officially."

She did not return the smile. "I have a few spies in the world. A few messengers. A few friends who still care what becomes of our future and our freedom. Unfortunately, none of them have a place among the high lords of empire. You were my hope for an entry there, Karel. Now even you are discredited and disempowered—"

"If you have no objection, lady, I'd like to die before you bury me. I'm still a good knight, and Konrad has need of allies. Desperate need of them, I think."

"Allies accused of sorcery and treason, when he himself is under the shadow of a worse condemnation? He can hardly risk it."

"That will depend," he said. "I've been in more wars than I care to remember, Raven. I've seen men lose land and honor over trifles, and I've seen others prosper in the face of accusations far worse than these. And it had nothing to do with guilt, proven or otherwise."

He took her by the shoulders, lightly. "I'll make you a wager—and if you win, you may name the prize. I wager I'll have a place among Konrad's captains an hour after I meet with him. Agreed?"

She smiled then, faintly, and brushed the back of her hand across his cheek.

"I'm beginning to understand why I chose you for this," she said.

"So am I, my Lady of the Mountain. You chose me for the same reasons Gottfried did."

"Some of the same reasons." She still caressed him, and the sweetness of it almost hurt. "Do you blame me for it?"

"No. You read me better than he did. Will you take my wager?"

"I'd probably lose."

"Then I will name the prize," he said.

"That could be dangerous."

He bent to brush his mouth across her throat. For a moment he thought she might draw away—Gottfried was in Mainz, after all, getting himself made king—but she only leaned her head back slightly, to let him play. He found the lacings of her tunic and began to undo them. Just to look at her, just for a moment, and kiss her there, through that fine scented silk . . . .

Every touch was a shock of remembered delight: wild hair tangling in his hands, the pulse of her throat against his mouth, the whisper of his fingers between her breasts, taking nothing, not yet, just tugging the soft leather strands from their eyelets. He would not make love to her, that was too much to expect, unshaven and bedraggled and dirty as he was, and she a highborn lady and a queen. Or so he told himself, quite aware at the same time that she was veela, and veelas were as wild as the forests they lived in.

"Raven."

The tunic fell open. He slid it softly back across her shoulders. He had forgotten how exquisitely voluptuous she was, forgotten it and never forgotten it, exaggerated it in his memory and his anticipation, and yet he was surprised, catching his breath at the sight of her. The shift she wore hid nothing, merely draped itself over the curves of her shoulders and the mounds of her breasts like a bit of wanton mist. Her nipples were hard without his touching them, pressing against the silk like copper pebbles. He thought of Lady Malanthine, and he wanted to laugh; in a thousand glittering veela years she would never equal this half-worldly witch—not in anything, and least of all in sheer sexual power.

"Lady." He was surprised at the rawness in his voice. "Would the queen of Car-Iduna consider bedding down with a bandit?"

"Just any bandit? Any ratty knave who happened by? Really, my lord count."

He caught her face between his palms, slid the tips of his fingers over the high line of her cheekbones. Her face was angular, sharply but very finely chiselled. Her skin was pale, and her eyes black like her hair. He had known many splendidly made women, and bedded more than one, but he had never been enchanted like this. Pauli called it sorcery. If it was, he truly did not care.

"Perhaps the queen could be seduced," he said. "If the bandit were a brave and highborn knight fallen on hard times."

"Queens are never seduced," she said.

"That, my love, is a singularly reckless challenge."

"Which any brave knight should bravely accept, hard times or not. Don't you agree, my lord bandit?"

He laughed and kissed her, just a few small kisses at first, teasing and playful. But he was hungry, so hungry it hurt; the kisses turned wild and shameless and the game was over before it properly began. He pulled her hard against his body, aware of nothing now except jasmine in his throat and blind greed in his loins, of her arms going round him, undoing in a heartbeat whatever had passed for hesitation or restraint.

He stopped finally, to look at her face, to see the pleasure there, the willingness. From the very first she had wanted him, in the midst of the storm, in the secret depths of Car-Iduna. To see it was like wine, and more than wine; it was like Wulfstan's potions, unraveling the boundaries of the world.

"What was it you said about queens, my lady?"

She smiled, her fingers tangled in his hair. Her eyes were wonderfully soft and smoky.

"They are never seduced," she said. "They *choose.*"

"I feared for you, Karel. Gods, but I feared for you." Her hand played across his face, lingered briefly on the scar where the young knight's lance had clubbed him. "Poor love. I promised you so much, and then I came too late. A whole day too late. Dead men were everywhere, and the manor burning. I heard you had escaped, and for a while I dared to hope. Then I saw them bring back your horse, exhausted and covered with blood—"

"Probably the blood wasn't all mine," he said.

"Probably. I thought of that. I thought of everything I could to keep from despair. But I couldn't find you. I searched . . . gods, Malanthine would have thought me a bandit, too, by the time I was done searching."

"You couldn't see through the darkness the shell made?"

"No. Possibly, just possibly, I could have undone it altogether—but then I would have had to find you before Gottfried's men did, and there wasn't much hope of that. It seemed I had done everything wrong. I trusted you, and so I didn't press you in your silence. So we waited too long, and then we found Gottfried could move faster than we could. I gave you the means to flee, and so, instead of being half-safe in one of Gottfried's prisons, where we could still hope to rescue you, now you were out of everyone's reach, wounded, maybe dying, and utterly alone. I grieved for my gifts to you, then. I grieved that I'd ever brought you to Car-Iduna.

"And the one person in the world who could have helped us we couldn't find, either, and I cursed him for it. Damned useless elf, I said, all these years he's claimed to be our ally, he's claimed to love the children of Dorn. But now, when the finest Dorn has ever bred has such bitter need of him, where is he? Chasing mountain sheep, no doubt, or lolling in some highborn woman's bed. Oh, I was bitter, Karel. I never knew I loved you so much."

He kissed her. It was almost worth half dying, just to hear her say it.

"You've forgiven that damned useless elf, I trust?" he murmured.

"A thousand times. As soon as I return to Car-Iduna I'll send messengers to thank him, and more presents than he'll know what to do with."

She paused, concentrating briefly as she plucked at a birch twig hopelessly tangled in his hair. He smiled when she scowled and gave up.

"The flower of chivalry," he said wryly. "Without fear and without dishonor. Just very, very dirty."

"You made a terrible impression on my sister, did you know?"

"Yes, it was rather obvious."

"Don't worry about it. She has no taste at all when it comes to men. She chases pretty eighteen-year-olds, and then complains bitterly when they turn out to be boring."

He laughed.

"Was she terribly rude to you?" Raven murmured.

"Not terribly. I think it's you she's annoyed at, not me."

"She's been annoyed at me for years. She could never understand why Car-Iduna was given to me. She's the eldest. She's pure veela, not a half-blood like me. But if she were queen, she'd never take care of the Chalice, or of anything else. She'd wander off for years at a time, and forget all about it."

"She isn't . . . ." He faltered. "She won't turn against you, will she?"

Her playful caresses stopped utterly still, and her eyes went dark.

"No. That kind of treachery is born of your world, not of mine."

He found he could not meet her eyes.

"I would have believed it of anyone else before him," he said. "Anyone, even Adelaide. Even Reini, I think, and Reini is like an oak, like the bones of the earth. I thought the whole world would turn on me before Pauli would."

"You should have killed him, Karel."

"I couldn't."

She did not ask him why and he was glad.

"I should have watched him more carefully, too," she said. "He made Marius terribly uneasy. But he was so obviously devoted to you, and you trusted him so much, so I did not mistrust him." She shook her head. "You might be dead now, because of my mistake."

"But I'm not. And we have a piece of Gottfried's willstone for our trouble. It may prove to be fair exchange."

"It will be dangerous beyond words to try to use it."

"But you will."

"Yes." She smiled faintly. If he had not been so utterly in love with her, he might have been troubled by her smile. "Yes, my bold summer stag, I'll use it. Carefully . . . ."

Her hand played softly across his belly, wandering downward with pretended indirection; her tongue brushed his nipple, over and over.

"Very . . . very . . . carefully . . . ."

He had been starving, the first time, and she had let him take everything he wished, as recklessly as he wished; let him lay her down on nothing but a ragged cloak and mount her without bothering to undress. And she had liked it well enough. But she liked this better, this game that would go on now for an hour, or for two, or for the rest of the day, wantonness mingled with talk and with wine, desire held like a nectar which could be sipped but did not need to be consumed, not yet; waiting made it sweeter, sharper, until at last the boundaries between desire and the rest of existence dissolved, and everything became desire. Darkness or light, music, wine, the sound of wind, the presence or the absence of other people—everything became excitement. Even an ill-favored lover was beautiful then, and an ill-favored place as magical as any other. If the bed was luxurious, he reveled in every thread of silk; if it was fouled straw, he reveled in its earthiness. Nothing mattered except to go on, to follow the spiral where it led.

Men asked him sometimes why he gave himself up that way—to passing strangers and paid harlots and even infidels—how could he bear to do it? Priests asked him, and the sterner and more Christian of his comrades in arms. He never had an answer. He never entirely understood the question. From the earliest years of his adolescence, sexual pleasure had been his one escape from violence. It took years before he understood that for many men the opposite was true: violence was their one escape from pleasure.

Pauli's, too.

XXXI

TO CHOOSE A KING

A little jargon is all that is necessary to impose upon the people.

SAINT GREGORY OF NAZIANZUS

I N NOVEMBER, IN THE YEAR OF 1104, it fell upon the consciences of seven men to name a new king of Germany, a new lord of the Holy Roman Empire. For it was the way among our people that the crown was never granted to any man solely by virtue of birth. A king's son was the likeliest choice, if he was brave and capable; indeed, as generations passed, the principle of hereditary kingship was growing stronger. But the old ways were still powerful, when the pagan tribes would follow their leaders through almost anything, but demanded in return the right to choose whom they would follow.

I will not say which way is better. Either way, evil men will come to power more often than good, for such is the way of the world. Kings must be chosen by God, and we've never learned to let him do so.

The seven who chose the king were these—two archbishops, from Mainz and from Cologne, and five princes: Ludwig, duke of Bavaria; the landgraves of Franconia and Swabia; the duke of Thuringia; and Gottfried von Heyden, duke of the Reinmark. Each prince brought with him a delegation of ten men—vassals and allies who represented differing interests within their master's domains. These followings had enormous influence, but they had no formal vote. Neither did the papal legate, who spoke for the interests of Rome.

They met in the great hall of the archbishop's palace, shielded by the dead king's honor guard and the bishop's own soldiery. By custom and by their host's command, those who bore arms left them on the wall, and sat at the council table unarmed.

It was a gathering of awesome rank and power, and of course I was not there. I had to piece the story together afterwards, from a dozen different tellers, none of whom seemed to be describing the same event.

Oh, on a few obvious things they agreed. Every day began with a solemn high Mass in the great cathedral of Mainz, and ended with the most unchristian bitterness, with even priests calling each other evil names, and more than one man ready to consign the whole assembly to the devil.

Certain positions were also clear to everyone. The archbishop of Mainz was the steadying influence; he insisted that no decision should be reached until all the facts were known.

He began by demanding that Konrad agree to accept the decision of the assembly no matter what its decision turned out to be. And Konrad, according to most accounts, went pale with anger, seeing he'd been backed into a corner before a dozen words were spoken. For if the prince said yes, he would in effect renounce his claim to hereditary right. And if he said no, he would alienate the assembly by denying its powers.

"I am his late majesty's only son," he said. "You know he chose me to succeed him. Every man of you knows it, for he commanded you all to come here in the spring, to elect me and crown me while he still lived. So he would see it done. So there would be no doubt about it."

"Yes," said Mainz, unperturbed. "But why summon us to elect you, if we had no power to do so? Do you, my lord, accept the authority of this assembly, or do you not?"

And Konrad, they said, did not answer for a time, and then threw the firebrand into the straw.

"I will accept the decision of this assembly," he said, "if the decision is reached without dishonor or deception."

This was a slur on the integrity of the council even before its deliberations were properly begun. Protests erupted on all sides, but Konrad overrode them.

"I have a reason for what I said, my lords. During the summer, soon after we returned from our visit to your domains, messengers came to my father with a warning. One of my father's highest lords, they said—one of the great princes of Germany—was planning to overthrow the king and seize the empire. He would do it by treachery, and would probably use sorcery to further his designs."

There was a stunned silence. Delegates looked at each other, and then looked back at the prince. They were hard men, and the memories and hatreds from years of civil war were still alive among them. Yet this was a terrible accusation.

"And did your messengers name this man?" demanded the prelate of Cologne.

"Yes. Gottfried von Heyden, duke of the Reinmark."

A dozen men shoved back their chairs, some of them threatening to leap across the table. Gottfried's followers, young Theodoric among them, shouted insults and challenges at the prince.

Then the duke himself rose to his feet, a towering, majestic man even in this gathering. He held up his hand for silence.

"And who sent these . . . messengers, my lord Konrad?" he asked. "Or shall I risk a guess? They came from Lys, did they not? From Karelian Brandeis, who has since revealed himself as a traitor and a demon worshipper. He sent the men you speak of."

"He did not," Konrad snapped.

"Then who did?"

Konrad was not a clever man, but he was bright enough to realize how unclever he had just been.

"I gave my word I would not name the man," he said.

"This is the highest authority in the land, my lord prince," Mainz said grimly. "And the matter at hand is one of treason. Tell us who sent you this warning."

"Indeed, I suspect that is the truth," Gottfried said, "for if he told you, he would lose what little sympathy he has left in this room.

"Let me explain, my lords, before you protest. There is a conspiracy abroad in Christendom—a conspiracy brought to sudden ferocity by our victories in the Holy Land. A conspiracy of men who have turned from God, and given their allegiance to evil. They are gathering demons to help them, and witches, the most vile and powerful of witches, women whom we in our complacency might have thought were creatures of the past, or even just creatures of legend.

"The wicked have always been with us, of course; Satan and his legions have never lacked for allies in the world. But now is a special time. On the one hand, the Church marches to new triumphs in the east, and so our enemies are raging and afraid. On the other hand, our borders are vulnerable, and the dark ways of paganism are still very much alive in our lands—in all our lands, my lords, whether you are aware of it or not.

"So they have chosen this time to gather all their forces and strike. I learned, by good fortune and God's kind favor, that I was one of the first targets of this conspiracy. My cousin, a man I once trusted and rewarded with the highest rank and honor, was chosen to be my betrayer. Karelian Brandeis has sworn himself to the lords of darkness. He worships Tyr the blood-drinker, and he has for his mistress the witch of Helmardin—who is no legend, my lords, believe me. She is real, and very dangerous."

At this, men looked from one to the other in black dismay, and soft ohhs rippled through the room.

"So I would ask this, my lords," Gottfried went on. "If the messengers Prince Konrad received were not from the count of Lys, or from his sorcerous allies, let the prince name them. And if they were, what trust can be put in their warning? Indeed, we must ask what warning they gave. What did they really tell you, my lord prince: that I meant to take your father's kingdom? Or that they wanted to take my duchy, and were hoping for your help?"

At this point—so all my storytellers agreed—the uproar barely stopped short of violence. Only the presence of the archbishops, and their overwhelming moral authority, finally restored a semblance of order.

"Your words are cause for the greatest concern," Mainz said then. "But you have given us, to this point, no proof for any of it. Karelian Brandeis may well be guilty of everything you say, but he has never been tried, nor is he present here to answer these charges."

"He has not been tried because he fled, my lord, conjuring up demons in order to do so, and leaving a field of dead men behind him."

"Flight isn't proof of guilt," Konrad flung back. "Least of all if a man has reason to believe he's already been judged and condemned!"

"And calling up the hounds of hell to slaughter us—what is that proof of? They slew my men, and caused so much chaos and confusion that he was able to escape—"

"He did this?" the archbishop asked softly, appalled.

"Yes." Gottfried then described the events in Lys. "And now," he concluded, "Karelian's castellan holds the fortress of Schildberge, and refuses to surrender it to my lawful authority. There is no question, my lords; he is guilty of both sorcery and treason. And therefore I say again, if he has been in touch with Prince Konrad, then his highness should admit it, and he should admit also that whatever Lord Karelian might have said to him, it must be disbelieved."

"And my father's murder?" Konrad demanded bitterly. "Should it also be disbelieved? My lords, we are getting nowhere. To begin with, we are not here to discuss the count of Lys—"

"We are here to discuss everything which may bear upon our decision, highness," Mainz interrupted. "And we will not be hurried. There are many things which are still unclear. How did you learn of this conspiracy you speak of, my lord Gottfried? Of Karelian's involvement with . . . with sorcerers? We all expected him to be here as part of your delegation—not to be told he is a fugitive, and a conjurer of devils."

"It is a long story, my lords."

"And will it bear upon our judgment here?" Thuringia demanded. "For in truth, I begin to share his highness's impatience with these digressions."

"It will bear upon our decision more than anything else we might discuss," Gottfried said. "My lords, you know well that there are times—rare times in the history of the world—when the affairs of men hang in so critical a balance that God, in his mercy and goodness, intervenes in some extraordinary way to give us help or guidance. So he parted the Red Sea for Moses. So gave us the Holy Lance on our journey to Jerusalem.

"We live now in such a time. I believe the next fifty years will determine whether Christianity ultimately triumphs in the world, or whether it will be cast back into the slavery of the catacombs. And everything will depend on who governs the empire of Germany.

"When I was in Jerusalem, I visited all the holy places, and spoke with the hermits and holy men who live there, who down through the years have protected our heritage against the encroachments of the infidel. And I was given, by one of them, a relic.

"And I will tell you frankly, my lords—when he gave it to me, and told me what it was, I did not believe him. He was a saintly man, but I thought he was also . . . well, shall we say, a little old? But I took it, because he insisted. It must go back with me to the heart of Christendom, he said. It belonged to Jerusalem once, he said; now it belongs to the empire."

"And what is this relic?" Mainz asked.

"He called it a truthstone. He said it was made of tears—the tears of the Virgin, and of John the Apostle, and of the angels—all the tears which were shed when Christ was slain, which turned into crystal and formed this miraculous stone. And because Christ by his dying gave his truth to the world, so will these tears speak truth to those who serve him."

"It is amazing," said Franconia, "the way relics turn up when men really need them."

Some told me he spoke mockingly, and others said his words were reverent. But he was always Konrad's man, so I don't think he was pleased with the direction of Gottfried's argument.

"What precisely are you trying to say, my lord duke?" the papal legate asked. "Did you bring this . . . object . . . back with you? And are you telling us it speaks?"

"It does not speak in words, my lord; it gives forth images—"

"By God's power?" Mainz demanded. "Or by sorcery?"

"That's what I asked myself," Gottfried said. "And so I gave it to the archbishop of Stavoren, so he could examine it."

At this point everyone looked at the archbishop, who sat among Gottfried's delegates.

"I also had grave doubts about the stone, my lords," the archbishop said. "And I told his lordship so. I kept it for more than a week. I tried many tests of its virtue, even to placing it on the altar beside a consecrated host. Finally, I gave it into the hands of our duchy's most revered exorcist, Father Mathias of Dorn, of whom you have all heard. He assured me there was nothing sorcerous in it—quite the opposite. It is a very holy thing, he said."

"And this stone is what revealed to you the treachery of the count of Lys, Duke Gottfried?" Mainz asked.

"Yes, my lord."

At this point, I have been told, the assembly fell into a brief and troubled silence. I am sure the same questions raced through the mind of every man there: *Is the thing a true relic, and trustworthy? And if it is, what else can it tell us? Can it tell us who murdered our king?*

"Where is the relic now?" asked the duke of Bavaria.

"I have brought it with me," Gottfried said. "For if ever God's guidance was needed in this land, it is now."

"I find it strange, my lords," offered the duke of Thuringia, "very strange, in fact, that this thing could have existed for centuries, and no one in Christendom ever heard of it. The cross was always known to us, and the shroud, and the lance—even the Holy Grail, though no one can say where it is, or prove he's ever seen it. Still we've heard of it. But this crystal of tears was tucked away right in the Holy City itself, all these years, and remained a secret? I find this hard to believe."

"It's God's privilege to hide or reveal things as he chooses," Mainz said. "That doesn't trouble me at all. What troubles me is how we can discover if it's genuine."

"Surely we've done so already!" the archbishop of Stavoren insisted.

"To your satisfaction, excellency," replied Mainz. "Not to mine. Nor, I think, to the satisfaction of this assembly. Will you show us the stone, my lord duke?"

And so Gottfried took out the crystal pyramid, and everyone marveled at its beauty. But they were very uneasy—not least because of all the talk of sorcery. How could they be sure the stone wasn't evil? Perhaps the prelate of Stavoren had been misled. He was old, after all, and he was known to be terribly devoted to his duke.

"My lords, in God's name!" Prince Konrad was on his feet. "This is precisely what we were warned about—that this man would use some sorcerous trick to get his hands on my father's crown! Can't you see where he's leading us? He'll twist the assembly any way he chooses with this cursed thing!"

"Enough, my lords, I beg you. Enough." The archbishop of Mainz got slowly to his feet. It was late, he said, and tempers were frayed to breaking. The meeting was adjourned. The pyramid, he said, would be carried to the cathedral, and kept there under guard. The bishops themselves, and other priests, and several holy monks from the abbey, would all remain to pray over it.

So it was done. Many believed the stone would shatter into fragments the moment it was taken inside the church, or that it would simply melt into smoke and blow away. But instead it seemed to brighten and grow even more beautiful. They sprinkled it with holy water, and laid a crucifix across it, and then a locket with a bone of Saint Martin of Tours. They called upon all the evil spirits whose names and kinds were known within the world, and commanded them to leave if they were present. The crystal remained serene and shimmering. As the night passed a kind of awe began to fill the watchers: if they could find no evil in the stone, in such an hour as this, with so much need and with so many prayers, then surely no evil could be there.

And although every member of the assembly had been sworn to keep the matter quiet, long before dawn crowds were gathering outside the cathedral, and hundreds of soldiers had to be called out to contain them. Cripples came, and blind men, and women with dying children, all of them begging to see the relic, or to be allowed to touch it. No one ever learned how the word got out, and many saw it as a miracle. There was a sacred presence in the stone, they said, a presence so powerful that people could discover it without needing to be told.

In the morning, the archbishop offered Mass with the truthstone shimmering on the altar. After the consecration, with great reverence and great fear he touched the Sacred Host against the stone.

And both glowed with a golden, mesmerizing light.

I wish I had been there. It was one of those moments, so rare in our vile and sinful history, when God reached into the mortal world and acknowledged us. From that moment on, there should have been no doubt about the authenticity of the stone. But of course, some men will always doubt. And others, to serve their interests in the world, will always pretend to do so.

The stone was carried back to the council room. And here all the tellers of the tale agree: several minutes passed before anyone would speak. It was awe, perhaps, but I think it must also have been fear. For they all had their secret sins, their secret ambitions. And most of them— as history would soon bear out—did not love truth or Christendom nearly as well as they loved their places in the world.

It was Mainz who finally led the prayers, and called upon God through his sacred relic:

"Tell us, if it be thy will, oh Lord, by whose hand our king, your beloved servant, died."

And the surface of the stone muddied, and took on a hint of color. Men gasped and stared, some rising to their feet, most crossing themselves; no one could have looked elsewhere to save his life. They argue to this day about what they saw—about the colors of the room, and whether the king was dressed or in his bedclothes, and whether the assassin smiled. But on this they are compelled to agree: Ehrenfried was alone with his son. And Konrad gave him a cup of wine, and while he raised it to his lips, the prince slipped like a footpad behind him, and drove a blade three times into his back.

"Cursed lying sorcerer!"

Konrad leapt to his feet, a dagger in his hand, shouting curses and denials and accusations all together, shoving savagely at the men who tried to restrain him. He would have tried to hack the stone to pieces with his blade, if he had been allowed to reach it.

Chaos erupted in earnest then—fury because Konrad had secretly retained a weapon, cries of sorcery answered with cries of treason and patricide, and the young prince vainly shouting challenges to men who could no longer hear him for the clamor.

"You'll fight me, von Heyden! By God and all his angels, you'll answer for this in the field!"

"Seize him!" commanded a voice. Whose voice it was no one could afterwards say. "Seize the murderer! Put him in irons!"

"Not just yet, by God!" roared the duke of Thuringia, flinging men away in both directions and leaping across the table to take his place by the prince's side.

Thus the assembly collapsed, as the empire would do within days. Men rallied to one side, or the other, or to none, as it pleased their affections or their hopes for gain. Some were ready to fetch their swords, but others kept their heads and restrained them. Then the great doors of the assembly hall swung wide, and everyone turned, expecting the bishop's guard. But it was Konrad's men who marched in, in full armor and bearing drawn crossbows.

And that, finally, reduced the electors to silence again. Aye, and according to some accounts, to a certain degree of pallor.

"My lord prince," Mainz said harshly. "This is an unforgivable outrage—!"

"Enough!" Konrad struck the table with his fist. "I've listened to the lot of you babbling long enough! You're so blind with this sorcerer's tricks you can't recognize an outrage when you see one!

"My father was warned about Gottfried von Heyden. He failed to heed the warning, and now he is dead."

His bitter eyes turned then to the Reinmark duke. "You expected a lot, villain, if you expected me to wait like a lamb for the second axe to fall. I will not let you slaughter me, nor will I let you take the crown of Germany, no matter what's decided in this room. You accuse me of killing my father—"

"It is not I who accuses—"

Three crossbows raised and leveled at the duke's chest, and his voice fell away.

"Thank you, my lord sorcerer; you will wait until I'm finished. Now, as I said, you accuse me of killing my father. And I swear to you, to all of this assembly, as God is my witness and my judge, I'm innocent of his death. And I'll defend my oath in the field. Will you stand behind your slander with your body, von Heyden?"

Gottfried, they say, met the prince's eye unflinching.

"I'm guilty of no slander. It is the stone of truth which accuses you, not me."

"Stop playing games, damn you! The stone is yours! You're the one who brought it here, and you're the one it serves!"

"My lord prince," said Mainz, "for your soul's sake, my lord, beware of blasphemy. It is a sacred relic—"

"Relic be damned! It's a piece of trickery and nothing else. Let me remind you of something, my lords. There is one person in this room who knows, without the smallest trace of doubt, whether or not I killed my father. I think there's more than one, but there is one for certain, and that one is me. So I know that damnable stone is lying—do you understand me, my lords? I *know!* It's no relic, and you can't threaten me with it. Now, by God, von Heyden, will you fight me or will you not?"

"We're a civilized and Christian nation," the archbishop said. "We don't judge men's guilt or innocence in duels—much less their right to govern us. This is not a matter for personal combat."

"Then it will be a matter for war!"

And the prince, they say, lifted the dagger he was holding, and drove it into the council table with such force that no one afterwards could pull it out. Which is a hard thing to believe, but that is what they say.

"I will fight this Reinmark traitor!" he said savagely. "And if I must, I'll fight you all! You speak of blasphemy, archbishop—beware of it yourself! Do you think God will allow the future of Christendom to be decided by a sorcerer? Do you really?"

At a signal his squire fetched him his cloak and his sword. He put them on, and spoke again.

"Decide as you please, my lords. But mark me: while I live, I am king. Lord Gottfried's stone makes clever pictures; we'll see if it's as clever at turning back an army."

"Do you threaten this assembly, highness?" the papal legate demanded. "Do you dare?"

"Call it a threat, call it a fact. I'll fight for what's mine. You may choose another as your king—but if you do, you're choosing war!"

And with those words, Prince Konrad left the palace, and rode out of the city in a great band of armed men, and set up a war camp on a hill beyond Mainz, and waited for the council's judgment.

They sat for three days more. I cannot hope to recount everything they said, or who said it, for it is clear they went around the matter and around it. No one was sure of anything except that one side or the other was evil beyond words.

But which side? Which man was the conspirator, the evil one?

—The prince. There's no doubt of it.

—Is there not?

—I can't see why he would he kill his father, when he was already heir, and almost certain to be chosen.

—They fell out. They were quarreling all the time; everyone heard them. He called his father names, and said he was unfit to be a king.

—And you've never quarreled with your father, I suppose? Or I with mine? Did we kill them afterwards? We'd be a room full of patricides in that case—and matricides, too, and Christ knows what else! The prince is young and hot-headed; quarrels like his mean nothing.

—The truthstone named him as the murderer.

—Aye, and what is this so-called truthstone? And where did it really come from?

—I will lay you odds it was forged in a demon's fire, my lords.

—That's utterly outrageous!

—Is it? Aren't any of you thinking straight? Ehrenfried is dead. If Konrad is disgraced and deposed, it's the end of the Salian kings, and Christ knows who will replace them.

—We don't lack for worthy lords in Germany.

—No, we don't. But what lord has Konrad's legitimacy? What lord can take his crown unchallenged? Don't you think other men will ask the same questions I'm asking? Don't you think other men will notice how damnably convenient this relic has turned out to be? In one fell stroke the royal line of Germany is undone, and the whole empire is in disarray. Is this God's will? Did he send that stone to enlighten us? Or did someone else send it to destroy us?

—But it was in the cathedral! It was touched with sacred relics, with the Host itself!

—What of it?

—Really, my lord Franconia, do you think God is less jealous of his honor than a man? To allow something so foul and deceitful upon his altar, against his sacred flesh?

—He allowed the Pharisees to humiliate him, and the Roman soldiers to nail him to a cross.

—That's not the same thing at all!

—And they challenged him just as we're challenging him now: if you're divine, put a stop to it! He had his reasons then; who knows what his reasons might be now?

—Maybe he's testing us to see if we can think.

—God's blood, it's not the same thing at all! You can't possibly believe it's the same.

—I believe God is a lot more complicated than you imagine. And ambitious men are always claiming to know exactly what's on his mind.

—And you're not an ambitious man, of course. You just happen to be blood kin to the Salian kings; Prince Konrad just happened to be fostered in your castle! If he were king you'd be first man in Germany. But of course, you're thinking only of the truth!

—My lords, I beg you, personal attacks will get us nowhere. We must try to determine God's will. If Konrad is innocent, why did he come armed to this assembly? Why is he gathering men, and threatening us with war?

—Oh, for Christ's sake, what should he have done? Walk in here like a lamb, when his father has already been murdered, and he's likely to be next? His actions merely prove he has enough good sense to be a king.

—Consider the possibility that he's innocent. Hard as it may be for you, excellency, just consider it for one moment. And then consider this: If he *is* innocent, then the relic is false. And if the relic is false, what are we to think of the man who brought it here?

—Can't we test the relic some more?

—How?

—We could ask it questions. Things no one knows but ourselves. Like what name my little cousin used to call me when we were boys. He's dead now, and I told no one, because it was embarrassing. If the stone could answer that, it would convince me.

—So ask it.

But the stone remained serenely silent—to this and to all their other questions. And at last Gottfried said to them:

"Really, my lords, why should it answer to such foolishness? You're not treating it as a holy thing, but as a magician's toy. You're mocking it with these questions. God will reveal to you what he judges necessary. He will not play games."

Even his enemies had to see some wisdom in his words. And though they went on quarreling about it until the end, it was already obvious that, unless some very extraordinary miracle occurred, those who believed in the stone were likely to go on believing, and those who doubted would go on doubting till they died.

At twenty I could not understand it. But I havé learned since that most people go through life believing what they wish. It does not matter what is obvious; they will shove aside a thousand proven facts, and close their minds upon a single supposition, because it comforts them.

So in the council chamber, and so after in the war.

The likelihood of war increased with every passing hour. Franconia's question, however self-serving it might have been, was a valid one: what lord could claim the crown unchallenged? They named perhaps a dozen, but from the first there were really only two: Konrad himself, and Gottfried von Heyden.

It was Ludwig of Bavaria who first put forward Gottfried's name for the kingship. He was an aging and saintly man. His enemies called him stupid, but he was really just unworldly, a man whose mind was always more on heaven than on earth.

God, he said, had clearly shown the duke extraordinary favor. The empire would surely be blessed if he were king.

Whereupon a great many rude, appalling things were said, and the old man was insulted to the point where he threatened to go home. Then the landgrave of Swabia stood up, and said he would support Duke Gottfried, and suddenly it was not an old man's silly notion any longer. It was a serious possibility. The room grew very still.

"Would you accept the crown, if it were offered you?" Mainz asked.

And Gottfried, to his credit, did not pretend to be reluctant.

"Yes," he said. "Not for the glory of it, or for the name of king. But there is a war to be fought, and I have always been God's warrior. So yes, if you want me to lead you, I will."

One day the empire will be dust, and men will still be quarreling over that election. Why did each of the electors choose as he did?—for in truth, only Bavaria and Franconia took positions which can be properly understood. The landgrave of Franconia was Konrad's cousin, a potential heir himself to the Salian crown. He would defend their hereditary rights to the bitter end. And Ludwig was genuinely drawn to the holiness in Gottfried. He was the only man there, I think, who either acknowledged it or truly cared.

Swabia was a venal man with a nasty personal reputation. He chose the right side, but probably for the shabbiest of reasons. Thuringia was a tribal chieftain of the old school. He spoke like a Christian because it was politic to do so, but more than one man believed he was a pagan in his heart; there was nothing he loved better than a fight. Both he and Swabia, I think, simply sided with the man they thought would win.

The night before the final vote, it seemed that Gottfried would be chosen. He had three certain votes: Swabia, Bavaria, and the Reinmark; and two probable ones: the archbishops of Mainz and Cologne, both of whom had shown nothing but reverence for the relic and hostility to Konrad's wilfulness and arrogance.

What passed between sunset and dawn no one knows. The archbishop of Mainz, they said, met long with Cardinal Volken, the papal legate. The legate opposed Gottfried's election—not because he doubted either the relic or Gottfried's qualities of leadership, but rather for the opposite reason—though of course he would never admit it. The Vatican did not want a strong king in Germany.

So it is said, and it may be true. It is said also that Konrad's agents found the prelate of Cologne in a private moment, and raised with him the thorny issue of his wife.

And said to him something much like this:

Did you know that Gottfried von Heyden particularly despises married priests? Oh, yes of course, we know, you're not married any more, you'd never have made bishop if you hadn't gotten rid of her—not in the great city of Cologne, anyway. Except you didn't really get rid of her, and all kinds of people know it. She still lives here, and you still visit her. And don't look at us like that; we have no objections. It's your would-be emperor who has objections. He's routed married priests out of every parish in the domain of Stavoren, just since he came back from Jerusalem, and he swears before he dies he'll rid the Reinmark of them altogether. He's even talked of using that old provision from the Synod of Toledo—you know the one we mean? Searching houses in the dead of night, and taking the priests' women and selling them for slaves?

Do you really want him for your emperor, my lord bishop? Do you really? Especially since we'll make a point of telling him about her. After all, if you vote for him, it will be no more than you deserve . . . .

No one but God knows what really happened, who really met by night with whom, what fears were bred and nurtured. But when they met and cast their votes in earnest, after high Mass in the morning, the archbishop of Cologne was Konrad's man, and the split was three against three.

And every man in the room—indeed, every man in Christendom—looked to the prelate of Mainz.

Who rose, and crossed himself, and said:

"I cannot vote."

"You *what?*" Fifty, perhaps a hundred voices shouted all at once.

"I cannot vote. There have been questions raised in this room, on both sides, which have not been properly answered. We're dealing with extraordinary events, my lords, and with a chain of astonishing coincidences. We are only men, trying to understand the will of God and the manifestations of supernatural power. We can't possibly do it in so short a time. I will cast no vote in this assembly at this time."

"Do you doubt the sacred relic, excellency?" Gottfried asked.

"No, I don't. But its arrival at this moment is remarkable, to say the least. My concern is for the future of the empire. I can't share the landgrave of Franconia's blind loyalty to the Salian house, but the questions of legitimacy he has raised are entirely sound."

"But we are dead-locked! You must choose, my lord—!"

"If we are dead-locked, then perhaps God himself is telling us something. Perhaps neither of these men should be chosen. Certainly I will not be the one to choose. We must seek further guidance. I think we should consult with Rome—"

"Rome be damned!" This was Thuringia, banging his great warrior's fist on the table. "Rome is not choosing our king, by God!"

And everyone—absolutely everyone except Mainz—agreed with him. Rome had nothing to say in the matter. *You must vote, excellency; there is no other way; you must vote!*

Mainz sat again, drawing his robe around him, and locking his hands before his chin.

"Forgive me, my lords, but I cannot. I cannot, and I will not."

"So be it," Thuringia said. "I've had enough. As far as I'm concerned, Konrad is king of Germany."

"He is not," the archbishop snapped. "No man is king without election. It's the law—and you, my lord, have always insisted on that law, more strongly than any man here."

The duke walked over to the wall, and took down his sword.

"Then we will elect him. The old way," he added grimly. "In the field."

XXXII

WAR IN THE REINMARK

But now, O mighty soldiers, O men of war, you have a cause
for which you can fight without danger to your souls;
a cause in which to conquer is glorious and for which
to die is gain.

SAINT BERNARD OF CLAIRVAUX

I DID NOT RUN FROM THE HIGHLANDS where I found Karelian; I crept
away like a thief. I longed to go west, to Franconia, to wherever
Gottfried might be, gathering men and glory for his kingdom. But I
did not have the courage to face him and admit my absolute defeat.

I sought shelter with the Benedictine monks at Karlsbruck, and I
stayed there until the winter was half gone, nursing my wounded pride,
my evil grief. For a time I thought about staying there forever, but
my heart and my mind were still in the world. Rumors came to us
steadily, even in our solitude. There would be war by spring, some
said. No, said others; Konrad would give up the struggle, and go into
exile. Or Gottfried would give up the struggle, and go into a monastery.
Or the matter would be placed in the hands of the pope for arbitration
(even the monks chuckled at that one).

There were questions, too, as well as rumors, and one of them
even I could not begin to answer.

Why would Prince Konrad kill his father?

Over and over I heard it asked, by the wise and the foolish alike,
by the rich and the poor. Why would the prince so recklessly endanger
his own secure position? He was young, legitimate, and widely admired. He was certain to be chosen king—indeed, more certain than

most heirs, for Ehrenfried had meant to crown his son while he still lived.

Such a murder was not only evil, it was stupid beyond belief. And therefore many people wavered, torn between accepting the overwhelming evidence of a sacred relic, on the one hand, and trusting their own common sense, on the other.

For myself, I did not waver. He *had* done it; therefore there was a reason. Evil had its own dread logic; it did not have to match the logic of the world. Perhaps the prince had made a pact with the devil. He would not have been the first highborn man to do so. Perhaps he was a secret unbeliever, and a secret catamite as well. It was common knowledge that he often failed to go to Mass, that all his favorites were young men, all of them beautiful, and one of them a poet. Perhaps Ehrenfried had learned some dreadful truth about him, and was planning to name another as his heir?

There were all sorts of possibilities—even, for some men, the possibility that he was innocent. Perhaps it was Gottfried who was the sorcerer. Perhaps his truthstone was something horrid and evil he had found among the infidels . . . ? Rumor fed upon rumor endlessly, and to all of them the abbot of Karlsbruck had only one reply:

"We don't know. We must pray, and God will make his judgment known."

I prayed more than anyone, I think, but prayer was not enough. When I learned just after Candlemas that Theodoric was mobilizing the whole of the Reinmark, raising an army to send to his father, I headed for Stavoren to offer him my service.

I caught up with him in Dorn, where he was urging loyalty on the margrave Ludolf Brandeis, Karelian's half-brother. I wish I could have been a mouse at that meeting.

Ludolf Brandeis was almost twenty years older than his youngest brother. They were not friends. According to Karelian's own accounts to me, Ludolf hated his father's last and prettiest wife, and bullied her children without mercy. When Karelian could, by the age of fourteen, outfight his full-grown brother bare-handed, or with any weapon man had ever made, Ludolf did not come to like him better.

Still, they were blood kin, and if the lords of Dorn were famous for anything, it was for their unpredictability. Theodoric could not take the margrave's loyalty for granted.

They ate and drank and hunted together. What promises Theodoric made to him I do not know, but they seemed to be on the best of terms when I came to Dorn, and begged an audience with the prince, and offered him my service.

Theodoric had not changed much since I'd seen him last. He was still impatient, still used to having things his way.

I told him everything I could about Karelian, and as little as I dared about myself. He did not seem interested in either.

"Your master," he said, "has already taken service with Konrad in Mainz. But since he brought with him no army and no gold, it seems the princeling wasn't much impressed." He smiled, and leaned back in his chair. "I never thought I'd credit Ehrenfried's son with having any sense, but in this he was wiser than my father. He gave the adventurer a hundred men, and sent him off to command the fort of Saint Orestius."

"Saint Orestius?" I said blankly. "Where is that?"

"Somewhere in the hinterland of Franconia. He can amuse himself there, hunting crows and chasing the odd bandit."

I was surprised at the malice in Theodoric's voice. He hated Karelian as a traitor against his father, of course he did, but there was something more in his hostility, something personal. And I knew there was nothing personal between them. Karelian had spent most of his life in the service of different foreign kings. He and Theodoric met only once, just the summer before, at the *Königsritt* in Stavoren. The meeting had been formal and friendly.

So why this remarkable hatred? Others noticed it besides myself, and offered reasons for it, but the only reason I could see was envy. Not envy of things, or even of honors. The son of the Golden Duke, the heir of the Merovingians and the empire, would never covet any man's place except a king's.

But no matter how much princes judged others as lords, they also judged them as men. Watched them and weighed them as men. Competed with them as men. And then a whole other set of rules came into play.

Karelian never needed to do anything in particular to earn Theodoric's hostility. He needed only to exist, and to be better than Theodoric at nearly everything which Theodoric considered important. A superior in rank could be forgiven that, perhaps, but an inferior, never.

Now Konrad had put the upstart in his place. It did not occur to Theodoric to wonder if Konrad was a fool. Or even to be grateful that his enemy had one good captain less. No. All Theodoric could do was gloat.

"So much for the champion of all Germany."

And then he looked at me, as though for the first time, and asked me what I wanted.

He knighted me at Easter. We were at war now, and he needed all the men he could get. But he did not send me west. There were too many good knights rotting in Lys, he said, starving that damned little traitor Reinhard out of his damned mountain fortress. He sent a ragtag army to replace them: some twenty fresh-dubbed knights, including myself; all of Stavoren's maimed and aging fighters; and a large body of common soldiers and peasant levies. We could easily maintain the siege, he said, and the skilled knights we replaced could go to Gottfried.

The first weeks there were dreadful. The spring was cold, and it rained almost every day. There was nothing to do. Simply being there was enough to keep Reinhard prisoner. We did not even have the stimulation of danger. Theodoric's brother Armund had the local population completely cowed, and any sortie from the castle would have been as vulnerable and exposed, coming down the long and winding road, as we would have been trying to go up. The defenders stayed safe inside their walls, and laughed at us. They had plenty of food. They had water. They even had revelry. Night after night we could hear shawms and drums playing merrily, and if the wind was right we could sometimes even hear the words they sang. War songs, mostly. Sometimes hymns, as though God was still on their side, treason and witchcraft notwithstanding. And tavern songs, too, especially when the summer began to flower, and the women would come out on the walls to dance and cheer on their warriors: *Chramer gip diu varwe mier diu min wengel roete* . . . .

It was one of the most popular songs of the day: Mary Magdalene persuading a merchant to sell her his prettiest things, so all the young men who looked at her would fall in love.

"It hardly seems fair, does it?" my companion said. "They do nothing up there but enjoy themselves, while we sit shivering in the mud."

"Till they get hungry," I said.

He grunted. His name was Wilhelm. He was a knight of forty or so, who had lost a hand in the civil war. From the first he had taken it upon himself to be my mentor, and give me the benefit of his wisdom and experience. I did not like him much; he was a rough-hewn, unimaginative man—a bit like Reinhard, actually. But he was kind to me, and I was grateful.

"They won't get hungry for a long while," he said.

He was right, of course. I had been in Lys all last summer; I had seen the loaded wagons, and the droves of pigs and cattle winding up the mountain road, day after day.

"We'll stay here as long as we need to," I said. And I tried hard to feel good about it, to look upon it as a willing act of penitence and self-denial. I deserved nothing better. I had no right to be with Gottfried in the west, in the heart of history. I was lucky to have even this small, unsatisfying place, and luckier still to be far away from the perilous shadow of Karelian Brandeis.

I would smile at my naiveté now, if I had a mind to smile at anything. It was the Reinmark, not the west, which was to find itself in the heart of history. It was the Reinmark where everything was decided: the fate of the empire, and the fate of the world.

As for Karelian, should I not have guessed he'd come to us?

He came with midsummer, as unlooked for as its sudden, black-winged storms. It was late in June; the day before had been warm and shimmering, drunk with a wildness of flowers. The slowly descending darkness brought no moon, only distant winking stars, the cry of owls, and a shawm wailing into the night from a high, unlighted battlement. Men sat by the fires and talked long into the night. When I came off my watch I curled up in my cloak and slept like a boy.

And woke to cries of alarm, to the sight of men running hither and thither among our tents, shouting of berserkers and Wends and I do not know what else. I sprang up dazed. It was barely dawn, and the world was patched with fog. I could see nothing beyond our own frantically waking cluster of tents, but I could hear war-cries and clashing iron, and the pounding hoofs of horses.

I thought of many things in those fragmented seconds before the attack reached us, but I did not think at all of Karelian. He was hundreds of leagues away, in some nowhere corner of Franconia. I thought instead of foreign invaders, and of the margrave of Dorn and his infernally untrustworthy house. Mostly I thought about ourselves, and what a makeshift force we were, green young men and worn-out veterans like Wilhelm. He was stumbling to his feet beside me, groping for his weapons and crossing himself with his one left hand. I thought I might be about to die, and the possibility was strangely calming.

Wilhelm's squire was shaking so badly I shoved him aside, fastened my comrade's armor myself, and handed him his sword. By then we could see our enemies, and I for one would rather have seen Wends. They stormed out of the half-light in waves, and swept everything that lay before them. We had no idea who or how many they might be. They were centaurs in armor, thundering out of hell. But every centaur carried a shield, and on every shield was painted a black tree without leaves. The winter tree of Dorn. The insignia of Karelian Brandeis.

The best of our men lost their courage then, for what we were seeing was not possible. How could he have come here, through the well-watched passes of the western border, past Gottfried's outposts along the Maren, and over the populated fields of Lys, in the full panoply of war, without anybody noticing?

How else except by witchcraft?

There is little more to tell about the battle. I was praised after for my bravery; Wilhelm and I and a handful of others managed to stay together and fight our way to the edges of the camp. By then our entire force was almost routed. The demon lord of Lys had come back. He had raised up armies of darkness and traversed the empire on horses of wind. Men caught a single glimpse of that stark winter tree and flung down their weapons and covered their eyes. Others, observing the debacle with a more worldly eye, shrugged and surrendered politely. Those who chose to fight went down; those who could still do so, fled.

A hundred of us, perhaps, made it back to Stavoren.

XXXIII

THE RETURN

The heathen never wearied of love,
and from that fact his heart was mighty in combat.

WOLFRAM VON ESCHENBACH

THEY WAITED FOR KARELIAN in a half circle just inside the gates. Reini. Adelaide. Father Thomas. The steward and the captain of the
guard. And immediately behind them, a great cluster of knights and
friends and servants.

From the battlements above, the sound of cheers and banging
shields welled out, crashing against the heights of the Schildberge and
echoing back across the valley of the Maren. Here below, for a brief
and blurring moment, no one shouted at all.

Grooms ran to hold his horse. He did not immediately dismount.
He looked at them, one after another. He looked up at the high walls
ringed with triumphant men, and he felt—for the first time in his
life—that he was truly lord of Lys.

Reinhard stepped forward and bowed deeply.

"Welcome, my lord. I thank God you are safe returned."

"And you were never so glad to see anyone in your life," Karelian
replied, smiling and sliding off his mount. "At least not since Acre."

"Not even then, my lord," the castellan said. His voice was unsteady. He would have knelt, he was so deeply moved; but instead of
letting him, Karelian wrapped him in his arms.

"Thank you, Reini. You are as I judged you, my friend: the very
best of men."

"I did no more than my duty, my lord."

"That is more than most men can manage, sometimes," Karelian said, and moved past him towards Adelaide.

She took a few steps forward, then stood absolutely still, staring at him as though he were a ghost.

"Lady . . . ?"

She touched his mail shirt lightly on the sleeve, like a child, and looked up, tears welling from her eyes.

"I thought . . . ." she whispered. "I thought you weren't . . . ever . . . ."

Ever coming back? He tried to smile. He was astonished by the pain in her eyes, the fog of bewildered longing. He took her face in his hands and kissed her mouth.

Just once, there in the courtyard. A hundred times more in her small stone chamber in the tower, naked and tangled on the bed, sating themselves in the broad light of day. Still she kissed him, and ran her hands over his flesh as though she feared he was not real.

"You were hiding for a long time," she whispered.

"Yes."

"There was darkness all around you. I was sure you were dead."

"I was close to it."

She pressed herself against him, as if her slender body could be a barrier against even the possibility of death. She was beginning to love him, to see him as she had once seen Rudi Selven, as someone different, someone strange and perilous and therefore . . . finally . . . safe.

It should have troubled him, perhaps, but it did not. She was his wife. With luck she would give him a child or two; with more luck he would live to see them grow. If he seemed to her more and more like Selven, if he came to be for her the elf-kin, the prince who would take her to the sea; if in the end the edges blurred altogether and she could no longer tell them apart, well, what of it? Men wove stranger half-truths than hers to bend the world till they could bear it.

They feasted that night in Schildberge castle—feasted and reveled with a wildness which bordered on ecstasy. Sometimes Karelian shared in the intensity of their triumph; sometimes he stood apart from it, marveling at it even as he understood its nature. Something had come unbound. The borders of the world had shifted, and something had come unbound.

They never stopped asking him questions: where had he been, would there be war in earnest now, how many men did Konrad have,

what of Gottfried's crystal, where had it come from and what could
it really do and why didn't the Church condemn him and how in the
name of all the saints had he, Karelian, come from Franconia to the
hills of the Schildberge without anybody seeing him . . . ?

They had heard rumors, of course, all sorts of rumors. Right from
the start Reinhard had been sending out spies, and most of them got
back safely.

"We heard what Prince Konrad did to you, my lord. I couldn't
believe he would be such a fool—"

"The king is young, my friends, and inexperienced. He will learn."

The wine was rich, unwatered. Karelian drank deeply, savoring it
all, the wine and the victory and the truth he kept quietly hidden like
a pearl. Konrad was hardly a fool. It would have been nice to tell his
people so, to let them laugh and slap each other's backs and pound
their cups against the table for the sheer delight of it. Tell them about
a winter night in Franconia, himself and Konrad while the whole world
slept, pacing about a quiet, carefully guarded tent, weaving their tap-
estry of war with exquisite cunning and care.

Konrad would have made him captain-general of the empire.

—I'm honored, my lord, but I can't possibly accept.

—Can't accept? Why? God's blood, isn't it enough? What the devil
do you want, then?

—I want the county of Lys back, when it's over, and your promise
that if I'm killed it will pass without question to my son.

—Your son? But . . . .

—I have a son, majesty, born in lawful wedlock. He is my heir.

—Yes, of course; so be it. Lys is yours. Now lead my army.

—You don't want that, my lord. At least not yet.

—You try my patience, Brandeis. I'm giving you a command as
your sovereign, and I expect to be obeyed.

—I have no wish to disobey you, my lord. But consider this: I've
been presented to the lords of Germany—and to the leaders of the
Church—not merely as a sorcerer, but as the agent of a great conspiracy against God. Too many people believe in Gottfried's stone, my
lord. That may change; I'll wager as the war goes on, more and more
disturbing questions will be raised. But right now, he holds the religious high ground. So claim a little of it for yourself, my lord. Keep
your distance from the likes of me.

—I need warleaders more than I need a halo.

—You have Thuringia. You have other good men. I beg you, my

lord, consider. Your father was a Christian king. He did nothing except insist on his autonomy within his own borders, and he was compelled to fight for twenty years to keep his crown. Harold of England was only half-Christian, and he is dead. You may find yourself an enemy of the Church no matter what you do, but there's no need to invite her enmity.

—I'm not an enemy of the Church, in God's name! This has nothing to do with the Church—!

—Quite beside the point, my lord. You will be *portrayed* as an enemy of the Church. That will be sufficient.

—Then be damned to them! If they can't see who the sorcerer in this quarrel really is, be damned to them!

—And be damned to the Salian kings as well, my lord? To the whole of Germany?

—Really Karelian, if I didn't owe you so much, I'd have you hanged.

—Then I will try to keep you in my debt, my lord. I have a plan.

—I'm listening.

—Treat me the way any honorable Christian king in difficulty would treat an ally accused of sorcery. Accused, remember, but not convicted. Later, if circumstances change, you may treat me better. For the time being, accept my service because I might yet prove innocent, but keep me out of sight. Surely you have a border post somewhere—

—A border post? Are you mad? We have a war to fight! I need you here!

—You need to destroy Gottfried von Heyden. If you do so, there will be no war. If you fail to do so, you will lose the war. That is the whole of your necessity, my lord.

—All right, if you put it so, all right. How are you going to destroy Gottfried von Heyden sitting in some infernal border post?

—I have no intention of staying there. His son Theodoric is stripping the Reinmark of men to fatten Gottfried's army. It's a reasonable thing to do. The duchy has always been loyal, and you're hardly in a position to invade.

—Go on.

—I won't take a large force, my lord. But I want good men. Well-trained men who'll understand the need for secrecy and speed. We'll take the duchy right out from under his feet. You won't know anything about it until it's over; and of course you'll grumble that I'm undisciplined and unpredictable. But you'll have the Reinmark. You'll name a new duke loyal to yourself—and if the electors accept him as legitimate, we'll have shifted the balance in the council.

Konrad had watched him very thoughtfully, for a very long time, until they began to notice the steps of the sentries outside, and the wind-blown snow scrabbling at the walls of the tent. He was not a philosophical sort of man, the young king, which fact made his silent contemplation all the more remarkable.

When he spoke again his voice was soft—half amused, half admiring, and deeply uneasy.

—You are shrewd, Karelian. So damnably shrewd I begin to wonder if what Gottfried says about you isn't true.

They were wondering everywhere, even here in the taper-wild hall of Schildberge castle. The night was soft as honey with midsummer coming down, the wine tasted of triumph, and something was loose in the Reinmark, an ancient passion cut free and running. Even a rock-hard crusader like Reinhard knew it was there, although he would never admit it, and still less would he ever put a name to it.

Father Thomas knew, too, and he was wondering most of all. The unsilenceable storyteller barely said a word, and barely touched his wine. He had been the one who slipped back to the manor house to rescue Adelaide's child. The one who saw the aftermath of carnage, who heard first-hand the tale of wolves leaping out of the ground. He was the one who reminded everyone of the story of Elijah, of the wolves God sent to protect his holy prophet. A perfectly reasonable connection to make, only. Thomas knew better than anyone that Karelian was not God's prophet, he wasn't God's man at all.

"Have you any word of Pauli?" Reinhard asked. "We heard rumors he escaped from Gottfried, but no one knows where he went. I thought he might try and find you."

"He did. But he's left my service," Karelian said.

Reinhard waited for him to explain. When he did not, the castellan asked bluntly:

"Well, why would he do that?"

"He thinks I'm a sorcerer."

"God's teeth! He *believes* Gottfried?"

"Yes."

It took a moment for Reinhard to absorb it. He had always thought Paul von Ardiun was a singularly bright young man.

"So where's he gone to, then? Over to *them*?" A southwesterly gesture, across the mountains.

"I don't know."

Reinhard spat. "If he joins up with that villain, he'd best not cross my path again."

Nor mine. And least of all hers . . . .

They walked on. It was full day now, the valley sun-drenched below them, speckled with cattle and goats, with ant-like wagons crawling the roads. Halfway up the mountain, on a broad plateau, the plundered ruins of the siege army's camp lay scattered in the sun.

"It must have been difficult for you at first," Karelian remarked. "Knowing nothing of what happened, or why. Not even knowing if I were alive or dead. Morale seems to have been good."

"It was. And is. And if I may give credit where it's due, my lord, you owe two unlikely people a lot for it. Father Thomas, and the lady Adelaide. He never lost faith in you for a moment. No matter what happened, he had a brave story to explain it. And she . . . well, in her heart I think she was certain you were dead. Even after we heard you were in Mainz, she never quite believed you'd be back. But it made her stubborn. And very brave—almost fey, if you'll forgive my saying it. It was as though she saw this fortress as her last stand. If the day had ever come when I saw fit to surrender, she would have forbidden it."

It surprised Reinhard to discover such qualities in Adelaide. It did not surprise Karelian at all.

"And you, Reini? Did you think I'd be back?"

"In truth, my lord, I didn't know. We heard you were badly wounded, but you'd gotten away. And then the rumors started, how the devil came and fetched you—that's why they couldn't find your body."

"He came with half a legion, did they tell you? And there's forty leagues of burnt forest along the edge of the Schildberge to prove it." Karelian chuckled. "I guess I kicked up a considerable fuss."

Reinhard put his elbows on the wall, stared across the valley for a time, and then looked at his liege.

"In all seriousness, my lord, will you tell me where you were?"

Karelian thought for a moment before he answered.

"Just between the two of us?" he said finally.

"Aye," Reinhard said. "I can hold my tongue, my lord."

"I was in the lair of Wulfstan."

There was a long silence. Reinhard surveyed the countryside again, even more thoughtfully than before.

"So which is it, my good friend?" Karelian murmured. "Do you think I'm bewitched or merely demented?"

Reini faced him, and met his gaze without flinching. "If that's where you say you were, my lord, then as far as I'm concerned that's where you were. Even a man like me can see the world is turning strange."

"It isn't turning strange, Reini," Karelian said. "It's always *been* strange. We just go for long periods of time trying not to notice."

Reinhard responded the only way he could. He began to walk again, and directed the conversation to practical matters.

"So what's your next move, then? We can't take Stavoren with just the men we have here."

"No. But we can isolate it. With this castle as a base, we can take every outpost and fortress Gottfried has between Ravensbruck and the mountains, and persuade the good burghers of Karn that Gottfried's wars will be bad for trade. We'll gather more men as we go."

"And the margravate of Dorn? Your brother has sworn allegiance to the villain."

"My brother would swear allegiance to the devil's painted arse, if he thought he would profit by it. And unswear himself again, just as easily. When we start rattling the walls of Stavoren, he'll go over to Konrad without blinking an eye."

They went down into the courtyard. Now that the siege was broken, and everything would be plentiful again, there was an air of exuberant activity: wagons and men coming and going, cook-houses pouring out rich smells, and clothing being scrubbed in great tubs of long-rationed water. He wandered among the guardsmen and servants, feeling very lordly and good about himself. Everyone was happy, most of all the children. The older ones worked; the younger ones played and harassed their elders for treats. But they all knew enough to bow to his lordship, and wish him good morning, and stand politely aside until he had passed them by.

Except one, who was scrambling across the cobblestones on all fours, right into the path of the count. A child of about a year, with black hair, and garments much too fine for any servant's child.

"Wulfi! Wulfi, you little wretch, come back here this minute!"

One of Adelaide's young women was running to snatch the child away. There was a distinct note of alarm in her voice. The youngster was too quick; he reached Karelian before the woman reached him. He stopped about a foot from the count's feet, and sat, and looked up. Here was someone the child had never seen before, someone quite magnificent-looking; he was intrigued.

"I'm so sorry, my lord," the young woman said desperately. "I only turned my back on him for a moment." She bent, reaching for the child. No doubt she had been cautioned many times to be careful: the youngster must never be a burden or an embarrassment to Karelian; he were best kept out of Karelian's way . . . .

"Wulfi, come!"

Karelian motioned her to be silent, to let the child be. He knew the whole of Schildberge castle was watching him. The cooking and the scrubbing and the loading of carts went carefully on—one did not stop working to stare at his lordship—but they were staring at him nonetheless.

At first he was angry about it, and then he wanted to laugh. It didn't take much, did it, to make the world stare?

He dropped to one knee. The child was beautiful, there was no doubt about it. And bright, too. His quick eyes were taking in everything. He scrambled closer, tugged briefly at the lacings of Karelian's boot, and then looked up and grinned.

All of the count's peers believed he should send this child away. Give him to the nuns to raise, or to the monks. They would feed him out of their Christian goodness . . . and they would put him to work in their vineyards or their stables or their sculleries, ten or fifteen hours of every day except the Lord's. They would fill his head with shame for being a bastard. And if he was bright—more importantly if he was obedient—they would let him study just enough so he could be a monk himself.

Two thoughts collided in Karelian's mind at the same instant. The first was of Wulfstan and Rudi Selven; of the tales and legends and whisperings. Perhaps they were true; perhaps they were not. But if they were, then this child might have as high a claim on the name and honors of Brandeis as Karelian did himself. The second thought was that it didn't matter anyway. He was done being ruled by the judgments of the world.

I had a father; he gave me his seed, for which I suppose I should be grateful. He gave me nothing else, not even his arm between myself and the rest of his savage get.

So be damned to them all. I like the look of you, little Wolfram, and I'm keeping you, and men can make of it what they will.

He brushed the back of his hand lightly across the boy's face, and then kissed him. His cheek was soft as a petal. Then slowly, the count got to his feet. The nurse was rooted to the stones, her eyes as big as saucers.

"Take good care of him, Magda," he said. "He will be lord here one day."

Then, with the greatest air of insouciance he could manage, he turned back to Reinhard, and went on evaluating the condition of his fortress.

XXXIV

THE WALLS OF STAVOREN

The demons are attempting to destroy the kingdom of God,
and by means of false miracles and lying oracles are
assuming the appearance of real gods.

LACTANTIUS

ONLY ONE OTHER TIME IN MY LIFE had I been so happy to see battlements—four years earlier, crossing the last sun-baked ridge of
an unending desert world, and looking finally upon the storied walls
of Jerusalem. I did not weep this time, looking on Stavoren, but I
did thank God almost as fervently.

The castle was not a warrior fort like Schildberge, aloof and inaccessible. It was the regal dwelling of a prince, lodged in the very
heart of the land. But it was nonetheless massive and secure, domi-
nating everything around it.

We could see it for hours before we reached it. We rode past
scattered villages and flourishing farms, finally past the broad fields
below the castle, where the flower of warrior Germany had gathered
just one year ago, at Ehrenfried's last *Königsritt*.

I remembered it all now: the vast army of tents, the feasting and
the revelry. The tournament. Karelian and Konrad meeting in the final
combat, and Karelian winning.

No one believed he would win—not even me, when I was being
honest with myself. But he won beautifully, magnificently. The Reinmark soared in triumph over the Salian princeling, there before the
whole world. And there, before the whole world, Karelian bent, and

picked Konrad's sword out of the trampled grass, and gave it back to him . . . .

I was exhausted, and maybe a little feverish—why else would I have remembered that moment with such an icy shiver of dismay?

I was grateful then for Wilhelm's chattering, for the nearness of the gates, for the sight of Gottfried's banners snapping in the wind. All I wanted to do was sleep, but I had barely crawled off my horse before a page boy came to fetch me. I was to attend the empress Radegund at once.

"The empress?"

I looked at the page boy, who nodded, and then at Wilhelm, who shrugged.

"Are you sure it wasn't someone else she wanted?" I asked.

"You're Paul von Ardiun, aren't you?" the boy said. He spoke scornfully, as if to remind me that he knew my name, even if I was too stupid to remember it.

I went to see the empress. She was waiting for me in the great hall, accompanied only by a pair of servants, and by her son Theodoric. I was exhausted and filthy. I almost stumbled as I knelt to her.

She saw my weariness, and ordered me to sit, and sent for wine.

"Have you been wounded, Sir Paul?" she asked. Her voice was kind.

"No, my lady I'm a little weary, that is all."

"My son Armund and his men speak well of you," she said. "They say you fought bravely and fled only when nothing else was possible."

A servant brought me a tankard. The queen insisted that I drink, and take a moment to collect my thoughts.

"There are some things I would like to ask you," she said then. "You were Lord Karelian's squire, I believe? You were with him in Ravensbruck?"

"Yes, my lady."

"You realize, I'm sure, the whole of the Reinmark is in danger from his rebellion. We must move quickly to defend ourselves. We need help, and the first place we would like to seek it is the march of Ravensbruck."

She was watching me carefully as she spoke.

"Count Arnulf of Ravensbruck has always enjoyed a good relationship with us," she went on. "My lord Gottfried speaks of him as the worthiest of his vassals. Not the best man, perhaps, as a Christian, but the most loyal ally."

She paused, very briefly. "He is now Karelian's father-in-law, which could dampen his loyalty towards us. On the other hand, we have heard certain . . . rumors. It is said Count Arnulf holds a bitter grudge against the lord of Lys. Perhaps you have some knowledge of this, Paul von Ardiun?"

Before I could think about how I might answer, she added sternly:

"Only facts, I caution you. Gossip we have in plenty, and speculation in cartloads. Tell us nothing but what you saw with your own eyes, and heard with your own ears."

I looked at her. She was a magnificent woman, not especially beautiful, but very regal. Though she dressed splendidly, as befitted her rank, there was no vanity about her, and not a trace of lewdness. Her gown was high-necked and heavy; her hair was coiffed with a splendid veil.

I honored her, and I wanted to be of use, but I hated talking about my time with Karelian. I wished the world would forget I had ever known him.

"When we first came to Ravensbruck," I said, "everything was fine. They got on very well. Though I don't think Karelian liked Count Arnulf very much."

"Really?" she murmured. "And why not?"

"Even before the wedding, he said he regretted the alliance. He said he wished he'd gone home to Lys and married a widow with a tavern instead."

The empress said nothing, but looked at her son as if she could not quite believe this of any highborn man, even Karelian.

"They were married nonetheless—my lord and Count Arnulf's daughter. And then, as I think you know, my lady, Adelaide was found with her lover, Rudolf of Selven, only a few weeks later."

"The whole of Germany knows about it. We want to know what happened afterwards. Selven was killed, was he not? By Count Arnulf's men?"

"Yes, my lady. We had all been out hunting when it happened. Count Arnulf put his daughter in the dungeon until we got back. He thought Karelian would want to punish her himself. But Karelian didn't. He said she was just a child. Arnulf was furious about it. He'd been shamed in his own house. And it's well known, lady, he is a harsh man. He kills . . . very easily. I thought more than once he would kill the lot of us, just to avenge himself on her. She was his favorite daughter, they say, so he took it very ill."

"So what passed between him and Karelian?"

"I don't know what passed, my lady. The only time they spoke, it was in private, and afterwards Count Arnulf would sit for hours in his chair, ignoring everyone. But when we left he spoke. He told us he would honor his alliance with Karelian for the sake of the duke—I mean his majesty Lord Gottfried. And then he gave a warning to Karelian I'll never forget, for it made my blood run cold. Never, he said, *never* fall out of favor with the duke."

The empress and her son exchanged another look.

For the first time, Theodoric questioned me, too. "Count Arnulf hates him, then? Is that what you're saying?"

"Yes, my lord," I said. "And it isn't just because of the lady Adelaide, it's—"

I faltered, realizing I had begun to speculate.

"Go on," the empress said.

"Karelian outfaced him in his own house, in front of his own vassals. Arnulf's men baited him. At the very end, Arnulf baited him, too. He even tried to stage another marriage, to his younger daughter Helga. But he couldn't get the better of Karelian, no matter what he did."

"But he was injured, wasn't he?" the empress protested. "We've been told he could hardly walk."

"Yes, lady, but he had his men there. He could have done anything to us he wanted. But Karelian was . . . Karelian controlled the situation from the first. He was utterly in the wrong, and he had only a handful of men, and still he controlled it. As though he only needed to decide how things would be, and they were so."

It had not, I reflected, been quite so easy or so straightforward. Control was the wrong word. Karelian had maneuvred his way through the threats of Ravensbruck, rather than controlling them. But that was, perhaps, the ultimate manifestation of control.

There was a brief silence. Then the empress rose, and spoke to her son.

"Send to Ravensbruck at once," she said. "He gave us only a token force to send west. Well and good; he has that many more men with him now."

She looked at me. "We are grateful, Sir Paul. For your knowledge, and for your loyalty."

Perhaps something showed in my face then, for she stepped closer.

"You find it painful, perhaps, to speak against the man who was your liege?"

I started to deny it, and then changed my mind. She would know. "Yes, my lady."

She smiled. For the first time, I remembered she was a mother. She had borne Theodoric and Armund, two other boys who died, and three daughters.

"Any fool can run downhill," she said. "It's the hard, bitter climb which is pleasing to God. But if we endure, in time it won't be hard. In time we won't even remember why it used to be so hard."

She was a wise lady, one of the few women in the Reinmark who were truly Christian, and truly chaste. She was a fit wife for Gottfried. Yet she was wrong in what she said. I endured, and the time she spoke of never came. I always remembered why it was so hard. I will remember till they carry me to my grave, and I greatly fear I will remember after.

Messengers hurried off to Ravensbruck to remind Count Arnulf of his feudal duties, and to summon him to the field against Karelian. On the way they would stop at the great trading city of Karn, and pass on a few reminders there as well. Like the margravate of Dorn, this city was traditionally a difficult place to deal with, not because its rulers were rash and unpredictable—quite the opposite. They were practical, canny, and pitilessly self-centered. Karn was the best place in Germany to buy anything—fine goods, weapons, mercenaries, whores. It was the worst place in Germany to find a friend.

I never learned precisely what inducements Theodoric meant to offer Karn for its continuing loyalty. But he was prepared to offer Ravensbruck a royal marriage. Arnulf had unmarried sons, and Arnulf was singularly ambitious. If he proved difficult, the princess Ludmilla, Gottfried's youngest daughter, would be held out to him as the ultimate reward.

We waited for his answer, and watched the war unfold. From the first it went strangely. Perhaps every war does. Ordinary human daring and ordinary human stupidity can combine in infinitely unpredictable ways, all by themselves, and our situation was far from ordinary. When the archbishop of Mainz folded his hands and refused to vote, Germany was left with two leaders, and with none. Both had allies and a measure of legitimacy, but neither could wield the full, acknowledged authority of a king. Predictably, chaos followed.

Swabian barons defied their landgrave and sent knights to Prince Konrad instead. In Konrad's heartland of Franconia, a visionary monk saw Gottfried on a mountain-top, receiving the crown from Christ himself. Peasants and tradesmen by the hundreds left their homes and followed the monk to Gottfried's camps. There, just like the common folk who marched to Jerusalem, they ate his food and got in his way, but added nothing to his military strength. The Bavarians prayed for his victory, but they had a great deal of difficulty finding either tithes or food. Konrad's proud warrior Thuringia swore he would drive the Reimnark usurper headlong into the realms of Hel, but when he called his vassals to arms, only half of them came.

In Stavoren, we heard these accounts one by one; our hopes rose and fell like the wind. There were battles, but they were small and they settled nothing. There were betrayals and sudden political reverses, but both sides suffered them. Uncertainty seemed to be the order of the day—uncertainty and something else, something elusive, which for months we sensed around us but could not begin to identify. A restlessness. A waiting. An uneasiness quietly mixed with anger.

Where was God in all of this?

This was his empire, his people, his king. The war was no ordinary struggle for power. There was evil in the land, a new and desperate peril, but only a handful of Germans were certain what it was, or how they might combat it, or even on which side of the quarrel it could be found. The others wanted to be told—by a miracle, or by the undivided authority of the Church, or by some kind of dazzling, absolutely conclusive victory. Unfortunately, miracles and churchmen were turning up on both sides, and victory on neither.

Where then was God?

Only in the Reinmark were matters changing decisively. Using his mountain fortress as a base, Karelian stormed over the whole interior of the duchy. He gobbled up Gottfried's scattered holdings one by one, overwhelming three small castles and placing the last one under siege. Some twenty barons who held modest fiefs directly from the duke he came to terms with, without battle.

The duke, he told them, was no longer duke, much less emperor. He had risen against his lawful sovereign, and all his lands and rights were forfeit. He, Karelian, would act as Konrad's agent and confirm the barons in their possessions, provided they swore allegiance and provided him with aid.

They were small nobility. They had already sent aid to Gottfried.

Not one of them could have put fifty knights in the field in his own defense. They swore.

Stavoren seemed to exist in a state of permanent crisis. Theodoric wanted to attack—to lead his men across the mountains and thunder into battle like the great Teuton warlord he believed himself to be. But we could get no reliable information about Karelian's forces. A thousand men . . . a few hundred . . . a vast, unstoppable army . . . everyone who saw him saw something different. As at Schildberge, his strikes were swift, sudden, and successful, and rumor raced on the heels of his victories like fear in a time of plague.

Viking berserkers had joined him from the north—so we were told—and bearded pagans from the east. They walked across canyons and rivers as other men walked on grass. Earthworks gave way before them; stone walls crumpled like those of Jericho, and hardened men fell dead of fear. The devil himself had been seen flying over the demon lord's forces, with some five hundred of his legion, and Odin's ravens, too, bearing messages and carrying off the dead.

And who was to wonder at it? The great witch of Helmardin herself rode by the count's side. She was seen in his camps, and on the march, and although no one in the world had ever seen her before, no one doubted her identity. A lady of rank, they said, finely dressed and marvelously beautiful. Surely it was she who called up the darkness and the fog to serve him, and so made possible his secret marches and surprise attacks. It was she whom they saw sometimes behind the battle lines, watching from a hilltop or a solitary cliff, mounted on a coal black horse, weaving death for all who came against him.

"Is this all you can bring me?" was Theodoric's usual response, roared out in front of some cringing messenger or exhausted spy. "Panic and imaginings? God's blood, are there no men left in the Reinmark, just battalions of rabbit-wits scaring each other half to death with stories? I don't want to hear another word about sorcery, by God! I want numbers, do you understand? You fools can count, can't you? Bring me numbers!"

But no numbers came, or rather they kept coming and they kept changing, and Theodoric did not attack. Radegund opposed it, but it was Gottfried, I am sure, who gave the final order: Wait! He himself had almost all of the Reinmark's best men, and he would not send them back. He needed them, no doubt, but more importantly he needed to diminish the political importance of Karelian's rebellion by pretending to ignore it. At the same time, he did not want Theodoric to play into Karelian's hands with some disastrous, ill-conceived attack. Stavoren was defensible, and Ravensbruck had always been able to look after itself. *So be patient, Theodoric; trust my power, and wait!*

The prince waited, but in a singularly wicked temper. He slept very little, and ate on his feet. He summoned his advisors at all hours of the day or night, and often dismissed them with explosions of rage. He was the sort of man who lived on action, whether there was an object for his action or not. Day after day he went around us like a wasp—angry, tireless, and full of sting.

My own circumstances had changed considerably. I was widely praised for my conduct at Schildberge, and that impressed Theodoric, at least a little. Or perhaps Radegund put in a word for me—or even Gottfried, satisfied at last that I had done my best. In any case, I was given a place in the prince's personal retinue at Stavoren. I stood guard in his council chambers, and accompanied him on journeys. Wilhelm and I both rode in his escort when he went a second time to Dorn, demanding further proofs of the margrave's loyalty.

This time I got to see Karelian's half-brother in person, although briefly and at some distance. I could not hear much of what passed between him and Theodoric, but Ludolf nodded and smiled a lot. Entirely too much, in fact. After, riding back, I asked Wilhelm what he thought.

"Ugly brute," he said. "Just like the old man before him."

"I don't mean his looks," I said. "I mean him. He seemed to be babbling a lot."

"He's between the hammer and the anvil," Wilhelm said. "And he's scared to death."

"Will he stay loyal, do you think?"

Wilhelm laughed and spat.

No one expected much of the margrave of Dorn, least of all Theodoric, who sent his men out to drain the granaries of the margravate, and empty the cellars and the smoke-houses, and drive back to Stavoren most of the goats and the cattle. My father's fief of Ardiun was raked bare like all the others.

"If we don't take it all," Theodoric said, "that accursed traitor will."

It was how wars were fought, of course. The first thing you took from your enemy was his food. But I could not help thinking that the only people likely to go hungry this winter were the people of Dorn.

On the other side of the mountains, Karelian had half the Reinmark to feed from.

The envoys came back from the north in August. It was late at night. The empress had retired, and came to the council room wrapped in a great cape, with slippers on her feet.

You needed only to see the men's faces to know their news was bad.

"Majesty." The spokesman, a knight named Friedrich, bowed deeply to the empress, and then to her son. "My lord. It grieves me beyond words to say this; I would willingly—"

"For Christ's sake stop grieving and spit it out!" Theodoric said harshly. "Where is the count of Ravensbruck? How many men has he sent us and are they ready to attack?"

"He's in his castle, my lord. He awaits your instructions, and your . . . reply."

"He has my instructions. He's to join me in putting down this damnable traitor in Lys."

"He can't pass through Karn, my lord. And he will not take the other route unless—"

The prince had seated himself formally when the envoys came. Now he jumped to his feet.

"Can't pass through Karn? What the devil are you talking about?"

"The city has made an alliance with Karelian."

"They've done what?"

"They've gone over to him, my lord. He's persuaded them that Konrad will be king, and told them they will lose their charters and their monopolies if they oppose him. His friend Lehelin has swayed the barons, and as for the merchants, they care for nothing except their trade. They've allowed Karelian's men to garrison the bridge."

"God *damn* him!" Theodoric spat.

"Did they allow you passage through to Ravensbruck?" the empress asked.

"No, my lady. They told us to come back here, and tell you—shall I repeat it, lady as they spoke it?"

"Yes."

"They said we should tell Gottfried's puppy there are wolves on the great bridge of Karn, and he should take care lest they bite his little head off."

"Indeed."

"We went west then, lady, to Karlsbruck. The bridge is gone there; it was swept away two harvests back, and has never been rebuilt. They have only rafts and homemade boats—"

"Get on with it," Theodoric snapped, pacing.

"Forgive me, my lord. We crossed with a local boatman, and went on to Ravensbruck, and met with Arnulf. He was not . . . enthusiastic, my lord. He can't use the bridge at Karn. And Karlsbruck has always been a dangerous crossing, even when there was a bridge. Now, to ferry his knights and destriers across on rafts, with steep wooded hills on all sides, where Karelian could hide his men and wait . . . he said he might as well hang them in his courtyard, and save them the march."

Theodoric glowered, but he did not disagree.

"There's another road south, you know," he said grimly. "Or is Arnulf afraid of it, like the rest of this damnable country?"

"He says he will march through Helmardin, my lord. But he has a price."

"He is our vassal," the empress said grimly. "It's not his place to set us terms."

"So I reminded him, my lady. And he reminded me that he was Karelian's father-in-law. Karelian wants to play kingmaker, he said; if he succeeds, he will be powerful indeed. He will be duke of the Reinmark at the least. Forgive me, my lord, I only repeat what was said—"

"Go on, Sir Friedrich," the empress said, with a tired glance at her angry son.

"Arnulf made a great show of his kinship with Karelian. You can hardly expect me to turn against so illustrious a son-in-law, he said, unless you offer me at least as much in return—"

"He hates his illustrious son-in-law, God damn it!"

"He does indeed. But it is Arnulf the man who hates him. Arnulf the border lord is pure survivor. He would like nothing better than to side with us. But he considers it a desperate risk, and he wants to be rewarded accordingly."

"Dear God, did you not offer him my daughter?" Radegund demanded. "What more does he want?"

"He wants your son. Armund. He wants Armund to marry his daughter, the lady Helga."

"My *son?*" This time it was the empress on her feet. "She should marry my son, and be a princess of the empire? And if fate proves cruel to us, maybe the queen? The mother of our royal blood? *Helga of Ravensbruck?* The man is mad! You told him it was utterly out of the question, didn't you?"

"Is it?" Theodoric asked flatly.

She spun towards him. "Yes! It's absolutely out of the question!"

Theodoric gave her a cold look, and addressed the envoy again: "Was there more to Count Arnulf's message?"

"No, my lord. But he says he will not take the field until Armund comes to Ravensbruck, and he sees them lawfully wed."

"The man's gall is beyond belief," Radegund said bitterly. "I suppose if Theodoric were not already married, Arnulf would have asked for him, and made his border baggage queen!"

"I expect he would have," Friedrich said unhappily.

"You may go," Theodoric said. "All of you, leave us."

So we left. What was said after I do not know, nor what message was sent back to Count Arnulf. As I went wearily towards my bed I thought about Helga of Ravensbruck, Adelaide's sister. She was fifteen, as I recalled, and already greedy as a young she-dragon, and just as cold. But pretty, and not at all stupid. She had longed to marry the glittering lord of Lys, and betrayed her sister's love-tryst in a futile attempt to replace her.

She would be smiling now, I thought, seeing there were even higher men who might be captured than a count, even finer and richer palaces to live in than the manor house of Lys.

It occurred to me, as I was drifting to sleep, that the empress might well call me to her council room again, and ask me what I might know about Count Arnulf's other unadmirable daughter. In fact, she did, but by then it scarcely mattered; we were ready to pay any price for help from Ravensbruck.

Karelian had crossed the mountains, and was riding into Dorn.

XXXV

DORN

Lasting honor shall be his,
a name that shall never die beneath the heavens.

WIDSITH —*Anonymous Anglo-Saxon poem*

THE VALLEY LOOKED EVEN POORER than Karelian remembered it: the houses more scattered and more hunched, the cattle fewer and thinner, the peasants wearier. They looked up at him and his passing soldiery with unsmiling and unadmiring resignation. They knew what his arrival meant: more fighting, more blood, more tribute.

But the landscape was as magnificent as ever, swept round by mountains on three sides, and shimmering in the late summer sun. Dorn had been rich once, richer than Lys, richer than Eden. It was the land of the winter tree, where the goddess-daughter Maris fashioned the Black Chalice of Car-Iduna, ages before, in the time of war among the gods.

The sky gods conquered in Dorn, and after them came armies, and then empires, and then the one-God and his priests, and with each coming Dorn grew less.

Now I come, he thought, *and what do I bring them, except more armies? Once the pyramid of power is in place, how do you undo it, except with still more power? . . . gods, I would have this over, over and done with forever . . . .*

He had returned to this valley only once since the day he left it. He was twenty-three, with a string of tournament victories and many battle honors to his credit, with silk on his body and gold in his belt. Everything he owned in the world was right there on his horse, and his honors were as unsubstantial as a dream. But his mother kissed him and praised him and laughed. She laughed as a woman might who had not laughed for many years. She wanted to believe he was halfway to a kingdom, and he let her believe it. In her presence he almost believed it himself.

Only once he came. Not to the manor house. Not to Ludolf or to any of them, but only to her, to the moody convent of Saint Kathrin, where like so many good wives and widows of the Christian world, she went to live out the last of her empty, passionless days.

I couldn't stay with him, Karel. I couldn't bear it after you were gone . . . .

Only once, to see his lovely mother. The world was broad. Its wars were scattered and went on forever, and some of them he lost. Before he could come again, she was dead.

He did everything very formally with faultless attention to form. He drew up his men well beyond fighting distance, and sent envoys under a flag of truce, asking the margrave Ludolf Brandeis to meet with him, with full guarantees of safe conduct and honorable treatment.

Ludolf, a great deal less formally, agreed. He sent a messenger of the lowest rank he dared, and obviously advised him to be blunt. The margrave would come, he said, but he would bring a proper escort, whether anyone approved or not. And he hoped his little brother would have the decency to provide a tent.

"A tent?" Reinhard murmured, looking at the sky. There did not appear to be a rain cloud anywhere in the length and breadth of Germany.

"Tell the margrave he may bring as large an escort as he wishes," Karelian said. "I will bring the same. We will set up a tent there—" he pointed—"below the hazel grove. I will meet him there in one hour."

"He can't possibly be ready in an hour, my lord," the messenger said.

"Then he may have two hours. And if he can't be ready to talk in two hours, then by God he'd better be ready to fight! Tell him so!"

Ludolf came to the hazel grove after two hours precisely. They rode towards each other, it seemed, across half a world and half a lifetime. It astonished Karelian to see that his brother was old, to realize he must be over sixty. The last time they faced each other he,

Karelian, had been fifteen. Strong, cunning, and singularly dangerous, but still only fifteen, still a boy, painfully aware of his brother's authority. The Ludolf he expected to see was the Ludolf he remembered—a tall man, copper-haired, watchful and mean.

The margrave of Dorn had a paunch now, and the pulpiness of too much wine about his eyes. He had lost much of his hair, and the rest of it was a yellowing grey. He had never been handsome. His father's first wife had given her husband a splendid dowry, and proven singularly fertile as well, but beauty she brought neither to her marriage bed nor to her offspring. As for Helmuth himself, he had always been ugly as a boar.

Ludolf resembled his father, now more than ever. But for all the signs of age about his body his eyes had not changed at all. His eyes were still watchful and mean.

He was scrutinizing Karelian intently, taking in every detail, from the fine boots to the fine, still-tawny hair. To his considerable surprise, Karelian felt vulnerable against his look. Memories of Ludolf's brutality settled into the pit of his stomach like small stones, grinding away his calm, political resolve. It would be easy to forget he was here on Konrad's behalf, not his own.

Do I still remind you of her, Ludolf? Your father's wife, younger than you the day he brought her home, so beautiful, and so hopelessly out of reach? Every time you looked at me you saw her. You saw your father rutting on her, wine-soaked and slobbering, and you hated us both.

Ludolf was smiling, but without a trace of affection in the smile. "You dress well," he said. "For a renegade."

Yes, Ludolf was still Ludolf in every way, most of all the malice—the dark, barely comprehended malice of a youth who had everything and nothing. He was the eldest, the heir, the one who mattered, yet he was coarse-made and clumsy and unloved. His father cherished no one, and his mother had eight more just like him and then died.

And this *brat* was gifted with everything he never had: with a warrior's body and a stag's grace and—most unbearable of all—with *her.* For Karelian she was always in reach, year after cruel year; always lovely and jasmine-haired, picking him up out of the dirt no matter how many times Ludolf threw him there, wiping the blood away and telling him it did not matter, one day he would be better than any of them, one day he would be a proud and splendid lord . . . .

They dismounted and embraced, formal as statues, and went into the tent, and sat. Servants brought wine. The margrave raised his cup in an ironic salute.

"You don't visit me for twenty-five years, and then arrive at my gates with an army. What am I to make of that, kinsman?"

"Consider it a gesture of nostalgia. For all the times I needed an army in your company and didn't have one."

Ludolf laughed, coarsely. "You always were a crybaby," he said.

Crybaby?

It was astonishing, Karelian thought, how men could transform the world to suit their own imaginings. As a boy he rarely wept, even in the bitterest pain, and never where this one could see him.

"I recall you made a bet once," Karelian said. "With Wilhelm. You bet him a solid gold mark that you could make me cry." He lifted his own cup, drank briefly, looked full into Ludolf's ice and iron eyes. "As I recall, you lost."

On the day of that bet Karelian Brandeis, aged twelve, became a soldier: a person who would consciously decide to carry out the task before him, no matter what it cost. He would not cry even if they rended him to pieces. A brutally pointless task, like so many of the ones which came after.

You never went to Jerusalem, Ludolf, did you? I went there for you. For all of you, with your arrogance and your bottomless appetite for power. I cried then, but by then it was too late . . . .

Ludolf's gaze had grown even more remote and cold. If he was so good at remembering things which never happened, no doubt he was equally good at forgetting things which had, and he did not like to be reminded.

"What do you want, Karelian?"

"I've been instructed, on the emperor's behalf, to accept your oath of allegiance—"

"Which emperor, little brother?"

"There is only one. To accept your oath of allegiance, and also on the emperor's behalf, your seal on this treaty of alliance—"

He nodded towards one of his knights, who promptly approached the table and unrolled a parchment. Ludolf glanced only at the first couple of lines:

In bounden duty to my liege and sovereign lord, Konrad, Holy Roman Emperor and king of Germany, etc., etc. . . . .

Then he shoved it aside, drank deeply, and wiped his sleeve across his mouth.

"You think your princeling's going to win, do you?"

"Yes."

"And what do you think the Reinmark will get out of it? We'll be third-rate citizens just like always. You haven't any loyalty, Karelian. You never did have. Everything you are, Gottfried von Heyden made you—"

"I made myself, Ludolf. Gottfried only bought me. Temporarily."

"And why shouldn't he? You sold to everyone else. For the first time, ever, we have a chance here in the Reinmark. We can see our own man as emperor—our own cousin, for God's sake. You could have been his closest ally. You could have done something for us finally, after spending your whole damn life serving everything and everyone except your own. Instead you stab him in the back, and offer the rest of us up as fodder for that high-handed Salian cock-sucker—"

"Enough!"

Karelian flung his chair back and leapt to his feet, slamming his cup down on the table. "Have you quite finished?" he said. His voice was low, but savage—more savage even than he had intended.

Ludolf seemed about to plunge on. He had never been a subtle man. But it did not require a great deal of subtlety to notice how the atmosphere of the room had changed, how men had shifted their positions and moved their hands closer to their swords. He shrugged, and poured down another vast amount of wine.

Dear gods, I think there is someone in the house of Brandeis who actually drinks more than I do . . . .

"There's no point arguing with you," the margrave said. "There never was. So what do you want? That I should swear allegiance to your . . . prince? Suppose I do? My oath will last as long as his pretensions to the crown. If he wins, so be it; I'll bow to God's will. If he loses, then God will have released me from my oath. Isn't that so, little brother?"

"I also want your seal on this treaty, and on everything it asks for. To start with, two hundred knights, fully armed and equipped at your expense."

"Two hundred knights? You're out of your mind!"

"Plus aid and sustenance for our attack on Stavoren: cattle, grain, wagons, tents, woolen cloth, oil, wine, candles—it's all very carefully itemized, and based on the war tribute we claimed across the rest of the Reinmark, neither higher nor lower—"

"But Theodoric has already taken everything!"

"While you smiled and bowed and kissed his pretentious von Heyden arse, no doubt."

"There was nothing I could do! I won't pay this! I can't pay it!"

"You don't have any choice. Listen, Ludolf. Forget I'm your little brother and just listen to sense for a minute. Konrad is the lawful heir to the imperial crown, and in the end he will be king. He didn't start this war. If you want to whine about the Reinmark's hard luck, or your own, whine to Gottfried. He had everything a sane man could want and it wasn't enough; he had to be king of the world.

"Well, he won't be. And there's one thing about the house of Brandeis—however many mistakes we make, we usually end up on the winning side. I'd hate to see you break the pattern."

Ludolf banged his fist on the parchment. "I don't have this kind of wealth, Karelian. Damn you, have you forgotten how much our father lost? The margravate is almost destitute—!"

"And do you remember how he lost it? By being stupid. Don't imitate him. You have plate and jewels you can sell; they will pay for half your knights at least. You can borrow the rest."

"And if I refuse?"

"Then I would have to take Dorn under my own authority. On the emperor's behalf."

There was a long, ugly silence. Once, Ludolf had come within a sliver of killing him. More than once, if he counted the traps and the tricks which, except for his own resourcefulness, could easily have proven lethal.

"So," Ludolf said bitterly. "It's like that, is it? You've sunk so low you'd make war on your own brother."

Karelian felt vaguely nauseous, and dangerously close to losing control.

"Our father the margrave never minded when we fought among ourselves," he said. "Don't you remember? He said it would toughen us up. The best of us would prove our worth, and the rest . . . well, it didn't much matter what happened to the rest, did it?"

He bowed, just a little. "I will come for your answer tonight, my lord. Have it ready."

* * *

She had been a Christian, his mother, and she was faithful still, sleeping under the eyes of a brooding Jesus and a chapel full of saints. Maybe that was why he had tried so hard to believe—so hard and for so many bewildered years, trying and quitting and trying again. Because she had been so good to him. How could she have loved a God less good than she was?

The tomb was simple, a stone slab in the chapel floor, no effigy, no epitaph, just her name, Gudrun Rath von Brandeis, as befitted a last and insignificant wife, mother of a last and insignificant son.

He wondered how she would judge him now. Count of Lys, and apostate sorcerer. Champion of a lawful king, and rebel against the established order of the world. Crusader knight, and bondsman of a pagan witch.

Probably she would smile, the way she always had, and brush his hair back from his face: *You will do splendidly, Karel. You will win, I know it! You will be a hero, a great lord the whole of Germany will look up to . . . !*

And then it would be paid for, made worthwhile somehow: the life which had been no life at all, the marriage without a whisper of joy, the years of unrelenting quiet fear. She had had so much potential for life, and so much hunger for it, and year by year it spilled through her hands like broken beads: her beauty wasted, her passions unspent, her daughters rushed into early, low-rank marriages to keep them safe, her son fled into mercenary exile.

But he would be a great lord.

He had imagined, in his youthful arrogance, that she was possessed of a dazzling and magnificent faith in himself. What she was possessed of was an obsession—a blind, life-sustaining fantasy of vindication and revenge.

It was she, more than anyone, who taught him to fight. Christian though she was, there was no turning the other cheek in the manor house of Dorn. And he went on fighting because of her, slashing his way across the world in a twenty-year pilgrimage to the blood-watered streets of Jerusalem. Because he was better than all of them, like she always said, and he would prove it.

But should he blame her for that—or thank her still, because he was one of the handful who understood what happened there, and walked away? She taught him the laws of rank and power, God and king and all the world in its place. But with every act of tenderness and impassioned sheltering she undid her own words. She loved him, and she would not give him up to the laws of power.

They can't hurt you, Karel. Not inside. They're older, they're stronger, they have authority; it doesn't matter. You know who you are, and no one can make you less.

Soft words and a safe place to sleep; a woman's hand in his hair; a last, wrinkled apple cut carefully in half and savored by candlelight, in the dead of winter—all worth more than power, more than the world's approval, even while the world's approval was held up as a banner to be won with blood and fire. It was a contradiction which took him twenty years to resolve, but without her, there would have been no contradiction at all. There would only have been them, Helmuth and his sons, and he would have grown up like them. It was she who made possible the questions she herself would never ask, the defiance she could give voice to only by giving it to him.

You know who you are, Karelian, and no one can make you less.

No one. In the end not even God.

The church of Dorn was large and old and gloomy, built by a missionary saint whose name Karelian had forgotten, probably on purpose. He felt alien in it, aware that he did not belong. He disturbed a presence here; he could feel it stir and watch him. *Why have you come to my temple, unbeliever? What is it that you want?*

There was no hostility in the question, only the aloofness of a sky lord looking down from an immense distance at a tiny, unimportant creature.

He made a small bow in the direction of the main altar. He meant no offense, but he would do what he came to do, and if offense were taken, well, so be it. Then he knelt before his mother's tomb, lifted the small clay urn in his hands, lit it, and held it high until the last scented petal had burned and curled into ash.

Honor to you, Gudrun Rath von Brandeis. I am and I am not the proud lord you dreamed I would be. I ride now by the shoulder of the king . . . and I may well die on the stake before I am done. But I loved you, lady mother, every hour that I lived, and I love you still.

The fire swayed and curled in water. For her, the masters of Dorn could still make him cry.

He was less inclined than ever to be patient with Ludolf when he returned to their meeting place. But Ludolf apparently knew when he was outmatched. He had signed the treaty. And stamped it with a great thump of anger, for the seal was badly smudged.

Karelian glanced at it, rolled it up, and passed it to Reinhard.

"Your oath, margrave," he said.

It would hurt Ludolf to have to kneel to him—hurt him more than a heated iron. And yes, Karelian was demanding the oath for Konrad's sake; it was the proper, necessary thing to do. That did not change a thing. The satisfaction it would give him had nothing to do with Konrad.

"My loyalty to Prince Konrad is guaranteed in the treaty," Ludolf said coldly.

"Do you speak of his majesty the king, margrave?"

"You know who I'm speaking of—!"

"Then speak of him with proper respect. As for your personal allegiance, I am commanded to receive it, and receive it I will."

"Do you do *everything* he commands, little brother?"

Karelian caught his breath. He was swept by a blinding, stomach-wrenching flood of rage. He had a fragment of his tactical good sense left—enough to know this was just Ludolf being Ludolf. It was not about politics, not about the empire or Konrad or the allegiances of Dorn. He had sense enough to know it, but not enough to care. Not any more. For fifteen years he had endured Ludolf just being Ludolf—being eldest, being bully, being permitted. Well, by the gods, not any more!

He swept forward and struck his brother savagely across the face with the back of his hand. And stepped back, in a silence so absolute he could hear his own heart hammering.

The margrave straightened, touched his cheek with a kind of lingering disbelief.

"You *dare?*" he whispered.

"Margrave." It was hard for Karelian to keep his voice calm, hard to stand there and behave like a lord. A boy, a common soldier, even a wandering knight could brawl sometimes, could fling a man across a room and batter him into the walls, use knees on him, boots, wine jugs, anything in reach, until he was a heap that his friends would have to come and carry away. He wanted that. More than anything in the world, just now, he wanted to break Ludolf into very numerous, very small pieces.

"I will say this only once," he said. "I am not little brother. I am the count of Lys, and his majesty's commander in the Reinmark. Until a new duke is named, I am the *de facto* ruler of this duchy."

He paused to let the reminder properly sink in. Then he went on.

"Since you are my kinsman, I'll overlook your disrespect towards myself—this time. Your disrespect towards my liege the king you will apologize for."

It did not seem possible the room could grow more silent than it was. But it did.

"I will apologize?" Ludolf was pale and almost trembling with rage. "You dare to strike me under a flag of truce, and *I* will apologize?"

"Yes."

"Never!"

"You will apologize, margrave, and you'll swear allegiance to your king. Or I will take Dorn—and when I do, I'll hang you from your own gates like a dog!"

"That's what you really want, isn't it?" Ludolf said bitterly. "To take Dorn away from me!"

"It's not what I really want. On the other hand, it won't grieve me much."

Ludolf steadied himself a little with wine.

"Men answer in the field for smaller insults than what you've offered me," he said.

"So challenge me. But consider this: you're too old to fight, and I am here on the king's business. I'm not about to waste my time duelling with one of your lackeys. So two men who've never met will try to kill each other on our behalf, in a quarrel neither of them started. Perhaps it will satisfy your honor, but when it's over, I'll take Dorn just as surely, and I'll hang you just as high."

He smiled. It was a fiend's smile, probably. He did not care. He was taut to his core with pure, shimmering hate.

"Surprise me, Ludolf. Show me you actually have enough good sense to stay alive."

The margrave looked at him briefly, turned away, walked a little, turned back.

"And what is the . . . king . . . offering me for my allegiance?"

"He will assure your hereditary right to Dorn, and overlook any past collaboration with the traitor Gottfried."

You signed the treaty, knave; it's all there.

"Then I apologize to his majesty the king." Ludolf moved forward, slowly, as if every step was painful. He knelt, and raised his hands palm to palm, and repeated the oath of allegiance. His voice was little more than a whisper, and his hands were ever so faintly trembling against Karelian's own.

He's old, Karelian thought. *He's old and he's never been wise and I am being cruel to him . . . and worse, I don't especially care.*

Ludolf stood up. "This will not be forgotten, Karelian."

Really? The small flutter of pity in Karelian's soul went out like a candle in a winter storm. *We have a very long way to go, Ludolf Brandeis, until you have as many things to forget as I do!*

The margrave of Dorn marched out of the tent with a great show of dignity. Karelian heard the voices, the jingle of bridles and clatter of hooves as they mounted, the thunder of them riding away. He heard it and did not hear it. The last of Ludolf's attendants had not left the tent when he waved at the servant who was holding the tankard of wine.

The boy started to pour some into a cup.

"Give me all of it, damn it!"

He lifted the tankard, drank hugely, and wiped his arm across his mouth. They were all watching him, all of his men, rooted to the earth and saying not a word. What could they say, or even think, after a demonstration like this one?

"Get the horses," he said.

They filed out, except for Reinhard, who moved closer to him.

"Are you all right, my lord?" he asked quietly.

"All right?" He made a brief, empty gesture, drank some more, and looked into the patient, troubled face of his seneschal.

"Yes, I'm all right. I'm just . . . God's blood, Reini, I've bargained with berserker Danes and kept my head. With Huns. With bandits. With Arnulf of Ravensbruck, and that's like bargaining in hell. But this one . . . ! A dozen words exchanged, and I'm his raging little brother again."

"You were unforgivably provoked, my lord."

"I've been provoked a thousand times. This was different." He shook his head. "I don't like forgetting who I am."

Or remembering too clearly, either.

"I didn't know there was such bad blood between you, my lord. I don't think anyone knew. There never was anything . . . public . . . ."

No. It was never public. The world was full of savagery that was never public.

He emptied the tankard and flung it away. "Be damned to it, Reini; we have a war to fight. Let's go."

* * *

He did not sleep well that night. Sometime in the depths of it he gave up trying altogether, and got up. Raven found him sitting by the table with a candle, some wine, and a scattering of maps. She sat across from him, tangle-haired and sleepy, wrapped in a great cape of black silk.

"What in Tyr's name are you doing, my lord? It's the middle of the night."

"I'm thinking."

She purred something. It sounded like bewilderment.

He did not really want to tell her what he was thinking. He wanted simply to act on it. But it was quite impossible. He was not only Konrad's vassal now; he was also hers.

"I think we should change our strategy in Stavoren," he said.

"Change it? Why?" Her voice was soft, and carefully even.

"It's too dangerous."

"We've tried it twice, Karel, in two different sieges. We know it works."

"Stavoren is different. Stavoren is Gottfried's ancestral castle, and the heart of Theodoric's defenses. Everything Gottfried didn't take to the west with him is there—all the men, all the secrets, all the sorcerous power."

"Yes. That's why we decided on this strategy in the first place—because Stavoren was different. Because Stavoren would push our skills, and our resources, and our courage to the limits. We've always known it was dangerous. We chose it because it offered the surest hope of success. Now success is a day's march away and you want to change your mind?"

"I don't want anything to happen to you."

"Nothing will happen to me."

"And if it did?" He stood up, restlessly. "You said it yourself, in Car-Iduna. We are none of us gods. I won't let you do it, Raven."

"You won't let me? Now there's an interesting idea."

She stood up, and moved around the table to his side, soundlessly, like a shadow.

"What did he do to you, Karel?"

"Do to me? Who? What on earth are you talking about?"

"Ludolf."

"This has nothing to do with Ludolf."

"I rather think it does. You're wiser than this, Karelian. Wiser and

far more daring. What old ghosts did your brother drag out of the
rocks of Dorn, and dangle in front of you? You know we're fighting
for our lives, as well as for the safety of the world. We will do what
we planned. We have no choice."

"We haven't looked at our choices."

"Yes, we have. So has the entire Council of Car-Iduna. All of this
was carefully studied, and all of it was agreed on."

He said nothing.

She brushed the back of her hand softly across his cheek. "Come
back to bed, my love," she murmured.

He took her by the shoulders, hard. "I'm as wise and as daring
as I ever was, my Lady of the Mountain. But I can't bear the thought
of losing you."

"And why have you suddenly decided you're going to lose me?
Here, in Dorn, when you never thought so before?"

"It has nothing to do with Dorn."

But that was a bare-faced lie. It had everything to do with Dorn,
with being young, and scared to death for all his defiant courage, in
a world with no shelter and no law.

Ludolf had stripped him of twenty years of armor in a day.

XXXVI

THE CAPTIVE

It is the height of piety to be cruel for Christ's sake.

SAINT BERNARD OF CLAIRVAUX

THEY CLOSED ON STAVOREN in the dead of night, and we woke to find ourselves besieged.

Oh, we had been warned; messengers galloped through our gates at all hours of the day or night, some with fact and some with rumor. Karelian's forces were on the move. He had swept down on his half-brother the margrave with a great body of men, demanding allegiance and aid. Ludolf, as we all expected, offered no resistance. Karelian gobbled up the last of his resources, took under arms the last of his men, and turned to march west.

That much we knew for several days. But numbers were still hard to come by, and precise locations were even harder. Peasants and woodsmen from the north reported seeing hundreds of well-armed knights picking their way along the southern edge of the Schildberge, presumably to circle around us and attack from the west. An even more disturbing rumor had a band of Thuringian mercenaries already approaching the borders of the Reinmark from the south.

Then the weather turned strange. Fogs rose out of the valleys of Dorn, so thick and cottony that Attila's Huns could have ridden right up to our gates, and they would have had to knock to be noticed.

When it cleared, we had numbers. Karelian's army lay all around us in sprawling defiance, a great forest of tents, hundreds of cook-fires kindled against the last receding fog. The world was drenched, but the sun was beginning to inch through breaking cloud, and everywhere it touched, it caught armor and high-flown banners. More of them and still more, till my eyes burned; till Theodoric, standing on the high rampart beside me, found himself—perhaps for the first time in his entire life—reduced to absolute, unmoving silence.

High over all the bright flags flew the eagle of the Salian kings, the banner of Prince Konrad. But it was not the one we were staring at. To the northwest of us, holding half the perimeter of the siege, was a force of well over two thousand men. There were few fine trappings to be seen among them; their tents looked ragged; their cloaks and surcoats were dark and plain. Their insignia was a square fortress with four high, stark towers.

A fortress and a banner I remembered very well.

"Ravensbruck?"

Men turned from one to the other, but no one spoke. I made myself look at Theodoric, and afterwards wished I had not. His face was pale and blank, like a man who had been clubbed.

More than anything, in the days which followed, I wished Gottfried could be with us. Theodoric was brave, but he lacked judgment. The empress was wise and good, but she was only a woman. I thought often of Gottfried's steadiness, of his capacity to stay separate and aloof, to carry his destiny with him like a beacon, an unmoving star around which a whole world could turn. If he were here, I knew, Stavoren would never fall. It was hard to remember that he was where God wanted him to be. He had more important things to do than coddle us.

I prayed a great deal; I suppose we all did. It was bitterly demoralizing to see the whole of the Reinmark ranged against us. Every one of Gottfried's vassals, without exception, had at least one company of men baying up at us, firing catapults and arrows at our walls, building their huge siege towers just out of bowshot, where we could watch them grow.

"When do you think they'll attack?" I must have asked the question twenty times at least. Every time Wilhelm's answer was the same.

"Soon."

The towers were growing fast. There were plenty of trees, plenty of men to work on them. And Karelian knew everything there was to know about siege warfare; he had been at Antioch and Jerusalem, not to mention all his little wars in Europe. He had stormed more castles than any of us wanted to think about.

"Look at it this way, Pauli," Wilhelm said. "At least it's men out there, not demons."

I gave him a sour look. "What do you mean?"

"All this talk about sorcery. I was getting properly tired of it; don't tell me you weren't. Demon armies, and live men walking on water, and dead ones picking up their severed heads and putting them back with a grin. The next thing we know, I thought, Karelian and his men will be riding around on dragons, and burning up whole cities just by going poof!"

"Just because there are men out there," I said, "it doesn't mean he isn't a sorcerer."

"So what did he do? Put a hex on the count of Ravensbruck to get all his knights?"

"It's not impossible."

"Do you think witchcraft would even take on that old Viking-killer? Or on all those fat burghers in Karn?" He laughed a little, shaking his head. "No, Pauli. No. Let's be sensible."

He sounded so much like my father just then, I wanted to scream.

"What about Schildberge fortress?" I demanded. "How did he get from Konrad's camps in Franconia all the way here, right up to our noses, and nobody knew anything about it?"

He shrugged. "There are ways. The world's mostly forest, you know. March by night, in small groups, stay disciplined, stay quiet . . . you can go a long way without being seen. I know. I did it once. With Prince William, in Lombardy. We gave the Normans one hell of a surprise.

"You told me yourself the man's a good strategist. Well, if he is, what's he going to do with all this demon-talk? He's going to take bloody good advantage of it, isn't he? Move fast, strike fast, make strange noises in the night. If it was me, I'd wear a set of fangs and paint myself bright purple. The more enemies you can scare to death, the fewer you have to fight."

"Are you defending him?" I demanded. It was a stupid question. But I was angry at his blindness, his refusal to see what any honest child could see.

All my life I would encounter it, even in my failing years, even here in the monastery. Years after the events in the Reinmark were over, I happened to be sitting one night by a campfire in the Holy Land. We talked of many things, and drifted by chance to the terrible day in the courtyard at Lys: to Karelian's capture, and his flight, and the wolves.

And I stared, open-mouthed and bewildered, as another man in our group said calmly:

"There weren't any wolves."

It was just a wild story, he said; a story with a kernel of truth, embroidered by fantasy and exaggeration and outright lies, until it turned into a legend. Karelian and his men had been out hunting, he said; the dogs had their blood up, and went crazy in a courtyard packed with too many strange men and horses. Panic and close quarters did the rest.

I stared at him. He was neither a boy nor a fool. He was a knight and a crusader, an experienced fighting man born of a renowned and noble house.

"They were wolves," I said to him. "I saw them. I was there."

"So was I," he said.

I had no answer for him then. But for days after I thought about it. First I thought only of the astonishing way in which men could delude themselves. Then I found myself wondering if perhaps it *was* what he had seen. Some seventy men, I reminded myself, had ridden into Helmardin, and lodged in the castle of a witch, but only two of them remembered it. Why then should we assume that an act of sorcery was a single thing? Perhaps it was many things, even layers of things, in which the final layer could not be distinguished from reality itself?

I grew very cold, thinking about it, and tried to put the question out of my head. Ordinary men could not hope to understand such things. That was why we had the Church and its priests: so we should always know precisely what was real. I knew what had happened at Lys. And I knew Karelian was a sorcerer, whether Wilhelm could see it or not.

He rubbed the stump of his arm, the way he always did when he was angry.

"I'm not defending anyone," he said. "I'm trying to keep a level head on my shoulders. You'd be wise to do the same."

He paused, and his voice softened again into the mentor-like tone he often used with me.

"I'm not saying he doesn't know any devil's tricks; maybe he does. It isn't a subject I know much about. I do know about war, and one thing I'm sure of, sorcery or no, we'll still have to fight them as men."

He grinned, and added: "Unless you want to start casting spells or something."

"Don't be stupid," I said.

"Just a suggestion," he said mildly, and slapped me lightly on the shoulder. He was only trying to cheer me up. We were all on edge, and fearful, and more than a little bewildered. None of this was supposed to have happened. The war had scarcely begun, and in any case it was far away. How had we come to be here, facing this totally unforeseen disaster?

I was asleep when it happened. I was dreaming, as I often did, of my wanderings in the forest when I searched for Karelian. The dark things which never found me in the wild always did so in my dreams; more than once I woke up screaming. So for a moment I thought the shouting belonged in my dream, with the black darkness and the smell of fog.

Then I woke, and saw it was the middle of the night. Torches were leaping everywhere to life and the whole of Stavoren was a-clamor. The alarm bell was ringing, and outside in the barracks yard someone was yelling "Treason! Treason, my lords, treason!" at the top of his voice.

I ran out like the others. A crowd had already gathered by the gate, and everyone was shoving and shouting.

—What is it? What's happening?

—I don't know! I can't see!

—I think they've caught a traitor!

—A traitor? Dear God, who is it?

—One of the sentries! They say it's one of the sentries!

Then Theodoric came, and as a pathway opened for him, I saw something of what had occurred.

Three or four bodies were lying near the gate. One man was being restrained by the guard, a young soldier I vaguely recognized. A great mailed arm was wrapped around his throat; two others pinned his own arms behind his back. But he was no longer fighting. An arrow was lodged in his shoulder, just high enough to have missed the lung.

"My lord." The captain of the guard stepped forward, bowing briefly to the prince. "This man . . . this damnable dog . . . has slaughtered the night watch, and was trying to open the gates!"

Theodoric seized a torch and lifted it close to the traitor's face. I was sure I had seen him before, a commoner whose name I was trying to remember even while something different was nudging itself into my mind, something out of the darkest places of my dreams. I swayed on my feet, foreseeing it an instant before it happened, before I could put words to it, or even thoughts. There was no time for thought, only for sheer, bone-melting terror.

The man's face was changing. He fought for a moment—fought with a terrible and desperate strength—so briefly and so hopelessly that I cannot say for certain if I saw a thing, or only a possibility, a shadow trying to take form, a flutter of wings, a greyness. Then his strength gave out. His armor melted like shavings in a flame, dissolved into blackness, into silk. The body beneath it was a woman's; the hair black, the face pale and spent and beautiful.

How can the same moment contain both clamor and silence? In the background, the alarm bell was still ringing, the cries of treason still answering each other in the night. But around us there were only soft gasps of terror, and the name of God whispered over and over: *God save us, sweet Jesus preserve us from evil . . . !*

Then the prince's voice struck like a crack of thunder: "Von Ardiun, come here!"

Theodoric waved me on, impatiently, until I stood at his side, directly in front of her. The arrow which brought her down had been broken off, but not removed; blood streaked her gown and ran from a cut on the side of her head. Theodoric reached and lifted her face. She was conscious; I saw at once that she knew me.

And I knew her.

I felt a brief stab of confusion. She had been a tall and powerful creature in her witch-court at Car-Iduna. Now, surrounded by all these men in the full armor of war, she seemed ordinary. Ordinary and utterly defenseless. Just a woman, caught in the path of an army.

"Well, von Ardiun?" Theodoric demanded. He had her jaws in one great hand, turning her face this way and that, as though I needed to see its every contour in order to be sure.

"Is this the witch of Helmardin?"

"Yes, my lord."

"You will swear to it? This is the traitor's necromancer, and his whore?"

"Yes, my lord."

"Good. Bring her."

He sent for a messenger, and motioned me to follow him. Shouts erupted all around us as we moved through the courtyard. The word was spreading like wildfire. *Witch! It's a witch! They have Karelian's witch!* Not only the garrison was out now, but the servants as well, sleepy grooms and terrified kitchen maids, running from their pallets and shoving through the crowd, greedy for a look at the sorceress—but most of them backed away when they saw her. Everyone was shouting. Everyone knew the best way to deal with witches: water and earth, fire and air. Drown them, bury them, burn them and watch them fly.

Under the fury and the triumph, though, was a clear note of fear. Even in the voice of Theodoric.

"What powers does she have, Paul?" he demanded. "What special devices should we use?"

"My lord, I have no knowledge of these things—"

He stopped in his tracks, and stared at me.

"You were in Car-Iduna, you damned fool! What did you see there?"

How could I tell him what I saw? It was all so uncertain. Oh, the power was real enough, the peril—but the forms it took, the possibilities—they melted even as you tried to give them names.

But Theodoric wanted names, and so I answered him:

"She is a shape-shifter, my lord, as we saw. And she can make things appear and disappear. After we left her castle, we couldn't see it; there was nothing around us but forest. They say she can turn men into creatures—"

"What about her demons? Her protectors?"

"I don't know, my lord."

"Christ, you don't know much about anything, do you?" He threw up his hands, and asked me nothing more.

We went into the castle keep, into the depths of the dungeons. For a while we clustered outside the door of a cell, while Theodoric decided how it might be safely guarded. He settled on a guard of fifty, ten by the door where we stood, ten more at the foot of the stairs, ten more at the top, and so to the gates, all of them bearing crossbows as well as swords.

No one wanted that guard duty, no matter how many of them there were, or how fiercely they were armed. What could any weapon do against the devil's power? Against a sorceress who turned men into gibbering birds and squeaking mice? Their faces were set; their eyes

looked carefully at anything except the eyes of their fellows. Some of
them audibly prayed.

I thanked God when they had all been chosen, and I was not one
of them. I forgot he would take guards inside the cell as well.

The messenger he had summoned came, bowing deeply, and asked
for his assignment.

"Listen well," Theodoric said. "I don't want this message to be
misunderstood."

The young man bowed again.

"Go out to the camp of the traitor Karelian, and tell him I have
his witch. Tell him he has two days to surrender the fortress of Schildberge, and to yield his army and his person to the emperor's justice,
or she will be burned alive. Tell him he has two days, but if he's wise,
he won't wait that long."

He took his dagger and slashed away the gold belt around the
witch's hips.

"Give him this."

The messenger went pale.

"He will kill me, my lord," he whispered.

"He might. But if you disobey me, I'll do it instead. Get your
horse now and go!"

"Yes, my lord."

The prince was not even looking at the messenger any more. He
was looking at the witch of Helmardin. At Karelian's whore.

"So, witch. We'll see how strong your spells are now." He motioned to the guards to drag her inside. And as God is my witness,
he smiled.

He made me follow with the others. Because I had been to Helmardin, he said. Because I had some experience of her power and her
ways. Perhaps he spoke the truth. Perhaps under his martial arrogance
he was just as frightened as everyone else, and really hoped I might
have some knowledge the others didn't have, some ability to warn him
of danger.

Or perhaps he merely thought it would do me good to see the
ways of men.

They gathered around her, and the place got very still. There was
a moment, how long I cannot say, a moment of uncertainty, of breathless tension. Wounded though she was, the two guards still held her
in an iron grip. I could not see the prince's face as he approached her.
I did not have to. Everything was clear in his words, in his motions:

the strange mixture of fear and riveted fascination as he stared at her body.

You who read this may well think me naive, but until that moment I believed the prince's taunt to Karelian was only a taunt. A lady's girdle was an acknowledged symbol of her honor; to take it from her, and send it to her lord, was the sort of gesture Theodoric could not resist. *Once it was your privilege to take her clothes off; now it is mine.* A sexual insult, I thought, cruder than a king's son should stoop to, but nothing more. They were Christian men. They were God's most favored knights. Theodoric was Gottfried's son.

Gottfried's son. Gottfried's blood, and heir to the kingdom of Christ . . . .

"They say forcing a witch is the surest way to undo her power," he said.

"If she's a virgin witch, my lord," someone replied. "Only if she's a virgin."

He laughed. "I don't think it matters. I can use the same rod to tame a filly or a mare. Isn't that so, witch?"

He pulled at her gown, and she cried out as it wrenched across the shaft in her shoulder.

"Isn't it?" he said again, savagely.

She looked at him. There were tears of raw pain in the corners of her eyes, and a kind of icy terror. Yet she defied him nonetheless.

"You will regret it," she said.

"And who will make me? Do you have some little fiend hiding with you, waiting to leap on my throat? Do you think we won't find him?"

I turned away as he began to maul her, tearing at her clothing, forcing his huge hand between her thighs.

"Where is the little devil, then? Is he here? No? How about here? He'd fly straight back to hell if he knew what was coming at him, wouldn't he, my friends?"

I tried to pray. I tried not to listen, not to look when they twisted her to the floor and pulled her legs apart. I tried not to hear him grunting and mocking her as he did it. I kept telling myself no, it was not happening, he would not lower himself to this, he would not . . . . Finally I heard him laugh, and growl a few words. I looked up; he was on his feet, wiping his arm across his face, and someone else was hunched over her in the torchlight.

They all took her, one after another while the others watched. And after a while I stopped trying to pray. I stopped trying to pretend it was someone else there, not Gottfried's son. I stopped trying not to hear her cries. Because I came to understand how it was possible—indeed, except for my conscience, I would say it was inevitable. And it was not because of lust.

Oh, certainly there was lust; she provoked it in men like a fever. There was a blind greed to possess her, to degrade her as an enemy; and even more, perhaps, a wish to degrade Karelian. But there was something else, and it was the most important thing of all. She was a witch. She was the disobedience which lurked forever at the edges of their consciousness, the loathsome carnality they resisted but could never free themselves from, not even now. She belonged not simply to an enemy in war, but to the lords of darkness, the enemies of Christ. To break her power—to break *her*—was somehow also a religious act. Sinful, yes, sinful and sickening, the endless heaving and thrusting of flesh, the sport they took in it, watching and laughing and urging each other on. Yet they all knew she was more than a woman, and it was more than a rape. Their laughter had a terrible edge, and their very greed had a ritual quality to it.

I cannot say it was not wicked. And yet there was something in it which I understood, as I understood why our knights walked ankle deep in blood through the streets of Jerusalem. Because of what *they* do to God, and to us.

They finished, finally, and dragged her to the wall. Heavy iron manacles hung there, cemented into the stone; they fastened these around her wrists, her ankles, her neck.

—I'll wager we've pounded the devil out of that one, my lord . . . !

More laughter. A few blows, to make sure.

—I thought they said witches feel no pain.

—Hey, Pauli, don't you want a go?

—Not a chance, Pauli's going to be a monk, aren't you, Pauli?

The dungeon was more than twenty feet below the surface of the ground. It had no windows, and as we left we rammed shut behind us a solid oak-and-iron door, with an iron bolt as thick as a man's arm. Nothing less than an army was going to get into her cell, and nothing less than a demon was going to get out.

Before we left, Prince Theodoric had a last word for the lady of Helmardin. He stood over her, and took a torch from one of his knights. She was still conscious, though perhaps barely. There was hate in her eyes, a kind of bottomless malevolence which reminded me quite suddenly of someone else, a woman in Ravensbruck, a Wend slave who slunk around the edges of Count Arnulf's court with the same burning darkness in her eyes. She too, they said, was a witch.

"My father spoke of you once or twice," Theodoric said. "The last of the whores of Odin, he called you. Then you corrupted his kinsman Karelian, and he spoke of you a great deal more. Do you know who my father is, witch?"

I caught my breath, not believing he would speak so. I looked at the other knights, milling about in the aftermath of their lust, wanting to be gone. I saw the question meant nothing to them—only to me.

And to her.

"Your father," she whispered, "is the son of a scorpion, and the sire of a dog."

He cursed savagely, and kicked her; it evoked a small gulp of pain, nothing more. He could have beaten her to death in her irons, and it would not have changed her eyes, or her inhuman defiance.

I wanted to warn him then, to tell him the devils had not left her. They would never leave her; she was too much theirs, too old and too hardened in their ways.

"You will burn, witch," he said grimly. He held the torch close to her face; she cringed away, the light dancing and shimmering in her hair. "The Reinmark is befouled while you are in it, and you will burn!"

Then do it now, my lord! You can't bait Karelian; you'll gain nothing by waiting. Do it now!

I wanted to say it. I even opened my mouth. But I was only Pauli, Pauli who was going to be a monk; Pauli who was loyal, no doubt, and maybe even brave, but who was not their equal as a man; Pauli who was too pure to hump a witch, Pauli who took everything too seriously, especially his conscience . . . . The words faltered in my throat, and stayed there. We left her to the darkness and her fiends.

When we emerged from the dungeon, we found the messenger had just returned from the lord of Lys. He did not bow to Theodoric and the empress. He knelt.

"The count ordered me to repeat his words, majesty, but they were terrible. Shall I do so, or say only that he will not yield?"

"We will hear his words," the empress said.

"He spoke thus. Tell the son of von Heyden I can surrender nothing. My fortresses, my soldiers, my life itself belongs to the king. But heed me, Theodoric: I will win this war. If you treat my lady with honor, and keep safe her life, I will return you favor for favor. Harm her, and the earth will not stretch wide enough, nor eternity long enough, to let you escape from my vengeance. I will call on heaven, and I will call on hell; I will destroy you and your blood; I will wipe your names off your tombstones, and cover your graves with salt. Carthage will rise again sooner than the house of von Heyden. Heed me, by whatever gods you choose, for it will be so!"

The messenger bowed his head almost to the floor. Perhaps he expected to be kicked, and perhaps he would have been, except that none of us could move.

The face of the empress was ash. "You dare?" she whispered. "You dare to repeat so foul a curse upon my husband's blood, before my very face?"

She rose. For just a moment she faltered, and her maid rushed forward to take her arm. She steadied herself, and looked bravely at Theodoric.

"She will burn, Theodoric. Pay no attention to this arrogance. God gave her into our hands, so we could rid the Reinmark of her evil. He will not allow us to be harmed. Call the chaplain. We will hear Mass, and exorcise this demon lord's words."

Only once in my life did I encounter what seemed to me a miracle. It was at first light the next day when our watchmen looked out sleepily across the sloping fields below the castle, and stared, and called their comrades over, and ran to other vantage points and wiped their eyes, and stared again. It took minutes before anyone really made sense of what they saw, before anyone ran down into the courtyard shouting for their lord, to tell him what they themselves could neither comprehend nor entirely believe. We had exorcised more than the demon lord's words. Where his tents and his long lines of tethered horses had been, grass rippled idly in the wind. The sky was empty of banners. A few spent fires smoldered in the pre-dawn light, and the great siege towers stood naked and abandoned. Karelian was gone.

Fled in the night like the fell creature he was, swift and soundless and defeated. Gone.

Theodoric, more cautious than I had ever imagined Theodoric could be, sent out twenty scouts, and pulled the drawbridge up behind them. But this time he had no cause for fear. They came back quickly, unharmed and unpursued. The fields were truly empty, and the army we so dreaded was vanished like a dream.

Or rather, the scouts told us, most of it had never been there.

"He had a thousand men outside our walls, my lord, or fewer—"

"A thousand knights, you mean?"

"No, highness. A thousand men, counting them all—knights, squires, foot-soldiers, grooms, servants—aye, and add in the dogs as well, maybe. You could set up a jousting field between one of his tent-sites and the next."

"What the devil are you trying to say?" Theodoric demanded.

"I don't know what I'm trying to say, my lord. But the army we thought we saw . . . wasn't there."

"And Ravensbruck? Were the men of Ravensbruck there?"

"Perhaps a few, my lord. Certainly not all of them."

"None of them were there. None of them! It was all sorcery!"

Theodoric rarely laughed, but he laughed now. It was a ringing, triumphant roar, half savage, half purely joyous.

"Don't you see? It was the witch's doing! He had nothing, just rabble from Konrad's army and mercenaries from Karn, and whatever leavings he could bully out of his brother the margrave. He had nothing and he is nothing, only the tool of a sorceress who's had her powers clipped! Dear Christ, we could have sent a sortie out of here and eaten him for dinner!"

He turned sharply to the scouts.

"Which way did they go?"

"East, my lord, towards Dorn."

"Yes, of course. And through the pass and back to Schildberge castle, where I'll have to smoke him out. Be damned to it, if I'd had my way in this he would be raven's meat by now!"

Perhaps, I thought. Perhaps. I edged away from the others, and looked across the empty, autumn-mellow fields of Stavoren, and I stood breathless, marveling at the audacity of Karelian Brandeis.

There is no other word to use. I marveled. He was evil, he was dangerous, he was Lucifer's own child, but dear Christ, he was brilliant. Because it might have worked. And if it had, the sorcery would never have been obvious. Our confusion over his numbers and his movements would be credited to his own tactical skill. Our opened gates and lowered drawbridge would seem a simple act of treachery from within. The lord of Ravensbruck, presented with an accomplished fact, would come to heel. Given credit and rewards for the victory, he'd be the last man alive to mention that his men weren't actually there. Oh, I thought, it was wonderfully clever and bold, and in a part of me . . . in a part of me I halfway wished . . . .

I caught myself, and made the sign of the cross. It was a devil's thought, but I halfway wished I were still with him. A devil's thought, and ridiculous besides. He was finished now. He could run for his mountain fortress, and take refuge there until Gottfried starved him out. Or he could run back to Konrad, who would have less use for him now than ever. No, I told myself, I wanted no part of him. I had made my choice, and he had made his. He had chosen sorcery, and sorcery had failed him. As it always would. Men were never brilliant when they stood against the power of God. They only seemed so—and only for a while.

Theodoric sent out more men, several hundred this time, to drag in one of the abandoned siege towers. It would make a magnificent stake, he said, sturdy and high and splendidly appropriate.

"Let the witch die on her demon lover's handiwork."

He looked eastward. He had given Karelian two days to surrender, but Karelian was not going to surrender, and in any case it did not matter—not any more, not when we knew he had no army worth mentioning. Theodoric probably did not even want his surrender now. He wanted to run his enemy down. He had held back and held back, and now he wanted blood.

"We will do it today," he added grimly. "At Vespers. See that everything is ready."

So we had a single day of triumph. One day in which every fragment of the world was fallen into place, and everything we believed in was vindicated. Gottfried had been proven right, if only by a thread. But that too was God's doing, that one sentry who was not in his accustomed place, who neither challenged the witch, nor approached her, but stood riveted in his tracks, watching long enough to be sure, and then taking his crossbow and firing.

We feasted in Stavoren castle, and we laughed. Some men drank too much; others made generous thanks to God. All of us watched the tower being prepared, and many talked about the coming execution.

Witches were always burned naked, so no demons could hide inside their clothes and succor them, so full and absolute justice might be done. But many of my comrades looked forward to the fire for reasons which had nothing to do with justice. Everyone had heard about the Lady of the Mountain, everyone knew she was beautiful, everyone knew she was a great harlot. And there was a pleasure in the eyes of some at the thought of her burning, an eagerness so sharp and so physical it seemed to me no different from lust. Indeed, some of them used the words of lust when they spoke of it—how the flames would caress her, how the arms of the tower would hold her fast. What they waited for was yet another rape. And it would be absolute this time, unlimited; the fire would violate what even they could not. And when it was done, there would be nothing left. The flesh would be ash; the soul would be in hell. The great harlot of the mountain would be gone.

And those same watchers would drink themselves into a stupor after, savagely sated and savagely empty. It would be days, perhaps, or weeks, before they noticed that she was not gone, that they lusted for her still . . . .

Paul von Ardiun put his quill down, and laid his head back against his chair.

Write what you will, he thought, *it doesn't matter. I know what is true. Maybe a few men felt that way, a tiny few, but most of us wanted only for the Reinmark to be free. What we did was for God, all of it, for the kingdom of God and for the right of Christian men to walk through the world without fear.*

"And what was it they were so afraid of, Brother Paul?"

He did not look up at her voice; he did not even open his eyes. He waited. She would say what she had to say, and then she would leave. And he would write again. Nothing else mattered. He would write, and come finally to the end of it. The end of everything.

"I'll grant you this," she said. "It wasn't quite the same for you as for the others. It wasn't me you desired, after all. But you were willing enough to see my body degraded and destroyed—the same body which enchanted Karelian, and rolled about with his in so much sinful pleasuring . . . full and absolute justice for *that,* dear gods—the flames wouldn't be halfway cruel enough."

"You were a witch," he said.

"Oh, certainly. But you never thought to pity me for Karelian's sake?"

"We don't pity the damned in hell; why should we pity them here?"

"Well said, Pauli. Why indeed? If your God takes such stern and righteous pleasure in destroying human flesh, those who serve him can hardly do less. That follows, I suppose. But you will understand, then, why some of us consider him unfit to be a god?"

He crossed himself quickly. He felt cold in the presence of this blasphemy.

"Yes, unfit," she said, "and don't bother to be so offended. You called *our* gods fiends for no reason at all. We honored yours when he first came here, because we honored them all, and he paid us back with broken altars, and massacres, and exile. And a bonfire now and then, for the stubborn ones, the ones you called the whores of Odin."

She moved close to his chair.

"Tell me," she murmured, "were you with them when they came to the dungeon to fetch me?"

"No."

"How disappointing."

No. Others had gone, a great number, he could not recall how many. And a priest went with them, not for the witch's sake, but to protect her guards and executioners—though of course if she had proven repentant, he would willingly have heard her confession, and given her absolution before her death. Even to one such as she, God would be merciful.

They went laden with weapons and warnings. She must be carefully searched, they were told, and carefully chained, and carefully guarded. All the inhabitants of the castle were by then in the courtyard, waiting, as well as hundreds from the villages below. The air was thick with anticipation, and hostility, and fear.

The guards came running back, white-faced and babbling. The dungeon was empty. The door was still bolted; the iron manacles still locked and rooted in the wall. But there was nothing in the cell except its few scatters of rotting straw, its stench of rats, its bloodstains.

And one thing more. Caught in one of the manacles was the small, blood-stained feather of a wren.

"All magic can be turned back upon itself by those who know how."

She spoke softly, as if she really wanted him to understand. He recognized the tactic. It was what Karelian always did, too—tempting him with cunning words, pretending to have some deep and secret gift of knowledge.

"Your master took so many precautions—the stone cell, the chains, the armed guards. But there were other powers there, powers of magic as old as the world. And he forgot about them, your Theodoric von Gottfried von Heyden von Clovis von Godfather Almighty. He didn't believe in magic; none of you did. You believed in devils, and that's not the same thing at all.

"It wasn't fiends who carried me off," she said. "If there were any fiends in Stavoren, they all worked for the duke. Pick up your pretty quill, Pauli, and I'll tell you how it was."

XXXVII

THE TURNING

Regard everything as poison which bears within it the
seed of sensual pleasure.

SAINT JEROME

It was after sin that lust began.

SAINT AUGUSTINE

ALL MAGIC CAN BE TURNED BACK UPON ITSELF BY *those who know how.*
Darkness wrapped her, darkness deeper than the deeps of the
world, darker than the lairs of the hunter elves when they died, when
the last coals of their fires melted out and their caves were lost
forever.

But it was an evil darkness, fouled with rot and desolation, with
memories of blood and murder breathing from the stones. There were
no elves here, now or ever in the past, no crystal and ruby walls; only
the souls of dead men weeping, and dead women too, all of them
nameless and broken and gone.

For a long time there was only darkness and pain, and a fog of
numbing disbelief. She could not believe the world had come undone
so easily, so brutally. A small misjudgment, a tiny moment of inatten-
tion was all it took. What did it mean to be queen of Car-Iduna, if
this were possible—this black failure, this terrible degradation?

Nothing is promised. The strands are woven and unwoven. We make of them the best we can, and what remains is shadow. Nothing is promised . . . .

She could not think; it was barely possible to pray. All she had strength for was the gathering-in of self; whether for action or for death, it did not matter. She would be whole; she would stand before them whole, as woman and as priestess of her gods.

Karelian, heed me! If you have ever loved me, heed me now! Take your men and go! Don't be foolish, don't try to save me, there's no hope of it! You must go! Go, my love. Just go. It's Gottfried who matters, only Gottfried, I command you to go . . . !

It was a long time, that time of pain and silence, but soft at the edges of it was a quiet, gathering knowledge. There was power here, ancient and mysterious and full of possibility. The power was not hers; hers was utterly exhausted and gone. It was theirs, twisted and befouled, reeking of cruelty and hate, but still magical. And all magic could be turned. All power was raw power in the hands of a witch, and the power of sexuality was very great.

From the very beginning, the Church understood that. Sex was humankind's great bond to the earth. Over and over it drew them back to her, back to the loyalties of kinship and passion, and away from the loyalties of rank and order and dominion.

Like so many of the sky gods who came before him, the god of the Christians was hungry for dominion. He dealt with the limitations of life by saying life did not matter. He had something better to offer than life: he had immortality. Before he came, the others had offered immortality in the world—monuments and empires, names graven into history, great lines of kings sired by a single conqueror. Now, for this last of them, the Christian, the world and all its glories were only rubbish; he offered immortality in heaven.

And yet in their blood all creatures born knew they died, and knowing it they craved to live. They did not want to build kingdoms, neither for gods nor for men, or to shiver night after night on their knees, grieving for sins invented in a book, living in terror of a hell none of them had ever seen. They did not want the transcendence of escape, the dream of a distant heaven where flesh and dying did not matter. They wanted the transcendence of connection. They wanted to know that flesh and dying had meaning in themselves, and that *that* meaning lay at the center of the world.

It was love which brought them back, love and lust and pleasuring, the enchantment of the ever-present body, and the ever-present possibility of delight. It was their own flesh, and the flesh of the other who must be cherished and not killed, which held them firmly to the earth, to the truths and the gods of the earth.

The Christians were quite right about it, and so were those pitilessly reasonable Greeks: the body was dangerous. The body interfered with the orderly obsessions of philosophers; it broke the icy mind-nets of priests; it rebelled against the endless war-mongering of kings. It reminded people that the world was here, and life was now, and if they had no rights over their own flesh, then they had no rights at all.

Worst of all, perhaps, the body remembered that once, not very long ago, sex had been a holy and magical thing. It was not sinful but sacred; it was the power of the gods in the world. Its fire was their hunger to connect and to create, its lawlessness their endless trying out and making new. And its wild and driven ecstasies were the measure of its sacredness; something so exquisite and so forceful could come only from the gods.

That was why the Christians hated it so much. How could lust be the work of their own Lord—their Lord who was not of this world? It was of the old gods, just like the people believed; and it was demonic, just like the gods were.

So it was forbidden, in every way it could be, and what the churchmen could not forbid they wrapped in shame. They said it was the most dangerous of sins, more to be feared than cruelty or violence or war. They said in Eden it never existed. They said God intended men to breed as they laced up their tunics, matter-of-factly, without a throb of passion or a thought of carnal lust. Only a fallen human being, rotten with sin, could possibly desire *that.*

They were terrified of sex, and they had reason to be—they knew its power.

They knew. But centuries had passed, and they had also forgotten. Not even priests could keep telling lies forever, without losing sight of the truth.

Like the wombs of women, the seed of men was still magical. And Theodoric and his men had all forgotten that. They thought she could change them into mice, that she might have demons hiding in her loins or in her mouth or in her hair. But they never imagined she could take their savagery—their gift of life degraded into death—and circle it, and take the power from it, and use it to escape. Like a fallen Amazon whose sword is broken and whose quiver is empty, and who looks about in despair, and sees that she does, after all, have one arrow left, and the enemy has given it to her . . . so did she take their cruelty, and feed it on the rage of centuries, and turn it back, and make it fly.

The sun was low, the prince's castle still clamorous with men and outrage, the valley below scattered with country folk going home disappointed. Karelian's army had fled, but he had not. She sensed his presence even as she cleared the walls of Stavoren, and though she knew it was unwise, she was glad.

So, my love, there are bonds you will not break, even to save the world. I commanded you to go, as you would have commanded me. And you stayed, as I would have done. May Iduna remember it forever, as I will . . . .

He was there, somewhere in the valley, but she had no strength to find him. She was wounded and already faltering; every pulse of energy she had went into staying changed, and trying to stay in motion. More than once she tumbled to the ground and simply huddled there, unable to go on, unable to think of anything except the thing she was, the small and feathered thing which must not change, must not, *must not!* or it would die.

They were safer now apart, both of them.

She flew on, north towards the forests at the base of the Schildberge. Veelas lived there, if she could only get close enough to summon them. She did not think about the distance. She noticed only the distance to the next stack of cut grain, the next village church, the next hedge where she could hide and rest.

A few search parties were out, first in Stavoren itself and then among the villagers. They stormed hither and yon to appease Theodoric's anger. They made impressive amounts of noise, but it was obvious they did not expect to find anything. The devil himself had come and fetched her away, through bolted doors and chains, past scores of armed men. What was the point in searching?

Only she knew how perilously close they were sometimes. And there were other dangers: hawks in the sky and foxes in the shrubs. As darkness fell and the danger from men diminished, the danger from the wild increased. And the forest was still far away.

Lady Iduna, do not give up my life, I beg you, keep it yet a little while . . . !

The world turned black and silver in the moonlight. She kept going, so weary she never saw the owl, nor sensed its presence, until its shadow passed across the moon, a few arm's lengths away. She dove into the swampland below, tumbling human into bracken and reeds. The hunter swept overhead with a small cry of bewilderment, and was gone.

She was a woman again, and she had no hope of changing back. No hope for anything now except her wild sisters. She struggled to her knees in the rank slough and wailed. It was a long and bitter cry, more eerie than a wolf's, and it shivered across the vale of Stavoren, once, and then again, and then again. Would they hear her? In the hunched black houses of the valley, men crossed themselves, and children pulled their pillows over their ears. No door opened; no man stirred from his house. Only veelas had such a cry, and only veelas would ever dare to answer it.

The swamp was cold. She shivered, huddling naked in the darkness. She heard only silence, and the small animal sounds of night, frogs and distant cattle, an insect buzzing around her hair. No veelas answered her. She cried again. And then, very faintly from the north, from very far away, came a cry like her own. And then from the northeast, another, and still another. The wild nymphs heard the summons, and hearing it, passed it on, so that all the skies of the Reinmark quivered with it, as with aurora on a winter's night; and even as they cried they came to her.

They came out of the forests and the lakes, out of the secret places of the Schildberge, out of the Maren shimmering by the golden fields of Lys. They came pale eyed and golden haired; they knelt and washed her wounds; they fed her healing herbs, and murmured charms of solace and revenge; they kissed her, and wrapped her in gossamer and down, and bore her home to Helmardin.

All but three of them went with her. Three she sent back into the valley of Stavoren.

"Go and find my lord Karelian, so he may know I'm safe. Tell him that so fiercely as I love him, so fiercely do I hate the son of Gottfried, and that is hate enough to burn a city. Tell him he shall find me where he sought me first, on the road to Ravensbruck.

"Send him to me, for I will do there a thing which few have the power to do, and fewer still the courage. But I will do it now, if the gods give me strength, and the house of von Heyden will be ash upon the wind."

XXXVIII

HEIRS OF THE KINGDOM

Christ left to Peter, not only the whole Church
but also the whole world, to govern.

POPE INNOCENT III

IT WAS TYPICAL OF GOTTFRIED VON HEYDEN to be ready first, whether for breakfast or for war. In late August he invaded Thuringia, leaving Konrad with no option except to field what men he had and hurry after to try to save his ally. Gottfried had time to plunder a great swath of the duchy, and to choose his battle ground as well—a high plateau near the town of Saint Germain.

There he camped to wait. And there, on a windy afternoon in September, a week after Karelian's flight from Stavoren, he received an urgent visit from Cardinal Volken, papal legate to the German empire. The legate had journeyed from the Vatican without interruption, stopping only to eat and to sleep; he looked utterly exhausted.

Gottfried did not especially want to talk to him. His mind was on the coming battle, on the thousand threats and possibilities of the landscape around him, on the readiness of weapons and armor and men. Not on Rome, with its nit-picking, clerical mind, its astonishing inability to see the world as it was, or to notice God for looking at the Church.

"My lord Gottfried . . . ." The papal legate cleared his throat. "Forgive me for addressing you so . . . so simply. But you must understand, my lord, until you are elected, I cannot in good conscience address you as king."

"And is your conscience as tender when you meet with the murderer Konrad, my lord cardinal?"

"I have not met with him since the council in Mainz. I've had no reason to meet with him. But if I do, I will not call him king."

"Then in your view, Germany has no king."

"Precisely so, my lord. A matter which is causing the Holy Father a great deal of distress."

Distress, my lord legate? Or merely anticipation? Gottfried leaned back a little in his chair.

"We will not argue the matter with you," he said. "God will make his will known." He paused, and went on. "As you know, Konrad's army is not twenty leagues away, and his captain-general Thuringia has promised him my head on a silver plate. You understand then, that our time for this meeting is short?"

The legate was not pleased. "Surely for a faithful Christian lord, there is always time to speak with Rome?"

"My lord, if you were building a palace, would you fit the stones in place while the mortar was wet, or would you stop for the afternoon and speak with Rome?"

"Mortar can always be made fresh," the legate said, aggrieved.

"Mortar can, perhaps. Battles usually cannot. What is your message from Rome?"

The legate looked about. Gottfried's tent was spartan and cool, but it was well guarded.

"It would be better, my lord, if we were entirely alone."

"Very well."

Gottfried dismissed his guards, and looked expectantly at the legate. Cardinal Volken was a thin man, pale from too much time indoors. He looked cold. Though it was only September, he had his cape pulled close about his throat. He was German by birth, but he was entirely Roman in every other way.

"It is a delicate matter, my lord Gottfried," he said. "I want to make it clear . . . very clear, right from the beginning, that the Holy Father holds you in the highest regard, as a Christian prince, and as a warrior of the Church. But there is a question of . . . how shall I put it? . . . of the proper use of relics. You see," he hurried on, "it is usual for relics to be placed in a church, so their blessings might pour forth on the entire community—"

"It is usual," Gottfried interrupted bluntly, "for relics to be everywhere. In churches, yes. Also in private chapels. Also on board ships, and on hearthstones; in sword-hilts, under the pillows of sick children, hung from neck-thongs and belts, and most anywhere else you could think of. Ludwig of Bavaria told me of a peasant in his duchy, a saintly and devoted man, who never goes out into his fields without wrapping a bone of Saint Martin on the harness of his horse. The saint knows he's honored by it; why should anyone else object?"

"My lord, we are not speaking of the relic of a saint. We are speaking of a relic more precious than anything in the world except the Grail. It should belong to all of Christendom, not to any one man. It should be safe in the finest church we could build for it, and not be carried about in war camps—"

"We carried the Sacred Lance under arms to Jerusalem, my lord legate; have you forgotten?"

"Yes. But not as one man's personal trophy. And after the city was liberated, those who bore it gave it up, and built a splendid chapel for it, to thank God for the victory."

"This victory hasn't yet been won."

"My lord." The legate put his elbows on the table and leaned forward. "My lord, have you considered the possibilities? Christendom has many enemies, many battles to fight, many decisions to make. In the east, as you know, the Saracens are beginning to regroup. We have the Huns on our borders, and the Wends. We have heretics in our midst. We have the empire of Constantinople to deal with, which calls itself Christian but denies the power of Christ's vicar on earth.

"Now, through our great efforts in the Holy Land, this relic has come to us, and could give the Church guidance in all its uncertainties. Everywhere, not just in Germany. You understand, my lord, what a blessing this would be for our faith. And you understand, also, those who give to God are rewarded seven-fold."

He paused, waiting for Gottfried to speak. When the duke remained silent, he went on:

"If the relic were given over to the Church, my lord, you would certainly reassure the Holy Father—and the archbishops of Mainz and Cologne—that you are worthy of the highest crown in Europe. On the other hand, if you keep it here in Germany, I fear all of us may wonder if perhaps you've placed your personal ambitions above the good of Christendom."

He made a small gesture with his hands. "I apologize, my lord, for being so . . . direct. I repeat again, it is not the Holy Father's intention to dispute in any way your claim to the German crown. That is obviously an internal matter. We are concerned only with the good of Christendom."

You are not concerned with Christendom. You are concerned with nothing except the universal mastery of Rome.

The duke waited a thoughtful moment, and then spoke wearily.

"Our trials here have been many, my lord legate. In truth, we've had little time to think beyond them. We are always, *always* the Holy Father's most faithful servant."

"I have never doubted it, my lord, and nor has he."

"But we would ask you to consider this. How many times has a saint been lying in some unworthy spot, and spoken from his grave: 'I am not honored here. Take my bones, and do them reverence in your own place.' Has that not happened many times, my lord?"

"Yes, but—"

"And as you said, this is the most sacred relic in the world. If an ordinary saint will not allow his blessed remains to be dishonored, do you think the tears of Christ and his dear mother will lie anywhere but where God wishes them to be?"

"Perhaps God is expressing his wishes through the words of his vicar the pope."

"Perhaps. But we believe God had a purpose in giving this relic to ourselves. We believe if he'd had a different purpose, he'd have given it to someone else. There were men from all of Christendom in Jerusalem with us. There were men from Rome. Yet God gave the stone to us."

"Perhaps so you might prove yourself his true disciple. By giving it up, as he gave up his life."

Oh, you are devious, Roman. Would you be less devious, I wonder, if you knew with whom you dealt? Rather more so, I think . . . .

"Then there is but one thing left to do, my lord," Gottfried said, rising. "We are obedient to God's will, and if he wants this sacred stone returned to Rome, then that's where it will go. We will summon our high lords, and we'll hear Mass together, and place the relic in our midst. Whatever God commands us then, we will do."

"My lord, I . . . that is not . . ."

"There is yet one authority higher than the pope. Surely you agree with me, my lord?"

"Yes, but . . . but what if there is no command?"

"If God is silent, we may assume he's already spoken. Through his vicar in Rome."

The legate smiled.

He did not smile when, an hour or so later, in the presence of

Ludwig of Bavaria and the Swabian landgrave, and many of their kinsmen and highborn captains, the stone began to shimmer, and an image formed within it, clear and magnificent: Gottfried seated as if on a throne, with a raised cross in one hand, and the crystal pyramid in the other.

Then, before they could properly catch their breaths at the sight, the image changed to a battlefield, to a great chaos of men and horses, a great and terrible slaughter, a man falling slowly from his horse, his face covered in blood. All around him, his knights were dead or in retreat. He fell to his knees, and dropped his sword. He looked up, and they saw his face.

—Thuringia . . . ?

—Thuringia! Thuringia is defeated! The victory will be ours!

—Praise God, the victory will be ours!

The image faded, and they saw Gottfried again, still holding the truthstone, and crowned as king.

The legate quietly departed for Rome, to consult again with the pope.

It was very late. A portion of the duke's tent had been partitioned off into a private chamber, and he sat there alone, his hands cupped around the willstone.

Today was the first time he had used it to prophesy. He had not planned to do so. It was an inspiration, received in one instant, acted upon in the next. He was confident of victory against Konrad and Thuringia, but until he saw his victory in the crystal, he had not been certain.

Now he was more than certain, he was impatient. There was so much to do. There would be many battles before the empire was secure. Many wars after this one, and many perils, and all the time the lords of Rome would be somewhere at his back, watching and wondering and fingering their knives. Already they were uneasy about him, demanding proof of his servility, as if he were just another worldly and dangerous prince.

He had known from the first that Rome would be a problem. The popes were only stewards of Christ's power in the world, but they had been stewards for eleven hundred years; they were used to it. They did not expect their master back before the end of the world. Still less did they expect to encounter his heir. They were sure he had no heir except themselves.

He did not want a quarrel with the leaders of the Church. Not ever, if it could be avoided, and certainly not now. The surest way to avoid a quarrel was to win—to win decisively and quickly. Enough victories, and he would not have to tell them who he was, and force them to accept it. Enough victories, and he himself would choose the man who was called pope, and choose the cardinals who advised him. Then Rome would come to him. All of Christendom would come to him, and know him without needing to be told. And they would finally understand what only half of them seemed capable of understanding even now, even after Jerusalem—that no true lord of heaven would settle for less than being true lord of earth.

He must finish it quickly. First Konrad here in Thuringia, and then the sorcerer in Lys. Theodoric and Armund would be in Ravensbruck in a matter of days. One day to marry Count Arnulf's little baggage, one night to bed her, and then they would march. Of course it was an unworthy marriage for his son, but what of it? He could annul it later on, if the good of the kingdom required it.

He'd had to argue about it nonetheless. Radegund did not want Count Arnulf's daughter in the family, not even temporarily. And Theodoric could not see why they should bother with Ravensbruck at all.

—We don't need Arnulf. Karelian has no army. All he can do now is dig in at Schildberge castle, and hope Konrad defeats you before he starves to death.

—Theodoric . . . .

Gottfried had stared at the face in the willstone, possessed by a terrible, undignified urge to slap it. It never mattered what he decided should be done, Theodoric always wanted to do something different. Theodoric was a bewildering, enduring disappointment.

He wondered what it might be like to have a perfect son, one who would never falter and never change. He prayed for it year after year, but his son remained flawed and unfinished, and he did not know why. Theodoric was like him in many ways. He was strong of will and body. He had the same absolute certainty of his place and his power in the world. But that other vital certainty Theodoric did not have.

He had listened with rapt attention when Gottfried told him of his discoveries in the Holy Land. He was a proud young man, and the astonishing account of his ancestry filled him with pride. Too much pride, sometimes. He readily forgot that God's son had a father. He wanted to have his way in everything, here and now, and raged at anyone who opposed his will or bruised his self-esteem.

Yet at other times, it seemed, he didn't really believe in his sacred ancestry at all. Not deep down. Deep down, something would always nudge him, always lift its cynical head and whisper: *Jesus Christ, my lord? You must be joking . . . .*

It was the same with the willstone. He wavered between treating it as a plaything, and believing it could do anything at all.

"I'm sick to death of preserves, my lord. The stone could make us a bowl of fresh peaches, couldn't it? No? Why are you so certain? Have you ever tried?"

He wanted peaches fashioned out of air. But when Gottfried told him they could use the stone for something which really mattered—to communicate when Gottfried left for Mainz—his son had simply stared at him. "That's impossible, my lord."

So Gottfried showed him, patiently, as he would have showed a child how to read and to count. He walled off a room in the castle of Stavoren, with a heavy lock to which only the two of them had a key. Inside he made a small stone chamber, shaped like a perfect pyramid, with a prie-dieu made of stone, and a place for one candle, and a silver bowl filled to the brim with water. He chipped a small piece of crystal from the bottom of the willstone, and dropped it into the bowl.

"Empty your mind of every thought but me, Theodoric. Bring nothing here; take nothing away. This is where we will meet."

Slowly, Theodoric learned. He learned to press his thoughts into the sliver of stone, to read Gottfried's from the water. But he never learned to do it just anywhere, with any simple scrying bowl. He needed the stone chamber, where there were no distractions, and where all the powers of the willstone were mirrored and multiplied. Even there, it exhausted him. Worse, he disliked it, and Gottfried knew why. It meant that his father's authority was never very far away.

—I'm not going to debate the matter, Theo. Take Armund to Ravensbruck, and marry him to Helga. Take every man you can beg or bully out of Arnulf, and bring the Reinmark to heel. I want every castle Karelian captured taken back, I want every oath made to him unsworn, and I want every whisper of treason in the Reinmark crushed. Do you understand me? I don't care what you have to burn or who you have to hang; I don't want to hear so much as a rumor of unrest from there again.

—I can't storm Schildberge castle, my lord.

—No, but you can lay siege to it properly this time.

—You asked for men, my lord. I sent you all the men I could. I had only boys and cripples left when Karelian attacked.

—Yes, I know . . . .

Gottfried shook his head. As always, Theodoric's image in the willstone was ill-defined. Fuzzy at the edges, like Theo's own princely self.

—It isn't always enough to do blindly what you're told. You have to think. You have to think about who you are, and who they are. And you never seem to do it. You didn't do it in the siege, and you didn't do it at Stavoren.

Least of all at Stavoren, Gottfried thought bitterly. At Stavoren God had placed victory in his grasp, and Theodoric, God forgive him, had not even noticed it. He had noticed nothing except the possibility of amusing himself with Karelian's witch. It appalled Gottfried every time he thought about it. How could Theodoric so debase his own high manhood, and endanger himself for such an empty, venal satisfaction? She was weakened, thanks be to God, or he might have found himself possessed, or filled with some wasting disease, or made impotent—he who was born to be king, and had yet no sons.

And his carnal folly wasn't yet the worst of it.

—You had the witch of Helmardin in irons; you might have made an end of her. But no. You left her in her cell unguarded, and she changed herself and got away—

—When we were done with her, my lord, no one thought she needed any guarding. She was too well tamed to swat a fly.

—Obviously.

—God damn it, father, how was I to know? I've never dealt with witches before.

—You knew she could shape-shift.

—She was in irons. In a bolted cell. With fifty armed men between her and the bastion gates.

—And what of it? You're dealing with sorcery, don't you understand? How could you forget what happened in Lys? I meant to try Karelian fairly and publicly. As it turned out, I had five minutes in which I might have driven a spear through his heart, and I didn't do it, and he escaped. You knew that. Why in God's name did you wait? You have to kill them. No trials, no bargains for surrender, nothing; just kill them where they stand!

—I understand, my lord.

—I hope so. This is no ordinary war, my son, and the rules of ordinary warfare won't serve us now. We have to go beyond them.

No ordinary rules would serve them now, in this one last rising of the armies of the Lord. Victory would not be easy, and he felt sadness sometimes at the cost of it. It was a cold, triumphal sadness, much like he had felt in Jerusalem, a sadness mixed with awe at the magnificence of a God who would demand so much, who was so absolute, so potent, and so terrible.

He did not know what other men believed of that day; he never asked them. But in his own mind there was no doubt: Jerusalem had been a sacrifice, a blood offering to a God who had given up his son eleven hundred years before, and still saw the human world filled with unbelievers and heretics and adulterers and thieves, with Saracens and pagans and idolaters and Jews, and said Enough! They will not serve me? Kill them!

There was an awesome purity to so much blood, and a special heroism in those who shed it. They did not falter, or try to refuse God even the smallest part of the offering; they accepted the hardness of it, the shock to their own merely human understanding. And they could stand afterwards and look on it, and marvel: It was God's work, and it was good.

He would remember Jerusalem. Every day, every battle, until it was done, until the kingdom flowered from the farthest edges of the earth to its very heart, one kingdom under God.

Always and everywhere Jerusalem.

XXXIX

THE RISING OF THE GODS

Difficult indeed it must prove to fight against a draugar.

POETIC EDDA

F ROM DAWN TILL DARKNESS Karelian rode without rest. His escort was
small, a mere eight men including his squire. They were good
men, the same eight he had taken into the heart of Stavoren, but they
were not his friends. Pauli was gone, Otto was dead, Reinhard was
again commanding the stronghold of Schildberge. Accompanied
though he was, he felt as if he rode through Helmardin alone.

The castle of Car-Iduna rose out of the darkness quite unexpectedly. It was not ablaze with lights, as it had been the first time. Only
two feeble torches marked its gates. Beyond rose a black and half-ru-
ined tower, a great shadow of stone against the moonlight, brooding
with power and stillness and decay.

This is not the right place, surely; I've gone astray somehow . . . .
He reined in his horse, his escort puffing up sharply behind him.

"What castle is this, my lord?" his squire whispered.

He did not answer. He let his eyes run across the battlements and
into the wood beyond. Nothing was the same. Everything was the
same. *Castle of love and revelry, castle of death. It's like all the priests
say, only they never understood the meaning of their own words . . . .*

Where was Raven?

He kicked his horse forward, aware of the dismay of his companions. Guards, shadowed against the castle wall, moved forward into
the flickering light, and bowed to him.

"Welcome, my lord."

Their faces were unfamiliar, but then, dear gods, what had he ever looked at here with attention except her?

"I am seeking the castle of Car-Iduna," he said.

"You have found it, my lord." The guard made a small gesture with his hand, and the gates began to open—slowly, as if they had not opened for a thousand years.

Somewhere within was a fire; he could see the glow of it, and the occasional leaping of flames over an inner court wall. There seemed to be nothing else here except a vast and crumbling ruin: weeds, and broken stone, and a terrible sense of emptiness which no light, no clamor, no numbers, would ever diminish beyond the moment. The presence of life here was temporary. He wiped icy sweat from his brow as he rode towards the gates, and felt it run in small rivulets down his body.

His captain Harald was tugging at the reins of his horse. He was a young man, rash and brave, but his voice was as unsteady now as the voice of a frightened child.

"My lord, what are you doing? You didn't tell us we were coming to a place like this!"

"You may wait outside the gates," the count said. "All of you."

"Not if you're going in, my lord!"

"Then precede me or follow me, Harald, but get out of the way."

It probably took every ounce of will the young man had, but he turned his horse, and led the way.

They trotted into the courtyard—or what had been a courtyard in some time before time, when men still lived here. It was tangled with briars and stones, and pieces of broken and rusting armor. It smelled only of woodland and midnight, but it *felt* of death so strongly that he shivered.

Harald crossed himself several times. "This is like a burying ground, my lord."

"Aye."

Servants were hurrying to meet them, friendly enough, smiling in the light of their small torches, taking the horses. Then at last a voice he knew, a hunched body padding quickly out of the shadows.

"My lord of Lys!" Marius the steward smiled, bowing almost to his feet. "Welcome to Car-Iduna, my lord. We hoped against hope you would arrive tonight."

"I came as fast as I could. Where is my lady?"

"She is waiting for you. Come."

Steps lay before them, and a wide stone door which Karelian remembered, which opened into the castle proper. Inside was the great staircase leading to the feast hall and the sacred chamber of the Black Chalice. But instead of entering, Marius limped back the way he apparently had come, alongside the inner bastion, towards the place of fire.

A second gate opened for them, narrow and high, through which a single mounted knight could pass if he ducked his head. They went inside, and there the fluid yet overwhelming presence of sorcery struck him with a physical shock. And with it, the realization that whatever they had begun here, they waited on him for its completion.

In the heart of the courtyard was an immense, hollowed-out stone with a fire leaping wildly in it. Some two or three dozen people gathered around it; many were in chain mail, magnificently armed; others in sweeping capes. Gold flashed everywhere, on arm bands and belts and jeweled torques; on the wrists of a young woman who approached him with a splendid goblet in her hands.

"Welcome, Karelian of Lys." She curtsied gracefully, and offered him the cup. Her breasts were almost bare, her hair as fair as moonlight. She was, he supposed, quite beautiful, but he could not see her face. Nor could he see anyone else's. The entire company was masked, and every mask was the same: the hollow-eyed, death-boned face of Hel, keeper of the realms of the dead.

He took the cup and thanked her, but he did not immediately drink. He bent, seizing the arm of Marius in an iron grip.

"What of my men?" he demanded.

"They will drink, and they will sleep, and they will remember nothing. She will hurt no one who belongs to you, my lord; surely you know that?"

"Where is she?"

"Coming," Marius said softly.

Somewhere within the castle, a drumbeat began; then, a few moments later, a shawm, howling as wolves howled, or the dead who could find no resting place.

"Don't approach her," Marius said. "Don't speak unless she commands you. And for your life's sake, my lord, don't break the circle."

The music soared louder, as though a door had opened; torchlight leapt into the sky. The procession came slowly, great hollow drumbeats tolling every step, shuddering into the midnight forest and echoing back. He looked for Marius, but the dwarf had already gone. A moment later Karelian saw a small hunched figure take its place in the circle, masked like all the others.

He drained the wine for courage, knowing there would be potions in it, and not caring. He had knelt, some sixteen months before—or sixteen lifetimes—on the banks of the Maren, in a circle of seven stones, and chosen his lady and his gods. Neither had yet betrayed him.

The procession moved closer. The musicians separated, curving around the circle, and he saw her. She was all in black, and pallid as a dream. And she was hurt—so hurt he caught his breath in anguish, and stared at her, unbelieving.

There were black marks on both sides of her face, and a long jagged cut on her cheek, which had probably been made by a boot. Her wrists were torn. The black silk which crept high to her throat hid the rest, but only until he thought about it.

He had not imagined she could be so wounded. The veela who found him in the woods of Stavoren said only she'd been shot with an arrow. He feared worse; he knew what was possible in wars; he had been through enough of them. And he knew the meaning of Theodoric's gesture. But he had tried desperately not to think about it. She was the Lady of the Mountain. She was queen and witch and veela, she was inviolable, she was *his* . . . *!*

Don't approach her. And for your life's sake, don't break the circle!

Except for Marius's command he would have swept men and fire and gods themselves aside to go to her. But even as he steeled himself, and held his place, he understood why he must do so. He understood why there had been no greeting from her, no kisses, not even a whisper of time to shelter or to talk. He could not even tell her how he had sent the army off with Reinhard, and slipped into the castle of Stavoren with a handful of men disguised as peasants, hoping to rescue her when her captors brought her out to burn. And how he had laughed when the soldiers came back empty-handed, and all damnation broke loose in the duke's splendid fortress, and it was himself who might have ended up a prisoner then, because he could not stop laughing . . . .

No laughter now, no chance to tell her anything, or to hold her even for a moment. Her pain and her dark fury were part of her strength now, part of the power she would use to forge their magic and their revenge. She looked at him. *So fiercely as I love you, so fiercely do I hate the son of Gottfried* . . . . She was already entranced, drunk on sorcery and passion. Maybe some of it leapt across the circle into his own heart. Maybe some of it came from the potions in his wine . . . some of this soft coiling hatred which was knotting his stomach and setting fire to his blood. It came from many things, even from this place which was and was not Car-Iduna, which was at once so sheltering and so fell.

But mostly it came from knowing—knowing now for sure. Theodoric had raped her. He had used her and given her to his men to use, to violate and torture and tear apart—she who was so lovely and so magical it seemed a butterfly should not light on her sleeve without permission.

For the first time since Jerusalem, he was glad he had been trained to kill.

She moved into the circle of light. Behind her, in their silver gowns and silver helms, came the Nine, bearing the Chalice, and placing it on an altar beside the burning stone. They too, took their places, and the circle closed. Raven was inside of it. She alone, besides himself, was unmasked.

"May the gods keep safe the world, and may the world keep safe the gods."

"So let it be."

The drum began to beat more quickly. She paid homage to the Grail, to the four corners of the world, to Karelian.

"Lord of Lys, be welcome in the circle of Car-Iduna, and be one with our power."

"So let it be."

She knelt, with her head bent forward. Her black hair and her black gown seemed a single darkness.

"The empire dies, the empire returns."

They began to chant. They called on the old gods one by one, called on them with such despair and passion that even the weariest, the most abandoned of gods must have heard and paid them heed. They called on Gullveig, the thrice-slain sorceress of the Vanir; they called on Hel. Sometimes he understood, sometimes everything was a rising and falling wail lost in the crying of pipes and the hammering of drums, pounding faster and faster, out of the night and out of time . . . .

"Out of the shadows—"

"Come forth!"

"Out of the time of forgetting—"

"Come forth!"

"You are unshriven—"

"Come forth!"

"You are still unforgiven—"

"Come forth!"

Raven was on her feet, a leaping brand held high in her fist, her head flung back, her voice a scream of power and defiance and driven need.

"Come forth! By the gods we command you! Come forth!"

Hoofbeats clattered softly across the courtyard behind him. For a moment he did not really hear them, and for yet another moment he thought in the world's terms, wondering what riders could have found the castle of Car-Iduna, and how they could have entered, and then he spun about as any worldly soldier would have done, his hand closing quickly on his sword.

They were filing through the narrow gate into the inner court, one by one, in full armor and on splendid mounts. The crest on their shields was familiar, and yet unfamiliar, as was the style of their helmets and the trappings of their horses. He looked at their faces, and his blood turned to ice.

He had never been afraid of Raven, never really. Oh, there had been moments of uncertainty. There were tales of nightmare and legend which had flickered across his mind, with a degree of genuine dismay and a greater degree of conscious irony: *Yes, and what really does happen to a man who binds himself to a witch—other than in bed, where everything that happens is what other men dream of?* There had been a few moments of uneasiness, and yes, one awful moment in the forest, when she had changed herself into a hunting cat, but it had been so brief, so playful.

Nothing was brief now, or playful. The chanting went on and the mounted knights came and gathered as to a liege lord's bell. And he knew from whence they came. Their faces were empty, hollowed out like the masks of actors, lit palely as with marsh lights. They were dead. She had raised the walls of Car-Iduna over some ancient butchering-ground, still scattered with broken armor and with ghosts, and she had called forth the dead.

To ride with him to Ravensbruck.

He was drunk with the sorcery of the night, and with his own deep hunger for revenge. Otherwise he truly might have faltered then; he might have given in to dread and despair and told himself this was not possible, this was not Raven or Car-Iduna, this was not anything he wanted to be part of . . . .

The chanting stopped. The dead men waited, looking past him as though he were not there, looking past everyone to the witch of Helmardin.

She called out names, and six of them moved forward. He did not know the names, but he recognized their marks of rank. They were all highborn men, captains in the emperor's service, leaders of the war band.

"Come," she said, and the circle opened to let them in.

"Behold your liege lord!" Raven cried, and flung her arm towards Karelian. "You will serve him, and obey him in all things. You will ride with him to Ravensbruck, as you were commanded to do. And you will destroy it as you destroyed Dorn. Such is the will of your emperor!"

Karelian caught his breath. These were not ordinary dead men. These were the flower of King Henry II's knights, the men who slaughtered Wulfstan's people and vanished in the wood of Helmardin, their planned attack on Ravensbruck never carried out. Now, for a different emperor, against a different lord of Ravensbruck, they would finish what they had begun. And in the very act of doing so, they would overturn the purpose of the original command—to destroy the pagans, and break the sacred circles of the world. They had slain the rebel heirs of Dorn. Now they would serve its most rebellious heir of all.

Oh, yes, this was Raven . . . ! Karelian smiled, and wished he had more wine, for ritual or no ritual he would have saluted her then.

The six captains turned to him. They did not dismount, but each touched a closed fist to his breast, and bowed. "We are at your command, my lord duke."

My lord duke . . . ?

Before he could wonder about it properly, Raven spoke again.

"You were cursed to this unrest by Alanas of Dorn. When Ravensbruck is taken, and your lord gives you leave, you may sleep. Till then he is your master and your hope. Shield him from harm, for if he does not return to me safe, you will wander to the last edges of the world, to the last broken scatters of time, and you will find no peace!

"It's long since you've ridden the marches of the north. I have summoned you a comrade who remembers them well."

She paused, turning towards the gathered army of the dead. "My lord of Selven, come."

Another man moved into the circle. He wore no armor, for he had died with none. He was young and very dark, and he carried himself with the same taut and thin-lipped arrogance Karelian remembered from his time in Arnulf's castle.

Rudolf of Selven. Adelaide's murdered love.

He moved towards Raven; then, as if from the corner of his eye, he noticed the count of Lys, and turned on him instead. He was dead, like the others, his face an unface, hollow and insubstantial, yet it twisted with a terrible, unbelieving bitterness.

"*This* is what I am to serve?"

"Aye, Selven," Raven said fiercely. "Serve him, or return to the shadows unrevenged! Return, and remember that Arnulf lives, and laughs, and readies himself for his daughter's marriage feast. Arnulf who broke his word to you, who gave Adelaide away, who chained you where you'd lain with her and drove his spear through your bowels—!"

"*Enough!*"

Could a dead man feel pain?—for it seemed he did. It seemed he would buckle from the weight of it. But his eyes never left Karelian's face, and his voice was as savage as the snarl of a wolf.

"What became of my lady Adelaide? I may serve you then, since it seems I must, but I want to know!"

"Answer him, Karelian!" Raven said.

"She is in Lys, and she is well. I did her no harm, save for the harm I brought to her unknowing."

"Does he speak the truth, witch?" Selven demanded harshly. Still staring at Karelian. Not believing his words, but hungering to believe them. He had been faithful to one thing in the world; he had loved Adelaide.

"He speaks the truth," Raven said. "He was never your enemy. You have but one enemy my lord Selven, and he sits in his feast hall with the sons of Lord Gottfried, boasting of his past and future greatness."

"Well then." Selven turned slowly, looked at Raven, at the waiting captains and the knights of empire, men who could still kill but could not die. He gave Karelian the faintest hint of a bow, and smiled bitterly.

"Well then, take us to Ravensbruck!"

The six captains as one drew their swords, and raised them high, and shouted: "Ravensbruck! Ravensbruck!" And the cry went up in a great pounding roar, like a sea against a cliff: "Ravensbruck! Ravensbruck!"

His lady came to him through thunder and dancing light.

"The pyramid thrives on the blood of its sons," she said. "So be it, Karelian of Lys. Bring me the blood of the sons of von Heyden. Bring me Theodoric's head. Sever it clean, and do not mark his face; I want to be sure his father can recognize it."

She offered her hand for him to kiss. Her wrist was raw and torn with manacles, the smallest of her wounds.

"My lady . . . ."

He longed to hold her, but he knew it was forbidden. Until she was avenged she would be sorceress, and nothing else.

She gave him a small, golden apple. "Your horse has been tended, my love, and will bear you without tiring. Eat this; you will need nothing more till you return."

She bowed to him, something she had never done before. So did each member of the circle always bow to the others, before they parted. He was now one with the witch-lords of Car-Iduna.

"Bring me his head, Karelian," she said again. "And then may his God help the man who holds the willstone!"

They rode like wind, like the storms of autumn, black-clouded and indistinct and echoing. It was four days' journey as the world measured; how long it took them he never knew. They did not rest and they felt no weariness. They pounded through wood and valley, past small brooding villages where everything living slept, or looked away. They splashed through icy streams and swept over hills where bare trees bent against the wind to let them pass. They rode, and the thunder of their hoofbeats sang in his heart. Black clouds rolled overhead, and he thought he heard sometimes the crying of Valkyries, at once harsh, and triumphant, and pitiful. He could have ridden for a thousand years; nothing contained his dark army, neither mountains nor rivers nor time. And the old gods rode with him, all of the old gods, Vanir and Aesir alike, and if he honored some of them more than others, and a few of them hardly at all, still in this they were allies; this night they would ride as one, for the honor of their priestess, for the honor of their wild and still defiant land.

After, a thousand tales would be told of what men saw, and did not see. But one telling was always the same. At daybreak after the night of the full moon, the walls of Ravensbruck were seen to *waffel*. The peasants saw it, and shielded their eyes and looked away. The woodcutters saw it, bringing their wagons of cut timber to feed the fires of the wedding feast. Guests saw it, arriving with their glittering retinues and gifts; a few of them took thoughtful counsel among themselves, and went away.

The high stone walls, square and solid as the mountain from which they rose, quivered and melted and reappeared, like a light behind a shifting curtain, like the Aurora of midwinter, the kind which did not leap and dance, but merely throbbed between being and not-being.

So ships were seen to do before they sank, and houses before they were consumed in fire.

XL

THE MARRIAGE FEAST OF RAVENSBRUCK

I see a channel and a chained wolf lying
Until the twilight of the gods:
Forger of lies, unless you be silent,
That fate will fall on you next.

POETIC EDDA

RAVENSBRUCK WAS AS DESOLATE AS I REMEMBERED it, a rough-hewn border stronghold in a sullen, half-settled march. Nothing, not even a royal wedding, could make it seem gracious, or soften the violence which seemed to lie everywhere beneath the surface of its life. It was a place where swords were drawn over trifles, where mastery depended on force, and where loyalty and rebellion were equally rooted in fear.

They called Arnulf of Ravensbruck the Iron Count, and even a half-wit would have understood why. He was bigger and heavier than Gottfried, but without Gottfried's aura of majesty, just a massive and dangerous beast of a man. Even his enemies admitted he was inde-structible, and even his friends admitted he was singularly cruel.

Two winters earlier, just before we arrived for Karelian's marriage, he had been thrown by a stallion and horribly injured. His wife Clara was accused by Adelaide of having bewitched his horse, but she was never tried. All he had for evidence was the statement of an adulteress, and a few charms and amulets hidden in her jewel case. Her sons objected to her imprisonment; her daughter Helga, apparently, did not. After some months passed Arnulf allowed her to retire to a convent.

"He wouldn't let her come to the wedding, though. And they say she was so mad about it, she howled and cursed and threw things at the nuns."

That was Peter, Count Arnulf's squire, wrapped in finery and talking with barely a pause for breath. We weren't five minutes in the great hall before he sought me out, renewing his acquaintance and smothering me with gossip.

"She set a great store by her little Helga, you remember," he added.

Oh, yes, I remembered. She wanted her little Helga to marry Karelian, and thought both fate and her husband were miserably cruel when they decided otherwise. Perhaps she thought better of them now.

"So how've you been?" he went on, seeing I was not going to talk about Lady Clara. "I see you've changed sides."

"I didn't change sides," I snapped. "The count of Lys changed sides."

He laughed. The hall was crowded, and we were some distance from the cluster of men around Theodoric and Arnulf. Nonetheless Peter lowered his voice.

"Is it true what they say? That he's turned sorcerer?"

"Yes," I said.

"Strange. He didn't seem the type."

"What is the type? Do you think the devil's men have cloven hoofs and tails?"

He laughed again. Perhaps he realized his comment had been silly. He drank generously from the cup he held, and leaned close to me to ask his next question, even softer than the first.

"You didn't notice anything, did you? While you were riding in?"

"Notice anything? What do you mean?"

"About the castle. They say every morning since the full moon— it's the servants saying it, and of course you can't believe anything they say—but they say it was . . . *waffeling.*"

"Oh, that. We saw it. Prince Theodoric was very amused."

"Amused?"

I looked at him. He was still a squire, and I was now a knight. Moreover, I was a knight who knew a great many things which he would never dream of. I felt very superior.

"Of course. It's just a foul trick of the witch of Helmardin, to try and frighten us away. She's very good at creating illusions. We thought Karelian had a whole army outside of Stavoren. We even thought he had the men of Ravensbruck—"

"Ravensbruck? But that's ridiculous—!"

"Of course. But you see, Peter, it's what they do. They fight with deception and trickery; it's the only way they can hope to win. But if she thought Theodoric would be frightened away by a mirage, she doesn't know him."

Peter brightened visibly. "The count didn't take it seriously for a moment, either," he said. "A whole lot of the servants ran off, though, before anybody noticed."

I suppose it was the mention of servants which reminded me. I had not seen the Wend woman at all since we arrived. I looked around, and could not see her now, either.

"What about the slave Count Arnulf had? The Wend with the scarred face? What became of her?"

"Sick. She's got a tumor." He patted his belly. "She's not allowed inside the hall any more. Lady Helga always did hate her, and the count doesn't like dying people anywhere near him. She sits in the wash-house and chews leaves—to kill the pain, I suppose. They say she sees things when she chews them."

I had cheered him up by saying the *waffeling* of Ravensbruck castle was just a shabby trick. Now, thinking of the hag Sigune, he grew somber again.

"A lot of things she sees come true," he said.

I wanted to ask him what she had seen that was bothering him, but there was a stir in the room, and we turned to see Helga coming down the stairs to meet her bridegroom.

She was pretty, there was no denying it, with the kind of full-breasted, pouty-mouthed prettiness men loved in peasant girls and whores.

Arnulf, leaning heavily on his cane, rose to his feet to present her to Prince Armund. She was the last of his children, he said, and the loveliest.

"She won't disappoint him like the other one did," Peter whispered. "The midwives made sure of it."

I looked at him, not understanding.

"She still has her maidenhead. Can you imagine—marrying the emperor's son—if she didn't?"

Frankly, I did not want to imagine anything where Helga was concerned. I understood Gottfried's necessity, and I accepted it, but I wished to God he might have found poor Armund a better wife.

I never liked the count of Ravensbruck. He was coarse and lecherous and brutal, and he had an equally bottomless appetite for vain-glory and for drink. He had gloated over the marriage of Adelaide and Karelian: *The duke's kinsman, by God, a man with royal blood!* That was all forgotten now, of course; the bride had turned whore and the bridegroom traitor. It was just a small mistake in the past, a small tumble on his long climb to greatness. Now he stood to make his fortune forever, to bind his house not merely to a ducal throne, but to the crown of empire.

He sweated pride now. He roared it out with his laughter, and washed it down with his uncounted cups of beer. One minute he would curse the servants roundly because, even by laboring day and night, they had not made his feast hall beautiful. And the next minute he would laugh and say be damned to it, Ravensbruck was a fighting castle, not a dancing one, and the whole world knew it. It was why they had come to him, why his daughter would be a princess, and maybe his grandson a king. Not that he wished it so, indeed not, God save your highness Theodoric, may you live as many good years as your father, and have as many fine sons . . . !

Other men got drunk. Arnulf simply got stronger, prouder, more unutterably Arnulf. I spent a very long afternoon, and an even longer evening, remembering everything I had forgotten about the man, re-membering how deeply Karelian despised him, and I had to admit Karelian was right.

And I had to ask myself—only once or twice, and very much against my will—where this place, these men, this absurdly vulgar marriage, all fitted in the empire of Christ.

The revelry, it seemed, would go on forever. The contract was read and signed, the gifts and vows exchanged, the marriage consum-mated almost immediately in broad daylight—a disgusting custom, but not uncommon in alliances of state, especially when armies were al-ready preparing to march. Then we feasted. The servants brought mountains of food, and kept filling our tankards from what must have been an ocean of good beer.

I cannot say when I began to feel uneasy. My brave words to Peter had been at least halfway sincere. Theodoric really had laughed at the wavering image of Ravensbruck castle. "Is this the best she can do now? No devils? Not even a few of Attila's Huns waiting at the gates?" He had laughed and ridden on, and I had been cheered by it. Besides, we were winning. Gottfried's invasion of Thuringia was going well. Konrad would either have to fight him there, with insufficient men, or let the duchy be gobbled up. Karelian was effectively disempowered. He could stay in Schildberge castle, or he could come down and fight and be destroyed. Either way, he was not going to be any help to Konrad.

Most important of all, the witch of Helmardin was wounded, and her wounds had obviously reduced her powers. So I thought yes, perhaps it *was* all she could do, make the stones wobble. Frighten us, if she could, and try to spoil young Armund's wedding day.

But even as those thoughts rested comfortably on the surface of my mind, underneath I still remembered Helmardin, I still remembered the courtyard at Lys. With witches there was no certainty, there was never a safe time or a safe place.

It was Theodoric, I think, who first began to kindle my unease. He was always a restless man, always on edge. As the evening wore on, he became almost desperate with tension. He tried to hide it. He laughed, he drank, he dragged servant girls onto his lap and pawed them. Once he left the hall for a considerable time, and I thought he was probably off coupling with some slut in a darkened corridor.

It was always hard for me to think of him as Gottfried's son. He had none of his father's moral qualities, and few of his powers.

But he had to have some of them.

Somewhere in the course of the evening I put all those facts together—his heritage and his tormented unease and the *waffeling* walls and the runaway servants and the hag Sigune who had apparently seen something no one wanted to talk about, and slowly, by the tiniest and iciest degrees, I began to be afraid. I began to think Theodoric knew something terrible, only he didn't know what it was. He didn't even know how or why he knew it; he never understood what it meant to be Gottfried's son. But he was afraid of *something*. And finally, so was I.

It is one thing to foresee disaster—or believe that you foresee it. It is quite another matter to actually confront it, to hear an alarm bell clanging frantically in the midst of a wedding feast, almost unnoticed at first over the laughter and the revelry. Then the clatter of overturned chairs, the pounding of feet, the sight of a blood-spattered soldier stumbling into the feast hall.

"Enemies! Enemies, my lord, we are attacked!"

We all remembered the omens then, the promise of Ravensbruck's doom. Even Arnulf must have done so, reeling to his feet, pale as I had never seen him. The soldier was almost by his chair, and the silence around them was deathly.

"My lord . . . ."

How had the man shouted? He had almost no voice left, and no strength. He held onto the table to keep from falling.

"What enemies?" Arnulf thundered at him. "Spit it out, man, what's happening? Who are they?"

"I don't know, my lord. But they're inside. They're coming over the walls."

"Coming over the walls?"

We stayed to hear no more. We ran for arms and armor. Some cursed the drink in their bellies, and some cursed the invaders, whoever they might be. I did not wonder who they were. I knew—or rather, I thought I knew. And I cursed myself for having dared to think there was ever such a thing as a disempowered sorcerer.

May God preserve me from ever again seeing what we saw in that courtyard! Even now, I cannot think of it without shuddering. Some of the attackers had already scaled the outer wall and were leaping down among us, landing lightly on their feet, as though their bodies were made of air, and their armor was only torchlight in a mirror. They looked like men, but they were not men. Their faces were empty and haunted, lit with a dim and horrid light. Nothing resisted them. Whatever they themselves were, their weapons were real; the men they cut down did not get up again.

For themselves, it was different. Spears pierced through their armor, and they laughed and plucked them scornfully away. One took a blow which should have severed his head from his body; the sword swept unresisted as through air, and the man who wielded it threw himself fatally off balance with the force of his blow.

In minutes the enemy had cleared the gates and swung them wide. The drawbridge came down with a mortal crash, and hundreds more of them poured in, mounted and headlong.

Karelian was with them.

Like everyone else I was afraid, I was appalled, I was all the things a man must be when in a single glance he sees both death and the fiends of hell coming at him. Yet for one frozen moment I saw only Karelian. Moonlight silvered his helm and flared on the trappings of his horse, moonlight and torchlight together, and for all my fear and his damnation I thought only of how magnificent he was. Outriders raced by his side, an honor guard of darkness and fire, with flaming brands in their hands and bottomless death in their eyes. I knew he would defeat us all, and a small, unpardonable thing inside me smiled.

So I stood breathless in my folly, a folly I think only a German could be guilty of, with our ancient and corrupting love of tragic heroes. So I stood, and a dead man came from the shadows and drove his sword into my back.

I remember falling, and barely understanding why. A horse leapt over me, another struck my shoulder with its hoof. Barely conscious, I tried to crawl towards the darkness, towards the shadows of buildings where there was no battle, no rearing beasts to trample me. I looked up once, and the sky whirled around me as though a child spun it on a rope, and I knew nothing more.

I could not have been unconscious very long, for when I saw the world again, the battle was still raging nearby. Someone had dragged me to safety. I was in a dark, wretched building where everything smelled of wetness and rot.

I tried to get up, and could not, and a woman's voice said quietly: "You're safe here, lad; lie still."

I sobbed something and dragged myself to my knees, looking about for the door. Gottfried's men needed me; I belonged in the battle. I saw light, and stumbled towards it, and fell. I crawled closer, and saw it was only a wide crack in the wall, left by a rotting timber which no one had troubled to replace.

It was all I could manage, crawling those few feet. I was done fighting for today and for some time to come. Perhaps I wept. I know I laid my head against the broken wall, wondering why God had brought us to this hour, wondering how we had failed him.

Then I heard a cry which would have rung clear through any battle, a voice I knew as well as I knew my own. Karelian's voice, fierce with triumph and raw with sorcerous power.

"Now, dog of von Heyden, it is over!"

I looked out. Theodoric stood among a scattering of fallen men. They had defended their prince, twenty of them or more, until the last one was felled by the creatures of Helmardin. Theodoric looked around, and saw that he was alone. The few remaining men of Ravensbruck were surrendering, or were backed into lofts and corners from which none would emerge alive. Somewhere to the left, among the storehouses, a flung torch caught a roof; flames were already shimmering through the windows of Arnulf's great hall.

Karelian rode slowly towards him.

"Over?" Theodoric cried savagely. "You think it's over? You'll never defeat my lord father! You're nothing but a damnable sorcerer—!"

"Yes, I'm a sorcerer. It's the one thing your lord father and I have in common."

"You *dare?*"

"We're cousins, Theodoric, have you forgotten?" As he spoke, Karelian began to circle his prey, slowly, riding deosil around him, as witches danced around their cauldrons, weaving spells. And nothing, not the fire or the butchery or the vulnerability of the prince horrified me quite as much as his strange, triumphant ritual act.

"A mere six or seven generations," Karelian went on grimly, "and we're both back among the witch priests of Dorn. And you don't even need any secret parchments dug out of the cellars of Jerusalem to prove it. It's a much simpler explanation for his lordship's remarkable gifts, don't you think? Simpler than counting grandfathers all the way back to Jesus Christ? Didn't that ever cross your mind?"

It had crossed Theodoric's mind. Even from here I could tell, in the way his body sagged for a moment, the way he snarled back an answer too outraged to be coherent, and almost stumbled as he turned, trying to follow Karelian's circling hatred.

God, how I wished for my crossbow then . . . !

"You're nothing, Theodoric von Heyden. You're no god and no prince, you're not even halfway a man. You're the shabby get of a cold-blooded, power-drunk trickster."

He reached, and took the javelin he carried on his saddle, and leveled it in his hand.

"God damn you!" Theodoric shouted. "God damn you for a coward! Won't you even fight me?"

"No. I've fought good men and bad. I've fought pirates and thieves and lunatics. I even once fought a wolf. But you I will not fight. I offered you your life for my lady's honor, and you shamed her and trampled her. I will take your head for it, villain, and I will take it *now!*"

His arm swept back. The javelin flew, with all his own strength and all the sorcerous power he could give it. Theodoric brought his shield up quickly, blocking his head and upper body from the blow. He did not see in the burning darkness that the aim was low. The javelin shattered his leg like a piece of willow, just above the knee.

He cried out, and faltered, reeling on his feet. Karelian rode at him with a howl of rage, crying something, the witch's name perhaps, and drove his sword into the side of Theodoric's neck, just below the helmet rim, piercing through mail coif and all, into his throat.

And he waited so, motionless on his horse, holding the prince on his sword, while Theodoric twisted and clawed at his neck. He held him so, until he was still, until he hung limp like a sack of meal from a nail. Then he wrenched away the prince's helmet and coif, and seized him by his pale hair, and cut his head off. And rode across the courtyard to where the undead were gathering in triumph to offer him their homage.

I sank to the floor and buried my face against my arms.

I did not want to live that night, but I did, for I was in the scrub house of the slave Sigune. All day she had soaked it down with tubs of fouled water, inside and out. Except for the stones, it was the only thing in Ravensbruck which would not burn.

She had water left. She poured some into my mouth, and over my hair. I recognized her then, in the small bit of firelight dancing through the broken wall—or rather, I recognized the scars on her face, the smashed cheek-bone, the watchful, malevolent eyes.

"It's over, Pauli," she said. "Don't fret yourself, your lord is safe."

My lord is safe . . . ? Dear Christ, I thought, what mockery was this? And then I understood. I wore no colors. Like most of the others I had run out of the feast hall with naked armor over my tunic. She was isolated now from the court. She had not seen me among Gottfried's men; she thought I was still with Karelian.

That was why she dragged me to safety. For his sake, not for mine.

"He is a lord among men, that one," she said. "Though when he came here the first time, I didn't think much of him. Nor of you, either, if you want to know the truth."

I lay still and let her tend my wound. She talked steadily; half the time I think she was talking to herself, rather than to me.

"Strange, lad, isn't it, how things turn out? All the years I waited for this, twenty years or more, to see that beast go down. I thought his wars would do it for him, but he survived them all. I thought his sons or his vassals would do it for him, but they all fell in line, and the ones who didn't, died.

"And then I tried, and it was still the same. I crippled his body but he didn't die. I broke what was left of his rotten heart, but he didn't die. Rudi died. Adelaide nearly died. And then I began to die . . . and he was still here. Still laughing, still rutting, still conquering the world."

"It was you?" I whispered. "The accident? It wasn't Lady Clara?" She laughed. "Lady Clara? That arrogant sow? No, Pauli, she picked on the weak, that one, not on the mighty. Like they all do in the castles.

"I thought it was over, all my hope of vengeance. And I grieved. It was the hardest thing of all to bear, thinking he might outlive me. I forgot he had other enemies. The whole of Europe must be peopled with his enemies. It's worth remembering, Paul of Ardiun. Men like Arnulf always have another enemy—the one they never counted on."

I grew colder still inside, listening to her babble. As far as she was concerned, none of this had anything to do with Theodoric or Gottfried or the fate of the world—only with Arnulf of Ravensbruck. With her petty slave's grudges and her bottomless hunger for revenge.

"After I saw how it would be, I didn't grieve any more. I just waited. They would all die, Arnulf and his sons and all his fine allies—"

"You knew?" I whispered, before I could stop myself. "You knew your own castle would be destroyed, and you did nothing?"

"And what should I have done, my pet, even if I'd wanted to? Go up to him and tap him on the shoulder? Excuse me, my indestructible warrior lord, but I've just had a vision of your most unpleasant end? Try it yourself sometime, and see what it gets you.

"Besides, one doesn't mess with the justice of the gods."

She stroked my hair. She hadn't noticed the horror in my question. She thought I admired her for keeping silent. "It wasn't hard to be silent, lad," she went on softly. "I have nothing whatever left to lose."

I shuddered. I suppose she thought I was in pain.

"Easy," she said. "I'd fetch your master for you, but the *draugars* are still out there. And grateful as I am for their coming, I don't like them much."

I told her no, there was no need. Karelian could not take his wounded with him now; I'd catch up with him later. And even as I spoke I thought of telling her the truth: *Call him then, God damn you, call the draugars, tell them you have the last of Theodoric's loyal men! I have no wish to live because of a lie . . . !*

Like a thousand other times, I was silent. She finished binding my wound, and pressed a piece of bitter foliage between my teeth. I took it, but the first chance I had I spat it away. After a time we heard a great clamor of hoofs, and then slowly, a great silence gathered over Ravensbruck, broken only by the sounds of burning.

She helped me to my feet, and shoved open the door of the scrub house. Karelian and his myrkriders were gone. We were quite alone in the courtyard. And yet she stood beside me staring, not at the flame-wrapped world of Ravensbruck, but beyond it, into the night and the wilderness, as though a king's procession marched there, or a legion out of hell.

"They will meet," she said. "Take care, Pauli, take good care, for they will meet."

I only half heard. I was hurting, and tired of her talk.

"What?" I said.

"Fenrir is riding from the south," she said. "They gather the cords of linen to bind him, and the cords of leather, and the cords of iron, and he will break them all. But the cord of magic he will not break."

"What are you talking about, woman?" I demanded. And then I wished I had been silent, for she would only speak more madness.

"The world eater," she said. "I see him at the hazelstangs."

Her face was awful in the shifting light, as though the scars she bore had come alive, and were moving and whispering among themselves.

"At the hazelstangs, Pauli. The wolf will open his mouth, and the hunter will thrust his hand between his teeth. And then it will be for the gods to judge between them."

"There is only one God," I said.

"We shall see," she replied, and made some gesture of magic against the burning night. "We shall see."

There were fewer dead in the ruins of Ravensbruck than I expected. A few of the servants had resisted, and some had merely gotten in the way. But most had hidden themselves from the first onslaught, and then fled once the gates were opened. Either the fiends had not cared, or else they had been commanded to let them go. Karelian was after finer prey: the princes of von Heyden, and all their retinues; the Iron Count and his sons; the knights of Ravensbruck who were loyal to their lord.

All those were dead, and little Helga too. We found her in the great hall, amidst a stench of smoldering tapestries and blood. An old servant woman crooned over her, stroking her hair. "Poor little thing, poor little thing . . . ."

The servant looked up. If she saw me at all, I do not know. Her eyes fastened on the Wend slave.

"He came back, Sigune. The lord of Selven. Just like you said he would. He came back and he killed them all. Poor little thing, she was so pretty . . . ."

"She was pretty," Sigune said. "But she had no heart. She was her father's child all through."

I stared at her, appalled. She did not even glance at the dead bride. She walked over to where Arnulf lay beside his chair.

He had not died easily, nor quickly. I found it hard to look at what was left. She did not. Yet to my surprise she did not smile. She looked sad.

"All gone now, my lord," she murmured. "A quarter century of conquering. More dead men than you could count, and dead women, too, Wends and Vikings and Frisians and Slavs. My life, and yours, and all your sons. All gone, and this to show for it. Was it worth it, my lord? Would you do it all again? But of course you would. How else could you prove you were a man?"

She paused, and her eyes turned to ice.

"May Hel find you a cold place, my lord; a cold place and an empty one. Farewell."

Three others of Theodoric's men survived the slaughter, all of them like myself by being wounded and having the good fortune (or bad fortune, perhaps, depending how one judged it) to fall somewhere secret, where the fiends did not notice them and the fire did not come.

I did not tell them what I had seen after I was wounded. There was nothing I could have done for Theodoric, or for anyone else. I could not have left Sigune's hut except on my hands and knees. Yet how could I admit the truth—that I had sheltered behind a scrub house wall and watched my own lord slain—my own lord, and the crown prince of the empire? I said I had been struck unconscious and did not revive till morning; and they told me stories more or less the same. We were all, I think, ashamed of having lived.

Two were too injured to travel, and we left them with peasants outside the ruined castle. Myself and the other, after a few days of recovery, disguised ourselves as common folk and picked our way back through Karelian's territories to Stavoren. It was a long and difficult journey made worse by the fact that we dreaded our arrival.

Then the news came from the south, and we began to live again.

Gottfried had met the army of Prince Konrad near the town of Saint Germain, in Thuringia, and beaten him. Only the heroism of the Thuringian duke prevented a rout, and saved young Konrad from being taken captive. Thuringia himself was badly wounded, and had lost an eye. Konrad was retreating to what was now the safest place in the empire for himself and his men: the Reinmark.

We reached Stavoren at the end of October. Like ourselves, the ducal fortress was torn between joy at Gottfried's triumph and blank horror at the fate of his sons. The news of the massacre had traveled faster than we had, and dreadful as the truth was, the stories were often worse. We were the first to come to Stavoren who had actually witnessed the attack, and we were taken at once to see the empress.

She looked at the two of us for a long moment, and I wished again that I had died in Ravensbruck. I know she blamed us in her heart—how could she not?—but in her mind perhaps she understood. War was chaotic. A man might easily be wounded and have a battle pass him by and his liege lord killed, with no fault owing to himself.

We knelt to her and spoke our grief. She did not answer. Her own grief was enough to drown the world. But beneath her grief I saw sternness, and unyielding resolve. This was a woman whom no amount of grief would ever break.

She motioned us to stand. There were only three guards in the room, I noticed, ones she held in particular trust. The archbishop of Stavoren, grey-haired and bent, sat in a chair by her elbow.

"What happened in Ravensbruck?" she asked. "It is said the necromancers conjured forth an army of the dead to destroy our house."

"It's true, majesty," I said. We told her of the invaders, how they had scaled the walls and leapt from them without harm, how weapons could not wound them. As we spoke, the archbishop became more and more distressed. He had heard it before; they all had. But until now he had not really believed it.

"I did not think it possible," he said. "I never thought God would permit such a thing."

She did not answer him. She was still looking at us.

"You know for a fact our sons are dead? You saw them?"

"We saw them, my lady, to our great sorrow."

"In what manner did they die?"

"In combat, as best we could judge. Prince Armund had a great wound in his chest, and Prince Theodoric . . . ." I faltered.

"What of Prince Theodoric, Sir Paul?" Her voice was calm, but under the calm was a terrible dread. "How was the body of my son?"

"He was . . . he had been . . . beheaded, my lady."

"And was his head beside him on the field, as it should have been?"

"No, lady. We could not find it."

The empress and the archbishop looked at each other. Her face was paler than before, and his was absolutely white.

"There is no doubt about it, lady," he said. "We are dealing with the full, unleashed powers of hell, such as has never before happened in Christendom. It may be the end of the world is upon us."

He paused. His voice fell almost to a whisper.

"With your permission, majesty—perhaps they should see it?"

"There's no need for every fool in the Reinmark to see it," she said bitterly.

"But they were in Ravensbruck, majesty. There may be something they know, something they would remember—"

"You're grasping at straws, archbishop. But very well. It scarcely matters now."

She looked at us again. "The night my sons were killed, I was seized by a terrible dread. I couldn't sleep, I couldn't pray. I wandered through the castle like a lost soul. I tried to believe I'd had a bad dream, and my terror would go away with the morning. It didn't go away. It grew more and more terrible.

"You know there is a chamber in the castle which his lordship has always kept locked. The chamber began to haunt me; I thought perhaps inside I would find some knowledge of my sons' fate.

"I have never disobeyed his lordship before. But this one time, for my sons' sake, I called the guard and made them batter down the door."

She stood up. "Come, and I will show you what we found."

The door to which she led us was guarded now. Inside was a room more strange than any I had ever seen. It was shaped like a pyramid, and made entirely of stone. No sound of the world beyond could possibly have reached it. It was utterly still, utterly closed upon itself. I experienced almost immediately an awesome feeling of constraint, and at the same time, an equal feeling of power. This was a place where one could not move outward at all, but one could move upward forever.

Then I looked down, instead of up. I saw the stone prie-dieu, the stone table in front of it, and all my being froze with horror. If I did not cry out, it was only because I had no voice at all.

A silver bowl lay on the table, and in the silver bowl, wrapped in a sheath of flame, was the head of Theodoric von Heyden.

Oh, my God, my God, my God . . . !

I crossed myself. I looked away for a moment, hoping it had been some mad hallucination. But the image was real, as real as those we see in mirrors, perfect in every detail. It lay on a pool of water, and except for the blank look of death in the prince's eyes, it might have seemed alive. The fire flickered and curled and smoked, lapping endlessly into his hair and across his face. Like the flames of hell, it burned and burned and consumed nothing.

I swallowed, and leaned on the prie-dieu to keep from falling. Pressed deep into the prince's forehead was a tiny wooden cross. A cross I recognized at once, from the shimmer of crystal in its heart.

They had used the crystal to work this evil. They had taken Gottfried's offer of grace to Karelian, and turned its power back on him.

I looked around, sick and bewildered. The room was always locked, the empress said. I did not know what it had been used for, but I was sure it was a sacred place. It was shaped like the truthstone itself; there had to be some link between them. I wondered if Gottfried now looked into his stone, and saw the same thing we saw here: this cruel image of his dead son.

"We have tried to exorcise this thing, and cannot," the archbishop whispered to me. "We've tried everything. Is there anything you can tell us, anything which passed in Ravensbruck . . . ?"

His voice fell away. He was, as the empress said, grasping at straws.

I told them I knew nothing, and I could not help. Gottfried would recognize the cross, and if he could not undo the sorcery, then this grey and palsied priest of Stavoren could not hope to do so, either.

They let me go. I went to my bed then, but I did not sleep. For the first time since it all began, I wondered if Gottfried might fail.

He cannot fail, I told myself, *unless it is God's will. And if it is God's will, then it cannot be misfortune.*

Then there is no misfortune, for all things are God's will.

Evil is misfortune. Evil is not God's will. God only permits evil.

But surely permission is an act of will. If a man said to me, do

you permit me to murder this child? and I have the power to say no,
then surely I must say no.
We cannot question God.

How could I reconcile those two things: a world filled with so
much overwhelming evil, and a world governed by a just and loving
God?

I tried then, and I have tried many times since. I have never been
able to do so, except by an act of decision. By saying: *I accept it. I*
do not question. It is a sin to question.

There is no other way. Our doubts are crosses, and we must bear
them without complaining. I look at my brother monks; I see how
contented they are, how confident and saintly, and I am almost reas-
sured.

Almost, but not quite . . . because I know they think the same of
me. Brother Paul, they say, how good he is, how pure, how admirable
in his virtue. Brother Paul, they say, is a saint.

Perhaps, in the secret places of their souls, they endure the same
emptiness, the same uncertainty, the same tormenting questions. *Who*
is this God for whom we have given up our lives? Did he ever ask
for the gift? Does he notice, does he care, does any of it matter? Does
he rule the world at all?

Perhaps their look of serenity is as carefully fashioned as mine.
Perhaps each one believes he is alone in his darkness, and so does
not speak of it, for fear of disheartening his brothers, as I do not
speak for fear of disheartening mine.

XLI

BETWEEN THE WORLDS

Here love will give him a shield which will be too
strong for his foe.

WOLFRAM VON ESCHENBACH

KARELIAN SLEPT FOR DAYS. From time to time he was aware of Raven's
presence, of her voice murmuring close by, and her hand in his
hair. He spoke to her, but afterwards he did not remember it. Twice
Marius brought him bowls of fine gruel, and made him waken
enough to drink it. He grumbled a few words of thanks, drained the
bowl down, and promptly went back to sleep.

When he woke properly it was day, but which day it was he did
not know. He was in Raven's tapestried chamber, suffused now with
soft autumn light, and she was sitting on the edge of the bed. She
was still hurt, wearing her shift laced high to her throat, but the marks
on her face had begun to heal.

She smiled.

"Are you alive, my lord duke?" she murmured.

"I'm alive. Why do you call me that?" He remembered, and added:
"Why did *they* call me that?"

"Because it's what you will be. You've given the Reinmark to
Konrad on a silver plate. Who else would he choose to be duke?"

"Frankly, I hadn't thought about it." He reached for her hand, and
drew it to his mouth. "Are you all right, my love?"

"I will be. I'm half veela, after all, and we can mend most anything in Car-Iduna. But I won't forget."

"I should never have let you go into Stavoren," he said bitterly.

"Really, Karel, it's been a very long time since anyone has let me—or not let me—do anything."

She bent, wisping soft kisses over his face. He reached to hold her, but she gently pushed his arm away.

"No, Karel. Not yet. Lie still and let me kiss you. All of you, my golden summer stag, every lock of hair, every sinew, every secret. I want to kiss you forever. I want to remember how beautiful can be the body of a man."

He was still wrapped in an easy languor, and it was lovely to take her gift, to let her have his body and worship it as she chose. She trailed kisses down the length of his arm, and back again, pausing to nibble at his shoulder, and press her face softly into the curve of his throat. Her hair whispered over him, smelling of jasmine; he would have liked to tangle his hands in it and pull her mouth to his own.

"Karel . . . ." She stroked his chest and his belly, let her tongue wander into the cleft of his navel; back to his nipples, where she feasted; back at last to his mouth, where she feasted more. It took a very long time, all of that, and she had only halfway begun.

"I love you, Karelian Brandeis." She ran her fingers over his cheekbones, over his nose and his mouth, almost as though she were blind, and wanted to discover him by touch. "You are fair, and you are brave, and I do love you."

"I'd gladly hold you, Raven, if you'd let me."

"After." She purred softly, the shameless purr of a veela pleasuring. "I want to have you first. All of you."

More kisses, right to the nails on his toes, back again. She lifted his knee, and began to nibble downward along the inside of his thigh. He had been aroused for some time, and even innocent caresses were exciting now. This was all but unbearable. She was whispering over his loins like a moth, idling away and coming back, tormenting him until he moaned.

"Lady, do you have it in mind to kill me?"

"No man has ever died of pleasure, my lord duke."

"That may be so, but I would hate to be the first."

She laughed, but she yielded to his hunger. She took him with her mouth, slowly and gloriously, and after he came she went on caressing him, treasuring him, taking back all her joy in his manhood and his grace, coming finally to lay beside him, her face tucked into his shoulder and her splendid body wrapped possessively against his own.

And he thought before he slept again that he did not want to leave Car-Iduna, not for Konrad, not for the duchy of the Reinmark, not for anything. In a part of his mind he knew it was enchantment, and it would pass. Men who strayed into the Otherworld always wanted to go home in the end.

But he also knew the common world could no longer satisfy him, either. He would hunger after Car-Iduna and its witch queen until the day he died. He would keep coming back, and if he could not come back the world would turn grey and empty, and he would break against its emptiness, and crumble, and blow away like dust.

That night he went alone into the chamber of the gods. He was permitted to do so now; he was no longer a guest in Car-Iduna.

It was dimly lit with candles, but the Chalice seemed to shimmer with its own light, dark and melancholy, yet suffused with an enduring, nurturing power. Like existence itself, he thought; like the very earth he walked on.

He felt the rush of a deep, long-thwarted wish to worship . . . or perhaps worship was the wrong thing to call it. Perhaps it was worship he had always objected to, the absolute self-abasement, the absolute surrender of identity and will. He did not worship these old gods; they were too bound up with the fate of the world. But he honored them, as he honored the sun and the snow, as he honored love and turning time, as he one day would honor death: because they were there, because they made everything else possible.

They were neither all-good nor all-wise, no more than a man could be. They were not omnipotent, for they yielded to each other and to the unfolding patterns which they themselves set into motion in the world. Yet they were powerful, and knowing, and deserving of honor.

It was these gods, strange and precarious and yet pitilessly real, who could stand at the world's center and truthfully say:

We are who are.

When he rode south again, the men of Ravensbruck who rode with him were real. More than half of Arnulf's knights had surrendered and sworn fealty to Konrad; they added substantially to his small army. He could have taken Stavoren now, with a good stiff fight, but neither Gottfried's lady nor her depleted garrison judged it wise to wait for him. He was advancing from one side of them, and Konrad from the other. They abandoned the ancient seat of von Heyden for the first time since their family had possessed it, and fled into Thuringia.

It was a golden day when they met again, Karelian and Konrad. It was early November, but it might easily have been early October. The world was still rich-hued with harvest and drunken with wine. The count of Lys took a moment to savor the sight of Konrad's banners flying everywhere above Stavoren; then he rode through the gates. And felt cold for a moment, remembering how Raven had almost died here.

The king did not send anyone to greet him. He was there himself, weary and troubled, but young enough to forget all his troubles in this moment of triumph.

"Karelian! God's blood, you've served me well, and I'm glad to see you!"

"My liege—"

He barely managed to bow; Konrad embraced him, and then stood back a little, gripping him hard by the shoulders.

"You keep your promises, by God! We'll take the Reinmark right out from under his feet, you said. And with so few men—you'll have to tell me how you did it. The stories are enough to make a man's hair stand on end. Come, you've made a long journey: let's have some wine."

"You are well, my liege?"

"I'm all right. My knights took a hard beating, though."

Servants stood nearby with a flagon of wine, two silver cups, a tray of pastries and chicken.

The king took only wine, but urged his vassal to eat. "Please, refresh yourself, Karel. Then we must talk."

"Thank you, my lord."

"All the signs are for a long, dry fall," the king went on. "We may have a month of good fighting weather left, perhaps even more. Plenty of time for Gottfried to come back and try to finish it."

"Plenty of time for other things to happen as well, my lord."

"Indeed," Konrad said grimly. "There's all manner of strange matters in the wind. Come, Karel. I've sent for Thuringia and my captains to meet us within the hour, but first I want to talk to you alone."

"The duke of Thuringia is still with you? I thought he was badly wounded."

"If that man were dead, my friend, and there was a war going on, he would insist on being carried around the field in his coffin, so he could at least stick his head out from time to time and give advice.

"He's rather disappointed in me, to tell the truth. He lost his duchy, and he nearly lost his life. If right and justice were on our side, it never should have happened. I swear to God he believes Odin is still riding the skies with his eight-legged horse, delivering victory to the most deserving."

"And is that so different from what we believe, my lord?"

Konrad looked at him a moment, surprised, and then he laughed.

They went to sit in Gottfried's pavilion, in one of the quiet inner courtyards of Stavoren. It was a lovely and graciously furnished place, open to wind and sun, but high above the courtyard, and therefore very private. Konrad ordered the servants to bring the wine, and then as an afterthought, the food as well.

He dismissed them, and sat.

"I owe you a lot, Karel," he said. "And I'm not ungrateful. Tomorrow morning you will be formally invested as duke of the Reinmark. I would rather have waited with the ceremony, so your lady and your vassals could be summoned, but with the war in our midst, it seemed wiser not to. If all goes well, we'll have another ceremony later."

So. She was right, my witch . . . as usual.

"My lord, I'm honored, and I will serve you willingly. But I was more than content with Lys."

"I know you were. It was the best reason I could think of for giving you more—that and your damnably good soldiering."

"You are very generous, my lord."

"Am I? It'll be a hollow honor if we don't stop Gottfried." He leaned forward a little across the table, moving flagon and plates aside so nothing lay between him and Karelian.

"Two things have happened of late, my friend, and I don't know what to make of either of them. I have spies in Gottfried's camps, as you must imagine. None of them get very close to him; there's a limit to what they can tell me. But there are whispers—from them, and from elsewhere—whispers which suggest there's something wrong with Gottfried's . . . what did he call it? . . . his truthstone."

He paused, and smiled faintly. "This news doesn't surprise you much, I see."

"I have reason to believe the stone is . . . altered, my lord."

"But how could such a thing happen? He must have kept it under guard, under lock and key. How could anyone have damaged it?"

"As I understand it, my lord, he was using it for divination. He tried to discover what was happening in Ravensbruck, and what he saw there is now sealed into the surface of the stone. I don't think it's a pretty picture."

Konrad was silent for a moment. Then he asked softly: "No offense, Karel, but is that really the truth?"

"It's close enough to the truth to serve, my lord."

"Very well. My other piece of news is fresh; I think it will surprise even you. The couriers came just last night, and they almost killed their mounts to get here. Cardinal Volken is back from Rome. The cardinal himself, the archbishops of Mainz and Cologne, and the duke of Bavaria, are calling for an immediate meeting of the electoral council—and presumably for a new election."

"Well." Karelian poured himself more wine. "The religious contingent wants a new election. That is interesting, to say the least."

"The religious contingent? Yes, I suppose you're right; I hadn't thought of it that way. Karel, what's maddening about this is the timing. If it were just a little later, I would think they'd heard about the stone turning strange, and decided it wasn't a relic and Gottfried was a liar and they wanted to elect me as they should have done in the first place.

"But even allowing for the marvelous good ears of churchmen, I don't think it's possible. Which means they decided to call a new election just around the time Gottfried was thrashing me at Saint Germain and you were said to be leading ghosts and ghoulies to the gates of Ravensbruck.

"I don't like it, Karelian. I don't like it at all."

"I don't know if I like it, either. But there's one good thing about it. By the time the council meets, and adjourns, it will be too close to winter for another campaign. By anyone. And we're in no shape for a major battle, my lord; delay can only help us."

"Provided they aren't meeting to make him king."

"If they do, will you accept it?"

Konrad laughed. "I'll kiss the devil's arse first."

"And so will I. But whatever happens in the council, the mere fact of it will give us time. And time is on our side at the moment.

"It's a peculiar situation, my lord. Gottfried has a fearful military advantage right now, but he's on the brink of an equally fearful political disaster. All his credibility depends on the truthstone. His very image as a Christian lord depends on it. If he can't use it—if he can't even allow it to be seen—people will start to wonder if it's really a relic. And if it isn't a relic, then he's nothing but a sorcerer and a usurper. His political support will erode, his soldiers will desert, the Church will condemn him—"

"So we could simply outwait him. Refuse battle, force him to chase us the length and breadth of Germany—"

"Except for one thing, my lord. He's a man of exceptional powers. I can't promise he won't get his truthstone back. And if he does, he'll have more credibility than before. He can tell the whole world how he wrestled a sacred treasure free from the clutches of the devil. He'll have the stone to use again, and he himself will be more powerful for the struggle. Sorcerers are like all strong warriors, my lord, only more so. If you wound them, and then fail to kill them, you're usually worse off than before."

"I suppose I shouldn't ask you how you know so much about it."

Karelian made a small, apologetic gesture with his hands. *I know, my lord; that is all. I just know.*

"We must finish it quickly, then?" the king demanded. "Is that what you're saying?"

"If there's any way to do so, yes. He's weakened now—not simply through his loss of the stone, but also through the loss of his sons."

"Sometimes grief only makes men more resolute and fierce."

"Grief, yes. Bewilderment, no. He had a very clear view of his destiny, my lord. He spoke to me about it at considerable length. He will find it very hard to believe he's lost the stone, and harder still to believe he has no sons. He cannot *be* what he thinks he is, without a son. If there's any way we can turn this council to his ruin, my lord, we must use it. If there's any way at all."

XLII

THE SECOND COUNCIL

The wretched world lies now under the tyranny of foolishness;
things are believed by Christians of such absurdity as no one
ever could aforetime induce the heathen to believe.

ANGOBARD

B Y THE TIME WE MET UP WITH GOTTFRIED'S slowly advancing army, news
of the impending council had already swept across the empire.
Whichever side of the quarrel they were on, most men seemed to be
happy about it. A long civil war was just behind us. The thought of
another was more than most Germans wanted to face. They wanted
it settled, and more than anything, the common people wanted it
settled without blood.

And because the council had been urged by the leaders of the
Church, everyone hoped it might sort through the tangle of doubts
and questions which hung over our rival kings. Both men had been
accused of dreadful crimes. Both had priests and princes of excellent
reputation among their followers. Both had suffered judgmental defeats
and won astonishing victories. Most important of all, both had been
helped by powers beyond the world.

In such a situation, among an ignorant and bewildered people, the
confusion was overwhelming. The right and wrong of the quarrel, so
clear to us whose sight was clear, grew muddier and muddier to most
of the rest of the world. Every question of personal or political morality was becoming secondary to one single question: *In which camp*
was the sorcerer? And it might well have been the right question to

ask, if people had looked at the right evidence—if they had looked
to God for guidance, instead of to superstition or the welfare of their
states.

Now we could have neither rain nor sunshine without someone
calling it an omen. If one king or the other passed by a village, and
someone died of an illness, or recovered from it, there was the true
king, or the false one. Other men, made cynical by all of it, shrugged
their shoulders and considered nothing except the political gains and
losses for themselves.

God, how we needed the Church then! It should have thrown the
whole of its moral and political authority behind Gottfried, and made
him emperor, and laid the foundations of a kingdom which could finally have brought the world to Christ.

But here it must be said: For centuries Rome has acted in the
world on behalf of God. Rome has put God ahead of dynasties and
nations, ahead of princes and priests, ahead of flesh and food and fire.
But Rome has never put God ahead of Rome.

If it was hard for me to face the lady Radegund, it was even
harder to face Gottfried, when we joined his army in Thuringia. I
wanted very much to see him, and yet I dreaded the summons to his
tent.

He looked haggard and weary, but not defeated. I heard after—
though I do not know if it was true—I heard he would sit every night
alone in his tent, staring at the image in the willstone. He looked upon
his son as a sainted martyr. Perhaps he even prayed to him.

He had also taken a concubine. I do not know, of course, what
passed between himself and the empress over this matter, but I never
heard from anyone the slightest indication that she was displeased.
She was past the age of bearing, and could give him no new son. And
I am sure he felt no passion for the wench he had chosen; it was
merely an act of duty, and therefore caused his lady no distress.

Like Radegund, he wished to speak with me because I had been
in Ravensbruck. Unlike her, he chose to speak with me in private.

"Tell me everything," he said. "Everything you saw, and everything you know."

I told him about the *draugars* and the battle, and the honors with
which we had buried his sons—poor honors indeed, but the best we
had to offer. When I had finished my meagre tale, he sat for a time
and looked at me; then he said flatly:

"I said you should tell me everything. Why do you not obey?"

Can you imagine my guilt, my burning shame? Or the rush of love I felt for him, the reverence? What a fool I was, to imagine I could hide anything from *him!*

I threw myself to my knees.

"Forgive me, my lord, forgive me! I was wounded, I couldn't walk or even stand; a slave dragged me to safety in a hut. And while I lay there . . . oh, my lord, forgive me—"

"You saw him killed? My son Theodoric?"

"Yes, my lord, forgive me."

"Who killed him?"

"Karelian. The fiends slew all the prince's defenders—all the men who stood with him, one by one. And when he was alone, the count of Lys rode up to him—"

"Don't call him that! He's no lord except in hell!"

"Karelian rode up to him, and insulted him—"

"What did he say?"

And so, as nearly as I could remember it, I told him everything which passed in the battle, including my encounter with Sigune, and her prophecy.

When I finished he was silent for a time. Never had he seemed so stern to me, so awful. My words had kindled a terrible wrath in him against the man who had killed his son.

They had kindled, also, a bottomless contempt for me.

"You worthless empty vessel," he said at last. "You clatter about the world making noise, but there is nothing inside of you! Nothing! I sent you to Helmardin to find Karelian. He had no army then, no risen ghosts to fight for him. You could have killed him as I commanded you—but no. You judged it too difficult, and wandered off to a monastery, and he lived to raise the powers of hell against me. He lived to take the Reinmark away from me with sorcery and blood. To murder my sons, and give my sacred relic into the hands of my deadliest enemy, so she could do me further mortal harm. If you had done your duty, Paul of Ardiun, none of this would have been!"

His words were knives in my heart, and yet strange as it may seem, I was glad to hear them. I was glad he knew me as I was, and would not tolerate my weakness.

"Then punish me, my lord! Whatever punishment you give me, I will accept it—I'll welcome it! I know I've failed you, and you can't despise me more than I despise myself!"

I sank even lower onto my knees. Every word I said was true. If he was my enemy, then I had nothing, I had no hope, I had no purpose, I had no self.

"Go. I have nothing more to say to you. In the days to come, I will give some thought to whether I still want you among my followers."

"My lord, please—"

"Be silent. You want to serve me, but only when it's easy."

"My lord, I will do anything, I'll die for you—!"

"Sometimes that's the easiest of all. Go. But consider this in your prayers. Either you are with me, or you're not; there is no third possibility. And if you're with me, then you will obey. You will not ask first if it's a good idea. You will not care if it's dangerous. You will not even wonder if it's possible. You will obey because I am your lord."

The electoral council met at Stavoren, late in November. The princes refused to accept Karelian as duke of the Reinmark, but they also refused to accept the new lord of Thuringia, who had been given the duchy by Gottfried after the victory of Saint Germain. Both appointments, they said, were in too much dispute. The electors would be the same ones who had met and voted in Mainz.

Konrad and his allies, as well as the princes of the Church, were lodged in comfort in the ducal fortress. Gottfried disdained to come as a guest into his own house, and kept regal court in his tent, amidst a large and well-armed body of his troops.

There was very little pomp. The delegates who had come from the west were weary from the journey and they faced an even more unpleasant journey home when it was over. They had two armies camped at their elbows, and the fate of the empire in their hands. They took only a single day to rest and plan.

The night before they met, I was summoned once more to Gottfried's tent. I went in fear and despair, wondering if I would be sent away forever. He greeted me with a measure of kindness—a very small measure, but it was sweet. He ordered me to sit.

"As long as a man is alive," he said, "he can repent. He can begin again."

I waited, half undone with hope.

"I will not take you back into my affections, Paul of Ardiun. Such acceptance is not freely given; it must be earned. But I will give you a chance to earn it. A final chance, I might add. If you fail me, you may still make peace with heaven. You will never again make peace with me."

"There is nothing I want more than to redeem myself, my lord."

"You know the traitor Karelian better than any of my captains do. And though he is my kinsman and my vassal, you also know him better than I do. You know his moods, his fancies, his habits—all the small and secret things which only a personal servant or a lover knows."

I cringed at his choice of words.

"You will attend the electoral council as a member of my delegation. Your only task there will be to observe Karelian. If he draws aside to whisper to anyone, I want to know who, and I want to know how they react to what he says. I want to know what pleases him in what is said, and what displeases him. Tell me when he drinks, and when he doesn't; who he smiles at, and who he doesn't. Notice everything, and be prepared to tell me what all of it means."

Tell you what it means? For a moment I was truly appalled; how could I possibly interpret anything to him?

Do not even ask if it is possible . . . .

"I will do my best, my lord. And I thank you. I truly thank you."

I went singing back to my own lodgings. Only later, in the midst of the council itself, did I come to understand the purpose of my task. There was nothing I could observe about Karelian which Gottfried's other men could not. There was little, if anything, which I could interpret more accurately than he could. I was not there to observe Karelian. I was there so Gottfried could observe me—in particular, so Gottfried could observe me in the presence of my former liege. So he could see how I responded, and what I saw, and what I left unseen, and whether my judgments of the man were sound. So he could know, finally, where my heart was.

Thus it came about that I, a knight of insignificant rank and even more insignificant accomplishments, came to sit among the electors of the Holy Roman Empire. Karelian was there too, in the heart of Konrad's party. He looked towards Gottfried when he came in, and saw me there. He took good note of me, I saw, but his face did not change at all.

The debate was begun by the archbishop of Mainz, as soon as the prayers and formalities were concluded.

"My lord Gottfried." There was something challenging in his

voice and in his mien, right from the beginning. "When we met in Mainz last winter, we received extraordinary comfort and guidance from the sacred stone of Jerusalem which you brought with you. Since our deliberations are now even more urgent, and time is short, we respectfully ask if you would share with us this gift which God has so graciously bestowed upon you."

He smiled, and looked hopefully at Gottfried.

Konrad, who had protested against the relic so bitterly in Mainz, did not say a word of protest now. On the contrary, he looked devilishly pleased.

Gottfried knotted his hands before him. "I regret, my lord archbishop, I can't bring the relic to this meeting, or I would already have done so. It has been stolen."

There was a rush of whispering and turning heads. On a few faces I saw looks of genuine dismay and horror, but mostly I saw looks of nodding confirmation: *Stolen, he says? Then the rumors are true! There's something wrong with it!*

"Stolen? How is it possible, my lord? A relic of such precious worth? How could you have allowed it to be stolen?"

Before Gottfried could answer, Karelian sprang to his feet.

"My lords, I doubt very much that this . . . thing . . . has been stolen at all. I wager it is lying where it's always lain—in his personal quarters, and under armed guard."

There was protest from Gottfried's followers, but Mainz silenced it quickly.

"But why should this be so, my lord Karelian? Are you suggesting the relic is now revealing things which Gottfried doesn't want us to know?"

"I'm suggesting it is no relic. It never was a relic, and it never revealed anything you could trust. It's a sorcerous tool and nothing more. He used it to deceive you. And now he's made some terrible mistake while using it, and it's been ruined."

"That's a lie!" The old bishop of Stavoren was almost shaking with anger. "It's a foul and demonic lie!"

"My lord Gottfried?" Mainz prompted.

Gottfried rose slowly, and even the small whisperings of his enemies gradually fell silent. He was still the most awesome of men. He commanded attention merely by existing. In some eyes he was already emperor; in others he was a powerful and perilous enemy to fear. He was also a man who had just lost both his sons—a personal and political tragedy which every man in the council room understood.

"My lords, what my enemies are saying does not surprise me. They steal a sacred relic—to blaspheme it, we must suppose, or to try and twist it to their own foul sorcerous purposes. And then they say no, it was no relic at all. They say I am the sorcerer. I will leave it to your own wisdom to judge. You all saw the truthstone in Mainz. You carried it into the cathedral; you saw it placed on God's holy altar. Do you disbelieve your own eyes, your own faith, and believe these lies instead?

"Consider who accuses me. Karelian Brandeis. A mercenary knight who all his life never cared if he served evil men or good, as long as they paid him well. A man who betrayed his liege lord, and gave his allegiance to a witch; who conjured the hounds of hell to escape from my justice, and conjured the very dead out of their graves to slaughter my son and his bride on their wedding day. Do you believe him?

"And then there is the man he serves. The man he would make king, so he can be underking and royal sorcerer. A man who murdered his own father because he grew tired of waiting for the crown. Do you believe *him*? A violent, vicious boy? A catamite?"

"I never killed my father!" Konrad's face was twisted with fury. "God damn you for a liar, Gottfried von Heyden! I never killed him! You arranged for it yourself, you bloody villain, like you've arranged for all of this, and I'll cut your dog's throat for it! By God, I will!"

More than once, during the meetings in Mainz, the assembly came close to erupting into violence. After a year, each side had hardened its position. Battles had been fought and men were dead; the possibility of total collapse was likelier now than ever.

The archbishop succeeded in restoring order, however, and made a plea for keeping it.

"If we cannot maintain peace within this room," he said, "even in so vital a matter as this, even for a day or two, what hope is there for the empire?"

That silenced everyone, even Konrad.

The archbishop began again; this time he spoke what was really on his mind.

"My lords of Germany." He fussed a little with his robes and with his ring. "We are a kingdom divided. We have no sovereign. We have no peace. We have neither legitimacy nor order in the land. One man follows his liege in the face of judgment, and says he obeys his conscience. Another abandons and betrays, and says the same. The people are bewildered and in despair. They look to us for leadership, and we give them chaos. If ever there was a time for the Church to speak, for its leaders to judge and act decisively, the time is now."

He had every man's absolute attention. This was what all of us had been longing to hear.

"His eminence the papal legate, my brother the archbishop of Cologne, the most Christian prince of Bavaria, along with myself and many other men, have given much thought and many hours of prayer to finding a solution for our unhappy kingdom. We are all agreed on this: both men who seek the crown have been accused of abominable crimes, and neither seems able to exonerate himself. We don't say they are guilty; but we do say they are irredeemably compromised. We are not satisfied as to what manner of man Lord Gottfried is, or what his purposes are in seeking kingship. As for Prince Konrad, even if he is not a parricide, his worthiness to rule has been called into question by other accusations, and by his alliance with Karelian Brandeis."

Outrage was coming at the archbishop from all directions, but he overrode it.

"We ask, therefore, that the electors reject both claimants to the throne, and choose another—a man whose integrity is questioned by no one, a man whom we all can willingly honor and serve. There is no worthier man in the empire than Duke Ludwig of Bavaria. We ask you to accept him as your king. Let us unite in this, my lords, and put an end to this futile and unconscionable war!"

I, like most everyone there, felt my stomach turn to water, and the bottom sink out of the world.

I will not recount what else was said that morning. Some of it I could not hear in the din of argument, and some I truly did not listen to. At one point Ludwig of Bavaria was asked if he was, in fact, a party to this clerical absurdity, and he said he was, and all of Gottfried's allies shouted him down for a traitor and a fool. He was the man who first put Gottfried's name forward for the kingship. He was the empire's most devout and Christian prince.

How could this be happening? It was Gottfried who was the best and worthiest lord, Gottfried whom the Church should be supporting. How could they reject him?

But even as I asked the question, I knew the answer. And he knew it, too. He sat in the center of the tumult, and said very little, the understanding of betrayal cold and ancient in his eyes. He was too good for them: too close to God, too pure, and too demanding. They did not want him for their king, any more than the Pharisees had wanted Jesus. They wanted an ordinary, malleable princeling of the ordinary world.

The meeting was adjourned. The archbishop asked the electors to take counsel with their allies and their supporters, and return to the hall at nones.

The mood of the afternoon was ugly. Men filed into the chamber in small, sullen groups, and spoke in low voices among themselves until they were convened. On almost every face was the same bitterness I myself was feeling, best described as the look of a man who has just been knifed by a friend.

We sat; we offered prayers. Then, before the lord of Mainz could speak again—which he was clearly preparing to do—the duke of Thuringia rose clumsily to his feet.

"My lords, I want to speak."

He was leaning on the arm of one of his men. His left eye and most of the left side of his face were wrapped in bandages. He spoke harshly; he was obviously in a good deal of pain.

"My grandfather came to Christianity late in life. When he was young, he used to say: There is no situation so awful that a priest of the One-god cannot make it worse. I'm a Christian as you know, my lords. But today I agree with my grandfather."

"This is insupportable!" cried Ludwig of Bavaria. "You will not insult our holy bishops—!"

"Be quiet, old man, and sit down. You're nothing but a prayer mat; you bend whichever way you're folded. I'm tired of listening to you. I'm tired of listening to all of you."

"If you do not respect this assembly," Mainz suggested coldly, "you are free to leave it."

"We heard your arguments, my lord," Karelian snapped. "We heard Gottfried's. Now by God we'll hear his!"

"Thuringia is raped and plundered," the duke went on. "The harvests are stolen, the villages burned. A usurper sits in the manor I built for my sons. I am a warrior; I can look upon both victory and defeat as fortunes of war. I will fight for land, I will fight for my king, I will fight for revenge. But I will not fight so the popes and cardinals of Rome can come after, when the warriors of both sides are dead, and lord it over us!"

He bent, and slammed his fist down on the council table.

"I say enough!"

He was unsteady on his feet, but his voice was rivetingly sure. His wounds seemed to make him not less but more formidable.

"Are none of you men any more? Are none of you Germans? We had two kings, and that was not enough to divide us; now we have three. We can tear ourselves to pieces between them, and when we are done, Rome will rule. Or we can take this bread and water duke of Bavaria for our sovereign lord—a man who's never had an idea of his own since the day he was born—and again it is Rome who will rule.

"And again I say enough! The lord of Mainz tells us we must put an end to this futile and unconscionable war. That is true. He tells us Gottfried and my lord Konrad are both tainted with infamy and neither can exonerate himself. That is not true.

"There is a way one of them can be exonerated—an ancient and honorable way. Let them go to the hazelstangs, and let God choose between them there."

He paused, and finished in a silence where even breathing seemed to be suspended:

"Let them fight!"

To my astonishment—and quite possibly to his—men from both camps leapt to their feet and shouted: *Yes! Let them fight! Let it be settled! Let them fight!* They did not wait for their liege lords to speak, or for their neighbors. It was an utterly spontaneous outburst, made without a moment's thought. Just as men in a burning building will turn and run wildly after anyone who shouts: *This way! This way!* so did they leap to approve the suggestion of Thuringia.

Konrad too. "Yes, by God, let it be settled! This very day if you will! What do you say von Heyden, will you fight me? Have you the nerve to face God with your lies?"

"My lords, my lords, in God's name, my good lords . . . !" Mainz was waving his hands and shouting for attention; it was some time before he received it.

"Trial by battle is a barbaric and heathen custom, my lords," he said. "It is tempting God, and we can't possibly consent to it!"

"You can't consent to it, perhaps," the landgrave of Franconia said flatly. "But this is a matter for the princes of Germany to decide—and especially, for the principals themselves. My lord Gottfried, you've said nothing yet. What is your answer to his majesty's challenge?"

Gottfried looked up. "His majesty hasn't challenged anybody yet," he said.

"God's teeth, this is too much!" Thuringia roared. He flung his arms out in gesture of frustration, and then almost crumpled in pain. His comrade helped him into his chair, and joined the debate himself. "We know you don't acknowledge my lord Konrad as your king. The question is: will you fight him?"

"We're all Christian men," Gottfried said. "We can't embark on such a course of action—nor will I do so—until we have considered it, and sought the guidance of God in our decision. I don't refuse Konrad's challenge, and I don't accept it. Let's meet again tomorrow."

"Will you answer us tomorrow?" Thuringia demanded, glaring at him.

"Yes. I will answer you."

There was a heady excitement in the air now, equal to the anger of the early afternoon, and equally frightening. Several of the comments I heard were hostile to Gottfried: *He's afraid. He doesn't know what to do. He's playing for time.* But one man seemed as uneasy about it as Gottfried himself seemed to be. As we dispersed, and the chamber gradually fell empty, Karelian sat motionless, his elbows on the table and a look of profound uncertainty on his face.

I could not decide which answer I wanted Gottfried to make. Like the others, I felt the attractiveness of the duel. It would be an awesome, public, and irreversible solution. Yet I knew it was forbidden. As Mainz said, it was a heathen custom. It was tempting God.

Nonetheless, I thought, in a certain sense we tempted God every time we made an offering, every time we asked for something and promised something in return. Was it so wrong to ask God for a mortal judgment, if in one hour it would end a war, and make Gottfried king?

It was much later—in the dead of night, I think—when I remembered Ravensbruck, and the wretched Wend woman and her babbling. *At the hazelstangs, Pauli. The wolf will open his mouth, and the hunter will thrust his hand between his teeth. And then it will be for the gods to judge between them.*

She saw things, Peter told me. And many things she saw came to be.

I do not know if Gottfried discussed his decision with his allies or with his empress; certainly he did not discuss it with me. He had no blood claim to the throne—at least none which his peers would acknowledge. Without the stone he had only his charisma, only his personal moral worth; he had to restore his credibility among them somehow. The morning came, and he gave the electors the only answer I believe he could have given in the circumstances.

"My lords, I have no doubts about the rightness of my cause. I have no doubts about the guilt of the man who challenges me. Perhaps he expects me to refuse, and to discredit myself by doing so. Or perhaps he is so corrupted by his own sins that he no longer fears the hand of God. But I will fight him."

He paused for just a breath.

"I assume the usual laws will apply. Since the crimes we are both accused of are capital, if the loser is not slain upon the field, he will be summarily executed, since his guilt will be proven. The victor will be declared guiltless, and may not be accused again. And since we are noblemen, we will fight in mail and on horseback. All of that is given, is it not?"

"All of that is given," Thuringia said grimly.

"Then let it be, and let God's will be done."

Mainz began to rise, but Karelian was younger and quicker.

"There is one other thing that's given. The life of the king belongs to the kingdom, and he can't be compelled to wager it in a duel. Both men claim the kingship; both must be permitted the services of a champion!"

"Why so?" growled the duke of Bavaria. "If they will engage in this barbarous, unchristian ritual, let them risk their own necks! Let them stand alone before God, with no intermediaries!"

"I am willing!" Konrad said defiantly.

"No!" Karelian cried. "It's out of the question!"

"And why is it out of the question?" Gottfried demanded. "Does it limit, perhaps, the possibilities for your sorcerous interference?"

"No," Karelian said. "It limits the possibilities for peace in the empire." And suddenly he was speaking with his enchanter's voice again, a voice soft as a cat's purr, and powerful as its claws. "This will be a bitter fight, my lords, with an empire and men's souls at stake. Even the victor may be gravely hurt. Whoever is king after this must be whole and strong to govern, or we may find we've only traded one fatal crisis for another. It's unfair to the kingdom to place the king's life in jeopardy. They must be permitted champions. That is the law. It has always been the law!"

"He's right," Franconia said. "It has always been the law."

No one contradicted him. It was indeed an ancient custom, applying not only to trial by battle but to any duel of honor, and even to challenges in war. The king's person was privileged, and that privilege could never be denied.

The king, however, could refuse to claim it.

"I need no champion," Gottfried said coldly, "and I will use none. If the Salian prince wants to hide behind some other man's sword, let him do so—but let it be a soldier, not a sorcerer of hell. The law forbids perjurers to act as champions; it forbids traitors; it forbids witches and infidels. My lords, Karelian Brandeis is all of those things, and he must be banned from acting on Konrad's behalf."

"Very clever." Franconia's voice was a snarl of contempt. "The greatest knights in the empire, save for Konrad and perhaps yourself, are the duke of Thuringia and the count of Lys. Konrad should not be risked, Thuringia is wounded, and you would have Karelian banned. Is there anyone else you want us to get rid of, my lord, before you think it's safe enough to fight?"

"Villain!" shouted one of Gottfried's company. "His majesty does not fear to fight any man alive! He should not be asked to fight devils!"

"Frankly, I couldn't think of a better match," Thuringia muttered under his breath, and a ripple of laughter spread among his men.

"My lords." The landgrave of Franconia wiped his brow. "Let us be done with this nonsense. We're not asking Lord Gottfried to fight sorcerers and devils. We have none to put forward. Dreadful accusations have been made against the count of Lys, it's true, but where's the proof? The only men who will swear to these things are men who serve Gottfried. We're told the count conjured deadly wolves in the courtyard of Lys—but there are plenty of other men who'll tell you they saw only maddened dogs. We're told a sorceress changed herself into a bird and flew into the castle of Stavoren to open it to the enemy—but all any man there ever saw was a woman spy who'd been shot with an arrow. One mere woman spy and to add insult to injury she escaped. So of course they say she was a witch. If it were me, I would think up a good story, too, rather than admit to such incompetence—!"

"Enough!" Gottfried cried. "You mock this assembly, Franconia! We all know what Karelian Brandeis has done. We have sworn statements from men who were in Lys, from men who were in Ravensbruck. They're not all in my service. And even if they were, they've sworn on the cross, on their very hope of salvation! Do you dare to say they're all lying? *Do you dare?*"

"They're not all lying."

Karelian's words caught me utterly unaware, like an arrow in the darkness. Perhaps they caught everyone so, for the room went very still.

"My lords," he went on, "men tell you they saw strange and dreadful things in the course of this war. And so they have. So have you all. In this very gathering, just a few months ago, you looked into a piece of crystal and saw a crime which never happened. Should it surprise us if other men see things which aren't real?

"So, yes. There are many who speak against me. Some of them, as my lord of Franconia suggests, are merely obedient servants of a man they hope will be king. Some of them tell truthfully what they saw—but what does it prove? It was clear in Aachen that Gottfried could conjure false images. Why shouldn't he go on conjuring them? It turned his campaign for power into one which couldn't fail. Every conflict he won, he was one step closer to the throne. Every conflict he lost, he cried sorcery, and heaped more disgrace on Konrad and his allies, and so in spite of losing, he was again one step closer to the throne.

"Consider this. Every time I've been accused, in every place where men claim they saw something sorcerous and evil, Gottfried was there, too. Or his son Theodoric was there, armed with his father's talents and his father's tools. Every time, both of us were present—*every time, my lords, except one.* I was not at the first electoral council, where this whole treasonous nightmare began."

Oh, it was intolerable to listen to him! It was intolerable to see the reaction of the delegates—the riveted attention, the sudden flash of insight: *Christ, we never thought of that . . . !* Gottfried protested, of course, and so did several of his allies, but the protests were distressingly ineffectual. Without the stone, or some other visible evidence of Gottfried's superiority, it was simply one man's word against the other's.

Once, for the briefest moment, Gottfried looked directly at me. I would willingly have died, I think, rather than speak in the council room. Nonetheless I hoped he would call on me. I could have told them where this treasonous nightmare really began—in Helmardin. I could have placed Karelian in a den of sorcery and evil hundreds of leagues away from anyone belonging to the house of von Heyden. I even considered leaping up on my own authority and doing so.

But I held my tongue. I knew what was likely to happen, just as Gottfried did. That was why he merely looked at me, and looked away again. They would ask me too many questions I could not answer without seeming stupid, irresponsible, or vile. I could almost see the smile curling Franconia's hard mouth as he ripped me to shreds.

—Why did you stay with your liege, if you knew he was dealing with witches? Why didn't you tell anyone? Why didn't you go to the bishop? To Lord Gottfried? To the king himself, perhaps, when you met him in Stavoren?

—I didn't really believe it. Not until what happened in Lys.

—Oh. Then you believed it. But you still didn't do anything about it. You disappeared for months. Why did you disappear, Paul von Ardiun? Where did you go? And if you were so horrified by Karelian's alleged sorcery, why did you promptly turn up in the camp of another man accused of the same crime? Did he offer you faster advancement?

No. I could say nothing. I had betrayed my liege in his own house, and then hunted him down in the wilds to betray him again. I could not deny it, and if I admitted it, I would render all my other testimony useless. Although these men were perfectly capable of reversals and duplicity themselves, they would use my own changed loyalties and my own deceptions to discredit every word I said. And I certainly could not tell them why I knew Gottfried was no sorcerer.

So, like many other times, I was silent. And this time I really do not think it mattered. There was already an abundance of evidence against Karelian. Those who wanted to believe it, did. Those who didn't want to, didn't. The arguments went on, but no one was really listening. They were only pounding on their own certainties. The face of Mainz was almost ashen with dismay, like a man watching his house go up in flames.

It was to him Gottfried made a final appeal.

"My lord, as a Christian prelate you must speak. You must oppose this! No man can be allowed to serve as champion who is so defiant of God, and so given over to sorcery! It would be a mockery of justice."

"I oppose all of this," Mainz said. "It is all a mockery of justice. I hear nothing in this chamber except the ranting of ambition, and the lash of malice. But you are both accused of sorcery, Lord Gottfried—

yourself and the count of Lys. If one of you is to be banned from the trial, so should be the other."

"Aye!" shouted fifty voices as one.

I stared at the archbishop in blank disbelief. It was a perfect Pharisee's judgment—legally flawless, logically sound, morally empty.

"Well said, my lord!" Franconia cried. "Are we agreed then? If Gottfried himself can take part in this trial, then there is no reason whatever why the count of Lys cannot?"

They were agreed. A hundred aye's drowned out the few, scattered no's. Gottfried made a brief gesture of angry surrender, and flung himself back into his chair.

So did they put stones in his path, and with lies they wove snares for his fret . . . .

Mainz tried one more time to sway them. "Do you really mean to do this, my lords?" His tone was heavy, and his body sagged as though his robe was made of chains. "To choose your king on the jousting field, the way you would wager for a coin? It's wicked and sinful, and it's lunacy besides! The more I see of these men, the more I think they're both unworthy of the crown. You can't mean to settle the fate of our holy empire with a travesty like this—?"

"You misunderstand us, my lord," Thuringia said. "We're not the ones who are going to settle it. It's obvious we can't settle it—and few men are more to blame for our dilemma than you. So we'll put it in God's hands, and let him judge. Perhaps, being a holy man, you can tell me what's wrong with that?"

"It's terrible presumption! It's utterly barbaric—!"

"Barbaric? Let me remind your lordship of our last twenty years. One year peace, the next year war. One day our emperor is excommunicated—and all his loyal vassals along with him, of course. The next day he's forgiven and restored. And then, by God, before half of us can be shriven or marry or bury our dead, damned if he isn't excommunicated again! One day we're God's people, and the next day we're the children of hell. And we haven't done anything different. The pope has merely changed his mind about our leaders, and how he wants to arrange things in the world. *That* is barbaric!

"We've seen the Roman way of settling our disputes. So now we'll use our own way and then it will be settled. For one thing I assure you, my lord of Mainz, when God has passed his judgment on these men, he won't come back tomorrow and change his mind!"

XLIII

THE KING'S CHAMPION

It is one thing for magicians to perform miracles,
another for good Christians, and another for evil Christians.

SAINT AUGUSTINE

THEY HAD ONLY A WEEK TO PREPARE for the trial, and Konrad began at
once. Before sunset his men were going over his armor and weapons with desperate care. There was no time to order anything new;
the old would have to do. It was battered somewhat by the war, but
it had been made for a prince, and it was sturdy. Other men occupied
themselves among his horses, trying to choose which would be the
strongest and healthiest and best-trained mount.

The prince himself was in the practice yard by late afternoon, and
it took all of the combined eloquence of his two loyal allies, Thuringia
and Franconia, plus that of Karelian himself, to drag him away to talk.

There was, he said, nothing more to talk about. He would fight
Gottfried von Heyden, and if there was a just God in heaven—and he
believed there was—he would defeat him, and clear his name, and claim
his crown. And would they now be so kind as to move out of his way?

"And will you, my good lord, stop being the haughty young king
for just a moment, and listen to reason?"

"You presume too much, Karelian!"

"If I do, it's only because I love you. My lord, your best captains
stand before you, and beg for your attention. Will you not listen to
them?"

"I know what they're going to say."

"Listen anyway, my lord," Thuringia said. "Karelian has earned that much from you, even if I haven't."

Konrad looked at the half-blind warrior and frowned. He wiped the sweat from his face, and swung down from his horse.

"I'll listen," he said. "For what I owe to the lot of you, I'll listen. But no more."

They went again to Gottfried's pavilion, but they had no wine, and only the wounded Thuringia troubled himself to find a chair.

"Well," Konrad said, "spit it out. You don't want me to fight."

"You must not fight, my lord," Karelian said. "You can't possibly win."

"I've been three times champion of Germany," the king said coldly. "If I can't win, perhaps you'll tell me who can."

"The man who defeated the champion of Germany," Thuringia said. "Right here on this same field, a year ago."

"A single joust proves nothing. I'm fifteen years younger than Karelian, and I'll wager you a hundred marks he'd never beat me again!"

"I'll take your wager," Thuringia said.

"A plague on you both!" Karelian cried bitterly. "This is not about jousting—in the name of all that's sacred, don't you understand? We're dealing with a sorcerer! You could be champion twenty times over and it wouldn't matter! You can't fight Gottfried on equal terms!"

"And you can? Is that what you're saying?"

"Yes! That's what I'm saying!"

The two captains looked at each other, and Konrad looked at something beyond Karelian's left shoulder.

"And if it's so," the king said finally, darkly, "what good will it do any of us? If the trial is decided by sorcery, it is no trial. Any trick, any treachery, even the wearing of a charm will condemn you, and I will be hanged by your side. Thank you, Karelian, but such championing I don't need."

"You're wrong, my lord," Thuringia said softly. "As I would judge it, the trial *is* going to be decided by sorcery. With Gottfried there, what else is possible? Surely none of you imagine he'll be restrained by the usual oath to use no magic?"

"Then he'll be condemned," Konrad said.

"Only if he uses magic which can be seen," Karelian replied. "A shield against wounds can't be seen. The power of a thought to ward off a blow can't be seen. Fear can't be seen. All those things he'll use, and likely others."

"And do you have such . . . weapons . . . at your disposal, Karel?"

I am too far gone in this to turn back now . . . . Karelian drew a long breath, and said simply:

"Yes."

"Thanks be to God," Thuringia murmured, and crossed himself. Then, in response to Franconia's look of dismay, he added:

"If they have cavalry, damn it, we want cavalry. If they have Greek fire, we want Greek fire. Well, if they have a sorcerer, then we'd better have one, too. I see no problem with it. I thought perhaps his majesty had arranged it so."

"Well, I didn't," Konrad snapped. "I accepted Karelian's service in good faith."

"I've not betrayed your faith, my lord," Karelian said calmly.

"No. No, you haven't. But God help us, you heard what Mainz said. My worthiness to rule is compromised merely by my alliance with you. If I name you as my champion, what will they say then? Will it even *matter* if you win?"

"It will matter," Karelian said. "Gottfried will be dead."

"I wouldn't worry too much about what the archbishop says, Franconia added. "His kind see devils in the bread basket. The knights and princes of Germany don't care a fig about most of the accusations against you. They care about whether you murdered your father. If that accusation is proven false, the rest is smoke in the wind. You're a good soldier, you're sound in mind and body. Those things—and good government—are what matter in a king. Nothing else."

"If I vindicate myself, yes," Konrad replied. "But if Karelian does it for me, what will they say, then? Won't they point to the courtyard of Lys, and to Ravensbruck—to every accusation made against you, Karel—and then say: Konrad was saved by a sorcerer; he is no king!"

"There are some things you must remember here, my lord," Karelian said. "One: you are the legitimate heir. Your vindication will have a rightness in itself. It will represent a return to order, and to the honored ways of doing things."

"Aye," growled Thuringia.

"And two: everyone wants peace. As long as the trial is concluded without treachery, without any open violation of the laws, most of Germany will be eager to accept it. And one thing more, my lord. In spite of all the fuss they make, not every man thinks it's wicked to have dealings with a sorcerer. As for those who do think so, let me ask you this: what's the difference between an act of magic and a miracle?"

"One is God's doing, and one is . . . someone else's."

"But how do we know which is which? How do we know if God did a thing, or if someone else did?"

"Before I met you, Karel, I would have said it was obvious."

"And what made it so obvious?"

"Well, if Jesus did it, or a saint, it was a miracle. Or if it came out of nowhere and helped us."

"So it wasn't the deed itself? It was the agent or the outcome?"

"Yes, I suppose so."

From the corner of his eye, Karelian could see the duke of Thuringia smiling. He went on:

"Have dead saints not appeared on battlefields, leading Christian armies to victory?"

Konrad made a small gesture of assent. *Yes. Or at least there are legends about it . . . .*

"It's said that dead men came to Ravensbruck, my lord, and it may be that they did. But I was fighting for the lawful king, defending his life and crown against a traitor, and those who came to help me were martyred warriors of the empire. Was it sorcery then, my lord, or was it the hand of God? The duke's followers will say one thing, no doubt, but yours will say the other, and nothing will be proved.

"If you are a just king, and govern well, and keep the law, nothing I have done or am accused of doing will unseat you. You will have enemies; no ruler is without them. And yes, they'll speak of Lys and Ravensbruck. And for every ten who speak of it, ten others will say it wasn't so, and twenty more won't care.

"They want a king, my lord. They want an end to the war, an end to being leaderless and torn apart. If you are vindicated in this battle, no one will take your crown because of me. If you want to lose it, you'll have to throw it away."

He stepped close to the young king, and dropped to one knee.

"My liege, I beg you: for your life's sake, and for Germany, let me fight!"

For a long time Konrad let him kneel. Then, slowly, he lifted him to his feet, and held him by the shoulders.

"Damn you, Karel, how do you think I'll be able to bear it? To stand aside like a worthless boy and watch?"

"You'll be able to bear it because it's necessary. And because you are a king."

There was another long silence. Neither of the captains intervened; everything they could say had already been said.

"All right," Konrad said heavily. He turned away. "Perhaps you're right; God knows you usually are."

Karelian's first preparations for the trial were not made in the practice field. He summoned a lawyer and a scribe, and with Konrad himself as a witness, along with Reinhard and several other men of rank, he acknowledged the boy-child Wolfram as his heir, arranged for his fostering and care, and appointed the priest Father Thomas as his tutor.

It is not enough, the scribe wrote under dictation, *for the boy to learn to fight and to govern; he must learn when to fight, and for what; he must learn how to govern justly. For that, let him learn to read; let him learn to think; let him be as much of a scholar as it is in him to be.*

The count provided also for Adelaide. She was to have the use of his property, and be allowed to live in comfort from its revenues, with the honor appropriate to her rank, for as long as she lived, whether she married again or not.

When it was done, he sat for a time alone, remembering his departure from Ravensbruck. He wondered if Rudi Selven would believe him now.

They had confronted each other among the ruins, one last time, in a world of fire and phantoms. If Karelian had believed in hell he might well have thought it lay about him. Selven rode up to him, stopping barely an arm's reach away. His clothing was drenched in blood. His eyes were filled with bitter, unsatisfied dreams.

"So, my lord of Lys."

Karelian nodded faintly. "Selven."

"It seems you are the last of my enemies left alive."

"I doubt you can kill me, Selven. Before you try, there's something you should know. Adelaide bore a child a year ago. A boy-child, with coal-black hair. The whole world thinks you fathered him, and they're probably right."

Selven stared at him, wiped his arm across his face, and stared again.

"He will be count of Lys one day," Karelian added, "if I live to hold it for him."

"Why would you do that?" Selven whispered.

Why indeed? It was a question he had never answered to his own satisfaction, much less to anyone else's.

"Why should I not? He's Adelaide's, and she loves him. He's healthy and beautiful. He never did me any wrong. Why should I throw him to the wolves?"

Strange, that in such a place, at such a time, there could be silence. No conflagration now, no war. Nothing seemed to exist but the two of them, motionless at the borders of the world.

"I would like to believe you, sorcerer, but I don't."

"I'm sorry for it."

"Is she happy?"

"She may never be truly happy, Selven. But she has a place in the world; she has a measure of security; she has the child. That is something."

"Will you speak to her about me?"

Karelian considered for a moment, and shook his head. "No."

"No, I didn't think so," Selven said bitterly. "Then say your accursed charms and set me free."

"You are free, Rudolf of Selven. Go, and be at peace."

He faded like a shadow into a greater and gathering darkness. At the last moment, before he was gone, he raised his hand in a brief, perhaps ironic, perhaps sincere salute. And went to whatever place they went, the dead who were truly dead and did not return.

Where I will go, perhaps, in a few more days . . . .

And if he lived? If he defeated Gottfried, and lived . . . what then?

He mostly believed his brave words to Konrad in the pavilion— though he would have spoken them whether he believed them or not. But in the quiet of his own reflections he knew them for what they were: just brave words. He had grown arrogant in an environment of war, surrounded by the powers of Car-Iduna and the loyalty of fighting men who cared little what their warleader did, or said, or thought, as long as he was winning and keeping them alive.

The council brought him sharply back to reality.

Oh, there was truth enough in his words: to the average citizen of the empire, highborn or low, the use of sorcery was not necessarily an evil, and if it was, they simply called it something else. A cross or a holy relic worn around one's neck was never called a charm, but it was a charm nonetheless. Priests made divinations by blindly opening sacred books, yet few men ever called the *sortes sanctorum* witchcraft. If he had only the Reinmark to live with, only the German empire, all his words to Konrad would have been true.

But there was the Church, and that was another matter altogether.

The Church also judged sorcery by the agent and the outcome; unfortunately, Konrad's vindication and his lawful right to rule—the outcomes which concerned Germany—did not especially interest the Church. And the agent would interest them entirely too much.

The archbishop of Mainz was not an evil man. Indeed, by ordinary standards of judgment, he was a good man. And yet, Karelian knew, if Mainz had the power to do so, he would try the lords of Brandeis and von Heyden on the same charges, and burn them on the same stake, with no concern at all for the real issues of their quarrel. To a faithful servant of the Christian hierarchy, the real issues *were* what a man believed, and how he served or failed to serve the dominion of the Church. By that standard, Karelian and his enemy were equally condemned.

They sent an army halfway across the world to slaughter unbelievers. Why should I imagine they'll ignore the Reinmark and its duke? I think it's just beginning, this passion for mastery, this drive to have the whole world submit, and every man in it, and every woman, in every thought and every dream and every whisper of our flesh. Gottfried himself was born of it, and so was the great crusade.

It's just beginning. Dear gods, what will become of us when it's truly unleashed?

The night before the trial Karelian was summoned to Konrad's private chambers—the rooms which had previously been occupied by the duchess Radegund. The king had taken Gottfried's quarters first, as was fitting; they were the finest in the castle. He left them again within the hour. "I don't find them pleasing," was the only explanation the proud and worldly young man would give.

Music filled the room when Karelian came in—a rich but melancholy music. Konrad half sat, half sprawled in his chair. He motioned Karelian to sit, but otherwise remained lost in the singing; his wine waited untouched by his elbow. Nearby a young man sat playing a flute. Another bent over a lyre, almost at the king's feet, and sang very softly: *Nu gruonet aver diu heide, mit gruneme lobe stat der walt* . . . . It was a long and lovely song, full of mourning for lost land and lost friends, yet filled with hope and reclamation. The exile, like the spring, would yet return . . . .

Finishing, the singer bowed his head over the instrument, and waited.

"God, but you have a gift, Wolfgang," the king said. He laid his head back. "Go now. I must speak with Karelian."

"My lord." The singer rose, and then bowed very low, taking Konrad's hand and touching it to his lips. "May God shield you, my lord, and keep you safe."

He backed away, not out of deference—Konrad never expected such exaggerated behavior—but as one backs away who cannot bear to give up the sight of what he is looking at. Even at the door he turned, and looked again.

"Good night, my good lord."

The door closed very softly.

"Have some wine," Konrad said, waving vaguely towards the tankard. He picked up his own cup, drank briefly, and looked hard at Karelian.

"Now I suppose you will be added to the list of people who wonder if that young man is my lover."

"If knowing would ever help me to serve you, my lord, or to shield you from some danger, then I would wish to know. Otherwise, I can scarcely think of a question which concerns me less."

"You have a wonderfully uncluttered mind, Karel." The king stared into his wine. "I suppose you still want to go through with this?"

"Yes."

"I'll have to wait under armed guard—did you know? Not with my knights, but under guard, like a felon waiting judgment. If you fail . . . if you fail I will be put to death."

"I don't intend to fail."

"I trust your intentions well enough," Konrad said wearily. "It's your alliances I worry about. You were not in Stavoren last night."

He noted Karelian's surprise, and smiled faintly. "I have no special arts for learning things. I'm only a king; I use spies. You were not seen leaving, but you were missed. You returned at dawn, very quietly and well disguised. Where did you go, Karelian?"

Karelian made a small, dismissive gesture. "To see a woman."

"The witch of Helmardin?"

"It's a duel to the death, my lord. I wanted some time with my mistress. Surely you don't begrudge me that."

"I begrudge you nothing, God damn it! But if your . . . mistress . . . has anything to do with this fight—if she so much as sets foot on the heath of Stavoren tomorrow, it will be the end of all of us! Don't you understand?"

I understand even better than you do, my lord. There isn't a shape she could assume which Gottfried wouldn't recognize, not even a rock. She won't be there. But she won't be far away.

"I will fight alone, my lord; you have my word. But I won't fight unaided. That was the whole point in my serving as your champion. We've already agreed on it."

"Did we?"

"Yes."

From somewhere in the castle came the sudden sounds of tramping feet, a clattering door, a shout. The king looked up sharply, tensely, and listened until the last of the steps had echoed away.

"I grew up in the coils of a civil war," he said. "From about age eight I recall waking up every morning and wondering if I would still be a prince when the sun went down. Or even if I'd be still alive. I thought my world couldn't get more insecure, or men more unpredictable. Amazing, isn't it, to have been so naive?"

"You have some faults, my lord, but naiveté isn't one of them. I doubt it ever was."

Konrad laughed, but there was no joy in it. When he spoke again he did not look at Karelian.

"Will you tell me something—just between ourselves?"

"If I can, my lord."

"Whom do you really serve? I mean, beyond the world?"

Karelian hesitated, but only for a moment. The Church made men into liars the way famine made them into thieves. And yet tonight, at this hour, with this man, he would not lie.

"I serve Tyr, the god of justice. Among others." He paused, and added softly: "Does that appall you, my good lord?"

"It would have once. Now I'm mostly appalled by the thought of dying. I'm innocent, Karel. Will God value my innocence above your unbelief?"

"If he doesn't, then is he worthy of belief?"

Konrad smiled, and this time the smile was warm. He raised his cup. "Well said, my friend, as usual. I'll say one thing more, and then I'll let you go. I have faith in you, Karelian of Lys. I would prefer to put my life in no man's hands, but since I must, then I'm glad the hands are yours."

He stood up, and wrapped his arms around his champion.

"May my God and yours both keep you safe."

XLIV

TRIAL BY BATTLE

Victory runes, if victory you desire,
You must etch on the hilt of your sword,
Runes on the sheath, runes on the blade,
And twice invoke Tyr.

POETIC EDDA

THEY WERE NOT YOUNG, THE MEN who fought that day; they were both ten years or more past the usual prime of knighthood. Yet none of us thought it strange they should meet—that it was these two, finally and no others, who would ride into the cold November morning and fight for the future of the world. We knew it would be more than a match of strength. Their years, their courage, even their skill as we normally understood it were less important than who they were, and what they fought for, and who would fight beside them.

For they would not be alone on the heath. We knew that too as we gathered, as we waited and watched the grey skies lighten without a trace of sun, and our knowledge left us pale. This was the match all of Germany might once have journeyed out to see; the one they waited for ever since the great tourney two summers past; the one they wagered on in the drinking halls and field camps, and quarreled over, and fought a thousand times in fantasy. If only Gottfried had taken part! they always said. If only he had met Karelian—then we would have seen a fight like no fight that ever was!

But there was no wagering now, no idle talk, no women blowing kisses at their favorites. And the boasting, what little there was of it, was raw-edged with fear.

They had chosen the great jousting field below the duke's castle as the place of trial, and there the armies gathered: the soldiers of God and the soldiers of rebellion—for such I call them, whatever men may call them now.

Reinhard, although a knight himself, served as Karelian's squire; indeed I am told he begged for the honor. I have never understood the man, so piously Christian, so mindlessly loyal, so unutterably stupid. He must have been tripping over Karelian's sins, so blatant they had become, and yet all he could say was yes my lord, of course my lord, whatever you wish my lord . . . !

Everything was done with unbearable formality: the marking out of the field, the placing of armored men in a solid wall of shields around it, the fanfare of trumpets, the slow advance of the imperial officers into the center of the field, accompanied by their herald. Gottfried rode to meet them from the east, Konrad and his champion from the west.

They stopped perhaps ten feet apart. Gottfried, they said after, seemed kingly and serene, Konrad arrogant. And the eyes of Karelian Brandeis burned hard and bitter, and no man wished to look in them.

"Lords of the empire, citizens of Christendom." So the herald began. "Today, under God's holy judgment, the guilt and innocence of these men will be resolved in trial by combat. Konrad, crown prince of Germany, stands accused of the murder of his father and his king, our great and beloved emperor Ehrenfried. Lord Gottfried von Heyden, duke of the Reinmark, stands accused of sorcery, of falsifying sacred relics, and of treason.

"Since no evidence can be found to establish guilt, save only circumstance and the accusations themselves, and since both men claim the crown of the Holy Roman Empire, we are resolved to put this matter into the hands of God. Lord Gottfried will fight against Karelian Brandeis, count of Lys, who will act as champion for the prince. May God now watch over us, and may his justice be done!"

The herald was singularly careful, I noticed, to name no man as king; to give each of them only the titles which they held at the hour of Ehrenfried's death. I did not blame him for his caution, but I noticed.

"This combat," he went on, "will be to the death, and none shall interfere. Any man who attempts to do so will be instantly slain.

"The loser shall be judged guilty, and shall suffer full and immediate punishment for his guilt: loss of rank, honor, and property—and, if he still lives, the penalty of death. All judgments passed by him against his enemies in the present war shall be void. All ranks, titles and honors given by him shall be void, and his followers shall disperse their armies and peacefully await the election of a new emperor.

"Is it so agreed, my lords?"

"It is so agreed."

Their eyes met then, Gottfried and the prince, and it was the prince who looked away uncertain, frightened like the rebel boy he was. They say he looked at Karelian, and Karelian smiled, and saluted him with drawn sword.

"I will not fail you, majesty," he said.

Konrad was then escorted from the field, to await the outcome under guard.

"My lords, will you now take the oath?"

One of the officers carried a bier; upon it lay a crucifix and many sacred relics.

In turn, Karelian and Gottfried placed their right hand upon the holy things, and swore to respect the laws of judicial duel:

That I shall use no charms or incantations, no ointments or magical devices, nor practice any act of sorcery to forestall the will of God. That I conceal no secret weapons. That I will use no act of treachery or deceit to gain an unjust victory. So I swear in the sight of God; may my life and soul be forfeit if I lie!

And what use was it, I wondered, to demand such an oath from a man like Karelian, who neither believed in God, nor feared his own damnation? Just the night before, one of Gottfried's young knights of Saint David had raised the same question.

"He will carry a devil's bag of tricks onto the field," the young man said bitterly. "All of his belongings should be searched, and he should be compelled to dress himself in front of witnesses."

Whereupon the speaker received so many insults and icy looks— and this from men of his own side—that he fled from the chamber. To the half-barbarian knights of those days, the thought of subjecting a highborn lord to such indignities was appalling. It was, perhaps, more appalling than sorcery itself.

So they took Karelian's oath, and he took what evils he wished onto the field.

Christ! Will they never get on with it?

All the excitement and bravado which had swept the council meeting was gone now. Men shifted in their places, tense beyond bearing, and afraid, all the thousands of them gathered to watch. Far too much now suddenly depended on far too little. Except for God, I do not think any of them could have faced it.

Karelian was eager to fight. Even his horse was stamping and restless, catching his master's mood. He had wanted no part in this war—or so he always said—but in this war as in all the others, once he began he hungered for the kill.

"Look at him," Gottfried's men growled to each other. "He would sink his teeth into the emperor's throat if he could!"

Or so I am told they said, for I was not with them. I was alone in the place I had chosen, waiting for the trumpets to blow again, signaling the beginning or the end of the world.

There was blood on the parchment. It was fitting, Paul thought. His own blood, finally, after all the others'. It would kill him to finish the chronicle. No other end was possible.

His whole life, since that day on the heath of Stavoren, had been built around forgetting. Slowly, year by year, he had woven his forgetting until it was almost whole, almost opaque. Only whispers of memory would come through, like shafts of light through a torn arras. Then *she* came, and the forgetting began to unravel, word by bloody word, and his life unraveled with it, crumbling as unearthed mummies crumbled in the light.

"Karelian . . . ."

Here was their final victory, the evil ones. Not his death, just a few more bitter words away. Not the blood on the paper from the quill which tore his hands. The memory itself was their victory; the face, the voice, the laughter, the earth-borne body of Karelian Brandeis, shimmering with silver and steel, racing across the sand and the heath and the history of the world, the only history which still lived, the one he could not refuse to remember. His own.

WHAT CAN I TELL YOU OF THEIR FIGHT? It was indeed a fight like no other we'd ever seen. Artists have painted pictures of it, sculptors have made statues, songs have traveled as far west as Wales, as far east as Jerusalem. Yet men do not agree on what they saw, or what they heard, or what any of it meant.

Were the ribbons Karelian wore on his lance black, for the witch of Car-Iduna and the devils whom he served? Or blue, for the Holy Virgin? That, you would say, is surely a simple thing to answer? Then go about the roads and villages of the Reinmark and ask. You will hear both answers, and seven more. Men still argue about every detail of the trial, except these: the names of the men who fought, and how it ended.

I watched alone from my chosen place. I knew how it would end, and my certainty should have been my strength, but instead it weakened me, filled me with an unforeseen and totally overwhelming regret. I could not take my eyes off Karelian, and to my shame I found them filled with tears.

He rode at Gottfried like a demon, black pennants flying (yes, by God! they were black!). They met with a shattering fury; both lances broke; Karelian's mount all but lost its footing. I imagined my comrades smiling.

It's just beginning, fools, I warned them silently. The duelists met again; this time Karelian parried the blow, and broke his own lance into the bargain. A great roar went up from Konrad's ranks. And I smiled.

Yes. I admit it. What is the use to lie now? It was still there, like a blackness in my blood, a rot in the very foundations of my being, upon which nothing whole could ever stand, not even Gottfried. It did not matter what my conscience commanded, or what my mind knew to be the truth. I admired him. I felt the power of his beauty as I had felt it the first day in Acre, a power as compelling as a sorcerer's, all the more potent for being damned. I could not make my eyes look elsewhere. I could not stop my breath from catching in my throat when the third set of lances splintered into the sky and they drew their swords.

"Now," Gottfried's men would say, "this witchspawn will be cut to shreds."

For the king was famous above all for his skill in mounted combat with the sword. He had the shoulders of a bear, an astonishing reach, and he towered over men of average size. He was a full head taller than Karelian. And he had, like Karelian, almost bottomless reserves of experience and will.

I have no idea how long it went on. We saw them strike, parry, and strike again; heard them shout; saw them wheel their mounts and circle and charge again with cries of rage; heard the clash of steel and the bursts of cheering which swept across the ranks, cheering which turned sometimes into soft waves of awe, and finally into silence.

It was a long time before I saw it, so trapped I was in my own confusion, my terrible blinding weakness. I may well have been the last man there to see it. It was the silence which made me understand, finally—the stillness of an entire world, where nothing moved except those two men, and God, and darkness.

Gottfried was going to lose.

Oh, it was not over, not nearly over, but a pattern had been set. Again and again the king would attack, smoothly, brilliantly. He used feints which bewildered us with their swiftness and cunning, and yet Karelian's shield was always there—or nothing was there at all. Again and again their swords met and held, and I would expect Gottfried's great strength to force Karelian off balance, and give the king an opening; yet somehow the count always eluded him, and always recovered.

And then, finally, he didn't.

Others, pushing and shoving at the edges of the field, did not agree on what occurred. But I had an unbroken view. I saw Gottfried strike. I saw Karelian parry the blow. They stood frozen, blade against blade, for what seemed an eternity. Then with a great burst of strength Gottfried broke the deadlock, and pulled his sword back and thrust again, under Karelian's shield. The count merely buckled a little, like a man who had been punched in the ribs, and spun away.

That was when the silence began. Men caught their breaths. Some looked to their neighbors and some looked to heaven, but each one judged the matter as it suited him—luck, or sorcery, or divine protection.

It was all happening just as Gottfried said it would.

—*Karelian will be shielded by his demons. And if he is shielded well enough, he will need nothing else.*

Nothing else at all. He could take all manner of risks, knowing he was safe. Or he could bide his time until he had worn the king down, until he had exhausted Gottfried's body and bewildered his mind, until in one carefully chosen moment he could slaughter even a god.

My confusion drained away and bitter anger took its place. I damned Karelian a thousand times more fiercely than I would have damned any devil out of hell, even Lucifer himself.

And I steadied my will, and my hand, and my eye, and I waited.

—He will not shield his back, Pauli. He will think there is no need . . . .

All those terrible days, waiting for the trial, I thought about what might come of it. On the fifth day I was summoned to Gottfried's tent. He wanted me to repeat to him the words of the hag, Sigune.

—I think she said: At the hazelstangs. The wolf will open his mouth, and the hunter—

—I recall all that. She said something else. Something about cords and magic.

—Oh . . . Oh, yes, my lord. Fenrir. Something about Fenrir riding from the south, and they will take cords of linen to bind him, and cords of leather, and cords of iron, and he will break them all, but the cord of magic he will not break.

—Ah, yes. The cord of magic he will not break. I am not Fenrir, Paul of Ardiun; they see all things as in mirrors, backwards. But it's clear they believe they're about to destroy me.

I had been watching him as we spoke. Never, at any time in Gottfried's life, would any man have described him as faltering. Yet he had been dealt, in short succession, three overwhelming blows: the loss of his sons, the ruin of the willstone, and the rejection of the council. Each was devastating, but the loss of the sacred stone was the one which was threatening to undo him—not only politically, but in his heart. For if the stone could be ensorceled, and he could not restore it, they had a power equal to his own.

What would happen, then, in the trial?

—Karelian will be shielded by his demons. And if he is shielded well enough, he will need nothing else.

I did not speak. Surely he could not doubt himself. He could not believe they would kill him . . . surely not . . . ? I swallowed, feeling sick with fear.

—Over and over you've sworn you want to serve me, von Ardiun. The last time, I recall, you said you would do anything. It's reckless to make such an offer until you know what a man might ask.

—I know you will ask me nothing evil, my lord.

—Evil in whose eyes?

—God's eyes, my lord. I care nothing for the world's judgments; I saw enough of those in the council chamber.

—Yes. So did we both. Tell me, then: should a Christian prince fight unarmed against the enemies of Christendom?

TRIAL BY BATTLE 489

—Indeed not, my lord!

—But if Karelian is shielded, then I have been disarmed, for my weapons can do nothing to hurt him. And he knows it; I've heard he hardly bothers to practice. And he's ridden twice from the castle of Stavoren into the wilds—to meet his witches, I suppose. To offer his foul rituals for their aid.

—I didn't know, my lord.

—I have more ways of knowing things than you do.

—Then I pray your majesty knows some way to defend yourself, for it cannot be God's will that you should fall.

—I'm not a sorcerer.

—No. But you're God's . . . you're God's holy king, and all things are possible to God.

For a long time he considered me. And then he said:

—You are sure of it, Sir Paul? All things are possible to God? And before you answer, think! For many men will leap up and say yes, but when they're faced with even a fragment of God's power, and see what it can do, they cringe away.

—I believe all things are possible to God, my lord.

—Even that I should discover a way by which I might defend myself; and bring this demon lord to justice?

—Yes, my lord.

Again he was silent, watching me. He knew how fond I had been of his mortal enemy. He knew I had failed him once already. He must have thought me the most insignificant, the most unworthy of men.

And perhaps that's why he chose me. Because he knew me so well. He knew my guilt, and my terrible need to expiate it. *You loved him once, this traitor who fouls our altars and plots against our faith. You didn't know what he was—or perhaps you did, just a little?—it doesn't matter. It's left tracks on your soul just the same. And you are the one who must erase them.*

If you really want to . . . .

He watched me from an immense height; I could have crawled for a thousand years and never reached his feet.

—Will you serve me in this, Paul of Ardiun? Be careful how you answer me, for any answer will be dangerous.

Dangerous? I almost smiled. What danger was greater than hell? And I do not mean the hell of fire, but the other hell, the hell of knowledge. It was beyond enduring, sometimes, to know what I was. To know what I had lost, and why I had lost it. I might have been

Gottfried's cherished friend; I might have stood at his shoulder and ridden by his side, if it had not been for Karelian, if it had not been for *them* . . . .

—I am at your command, my lord. Do with me as you will.

I held the crossbow steady, judging aim and angle by feel. I was a good shot, and I had chosen an excellent position.

—*Just after a pass, von Ardiun, so when he falters it will seem I have dealt him the blow* . . . .

Do you think it was base of me to watch there, unseen? No doubt you do. And no doubt like the fools who spoke of it afterwards, you think I was hidden by sorcery. You may think what you please. I did only what my lord commanded.

I touched my finger against the tip of the shaft; it was deathly sharp, and it seemed harder to me than any metal could have been, hard as the edge of a diamond, hard as the crystal pyramid from Jerusalem.

Hard as the eyes of a god who looks into your soul and sees it as it is, corrupted and empty. He knew I was not free of Karelian Brandeis. I would never be free of him. I loved him, and I hated him. Because he was hateful I loved him better. Because I loved him more than Gottfried, I hated him more than anything that lived.

As I hated him now, so proud in his godless power, slashing at Gottfried and wheeling away and coming at him again, all for his witch queen and his catamite prince. What was righteousness to him, or the empire of Christendom, or Gottfried's sacred blood? He would glory in bringing them down; he would laugh, and raise his bloody sword, and drink a toast to his demons and take their foul honors and couple with them after in the howling darkness . . . !

The bolt flew silent, unseen—invisible as the man who fired it, hidden by God's power in a bare November oak, a winter tree, stark as death against the sky. Karelian jerked upright in his saddle, and I knew my bolt had struck him. He swayed a moment, his sword arm dangling. Those men who were privileged with seats leapt to their feet. Konrad sprang forward in fury and dismay and had to be restrained by his guards. A great moan passed over his men; some fell to their knees, and soldiers though they were, many turned their heads away.

For a moment, for a few brief heartbeats, it seemed Gottfried had dealt the count a mortal blow. The king was already turning his mount to charge and strike again. At the last possible moment Karelian wheeled out of his way, clinging to his shield, and his weapon, and his life.

And all the powers of hell gathered then, all the fiends and minions who served him, all of them rising black to his summons, so great in his sorcery he had become. They came to him, numberless, and closed him round; they shattered the grace which Gottfried placed upon the shaft, and I saw it.

Oh, God, no, this can't be happening, it can't . . . !

But it was. Everyone saw it. Princes and soldiers and commoners and priests, all of us saw it, and Gottfried, too, as he reared his mount backwards and stared. The prince's champion had been shot in the back. The justice of the trial had been broken. Men spun one way and then the other, trying to see from whence the treachery had come, but they could see nothing, and it only made them angrier. The moan of dismay turned into a tumultuous roar of fury. Konrad was battling his guards, and dozens of Karelian's men, led by Reinhard, had by sheer force of numbers broken through the armored guard, and were pouring onto the field. It might have been blood and butchery then and there, that very day, but Karelian's voice rang clear above the breaking chaos:

"Stay in your ranks!"

He had gathered all his strength for the command. He was the only man there whom anyone was prepared to obey.

"This is a fight to the death, and by the gods I'm not dead yet!"

Yes, he said gods, though of course there are a thousand men who'll swear they heard otherwise. And they'll tell you that even as he turned and raised his sword again, the clouds divided, and a burst of winter sun caught against the blade like fire; that was why it shimmered so. They will tell you a dove flew over his head, too, and every other kind of nonsense you might wish.

But I know what I saw. He yanked the pouch from beneath his surcoat, and took the black feather from it, and touched it to his lips, and flung it into the air. It fluttered there for a moment, and turned suddenly into a raven; before the eye could properly discern it, it was gone, flying hard towards the east and the high pass of Dorn.

Why did Gottfried not attack him then, in those moments while Karelian was gathering his powers? Did he think God had abandoned him? That judgment had already been given, and there was nothing further he could do? Or was he praying and restoring his own strength?

Down through the years I have wondered, and I have no answer; I know only that he waited, like we all did.

Karelian lifted his sword. There was no sun. I care nothing for what the tales may say; there was not a break in our brooding, ashen sky, not a whisper of God's light to explain the orange shimmer dancing on his blade. I will not say from whence it came, but I have seen it since.

"*Tyr!*" he cried savagely. "*Tyr, wield my sword!*"

And he rode at Gottfried.

I see it still, oh so clearly, as though I stood even now on the heath of Stavoren. There was no other sound in the world then, only the crashing of hoofbeats and iron. We all stood as stone men, except for the witless ones who imagined they were in the presence of a miracle, and knelt. Karelian's first blow struck the king's shield, and it shattered as though it had been made of clay; all my hopes shattered with it.

He struck again. Gottfried parried the blow with his sword, and the sword broke, three grey splinters scattering wide like startled birds. Karelian flung away his shield; he had no need for it now. He seized his weapon with both hands, rising in his stirrups, and dealt the king his death-blow. It caught Gottfried at the base of the neck on the left side, and emerged on the right, below his armpit, severing all which lay between.

Armor and bones and blood and sacred life, all in one fell stroke undone. I stared, unbelieving, as the king's trunk hovered a moment in the saddle, gushing blood; Karelian dragged it down as though it belonged to a beast, or something less than a beast, and reared his horse to trample it into the earth.

And stood so, over the broken body of my lord, and raised his sword again.

"*Konrad! Hail Konrad, king of Germany!*"

A thousand voices took up the cry, or maybe ten thousand; it hit the black sky and thundered back; it echoed off the walls of Stavoren, and rolled back seconds later from the brooding heights of the Schildberge. It echoes still, even now, in the stone walls of my cell. I did for Karelian the one thing he could never have done for himself.

I gave him an absolute victory.

Oh, there are men who say he was a sorcerer. There are men who hate Konrad, and he will be quarreling with the Church through every day of his reign. But from that hour onward the prince was a king, and his champion was a hero. Maybe not a saint, but a hero, and in Germany that's a far better thing to be. His enemy had proven treacherous, and he had won even against treachery. He had won even with a death wound in his body, and to the whole world of our day, except for a tiny handful, his victory was taken as the clear and final judgment of God.

I looked down, weeping, and I saw my own hands; I saw a vagueness forming in their grasp, and recognized my own crossbow. The sight of it, even more than the horror on the field, made me realize that Gottfried was dead, and his power utterly undone.

Even as the bow took its shape I flung it savagely away to crash wherever it might upon the heads of the cheering fools. I slithered down from the tree, hidden by its massive trunk from the ranks of men behind, unnoticed by the ranks of men ahead. I could not hear my own sobs for their shouting:

"Hail Konrad! Hail the king of Germany!"

The cries went on. Somewhere across the field, where I could no longer see him through the crowd, Karelian fell forward over the neck of his horse, and slid into Reinhard's arms.

What happened after I know only from the words of others. The seneschal, they say, wept like a boy cradling his lord against his knees. Some ran for the surgeons, and others for a priest, but Karelian wanted nothing of either. Nor would he let anyone touch his wound.

"Take me to Lys," he said.

They looked at each other in dismay: *Dear God, he is raving, he's already gone . . . !* But he was not raving. His eyes were still clear, and his voice was steady although losing its strength.

"Reini, if you've ever loved me, do as I say. Don't argue. Make a bier to carry me, and take me back to Lys."

"It's several days' journey my lord, even for a healthy man. You can't do it; you will not live—!"

And then Konrad was there, shoving everyone aside, men stumbling over each other to give him place as he swept close and knelt. He cursed when he saw how the arrow was placed; like the others he could see it was mortal.

"Karel . . . oh, God save us, Karel . . ."

"Will you grant me a favor, my liege?"

"Anything, my friend, only name it!"

"Order these men to obey me."

"Do what he commands you, villain!" the king snarled at Reinhard. "Have you no decency at all?"

"Majesty, he wants us to take him home."

"Home? Back across the mountains?"

"My lord," Karelian said, "no surgeon can help me. You're a soldier, you know as much yourself. If there's help for me, only my lady can give it. If not, then I would die in her arms." He coughed harshly, and there were flecks of blood on his lips. "My lord, I beg you."

None of them knew what to say then, or what to do. Some who tell the story say Karelian motioned the king to bend close, and whispered something into his ear. Others insist that nothing private passed between them, and nothing had to. They were neither kinsmen nor old friends, yet in this hour of blood-bought fealty, they were better loved than either.

"You're sure of it?" Konrad asked him. "This is what you want?"

"Yes."

The king got to his feet.

"Do as he says."

So a bier was fashioned, and he was lain upon it gently. They had removed his helmet and coif; his fine hair was matted now and stained. Konrad ordered men of his own guard to accompany him, and kissed him farewell.

"I would not have you go like this," he said. They say he wept as the small procession wound away, across the valley of Stavoren towards the borderlands of Dorn.

Just past the first of the villages, while the great castle of von Heyden was still looming at their backs, they passed through a heavy wood, and there their path was blocked by riders. At first Reinhard thought they were pilgrims, for they were all dressed in plain brown, with hooded capes pulled low across their faces. But their leader was a woman—a woman too beautiful, he said after, to belong to the ordinary world. Her followers were armed with swords and bows.

She slid quickly and gracefully from her mount, and came to the bier where Karelian lay. And he saw they knew each other. She was the lady of whom Karelian had spoken. She held him, and kissed him many times, and turned to Reinhard a face covered with tears.

"We will take him now," she said.

The seneschal did not argue; the world had passed far beyond his meagre understanding.

"Can you save his life?" he pleaded. "Please God can you save him?"

"Perhaps," she said. "All the power I have will be spent on it, and I have much. But you must know, faithful Reini: whatever comes to pass, he will not return to you."

"But he is a great lord," Reinhard said.

"Yes," she said bitterly. "Greater than any in the land. And he is mine."

She left the seneschal little time for his farewell. She signaled to her followers, and they came and took the bier, and she mounted to ride alongside of it.

"Go now," she said to Reinhard. "Go quickly and don't look back."

But of course he did, after a time; he could not help it. And all he could see, as far as the earth and the sky and his heart and his prayers could reach, was grey cloud and black trees shivering in the wind.

Did he live that day my Karelian? Is he with her still, in the depths of Car-Iduna? Sharing her bed, and feasting by her side, surrounded by harpsong and dancing women and sorcery? There are many who say they see him riding to the hunt on stormy nights. The serfs of Lys swear they see his fires in the woods, in the dead of winter, and there are tracks there after—tracks which lead to no place within the world. The countess smiles and tells her women that he comes to her by night sometimes, to lie with her. But the countess, God knows, is mad . . . .

What more is there to write? Gottfried is dead, and for all the love I bore him, and all the honor he deserved, I cannot keep him living in my mind. He stands as if in shadow; it is effort now even to remember the color of his eyes.

But that one, shimmering in the desert sun of Acre, snow-kissed in the storms of Helmardin, falling on the torn heath of Stavoren, against the death-bolt I dealt him, against my heart, soaking both in blood . . . that one I do not forget.

Karelian . . . .

A lovely name, Karelian. It plays on the tongue like a kiss, and I do not forget.

EPILOGUE

PAUL VON ARDIUN was found dead in his cell in the Benedictine monastery of Karlsbruck in November of the year 1135. The only writings in his possession were devotional works inspired by the teachings of Honorius of Autun. He had deep wounds in the palms of his hands, which were believed to be the stigmata of Jesus Christ. Because of this, and because of his exceptionally austere and penitential life, he was canonized as a saint in 1187.

The same year, Saladin destroyed the crusader army at the Horns of Hattin, and took back the city of Jerusalem. It had belonged to the domain of Christendom for less than a hundred years, and it was never to return.

AUTHOR'S NOTE

This is a work of fiction. The duchy of the Reinmark is entirely my own creation. All characters are fictional, including the emperor Ehrenfried and the various high German lords, who are not intended to resemble the actual, historic persons who held those ranks and offices at the time. There are some minor anachronisms in the text, and a certain vagueness of geography which becomes inevitable, I believe, when you drop a non-existent territory down in the middle of a real one.

Nonetheless, though the story is always fiction, and sometimes fantasy, the world into which I have placed it is mostly real. Like the indigenous people of the Americas, the people of Germany were Christianized in large part by conquest. Many accepted baptism merely to avoid punishment, and went on quietly believing in the old ways. Political resistance to Church authority remained strong. My fictional twenty-year quarrel between Rome and the Emperor is very similar to one which actually took place. All the material on the First Crusade is drawn directly from eye-witness accounts. Trial by combat was a time-honored tradition among the Germans, used for resolving not merely personal disputes, but legal and political ones as well.

Most important of all, my portrait of the Church is also drawn from contemporary sources: the sermons, penitentials, and theological writings which shaped medieval moral thought. However worthy these writings may in some respects appear, they reflect a pervasive dread of hellfire, disgust for human physical life, and an astonishing compulsion to dominate, even in very small things, the minds and bodies of others—factors which contributed significantly to three hundred years of violent crusading, and three hundred more of witch burning and sectarian warfare. In his views of sin, sex, and sorcery, Paul von Ardiun is not untypical; he is a mainstream Christian soldier of his time.

But in the medieval world, as in every other, there was dissent. Heresies sprang up faster than they could be suppressed, challenging every aspect of orthodox belief. Many ideas which we consider uniquely our own are hidden away in the half-forgotten books of our ancestors.

Knight and poet Wolfram von Eschenbach condemned religious intolerance in a statement as powerful as anyone, in any age, has ever made: "Those who never received baptism: was it a sin to slaughter them like cattle? I deem it a great sin, for they are God's handiwork, all two-and-seventy languages of them that are His." While Christian theorists denigrated women and vilified pleasure, he created proud and splendid female characters, and celebrated sexual passion, not as a courtly game, but as a vital, nurturing power which healed and matured the human person. Medieval in some ways, he is so modern in others that we catch our breaths. In spite of this (or perhaps because of it?) his finest and most daring work, *Willehalm,* was not translated until the 1970's.

A NOTE ON THE EPIGRAPH SOURCES

Saints Augustine and Thomas Aquinas were (and still are) ranked as two of the giants in the history of Christian thought. Saints Jerome and John Chrysostom, though less eminent, are major figures. Saint Bernard of Clairvaux preached the Second Crusade and drew up the rule for the military Order of the Knights Templar. Though little known today, Honorius of Autun was one of the most influential and widely read theologians in Europe in the 12th Century. Huguccio of Ferrara and William of Auxerre, also theologians, were his contemporaries. Innocent III was pope from 1198–1216; he instituted the death penalty for heresy and launched the first crusading wars against fellow Christians, which ended in the sack of Constantinople and the virtual extermination of the Cathars in southern France. Erasmus was a Christian humanist writer of the Renaissance. Saint Gregory of Tours, a sixth century bishop, wrote *The History of the Franks,* recounting the lives, loves, and wars of the Merovingian kings. Saint Gregory of Nazianzus was bishop of Constantinople in the 4th Century; he and his contemporary, Lactantius, achieved fame for their attacks on paganism. The various penitentials were guidebooks used by the clergy to counsel their flocks and to assign standardized penances for sin. The *Liber Exemplorum* and the "Revelations to a Monk of Evesham" were popular works of unknown authorship. Also anonymous, the *Gesta Francorum* was a documentary account of the First Crusade, written by one of the participants.

The *Poetic Edda* is a collection of traditional Norse poetry originating in pagan times. The *Volsunga Saga, The Niebelungelied,* and the writings of Saxo Grammaticus, are all medieval works, recounting inter-related legends from Nordic myth and history. Marie de France was a poet writing in England in the late 12th Century; her precise identity is unknown; some believe she was a daughter of Eleanor of Aquitaine. Ludwig Uhland and Rainer Maria Rilke were German poets of the Romantic and Modern eras, respectively. The Wolfram excerpts are from prose translations of his epic poems, *Parzival* and *Willehalm.*